PERFECT

Carole McKee

AuthorHouse™
1663 Liberty Drive, Suite 200
Bloomington, IN 47403
www.authorhouse.com
Phone: 1-800-839-8640

First published by AuthorHouse 7/18/2007

ISBN: 978-1-4343-1890-9 (sc)

Printed in the United States of America
Bloomington, Indiana

This book is printed on acid-free paper.

Katrina

1-1

From the day she was born her parents referred to her as their miracle baby. She was preceded by two older brothers. Danny, her oldest brother was nine when she was born, and Michael was seven. Since Michael's birth had been so difficult, the doctor strongly advised that there be no more children. Mary Kitrowski was heartbroken over this, since she always looked forward to having a daughter. When she discovered that she was pregnant again, there were mixed feelings of joy and fear that either Mary, the baby, or both would not survive. Joy overcame the fear when it was learned that Mary was carrying a girl. She knew that it was meant to be. She wanted her baby girl to have everything to make her life perfect. She and Ed poured over baby name books, trying to come up with a perfect name for her. When Mary came across the name Katrina she knew that was what it had to be.

Katrina Leigh Kitrowski entered the world on April 14th in the year of 1977. The birth had been as easy as the pregnancy, and little Katrina was perfect in every way. Mary and Ed were thrilled with their beautiful baby girl. Danny and Michael fell in love with her as they stood by her crib and just watched her sleep. When Katrina was one month old, Danny turned to Michael and said, "Nobody better ever hurt our baby sister." Michael nodded in agreement. From that day forward, they became Katrina's protectors—guardians. No matter where she went, Katrina had two big brothers keeping an eye on her.

By the time Katrina began sitting up by herself, everybody who saw her knew that she was special. She had a delightful laugh and a radiant smile that nobody, especially her brothers, could resist. It was her beauty that turned most heads, though. Her very blue eyes fringed with thick dark eyelashes sparkled when she smiled, and her shiny light auburn hair was thick and manageable even at an early age. She was blessed with a perfect, tiny nose that just turned up ever so slightly at the end, perfectly shaped lips, classic jaw line, and high cheekbones, all set in an oval-shaped face, with a dimple in each cheek. Mary and Ed beamed when strangers gushed over her. Danny and Michael didn't mind taking a back seat to the attention she got, but they always made it known that they were going to "protect her forever", as they put it. This always won the approval of those who were around at the time.

1-2

Katrina went from a beautiful baby to an adorable toddler, and then to a darling pre-school aged child. Her parents noticed three outstanding qualities about her: One was that she had a very gentle nature about her; two, she was self-reliant and could spend many hours playing alone; and the third quality was that she was artistic. By the time she was four years old she could draw animals and people in correct proportions. Her drawings showed that she had an eye for detail and geometrics. Ed believed she was a "born-artist". Mary enrolled her in dance classes, which Katrina took to quite well, leading Mary to believe that she was born to be a dancer. When Katrina entered kindergarten Mary added piano lessons to Katrina's development; but Katrina wouldn't go unless Michael went, too, since she was particularly close to Michael. He agreed to take lessons when Mary asked him, so both Katrina and Michael went together once a week to piano lessons. To Mary's delight, Michael excelled at the piano, as did Katrina. There were now two musicians in the Kitrowski family. Michael began playing the guitar in addition to the piano. Danny was fourteen by now, and playing junior varsity football. He was looking forward to getting into high school and playing varsity football. At fourteen he was five-feet-seven inches tall, and muscular. He was becoming a handsome boy and the girls were starting to notice. He kept his grades above average with very little effort, and he was active in school clubs. Mary and Ed were proud of him, Michael looked up to him, and Katrina adored him. He still referred to her as his baby sister, and always got her response, "I'm not a baby!" This never ceased to amuse him. He adored her as much as she adored him.

As a grade-schooler, Katrina excelled at everything, but was particularly good in art class. She brought home report cards with all A's and an A-plus in art, every semester. Her dancing lessons and piano lessons continued on a weekly basis, and she was a star pupil in both.

1-3

When she was in the third grade, her school was planning a talent show. Mary and Ed couldn't wait to enter Katrina, since she was so talented.

Mary asked, "Katrina, what are you going to do for the talent show—dance or play the piano?"

"Neither," was the response. "I'm going to sing."

Mary drew in her breath, and asked, "Can you sing?"

Michael came to her defense. "Yes, Mom, Katrina can really sing. She sometimes sings for me when I play a song on the guitar. She's really good."

"What are you going to sing, Honey?"

"It's a surprise." Katrina then added, "I can't tell you. It would ruin the surprise."

Mary bit her lip, and then nodded.

During the next couple of weeks Mary asked her daughter more than once if she wanted to practice her song so Mary could hear it. The response was always the same. Katrina did not want to ruin the surprise. Mary was both amused and disappointed at this, but knew that she wouldn't change Katrina's mind.

On the night of the talent show, Mary and Ed, Michael, Danny and his new-found girlfriend found themselves sitting in the second row of the auditorium. Mary was nervous. She felt that Katrina should have chosen a dance number rather than sing. She really never heard Katrina sing. She and Katrina chose her outfit carefully for this night. She would appear onstage in a long dress of mint green silk. Her long auburn hair was braided loosely with a mint green ribbon to hold the braid together. Just a dab of lipstick for color, (and courage) was added.

Her family sat through eleven performances before her turn came. There were some talented dancers, a pianist who showed promise, a couple of singers who were not so talented, and a cellist who just bored everybody. When Katrina's name was announced, both Mary and Ed sat forward in their seats. Michael and Danny sat very calm and relaxed. They knew their sister would be wonderful. Her song choice was one that she sang when she thought nobody could hear her, but her big brothers always heard her. They knew she could do it. The stage went dark, and one small spotlight came on. Katrina entered that spotlight and all became quiet. Mary let out a small breath of air. The dress that Katrina had chosen had been slightly altered. The left side of the dress had been pulled up and pinned, exposing Katrina's left leg. Mary looked over at Michael. She knew that somehow, someway, he was partly responsible for that. She turned back to the stage to concentrate on her daughter. Katrina was ready. Out of her mouth came the sweetest, clearest tones that one could imagine for such a small person, as she began her song, "Start spreading the news, I'm leaving today." As her song went on, her voice got stronger, giving Mary goose bumps. The audience was mesmerized. She ended her rendition of "New York, New York" in a powerful crescendo, and the audience exploded with applause. Mary and Ed were overwhelmed with pride. Mary looked at her two sons and quickly looked away. Neither of them could hide the tears of pride running down their faces. Michael looked over at her and smiled, "See, mom? I told you she was good." Mary nodded her agreement. Katrina won first prize.

Mary thought, "Of course she did. My baby will always be in first place. She's perfect—a true gift from God. But where did she learn to sing like that?" Mary was so involved with these thoughts that she almost forgot about the dress alteration.

As soon as they got home she asked Katrina—and Michael—about the dress.

Katrina offered her explanation. "Well, it was easier to do the chorus line kicks if we tied the dress up like that." Then she demonstrated the kicks in time with the words, "It's up to you, New York, New York."

"Oh." This was all that Mary could say. Of course, it made sense.

14

When Katrina entered the fourth grade, Danny went off to his first year of college. For the first time in her young life, Katrina felt sadness. "I feel like I'm never going to see him again," she told Michael.

"You will. He'll be home for Christmas," Michael assured her. "Just think. In two more years I'll be going, too."

Losing Danny was tough enough, but the thought of Michael going away was almost too much for her to bear. "Oh please, Mike! Don't go away!"

He laughed and hugged her. "Katrina, me and Danny will never be far away from you. You know that. Whenever you need us we will be there. You'll get sick of it, but we won't go away." She couldn't imagine ever being sick of having her brothers around.

The semester went by and, sure enough, Danny came home for the holidays. All was right with the world, as far as Katrina was concerned. Danny teased her as always, and they all went ice skating together. It was Katrina's first time, so the boys were ever watchful that she didn't fall and hurt herself.

Michael had a girlfriend. She came for dinner on Christmas day. She was Michael's first girlfriend, because even though he was good-looking, he was shy around girls. Kim seemed to like him a lot. She made a big fuss over Katrina, and Katrina thought it was probably because she thought she had to. It was obvious that Michael adored his little sister.

The holidays came and went and Danny returned to school. Before he went back he gave Katrina his phone number. "If you ever need me, just call this number. I'll be there." He winked at her and jumped into his car and drove off. Katrina looked forward to summer when his classes would be over and he would be home for the summer months. She didn't have to wait that long to see him, though. Danny surprised

Katrina by coming home for her 10th birthday in April. He had a special present for her.

"Close your eyes," He taunted. "Keep them closed until I say 'open them', okay?"

"Okay," Katrina was giggling with excitement.

"Open them."

There in front of her was a white kitten with a blue ribbon around its neck.

"Happy birthday, Little Sister," he whispered in her ear. Katrina squealed with delight.

"Thank you! Thank you, Danny! It's just what I wanted! I'm going to name her Sugar!"

Katrina was beside herself with excitement. This was her first pet. She loved all animals, but especially kitties, and anything associated with them. In school, kids called her Kit-Kat because of her name, and she never minded it. She even wrote that name on her book covers. It was becoming her 'logo'.

1-5

In 1988, Katrina entered her 6th grade year. She was growing up. It was the year for the discovery of boys—and the boys were certainly looking at her. By now, her thick light auburn hair had grown down to her waist. Sometimes she wore it straight and other times she put some curls into it. She was lucky to have hair that would do whatever she wanted it to do. She still had that twinkle in her blue eyes and her smile was still sweet enough to melt the heart. Her laugh was still that melodious laugh that brought joy into a room. She was popular and well liked by both girls and boys. What worried Mary was that Katrina seemed to have no close friends. She never asked to go to a sleepover and she never asked if she could have one. No friends ever came to visit. Was there a problem? She felt that she should ask Katrina about this, but wasn't sure how to approach it. She thought maybe a birthday party. Katrina's twelfth birthday was coming up. Maybe she would like to invite the kids from her class to a party. She called Katrina into the kitchen.

"Katrina, how would you like to have a birthday party this year? Maybe invite kids from school? What do you think?" Mary waited for her daughter's response.

"N-no, mom, that's okay. I don't want a party. Just with you and Dad and Michael. Maybe Danny, if he can come home. That would be the best party ever."

Mary looked at her daughter intently. "Honey, do you have friends at school?"

"Well sure, mom, I have friends."

"Well, why don't they ever come here? Or why don't you ever go visit them? You don't ever go anywhere, or ever do anything with friends. Why?"

Katrina looked at her mother.

"Mom, it's because I have everything I need. I mean…I think….." For a moment she looked helpless, trying to find the right words. She reached into the refrigerator for a bottle of water, opened it, took a gulp, and sat down across from Mary. She didn't say anything for a minute or two, then looked into Mary's eyes and sighed.

"Mom, I could do all that stuff. Go to parties, the mall, sleepovers. I don't, because, well…..I don't want to. Friends are okay, but family is important. I would rather be with my family. Besides, some of the things that the girls want to do are stupid."

"Like what?"

"Like hide and wait for boys to go by; then follow them. Or try to make boys kiss them."

"And you don't want the boys to kiss you?'

"No."

"How about a special boy?"

"There isn't a special boy. Yet. Someday, Mom, there will be. I just know it. And when there is, I will want him to kiss me. But it will be special, just like he will be special."

Katrina stopped, suddenly embarrassed by what she had just told her mother.

"Baby, he will have to be very special, to be anywhere close to being good enough for you." Mary swallowed the lump in her throat, and added, "I love you, Katrina, so much."

Mary was suddenly very relieved. Her daughter was indeed very special. God had truly blessed her with this wonderful child.

1-6

Katrina was now going into seventh grade. Danny was beginning his senior year in college, and Michael was just starting his second year at the local university. Katrina was relieved when Michael decided to stay at home and go to the local university. She still had him around and was not sick of it yet, as he said she would be. Kim was still his girlfriend, so Katrina got used to seeing her around the house, too.

In the first week of the new school year, Katrina brought home a sealed envelope addressed to her parents. She had no idea as to the contents of the envelope, but she hoped she wasn't in trouble for something. Her mother opened the envelope, read the contents, then put it back, and said nothing.

"What is it, mom?"

"Later, Honey. We'll wait for daddy to come home. Then maybe we can talk at dinner." Mary smiled at her daughter. "Don't worry. It's nothing bad."

Katrina was relieved by that, but still....she was very curious. She knew she would have to wait until dinner, though. She hurried and finished her homework, got out what she would be wearing for school the next day, then curled up on the bed with Sugar. She must have fallen asleep because the next thing she heard was her mother calling her for dinner. The envelope! Now she would know what was in it! She jumped up off the bed, grabbed a hair tie, tied her hair back, stopped in the bathroom to rinse off her face, and then ran down the steps to the kitchen. This all took less than a minute. She kissed Ed on the cheek and sat down. Michael and Kim were there at the table, too. Food was passed around, grace was said, and everybody began eating. "What about the envelope?" she silently prayed that her mother hadn't forgotten about it. The meal was finished when her mother announced that there was dessert. She got up and helped clear the dishes from the main course, and got out the dessert plates. She spotted the lemon meringue pie......her favorite. Her mother was pouring coffee for the adults, Michael and Kim being included as adults. She got out the milk carton and poured herself a glass of milk.

"Go sit down, Honey. I'll take it from here." Mary smiled at her, reassuringly. It was then that Katrina noticed the envelope in Mary's apron pocket. What a relief! She was going to read it over dessert!

When everybody was seated with a piece of pie and a cup of coffee (milk for Katrina) in front of them, Mary said she had some news for everybody to hear.

Finally!

Mary pulled the envelope out of her pocket, opened it and began to read:

"Dear Mr. and Mrs. Kitrowski.....It is our pleasure to inform you that your daughter has been accepted into the "gifted child Program".

The letter went on to say that Katrina would have to option of taking advanced courses and that in her last year of high school her classes would be accepted as college credits. Her parents were supposed to discuss it with her, and then set up a meeting with the school guidance counselor and a couple members of the school board to discuss her curriculum. Katrina looked over at Michael. He was grinning from ear to ear. He winked at her, and she smiled. She knew he approved.

"But there's another page here," her mother continued on. "Not only is she accepted into the gifted program for scholars, but...... Katrina, Honey.....they are awarding you a scholarship for art. It's a special program for kids with artistic ability. They want you to go to the Art Institute every Saturday morning for art classes. The classes are paid for through this scholarship set up by the school. Oh, Honey...." Mary trailed off.

This time Katrina looked at Ed. He wiped his eyes, and all he could say was, "Perfect."

Mary and Katrina cleared the dishes off the table and stacked the dishwasher. Mary turned to her daughter and put her arms around her neck.

"I'm so proud of you, Baby. I feel blessed that you are my daughter."

"Now do you see why I don't want to do what other girls my age do? I want a future, a career, a place in life, but most of all, Mom, I want you and daddy, Michael and Danny to be proud of me. Remember

I told you.....I have all I need? Well, I do. I think when you have everything you need, it's possible to focus on what you want. I don't want to settle. That's what I think the girls at school are doing. They just settle for what's here and now. I don't want that. Somewhere out there in the world there is something, and someone, very special waiting for me. I can feel it. I have to focus on that. Don't worry, Mom. I'm certainly not unhappy." She smiled and hugged Mary.

"How did you get so wise?"

"It's in the genes," she smiled and winked at Mary, and then ran into the family room to watch television with Michael and Kim.

1-7

The next couple of years were full for Katrina. She still had dance classes on Wednesday evenings, piano lessons on Thursdays, and art classes at the institute on Saturdays. Her classes at school required lots of homework. The homework sometimes kept her up past eleven at night. She was maintaining an A average, but it was work. When she needed help with algebra, she got Michael to help her. Math was his strong point. She never complained about the grueling schedule she kept. She stayed focused, as she told her mother she would.

At the end of her seventh grade year, the family made the trip to watch Danny graduate and receive his Bachelor's Degree. Oh, how proud of him Katrina was! He looked so handsome! She watched as he received his diploma and her heart could have burst from pride! It was when Michael slipped his arm around her that she realized that there were tears on her cheeks. They were tears of happiness and pride. She wondered if Danny would be coming home for good. Nothing had been said so far. After the ceremony, they met up with Danny. He hugged Katrina and lifted her up off the ground.

"My baby sister is not a baby any more. Look at you! You're gorgeous!"

Katrina blushed. It was the first time either of her brothers had ever referred to her as 'gorgeous'. She was aware that she had grown up, especially in the last year. She was wearing a bra now, and had started her cycle that year. Her waist seemed to be smaller than it used to be, or maybe her hips were bigger, she wasn't sure. She began shaving her legs and underarms, but she still didn't wear makeup. She really didn't think she needed it. Her hair was still waist-long and as thick and rich-looking as ever. She was now five feet, three inches tall. Since Danny and Michael were both six feet, she knew she would probably grow taller than she was. Not too much taller, she hoped. She was thirteen now, and looking very much like a beautiful young woman.

The family went looking for a nice restaurant to have dinner. Katrina was looking forward to sitting there, all of them together, and hearing of Danny's plans for the future. She had grown up over the past four years, and she was able to keep her thoughts realistic. There was always that possibility that Danny wouldn't be coming home.

Danny got accepted into law school—in Florida. "That's so far away," she thought. She looked at Danny and saw how happy and excited he was. She had to be happy for him. She was, but she was unhappy for herself. His college had been three hours away. "Florida! That's over a thousand miles from Pennsylvania!" She felt like bawling out loud. She couldn't look at Danny any more. 'Why so far away?' She was thinking.

Michael reached over and grabbed her hand. "You still have me," he reminded her.

"Oh, Mike! I never thought that any of us would ever be separated by that many miles!"

"Me neither, Kat.....Hey, we can always go visit him. He'll be living in a vacation spot! White sand, beaches....I'm there...how about you?"

"Sure." She smiled at Michael. How she loved him! He had always been her rock. She would have to get used to the idea that Danny would be miles and miles away. Thank goodness Michael wasn't going anywhere for awhile.

Eighth grade was uneventful for Katrina. She continued all of her classes and lessons without a hitch. She was at the top of her eighth grade graduating class. Her speech was all about focusing on goals and seeing the 'big picture'. Most of the adults understood it, and most of them were impressed. Katrina's parents didn't think that any of her classmates had a clue as to what she was talking about.

1-8

Ninth grade.....she was nervous. She would be going to the high school. During the summer she tried out for the drill team, and made it. With all the years of dance lessons, she was a natural at it. She tried out because she thought it would be good exercise. That was how she looked at it....exercise...not a path to the in-crowd. That still was not her 'thing'. She still had the dance classes, the piano lessons, and the art classes. She had become quite accomplished at the piano, and her artwork was hanging in various places around the school. In addition to the drill team, she joined the school newspaper and the school choir. She had very little free time but she never complained. She stayed focused because better things were coming. She knew it.

The year flew by. Katrina turned fifteen in April. She was stunning. Every boy in school fantasized about her. Some went out of their way to sit next to her, or to talk to her, but she seemed unaware of any of this. It wasn't as though she ignored it....she really didn't see it, because she was focused on other things.

It was Michael's turn to graduate from college. The day was lovely. It was unusually warm for May in Pennsylvania. She and her parents were attending the graduation. Kim was graduating too, so the plan was to have dinner with Michael, Kim and her parents. It would be the first time meeting for the parents. Katrina wondered just how serious it was between Michael and Kim. Michael told her everything, but he never said he was in love with Kim.

She sat and watched as Michael accepted his diploma. 'Oh Mike! I love you! I'm so proud of you!' As she thought these words, she had tears in her eyes. She felt Mary's arm slip around her.

"You'll be next, Sweetie." Mary hugged her and kissed her forehead.

"I wish Danny could have been here."

"Me, too....but he has finals this week."

Mary bit her lip because she didn't want to spoil the surprise. Since Danny had taken a job near the campus, he wouldn't be able to come home for the summer. Katrina knew that. The surprise was that they were traveling to Florida to see Danny after Katrina's school year was completed.

The two families had reservations for dinner at a restaurant called The Red Bull Inn, a restaurant that had a reputation for serving a fine cuisine. Nobody was disappointed....the food was delicious. Michael and Kim had a surprise of their own up their sleeves. When they came into the restaurant together, she was sporting a diamond on the third finger of her left hand. Everyone gasped and the congratulations started. Katrina was stunned. She felt hurt that Michael hadn't shared this with her first. They shared everything else. She even knew the first time that Michael and Kim slept together. Michael told her. When Michael came over to hug her, she stiffened a little. It was the first time in her life that she felt angry with him. Michael felt her stiffen and he was puzzled and hurt. He wanted her to be happy for him. "Kat," he whispered, "what's wrong? You like Kim, don't you?"

She *did* like Kim.

"Yes, Mike, I like Kim. I'm hurt that you didn't tell me you were going to do this. You tell me everything else."

"I know I do. I tell you everything....but I did this on the spur of the moment. I hadn't planned it. I walked past the jewelry store and saw the ring. When I saw it I knew that I wanted to buy it for Kim. Kat, please be happy for me, because I'm so happy! Please?"

She looked at him and just burst out laughing. "Okay.....I'm happy if you're happy! I love you, Dork!" They both hugged and laughed some more.

1-9

Katrina bounced into the house and dropped her purse on the kitchen table. School was over until the end of August. Mary heard Katrina come in and ran down the steps and met her in the kitchen.

"Ready to go shopping?" Mary's eyes were twinkling.

"Shopping? For what?"

"Oh......shorts, swim suits, sandals.....Ready to go?"

"Mom?"

Mary couldn't hold it in any longer. "Okay...Okay....we leave for Florida in two days!"

"To visit Danny?" Katrina squealed.

"Yep."

Mary drove toward the mall. She could feel Katrina's excitement.

"We shop for clothes today, and tomorrow we get our nails done, get a pedicure, and then to a tanning session. We don't want to be ghost-white when we get there, do we? Whatever we don't find today, we can search for tomorrow. How does that sound to you?" Mary teased.

"Can I get a bikini?" Katrina stared at her mother's profile.

"We'll see." Mary answered.

They went to what seemed to Mary like a hundred stores. Katrina was thrilled with all the purchases so far, especially the bright yellow bikini that Mary agreed to, reluctantly. It was a solid taxi yellow held together by brass hoops on each side and in the back of the bra. Her brothers and her father were going to have fits! She looked so gorgeous in it, though! How could Mary resist? It covered where it needed to cover, so it was fine. Mary sighed as she thought about the future. How long would she be able to keep her daughter safe? She was so beautiful; so perfect....but so innocent.

"Mom? Which one do you think I should get?" Mary shook off her thoughts and looked at Katrina, holding up two sun dresses. One dress was a lovely shade of blue with ivory colored lace trim, and the other was a lime green with pale yellow lace trim. The styles were almost identical—strapless and princess style lines that would be flattering on anyone. The material was what Mary thought of as 'that mystery material'—sort of crinkly, sort of pleated. You could almost see through it, but not quite. Both colors suited Katrina.

"Get them both. You'll need more than one dress." Mary smiled at Katrina. "You should probably get at least two more dresses. Let's see, you got three swimsuits, five pairs of shorts, seven tops, so two more dresses should do it. Then we have to go find some sandals." Mary bought two dresses, two swimsuits, three pairs of shorts and three tops for herself. She and Katrina would both need at least two pairs of sandals.

1-10

Katrina was sitting in the window seat. This was her first flight, which made her both nervous and excited. It was her first real vacation, actually. There had been three-day weekend trips to the lake in the past, but not actually a real vacation. Her father's business had always been so demanding on him that he very rarely had time away from it. In the past two years, the business had begun to grow at a rapid rate. Ed hired an assistant who was quite competent, so Ed felt comfortable taking a well-earned vacation. He looked over at Katrina.

"Excited?" He asked her.

She had been staring at her beautifully manicured nails. She chose a French manicure like Mary's, and she thought her nails looked magnificent. She nodded her head in answer to Ed's question, and turned back to the plane's window. There were a few clouds in the sky. The clouds below the plane reminded her of snow. She looked down and watched the ground whiz by. The buildings all looked so small. While she watched the outside world go by, she listened to her parent's conversation.

"I rented two convertibles, one for us and one for Mike and Kim. So you will have to do most of the driving. I'll sit in back. I don't worry about my hair getting messed up."

This brought a giggle from Katrina. "You don't have much hair to worry about!" She laughed.

"Okay. That does it. As soon as we get back I'm going to get a rug for my head…a toupee." Katrina and Mary were both giggling. Michael and Kim were sitting across the aisle. They leaned over to ask what was so funny. Ed looked at Mary and Katrina and put his index finger to his lips. "Not a word." He looked over at Michael and Kim and said, "Nothing!" Mary and Katrina stifled the rest of their giggles.

The plane touched down in Tampa at eleven-ten in the morning. Danny would be at work so they would just claim their baggage, pick up their rental cars, and make their way to the hotel. They had reservations at a hotel on the beach. Katrina picked up on another conversation between her parents.

"One room is a suite. There are two bedrooms and a sitting room. The other room is one bedroom and a sitting room. I know Mike and Kim want to stay in the same room, but do you think it's a good idea? I mean, what will Katrina think? I think maybe Mike and I could stay in one room and you and Kat and Kim can stay in the other room. What do you think?"

Ed looked at Mary, waiting for her response.

"I don't think Mike and Kim will like that idea," Mary answered.

"Well, hell, I'm paying for the trip! Like it or not, I'm concerned about my fifteen year old daughter seeing her *unmarried* brother spending the week in a hotel with his *unmarried* girlfriend."

Katrina decided to step in. "Daddy, I know they sleep together. It doesn't matter to me, and it doesn't mean that I will go out and do the same. Michael is Michael, and Kim is Kim, and I'm *me*. It won't bother me if they stay in the same room, and besides....if you, mom and me stay together, we can do what we want to do and they can go do what they want to do. You know they probably want to go to the clubs at night. They would wake us all up when they came in late at night."

Ed looked at his daughter. His heart swelled with pride. "You may be only fifteen, but your logic is way beyond your years. You're right. So we all turn our heads the other way, right?"

"If you say so, Daddy," she answered demurely.

They checked into the hotel around one-thirty. It was too early for Danny to join them, since he worked until five, so there was plenty of time to start working on their tans before dinner. Katrina and Mary bought sun screen when they were at the tanning salon, and they both knew how important it was for everyone to use it. They quickly unpacked and put on their swim suits. Katrina put on the yellow bikini and walked into the sitting room where Michael, Kim and Mary were already sitting and waiting.

"What the hell is that?" Michael yelped.

"It's my new bikini." Katrina answered.

"You're not going to wear that in public, are you? Gees, I'll be punching people out all week!"

Mary jumped up and tapped Michael's hand. "Michael Raymond, may I see you in private a minute?"

"Yeah, sure."

Mary and Michael went into Michael and Kim's adjoining room. Mary turned on Michael and warned, "Enough, already. She looks great in that suit."

"Too great, Mom! Come on! Guys are going to be drooling!"

"Michael, guys would drool if she wore a nun's habit. Look at her! She's beautiful! And Michael....she's growing up. Give her some breathing room. By the way, Dad didn't think the sleeping arrangement was right. Kat went to bat for you. So you and Kim are together because Kat made Dad see the logic in it. Show your sister the same consideration, for God's sake. Okay?"

"Yeah, all right," Michael gave in reluctantly.

Mary started back into the adjoining room, but turned back to Michael. "Don't worry. We will *all* be watching out for her. It's okay to watch out for her. But we have to let her grow up, too."

Michael nodded.

Katrina tied her little beach wrap around her waist and the family made their way to find a spot on the beach. Michael's prophecy was accurate. Mary and Ed watched the heads turn as Katrina made her way past the sunbathers. Ed laughed out loud when he saw a young man trip over a beach chair because he was watching Katrina instead of watching where he was walking. This was going to be some vacation.... with Katrina in her bikini.

1-11

The family came in from the beach to shower and dress for dinner. Danny left a message that he would be there around five-thirty. Katrina decided to wear the green sun dress. She was drying her hair and thinking about Danny. It had been almost a year since she had seen him. How she missed him! She wouldn't have to wait too much longer—it was already after five.

Katrina was the first to the door when the knock came. She flung open the door, smiling from ear to ear. "My God, look at you! You're a vision!" Danny reached out and grabbed her to him. "I sure have missed you. Wow! You're growing up on me!"

"I sure have missed you, too. You look so handsome! And.... older...," Katrina trailed off. Danny had matured in the past year. All of his boyish features had been replaced by manly ones. He was twenty-four now.

Danny chose the restaurant. The family, sitting at a large round table, perused the menu. They had already ordered their beverages, and the waiter was distributing them at the moment. The waiter, probably a college student, was staring at Katrina like a hungry puppy. Michael was glaring at him like a junk yard dog. "Hey, Punk...the meat's in the kitchen...not out here at this table." Mary, Katrina, and Kim released "Michael" and air from their lungs in unison. The waiter turned crimson and stumbled away from the table. Danny laughed. Katrina was embarrassed, and she could tell that Kim was angry. She tapped Kim on the arm and asked, "Bathroom?"

Kim and Katrina made a bee-line for the bathroom. Once inside, Katrina looked at Kim. "You're really upset, aren't you? Are you angry with Michael or with me?"

Kim sighed. "Not you, Kat. It's not your fault. But, Damn! Just once I would like for him to be worried about someone staring at me, instead of you."

"Me, too. I mean...I don't know how you feel, but I know how I feel. It's embarrassing. You know what I worry about? What if I want the boy to look? What if I want to look back at him? That can't happen with my two pet Dobermans standing there glaring and growling." Kim broke up laughing, and then so did Katrina. "Maybe I should become a nun...or at least dress like one. What do *you* think?" Kim laughed again. "I don't think it will help. Let's go eat."

The week went by too fast. The family soaked up as much sun as they could that week. Katrina's skin was a beautiful copper color. She loved Florida. The beach, the water, the foliage, the wildlife, and the tropical temperatures suited her. She had her sketchpad with her, as she usually did, and while sitting on the beach, she sketched a little boy playing with his trucks in the sand. When the little boy and his parents got ready to leave, Katrina took the sketch over to them. They were impressed with the sketch and thanked her for it. The boy's father offered her money for it, but she turned it down. She signed it for them. Someday that may be a famous piece of art, she thought. She hoped.

The vacation was ending the following day. Katrina was saddened by this. It was more than leaving Danny…it was leaving Florida, too, that made her sad. She felt more alive here. She sat up and brushed sand off of her knees and smoothed down the bow on her swimsuit. She was wearing the black one-piece today. It won Michael's approval, she was sure, even though it was cut very low in the front and back and very high up on the thigh, showing part of her hip. He had lightened up since that first day. Katrina guessed it was because Kim told him how she felt.

"Kat? Want to go shopping for souvenirs?" Mary was standing beside her.

"Sure. Now?" Katrina stood up and grabbed her towel.

"We have about four hours, so let's hit the shops!"

Mary, Ed, and Katrina didn't even bother to change clothes. They each grabbed a tee-shirt from the room and of course, Katrina and Mary had their beach wraps around their waists. They had the time of their lives, going from shop to shop. Katrina bought a toy for Sugar, who had been left behind at a boarding kennel for pets. She also bought a pair of shell earrings for her piano teacher and a dozen shell bracelets to pass out to the drill team when practice started in July. She almost forgot something for herself, until Mary showed her the really great tee-shirts the shops had on display. She bought three of them. They hurried out of the last shop, laden with bags of items. Mary wondered how they were going to fit everything in the suitcases. As they rounded the corner of the last shop, they almost ran into a teenaged boy, who was rounding the corner at the same time. He was almost nose to nose with Katrina when his eyes got wide and he gasped and said, "There *is* a God!" Mary, Ed, and Katrina roared with laughter. They hurried back to the hotel to get ready for their parting dinner with Danny.

Tonight they had decided on a revolving restaurant on the top floor of a hotel. It was fun to sit there and watch the beach come and go while they ate. Katrina saved the blue dress with the ivory lace for tonight. She pulled her hair back and fastened it with a pearl clip and let it fall down her back. Around her neck she wore a thin chain with a single pearl attached to it, and matching pearl earrings in her ears. She looked magnificent. They were seated and handed menus to study. Katrina felt someone standing next to her. She looked up into the freckled face of a boy of about ten years old. He stared at her and asked, "Are you someone famous?" Katrina smiled sweetly at him. "Not yet," she said. He came back with, "My mom says anybody who looks like you must be famous."

"Tell your mom 'thank you' for me, but I'm really not famous. Sorry to disappoint you. Hey, if I ever become famous you can tell people you met me when I wasn't. My name is Katrina. What's yours?" She asked, as she extended her hand to shake his.

"Patrick Colin Sullivan," he answered. "Well, Patrick Colin Sullivan, now that we know each other, when one, or both of us get famous, we can say we knew each other when."

Patrick seemed satisfied and went back to his parents' table. Katrina could see him telling his parents of the whole conversation. When his family got up to leave, he turned around, waved, and yelled, "Bye, Katrina!" She waved back and blew him a kiss.

Michael sat there looking amused by this exchange.

"All ages....are there no boundaries? Kat, you are definitely a guy magnet." Katrina made a face at him and continued her meal of filet mignon, done rare.

They made an early night of it since they had to get up early to catch their flight. Danny was taking the morning off to go to the airport with them. At the airport, Katrina hugged Danny fiercely. Danny promised to come home soon and she promised to come back to Florida to see him. That promise came easily, since she loved Florida.

Katrina was quiet on the flight home. Ed leaned over Mary and asked, "Did you have a good time, Kat?"

"Yes, I did. I think that was the best week of my life. Thank you, Daddy. It was a wonderful trip." She turned back toward the window and closed her eyes. She was thinking, not sleeping. After a time, she opened her eyes and looked over at her mother.

"Mom? I think I would like to live in Florida."

Mary silently said, 'Ouch!' To Katrina she said, "You have a few years before you can decide to do that."

"Oh, I know," Katrina answered her. "But I think that's where I want to spend my life. I think Danny likes it there well enough to stay. Maybe Michael will, too. You and daddy could retire there."

Mary and Ed laughed. "You have it all figured out, do you? Let's just get through the next couple of years and see what we think then. Okay?"

"Okay. Wasn't it great seeing Danny?" Mary and Ed nodded their agreement.

1-12

It was a gloomy August day. It had been raining all morning and well into the afternoon. Katrina was sitting on her bed sketching Sugar while the cat slept on its back with its back legs extended outward. Mary had just come in from grocery shopping and was busily putting things away, when the phone rang.

"Katrina? Phone, Honey!"

Katrina picked up the receiver next to her bed. "Hello?"

"Yes, Hello, is this Katrina Kitrowski?" A man's pleasant voice asked.

"Yes, it is. Who is calling?"

"Katrina, this is John Chambers from the Art Institute. I have a buyer for a couple of your paintings that are hanging in the gallery. Are you interested in selling any of them?"

"Which ones?" Katrina asked. Her heart skipped a beat. Wouldn't that make her a real artist?

"Well, the couple is furnishing a home and an office. They liked the couple of wildlife scenes for the office, and the wife went wild over your jungle paintings. There are five paintings in all, and they are offering two thousand for them." Mr. Chambers told her.

"Dollars?"

"Yes."

"Well, wh-what do you think? I mean....I-I never did this before."

"Okay. Well, it would mean that you have made money as an artist...therefore your price for artwork would go up after this. Not to mention the exposure. Your paintings will be seen by people.... potential buyers. And that's not a bad price for the first sale."

"Okay, then. Sold! Now what?"

"Well, I'll handle the deal for you. They have agreed to pay my fee for selling them, so you will keep the whole two grand. I'll write up the bill of sale, have them sign it, then collect the money for it. You can swing by here any time the gallery is open and pick up your money. Sound good?"

"Sounds great! Thank you, Mr. Chambers!"

"Hey, don't thank me....you're the one with the talent. And, Katrina? From what I can see, you'll have a lot of buyers in the future."

Katrina hung up the phone and squealed as she ran down the steps to tell Mary.

"Oh, Honey! You're an *artist* now! Not an art student, but an *artist*! That's wonderful! I can't wait for Daddy to hear this!"

"And Danny and Mike! Where is Mike anyway?"

"He had some errands to run. He needed to buy a couple of dark suits and some black shoes for interviews. He hasn't heard anything on his application to the FBI, so he thinks he should go out looking for work. I agree. He should be home any minute now."

"Is it still too early to call Danny? I can't wait to tell him!"

"You won't have to wait to tell Michael. His car is pulling into the driveway right now."

Katrina ran out the door to greet Michael as he was getting out of his car. Mary could see them from the window. Katrina was talking animatedly and Michael was standing there grinning at her. Mary watched them hug each other, and tried to swallow the lump in her throat. She was so lucky. She had two great sons and a marvelous daughter. What more could anyone ask for?

At dinner that night Ed asked Katrina, "What are you going to do with the money, Honey?"

"I'm going to put it toward my college fund." She smiled at her father. "Isn't it great, Daddy? I actually earned money as an artist."

"It won't be the last money earned from your artwork, I'm sure of that. Hey, you may be supporting us some day." He smiled at her with a twinkle in his eye. They both laughed.

The year was 1992. Mary and Ed Kitrowski knew how fortunate they were. They knew that quite a few households were being disrupted due to problems between the parents and children. They also knew that many teens were getting involved with drugs, alcohol, cigarettes, and sex. Their little nucleus was untouched by any of these problems. Later that night, Mary turned to Ed and expressed how lucky they were. Ed turned on his side to face her.

"Honey, some of it is luck, but remember, we are good people. We never hurt anybody, nor did we ever do anything that would harm ourselves. Our kids are a product of us. Look at Danny...he got my athletic ability. Katrina got my art talent, and both Michael and Katrina got your musical ability. I remember when you played the piano at school and the organ at church. We both got good grades in school, so why shouldn't our kids be bright? We have no addictions to pass onto them, so there isn't a problem there. Our kids are good kids because we put effort into raising them. We love them, and it shows. Baby, the blessing started with us." He reached for her, and added, "Between the two of us, we have a hell of a good gene pool." He kissed his wife tenderly and passionately. Mary felt the same excitement she felt more than twenty-seven years ago when they shared their first kiss.

1-13

Katrina began her tenth-grade year. A sophomore! Her class was no longer considered "the babies" of the school. She looked forward to that.

Two major events occurred during her tenth-grade year. She turned sixteen and learned how to drive, and Danny fell in love. The latter came to light at Christmas that year. Danny called to say he was coming home for Christmas and that he was bringing somebody with him. Two days before Christmas Danny came through the door, laden with suitcases and shopping bags full of gifts. Right behind him came a five-foot-two, pretty, green-eyed blonde girl. She was small enough that she was hidden behind Danny. Katrina bounded down the steps and threw herself at Danny, wrapping her arms around his neck. Danny reciprocated with a bear hug that raised her up off the floor. Katrina spied the girl behind Danny and said, “Oh! Hi!”

The blonde girl smiled up at her and said, “You must be Katrina.”

“Yes, and you?”

Danny kept one arm around Katrina and put the other around the blonde girl. “Kat, this is Kathy. Kathy, meet Katrina.”

“Hi. I’ve heard so much about you. Danny tells me you are very talented. He says you sing, dance, play the piano, and you are an artist, as well. He has told me so much about you that I feel like I know you already.”

“Well, you’re at an advantage, because all I know about you is your name. We have two weeks to change that, right? So let’s get started. Come on into the kitchen and meet mom.”

Katrina hooked her arm through Kathy’s and steered her towards the kitchen, with Danny following. “Danny, you can put that stuff down. Take the suitcases upstairs. The gifts can go under the tree. By the way, I did the tree by myself this year.”

“Nice job, Kat. Mike didn’t help?” Danny asked.

“No. Not one ornament, light, tinsel, nothing.”

“Well, you did a fine job by yourself, then. Where is Mike?”

“Over at Kim’s. He’s helping her do her tree. Don’t say it! I know what you’re thinking!”

Danny chuckled and took the suitcases upstairs. He yelled down the steps as he was going up, “Kat, do you mind if Kathy sleeps in your room?”

“No! Not at all!” Katrina caught her mother’s eye and saw that Mary approved of that arrangement.

“Mom, this is Kathy.” She turned to Kathy and asked, “Are you Danny’s girlfriend? Fiancée? What?”

“Girlfriend, I guess you might say.” Kathy answered shyly.

“Cool” was Katrina’s response.

The Christmas holiday was a happy one. Kathy took to the family and they certainly took to her. She and Katrina were becoming friends. Katrina learned that Kathy was going to be a lawyer and that she and Danny talked about practicing law together. Kathy was originally from Kansas. She moved to Florida after her parents had died in a plane crash. She had a married sister who she rarely talked to, since the sister had four children and was always busy. Katrina learned how Kathy and Danny met. They were in a grocery store and Kathy was trying to reach for something on the top shelf when a hand went over top of her head and grabbed what she was reaching for. She turned around and there was Danny, grinning as he handed her the item. Kathy said it was love at first sight for her. Katrina thought that was so romantic, like something in a movie. Kathy told Katrina that they talked for a couple of minutes and learned that they both went to the same law school, had the same likes and dislikes, and that they were both hungry. So they quickly went through the check-out line and went to the local pub for burgers and beer, and had been dating ever since. "Wow, Kathy, that's so cool. So you love Danny?"

"Oh yeah, Kat! Big time!"

"Then welcome to the family!" Katrina hugged Kathy. "Danny wouldn't have brought you home if he didn't feel the same way."

Christmas couldn't have been better. The whole family was together, and both Danny and Michael had someone they cared for beside them. Katrina was happy for both of them. Danny and Michael gave everyone lovely gifts. Danny surprised Kathy with an engagement ring. Ed and Mary presented everyone with expensive gifts that year. Business was booming, so they could afford it. Katrina's gift sat in the garage. A white Mustang convertible sat waiting for her to discover it. She still had a few months before she could drive it, but Ed was offered such a good deal on it that he had to take it. Danny gave Katrina a warm-up suit and running shoes. The warm-up suit was blue with white trim and the shoes were white with blue trim. Together they made a stunning outfit, and looked great on Katrina. Michael's gift to Katrina was a gold herringbone chain. She loved it. Katrina bought each of her brothers two pastel shirts with coordinating ties. She knew they would need them for work. For Kim, Katrina had a pair of opal earrings, and for Kathy, a pair of pearl earrings, which she managed to purchase the day after she met her. Mary and Ed got a gift certificate to their favorite restaurant and movie tickets from Katrina. Sugar got some new toys. Everyone was in a festive mood which was only brightened even more by the wonderful Christmas meal Mary had prepared. Mary had the camera on the coffee table for anyone to pick up and take pictures. Many candid shots were taken as well as posed shots. Katrina took one of Danny and Kathy, then Michael and Kim. Kathy and Kim seemed to get along well, and Katrina liked them both.

Dinner was served early so everybody could eat then go visit friends. Before dinner Ed sent Katrina out to the garage to get a bottle of wine. The family crowded into the doorway to hear her reaction when she opened the door to the garage. Ed had rigged a large red bow on top of the Mustang and put a sign on the windshield that said, "Merry Christmas, Katrina, from Santa Claus". They all awaited her reaction. It was worth the wait.

"Oh, my God!!!! She squealed. "Mom! Dad! Oh my God!" She came running from the garage and threw her arms around both of her parents. She was crying and laughing. "Oh, thank you! Thank you! I can't believe it! My own car! Wow! Now I can't wait until I'm old enough to drive."

"Kat, I'm glad you're so excited and happy about it, but remember, we will go over all the rules before you get your license," her dad reminded her.

"Oh, I know. And, Daddy, you know you don't have to worry about me not following them." She hugged him tighter. Ed knew that was true. She was such a delightful, perfect daughter.

On Christmas evening, Katrina and Michael sat down at the piano and played Christmas carols together. Soon everyone was gathered around the piano singing along with them. Michael urged Katrina to sing "*Silent Night*" as a solo while he played. Her clear voice made the evening seem magical. When the song ended no one could speak for a minute or two. Katrina's voice was marvelous.

The week between Christmas and New Year's went by quickly. The house was filled with visitors who came by to say hello to Danny. Michael's friends came to visit and a couple of the drill team members came by to see Katrina. On New Year's Eve the Kitrowski's hosted a party for friends and relatives. Katrina and Kathy helped Mary prepare food in the kitchen. The two girls were good friends by now, and very comfortable with each other. Mary liked Kathy, too. She was glad that Danny had chosen a girl that fit into the family as well as she did. Kim came into the kitchen. She got there early so she could help out, too. The three girls sat at the table cutting and chopping, while Mary stood at the stove.

"Hey, You know what I think is cool?" Katrina asked.

"What?" the other three women asked in unison.

"All three of us have names that begin with K. We will all be K. Kitrowski at some point. My middle name is Leigh. What's yours, Kim? Kathy?"

Kathy answered first. "I was christened Katherine Ann, after both of my grandmothers."

"How nice." Mary contributed, smiling.

Kim went next. "I was christened Kimberly Louise. Kimberly... because my mom loved that name....and Louise for her sister that died when she was fifteen."

"Well, anyway....I think it's cool that we will all be K.K."

"But, Katrina, someday you may be changing yours." Mary looked at her daughter.

"Not for a long time, Mom. And, anyway, who says I have to change it? Lots of women get married and keep their names."

"That's true." Mary Agreed. "Speaking of marriage, Kim, have you and Michael thought about setting a date?"

"We're talking about it. We will let you know when we decide for sure. We don't plan on having a really big wedding. Which reminds me, Kat, I haven't asked you formally, but you will be in the wedding, won't you?" Kim's eyes were on Katrina.

"I don't know...I may be busy that day."

"Katrina!" Mary looked at her, shocked. She didn't see the wink Katrina gave Kim. Kim laughed, threw a piece of carrot at her and said "Brat!"

1-14

Katrina awoke feeling very special. It was her sixteenth birthday. Soon she would be able to drive her car. She had already applied for her permit to drive and was anxiously waiting for the permit to arrive. It would be there any day. She swung her long legs over the side of the bed and stood up. She had reached what she hoped was her adult height. She was just under five feet, six inches and very well-proportioned. She stretched, and then walked over to stand in front of the mirror to scrutinize herself. She was a little disappointed that she didn't look any older than she did yesterday, but was happy with the curves she saw on her slender frame. Her figure was, in fact, perfect. All the years of dancing kept her muscles well toned and there was very little fat on her body. She took one last look and headed for the shower.

She was wearing her favorite jeans and a pale yellow sweater, and had just finished drying and brushing her hair when Mary called her for breakfast. She decided to wear her hair down today, but put a couple of curls in it with the curling iron. Her hair was still very long. It just touched her waist. She wondered if she should get it cut—not short, but maybe get it shaped better.

"Kat? Breakfast is ready. Are you coming down?" Mary called up the stairs.

"Yeah, Mom, I'm coming!" She tied the laces on her white Nikes and jaunted down the steps. She slipped into her seat and saw an envelope leaning against her orange juice glass. She grabbed up the envelope and opened it. It was from Michael. He came up behind her and kissed her on the cheek as she was reading it. "Happy birthday, Kat," Michael said to her as he put her in a loose choke-hold from behind.

"Thanks, Mike. This card is cute." She read aloud, "I had the money to buy you a really expensive gift...." She opened the card and finished, "But I spent the money on myself." She smiled up at him. "Well, I guess you just owe me."

"Later...after work. Gotta run now." He tweaked her chin, gave his parents a weak wave, and departed.

"He's in a hurry." Katrina stated, as she watched him go out the door. He looked so handsome in his police uniform.

"Yeah, well, there are things going on at work. He wants to get there early today." Ed told her. "So happy birthday, Sweet Sixteen! Where do you want to eat dinner tonight? You pick the restaurant, okay?"

"Okay, I'll think about it and tell you after school. Thanks, Daddy. Mom? Did you sign that permission slip for me to go on the field trip next week?"

"Yes, I did, Honey. It's with your books, and happy birthday!"

"Thanks, Mom." The three of them finished their breakfast, and Katrina grabbed up her books, blew kisses to her parents, and headed toward the door.

Ed called her back. "Hey, let me drive you to school today, okay?"

"Sure," she smiled at him.

This was always a special time with her dad. It was a twenty minute ride to her school and in that time she and Ed would have conversations about things that were important to her, like her artwork, college, and where the money for college was coming from. It was during one of these conversations that she learned about Grandma Kitrowski. Ed's mother had set up trust funds for her grandchildren before she passed away. Danny and Michael had used a good portion of theirs for college, but Katrina's had grown considerably over the years. College money would not be a problem for her. On this day, the conversation was about driving a car.

"Your permit will be here soon. Are you ready to learn how to drive?"

"Yes, I am!" Ed didn't know that Michael had been letting Katrina drive his car up and down the driveway for the past three months. "I hope it gets here this week."

Ed turned and smiled at her with a mixture of pride and sadness. She was growing up. He knew that someday she would be out there on her own, a grown woman. It was going to be hard to let her go when that day came. "So is there anybody special in your life yet? Maybe somebody you want to invite to dinner tonight? You know, to celebrate your birthday with you?"

"Nope, just the family, and Kim, of course. She's family."

Ed smile again. He was relieved. No boys in her life yet. He slowed the car in front of the school, and pulled in close to the curb. Katrina leaned over and kissed his cheek. "See ya later, Daddy." She opened the door and stepped out onto the sidewalk that led to the main entrance. As Ed drove away, he heard a couple of girls calling her name.

Katrina chose the Red Lobster for dinner, since she was especially fond of seafood. After dinner they would go home so Katrina could open her birthday presents. She spied quite a few wrapped presents sitting on the dining room table, along with a birthday cake that Mary had so painstakingly decorated while Katrina was at school. Sitting at their table in the restaurant, Katrina let out a happy sigh. She knew how lucky she was to have this wonderful family. In sixteen years she had never had to worry about anything. She knew she was loved, and oh, how she loved each of them.

"Earth to Katrina! Earth to Katrina!" She quickly cleared her thoughts away. Michael was smirking at her. "Where were you just now? Were you on the beach or in outer space?"

"Sorry, I was thinking. What did I miss?"

"Nothing, yet. I was just about to make a toast to you for your sixteenth birthday, and I asked you if you wanted some ginger ale in your champagne glass."

"Oh....sure, why not?"

"Are you okay?"

"Never better. I...I was just thinking about how lucky I was.... that's all."

"We all are, Kat. You, me, and Danny lucked out to get the kind of parents we have. When you hear of all the things that other kids go through growing up, you really know how lucky you are." Michael and Katrina locked eyes and smiled at each other. She couldn't have been happier than she was at this moment.

The dinner was wonderful. Katrina ate shrimp, which was her favorite seafood.

The telephone was ringing as they filed into the house. Michael grabbed it in the middle of a ring. "Kat, it's for you!" He handed her the phone, raised his eyebrows and shrugged his shoulders simultaneously.

"Hello? Oh, thank you. How did you know it was my birthday? Oh....well, thank you for calling. Yeah, see you tomorrow....bye."

Michael was still standing there waiting for her to tell him who the caller had been. "Well? Who was it?"

"Oh, just some kid from school. He's in one of my classes. Shelley, a girl on the drill team told him it was my birthday, so he called to say 'happy birthday', that's all."

"How did he get the phone number?"

"Mike, we are listed in the phone book."

“Oh….right.” Michael let it drop, but it still bothered him that the boy called her without her permission.

Mary called for Katrina and Michael to come into the living room so Katrina could open up her presents. She opened the gifts from Mary and Ed first. These were new clothes and shoes. Kim gave her a new purse, and Katrina loved it. Michael’s gift was one he put a lot of thought into. He paid for driving lessons for her. He thought it would be wise for her to get professional training before she drove off in her Mustang.

“Mike, what a great gift! I love it!” She leaned over to Kim and whispered, “I was afraid it was going to be a gift certificate for a chastity belt.” Kim roared with laughter.

Danny sent her a hundred dollar gift certificate for her favorite store in the mall. It came in a beautiful card. He also sent a funny one. Kathy sent a card with another gift certificate. When all the gifts were opened, Ed pulled an envelope out of his breast pocket.

“Here, Kat, this came in the mail today.” He handed her the envelope with her driving permit in it. Katrina’s face lit up. “Oh, wow! Perfect!” Mary called them into the dining room for the birthday cake. And what a beautiful cake it was! Mary had spent a good part of the day decorating it, showing all of Katrina’s accomplishments. There was a piano, an artist’s easel, dancing shoes, a drill team outfit, a choir robe, and a newspaper drawn on the cake. The sixteen candles were lit, everybody sang, and Katrina blew them out. The phone rang again. This time it was Danny.

“Happy birthday, Beautiful! Sixteen! Wow! Getting up there, huh? Kathy wants to say ‘hi’.

“Katrina? Hi! Happy birthday!”

“Thanks, Kath. Oh, and thanks for the gift certificate. It will get used, I can assure you! How are you?”

“Good. Fine. Everything is great. Here, talk to your brother! Can’t wait to see you again!”

“Same here, Kath. Danny? Thank you for the cards and the gift certificate. They’re great. How is everything going?”

“Couldn’t be better, kiddo. I miss you!”

“Miss you, too. I got my driving permit today! Michael is paying for me to take driving lessons!”

"Great! You be careful, you hear? Gotta run, Kat. Love you!"

"Love you, too, Danny. Bye!"

The day was now complete. She was surrounded by everybody she loved, and those who couldn't be there, called. Again, she thought about how lucky she was.

1-15

Katrina passed her driving test! She was thrilled. Ed took the morning off so he could take her to the driving test. He watched as she drove off in Mary's Toyota with a state trooper in the passenger seat. He could see the entire course from where he stood. She was grinning ear to ear when the trooper stamped her permit. Ed let her drive home. "Remember, Kat, when you are behind the wheel, concentrate on driving. Don't play with the radio, don't watch the scenery, concentrate on the road."

"Okay, Daddy, I will. I'm just so excited! Oh, and Daddy? I can afford to pay for my part of the insurance. I've sold a few more paintings, so I can pay my portion."

"Sounds good. How many have you sold so far?"

"Well, let's see....there were the first five...then two more. I just sold three more yesterday. That's paintings. I have sold twelve black and white sketches as well. The paintings I sold yesterday? I made twenty-seven hundred dollars. I'm glad I earned a spot for my work in that gallery. I wouldn't be selling anything if I didn't have that exposure."

"That may be true, Honey. But I'll tell you what....if you didn't have that spot, I would probably buy a gallery for you, just to show your work. That's how good I think it is."

"Thanks, Daddy!" She rewarded him with a smile. She pulled into the driveway, shut the car off, unfastened her seatbelt, jumped out of the car, and ran to tell her mother that she passed.

Later that evening, Ed told Mary that she did well.

"It's a good thing I was watching, because that trooper wasn't watching anything but her. She could have turned out into the middle of the highway and did donuts, and he wouldn't have noticed. She's a good driver, though."

Mary just had to laugh. She could just imagine how the trooper must have felt sitting so close to her beautiful daughter. It probably made his day.

All through May Katrina drove her Mustang to school. True to her word, she paid her portion of the insurance, she drove carefully, and she took care of the car. She didn't neglect her studies, nor did she forget her piano lessons or dance classes, and she continued to attend the Art Institute classes on Saturday. Katrina completed her tenth grade year with a 4.0 grade point average. Summer was upon her. Although there would still be piano lessons, dance classes were off until September. There would be no classes at the Art Institute until fall classes began. Katrina toyed with the idea of getting a job for the summer. It had been a long time since she had actually had so much free time. She made a mental note to bring it up at breakfast the next morning. As it turned out, she didn't have to.

It was the first day of her summer vacation. She was sitting at the table eating breakfast with Ed, Mary and Michael when someone rang the doorbell at the front door. Ed went to open the door while the rest of the family leaned toward the door to see who would be visiting at eight in the morning. Katrina recognized the voices of one of her dance instructors and the owner of the dance studio. She gave Mary a puzzled look. The words were getting clearer as they moved toward the kitchen. "I hope we aren't disturbing you. We wanted to get here before you left for work, because we need to have parental approval." The two women were now entering the kitchen, and Michael was up and pulling out chairs for them.

"Would you ladies like some coffee?" Mary offered.

"That would be wonderful. Hello, Katrina! How are you today?" Victoria Vallas, the owner of the dance studio smiled broadly when she spoke to Katrina.

"I'm fine, Miss Vallas. How are you?" Katrina returned the pleasantry.

"I'm fine, also. I guess you're wondering why we are here, aren't you? We aren't going to keep you in suspense very long. We know your father has to get to work so we will be quick. Our school of dance has been one of the schools selected by the county government to participate in a program that introduces the arts to underprivileged children. It is a summer program. The children from poor neighborhoods must be enrolled in the program. We have been contracted to teach these children dance. We are paid, and so are our dance instructors. Katrina, you qualify as an instructor since you have danced for so many years. You would be teaching beginners the basic steps and little dance routines, and you would be paid for your effort. Are you interested, Katrina? You must have your parents' permission, of course."

Michael was the first to speak. "Where are these lessons going to be taught?"

"There has been a location chosen in the area where these children live."

"In the ghetto, you mean?"

"If that is what you call it, yes."

"Then, no, she can't."

"Mike! Miss Vallas, I am interested. Mom? Daddy? It's a noble effort! It's a chance for me to give something back. I have so much! If I could just make one child see…feel….the beauty of dance! It would be worth it!"

"W-well, how bad is the neighborhood?" Mary didn't want to say no, but she cared about her daughter's safety. She could see how much this meant to Katrina.

"It's bad, Mom. There are shootings, robberies, rapes and murders down there, and that's on a good day." Michael's jaw was clenched. "Mom, you can't be seriously considering letting her do this!"

"There will be police protection. We have already established that we will have a policeman on the premises while we are there." Miss Vallas assured him.

"Well, that seems…safe, Mike, don't you think?" Mary looked to her youngest son. "It's a good opportunity for Katrina. I care about her safety, but, Mike; honestly, she should get a look at the other side of the world."

"The classes are on Saturday, between the hours of ten and three." Victoria Vallas offered. "That's all daylight hours."

Michael sighed. "Well, I'll tell you what. If my parents are going to let her do this, then there is one more safety feature I want to add.

Saturday is my day off. I will be there, too. Agreed? Mom, Dad, Kat? Miss Vallas?"

Victoria Vallas smiled at him. How noble he was that he cared that much for his sister's safety. "We would be honored to have your presence."

Ed spoke up for the first time since the women entered the room. "You ladies are asking my permission to take one of my most prized 'treasures' into an unsafe area. If I agree to this and something happens, I will never forgive myself."

"Daddy, please!"

"Wait, Sweetheart. Just answer me this one question....who else from the dance school will be there?"

"Miss Vallas spoke immediately. "I will be there, Marla here, will be there, and so will my daughter. We have one other student teacher besides Katrina. That's Sarah Fenton. You know her, right, Katrina?" Katrina nodded.

"Okay. So you will have your own child there as well, huh? Well, Mary, what do you think?"

"Well, if Michael goes, I'll feel better about it. I know he won't let anything happen to her. I think it would be good experience for Kat. It's actually a summer job."

Katrina loved her mother, but she especially loved her more at that moment. Her mom understood.

"So is it a 'yes'? Miss Vallas asked.

"Yes!" came the four voices in unison.

"Good. Katrina, we start this Saturday. Be there at this address, at nine-thirty." She handed Katrina a card with the address written on the back. "See you then. Oh, and did I mention that you will be making ten dollars an hour?" The surprised looks on all of the Kitrowski faces gave her much satisfaction, as she left the house.

Michael and Ed scrambled to get to work. Ed stopped to kiss Mary and Katrina on the check, and Michael stopped to whisper in Katrina's ear, "You're not driving there either. No arguments."

1-16

Saturday morning, Michael and Katrina left in Michael's car. Michael knew exactly where the place was. Since he had been working for the city as a detective, he had learned many of the addresses in the poor neighborhoods. Katrina sat beside him watching the scenery change from lovely to horrific as they got near the center where she would be teaching. "It's right up here around the corner," Michael told her. He made the left and pulled to the curb. Katrina saw Miss Vallas' car parked in front of Michael's. She was already inside. Michael got out, put his 'police' placard in the window, and ran around to open her door.

"Why that?" Katrina asked him, pointing to the placard.

"Because they generally won't try to steal a police car." He answered her.

"You're incorrigible!" She retorted.

"Nice word. I'm being honest, though." He looked down the street, appeared to be satisfied, and held the door open for her. Thank goodness she didn't see the two extra police cars, one a K-9, he had posted there for the day.

The center was buzzing with excitement. "There must be a hundred kids here." Michael whispered to Katrina.

"Actually a hundred and two!" Miss Vallas' came from behind him. "Katrina, you will start a tap class for beginners. They are getting their shoes, leotards and tights right now. After the tap, you will have a jazz class for a little older group, okay? Michael, you may sit anywhere you like."

"Thanks."

Katrina found the room that was designated for her class. She went there to look it over and wait for her class to show up, fully dressed. Michael watched where she went and placed himself just outside of that room. He could see inside the room from his angle, and that satisfied him.

Soon Katrina's class began filling up. She checked the roster and discovered that she would have twelve children to teach. As they came in she checked off their names. When all had arrived she found that she had quite a mix of children. Two Caucasian girls, two Asian girls, five

African American girls, two Hispanic girls, and one African American boy made up the class. They were all within the age range of six to eight. Katrina began by telling them to line up. They complied.

"Okay. We are going to learn to dance. Does everybody have their tap shoes on?" The replies were unanimous.

"So let's start! Do as I do. Right tap!" She extended her right foot, pointing her toe downward. "Left tap!" She extended her left foot in the same fashion. "Now do what I do! Right foot....shuffle, step. Left foot...shuffle, step. Now, let's put it together. Tap! Tap! Right, shuffle step, left shuffle step! Good! You are all dancing! Now let's do another one. Right foot, shuffle ball-change...left foot....shuffle ball-change. One more time! Now let's put it together with the other steps!"

Michael sat there amused. Katrina was good with these kids. She was a natural! He sat through the entire hour class and watched, fascinated. His sister was a dance teacher, and a good one at that! These children were learning from her and listening to her every word. She had total command of the class! It was amazing! The class was almost over and Katrina was lining the children up. "Now we are going to dance out to where you parents are sitting. Get ready! Remember... tap, tap, right shuffle, step, left shuffle, step....two shuffle ball-changes, two shuffle hops, then march, march, march! Then we do it all over again until we get out there to the middle of the room, okay? Ready? Here we go!"

She led them out and almost every child was in step and remembered the order of the steps. "Let's give the little dancers a hand!" She began applauding them as did the parents. "Same time next week, right?" Twelve little voices yelled, "Yeah!" and then disbursed. One lady stopped beside Katrina and said, "You are marvelous."

"Thank you!" Katrina was both surprised and delighted.

"Get ready for the jazz class! All those in the jazz class please come into this room!" Katrina pointed toward the room she had just left. Michael watched this class with interest. These girls were a little older. There were only eight in this class, seven of which were African American. Katrina put on music and danced a routine for the girls. They were in awe of her. So was Michael. Wow! She could dance! He heard her telling the girls that they too, would dance like that if they practiced hard. He watched her teach the steps and moves to the girls. They were eager to mimic her every move. When the class was over she had them line up and dance their way out to their parents as she had with the tap class. Again, she applauded them and encouraged the parents to applaud as well. As the girls were heading toward their parents, one of them ran up to Katrina and threw arms around her. "I love you," she said, and then ran to greet her parents. Katrina stood there smiling after her. Michael came up beside her.

"You're pretty special, do you know that? I'm awed!" She smiled at him, and said "Let's see if I'm done for today."

She caught up with Miss Vallas. Victoria told her that she would have the ten o'clock tap class she taught today, and that the jazz class she had would be at noon every week. That would be her two classes, and she was free to go after them. She and Michael gathered up her things and they left. Michael opened her door, and then came around to his side of the car and got in.

"Lunch? I mean somewhere out of this neighborhood, okay?"

"Okay, I'm starving!"

"I'll bet! You put a lot into that, don't you? I mean, it's a regular workout, isn't it?"

"Yeah, pretty much. Why do you think I stay so thin? I think if I quit dancing I could weigh two hundred pounds."

"Well then at least I wouldn't have to worry about guys taking advantage of you. Ever think about quitting?"

"No.....okay, Mike, I get it. Ha-ha!"

They ate lunch and got home around two. Katrina ran up to take a shower and Michael found his parents in the den. They looked up when he walked in. "How were the dance classes?" They asked in unison.

"Mom, Dad, do you two have any idea how good Katrina is? Not just with the dancing...I mean she's a spectacular dancer, but...with teaching kids. She had two classes today. There were twelve in one class and she taught them almost an entire dance routine. She's great with kids and she's a good teacher. They all looked up to her. I was awe struck. I know I objected to the whole thing, but I can see where she can make a difference in someone's life. Wow! I don't mind going with her every week either. She's wonderful to watch. Maybe you guys should go at least once to see her teach these kids. Think about it."

Mary and Ed looked at each other. "We will, Mike. We love watching her do anything she does."

1-17

The dance program lasted twelve weeks, with the last week planned as a recital for the families of the participating children. Mary and Ed showed up on week ten of the classes, just to watch Katrina. They spotted Michael before they saw Katrina. Admiration was written all over his face as he watched her. They moved quickly toward him and sat down. All three of them watched while she taught the class. Mary and Ed were impressed. "She's something, isn't she, Mom?" Michael whispered in Mary's ear.

"Yes, Michael, she's something." Mary was smiling as she watched Katrina work with the children. She glanced at Ed and saw the pride shining in his eyes. She was very glad that they had agreed to let Katrina do this.

Week twelve had arrived. Katrina chose a sleeveless, black chiffon high-necked dress with fitted bodice. The skirt was pleated and just touched the top of her knees. She looked elegant. She had worked for three weeks designing and creating a simple addition to the leotards and tights the children in the tap class could wear for their dance number, since costumes were not in the program's budget. She bought twelve red, white, and blue cellophane top hats and red, white, and blue material to make banners for the children to wear draped from the shoulder across the chest to the waist. The additions were to be a surprise for the children on the day of the recital. The surprise went over well. The children were thrilled to have something different to wear when they appeared on stage. She had her group ready to go and would lead them out on cue. They would start with the march she taught them, and then do the dance routine. The number would end with the ending pose she taught them. She was as excited as they were! They had worked so hard and wanted to show off their ability to dance. Katrina searched the audience and saw many of the children's parents patiently waiting for the show to begin. Her own parents were there, along with Michael and Kim. She knew her family always supported her, and she was glad to see the other families supporting their children.

Katrina caught her cue. She made sure the class was ready, and then started out onto the stage. The children were wonderful! The dance went very well, with nobody missing a step. How proud of them she was! When the number was finished, the applause was loud. She saw a couple of the mothers wiping their eyes. This program was a success! Her jazz class did equally well. When that number was over she went out into the audience and sat with her family until the show was over. She was called up on stage to receive recognition and credit for her teaching at the end of the show. Her tap class and jazz class both presented her with bouquets of flowers. Now it was Katrina's turn to wipe her eyes. Every ounce of work that she had put into this program paid off at this moment. She knew that she had really given something back to society. She had so much! What a pleasure to share with others who had so little. She looked at the sea of happy, smiling faces. The children's smiles were because they accomplished something wonderful, and the parents smiled because they were delighted at seeing their children succeed at something so beautiful. She knew that she would always remember this day.

1-18

School started for Katrina the Wednesday after the recital. Her junior year was going to be another busy one. She still continued the piano lessons and the dance classes, but now she was considered a student teacher at the dance studio, so would be paid a small wage for teaching classes. There would be no charge for her ongoing classes. Once again she would be attending the Art Institute on Saturdays. Friday nights were reserved for football games since she was on the drill team. She attended school newspaper meetings and was involved in the monthly publishing of the paper. Though none had been scheduled yet, there would be choir practices for upcoming concerts. Yes, this would be a very busy year for Katrina. She looked at her class schedule with some apprehension. Calculus! Along with Calculus she had been given English, History, fourth-year Spanish, and Physical Education.

This was a full schedule that would require a lot of effort. "Oh well," she thought, "I will just have to deal with it. Kat, you can do anything you put your mind to...remember that." So began her school year.

She was looking forward to the Art Institute classes this term. They would consist of photography, technique and darkroom, and also a class in cartooning. She bought herself a 35mm camera and a few lenses, along with other equipment and film. She thought it might be fun to learn how to take really good photographs.

It was the first Friday night football game. Katrina, dressed in her drill team uniform, was eating an early dinner with Mary and Ed. "What time do you have to be there?" Ed asked.

"Seven. Are you two going to the game?"

"Yes, we are. Wouldn't miss it. I hear the drill team is pretty good." Ed's eyes were twinkling as he said it. "I hear Mike's car. Is he going"?

Michael came crashing into the kitchen holding a white envelope in his hand. He had a grin that exposed all of his white teeth. "Hey! Look! I'm in!! I'M IN!!"

"What are you talking about?" They all stared at him, but it was Katrina who asked the question.

"I made it! I'm going to be an FBI agent! Read it! I will be going for training....oh, here, you read it."

"Does Kim know, Mike?" Katrina wanted to know.

"Yeah, I just came from there. We are getting married December the eleventh, by the way. We decided that when I got this letter."

"You were supposed to wait for me to get here before you told them!" Kim was out of breath when she got into the kitchen.

"Sorry, Honey! I guess I was just so excited. Go ahead, you tell them some details."

Kim looked around at her soon-to-be family. "Well, we are getting married on December eleventh. Mike will be back from his first training by then. We will have a small wedding, with just Kat and my sisters as bridesmaids. My sister Katie will be the maid of honor, and Karin and Kat will be the bridesmaids. There isn't much time so I thought my mom, my sisters and I could come over tomorrow morning and put the thing together. What do you think?" Kim looked toward Mary with anticipation.

"Sounds good! Now we have to get going or Kat's going to be late. Are you and Mike going to the game?"

"Yeah, Mom, I wouldn't miss it!" Michael yelled from the top of the stairs. "I hear the drill team is pretty good!"

"That one's already been used, Mike!" Katrina yelled back.

The family all went in one car, with Michael driving, Kim in front beside him, and Mary, Ed and Katrina in the back seat. Katrina was unusually quiet. Michael was leaving. Danny was in Florida and Michael was leaving. An FBI agent! Wasn't that dangerous? Katrina knew how badly Michael wanted to work for the FBI, but she was frightened for him. What if something happened to him? She wondered how Kim felt about it. She would ask her about it when they were alone.

The car stopped near the area where the game participants waited and Katrina got out, running to catch up with the rest of the drill team. She was quickly surrounded by the other members, all of which were talking and laughing at once.

"She certainly stands out among them, doesn't she? Or do I just think so because she's my daughter?" Ed asked his wife.

"Well, I think so, but she's my daughter, too." Mary smiled at Ed. "I think she's the prettiest one, but I may be biased."

"Homecoming is in a few weeks. Has she said anything about going to the homecoming dance? She's on the drill team, and that's part of football." Ed looked to Mary for a response.

"No, she hasn't said a word."

"Mom, are you going to let her go?" Michael asked, as he searched Mary's face in the rear view mirror.

"No, Mike, I thought I would tie her up in the basement to keep her home."

"Very funny. Hey, I can't help that I'm overly protective of her. Danny and I made a pact that we would always watch out for her." Michael got quiet as he concentrated on parking the car.

"Mike," Mary began, "I know you love her and want to protect her, but she's sixteen, Mike! She has never had a date. I think it's time she did. I trust that she has enough sense to choose a decent boy to go out with, especially to homecoming. You have to back off a little."

"Mom, she is so innocent! She doesn't know what guys are like! Damnit! I won't be here for homecoming either!"

"Well, don't jump the gun. She hasn't said anything, so I guess she hasn't been asked."

"I hope not." Michael muttered.

The game was exciting. Their school was victorious by two touchdowns. The family joined quite a few of the other spectators at a local hangout called Bear's Place. It was here that Michael's hopes were dashed. Many of the players on the football team and their families were there for after-game burgers and drinks. Bear served beer, wine, wine coolers, and soft drinks only. Ed and Michael ordered draft beer and Mary, Kim and Katrina ordered diet soft drinks. There was plenty of laughter to go around. The win had put everybody in good spirits. At one of the tables near theirs, the Parks family sat. Sean Parks played on the team as a receiver. Many of the girls in school had a crush on him, since he was very good looking. He stood about six feet tall, had broad shoulders and a trim waist. His dark hair was slightly curled just above his collar and framed his face accentuating his dark blue eyes. He was in a couple of Katrina's classes, so they knew each other. He waved at her and she smiled and waved back. He excused himself from his table and got up and walked over to the Kitrowski table. "Hi, Katrina!" He smiled down at her.

"Hi, Sean! Good game!"

"Yep! Did you see my T-D?"

"Yeah, I did. Nice going!" This made Sean's smile broaden, showing even, white teeth.

"Hey, Katrina, I was wondering....I mean....the homecoming game is in a few weeks. Uh....I mean...would you like to go to the homecoming dance with me?" Sean stammered.

Mary noticed that he was blushing. Unbeknownst to anyone else, she had her sneaker on top of Michael's foot, and was digging her heal into him. Michael knew, of course. He felt the pressure. He kept silent.

Katrina looked at Mary and caught the signal that it was okay with her. She quickly looked at her father, and saw the hint of a smile and a quick wink, that only Katrina saw. "Yeah, sure, Sean, I'd love to." She looked up at him and smiled.

Sean's broad smile turned into a smile akin to a toothpaste ad. "Great! I have to get back to my parents, but it's a date...right?"

"Right." Katrina confirmed.

"He's cute, Kat!" Kim said with a lilt. "And I think it's sweet that he asked you in front of your family like that. That took some courage."

Michael got up from the table and started walking toward the table where Sean and his family were sitting.

"Mike! Mom, what's he doing?"

"I don't know. I better not have to grab him back here!"

Katrina and Mary watched Mike extend his hand to Sean's father, who smiled broadly and stood up. He pumped Mike's hand and clapped him lightly on the back.

"I think he knows him, Kat. I hope that's what it's all about."

Michael sat down at the Parks' table and talked animatedly with Mr. Parks. They were both laughing over something. Mary and Katrina gave a sigh of relief, and went back to enjoying the evening. Michael sauntered over after a few more minutes and sat back down with his family.

"Do you know Mr. Parks, Mike?" Katrina wanted to know.

"It's Officer Parks. He's a uniform."

"Oh....I didn't know Sean's dad was a cop."

"Yeah, well, he heard today that I will be leaving the force, so he was congratulating me. He's a good guy. I like him. Oh, he always said that the reason they let me wear a suit is because my name wouldn't fit on the name tag. He was one of the few guys who didn't get all pissed off when I made detective so soon after joining the force. I worked the required time in uniform, but having a college background helped me. Also, I passed the test with a really high score. Parks never resented me for it." Michael concentrated on his beer again.

"Mom, I don't think that was all of it."

"I'll try to find out, Honey. I hope he didn't intimidate Sean."

"....or threaten him." Katrina added.

1-19

Kim, her mother and sisters arrived early on Saturday morning. Mary had fresh coffee and Danish ready when they got there. It seemed to be utter chaos to Ed when he entered the kitchen. "Since you females have taken over the kitchen, do you mind if I take my son out for breakfast?" He looked around at the women who were getting ready to settle into the kitchen, completely taking it over.

"I think that's a wonderful idea, Honey." Mary smiled at Ed. "Go ahead, and take your time! All this may take awhile."

Katrina and Kim were pouring mugs of coffee and setting pastries on plates for the center of the table. Meg, Kim's mother sat at the head of the table. "Let's get started. We have a lot to cover in so little time."

Kim was full of excitement as she told the girls they would be dressed in Christmas colored dresses. Katie would wear red and Katrina and Karin would wear green.

"It sounds wonderful, Kim!" Katrina's face was radiated with a smile.

"Thanks, Kat. Now, we have the chapel at the church reserved. It holds about fifty to seventy-five people, so we have to work on the guest list. Michael rented the F.O.P. hall for that night, so that's taken care of. We have to find a caterer, a DJ, and invitations. Girls, I want to go shopping for dresses, like now....today or tomorrow. Is that okay?"

Everybody nodded an agreement.

"Kat, you didn't go to classes today."

"Next week....class begins next week."

"That's good, because we have a lot to do this weekend. Now let's start on the guest list." Kim handed everyone a small tablet to write down the names of people they thought should be invited.

"Don't forget Danny and Kathy," Katrina reminded anyone who might have heard her.

"Kat, don't worry. Michael called Danny yesterday. They are getting their plane reservations today." This news made Katrina smile.

The day was a flurry of activity as the wedding plans were formulated. The girls made plans to go shopping for dresses on Sunday. There was no time to order dresses that might require alterations. They were going to have to rely on one of the better department stores or small bridal shops to carry dresses nice enough for a small wedding. The first priority was to shop for Kim's wedding gown. Both Meg and Mary were feeling a little nostalgic and looking forward to this shopping trip.

"Mike will take care of the flowers and the tuxedos." Kim affirmed. "There will be three, plus Mike's, then one for each of our dads."

"Kim, do you know who the groomsmen are?" Katrina asked as she began clearing the table.

"Well, the best man will be Danny, I know that. Mark is Mike's best friend. I'm sure he asked him. I don't know who the third one will be. Why?"

"Oh just curious."

"You're worried about who your partner will be…admit it." Kim was laughing.

"No, not at all…just wondered." Katrina defended herself, laughing.

"What do you think about the flowers, Kat? You're the artist, so give me some ideas."

Without hesitation, Katrina said, "Holly…..white carnations with sprigs of holly in the bouquet. Yours can be red and white roses with holly. Some tinsel, and a candy cane, in the bouquets might be a nice touch. What do you think?"

"I think I know why I asked you! That sounds so perfect!" Kim hugged her future sister-in-law. "Thanks, Kat!"

* * *

Mary and Katrina left early on Sunday. They were going to Kim's house for morning coffee before they all left for the mall. The McKean family lived in a ranch house on a lovely street not too far from where the Kitrowski family lived. Katrina had been there with Michael on a couple of occasions, but this was Mary's first visit. Her first thought was that the house was lovely and very well maintained. Bill McKean, Kim's father was very handy around the house, she knew. By trade he was a carpenter. He was the one who answered the door when they rang the bell.

"Come on in!" He boomed. Mary and Katrina liked him. He was a big man with a heart of gold, always laughing and hugging when he could get away with it. At this moment he was hugging Katrina. "Hi,

Princess....Beautiful as ever, I see! Coffee's ready......made it myself. I make the best coffee in the house. They are all down the hall getting dressed. I tell ya, you have no idea what it is like living with all these women! I had to put a bathroom in the basement just so I would have one. There are three on this floor and it's not enough. Here, sit down. I'll pour the coffee. Katrina, do you drink coffee yet?"

"Sometimes I do." Katrina answered him, smiling.

"Probably not good for you, but hell, I guess you have to have one vice, at least."

Mary started to open her mouth to protest this, but changed her mind. She knew he meant no harm.

Katrina and Mary sat down and Bill put coffee cups of steaming, hot coffee in front of them. "Cream and sugar is on the table." He needlessly pointed out.

Meg was the first into the kitchen. "Sorry, we're running behind schedule.....so many of us to be ready at the same time." Meg apologized.

"It's okay. I guess I never really realized how lucky I am that I have no sisters. I always get a bathroom to myself." She said this to Meg, but looked at Bill to get his reaction.

He chuckled and winked at her.

It was still early when they got to the mall. Many of the stores hadn't opened yet, so they walked around looking into the windows, trying to see what the stores had to offer. Kim let out a little shriek.

"There! Those dresses are exactly what I had in mind! Look, they come in both red and green. How perfect!"

They were all looking into the window at the dresses that Kim pointed out. They were beautiful soft velvet gowns, in both green and red. The dresses were strapless and had a short nylon cape that dropped from across the back of the shoulder blades to just past the waist. Around the bottom of the cape was a row of white faux fur trim. The dresses themselves just dropped to the floor from the bodice. They were both elegant and Christmas-like.

"Let's hope they have everybody's sizes in the right colors." Kim crossed her fingers.

They were in luck. Katie tried on the one in red in her size and it was lovely on her. She and Kim both had shiny black hair and looked very much alike. Karin got the lighter hair, which was brown with lots of red highlights. She looked more like Bill while the older girls resembled Meg. Karin and Katrina tried on the green velvet dresses in their sizes. They looked lovely in them. Kim was delighted.

"We'll take them! They are exactly what I want you to wear, and they look great on all of you!" Kim was breathless with joy and excitement. "Now let's hope we have the same kind of luck with my dress."

They did. Kim found a dress that couldn't have been more right if it had been made for her. It was velvet, too. The material was a thin, soft, white velvet. The style was a simple princess cut with a beautiful, small satin and velvet train that was detachable. This dress was also strapless, with pearls trimming the bosom and bodice, and around the bottom of the skirt. The saleslady recommended a veil for her. It was a pearl crown that sat high on her head and had nylon layers coming from it. The very bottom layer had a white satin strip sewn around the end of it. It went with the dress perfectly. Kim was delighted.

"Shoes! We need shoes!" She was practically jumping up and down.

"But lunch first." Mary interjected. "My treat."

"You're on!" Kim countered. "Where do you want to eat?"

They settled into a large booth in one of the mall restaurants. Katrina was starving. She ordered a double cheeseburger and fries.

"You better be able to fit into your dress!" Kim threatened her. "Eating like that could change your dress size!"

"Don't worry; I'll dance it off in dance class this week. And besides, Michael would like it if I got fat. He says he wouldn't have to worry about me as much."

"Oh, Katrina, speaking of which....you're on the drill team, right?" Kim's sister, Karin wanted to know.

"Yes." She answered.

"So you know Allison Kinsey, right?"

"Yes, of course," Katrina answered.

"I hear she's pregnant. The girl who lives next door to us told me. She says it's all over school."

"I don't know anything about it." Katrina concentrated on her food. She took a big bite of her burger and chewed.

The day of shopping came to an end. It was a complete success. Katrina and Mary would work on the guest list so Michael could take it over to Kim's later that night. Everything was coming together perfectly. It would be a beautiful wedding even if it was put together on short notice.

Mary and Katrina sat at the kitchen table writing names and addresses for the invitations. Mary looked over at Katrina and asked, "Do you think there is any truth to that rumor about Allison?"

"I don't think, I *know*. It's not a rumor. She is pregnant, and she is starting to show. She will not be able to stay on the drill team much longer. Her uniform is getting way too tight."

"What will she do?" Mary wanted to know.

"I don't know, Mom. How stupid, though! Why would you ruin your life that way? She is actually happy about it. She's nuts! Her boyfriend is just as goofy. He's all proud of himself....they're both idiots! But anyway, I didn't let on that I knew anything about it to Karin, because I don't like to gossip. It's not her business."

"Good girl! Who lives next door to the McKeans?"

"I think Jessica Woods does. She has nothing going for herself, so she has to talk about somebody else. I feel sorry for people like that." Katrina added.

Mary just smiled. Her daughter was something else.

Michael was getting ready to leave for Kim's house, so they quickly finished their list. He was taking her out to dinner at one of the finest restaurants in the area, since he would be leaving for training in Georgia in the morning. Katrina was skipping the first two classes so she could see him off. The house was sure going to be empty without him.

1-20

Katrina hugged Michael at the airport. The Kitrowski's, as well as Kim, were there to see him off. Katrina bit her lip to keep from crying in front of him. She was happy he was getting the job he always wanted. She watched for a moment as he and Kim clung to each other, then she had to turn away. Biting her lip wasn't working. They watched him disappear through the door before they left the airport. Kim ran up and put her arm around Katrina and they were both crying. Michael had been there for both of them for so long! Now he was gone. He would be gone for almost three months, come home for the wedding, and then go for more training. Katrina glanced back at her parents. Mary and Ed were holding hands and talking as they walked out of the airport. She didn't feel like it, but she had to get to school. She kissed her parents' cheeks and drove off toward the school.

Katrina slipped into her second-period class and slid into the closest seat. Sean Parks was in that class. He noticed that she had been crying, so he waited for her when the bell rang.

"Katrina? Hey, are you okay?" He fell into step beside her on the way to the third-period class. "What's wrong?"

"Oh, Sean, hi....I'm okay. My brother left for Georgia this morning. He's going to be an FBI agent."

"Oh yeah, my dad told me. I guess you're going to miss him?"

"Yeah, I'll miss him a lot. He's always been there for me, and..." Katrina's voice began to falter. "I don't know what I'm going to do without him." Tears were falling on her cheeks. Damn! She didn't want to cry...not in front of Sean, or anyone, for that matter.

Sean put his arm around her shoulders, and pulled her to him. "Hey, that's rough. When will he be back?"

"For his wedding...that's in December." Katrina was wiping her eyes with a tissue.

"Well, that's not too far off. He's lucky he has a sister that loves him like you do, you know that?"

"Well, I've been lucky, too. Both of my brothers love me and watch out for me. They always have. Michael promised me that he and Danny would never be farther than a phone call away from me...ever."

"That's really great. You stopped crying, too. That's even better. Can I call you tonight? I want to talk to you."

"Sure. I guess...if you want." She answered.

"I want. Talk to you later." He smiled at her and disappeared into his next classroom. She walked on down the hall to her next class. There were no more tears the rest of the day.

Katrina and Mary were clearing the table and stacking the dishwasher when the phone rang. Katrina lifted it off the hook.

"Hello?" She greeted.

"Hi. Katrina?" It was Sean.

"Hi, Sean. How was the rest of your day?" She asked him.

"Good. Yours?"

"It was okay." She answered.

Mary made a pretense of being busy. She didn't want to eavesdrop, but this was the first time a potential suitor had called the house.

"Katrina, I was wondering....I have to whisper....sorry. Uh, my parents' twenty-fifth wedding anniversary is next week. On Saturday, my aunts are having a surprise party for them in the Holiday Inn banquet room. They say I can take somebody....I would like to take you. Would you go with me? If you're not busy, that is...."

Katrina let what he was asking sink in. She said nothing.

"Hello?" He prompted. "Are you still there?"

"Yes, Sean, I'm here. No, I'm not busy....and yes, I'd love to go with you. I think it's sweet of you to ask me." She could see Mary doing a silly little dance from the corner of her eye, and she almost laughed into the phone.

"You will?" He sounded surprised.

"Yes, I will." She answered him.

"Wow! That's great! Oh, remember...it's a surprise." His voice got lower. "Just a minute, okay?"

Katrina held the receiver to her ear and waited.

"Okay. I had to go down the hall to my room so they wouldn't hear me. My aunts are so excited about this party. My parents think they are going to dinner with my aunt and uncle. They will be surprised when they enter what they think is the restaurant, but is really a private banquet room. All the guests have to be there at six-thirty. Is that a problem for you?"

"No, not really. I have art classes in the morning but I'm home by one. I get all my homework done, and then I'm free for the rest of the weekend."

"Oh, cool. Speaking of which, I have to start my homework for tomorrow. See you in school tomorrow?"

"Sure. Bye, now."

"G'night, Katrina," He said as he hung up.

She laid the receiver back in its cradle. When she turned she almost stepped on Mary.

"Well? Come on! Don't keep me in suspense!"

Katrina gave one of her melodious laughs. "He invited me to his parents' anniversary party. That's all."

"Oh wow! That's huge! What are you going to wear? I guess you need a gift, too, right?"

"Don't know what I will wear, and yes, I will need a gift, I guess. What do you buy for a twenty-fifth anniversary?"

"Something silver. How about a silver picture frame?"

"That sounds nice. Hey, has Kim called?" Katrina trotted up the stairs to her room to check out her closet, and then to do her homework.

1-21

It was almost time for Sean to pick her up. Katrina chose a royal blue silk jumpsuit to wear to the party. She was just finishing her hair, and all she had to do was step into the jumpsuit and she was ready to go. Her hair was pulled back and fastened with a silver clip. She used a curling iron to put four or five long curls into it, and then left the rest of it straight.

Sean pulled up into the driveway. He was nervous. He had ridden past her house many times, but he had forgotten how nice it was. It was a much bigger house than his, and just....nicer. It looked like they had a gardener or a personal landscaper. Katrina didn't act snooty or anything, but it was obvious that her family had some money. He hoped it didn't matter to her that his family didn't.

As she was slipping into the jumpsuit she heard the doorbell. She stopped in front of her mirror to check out the finished product, and as an afterthought, picked up a bottle of perfume and sprayed some on. Ed was calling her name as she got to the landing.

She heard her dad talking to Sean, when she got to the bottom of the steps.

"Now you will drive safely, won't you?" Ed was asking Sean.

"Yes, Sir." Sean countered.

"No alcohol, right?"

“No, Sir. I don’t drink or smoke, Sir, or do drugs. I play football. We will be with my parents, anyway.” Sean seemed so nervous that Katrina almost laughed.

“Oh, very good,” was Ed’s response. “Have fun.”

Katrina picked up the beautifully wrapped silver picture frame with a card attached, and reached for her coat. Sean came around behind her and took the coat from her hands and held it for her to put her arms into the sleeves. “What’s this?” He asked, pointing to the wrapped package.

“It’s a silver picture frame. Silver is what you give someone for their twenty-fifth anniversary. You knew that, right?”

“No, but you didn’t have to get them anything. I didn’t expect you to.”

Mary heard Sean as she came into the living room. “A gift is appropriate, Sean. Katrina would have felt bad if she didn’t have anything to give them for their anniversary.”

Katrina was grateful to Mary. For a minute, she thought she had committed a faux pas. Sean just shrugged his shoulders in agreement.

Sean made an attempt to hide his car in the parking lot of the Holiday Inn. He didn’t want his parents to recognize it. When he was satisfied that they wouldn’t see it, they got out and walked into the banquet room. Many people had arrived already. Sean introduced Katrina to his relatives as they greeted him. “Some of these people I don’t know. I think they work with my dad.” Katrina knew his dad was a police officer, so she wondered if any of them knew Michael.

At a few minutes to seven, they were instructed to form a semi-circle around the door, and yell ‘surprise’ when Sean’s parents came into the door. Sean stood next to Katrina and lightly put his arm around her waist. She noticed a couple of his aunts looking in their direction, smiling approval at them.

The Parks’ were quite surprised by the party, and the party itself was lots of fun. A buffet table, laden with food, had been set up and there was a bartender serving drinks at an open bar. A disc jockey had been hired for the evening and many people were dancing to the music he was playing. Sean asked Katrina to dance a slow one with him. It was the first time she had ever danced with a boy, although she knew how to dance.

"You're a really good dancer, Katrina." He spoke shyly to her.

"Thanks, and you can call me Kat. A lot of people do. It's less formal."

"Okay. Kat....that's really a cute nickname. How about some food?"

"Sounds good to me." She smiled up at him.

Halfway across the room, Sean's father was standing with a fellow police officer.

"Your son has excellent taste in women, Tim."

"Oh, you know who that is, Frank? That's Kitrowski's little sister. You know the young guy that made suit so fast because he had college? That's his sister. Sean goes to school with her. Says she's a straight A student, on the drill team, a really good artist, sings, dances, and plays the piano. A complete package. Sean's nuts over her. Says most of the guys in school are. Those who aren't are fags."

"Think he's getting any? God, she's beautiful!" Tim's colleague asked.

"Doubt it. From what I hear she doesn't date much, if at all. Well, Kitrowski is very protective over her. I hear the older brother is, too. Look at my son. He acts like he just discovered some rare treasure every time he looks at her. That ain't the look of someone who is getting any."

"True. Hey, I hear Kitrowski is going to be an agent. That means his spot is open, right? Think I'll apply for it. Can't hurt. Damn, that girl is beautiful!" Officer Frank Adams couldn't take his eyes off of Katrina.

"Remember how old she is, Frank. Behave." Tim Parks reminded him.

"You mean, 'how young she is', don't you?" Adams corrected.

"Yeah....whatever."

Sean pulled into Katrina's driveway at eleven-thirty. He hesitated, and then got out of the car. Most of the girls he dated didn't require that he walk them to the door, but he knew that Katrina was not like most girls. She was a treasure. He wanted to be with her, and he also wanted to be seen with her. The guys would envy him for that. He still couldn't believe that he got up the nerve to ask her to go out with him. She was so beautiful! That she actually said she would go out with him still amazed him. He had gone out with plenty of girls, some of them prettier than others, but Katrina....Katrina was incredible. He heard that he was the first boy she ever agreed to go out with. He wondered if that was true. He came around to the passenger side of the car and lifted the handle of the door, and reached in for her hand to help her out of the car. He didn't let go of her hand when she was out of the car, but instead walked her to her door, her hand in his.

"Thank you for coming with me tonight." He thought he sounded stupid.

"Thank you for asking me. I had a really nice time. It was a great party."

"Old people, and all, huh?" he chided her.

"That made it special. Did you see your grandfather and grandmother doing the twist? It was great!"

"I wouldn't take most girls to something like that. They would think I was a dork, or something. You seemed to like it." He really wanted to kiss her.

"I'm very family oriented, Sean. I love being with my family. Having a family means more to me than anything. When it comes to being with my family or going out with friends, my family wins."

"Oh wow! I feel the same way! I go out, but only if there is nothing going on at home. We must be weird or something. I don't know of too many kids our age who feel that way. Actually, I only know two.... you and me." With that being said, he took her chin between his thumb and forefinger and lightly kissed her on her lips. She didn't protest. It was a quick kiss. It was her first kiss. Sean stared down at her for a second or two, then cupped her face in his hands and gently kissed her. He let out a quick sigh. "You're so.....different." He said.

"Is that good or bad?" she taunted.

"It depends."

"On?" She was looking up at him, the corners of her mouth just slightly raised.

He looked into her eyes and smiled. "Let me get back to you on that. Okay?"

He lifted her chin with his thumb and forefinger again, quickly kissed her and jogged toward the car. "Call you tomorrow, okay?"

"Okay." She answered, and opened her front door. She could hear her parents in the family room, so she went in to tell them about her evening.

1-22

The homecoming game was scheduled for Saturday afternoon at two o'clock. Katrina cut her art classes short so that she could get home to get ready for the game. There was an air of excitement in the entire town. The football team was undefeated so far this year, and many people were talking 'championship'. She jumped out of her car and ran into the house to get ready. She had to be at the field with the rest of the drill team in an hour. Mary had helped her out by getting her drill team uniform ready for her. It was hanging on the back of her closet door when she ran into the bedroom. Mary had also placed the huge bouquet of giant chrysanthemums on her nightstand. On Friday, the cheerleaders sold the flowers wrapped in black and gold ribbons, since black and gold were the school colors. Sean bought one for Katrina, as did several other boys. She ended up with such a huge bouquet that Mary actually had to buy an over-sized vase to put them in. Katrina laughed when she saw that the one Mary found happened to be black and gold.

She was almost ready when she heard Mary coming up the steps. "Hi, Mom!" She yelled. "You and daddy are going, aren't you?"

"Sure are, Sweetie, and guess what! I hope this doesn't upset you… but," Mary was leaning on the door frame of Katrina's room now. "Dad and I got a call to chaperone the dance tonight." Mary waited for a response.

"Great! What are you going to wear?" was Katrina's response.

"Oh, I have something nice. Daddy will wear his newest suit. We won't embarrass you, I promise!"

"Oh, like I have ever felt that way! I'm glad you'll be there. Hey, I'm almost ready. Where's Daddy?"

"He's downstairs getting the camera loaded. I have the movie camera ready. Oh, and Kim's down there, too. She's going with us."

"Oh, good!" Katrina took a last look in the mirror, was satisfied with her appearance, and headed down the stairs. They had a whole twenty minutes before they had to leave.

Katrina hugged Kim and ran toward the kitchen to grab a bottle of water out of the refrigerator. The telephone rang just as she shut the refrigerator door. She grabbed up the phone on the first ring since she was so close. It was Sean.

"Hi, Kat! Are you about ready to leave?" He asked her. He had become a regular caller since his parents' anniversary party. Since that night, he and Katrina went out every Saturday night, and sometimes saw each other on Sunday. Friday nights they went with everyone else to Bear's Place. At school they were considered an item. Wherever Katrina was, Sean was not far behind. They were linked together by both students and teachers. It was 'Katrina and Sean' or 'Sean and Katrina' to everyone. She wasn't sure how she felt about this. She liked Sean, but she wasn't sure she was ready for this exclusive relationship. She knew their relationship was not going to go further than a few kisses, but she wasn't sure if he was aware of that. Lately his goodnight kisses had become more ardent and demanding, and she didn't like how he always had to have his arm around her in school, like she was his possession....."Katrina? You there?"

Katrina snapped back to the present. "Yeah, of course I'm here. Sorry...I was fixing a tassel." She lied.

"It's okay. I just called to say 'good luck today'. I know the drill team has a special presentation planned."

"Thanks, Sean. Good luck to you, too. Hope we win today!"

"Yeah, me, too. See you after the game? I know we have to get home to get ready for the dance, but maybe for a few minutes?"

"Okay. The Alumni have something planned in the cafeteria anyway. I know my parents will want to stop in. Just meet me in there, okay? See you later. Bye." She hung up and called out to everyone that it was almost time to leave.

The air was full of electricity. Katrina could feel it the moment she stepped out of the car. She saw that some of the drill team members were already gathered together in their special area where they always waited. The stadium had been decorated in black and gold, and many people milled around in the school colors as well. The stands were already filling up even though game time was an hour away. She could hear the band instruments warming up at the other end of the field, as well as laughter and shouting from the stands. There were squawks coming from the P.A. system indicating that someone was working on it. She hugged her parents and Kim and headed toward the drill team. The director, Ms Patterson was handing out banners to those who had been nominated for homecoming queen. "Here, Katrina, this goes over your left shoulder, okay?" she advised as she handed Katrina hers.

"Thanks, Ms Patterson," Katrina answered, as she slid the banner over her shoulder shyly. She felt a little uncomfortable about wearing it since it seemed as though she were bragging about being nominated. The other nominees didn't seem to feel uncomfortable wearing it, so she felt a little more at ease. It was just before game time. One day during the week she had been asked to sing the National Anthem, and she just remembered that she forgot to tell her parents. "Here goes another surprise for them," she thought, as the school principal came over to escort her to the center of the football field. The football players were running onto the field as their names were announced. She couldn't help but hear Sean's name. When both teams were assembled on the sidelines of the respective sides, she and Mr. Wilkes walked out onto the field and stepped up onto a newly erected platform on the sideline of the center of the field.

"Ladies and Gentleman," boomed the announcer's voice. "Please stand for the National Anthem, sung by our own Katrina Kitrowski!" There were a few cat calls and cheers, but then all got quiet. She sang it beautifully and never missed a note. The grandstand exploded with thunderous applause at the end of the anthem. She stepped down into the electric cart waiting to drive her back to where the drill team waited. Katrina looked straight ahead as the cart whisked her off of the field. If she had looked to the right she would have seen Sean waving to her, Mary dabbing her eyes with a tissue, and Ed boasting that she was their daughter. The game began.

It was another victory for the team. This time they won by four touchdowns, two of which were scored by Sean. He met her in the cafeteria after the game and was quickly swallowed up by fans congratulating him. Katrina was happy for him, and yes, she even felt some pride that she was considered his girlfriend.

She smiled to herself as she got out of the shower. Sean was considered quite a catch. So many of the girls in school liked him, but it seemed obvious that he only had eyes for her. She began drying her hair. Tonight she would wear it piled on top of her head.

Kim knocked on her door while she was working on it. "Hi! Can I help?" Kim asked, as she took the brush from Katrina. Katrina was glad to see Kim. They hadn't had much time to talk since Michael left for training, so this would be a good opportunity.

"So do you miss Mike?" Katrina began.

"You bet I do!"

"Kim, are you worried about this job? I mean the danger in it."

"Yes, of course I am. Mike really wants this. It's all he's ever talked about doing. I can't let him know how I object to it because it's dangerous."

Katrina sighed. "I just hope nothing ever happens to him."

"Well, me too, but I guess any job can be dangerous. So now tell me about you and Sean."

Katrina groaned. "I don't know, Kim. I like him, but....well, it's not going to be forever. He's possessive, and I can't handle that."

"So has he made a move on you yet?"

"You mean sexually? No, not yet, but that's coming, I can tell."

"And how are you going to react?"

"He better know what 'no' means. Kim, I like him, he's nice and all, but he's not 'the one'. You know what I mean?"

"You bet. I know exactly what you mean. When I met Mike I knew instantly that he was 'the one'. Hey, do you think you'll be homecoming queen?"

"Oh, I doubt it. It will probably be a senior. It should be, anyway. I still have next year."

"But you're so popular, and that's what counts. It's how many vote for you."

Katrina shrugged. "We'll see."

"There, your hair looks gorgeous!"

"Thanks, Kim!" Katrina surveyed Kim's handiwork and was satisfied with the results.

"Kim?"

"What, Honey?" Kim sat down next to her.

"Please don't mention what I told you about Sean to Michael. I don't want him going off on him. Nothing is going to happen between Sean and me, even if I am the last virgin in school!" She looked at Kim mischievously.

"I don't think you're the last one in the school. There's old Miss Bachman!"

Katrina and Kim laughed at the reference to the old-maid English teacher. "Well, I know I'm the last one on the drill team. I think I'm supposed to care about that."

"Says who?"

"I don't know....everybody. But you know what? I don't. All of my life, I have always had what is best for me. I have always done what is best for me. I'm focused on a future, you know what I mean?"

"Yeah, I do....and *you know what?* You have more intelligence in your little finger than most of that drill team has put together. Stay that way...promise?"

"Yes, I promise. I guess I better finish getting ready. He'll be here in about fifteen minutes." She reached behind the closet door and pulled out the dress she bought for the occasion. It was a black stretchy material with silver threads going through it. The top of the dress was a halter that tied at the nape of the neck and plunged into a V down the front. The bodice clung to the waist, where it flared out slightly and dropped to the floor. There were more silver threads at the waistline than anywhere else on the dress. The threads fanned out from the waist up and from the waist down, giving the dress a sunburst effect.

Kim gasped when she saw it. "That dress is gorgeous!"

Katrina smiled at her. "Isn't it? I love it." She said as she slipped the dress over her head. It looked magnificent on her. "Wait until you see these..." She pulled a shoebox off of the top shelf. "They're almost a perfect match." She took her shoes out of the box and slipped them onto her feet. The shoes were sling backs covered with a black material that had silver threads going through it. The open toed front had silver threads that formed a small sunburst. They were perfect for the dress.

"Wow! They are! You look sensational! I don't know if that dress flatters you, or if you flatter the dress. I can't tell."

Katrina fastened the clasp of the silver chain that held a small oval black onyx with a diamond chip in the middle of it. She inserted earrings that matched. She smiled at Kim.

"See? It's what I'm talking about! When I saw this dress I knew it was 'the one', so I got it. And look. It compliments me and I compliment it. When I find 'the one', we will be perfect together. He will compliment me and I will compliment him. You know, bring out the best in each other. There. I'm ready. And as on cue, there's the door bell!" She posed her arms to the left like she was introducing a small child.

Kim was laughing so hard she had tears in her eyes. "I can't believe you just compared a guy to a dress! Oh, that's funny! But wow! You look beautiful! Sean is going to lose his mind tonight."

Katrina gave a quick laugh through her nose. "Let's find out!" She headed down the stairs with Kim trailing behind her. She heard Mary talking with Sean as she hit the bottom step.

"Hi!" She smiled at both Sean and Mary. "Where's Daddy?"

"He's getting dressed." Mary answered her.

Kim looked at Sean and put her hand over her mouth to keep from laughing. He was stunned and rendered speechless when he saw Katrina. His eyes looked like dark blue sponges trying to soak up all the water on a beach. He couldn't take his eyes off her.

Finally he spoke up. "Wow! Wow! You look....you look....WOW!" He let out a low cat call whistle. "You look unbelievable!"

"Thanks. Are we ready to go?" She grabbed up the black faux fur wrap she had chosen for the evening, along with the small clutch purse that matched her shoes. "Mom, I guess I'll see you and daddy there." Mary was handing her the 'Nominee' banner that she was supposed to wear until they crowned the queen.

Sean turned around and looked at Mary with surprise. "Oh, are you chaperoning? My parents are, too."

"I didn't know that." Katrina interrupted.

"Yeah, they were called on Friday. Another set of parents was supposed to but they had to go out of town for a funeral. So my parents took their place."

"Oh, well then maybe we will get to meet them." It was Mary's turn to interrupt.

"Oh you will. I'll bring them over to your table. Ready to go, Beautiful?" He held out his arm to Katrina, which she accepted, and they walked out the door toward the car.

Even though they were not arriving late, the dance was in full swing when they got there. They could hear the music from the parking lot. The ride over had been quiet, with Katrina making most of the small talk. She didn't seem to notice that Sean was unusually quiet. He got out of the car and came around to her side and opened the door for her. He held out his hand and she grasped it and slid out of the car. He stood in front of her staring into her face for a few seconds.

"Katrina.....Katrina, I.....uh, good luck. On winning tonight, that is." Sean faltered. He appeared to be tongue-tied.

"You, too, Sean....you're a nominee, too. We probably won't win because we're not seniors. But that's okay...we have next year."

Sean kissed her very gently and softly on the lips. "Been wanting to do that since you came down your stairs. Sorry. I didn't mess anything up. You still look perfect."

She let out a small laugh, and they walked into the gymnasium, hand in hand. They were immediately surrounded by drill team, football players, majorettes, and cheerleaders. Sean took Katrina's wrap and went to check it in the coat room that was created for the event.

"You look fabulous, Kat!"

"Thanks, Morgan, so do you! I see we both have that black and silver thing going on." Katrina's friend was wearing a black gown made from the same stretchy material as Katrina's. It also had silver threads going through it, but they were patterned like leaves around the waist of the dress, followed by the stems that ran down the front of the dress. Morgan's dress was strapless with a fuller skirt. It suited her blonde friend quite well. In an instant, Sean was back at her side. "Where are we supposed to sit?" He asked Morgan.

"Homecoming nominees sit at that front table. Kevin is already over there." Kevin was Morgan's boyfriend, and had been for the past two years. He was the team safety. The three of them made their way to the table as quickly as they could, considering that they were mobbed by other students who wanted their attention, if for no other reason than just to say hello. The nominee table was being served this evening by underclassmen. They quickly put beverages in front of Katrina and Sean, and asked if there was anything else they could get for them.

Sean and Katrina danced a few dances together, and then Kevin and Morgan cut in. When they separated and went back to their respective dates, Sean spied his parents coming through the door. "My mom and dad are here. Let's see if we can get them a table big enough for your parents to sit with them, okay?"

As they were seating Sean's parents at a table big enough for eight, Katrina's parents came through the door. She waved them over to the table, and Sean introduced them to each other. Principal Wilkes was on the stage with microphone in hand. This was Sean and Katrina's cue to get to their table. "See you all later." They both whispered to their parents, as they turned to go sit down.

"Good evening, everybody," Principal Wilkes began. "Good game today, I'm sure everybody agrees. We are still undefeated this season." The principal waited for the applause to die down. "Tonight we crown the homecoming king and queen for the school year 1993-1994. Let's start by bringing the ten nominees up here on stage. Please come up here as I call your name." Principal Wilkes paused for effect, and probably to catch his breath as well. He opened up a scroll and began to read aloud.

"Morgan Butler, drill team." Morgan climbed the two steps to the stage and was directed to her seat. After the applause, Wilkes continued. "Kevin Glass, football, safety..." The clapping continued. "Candace Dunn, cheerleader captain." Mr. Wilkes stopped for the whistles and applause. "Jeff Hall, quarterback and captain of the team..." Jeff took his seat and again the principal waited for quiet. "Katrina Kitrowski, drill team..." The applause and the whistles were deafening. When it was quiet once again, Principal Wilkes continued, "Sean Parks, football, receiver...by the way, he has scored eleven touchdowns this year." The student body, the faculty, and the parents gave Sean a standing ovation. "Brittany Schultz, majorette...." It appeared that Brittany had her own fan club, since there seemed to be screaming and cheering from one section of the gym. "Jim Burton, football, linebacker...(applause) Lori Lysowski, cheerleader...(more applause)...and last but not least..... Dave Sipinski, football, running back.....and there you have our homecoming court! Let's give them all a hand one more time."

The gymnasium rocked with applause and cat calls, and whistles and screams. Then the gym got quiet.

"Are we ready?" Principal Wilkes prompted. "The runner-up for king will take the place of the king if for some reason he cannot fulfill his role as Homecoming King. There was some laughter from the audience, which pleased the principal, since he meant for the remark to be humorous. The runner-up is........" Again, he paused for effect, while he opened the envelope. "Sean Parks!" Katrina was as surprised as Sean was. She looked over at him and grinned. "The runner-up for queen is........Morgan Butler! If for some reason the queen cannot fulfill her duties, Morgan will take her place." Again, Katrina grinned, and hugged Morgan.

"Okay, let's move on. The homecoming king for this year is..... drum roll, please....Jeff Hall!" After a deafening applause he called, "Jeff, come up here and stand beside me....right here. Are you ready to meet your queen?" Jeff nodded. "Is everybody ready to meet the new homecoming queen?"

"Yes!" The crowd cried.

"May we have the king and queen from last year up here?" The two former students stepped up on stage.

"Okay. This year's homecoming queen is.........Katrina Kitrowski!!"

Katrina's hands flew to her face as she let out a squeaky gasp. Her eyes were wide with surprise. The gym exploded. There were screams and whistles and hands clapping, feet stomping, and cat calls, and Katrina just stood there in shock. Somehow her feet began to move forward. She was having a hard time seeing. 'Great time to go blind,' she thought. Then she realized that she was crying. Flashbulbs were going off everywhere as she made her way to the front of the stage. She had to stoop down so the former queen could place the crown on her head.

"Jeff and Katrina, I congratulate both of you. Would you so kindly step down onto the floor and dance the royal homecoming dance together?" Jeff took Katrina's hand and led her down the steps to the dance floor. He encircled her waist and took her hand as the music started. He looked down at her and smiled. "You're the most beautiful queen I have ever seen. But you know I now have something to worry about."

"What's that?" She asked him.

"Well, you heard that if something happens to me the runner-up takes over as king. Look who the runner-up is. I think I'm in danger." He made his face into a grimace. Katrina broke up laughing.

"I did *not* think I'd win." She spoke honestly.

"Ah, and that's why you did win. You're gorgeous and talented, but you're also damn nice. Everybody likes you because you're not conceited or stuck on yourself. To tell you the truth, I'm surprised that Candy was up there at all. She's such a snob and she refuses to be nice to people who she considers beneath her status, even though she's a slut. What she doesn't realize is that everybody gets to vote, not just those she sleeps with. They voted for you, because you will talk to the nerds and the geeks and the burnouts. And you're nice to them, and treat them like people. You're such a genuine person. Hell, if Sean hadn't grabbed you up, I sure would have."

The song ended as Katrina thanked Jeff for his kind words. Sean appeared at her side. "We should go over to our parents' table. Your parents are just....well, you'll see."

Katrina saw what Sean meant. Mary and Ed looked like they were going to burst. Mary's eyes were red and she was still holding a tissue. They got up to hug their daughter—their pride and joy—as soon as she got to the table. More flashbulbs went off as people were taking pictures of Katrina with her parents. She saw the newspaper cameras honing in on them to get good shots. "Congratulations, Baby!" Mary gushed, and the tears started all over again. Ed hugged Katrina and didn't want to let her go. "God, I'm proud of you! So damned *proud!*" He let her go in order to get his handkerchief out of his back pocket. Sean's parents told her she looked beautiful and congratulated her on winning. Morgan came over and asked her if she wanted to run to the bathroom. She excused herself from the crowd, told Sean to wait there for her, and ran into the bathroom with Morgan.

Inside the bathroom, she leaned up against the wall. "Morgan, I can't believe I won!"

"Why not? I don't have any trouble believing it. Candy is pissed, too. She thought it should have been her."

"I do, too. I mean, she's a senior. We have another year."

"She may be a senior, but she's also a bitch! You know that, even if you don't ever say it."

"Well, you know I would never say that about anybody."

"And that's exactly why you won! You don't bad-mouth anybody, and you're nice to everybody. Hell, you're even nice to Candy, who hates you because you're beautiful...then hates you even more because you're so nice to her! I love it when I see you talking so nice to her. I know how it pisses her off. And I know another secret." Morgan smirked and rolled her eyes at the ceiling, causing Katrina to laugh.

"Okay, I know I'm going to be sorry I asked, but what's the other secret?"

Satisfied that she had her friend's attention, Morgan lowered her voice, but spoke dramatically, "Well, she's in love, *in love,* with Jeff Hall! But....Jeff is nuts, *off the deep end-nuts,* I mean, about *you!"*

"No way!"

"Yep."

"I didn't know that. Until tonight, I don't think he has ever even said anything to me. Tonight, while we were dancing, he told me that if Sean hadn't grabbed me up, he would have. I thought he was just saying that to be nice. Come on, we have to get back out there. Sean will think I fell in." Both girls laughed at that thought.

"Yeah, and he would come running in here to check, too." Morgan added, as they pushed open the bathroom door, laughing.

Sean was waiting right where she told him to be, so she went over and joined him and their parents. He immediately took her hand into his and asked if she would like to dance again. Off they went onto the dance floor, where they spent most of the night. Many boys cut in to dance with Katrina. Sean had to be gracious about it because everybody had a right to dance with the queen. After all, they all voted for her to put her there. Katrina was exhausted when the dance ended, and her feet hurt, too. Sean was exhausted, too, thank goodness! They were both quiet for most of the ride to her house.

Sean broke the silence. "Tired?"

"Very. I'm exhausted, actually." Katrina admitted.

"Me, too. You looked so beautiful tonight...outstandingly beautiful."

"You looked pretty good, too, you know."

"Kat, you're so…different from anybody I have ever known. It's like you came from another world, almost."

Katrina sat up straight in her seat. "You're calling me an alien? An E.T., maybe?" She laughed her melodious laugh. "My neck isn't that long!"

Sean laughed with her, as he pulled into her driveway and shut the car off. "Come here, E.T." he ordered as he reached for her. He put his arm around her and pulled her close to him and cradled her face with his other hand. He looked down into her eyes, and slowly lowered his face to hers. He kissed her passionately….more passionately than he ever had before. Katrina could hear his breathing quicken and become heavy. She stiffened a little, and backed off.

"Sean, it's late and I'm really tired."

"Yeah, okay," He said as he reached for her again. She dodged his arms this time.

"Really, Sean, I'm tired. I want to go in and go to bed."

Sean was looking down at nothing in particular, and let out an agitated sigh. "Okay. Sorry. It's just that…you drive me crazy, Katrina. The way you look, your laugh, your smile…just makes me want you, more and more."

"I also have brains and talent. Don't forget that. To me, those things are most important. But then, I guess a guy has never been turned on by the looks of a brain. They are kind of gross looking. Now if the human brain looked more like a set of boobs, a guy could get turned on by it…right?" She teased.

"Oh, you're being funny, huh? I know you're intelligent and that you are very talented. I appreciate all of that, too. Like I said, you are just so different…from all other girls. You shine. You stand out. No guy, in his right mind, wouldn't want to be with you. I'm so grateful that you are sitting in my car next to me." Sean paused for a moment. "I just don't ever want to lose you, Baby."

"Well, then let me go in to bed, before I die of exhaustion, okay?"

"Okay. Come on, I'll walk you to the door." Sean got out and went around to her door and opened it for her.

Something had to change here. He wanted her so badly that it hurt. It hurt when he walked up to the door with her. She held the door knob in her hand as she kissed him quickly and slipped inside. He walked slowly back to the car. Damn, how he wanted her. As he drove toward his house, he thought, 'What the hell? Was she the last virgin in the school?' Most girls he had been with gave in easily. Katrina...well, she was...different. He didn't want to hurt her. Damn it, he loved her; he was sure of that. He was nearing his street and was about to signal a left to turn in, but changed his mind and kept on going straight. He needed to clear his head, and a little drive would be good for him.

Kim rolled over to answer her ringing phone, and glanced at the clock. It was eight o'clock Sunday morning. It had to be Michael.

"Hello" Kim spoke softly into the received.

"How is my future bride this morning?"

Kim smiled. "I'm just fine, Mike. I still miss you. I can't wait for you to get back here."

"Another few weeks of training and I'll be home. Anything new?"

"Have you called your parents' house?"

"No, is there something wrong over there?"

"No-o.....I just thought you would want to congratulate the homecoming queen." Kim came back coyly.

"Katrina is homecoming queen?"

"Well, somebody in that house is. It's either her or your mother... now which one do you think it is?"

"Wow! Kat made homecoming queen." It was a statement. "I wish I could have been there."

"Oh, your dad has a million pictures. When you see them it will be just like being there. Her picture should be in the newspaper today."

"Can you get me one?"

"I'll try. That is if your dad hasn't gone out and bought them all up." Kim laughed. Mary and Ed had called her last night when they got home. They were ecstatic.

"Is she still going out with that Parks kid?"

"Sean."

"Whatever. Is she still going out with him?"

"Yeah, he was her date last night. He was runner-up for king. Your parents sat with his parents last night."

"He better not be touching her...

"Mike, whoa! Don't worry about it. Katrina and I talked about it. Nothing has happened. Katrina won't let anything happen. The way she put it, he's not 'the one'. She likes him, but that's about it."

They drifted off the subject and talked about other things before they hung up.

* * *

The three of them were having breakfast when the phone rang. Mary answered it on the second ring.

"Are there any queens living in that house?" Michael's voice came over the line.

"Only one. Would you like to speak to her?"

"Yep! You bet!" Mary handed the phone to Katrina.

"Hi, Mike!"

"So the princess is now a queen, huh?"

Katrina laughed into the phone. "I was so surprised when I heard my name! I never thought I would win! I'm not even a senior. Mike, how is training going?"

"It's going fine. And for the record….I'm not surprised you won. Congratulations, though." She knew Mike was smiling on the other end of the phone.

"Daddy wants to talk to you for a minute, okay?"

"Okay. Hey, how are things with Sean, by the way?"

"Oh, okay, I guess."

"Love you."

"Love you, too." Katrina made a kissing sound into the phone and passed it to her father. Mary walked from the front door with the newspaper in her hand. The tears were welling up again as she looked at the picture of her daughter on the front page of the paper. She held it up for Katrina and Ed to see.

Ed nodded and said, "We have to get more of these. I'll run to the store and buy some more papers. "You want a copy of this paper, Mike?" Ed spoke into the phone. "Your sister's picture is on the front page."

"Yeah, send me the pictures and the write-up. I'll have something to brag about down here. By the way, it's hot here!" Ed laughed.

"Send some heat this way! Your mom wants to say something." Ed handed the phone to Mary, and grabbed up the paper….

1-23

The days had passed quickly. Thanksgiving had been a quiet affair with just Katrina and her parents. Not having Danny and Michael there was painful for all of them. They were truly looking forward to the wedding when everybody would be together again.

* * *

Katrina came in from Wednesday night dance class and shook off her heavy parka. "Mom? What time will Danny and Kathy be here?" She yelled toward the kitchen. She knew her mother was in there because the light was on. From the darkened living room she heard a masculine voice say, "About an hour ago."

"DANNY!" She screamed. She raced at him, jumped into his arms and threw her arms around his neck. They were both laughing as he spun her around in a circle. "I sure have missed you! I'm so happy you're here. Where's Kathy?"

"Right here." Katrina turned her head toward the kitchen and saw Kathy and Mary standing in the doorway. She let go of Danny and ran to hug Kathy.

"So I hear you're a queen now." Danny teased her.

"Oh, that's all over and done now. It was exciting for a couple of days, but…eh…who even remembers now?"

"Well, I think it's a big deal. Dad promised me he had lots of pictures and I want to see them all. Also, I hear you sang the anthem at the homecoming game."

"And she sang it perfectly." Mary chimed in. "She forgot to tell us that she had been asked, so imagine our surprise when it was announced over the P.A. system. Oh, we also have pictures of the drill team….. movies and prints. The movies are really good."

"Can we watch them tonight? We have nothing planned except to get some sleep. Kathy is in your room again, Kat. Okay? Let's call Mike and Kim and have them come over to watch." Michael had come home the day before. Katrina and Michael hugged each other when she picked him up from the airport and dropped him off at Kim's. Kim brought him home later that night. He slept until past nine that morning, so Katrina hadn't really seen very much of him.

"Sure. I'm starving. Is there food?"

"Dinner is all ready." Mary was carrying bowls into the dining room as she spoke. "Kat, Honey, why don't you call Sean and invite him over to watch the movies? I'm sure he would like to see them. We can make a little party out of it. That's if it's okay with Danny and Kathy. You may be tired..." She looked over at them.

"No, that's a good idea. I want to meet Romeo anyway." Danny winked at Mary.

"Okay," Katrina answered. She went to the kitchen to call him. She was back within five minutes. "Mom, I called Morgan and invited her, too. She and Kevin are going to come over. Is that okay? I told them eight was good, okay?"

"That's fine, Honey. One of us should run out after we eat to get some snacks and drinks for everybody."

"I'm in." Ed volunteered himself.

* * *

The group crowded into the family room to watch the home videos. There were two of them to see. One was of the game and the other was of the homecoming dance. Sean had showed up with chips and dip, and Morgan and Kevin came with soft drinks. Ed and Danny went out after dinner and stocked up on cheese and crackers, chips, corn curls, and anything else that might be devoured. They each carried in a case of Pepsi and Diet Pepsi, and a six-pack of beer. When everybody was sitting with something to drink and within reach of a bowl of snacks, Ed put the first video into the VCR. It began with the National Anthem, sung by Katrina.

"Oooh, I have goose bumps!" Kathy swooned. Katrina laughed.

The sound was very good on the VCR, so it was easy to hear everything. They could hear the announcer of the game. Sean got to see his touchdowns for the first time. He was blushing when he heard his name. The rest of the audience was cheering and clapping like they were watching the game for the first time. The halftime show was wonderful. The drill team's new routine looked terrific on video.

"Hey, we look good, don't we, Kat?"

"Yeah, we do. I wonder who thinks this stuff up knowing that it's going to look good on tape."

"Choreographers do it" Both Danny and Kathy piped up. "They have an eye for stuff like that." Danny finished.

Ed and Mary both had the same thought, but this time they kept it to themselves, since there were others besides family in the room. They both thought Katrina looked the best and danced the routine better than any of the others. Little did they know that all company present, including Morgan, was thinking the same.

The first video was over. "Let's have an intermission before we put the second one in. There are four bathrooms, gang. Help yourselves." Ed instructed them.

Kathy, Katrina, Kim, and Morgan headed upstairs to Katrina's room. "So that's Sean, huh, Kat?" Kathy spoke with an amused look on her face. "He's cute."

To that, Katrina shrugged. "He's okay, I guess."

Morgan covered her face and put her head down. She was snickering.

"What's so funny?" Katrina wanted to know.

"Oh, nothing....it's just that all the girls in school think Sean is gorgeous, and all you say is 'he's okay, I guess'. Morgan started laughing, and Katrina joined in.

"Let's get back downstairs before Danny and Michael gang up on Sean, okay?" Katrina started out of the room first.

"Okay, the second half of the home videos is beginning." Ed called to everyone. "This one is the homecoming dance."

"Just wait until you see Candy's face when she realizes that she didn't win. It's hilarious!" Morgan's face was full of mischief at this point.

Sean stared at her curiously. "What do you mean?

"You'll see." Morgan leaned closer to Sean and whispered, "She hates Kat." Sean stared at Morgan for a moment and then turned to watch the video.

At the point where Katrina's name was spoken, Morgan said, "There! See her face? See how shocked she is that she didn't win? Now look how mad she is!" It definitely looked that way on the video. Sean was staring at the video and not believing what he was seeing. The rest of the spectators found it amusing that someone could be so angry over something so unimportant to the future of mankind. Mary, Kathy, and Kim cried when Katrina's name was announced on the video. Katrina looked so beautiful. Sean was very quiet through the rest of the video. Nobody seemed to notice.

1-24

Everyone awoke in good spirits on Saturday. Michael and Kim were getting married. The rehearsal was held on Thursday evening, with a dinner following, so that everyone could attend the football game on Friday night. The entire family went to Bear's Place after the game. It felt great to be together again. The atmosphere at Bear's Place was wild on this night. It was the last game of the season and the team had a perfect winning record. They were the champions this year, and it was the first time in over twenty years. Sean and his family joined them at their table. "Great game, Sean!" Ed was the first to speak to him. "Three touchdowns! With a record like that you're going to get into a good college; maybe have a shot at the pros…you think?"

"I hope so!" Sean beamed at Ed's remark.

Kim looked over at Katrina and mouthed the words, "Bathroom." Katrina nodded. It had become their little signal that something needed to be discussed. They both got up and headed toward the rear of Bear's.

There were three stalls in the bathroom but they were all empty at the moment. Kim asked Katrina, "Is Sean going to the wedding with you?"

"Yeah, that's okay, isn't it?"

Kim let the air out of her lungs. "Yes, it's more than okay. You see, your brother invited the Parks at the last minute. I didn't want any embarrassment for you in case Sean wasn't invited, or even worse, if you had invited someone else."

Katrina tipped her head back and laughed. "Let's just pee and get out of here."

Katrina wandered down to the kitchen where Mary was already cooking. "Morning, Mom. Is anybody else up?"

"No, you're the first. Are you excited about the wedding?"

"Yeah, a little. Kim's going to be beautiful, isn't she?"

"Yep, she sure will," a voice from the stairs piped in.

"Mike! Are you ready for breakfast?" Mary asked him. It felt good to have both Michael and Danny home in their own rooms. With the boys gone and Katrina almost grown, she was feeling a little melancholy at times. She heard the stairs creaking again, and looked up to see Danny and Kathy, followed by Ed. "Let's all have a nice breakfast together. I'm so happy to have all of you together again."

* * *

Katrina came down the stairs dressed in her bridesmaid gown. Danny whistled at her from the living room. "Looking good, Baby! Looking good!" He walked out of the living room and met her at the bottom of the stairs. His Tuxedo was black with a red cummerbund and bow tie. She knew the other tuxedos had green rather than red.

"Well, you look pretty terrific yourself. Is Mike ready yet?" Katrina looked up toward the top of the stairs.

"Coming!" Michael yelled down the stairs. His tie and cummerbund were white.

Mary and Ed came from the direction of the kitchen. Ed looked quite handsome in his tuxedo. Katrina could see how much Danny looked like him. Mary's dress was lovely. She and Meg McNeal had gone shopping together in order to get dresses that didn't clash with each other. Meg's dress was a pale pink, while Mary had chosen a light blue. The color was perfect for Mary. The dress had a high waist with an inverted pleat in the front, a high neckline with a stand-up collar. She wore shoes to match.

"Mom, you look beautiful!" Katrina was awed by how pretty her mother looked.

"You do, Mom!" Both Michael and Danny said it in unison.

Ed put his arm around Mary and said, "She is beautiful. She's still my bride."

Kathy was standing at the foot of the stairs, smiling. "What a nice family I'm getting into." She thought to herself.

The wedding was lovely. Kim and Michael stated the vows they had written for each other, and they were so moving that everyone must have felt the love. Mary cried. Katrina cried. Meg cried.

The bridesmaids' dresses and the tuxedos went well together, and the flowers were perfect. Each bouquet had holly sprigs and a candy cane mixed in with the white carnations. Kim's bouquet was red and white roses with holly springs mixed, just as Katrina had suggested.

The cars were decorated like Christmas. Instead of tin cans or shoes or whatever anybody else put on the back of a car, the bridal limo, a gift from Ed, had unbreakable Christmas ornaments attached to the bumper. The 'Just Married' sign on the back of the limo was done by Katrina, herself, and of course, the ornaments were her idea, as well.

The reception followed the ceremony. Guests were greeted by the wedding party at the door of the hall. Sean came in with his family, and his eyes immediately honed in on Katrina in the receiving line.

"You look beautiful, as usual." He stated, as he took her hand and kissed it. "Can I do anything for you? Do you want something to drink while you're standing here?"

"Oh, Sean, that would be great. Just a glass of water would be good. Thanks." She rewarded his thoughtfulness with a smile.

He came up behind her and handed her the glass of water. "Thanks", she said again. "Uh, Sean.....I have to sit at the bridal table for the dinner, but I'll be over to sit at your table as soon as I can, okay?"

"Sure, that'll be great." He answered her. He made eye contact with her, and then went to sit with his parents. "He sure is acting strange," Katrina thought, and then mentally shrugged it off.

After the dinner was served Danny got everyone's attention and made a toast to Michael and Kim, and made his best-man speech. There was dancing after the dinner. Katrina went over to Sean's table and dropped down into a chair.

"Hi, how was the food?" She made it a point to include everyone at the table with that question. Everyone agreed that it was good.

"Dance, Kat?" Sean asked, and held out his hand to her.

"Okay." She stood up and they walked out to the dance floor.

"That color looks great on you. But everything looks great on you, I guess." He was peering down into her face. "Kat, are we okay? I mean, you and me, are we okay?"

"I think so. But you have been acting strange lately. You know if there is somebody else you would rather go out with, you can just tell me." Katrina waited for his answer.

"Oh God, no…there is nobody I would rather go out with. Why would you think that?"

"I don't necessarily think that. I'm just letting you know that you can see other girls, if that's what you want, that's all."

"I don't want to. Do you want to see someone else?"

"No….I don't even think about it." She answered truthfully.

He let his breath out slowly. "I was scared you were going to break up with me." He started to pull her closer to him.

"Careful!" She warned him. "Unless you want my two Doberman brothers on your back!"

"Oh yeah, right….I forgot." He loosened his grip on her. "Can I drive you home tonight?"

"Okay." The song ended and they walked back to the table.

Kathy caught the bouquet and Danny caught the garter. Katrina thought that might have been planned, but didn't know for sure. She was glad, though. Tomorrow morning she was going to ask them about their wedding plans.

She was exhausted when they left the hall. Sean helped her into the car after he got the engine warm and the heater working. On the way home she dozed off with her head on Sean's shoulder. She awoke when he stopped the car, and looked around.

"This isn't my house. Where are we?" She looked up at Sean.

"The Point. I just wanted to come here for a few minutes. I haven't had you all to myself for almost a week. Just a few minutes, okay?" The Point was where couples came to make out, and more. Katrina had never been here before.

"I-I don't know, Sean. I think I should get home."

"Just a few minutes, okay? I just want to sit here and put my arm around you for a few minutes. Please?"

"All right. But just for a few minutes..." Katrina pleaded.

Satisfied with this, he settled down and put his arm around her shoulders and leaned his head toward hers until they were touching. "It was a nice wedding. Who was that guy that was your partner? Is he from around here?"

"Oh, no....Mike went to college with him. His name is Terry. He's from Philadelphia. The other guy is Mark, Mike's best friend."

Sean tuned his face to Katrina's and lifted her face up by her chin. He covered her mouth with his and gently, but firmly, kissed her. This time she responded to him, and returned his affection. His tongue darted around her lips and tentatively, he slid the tip into her mouth. She met his tongue with hers. He pushed his hand up into her hair and crushed her curls, while he continued to kiss her. His breathing became heavy and he ran his hand down her throat to her chest, and almost to her breast. She grabbed his hand and pushed it away.

"Let's go. I want to go home...now." She was getting angry.

"Come on, Kat! Please don't be like this! Okay. I'm sorry. I got carried away. But please, don't be mad." He was pleading with her.

"Sean, I want to go home...now. If you aren't willing to take me home, I will get out of this car and walk!"

Sean sighed, and started the car. They did not speak at all on the way to her house. He pulled into the driveway and quietly apologized. "I'm sorry. It won't happen again. I promise. Forgive me...please?" He looked at her and could see there were daggers still coming out of her eyes. His heart sank. She gathered up her stuff and he got out and went around to her side of the car and opened the door. He offered his hand but she refused it. They walked to the door without touching or speaking.

"Can I call you?" His eyes were pleading with her.

"Sean...." She sighed. "I'm not going to go through this every time we go out. No means NO."

"I promise it won't happen again! Please? Can I call you tomorrow?"

She nodded and slipped inside the door and shut it.

Katrina was the last one downstairs in the morning. She went over to the counter and poured herself a cup of coffee, and sat down beside Danny.

Ed spoke up. "You were kind of late last night, weren't you?"

"Sorry, Daddy," She apologized.

"It's okay, since you don't do it very often. I don't want to see it become a habit, that's all."

"Where did you go?" Danny asked her. "I thought you left when we did."

"Oh...yeah, we did, but we had to stop for an argument." Katrina made a face and rolled her eyes at Kathy across the table. Kathy burst out laughing.

"What were you arguing about?" Danny wanted to know.

"He can be a real idiot." Katrina answered. "It was nothing."

"Is everything okay?" Danny prodded.

Katrina nodded.

"Hey, Mom, I was thinking. Instead of buying a new gown for the Snow Ball I thought maybe I could just wear the gown I wore yesterday. I would take the cape off of it, of course. It's definitely a Christmas look. What do you think?"

"If you want to, Honey. I can help you do the little bit of alterations."

"Of course, I may not even have a date for it, now."

"Oh, you still have a date." Danny was standing at the dining room window. "He just pulled into the driveway, and he's not empty-handed. Beware of geeks bearing gifts!" Danny was smirking, and Katrina was laughing. "I think I'll answer the door." He was full of mischief as he went toward the door when the bell rang.

"Hi. Uh, can I come in?" Sean was standing at the door, holding a bouquet of flowers, looking very unsure of himself.

"Are those for me?" Danny asked, indicating the flowers.

"No, they're for K-Katrina." He stammered. "We s-sort of had an argument."

"What do you mean, 'sort of'? You either did, or you didn't." Danny crossed his arms, leaned on the door frame and stared directly into Sean's face. He was enjoying this moment of making Sean uncomfortable.

"We did. It was my fault. I came to s-say I'm s-sorry."

"Well, I should hope so. KAT! You have company!"

Katrina came out of the kitchen trying to keep a straight face. Danny was terrible! Sean was standing there looking very sheepish, holding a bouquet of flowers. It reminded Katrina of a Norman Rockwell painting. Sean was staring at her like it was the first time he had ever seen her. She looked down and realized that she was wearing old sweatpants and a tee-shirt. He had never seen her that way.

"I guess I'm not exactly dressed for company. I didn't know you were coming. Come on in."

"I think you look cute like that. I never saw you in sweatpants."

"You're just lucky, I guess, because I have them on most of the time when I'm home."

"Maybe I should come around more often, then, because you sure look cute in them." He smiled and tried to look into her eyes. "I'm sorry, Kat. Honest, I am. Can we talk for a couple of minutes?" He was pleading with her.

She raised her arms, palms up, in a small shrug. "Do you want some coffee? We can sit in the dining room."

"Coffee would be great." He smiled tentatively.

She went into the kitchen to get him the coffee, and noticed that everyone had vanished.

"Sean, come on in the kitchen, okay?"

He followed her into the kitchen and sat down at the table. She poured his coffee and put the cream and sugar in front of him. Sugar was winding herself around Katrina's legs, so she stopped to pour some dry cat food into her bowl.

"I didn't know you had a cat."

"Yeah, since I was little. Danny bought her for me for my birthday one year. I really love cats, especially mine." She reached down and scratched behind Sugar's ears and smiled. She got herself another cup of coffee and sat down at the corner of the table next to him.

"Kat, I'm sorry. I need to know that you forgive me." He looked at her with anticipation.

"Sean, I told you last night that I am not going to go through a hassle every time we go out. No means exactly that. No!"

"I know, Honey. I'm sorry. I try to behave, but then you always look so damn good! I can't help myself. Please give me another chance. Please?" He looked like he was going to cry.

Katrina sighed. "If it happens again, that's it. Okay? Sean, look at me! It's not going to happen. Do you understand that? It's...not... going...to happen. If you can't accept that, maybe you should find someone else."

Sean gasped sharply. "No! I mean, I-I don't want anybody else. Please don't say that. I promise, I *promise* you it won't happen again." He reached for her hand. "Okay? Only hand-holding and kissing, from now on, I promise."

Katrina looked into his face. He looked sincere, and she was sure he meant it, but would he keep his promise? If not, they would not be going out for very much longer.

1-25

The Snow Ball was wonderful that year. The gym had been transformed into a winter wonderland, with mounds of snow and snowmen made out of Styrofoam. There were Christmas lights hanging from everywhere, and a huge Christmas tree stood in the corner of the gym. Katrina wore her bridesmaid dress with the few alterations that Mary helped her complete. Sean was a perfect gentleman that evening. He was attentive as always, he danced with her most of the night, except when Candy cut in twice, and he took her straight home afterward without a hassle. He walked her to her door and lightly kissed her on the lips and on her forehead and went back to his car and left. She was relieved that the on-going struggle appeared to be over.

Christmas followed the dance a week later. Mary and Ed gave Katrina a computer for Christmas, and Katrina was delighted about it. It was a quiet Christmas since Danny was in Florida and Michael had been sent to a training class for another month. Kim visited on Christmas night and they all enjoyed homemade Christmas cookies and eggnog. Sean spent Christmas Eve with Katrina, but said he had to spend Christmas Day with his parents. His gift to Katrina was a lovely white sweater and a silver bracelet. She gave him a blue, woolen sweater that matched his eyes perfectly. The tension between them seemed to be gone, at least for Christmas Eve. They laughed together and they talked. Since he was there early in the day, he helped her put the finishing touches on the tree, helped Ed carry in logs for the fire, and offered to 'taste-test' the cookies in the kitchen. Mary and Ed were enjoying his company as much as Katrina was. It snowed during the night and had been snowing off and on all day, so there were quite a few inches on the ground. At mid-afternoon, Katrina and Sean went outside to build a snowman. They were met by Mary and Ed, and engaged in a snowball battle with them. All four of them, cold and wet, went in through the kitchen for hot chocolate. They sat in front of the fire in the fireplace discussing who had won the snowball battle, and laughing about it.

Christmas Eve dinner was comprised of roast turkey, stuffing, mashed potatoes and gravy, broccoli, and biscuits, with pumpkin pie and whipped cream for dessert. Ham was their traditional Christmas Day dinner, so Mary always went with turkey on Christmas Eve. They usually ate both ham and turkey leftovers for a week, but nobody ever complained. Sean insisted on helping Katrina clean off the table and load the dishwasher. Mary cleaned the rest of the kitchen while they worked. When the dishwasher began to run, Katrina and Sean went into the living room and lit up the lights on the tree. The outside lights were turned on as well. Katrina sat down at the piano and began to play. Sean slid onto the seat with her and admired her ability for a few minutes. She played Christmas carols and they both sang. It was the first time she had ever heard Sean sing and she was surprised at how good his voice was. She changed the music into a modern pop song and they sang that together. Soon Mary and Ed joined them for the traditional Christmas carol singing they had done every year since they bought the piano. Sean left just after midnight. He gave her a gentle Christmas kiss under the mistletoe, and kissed her cheek before he went.

* * *

The holiday week passed quickly. Mary and Ed visited local relatives all week. Sometimes Katrina went with them, but mostly she stayed at home to play with her new computer. On New Year's Eve she went to Sean's house. His parents were hosting a New Year's Eve party and Sean had invited her. While she was getting ready for the party, it dawned on her that he had not come over at all since Christmas Eve. He called her every day during the week, but had made no effort to see her. She shrugged it off, thinking he probably had things to do, and besides, seeing too much of each other usually made his hormones rage out of control. Maybe he realized this, too, and decided to put some space between them. She was dressed in a two-piece berry-colored dress that accented her figure. The neckline came down to a V in the front, and just showed the slightest bit of cleavage. The dress top had long sleeves that zippered closed at the wrist. The A-line shirt, which stopped at mid-thigh, had two zippers in the front, one on the left and one on the right. She pulled on black boots, and stood in front of the mirror, where she pushed her hair behind her ears and fixed a black tam in place. She was satisfied with the look.

Sean picked her up at eight o'clock. When they got to his house, the party was already started. Many off the guests were off-duty police officers, some of whom she recognized. A couple of them asked her how Michael was doing and where he was at that time. Michael was in Virginia for training, she told them. She recognized Rob Sammond, because he went to school with Danny and they played football together. He asked her about Danny and she filled him in. Danny would be graduating from Law School in May and he would be coming home with his fiancée to get married. They would be living in Florida after that, since both of them were offered positions in local law firms down there, contingent on their passing their exam, of course.

The party was loud and getting very much out of control, Katrina felt. She noticed Sean was drinking some beer, so she slipped down the hall and found a phone. She called home and asked that either Mary or Ed pick her up around twelve-thirty. They agreed to this without hesitation. At midnight, Sean grabbed her around the waist, and pulled her close to him. She could smell the alcohol on his breath and she almost gagged. He began to kiss her gently, but soon his kiss got demanding. "Sean, stop! You're hurting me!" She pleaded with him.

"Sorry, Kat." His speech was slightly slurred. "I just love you so damned much! I can't help it if I want you every time I see you."

She stiffened. 'He didn't just say the L-word, did he?' She thought to herself.

He was looking down at her, with a smirk on his face. "You love me, too, don't you?"

Before she had to answer, Sean's father came up and grabbed both of them around the waists. "Hey, you two, Come get some food! Sean, You're not drinking, are you?" He led them both out to the kitchen where there were platters and bowls filled with foods of all kinds. Katrina whispered to Mrs. Parks that her dad was going to pick her up, since Sean had been drinking. Beth Parks seemed relieved.

True to his word, Ed was there at twelve-thirty to pick her up. She looked for Sean to say good-night and found him passed out across his bed. She shut his door, grabbed her black wool coat and the tam she had worn from Mr. and Mrs. Parks' bedroom, and left with her father. Thus began the year of 1994.

A very sheepish Sean called her on New Year's Day to say how sorry he was, and that he was grounded for a week, because he had been drinking, and he also told her he wouldn't do it again, since he had been sick several times during the night. She couldn't help the triumphant smile that spread across her face when he told her about being sick. "Good!" She thought. Sean left out the part where his parents told him he was going to lose that nice girlfriend if he didn't straighten up. He couldn't bear to say those words out loud, so he eliminated them.

The new school term began the Monday after New Year's Day. The day was bitter cold and ice covered the driveway and part of the road. Ed insisted on driving Katrina to school rather than let her drive. She agreed, since she had never driven on snow or ice before. At school Sean met her in the entry hallway and walked with her to her locker. She was wearing a new black and white running suit that Danny had sent her for Christmas. Sean told her she looked great in it. He walked her to her class, and headed toward his first period class. They had the second period class together so they would see each other then. Morgan was in her first period class and they were happy to see each other. They talked about what they got for Christmas before the teacher entered the classroom.

January led into a bitter cold February. The St. Valentine's Day Dance was scheduled for February the twelfth, and of course, Sean had already asked Katrina to go. She and Morgan had gone shopping together for their dresses. Morgan's dress was pink and ivory and looked lovely on her, particularly with her blonde hair. Katrina found a red and white one. It had two-inch wide red and white stripes that fell diagonally from top to bottom. One side had a long sleeve and the other side was strapless. Both dresses were just past mid-thigh.

Sean picked Katrina up at seven-thirty and was bowled over when he saw her.

"Nice freaking dress!" He looked her up and down.

"Do you really like it?" She hoped it looked good on her. Although her hair was a shiny copper color, not actually red, sometimes red was not her color. Sean assured her she looked smashing in it.

The dance was a romantic affair. The gym had been decorated with pink, red and lavender hearts, and there was a gold gilt statue of Cupid surrounded by a white picket fence. The lighting gave off a soft pink glow that flattered even the palest of complexions. Sean and Katrina danced together most of the night. Since their first date Sean had learned to dance more than a slow dance, so he was much more fun to be with. Katrina, of course, with all of those dance classes under her belt, was an excellent dancer. She picked up the newest moves easily. They were really enjoying themselves on this Valentine's evening. Candy came over to their table and asked Sean to dance a few times, but Katrina didn't mind. She was beginning to think that Candy now had a crush on Sean since she couldn't have Jeff. It was all over the school that Jeff told her to get lost right after homecoming. Morgan and Kevin sat at their table with them. Morgan leaned over and asked Katrina why she was letting Sean dance with Candy.

"Why not? I don't own him. Besides....she apparently has nobody to dance with." Katrina told Morgan.

"That's because she's a bitch," was Morgan's answer. They both laughed.

The dance ended with the last song being a slow romantic song from the 1950's. Katrina and Sean danced it together. Sean held her tightly around the waist and whispered into her ear, "Kat, I love you."

Katrina looked deeply into his eyes and said, "No, Sean. Don't say that. We are too young to feel that way. We both have another year of high school and at least four years of college. We can't talk about love, and we can't be in love."

Katrina saw the hurt and disappointment in his eyes. She didn't want to hurt him, but damn it! Why did he want to be all wrapped up in love like that? She was going to make her decisions about her future based on what was best for her. They probably wouldn't even go to the same college. Wasn't it futile to fall in love now? There would be so many new people at college. She was sure they would forget about each other once they began their college years.

After the dance, Sean drove her home. He walked her to the door where he held her for a moment, and then kissed her forehead before he kissed her lips.

"You drive me crazy, Woman." He said to her as he waved and walked toward his car. She slipped inside the safety of her home.

* * *

It was February twenty-sixth, just two weeks after the dance. Sean and Katrina went to see a movie and stopped at Bear's Place for cokes afterward. It was still early, so Sean suggested they go for a drive. The night was cold and clear and the lights of the city sparkled like stars. He pulled the car up onto a dirt road where they could view the city down below.

"Beautiful, isn't it?" It was barely a whisper.

"Yes, it is." She answered.

"Like you." He said. "You're beautiful."

"Thanks." Her breath caught in her throat. "It's so cold out."

Sean accommodated her statement by turning up the car's heater. "Better?"

She smiled at him and nodded.

"Have you thought about where you want to go to college, yet?" He locked eyes with her for a moment.

"Well, sort of. I mean, I want a school that can offer me enough business courses to help me handle my business affairs, but also offer me liberal arts courses. What about you?"

"I don't know. Dad wants me to apply at Penn State. I guess I will. Sounds like it might be Carnegie Mellon for you, huh?"

"I don't know. I might consider an out-of-state school."

"Do you have money for that?"

"Uh-huh. I have a great college fund, not to mention how many paintings and sketches I've sold over the past two and a half years."

"Wow. Oh, I almost forgot. I have something for you." He reached past her to the glove box and opened it. He pulled out a five-by-seven envelope and handed it to her. "My dad took this picture at one of the games and had it enlarged for you."

She took a picture of herself in her drill team uniform out of the envelope, and smiled up at Sean. "This is a great picture! Tell your dad I said 'thank you', okay?" She slipped the picture into her purse.

Sean slipped his arm around her at the same time. When she turned to face him, he quickly put his lips onto hers and began kissing her, softly at first, but the kiss became more demanding. She started to push him away, but her hand slipped on the nylon of his jacket, and her arm went around him. Sean mistook that as a sign of consent. He wrapped his arm around her, almost pinning her to the seat. His other hand was holding her face in place as he forced his tongue into her mouth. She tried to move, but she couldn't. He loosened his hold on her a little as he slipped his hand under her sweater, and quickly found her nipple. She gasped and began to struggle. She jerked her face away from his and hissed, "NO!" She freed her arm and began pushing his hand away from her breast. "NO, SEAN, STOP! PLEASE!" She pleaded, while she struggled to get out of his grasp. His arms tightened around her.

He was breathing heavy and ragged. "Oh, Baby, Baby!" He moaned. "Don't stop me, please."

Katrina was beginning to panic. He was so much stronger than she was. She was pushing him away with all of her strength. "SEAN! STOP IT!" She suddenly found her right arm free. Without thinking, she balled up her fist and punched Sean square in the face. His head snapped back.

"Ow! Son-of-a-bitch!" With this he released his grip on her.

In a flash she was out of the car and running as fast as she could.

Sean sat behind the wheel, stunned. He punched the steering wheel, and uttered, "Fuck." Again he punched the wheel and hollered, "Fuck!" He looked into the rear view mirror and couldn't see Katrina anywhere. It was like she had vanished. He sat there in the car for what seemed like a long time, then put the car into gear and drove away.

Katrina was running, running as fast as she could, and crying. She was crying so hard she couldn't catch her breath any more. She stopped and leaned up against a lamp post to catch her breath; the cold air painfully searing into her lungs. She turned her back to the street in case a car came along. She wouldn't want a passing motorist to see her this way. "But what if it was Sean driving past?"

She began to panic again. She forced herself to calm down once again. Her body was trembling and when she looked down at her hands she saw that her right one was bruised and swollen, and bleeding a little. Thank goodness she had the presence of mind to grab her purse. She got out her brush and brushed her hair. When she looked into her compact mirror she wasn't too happy with what she saw. Her face was pale and blotchy and her eyes were swollen from crying. She felt herself on the verge of crying again, when she saw headlights coming. "Please don't let it be Sean," she thought. The car glided by her. It wasn't Sean's. She realized that she was shivering. Up until now she had forgotten how cold it was. It was at this moment that she remembered that she had no idea where she was. She raised her head to look around and saw that the windows on the buildings were covered with plywood. Someone had spray-painted graffiti on most of them. Somewhere not too far away, someone was yelling profanity. A woman standing across the street hollered to her.

"HEY BITCH! YOU ON MY STREET. GET LOST!"

To make matters worse, the car that had gone by a second ago was backing up. "Oh, God. Don't panic." She told herself. She couldn't breathe and there was a roaring sound in her head. Her tears were uncontrollable now that she was experiencing pure fear. "I can't even scream," she thought. She also thought she heard her name.

"Katrina? Is that you?" The passenger window of the car was halfway down. "Katrina, are you okay? It's me, Jeff. Jeff Hall." He climbed out of the driver's side door and came around to the sidewalk to her.

"Hey, are you okay? What's wrong? You're shivering! And you're crying! What's wrong, Sweetie? What happened?" Jeff put his hands on her shoulders, and that was all it took for her to fall against him, crying.

"Come on; get in the car where it's warm. Your teeth are chattering." He put a protective arm around her shoulders.

Jeff helped her into his car and it was warm, just as he said. He slid behind the wheel and reached for some tissues out of the glove box. As he handed them to her, he asked, "Have you eaten? Are you hungry?"

Katrina shook her head. Jeff turned on the overhead light and flipped down the passenger seat visor, exposing a mirror. "Here you go. Sorry I don't have better lighting, but it should be sufficient to fix your face up. Look at me."

Reluctantly, she turned to look at him.

"You don't look too bad. Come with me. I'm starving. I know a nice quiet little restaurant not far from here. The lighting is dim and the food is excellent. Once you smell it, you may get hungry. Okay?" He reached for her hand and squeezed it. She winced. He looked down at her hand and said, "We need to get some ice on that." He reached into the back seat and pulled a blanket over the back of the seat. "Here, wrap this around you so you'll warm up faster." He actually wrapped the blanket around her as he spoke. He put the car into gear and drove away.

* * *

The parking lot of the restaurant was nearly deserted. The restaurant's lights were shining through the windows onto the icy parking lot. Jeff turned the car off and turned to face Katrina.

He let out a small sigh and raised the corners of his mouth into a small smile. "Before we go any further, I want to set your mind at ease about me, okay?"

She nodded.

"Here goes. I work. I work every day after school and on most weekends. I have to. Since my dad died my mom has a tough time making ends meet."

Katrina started to say something, but Jeff stopped her.

"Hear me out. I want you to feel comfortable and safe with me, okay?"

She nodded, again.

"Anyway...It's just me and my mom. My sisters are married and living on their own. I want to go to college and I'm hoping to get a scholarship, but if I don't, my boss has taught me a fine trade. If I don't get the scholarship, I can work full-time at my trade and go to school at night. I divide my paycheck into thirds. One third I give to my mom, another third I put away for school, and the other third is mine. At any rate, I will get to go to college, but I need this job to help me. I have a wonderful, supportive boss who trusts me and is willing to help me any way he can, and I would not jeopardize my position with him. Now...the question is, can my boss trust me with his only daughter? You bet he can! I will be your knight in shining armor, I promise. So you just tell me where the dragons are and I'll slay them for you!"

Katrina stared at him for a moment. "You work for my dad?"

Jeff nodded. "I have for a year now."

"My dad never said anything."

"Your father is a gentleman." Jeff grinned at her. "I wouldn't want to lose his respect. Let's go inside. You are going to love this place."

"Uh, dragons, Jeff? I can think of one at the moment."

He was certainly right about smelling the food. She didn't even know she was hungry until they were seated at a small booth in the far corner, away from everyone. The restaurant was small and cozy with a country décor. The tablecloths and matching curtains were blue and white checked. The decorations on the walls were shapes of barnyard animals, including cows and roosters and pigs. Each table had a lit candle in the center. The salt and pepper shakers on the table of their booth were a set of matching cows. The waitress brought them glasses of water and menus. She was an older woman, probably past fifty, and very pleasant. She smiled and greeted both of them like they were family, but it was obvious that she knew Jeff. Katrina wondered for a moment if she were Jeff's mother, but it soon became clear that Jeff was just one of her favorite customers, and that was all there was to it. After joking with her for a couple of minutes, Jeff introduced her to Katrina as Clara, 'one of the sexiest waitresses ever.' Clara loved the reference, and winked at Katrina. "He's one in a million, Honey. I can tell you that."

"Clara, can you bring us some ice in a towel? My friend here caught her hand in the car door."

"Sure, Honey. Let's see it, Sweetie."

"Oh yeah, you're going to need ice. I'll bring it right over."

She hurried away and Jeff looked at Katrina and smiled. "I'm a sucker for older women, did you know that?"

Katrina laughed.

"There. I like that so much better than you crying." He hesitated while Clara handed him the ice wrapped in a towel. "Thanks, Clara. How about some coffee? Katrina? Coffee for you?"

"Oh, yes, I could use a cup. I'm still freezing."

"Okay, two coffees coming up." Clara hurried away again.

Jeff took Katrina's hand in his and placed the towel on top of it, and held it there.

"Now...can you tell me what happened?"

Katrina related the story to him, and all the while he sat there staring at her with an intense look.

".....And I hit him. I punched him in the face. He swore at me, and then I jumped out of the car and ran...and ran...and ran."

Jeff looked angry. "He's an idiot, a real idiot. Even after you said 'no' he wouldn't stop?"

"No. That's why I had to hit him." Tears began to well up in her eyes again. "I never hit anybody before."

Jeff reached over and wiped the tears from her cheek with his thumb. "He deserved it. I may have to hit him, too. Ignorant asshole! Sorry. So did you hit him hard?"

She raised her right hand slightly as a reminder.

"Do you think he'll have a black eye? I hope he has a black eye! I think I'll give him one on the other side so he has a matching pair." Katrina was laughing quietly.

He stopped and looked at her seriously. "Has it always been like that with the two of you? I mean, Sean always trying to get somewhere, and you always saying 'no'?"

She nodded. "I didn't realize it until tonight, but I'm always afraid to be alone with him. Jeff, it's not that I'm frigid or prudish....well, maybe a little prudish, it's just that I think sex should be special between two people who really love each other. I think the first time should be in a special place…not in a car. But most of all, I have goals. I'm not about to settle for what Sean or anybody else thinks is the right thing to do. I have a future. There are so many things I want to do, and none of them include having someone jump my bones in his car, simply because he can't control himself."

Jeff pinched his chin between his thumb and forefinger and stared at her silently.

"You're incredible, you know that? Sean's a jerk. You know, there are girls who put out all the time, there are girls who put out for someone they think they love, and then there are those rare treasures like you. What a prize you are, Katrina! When a guy has a girlfriend like you he should thank his lucky stars. Of course, any guy would want to make love to you. You're so beautiful. But with someone as special as you are, a decent guy learns how to control himself and doesn't overstep his bounds. It's not like he's not getting any. He's been banging Candy on the side for five months now."

Katrina snapped her head up and stared at Jeff. "What?"

"I'm sorry. I guess it wasn't my place to say anything. But that's why I don't go near Candy. It started after the homecoming dance."

Katrina thought for a minute, and then began to laugh.

"You're taking this well. Better than I expected."

"No, I was just remembering that he stopped trying to force the issue for awhile after that night. I thought I had finally gotten through to him. I guess I can call Candy as his secret outlet, then. I wonder what changed things tonight."

"From what I hear, Candy told him either he had to break up with you or she was shutting him off."

"Well, she can have him all to herself. We are over." Katrina was suddenly ravenous. "Let's order that food you promised, okay?"

Jeff grinned and called Clara over.

They enjoyed the meal they ordered and Jeff drove her home. He walked her to the door and hugged her. "Can I call you?"

Katrina looked up into Jeff's handsome face and simply said, "Yes."

He started walking to his car and she called him back. "Jeff, wait. Thanks for getting rid of those dragons for me."

He grinned from ear to ear, showing his even white teeth. His grey eyes sparkled in the light from the porch. He removed the ball cap he always wore and his straight brown hair fell forward. He swooped forward into a gentleman's bow and said, "Any time, my lady....any time." He threw her a kiss and jogged to his car. She watched him go, and realized she was smiling.

On Sunday morning, Katrina awoke feeling ill. Her throat was scratchy and her head hurt. She got up for awhile but went back to bed when she couldn't eat breakfast. Mary and Ed worried that she might be coming down with the flu. Around mid-day Mary went up to her room to check on her. She felt very warm to the touch, so she sent Ed out for cold and flu medicine. When he returned Katrina awoke for the second time that day. "Daddy, I didn't know that Jeff Hall worked for you." She croaked out.

"Yeah, Honey, he's a fine boy, and a hard worker, too. There aren't many kids like him nowadays. He's a good-looking kid, too. I'm surprised you two never got together after homecoming last year. I'm fairly sure he likes you. Get some rest, Honey, okay?"

By evening, Katrina was very sick. Her breathing was ragged and she was burning with fever.

Mary was worried. "If this keeps up, I want to take her to emergency, Ed."

Ed frowned down at Katrina and watched her labored breathing. "Let's give the medicine an hour or so. If there's no change, we should take her."

Mary sat down on the bed beside her daughter. "Oh, God, please... make her well again." The phone beside Katrina's bed jingled, and Mary grabbed it up before it could wake Katrina. It was Jeff Hall.

"I'm sorry, Jeff, but Katrina is very sick. She's sleeping right now..."

"Mom, let me say 'hi' to him." Her voice was barely there. Mary handed her the phone.

"Hi. I think it's another dragon, Jeff." Her voice was barely recognizable and the words were hardly audible, but Jeff knew what she said, and he smiled in spite of his concern for her.

"Put your mother back on, Sweetheart, Okay? You need to go back to sleep, got it?" She nodded, but could say nothing. She gave Mary the phone.

"Mrs. Kitrowski, what's wrong with her?"

"I don't know for sure. She woke up sick this morning. Her breathing is terrible."

"Maybe you should take her to the hospital."

"That's going to be our next move, I think."

"Mrs. Kitrowski, I know you're worried about her, and it's probably all you can think about right now, but will you keep me informed on what's going on with her?"

"I'll try, Jeff, but if I don't call you, feel free to call me or my husband, okay?"

"Okay, thanks, Mrs. K. Bye now."

He hung up, and said aloud to the mirror in the hall. "This is that fucking Sean's fault. Thinking about Katrina running through the streets in the below zero weather, just to get away from him, just pisses me off."

Katrina's breathing worsened. Mary called to Ed to get the car out of the garage. He ran to the garage, started the car, pulled it up next to the side door, and ran into the house to get Katrina. He picked her up and Mary wrapped a blanket around her. Katrina appeared to be unconscious. Ed told Mary to drive while he held Katrina in his arms. She wasted no time getting behind the wheel and getting the car into gear. She sped off into the night to the closest emergency room.

They waited outside while the doctor examined her. He ordered chest x-rays and they sat and waited some more. It was almost three o'clock in the morning when the doctor met them in the waiting area.

"I'm going to admit her. She has acute bronchial pneumonia. I'm ordering oxygen for the next twelve hours and hopefully, with the antibiotics, she will start to improve. Tell me, was she exposed to those sub-zero temperatures for any period of time?"

"I-I don't know. She had a date with her boyfriend on Saturday night. I don't know what they did. She was home a couple of minutes before midnight. They went to see a movie and probably to eat afterward. I'm not sure."

"Well, we'll ask her. In the meantime, you two should probably go home and get some sleep. There's really nothing you can do for her here. You'll probably have to call her school and report her absent. She'll be here a few days. I'll be in to check on her around eleven o'clock when I make my morning rounds. If you're here then, we can talk some more. Okay?"

They thanked the doctor, went in to kiss Katrina, who had already been moved to a hospital room, and went home.

"Get some sleep, Ed. I know you are tired."

"Something's not right, Mary."

"What are you talking about?"

"I'm not sure, but I smell a rat somewhere. Did Sean even call the house all day today, well yesterday, I mean.....Sunday."

"No, he didn't, but that's not too unusual."

"Maybe not, I just have this gut feeling that he may be responsible for our daughter being that sick. Mary, if he hurt my girl in any way, I'll....."

Mary looked at him and said nothing. She hoped not, but Ed was rarely wrong about these things.

In the morning she made coffee and breakfast for Ed to go to work, and she began getting ready to go to the hospital. She jumped when the phone rang. It was Jeff. She told him that Katrina had been admitted into the hospital with bronchial pneumonia, and Jeff sounded deeply concerned. "Is it okay if I visit her?" He wanted to know.

"Yes, of course, Jeff. Her room number is two-twenty-four."

"Thanks, so much, Mrs. K. I hope she gets well soon."

"Thanks, Jeff. I hope so, too. Have a good day." She placed the receiver back into the cradle and finished getting ready. She called the school before she left and let someone in the office know that Katrina was in the hospital.

* * *

She found Katrina with her head propped up on pillows and she looked slightly better. She had tubing going into her nostrils for oxygen purposes, but other than that, she looked like she was sleeping comfortably. Mary pulled a paperback book from her purse and sat down in the most comfortable-looking chair and began to read. Around eleven o'clock the doctor came in to examine Katrina again. He listened to her lungs, seemed satisfied, and sat down in the other chair next to the bed.

"The lungs are improving already. That's what acute means. It comes on suddenly, attacks hard, responds to treatment, and goes away quickly with no after-effects…usually. Sometimes there are complications, but not with someone so young and in such good health. She's going to sleep most of the day. The drugs we have given her will cause that. Take a nap, yourself. You look like you could use it."

Mary laughed. "I may take you up on that."

1-26

Jeff walked into the cafeteria after his fourth period class, and the first person he saw was Sean. He was quietly eating his lunch with not one ounce of guilt on his face. In fact, the only thing on his face was the shiner that Katrina had given him. 'Boy, I'd love to do the other side.' He thought.

He walked up to Sean's table and asked, "What happened to your eye?"

"I bumped it getting out of the car over the weekend."

Jeff leaned down and put his forearms on either side of Sean's lunch tray, and in a low growl, asked, "Was that before or after Katrina nailed you when you attacked her?"

Sean blanched. "That's none of your business."

"Well, I just made it my business. You know she's in the hospital, don't you?"

Sean looked as though he were going to faint. "No. Wh-what happened? Why is she in the hospital?"

"You fucking bastard! She jumped out of your car and ran off because she was afraid of you, and you didn't even try to look for her, did you? Did you think about what could have happened to her? Did you care? Did you even call her yesterday to see if she got home okay? NO! You didn't. You fucking didn't. You couldn't get a piece of ass, so you just fucking let her run off into a bad neighborhood by herself, and you didn't even care what happened to her. You're a piece of shit, you know that?"

Jeff said all this with his face six inches away from Sean's. He stood up and looked at Sean with disgust, shoved a cafeteria chair, slamming it into the table, and walked away.

Sean sat there staring after him. He had wondered why Katrina hadn't shown up in their second period class, and yes, there had been a pang of guilt that he hadn't called to see if she got home okay. He was afraid that she would have hung up on him if he called. He wanted to give her time to cool down. Contrary to what Jeff had said, he did care. He really loved Katrina. Now she's in the hospital! What happened? He had to go to her…tell her how sorry he was….

Jeff stormed out of the cafeteria and Morgan caught up with him.

"Jeff, what's going on? Jeff, wait…." Morgan was practically running to catch up with him. Jeff stopped and leaned against the wall to get his composure back.

"Tell me. Do you know where Katrina is today? What's going on?" Morgan looked concerned.

"Morgan, Katrina is your friend, right?"

"Yeah, my best friend, I think."

Jeff told her all he knew about Saturday night, and how he found Katrina that night. He let her know that Katrina was in the hospital with pneumonia because of Saturday. "And another thing, Morgan….. did you know that Sean was sleeping with Candy?"

Morgan gasped. "No!"

"It's been going on for a few months. I found out about it the day after the homecoming dance. A lot of kids here know about it. I'm surprised that nobody told Katrina."

"Nobody would want to hurt her, except Candy, maybe. Why would he sleep with her? Everybody knows what she is."

"It's because Katrina always said 'no'. Funny how he kept trying, huh? Katrina told me that she was afraid to be alone with Sean."

"Is Katrina going to be okay?" Morgan was genuinely concerned. "Is she allowed visitors?"

"Yes to both questions….I'm going to go see her after I get off work tonight."

"Jeff, you really like Katrina, don't you?"

"Uh...yep. I never wanted to interfere with her and pretty boy though."

"Maybe you should have."

"I'm going to, now." Morgan saw him smile for the first time since he left the cafeteria.

* * *

Sean was nervous as he walked down the corridor of the hospital. "She's in room two-twenty-four." The receptionist told him. He had ducked out of his last three classes, stopped to buy flowers, and had come directly to the hospital. Outside of her room, he hesitated. He couldn't see into the room, so he listened to see if there were other people in the room besides Katrina. He couldn't hear anyone talking. He hesitated for a few more seconds, took a deep breath and walked into the room.

Mary was just getting off the elevator from the cafeteria. She was holding a cup of coffee for herself and a diet soda for Katrina. She spied Sean standing in front of Katrina's room and she stopped. He hesitated for only a moment before he went into her room. Mary hurried down the corridor toward room two-twenty-four. 'I hate to eavesdrop, but she's my kid. I have to know what happened to her.' Mary thought as she stepped into the short hallway that separated the room from the corridor. She knew she couldn't be seen from the room but she could hear what was being said inside.

"Katrina, I....I'm so sorry." Sean set the flowers down on the bed and looked at Katrina.

Katrina turned her head and stared at Sean like she was seeing him for the first time. She immediately noticed his black eye, though.

"This can't be fixed with flowers this time, Sean. This is your fault! Some of it's my fault...I should have ended it with you when I realized I was afraid to be alone with you."

At this, Sean sucked in his breath in a short gasp. "Afraid to be alone with me?"

"Yes....afraid. How many times did I tell you that '*no*' means '*no*'? But it was always the same struggle. What made you think that you were going to be able to change my mind? I told you that it was never going to happen. I even told you that if you couldn't accept that, to find someone else. Which you did…..oh yes, I know about Candy… but you still couldn't keep your hands where they belonged. Well, it's over. You and I are done, finished." She had to stop talking just to catch her breath.

"Katrina…no…let me explain…Candy came on to me…I…I didn't…."

"This is not about Candy!" Katrina hissed at him. "This is about you….and me. I will not be compromised just because you can't control your raging hormones! I will not be put into a position to where I have to punch someone to make him take his hands off me…. ever again! I'm sorry that I hit you, but I am angry that you forced me to hit you!"

Mary had to put her hand over her mouth to keep from laughing. Katrina punched Sean?

"Now, get out! Take the flowers. Give them to Candy, for all I care. From now on, we don't know each other!" Katrina was beginning to cry and Sean made an attempt to reach for her. "Get out, Sean!" She hissed as she shrank back from him.

Sean turned on his heel and quickly got out of the room, almost slamming into Mary who had been standing there all that time. Mary immediately went to her daughter to comfort her. She put her arms around Katrina's narrow shoulders and cradled her against her shoulder. She held her long after Katrina stopped crying. Mary was trying to put the pieces together, when she looked down and saw Katrina smiling up at her.

"Do you want to talk about it, Honey?" Katrina nodded. She told Mary everything that happened between her and Sean, and how she punched him and ran. She was going to tell her the part where Jeff came in, but just then, Jeff came into the room. He was carrying a large stuffed dragon with a red rose in its mouth. Katrina laughed at it.

"Hi Jeff, I was just filling my mom in on what happened Saturday night. I was just at the part where you came in. Jeff came to my rescue, Mom."

"Well, I thank you for that. What happened next?"

Jeff told Mary how he saw Katrina on the street, and that he stopped for her. "She was shivering and crying, her teeth were chattering, she was shaking so bad. I made her get into the car and I wrapped her up in a blanket. Then I took her to my favorite restaurant…"

"And flirted with the middle-aged waitress…" Katrina interjected.

"….And yes, that I did….but that also got us some ice for your hand, didn't it?"

Mary shivered a little, just thinking of her daughter being in the condition that Jeff just described. She looked at Katrina's hand and saw that it was still bruised. She had noticed that on Sunday morning, but didn't think to ask about it since she was preoccupied with Katrina being ill.

"Well, anyway, then I took her home." He looked at Katrina and asked, "Did you see his eye? Nice work!" They both laughed.

"So….how do you feel?" Jeff wanted to know. "You sound better. I can understand what you're saying now."

Katrina looked at Mary and then at Jeff. "I'm feeling a little better." She saw the look of relief on both of their faces.

"Aha! I caught you!" All eyes turned toward the hallway, and there stood Ed. He was smiling at Jeff. "I should have known why you called off work! I knew it had to be something important, and nothing is more important than my daughter!" Ed's eyes had a twinkle in them as he spoke. He came around the bed and clapped Jeff on the back. "Glad to see you here."

"Thanks, Mr. Kitrowski, and yeah, you caught me. I confess…I'm interested in your daughter."

"Well, if it's okay with her, it's okay with me. How are you feeling, Baby?" He turned to Katrina.

"A little better, Daddy, and mom can fill you in on everything that's happened, and why Jeff is a hero."

"Okay, can I get you anything? Do you need anything? How's the food? Are you eating?"

"No…No…Okay…and yes! Any more questions?" She was laughing her melodious laugh and it was music to everyone's ears.

Morgan and Kevin came to visit. Morgan joked that even when she was sick, she still looked better than most of the girls in school.

"Jeff filled me in on everything." She whispered to Katrina. "Sean sucks." Katrina just chuckled a little.

Katrina recovered quickly. She was released from the hospital on Thursday, with the doctor's okay to go back to school after a week of rest at home. Jeff and Morgan visited her almost every day, bringing her assignments so she wouldn't get behind. She gave Jeff the combination to her locker so he could get what books she needed. Morgan visited after school and Jeff came later in the evening after work. Ed began treating Jeff almost like a son after he found out what Jeff had done for Katrina after Sean had treated her so badly. He still brooded about that. Mary stopped him from going over to Sean's house, but she couldn't stop him from telling their sons about it. He told Kim all about it and he was sure it would get to Michael. It did. Michael called to talk to Katrina. Just hearing her voice made him feel better. "You're okay?" He wanted to know. She assured him that she was. "You punched him?" She affirmed that she had, and elaborated about the black eye he had. "Good girl!" was Michael's response. It wasn't over as far as Michael was concerned, and he was sure that Danny would agree.

Kim was sitting on Katrina's bed just visiting and offering whatever support or solace she could. "Michael never trusted Sean, did you know that?" Kim asked her.

"No, I didn't. Michael wouldn't trust anyone with me though."

"Oh I don't know...he likes Jeff."

"Jeff? How does he know him?"

"From working at your Dad's company....Michael went there a couple of times to see your dad and he met Jeff then. When I told him about Jeff rescuing you and that he had been coming over to visit you every day, Michael was happy about that. He said Jeff is a stand-up guy."

"Oh..." was Katrina's response. Michael was right about Jeff. He truly was a stand-up guy. Katrina really liked Jeff, but more than that, she felt safe with him.

1-27

Katrina returned to school and was greeted by a lot of well-wishers. Many had heard about the incident with Sean, and many of them knew about Sean and Candy. Katrina halfway expected to see them together as a couple, but it didn't appear that way. It looked more like they avoided each other. In second period class, Sean dropped down into the seat next to her, and she didn't even glance at him. He was hurt but he knew he had that coming. He blew it, he knew. His actions were something he would always regret. He told Candy to stay away from him. 'What was I thinking, cheating on Katrina with her?' he thought to himself. He felt so miserable and embarrassed that he truly wished that the earth would open up and swallow him. What made it worse was that he saw Katrina and Jeff Hall holding hands in the hall. 'He didn't waste any time moving in, did he?' Sean grumbled to himself.

Katrina went to the St. Patrick's Day dance with Jeff. They made it a foursome with Morgan and Kevin, and it was fun. They laughed and laughed all evening. Jeff was so funny that Katrina thought he should become a comedian. They were all wearing the traditional Irish green topped with green cellophane hats. For once she was truly enjoying a date.

* * *

Her seventeenth birthday was approaching. Sitting at the kitchen table having breakfast one morning a week before her birthday, Katrina asked her parents if it would be okay if Jeff joined them for her birthday next week. "I mean, I know we always go out to dinner, so I thought maybe he could go, too." She looked at her parents expectantly.

Ed was the first to speak. "Of course.....it's fine with me. I like the kid, myself."

Mary nodded in agreement.

"Great!" Katrina responded. "Oh, that would mean he would need to get off work a little early to get ready...."

"I think I can take care of it, Honey." Ed smiled at her. "I won't ever forget what he did for you...how he was there for you. No matter what happens with you and Jeff…if you go your separate ways or stay together…I will always hold a special place for the boy who cared enough to take care of my daughter when she needed someone."

"Thanks, Daddy." She smiled at her wonderful, loving father. He nodded and turned back to his breakfast. He had a little secret of his own they were all going to discover before too long. He smiled to himself.

For her birthday they went to Jeff's favorite place—the place he had taken her to on the night fate took over. They sat in a larger booth, of course, but had the same waitress. Katrina pointed her out and said to Mary, "There's my competition. That's Clara." Jeff laughed and squeezed her hand under the table.

Clara made it over to the table. She instantly recognized Jeff, then Katrina. "How's your hand, Sweetie? Did it get better?"

"Yes, it did. Thanks for asking."

"Still with this guy, huh? I told you, he's one in a million." She was indicating Jeff.

Katrina introduced her to Mary and Ed, and Clara told them they had a beautiful daughter. Jeff told them they wouldn't be disappointed with the food, and that earned an appreciative glance from Clara. The evening was comfortable and enjoyable. They left the restaurant and headed back to the house for cake and ice cream. Katrina still had presents to open, too.

Katrina received clothes, clothes and more clothes, from Mary and Ed, and gift certificates from Michael, Kim, Danny, and Kathy. Kim slipped in for a visit while they were eating cake.

"Don't forget, we're going to Florida for Danny's graduation, so you'll need things for the trip." Mary reminded her.

"Yeah, another trip to Florida with Katrina…..Whoopee….Jeff, let me tell you about the last time we all went to Florida." Ed began.

"Daddy!"

"Ed!"

"What? Jeff, walking across the beach with her in her bikini was like walking through a war zone. Every male was a testosterone grenade."

"DADDY!!"

Jeff was roaring with laughter. "I can imagine." He got quiet for a moment. "Kat, I haven't given you my gifts yet."

"Je-eff! I told you that you didn't have to get me anything. You need to save for school."

"I know you did. You said not to get you a gift…so…I got you two! Get it? Not a gift, but two gifts."

Katrina rolled her eyes. "Got it."

He reached in his jacket pocket and pulled out a small oblong box wrapped in blue foiled paper, and handed it to her. She opened it quickly and found a fourteen karat heart-shaped gold locket on a chain.

"Jeff, it's beautiful!" She looked up and smiled at him.

"Open it." He urged her.

She opened it and found a small photo of the two of them. It had been reduced in size to fit the locket. "I love it. It's great, Jeff. Thank you." She leaned over and kissed his cheek, and then put the locket around her neck and secured it into place.

"Okay, the other one is already on your car. Go look." She ran outside and saw the vanity plate on the front of her car. Jeff had it specially made. The pale pink plate had, 'Kit-Kat' written on it and had a picture of a sleek white cat holding a red rose.

Her eyes showed how she felt about it. They lit up and sparkled. "How did you know about that name? And the cat is…perfect" She stared at Jeff.

"I remember from grade school….and that is your cartoon character's name, isn't it?"

"Yes, it is." She smiled up at Jeff. How appreciated he made her feel.

Mary and Ed stood there wondering what they were talking about. What cartoon character? "Would you like to clue us in on all this?"

Katrina told them about her cartooning class at the institute. She invented her cartoon character and developed a cartoon series based on it. It was a sleek white cat named Kit-Kat.

"How cute, Honey." Mary was impressed. Ed was curious and wanted to see it.

Katrina offered to get it from her room, leaving them all standing inside the kitchen. They sat down when Katrina produced the cartoon portfolio.

"This is very good, Sweetheart." Ed was impressed. Mary and Kim were looking over his shoulder at Katrina's cartoon.

Jeff looked at Ed, and then he turned toward Katrina. "I got the license plate because....well, I have a feeling that will be your trademark in the future, and someday the name Kit-Kat will be known to everybody in America."

"Thanks, Jeff....it means a lot to me that you feel that way." Their eyes met and they connected in a very special way.

* * *

The Awards Banquet was scheduled for May fourteenth. Katrina and Jeff would be attending it. Since it was a family event, Mary and Ed and Jeff's mother would also be there. Katrina had not met Jeff's mother so she had no idea what to expect. They were all seated at a table together. Mrs. Hall was very pleasant and seemed to like Katrina. Every student in the room was there to receive an award of some kind. There were sports awards, achievement awards, and scholarships to be passed out. The air was thick with excitement and expectations. Katrina looked across the room and spied Sean and his parents. At the table next to Katrina's, Morgan and Kevin and their parents were seated. She knew that she and Morgan, as well as the rest of the drill team, were going to be receiving letters or additional pins to attach to the letters they already earned, for their participation on the drill team. Katrina and Morgan already had the letters, so they would be receiving pins to put on their letter jackets.

The dinner was served first and the banquet servers were clearing the tables so the awards program could begin.

The achievement awards were first. Katrina's name was called to receive a pin for being in the choir, and again for her work on the newspaper. She was called up on stage a third time. This time it was a surprise to her. She was given a plaque and a certificate for outstanding academic achievement and for maintaining a 4.0 grade point average for five consecutive years in the gifted child program. As usual, Mary had the tissues out. Ed grinned and Jeff fell in love with her for the millionth time.

The next category was for sports. All of the players of all the sports in the school received sports letters for their jackets. Morgan and Katrina, along with the rest of the drill team, went up for their letters or pins for drill team participation. The cheerleaders went up for theirs after the drill team. For a brief instant, she and Candy locked eyes. Candy looked away first.

The last category, and the most important, was the scholarship awards. Kevin was awarded a scholarship to UP. Morgan was glad because now he wouldn't be going far away. WVU was offering a full football scholarship. There were people there from WVU to present their scholarship. Everybody waited breathlessly to hear who was getting the scholarship.

"This year's full football scholarship to WVU goes to—JEFF HALL!"

Katrina's hands flew to her face. Her eyes were wide with excitement. Jeff seemed unable to move. "GO! Go up there!"

His eyes connected with hers and all he ever wanted to say to her was conveyed at that moment. Katrina reached for Mary's ever-ready tissues. Jeff's mother reached for them, too. All three women looked at each other and laughed lightly. Jeff accepted the scholarship and came back to the table, cheeks flushed. When he sat down, Ed got up and went up to the microphone.

The room got quiet as he got the audience's attention.

"My name is Ed Kitrowski, and I am the owner of Kit Design, Inc. Every year we give an award to someone who deserves the title of 'hero'. Our award has become known as the 'Hero Award' and I'm sure some of you have heard of it. In order to receive this award, the chosen person must be an upstanding citizen, an asset to the community, and must have committed some heroic act where he or she saved someone from harm, or protected someone in an hour of need. This person, even though heroic, is humble and down to earth. He is not a glory-seeker, but just a good person following a good path of life. Every year my employees cast their votes for the person in the community that they feel should win. This year it was unanimous, except for one vote. That one vote was from the person who didn't vote for himself. Ladies and Gentlemen, I am proud to present this plaque of honor and a check for five thousand dollars to that person tonight. I have a personal interest in this, I must say. For saving and protecting my daughter when she needed you, this award goes to you, JEFF HALL!"

The applause was deafening. Mary, Katrina and Mrs. Hall were again reaching for tissues. Jeff went up to Ed, reached out his hand to shake Ed's, then thought better of it, and grabbed Ed in a bear hug. "I love her....you know that, don't you?" Ed nodded.

Sean witnessed all this and turned away.

"You wouldn't know what he was talking about, would you, Sean?" Tim Parks' eyes were boring a hole into his son's face. He had been suspicious about Sean and Katrina's breakup ever since it happened. Sean came home with a black eye, and Katrina's name was not mentioned in the house since then. 'That girl is a real class act,' he thought to himself. 'I hope he didn't hurt her in any way.' Sean just looked at his father and shrugged.

The Prom was the following week, May twenty-first. Katrina was excited about going with Jeff, just as much as Jeff was excited about taking her. He knew his date would be the most beautiful girl there. Katrina's gown was a lavender lace with lace straps. The dress was cut straight across the top of the bosom, where an overlay of lace ruffle dropped down across the top. The five-tiered lace skirt was full because of the petticoats attached inside it. She was a vision of femininity, right down to her high heeled white sandals. Her hair was piled high on her head save for some curly wisps that hung down at the sides and at the nape of her neck. She chose an amethyst stone necklace and matching earrings. Mary and Kim were up in her room with her helping her with the final touches, and Ed and Michael were downstairs when Jeff's car pulled into the driveway.

"Wait until he sees you!" Kim whispered. "You look heavenly!"

Michael asked Ed, "This guy really is okay, right, Dad?"

"Don't ask me...you're the FBI guy!" Ed retorted with a smile. The he added, "Mike, I would trust this guy with Katrina's life. You know Jeff, anyway. When you see him, you'll remember who he is. He works for me. After they go, I'll tell you what happened between Katrina and that Sean. Jeff stepped in, and I'm damn glad he did."

Jeff tapped on the door and Ed went to let him in. Jeff looked very handsome in his pearl gray tuxedo with the lavender cummerbund and tie.

"Jeff, you remember Michael, don't you? My son?"

Jeff extended his hand to Michael and he accepted it with a handshake. "Good to see you again. So you're an FBI agent now?"

Michael nodded. He remembered Jeff from his dad's shop. He was thinking about what his dad was going to tell him. He knew part of it, but he wanted to hear the rest. He hadn't had time to talk to anybody about it, since he had just arrived in town the day before. He would be in the area for quite a while, so he and Kim were apartment hunting all day. He came out of his reverie with the sound of rustling skirts. He looked up and gasped. Katrina was a vision of beauty. He caught a look at Jeff from the corner of his eye. 'Yep, that boy is definitely in love,' he thought to himself.

"Wow!" was all that Jeff could muster. He stared at her, and just drank in every inch of her before he regained his composure.

"Here, this is for you. You look....amazing!" He handed her a wrist corsage of white roses mixed with lavender colored daisies, which matched the color of her dress perfectly. She put it on, and Mary had the camera ready. Kim had her camera, too, so there would be lots of pictures of this night.

"The lavender tie and cummerbund match my dress perfectly!" Katrina laughed with delight.

"What time do you want her home, Mr. K?" Jeff asked Ed.

"What's the agenda?" Ed wanted to know.

"Well, there's the Prom dance at the country club, then there's the after-prom party at the gym. If we go there, we have to stay until five o'clock in the morning. Once you go in, you can't get back out until then. It's school rules."

Ed gave Mary a questioning look. Mary raised her eyebrows at Ed, letting him know it was his decision.

Surprisingly, Michael stepped in. "You know, Kim and I can go at no charge since we are Alumni. Kim? What do you say we get dressed up and to go the after-prom party?" Kim smiled at him and said, "It's a date! Pick me up at eleven. I'll be ready."

Katrina hugged Michael. "I love you." She whispered in his ear.

"You owe me." He whispered back, and smiled at her. "You look... fabulous."

"Well, we better go. We still have to stop at my place and be tortured with more flashes. Mom brought film home. She got off work early to be there for us." Jeff spoke as he placed Katrina's lavender lace shawl that came with the dress over her shoulders.

"Have a good time, you two," Someone said as they went out of the door.

After they were gone, Ed and Mary filled Michael in on what had happened between Katrina and Sean. Michael laughed again when they told him Katrina punched Sean. Kim had already told him that part, and so did Katrina, but it was still funny.

"I just don't think he should get away with it."

"Well, Morgan says he's really suffering because Katrina won't even look at him. Maybe that's punishment enough…." Mary's voice trailed off. She could see that wasn't cutting any ice.

"I think I'll pay a visit to Parks tomorrow. He's really a decent family guy. I don't think he will be too happy to find out his son is a jackass like that."

* * *

The Country Club was decorated beautifully for their magical night. There were flowers and small twinkle lights everywhere. The dance floor had been separated from the tables with lattice-work fences that had flowers entwined in them. There were plenty of dim lights everywhere so that it wasn't too light, but not too dark. In fact, the lights created a golden glow in the room. Jeff and Katrina walked hand-in-hand into the area designated for their prom. Jeff noticed how everyone's head turned to gape at Katrina. She really looked magnificent. She looked up at him and smiled that beautiful smile, and his heart melted as it always did when she smiled at him. He smiled back, and hoped he didn't look too stupid.

Morgan appeared out of nowhere wearing a slinky black strapless gown. She grinned at Katrina. "You look smashing! I knew I should have gone with ultra-feminine instead of glamorous and slinky!"

"You definitely look glamorous! Hey, you do glamorous so well! I happen to be in touch with my feminine side." They both broke up laughing.

When Kevin appeared they found a table for the four of them. A waiter approached the table almost immediately. They gave him orders for drinks and began laughing and joking with each other while they waited for the non-alcoholic beverages to arrive. The room was filling up with high school students all dressed in their finery. On each table were ballots for voting for the prom king and queen. They checked their ballots and Jeff took all four of them over to the ballot box.

Morgan touched Katrina's arm and said, "Don't look now, but Sean and Candy just walked in together."

"I hope they have a good time," Katrina gave Morgan a big, fake grin, and Morgan laughed.

"I hear she asked him." Morgan confided.

Katrina rolled her eyes upward. "Oh, God...please don't ever let me get that desperate."

Morgan laughed harder. "Stop! You're going to make me ruin my make-up!"

"However," Continued Katrina, "At the after-prom party...my brother Mike and his wife will be there. I have a feeling that Sean will be made very uncomfortable. I've told Mike to just drop it and leave it alone, but I know my brother, and he won't."

The music began and the prom was definitely underway. Jeff took Katrina's hand and led her to the dance floor, where he encircled her waist and tucked her hand in close to him. He rested his chin against her head and whispered, "Everybody in this room wants to be me right now."

She raised her eyes to meet his and simply said, "Nobody else could be."

Once again Jeff and Katrina were king and queen, only this time they were prom royalty and they were a true couple. Morgan joked that the only way she would ever be voted in as any type of queen would be if she moved away to another school. Kevin—wonderful, loving Kevin—told her that she would always be his queen and that seemed to appease her.

The prom ended at eleven-thirty, giving them all time to get to the gym before midnight. True to his word, Michael and Kim were at the gym whey they arrived. He was talking to some of his former teachers when Katrina and Jeff walked in. He smiled when he saw them both wearing the crowns. He ran up to them and hugged his sister.

"Want us all to sit together, Queenie?" He teased.

"Yes, but Morgan and Kevin are with us, so we have to get a table big enough for them to sit, too." Katrina countered.

"No problem....Kim and I have found a table for six....is that good?"

"Perfect," Both she and Jeff answered simultaneously. They looked at each other and grinned.

The after-prom party was loads of fun for everyone. The disc jockey had a Karaoke machine and Katrina and Morgan got up and did a rendition of "My Guy" together. Kevin and Jeff agreed that they were cute, and both of the guys felt good about their song choice. A couple of boys who couldn't carry a tune in a bag got up and made complete fools of themselves, but brought the house down with laughter. Morgan and Katrina kicked off their shoes and danced in their stocking feet, and the guys loosened their ties. They all listened to anecdotes about training class from Michael, and were fascinated by his recount of things that happened during the trainings. The three girls all went to the ladies room and left the three guys sitting there.

Michael looked over at Jeff and asked, "Have you thought about doing anything to Sean for what he did to Katrina?"

"Oh, many, many times...but Katrina doesn't want me to do anything. She says it's not worth it since I could get into trouble." Jeff answered him.

"Yeah, she's got a point, especially with you getting that scholarship. I hear she punched him. Was his eye marked up at all?"

"Oh hell yeah...he had a very black eye for days. You don't know how badly I wanted to do the other side, so he would have a matched pair." Jeff sneered.

"Well, I was on the local force with his dad. I think I'm going over to see his dad tomorrow, and I don't think he's going to like what I have to say. In the meantime, I'm just going to intimidate the hell out of Sean all night tonight. He just walked toward the bathrooms, and wouldn't you fucking know it...he's staring at Katrina coming out of the bathroom. I'm about ready to get up...now." With that, Michael stood up and looked over the crowd right into Sean's face. Sean quickly retreated.

The three guys stood up when the girls got back to the table, and pulled out their chairs for them. The rest of the night went without incident, and when five o'clock in the morning came around, they were all ready to go home to bed. On the drive home, Jeff held Katrina's hand. To him, it was truly a magical night. At her house, he got out and walked her to the door, where he pulled her to him and just held her. He looked down into her face and brushed her cheek with his thumb. He couldn't trust himself to speak at that moment, so he said nothing. He kissed the tip of her nose, and then very softly kissed her lips.

"G'night, my lady," He spoke softly.

"Goodnight, Dragon-slayer," she answered just as softly, and went inside.

1-28

The following weekend the Kitrowski's traveled to Florida to see Danny graduate. Graduation exercises were held on Saturday, which would give them a full day on the beach on Sunday and some time on Monday, since their flight out of Florida wasn't until seven in the evening on Monday. It was just Mary, Ed and Katrina, since Michael was 'on the clock' that weekend. The graduation ceremony was long, with many speeches. Katrina spotted Danny first, and then Kathy as the graduates filed in. After what seemed like hours, the ceremony was over and Danny and Kathy joined them. There was a reception for the graduates and their families, so they all headed in that direction. Danny introduced them to many of the graduates in his class and a few of the Professors. The dean, who looked to be close to one hundred years old, asked if he could be introduced to Katrina. He was a sweet, elderly man who appreciated perfection, as he put it. He kissed her hand and told her that she was lucky that he was a faithful, married man. They all laughed over that.

The weekend ended too soon. Danny and Kathy told them they would be flying in on the twentieth and getting married on the twenty-fifth.

* * *

Katrina managed to get a golden tan, in one day, to take back to Pennsylvania with her. She also managed to get small gifts for Jeff, Morgan, and Kevin. Their plane had been in the air for half an hour when Mary mentioned planning a small wedding and reception for Danny and Kathy.

"Kathy has no family to speak of, except for a sister. I think we should throw something together for them. What do you think?" She looked back and forth from Ed to Katrina. Of course, they both agreed it would be nice. They began the planning on the plane, when Mary pulled out a pen and notepad out of her purse.

* * *

The following weekend was consumed with the Arts Festival. Katrina had several entries on display, some of which had been selected to receive ribbons. She had to be there most of the time that first weekend, so Mary and Ed went with her during the days. Jeff showed up after work in the evenings, helped her close her portion of the festival down, and drove her home. The festival was a full week's event, but because of school and lessons, Katrina could not be there all the time. She and Jeff showed up on a few of the evenings. Every time they went to the area where her work hung, there was a new 'sold' sign on one of the paintings. On the last night, Mr. Chambers was there to greet her. He wanted to know if it was okay to sell all those he had sold for her, since they were all sales pending her approval. She agreed to all sales, and was amazed and shocked at the amount she would be earning. Mr. Chambers agreed to handle all the details as he had done in the past. Katrina was well on her way to becoming a renowned artist, and she was only seventeen!

* * *

Katrina attended Jeff's graduation ceremony with his mother. Her eyes shone as she watched Jeff accept his diploma. She really liked Jeff a lot. He never put any demands on her, and when they were together, they enjoyed themselves. She recognized the longing in his eyes many times, but he never went any further than kissing her.

When the ceremony was over and Jeff joined her and his mother, they walked through the parking lot with Jeff in the middle and their arms around him, and his arms around each of them. They went to Jeff's favorite restaurant and were disappointed that Clara wasn't working. After they had dinner, Jeff wanted to go to a few graduation parties.

"You go ahead, Jeff. I have school tomorrow." There were still two more days of school for her. Jeff drove her home and promised her he would be careful.

"No drinking....please, Jeff?" She begged.

"Scout's honor," He promised, as he held up two fingers. She smiled and kissed him on the cheek. He put his arms around her and held her close for a moment, and kissed her on her lips.

"Congratulations, again. Oh, and I have a graduation present for you. You'll get it at your party on Saturday. She promised. "Have fun tonight, but please, please be careful."

"Hey, you didn't have to get me a gift." He smiled at her and kissed her nose again.

"I didn't get you a gift....I got you two gifts." She countered, and gave him a mischievous smile.

1-29

Danny and Kathy arrived. They were pleased that there had been plans made for an informal wedding and reception. Kim and Katrina volunteered themselves as bridesmaids, and already got their matching dresses, both blue voile peasant-styles with off-the-shoulder elastic necklines, and skirts that almost touched the floor. They looked adorable in them. They whisked Kathy out to the mall to find her a suitable white dress, while Michael and Ed took Danny and Jeff to get tuxes. Since they had two bridesmaids, Jeff was asked to accompany Katrina as her escort. At the mall, they found a lovely white peasant-style dress for Kathy. They bought pastel and white flowers, and netting and rushed home so Katrina could make head pieces for her and Kim, and a veil for Kathy. Once again, a wedding thrown together on short notice would be a lovely affair. Michael got the FOP hall again for the reception and the chapel where Michael and Kim got married was available. Katrina, once again, made a 'just married' sign for the back of the car. Invitations had been sent out two weeks in advance.

"Yes, it's on short notice, but so what? Either people show up or they don't." Mary told Ed. The positive RSVP's were steadily being called in rather than mailed. It looked like there would be around fifty people attending. The caterers were called, the chapel and hall were secured, the dresses were bought, and it was going to be lovely.

The wedding was more than just lovely; it was fun as well. Everyone enjoyed the dancing and the food was delicious. Mary made a mental note to always call this particular caterer when she needed one. On such short notice, he came through with a delicious assortment of foods and a lovely buffet table as well. She looked out over the dance floor and saw Katrina and Jeff, Michael and Kim, Danny and Kathy all dancing a fast dance. 'Where did all her kids learn to dance?' She wondered. She felt a hand on her arm. It was Ed, smiling at her. "Let's go, Sweetheart, and join the rest of our family." She grinned at Ed and hurried to the dance floor to dance with her husband.

* * *

The wedding was over, Danny and Kathy flew back to Florida, and life went back to normal. Kim and Michael found a small house for rent on a nice street not far from either of their family's houses. They were planning on having both families over for a cookout since there was a small yard and patio in the back of the house.

Katrina was spending her summer working on her artwork. She was enjoying the photography part more than she thought she would, and was taking some beautiful shots worthy of framing and selling. She was permitted to use the darkroom at the institute for a nominal fee, since she had been a student there for such a long time. Ed found her a small storefront for her to work in and sell her work. Since she was still underage, Ed put everything into his name, but profits went to Katrina. She and Jeff cleaned, scrubbed, painted and decorated the little store to get it ready to open to the public. The grand opening was scheduled for August the first. Mary's new favorite caterer provided punch and canapé sandwiches and cookies for the opening. He was excited to do this because of the exposure he would receive. Katrina allowed him to place business cards on the food table. For this, he gave Mary a discount for his services. Katrina appeared at her opening in a simple white long dress, and she looked elegant. Jeff—bless his heart—appeared in a tuxedo and acted as a guide through the gallery. Mary and Ed were present as supporters, as were Kim and Michael. The response to the gallery was overwhelming. The storefront was at its capacity most of the day, and the sales were amazing. The press showed up for pictures and a story for the newspaper that would be printed in the following Sunday edition. The story would include the store front hours, which were Monday, Wednesday and Friday, ten until three—private appointments upon request. On the other days, Katrina would be working on additions to the gallery. She was still in high school and she was already a semi-successful business woman. She didn't think about the business part of it, since she was just doing what she enjoyed. All through August, she spent her days either working on something for the gallery or being at the gallery showing her work. Sometimes Mary went with her to keep her company for those times when nobody was in the gallery. She and Mary would dust and tidy up, and rearrange the art on those days. Since the gallery was near Ed's business, many times Jeff or Ed, or both of them, would visit for lunch.

Jeff was working full-time all summer before he left for college, so they spent a lot of their evenings together. In mid-August, Jeff's mother invited Katrina over for dinner. Jeff left the house before his mother got home from work, and went to pick up Katrina. When they got to his house his mother was not there yet, but the phone was ringing. It was Mrs. Hall. She apologized to Jeff that she was not going to be able to get home for dinner. Mrs. Hall was a nurse. There was an emergency disaster at the hospital where she worked, and all personnel were required to stay. 'A train derailment or something,' Jeff said. Jeff put Katrina on the phone and Mrs. Hall apologized to her, and asked if she would take a rain check.

"Of course, Mrs. Hall…I understand," Katrina assured her.

"So what do we do now? Go out to eat?" She asked Jeff.

"Nope….you were invited to dinner here, and that's what you're going to get. I'll cook." Jeff was reaching for the cookware as he spoke.

"You're going to cook? Can you?"

"Honey, I can do many things around the house. Mom always needs help doing stuff, and she works long hours, so I have always been elected to do what had to be done around here. My sisters bailed and left the chores for me. Get ready for a tantalizing, mouth-watering omelet masterpiece like you have never had before in your life. I do an egg proud!" He smiled down at her surprised face. "You can set the table and then watch the master at work!"

They both laughed, and she got the dishes and silverware out, while he heated the pan. She sat on a stool and watched him create his 'omelet masterpiece'. It amazed her that he was as adept as he claimed to be with a frying pan. He turned out two beautiful omelets, and put them on the plates she offered to him. He poured the cheese topping he created over the top of the omelets.

"Wow! This is delicious, Jeff!"

"Thank you! I accept your praise, because I agree. If we should get married some day, you will appreciate the fact that I can cook and do housework."

"Wow….I never even thought of getting married…..I mean, we both have to work toward our careers and everything first. It seems that it's all I've ever focused on." She bit her lip and stared at him. "Do you think about getting married?"

"It seems that you have your career already started and you haven't even finished high school yet. And yes, I think about getting married…. to you. I've loved you since the third grade." He confessed. "Wait here. I want to show you something."

He disappeared through the doorway and she sat and waited. Marriage was something she *really* never thought about. It surprised her that he thought about it. 'I've loved you since the third grade,' he said. She had no idea he felt that way. Third grade! She didn't even remember him from grade school. She would have been in second grade.

He came back into the kitchen and put a worn piece of notebook paper in front of her.

"Look at this. These were my goals in the third grade."

He handed her a piece of notebook paper, and there, in third-grade penmanship, was written:

My Goals when I grow up.

1. Go to college
2. get a good job.
3. Marry Katrina

"I see the handwriting hasn't changed much," She teased. "I'm flattered, though."

"Now look at this one."

It was a large piece of construction paper with a drawing on it. There was a house and two people holding hands, one of the people had long red hair, and then there were five other mini-people standing beside the bigger third-grade-style people. 'Katrina' was written above the red-haired figure and 'me' was written above the other.

"What are these? Some of them better be dogs and cats." She laughed, as she pointed to the five smaller figures.

"Well, remember, I was in the third grade. I thought it would be cool to have lots of kids. I didn't know where they came from then. Since then, I've thought maybe two would be nice."

"That's better," She nodded in agreement. She stared at the drawing while she chewed on the nail of her thumb on her right hand. She was pensive for a moment, and then she looked up at him, smiling. "You forgot to put the cats and dogs in the picture, then?"

"I guess I did," He conceded, and began to clear the table.

They did the dishes together; she washed and he dried and put them away.

"Want to watch a movie? Mom just picked up a couple from Blockbuster last night."

"Sounds good…what did she get?"

They walked into the family room, chose one of the movies, and settled on the couch in front of the television. Soon they were kissing, soft and gentle at first, but then the kisses became more heated. Katrina was responding to Jeff's kisses in a way that she had never responded before, and it surprised both of them. Jeff was the one to pull back first.

"You're making me sweat." He told her, teasingly. "I'm going to get us something to drink."

He brought back two cans of soft drinks from the refrigerator, and opened them both. He handed her one, and drank a huge gulp from his before he sat back down.

"I love you." He simply stated. He leaned back, rested his wrist on his forehead, and stared at nothing on the ceiling.

"Jeff?"

He turned his head slightly to look at her.

"I love you, too."

It was a whisper that was barely audible, but to him it was like cymbals crashing or like rain slamming against the window, or the roar of the waves at the beach. Every fiber of his body reacted to those words. He reached for her, and ran his hands up through her hair, and then held her head in his hands while he kissed her. He slid his arm around her, and held her face with his other hand, and kissed her again, this time parting her lips with his tongue. He was getting a head rush from kissing her, and she must have been feeling the same thing, because they both slid down on the couch and were lying side by side.

"Katrina." Was all he could say before she pressed her lips to his, her tongue darting in and out, and then teasing his lips. She slid under him and ran her hands down his back, and he moaned. He kissed her chin, then her throat, and then moved down to her chest. She felt his hardness pressing against her. His hand slipped under her blouse and began to caress her breast until he found her nipple. His mouth covered hers again, and he drew her tongue into his mouth and held it there. He unbuttoned her blouse and unhooked her bra, and his mouth moved to her breast. He teased her nipple with his tongue, and then moved back up to her mouth. "Stop me, if you want." His voice was ragged. He ran his hand down her belly and touched the band of her jeans, and undid the snap. The zipper slid down, and his hand slid into her panties. He felt her mound of pubic hair and caressed it for a few seconds. He felt her jerk and stiffen. Slowly he removed his hand and moved to a sitting position, pulling her up with him.

"Jeff....I-I'm so...sorry." She covered her face with her hands.

"It's okay. I'm sorry I went that far."

"No, you told me I could stop you, but I didn't...until now. I just got....scared, I think" She looked like she was going to cry. "That was...I don't know....mean, maybe?"

"Torturous would be a better word...but that's okay." He encircled her in his arms. "Honey, I meant it when I said 'I love you,' and when you said you love me....wow! I mean, it's something I've dreamed about....for years. I don't want you to do anything that you'll regret, okay? You said the words I have always wanted to hear you say. That's what matters to me."

He looked into her eyes and the corners of his mouth twitched upward, preparing for a smile, in case he got one out of her. He pulled her to him and just held her, his chin resting on her forehead. After a few minutes, he felt her relax against him.

"Are we still friends?" He whispered into her ear.

She sat up and looked at him, wide-eyed.

"Friends? Is that all we are?"

"No, no, no......we're more than friends....but we have to be friends before we are anything else. Come on, of course I consider you more than a friend. You're my best friend, you're my girlfriend, and you're my future wife some day, I hope." He was chuckling at her reaction.

"Oh...." She looked up at him and smiled, and then began laughing. She grabbed him and hugged him fiercely.

"Whoa....whoa...stop, or we'll be at it again." He made a mockery of straightening his shirt. "One of us has to have some self-control." She began laughing again.

He looked at her intently.

"Seriously, though....I don't know if I want to be your first. But I know I want to be your last."

He took her chin between his thumb and forefinger and kissed her nose. "Let's get you home before you take advantage of me."

His eyes twinkled when he said it, and she hit him with a throw pillow. He took her hand and pulled her to her feet, hooked her bra back up, buttoned her blouse, and once again, pulled her to him and hugged her.

* * *

Jeff was packing for college, since he was leaving in the morning. Katrina sat on his bed and watched. He caught her eye and winked at her. Since that night, he was careful not to put them in a situation like that again, but here they were in his room, alone. "You look sad." He said to her.

"No, not really sad….just a little…oh, I don't know….melancholy, maybe." She looked at him and gave a wistful smile. "I'm going to miss you." She sighed.

"Well, you know I'll be home for homecoming, right? I have to. I have the crown. And you have the other. You will go to the dance with me, won't you?"

Katrina grinned at him and said, "You bet."

She watched him pick up a framed picture of her and put it in his suitcase.

"Rats in the dorm?" She teased.

He nodded.

"Did I tell you I met my new roommate when I went down there on Wednesday?"

He was studying her face.

"No, what's he like?" She replied.

"I guess he's okay. He's from Ohio. I think we will get along fine."

"Good….Jeff? If you have loved me since the third grade, why is it I just found out about it this year?" She was sitting with her heels resting on the bed frame, chewing her lip.

"Why, you ask? Because…..I didn't want to embarrass myself; or worse yet, if you would have laughed at me, I would have been crushed. You were always the queen of my dream"

"I wouldn't have laughed at you! I've never done anything that cruel, except hit Sean, maybe."

"He deserved that, and no, you are not a cruel person. You probably would not have done anything to hurt my feelings…intentionally, that is. But if you wouldn't have said it back, my third grade heart would have been destroyed." He sat down beside her and put his arm around her. "Then in high school, you seemed aloof, and then you were Sean's girlfriend. That made you off-limits. I was going to ask you to the homecoming dance last year, but I heard he already did."

"Yes, he asked me on the night of the first football game last year. Do you know I really never thought of myself as Sean's girlfriend? I was never really comfortable with him."

"And now? Are you comfortable?" He waited for her response.

She smiled at him and snuggled into his shoulder. "I'm very comfortable."

They fell back onto the bed, and this time she took his head between her palms and kissed him. He responded by pulling her close, and kissing her neck and throat. It was his turn to pull back. "No, Sweetheart, we aren't going to let this happen. I love you so much. We'll wait until the time is right." He sat up and pulled her up by her hand.

Katrina watched as he continued to pack, and she listened as he continued to talk to her, while he was taking things from drawers and shelves.

"You know, you're the only girl I ever wanted in my life. Any time anything good or bad happened in my life, my first thought was always you. What would you think? How would you feel? What would you say? I remember when I made the all-star team in little league. I hoped you would hear about it. I even hoped you would be at the all-star game. Hell, I even thought about you when I hit my first homerun. I was hoping you would hear about it." He reached up on the top shelf for some sweatshirts, grabbed two to put into a suitcase, and threw one at her. "Here is a souvenir for you."

It was one of his football jerseys. It had his number and name on it. She grinned at him and folded it into her lap.

"Now, let me tell you why Candy hated you. I'm sure you wondered what you ever did to her." He looked at her and she shrugged. "Well, when I got to the high school, and you were still in middle school, I met Candy. She came on to me like a cat in heat. Well, I was a young teenaged boy....damn, it was flattering as hell. She was good-looking, and hell, she had big boobs. But.....you were in my heart, so she didn't mean anything to me. Anyway, she kept coming around me, asking me to come over to her house, and I kept making up excuses why I couldn't go. Well, she showed up at this house one day and nobody was home but me. One thing led to another, and well, to be blunt, I got my first piece of ass."

Katrina stared at him as though she were in shock.

"I'm sorry, Honey, but it's the truth."

She shrugged and nodded.

"Well, it certainly wasn't her first time, but anyway, she said she loved me, and asked me if I loved her. Of course, I said 'no, I love Katrina'. She had no idea who Katrina was, until you arrived at the high school the following year. It was instant hate, because you had what she wanted."

Katrina stared at Jeff, not quite sure what to say. "Jeff, I...never really cared why Candy hated me. You know, it just dawned on me.... I've had two boyfriends and both of them have slept with Candy. Why did you have to tell me that?"

"I told you because I don't want any secrets between us. I don't ever want you wondering about whether I'm truthful, faithful, or sincere. Maybe it was too much information, but I know how much I love you, and Sean, in his way, loved you, too. Neither of us gave a rat's ass about Candy. She was just there, throwing herself at...both of us. The difference between me and Sean is that I would not even dream of being with Candy now that we are together. Candy and I were before I ever even kissed you. I would never touch her, even if she walked into my bedroom stark naked and offered me a thousand dollars to sleep with her, now that I have you. Sean? Well, he's a stupid, stupid kid." And with that said, Jeff zipped one of his suitcases shut.

"It's just that so much time has been lost. Time we could have been together." Katrina spoke softly and wistfully.

He reached his hand out to her and she accepted it, and he pulled her to her feet. He grabbed her free hand with his other hand and, while holding onto her hands, brought them around to her back, and looked down into her face. "We still have lots of time to make up for that. How about getting burgers at Bear's? I'm starving."

"Okay." She nodded her approval, and smiled up at him. They stood like that for a few moments, eyes locked, drinking in each other's thoughts. 'I want you so badly,' he thought. 'I want you, too.' Her thought came back at him, and he mentally perceived it.

1-30

Jeff left for college. Katrina was so happy for him, but sad at the same time. She would miss him. She realized that night he made the omelets that she really did love him, and she believed that he might be 'the one.' They got through the summer with her virginity still in tact, but now she had experienced the desire. She wanted Jeff, and sometimes she ached for him to touch her. He was so self-controlled, and she was glad of that. She liked it that she could feel safe with him. He didn't put pressure on her, even though she knew how badly he wanted her.

School started a few days after Jeff left. She was now a senior—her last year before college. She thought about what school she would like to attend, and Carnegie Mellon seemed like a good idea. She would get the education she wanted, be able to stay close to her family, and of course, she and Jeff would not be all that far away from each other. She had time to think about it, though, and she delved into her senior year. It was strange not to see some of the people who graduated the year before. She still had Morgan and there was Brittany. Sean was still lurking around somewhere, but he knew not to talk to her. Michael, true to his word again, went to Sean's house and spoke with Tim Parks about what Sean had done. Both Michael and Tim Parks agreed that it wasn't so much that Sean tried to get to first base, as it was that he left her in a bad neighborhood where anything could have happened to her. They made Sean sit down at the kitchen table and both men grilled him on his behavior. They broke him, after a while. He began sobbing and said he was sorry, and that he would never want to hurt Katrina, ever. He looked at Michael and told him that he really loved Katrina. Michael's answer was that he had a hell of a way of showing it. He told Michael he didn't give a damn what he thought of him, but he just wanted Katrina to forgive him. Michael ordered him to stay away from Katrina. Tim Parks took the car away from him. He told Sean that it was transportation, not a 'booty box.' If Katrina had known all of this, she would have felt that it was a little much to put him through all that. She might have felt bad for Sean.

Katrina's life returned to a routine that had been normal for her, except that her classes at the Art Institute ceased. She was no longer a student of art since she had sold so much of her work. In many cases, the art instructors at the institute considered her a colleague now that she was paid for her work. She still had her dance classes and piano lessons. Dance classes were on Tuesday nights now, and piano lessons were on Wednesdays. Friday nights were reserved for football games. She was voted captain of the drill team, which didn't really require much more responsibility. She wore captain's bars on her shoulders, which was really the only difference.

Her art gallery was now closed except for Saturdays. She was used to being at the institute on Saturdays, so keeping the gallery open on Saturdays was close to her normal routine. She still had appointments, but they were after school. She was making money at the gallery, but of course, not as much as in the beginning when it was newly opened.

One Monday after school started, Katrina drove to Michael and Kim's after school. Kim was home already, which was good. Katrina ran in, yelling, "Kim! Guess what!!" Kim appeared in the kitchen doorway, wiping her hands on a towel.

"What? What's wrong?" Kim was alarmed.

"Nothing.....except that I am the only virgin in school! Miss Bachman got married!"

Kim threw her head back and laughed, "No way! To who...?"

Katrina shrugged, "Don't know. Some guy...." Then she began to laugh. "Do you believe it?" She followed Kim through the doorway into the kitchen, and sat down at the counter.

"Well, maybe Miss Bachman will be nicer now. What's her married name?"

"Lennard...."

"So.....my young sister-in-law.....you are still a virgin? I wasn't so sure....I mean, I saw the way you and Jeff looked at each other...."

"He...wouldn't. I mean, he has so much self-control...more than I do."

"*HE* wouldn't? You would have?"

"I…think so. Maybe not, though….put it this way….I know what it is to want someone….so bad that it hurts. But we didn't….he said not until the time is right."

"….Kudos to Jeff!" Kim chirped. "I knew he was a great guy! See, Honey, that's love. He did what was right for you, not what would have made him feel great. He gets an A-plus in my book."

"Mine, too….he's so….wonderful. He's coming home for homecoming. He has the crown, so he has to."

"You'll be his date, right?" Kim asked.

"Of course…..I can't wait to see him. We have only talked on the phone once since he's been there because of the expense, but we write to each other."

"Writing….it's a dying art." Kim philosophized.

1-31

Jeff pulled into his driveway and ran into the house, kissed his mom's cheek and grabbed the telephone. Katrina answered on the first ring.

"*I'm home!*" He sang into the phone. "Can I come over? ….I'll throw my stuff into my room, and be right there. I brought you something."

"Hi, Mom…" Jeff finally said to his mother. "Sorry…I have really missed Katrina."

"I know. Go….just promise I get you for breakfast tomorrow, and breakfast, lunch and dinner on Sunday. Katrina's welcome, too…. okay?"

"You got it, Mom," With that, he ran out the door and headed for Katrina's.

Jeff pulled into the driveway and was out of the car in a flash, as Katrina was floating through the front door. They met in the driveway somewhere in between. She jumped into his arms, and he spun her around, laughing. "Damn, I've missed you!" They spoke the words simultaneously, and laughed at themselves. He put her down, and gathered her into his arms and stared into her eyes for a moment. He lowered his face to hers and kissed her, and she kissed him back. Mary was standing at the window, not wanting to spy, but she was intrigued by the way they melded together as one. "I think this may be it for her," She said to no one in particular. She jumped when she heard Ed's response, "She could do worse."

They entered the house, Katrina pulling Jeff by the hand, both of them chattering away to each other. It was good to see her so happy. They went into the kitchen, and Mary heard the refrigerator open.

"Hey, Mom! Can Jeff stay for dinner?"

"OH, of course he can! I wouldn't have it any other way." She came into the kitchen, and said, "I thought he might be here, so I made plenty. How is college, Jeff?"

"It's great, Mrs. K. My classes are going well, and my roommate is a really cool guy. We get along well. The only thing is that I miss Katrina so badly."

"Well, I can't speak for her, but I think she misses you, too." Mary assured him.

"You know I do. I couldn't wait for homecoming. Oh, I withdrew my name from the ballot this time. I don't think it's fair to be on every queen ballot and win. Besides, I'm hoping Morgan wins. I campaigned for her...and this way, I get to be with you all evening."

"I like the sound of that." Jeff mouthed a kiss to her. "Oh, here... I almost forgot." He handed her the WVU sweatshirt he had been holding the whole time. "I got you this."

Katrina took the sweatshirt, thanked him and promised to put it on after dinner.

After dinner, Jeff and Katrina drove off to Bear's Place, knowing everybody would be there. Sure enough, Morgan and Kevin were there together, as were many of the former and present football players. Morgan called them over to their table, and hugged them both after they threaded themselves through the crowd to get to the table. There was only one chair, so Katrina sat on Jeff's lap. She was wearing the WVU sweatshirt.

"Are you going to talk about the first thing that pops up?" Kevin teased them.

"Why would we want to talk about *your* wang?" Jeff shot back at him.

Everybody at the table laughed. They were all together again and having a wonderful time. Jeff kept his arm around Katrina, and she draped her arm around his shoulders. They stole kisses whenever they thought no one was paying attention. Sean was sitting with a girl named Taylor, just four tables away. He was paying attention, and it hurt him every time he saw them kiss. He was still beating himself up for being so stupid, and losing her.

* * *

The day of the homecoming game was crisp and clear. Katrina got out of Jeff's car, kissed him, and joined the rest of the drill team. Jeff got out, too, and ran to her holding her captain's bars. "OOPS! I can't forget to put these on…thanks, Sweetheart."

"No problem…good luck… and I'll be in the stands watching. Love you!"

"I love you, too." She smiled and winked at him, and then stood there watching him walk back to his car.

Morgan sidled up to her, smirking. "Love? You *love* him? Kat, have you been holding out on me? You and Jeff…..are doing the nasty?"

Katrina looked at Morgan, and laughed lightly. "No, we're not…. but it could happen. I mean, we both want each other, but well, the time has to be right. But don't worry…you will be the first to know."

"Cool! Me and Kevin did it….last weekend." She whispered to Katrina.

"I thought you have been doing it!"

"No….everybody suspected that we did, and I let them believe it, but, hey, Kat, I was a virgin up until last weekend." Morgan confided.

Katrina looked at her friend with surprise, but she was happy to hear that. She was also very happy for Morgan that she and Kevin *had* waited that long before anything happened.

The team lost the game that day. They did not have a very good record this year, only having won two games so far this season, but it was because all of the best players graduated the previous year. Many times she heard how they wished they had Jeff Hall back to quarterback.

Jeff was playing second-string quarterback for WVU, which meant he didn't get to play at all. His turn would come, Katrina felt sure.

* * *

Katrina was ready to go when Jeff pulled into the driveway. She was wearing a sleek, gold lame dress, sleeveless with a mandarin neckline. Her hair was pulled back, with a braid wrapped around her mane like a clasp. Her long copper tresses hung down the length of her back. She slipped into her gold shoes and made her way down the stairs. She heard his whistle when she stepped around the corner into the living room. She smiled up into his handsome face. His gray eyes were shining as he looked her up and down.

"You look…like a queen." He laughed as he said it. "You have to put the crown on, you know. You still are the reigning queen."

"Well, where is yours?" She demanded.

"It's in the car. I'll put it on when we get there. They are going to make me do that anyway."

She grabbcd up thc crown, went to the mirror in the hallway, and fitted the crown into her hair.

"Perfect!" The group in the living room chorused.

The homecoming dance was more elaborate than the previous year. As king and queen, she and Jeff were escorted to a special table with velour high-backed chairs. Katrina thought that they probably belonged to Miss Bachman before she got married, and laughed to herself. The underclassmen placed drinks in front of them immediately. She reached over and grabbed Jeff's hand. "You look so handsome tonight." She whispered to him. He smiled at her appreciatively.

The crowning of the new king and queen went off without a hitch. Dave Sipinski and Morgan Butler won the rights to the crowns. MORGAN! Katrina was ecstatic about it. She placed the crown on her friend's head and hugged her. "It fits." She mouthed at her over the noise of the crowd.

Katrina and Jeff danced every slow dance together all night, talking softly and gazing into one another's eyes. They danced fast dances, too. They were sitting out for a couple of fast dances, just holding hands, when Morgan approached them. "All right, enough of this love- fest over here! Are you two going to join your friends, or not?"

Both Katrina and Jeff laughed, and got up to go sit at the table with Morgan and Kevin, Dave and his girlfriend, Lori. They talked and laughed with them, and never let go of each other's hand. Sean walked past their table, holding hands with Taylor Mitchell, the girl who was at Bear's with him. Katrina didn't notice, but Jeff noticed Sean staring at Katrina. When he saw Jeff staring back at him, he turned away.

It was almost midnight when Jeff pulled into Katrina's driveway. He shut the car off and turned to her with a serious look on his face. "Katrina, look....I know we both have lots to do before we settle down. We both have to finish college, get a Master's Degree perhaps, but I know how I feel about you....how I've always felt about you. That's not going to go away. When I say 'I'll love you forever' I mean it. What I'm trying to say is....well, what I'm asking is....when we both are finished with school....will you marry me?"

Katrina didn't trust herself to speak. She looked into Jeff's eyes and nodded, smiling. Jeff grabbed her up and hugged her, and then let her go as he reached inside his jacket pocket. He extracted a small velvet box and opened it. There was a small gold ring with a tiny diamond in a raised setting. "It's a promise ring, not an engagement ring. It means that I promise to get engaged to you after we are finished with school....or something like that. Will you take it?" He was watching her intently. He couldn't see her eyes since her head was tilted down looking at the ring. She slowly lifted her head and met his eyes.

"Yes..." There was a tear rolling down her cheek, and he wiped it away with his thumb. She took the ring from the box, he took it out of her hand, and slid it onto the third finger of her left hand. Neither of them could trust themselves to speak at that moment. Jeff gathered her up in his arms and just held her. He swallowed hard, in order to say to her, "Remember, you are the queen of my dream. Everything I do from this moment on is to ensure your happiness and well-being. Now let me get you inside. Remember, breakfast, lunch, and dinner at my house tomorrow. Okay?"

"Call me in the morning? Do you want me to drive over instead of picking me up?"

"Yeah, that way I can see you up until the moment I have to leave."

She smiled at him, and they walked hand-in-hand to the door. He kissed her, lightly, and then passionately. Their night ended with a big bear hug.

She spent Sunday with Jeff and his mother. They taught her how to play Hearts, and then they sat in the kitchen just bantering back and forth, laughing. Jeff's mother noticed the ring, but didn't say anything. She felt that they would tell her what it meant when they were ready. She really liked this girl. She remembered how Jeff used to talk about her all the time in grade school. She knew he had been in love with her since then, and now it appeared that the feeling was mutual. 'See what perseverance can accomplish?' she thought to herself, and silently chuckled. The three of them took a walk through the woods when the sun warmed the day up a little bit. Janice Hall loved the sound of Katrina's laugh, and it got even better when she and Jeff laughed together. When she watched them together, the phrase 'pure love' came to her mind. It was true love, all right, but there was something so pure about it....pristine. It was actually beautiful.

Too soon it was time for Jeff to leave. He hugged his mother and grabbed Katrina's hand and led her outside. He threw his oversized duffel bag in the car, and reached for Katrina's hands and wrapped her arms around his waist. He pressed her up against the car, and gave her quick kisses on her nose, her cheeks, her forehead, and then her lips. Her blue eyes were shimmering with tears. He let go of her hands and wrapped his arms around her and held her tightly. He whispered in her ear, "I'll be home in a couple of weeks, for Thanksgiving, okay?" She nodded.

They stood there looking into each other's eyes, as they melded together in a passionate kiss. "I love you, my queen. I love you so much!"

"I love you, too, my Dragon-slayer....so much." She let him go, and he got into his car and started the engine. She watched while he drove away. Little did she know that it would be the last time she ever saw him.

1-32

The telephone woke Mary. She looked at the clock and saw that it was six in the morning. "Who could be calling at this hour?" She whispered as she reached for the phone in a panic. Danny? Mike? Oh, no!

"Oh God! NO! I-I don't know what to s-say. Yes, of course, I'll break it to her. Janice, we'll be there later."

"What's that all about?" Ed rolled over to face Mary, who was sobbing already.

"Honey, what's wrong?"

"There's been an accident. Jeff was killed. Oh, God! Katrina! We have to tell her! How do we tell her?" Mary was bawling. "Ed, she loves him!"

They got up and went downstairs to make coffee, and sit and think. "Let her wake up first. When we hear her alarm, we can call her down here." Mary nodded.

They heard Katrina jump up out of bed, and Mary went to the bottom of the stairs and called to her. "Katrina? Honey, come down here, please...now?"

Katrina came to the top of the stairs and saw her mother standing at the bottom. Something was wrong! She ran down the steps, asking her," Mom, what's wrong? Something happened, didn't it? Mike?" She saw her dad standing in the hallway, looking uncomfortable.

"No, Honey, it's not Mike...or Danny. There's been an accident. Jeff....Janice said he never stood a chance...." Mary's voice trailed off.

Katrina felt like she had been hit with lightning. She heard a blood-curdling scream, over the roar in her head. The scream was coming from her, but she didn't realize it. She felt herself being slammed against the wall by a bolt of something, but she didn't know what.

"NO!! NO, NO, NO-OO!" She screamed between sobs.

Mary and Ed both grabbed her. Ed crushed her to him, and held her as tightly as he could.

"Easy....Easy, Baby Girl..." He held her and rocked her back and forth, and he felt her pain. He looked at Mary through tears, and saw she was feeling Katrina's pain, as well.

Katrina was shaking. "Daddy, I have to go….go to Jeff's mom…"

"I know you do, Princess. We're all going to go. We all loved Jeff." Katrina's sobs began once again.

Mary walked into the den and called Michael's house. He was already gone, but Kim answered. Mary related the terrible news to Kim, and she said she would be right over. Ed helped Katrina up the stairs and told her to lie there for a few minutes, and that they would bring her coffee up for her. Mary took her coffee, and Ed let Kim inside. Kim ran up the stairs into Katrina's room, grabbed Katrina and hugged her fiercely. Katrina began crying again.

"Oh, Kim…." She sobbed. "I loved him so much!"

"I know you did, Sweetie. I know." Kim rocked her back and forth. "I have to get to work, but I'll be back with Mike later, okay?" Katrina nodded.

Mary called the school and reported Katrina out for the next few days. She let the office know about the accident, and how distraught Katrina was. The secretary expressed her concern and said she would get the information to the school counselors, since Katrina may have to talk to one of them. She was hanging up the phone when Ed came in from outside. He looked like he had lost his best friend, and maybe he had. Ed thought the world of Jeff.

"Where is she, Mary? Where is my baby girl? She's so young to have to feel pain like this"

"Upstairs. Oh, God, Ed! This is awful for her. She's in pain, you can see that. She's really suffering." Ed nodded.

Katrina came down showered and dressed. Her hair was brushed, and her skin looked very pale. Her eyes were swollen from crying, and she was quiet and subdued. She jumped when the phone rang. It was Morgan. Mary confirmed to Morgan that what she heard at school was correct. Morgan wanted to know if Katrina was okay, and Mary told her she was taking it hard. Morgan told Mary that she, and Kevin, would be there for her later. Mary hung up.

The announcement came over the P.A. system. "We regret to inform the students that there has been a tragic accident……last year's quarterback………Jeff Hall….killed….sadly missed….drunk driver"

Sean felt the bile rise in his throat. He ran to find Morgan. He had to know.

"Morgan!" He called to her.

She stopped and turned around to face him.

"Is…is it true? Morgan? Where is Katrina? Was she …..there… with him?" Sean was trembling. "Morgan, tell me! Is Katrina okay?"

"Katrina wasn't with him, Sean. She's not here because she's taking it hard. She's pretty hysterical right now."

Sean looked relieved. Morgan looked at Sean for a moment, and then turned away. 'In his warped little way, he loves her.' Morgan thought to herself.

Ed, Mary, and Katrina stood in front of Hall's front door. Ed knocked lightly, and the door was opened by a young woman. She stared at them, and a light of recognition came into her eyes. "You're Katrina, aren't you? I'm Judy, Jeff's sister. Come in."

Katrina spotted Mrs. Hall and went to her immediately. Janice Hall grabbed Katrina and hugged her tightly, crying on her shoulder. "Oh, Katrina, he loved you so much!" Mrs. Hall put her hands on Katrina's shoulders and looked into her face.

"I know he did. I loved him, too." Fresh tears were coming out of Katrina's eyes, and sobs were wracking her body again.

"Did you get the chance to tell him that?" Janice Hall wanted to know. "Did he know you loved him, too?" Katrina nodded, still sobbing hard. "Oh, Thank God. I know you made him so happy when you said it."

Katrina remembered the ring. She held it up for Janice to see. "It's a promise we both made to each other. When we were done with college, we were going to get en-engaged."

With these words, Katrina broke down again. Ed came up behind her and took her into his arms and stroked her hair. Mary was making coffee for everybody. Ed helped Katrina to a kitchen chair.

Katrina looked around. Until now, she hadn't realized that there were other people in the house. Judy, and Jeff's other sister, Joanne were there with their husbands and children. There were three small children in all. From talking with Jeff, Katrina knew that Judy had two and Joanne had one—all were boys, ages five, four, and four.

Mary poured coffee for everybody and sat down. No one spoke. Katrina and Janice were quietly sobbing. Judy and Joanne's husbands went to make funeral arrangements.

It was Judy who spoke first. "Katrina, you're all he ever talked about when he was little. My dad used to call him Charlie Brown, in love with the little red-haired girl." This made Katrina laugh a little.

"He showed me the drawing of us, married with five kids!" Katrina broke down again. "Now that will never happen." She buried her face in her hands, and cried, and cried, and cried. Everyone at the table cried with her, including her father, who kept his arm around her.

After a while, she stopped again. They began exchanging anecdotes about Jeff, laughing and crying as they remembered them. Morgan and Kevin showed up, which brought fresh tears from Katrina as she and Morgan cried together. Kim and Michael came in after Morgan and Kevin, said their condolences, while Michael hugged Katrina from behind, and kissed the top of her head. He could feel her pain, and he would have done anything at that moment to ease it for her.

Somehow Katrina got through the funeral. There were a sea of faces offering her sympathy and condolences. Mostly they were all blurred by tears, so she didn't recognize a lot of them. She remembered seeing Sean come in to pay his respects, and she remembered that he offered her his sympathy. She remembered seeing the drill team members, football players, and some faculty members. Relatives of Jeff's came in droves. She had no idea Jeff had so many relatives. They all came up to her and called her by name. She was no stranger to them, since they heard of her so often over the years.

Suddenly it was over. Jeff was laid to rest in the family burial plot beside his father, and it was over. Katrina walked away from the cemetery with her head bowed, flanked by Mary and Ed. Life would never be the same. She felt the pain of losing someone she dearly loved, and there would be a void there forever. They stopped at Jeff's house to say hello and goodbye to those who came to offer support, and then went home. Katrina went upstairs and curled up in the fetal position with Sugar tucked in at her stomach. She awoke when Kim came in, followed by Morgan. She sat up and stared at them with hollow eyes.

"Hey, are you doing okay?" It was Kim who spoke. Katrina just nodded.

Kim sat down on the bed next to Katrina, and Morgan sat on her other side.

"Kat, I know how painful this must be. You'll get through this, I know you will."

"It's not about me." Katrina spoke up. "It's about Jeff. He had everything to live for. He had a future, we had plans, and he had dreams. He called me 'the queen of his dream'...did you know that?" New tears once again welled up in her eyes.

"No, I didn't." Kim admitted. "Kat, is there any chance that you... I mean, did you two ever...."

"No, we didn't. I wish we had, though." And once again, Katrina was crying. Morgan and Kim held her, crying with her, while Kim gently stroked her hair.

Life did go on. Katrina returned to school and threw herself into her busy life. Evening lessons continued for her, and the art gallery remained open on Saturdays. She hung a new portrait in the gallery that was not for sale. It was Jeff's portrait that she hung in his memory. Many people recognized his likeness when they visited the gallery, and some recognized that he had been Katrina's first love.

Drill team activities continued until football season ended, and Katrina hung up her uniform and said goodbye to another part of her life. Yes, life did go on, and it was ever-changing.

Christmas came and went. It was uneventful for her, and the family didn't play it up too much. They knew she was still hurting very badly. She wore Jeff's football jersey to bed every night and on many nights she cried herself to sleep.

Jeff's nineteenth birthday would have been on February first. She went to the cemetery and cried on his headstone. "Oh Jeff...." She hugged her coat to her trying to fend off the bitter chill. "Jeff, I miss you. I know what we planned can't happen any more. But, Jeff, I promise you if I ever get married, he will be like you. Oh, God, how I miss you! I'd give anything to see you again. I love you so much." She closed her eyes, and at that moment she could have sworn she felt someone touch her cheek. She opened her eyes and no one was there.

* * *

Katrina's SAT scores came in the mail. "With those scores you can go to any college you want." Ed told her. "You should probably start applying."

Once again, it was time to think about the prom. Katrina had no desire to go, but Mary coaxed her into going when Josh Barnes asked her. "It's your last year, Kat. Just go, if for no other reason, to be around Morgan and the other kids who care about you." Katrina agreed to go. She missed the Snow Ball, the Valentine's Dance and the St. Patrick's dance. She told those who asked her to go that she was still in mourning.

The awards banquet was coming up right before the prom. Katrina, Mary, and Ed planned on going. This year they sat with Morgan and her family. The drill team received their usual awards, and Katrina got her kudos from the choir and newspapers, as she did the year before. Sean got his scholarship to Penn State, and she was glad for him. Morgan got a five thousand dollar scholarship to the school of her choice. She applied at UP and IUP, but hadn't heard back from either of them yet. Katrina received a scholarship of five thousand dollars for academic achievement, to the school of her choice. She had applied at Carnegie Mellon, and several others, including University of South Florida. She had not heard from any of them yet, either. She and Morgan hoped to hear something before June.

The prom came and went. Katrina was just not 'into it', as she put it. She wore a turquoise gown with a white lace panel down the front. The color suited her. She did her hair in a French braid and threaded a turquoise ribbon through it. She looked lovely, save for the hollow haunted eyes. Unless one knew her well, that went unnoticed. To Josh, she looked fabulous. He was a good date, as far as dates went. He was attentive, polite, mannerly, and he kept his hands to himself. He told someone weeks later that she was gorgeous, polite, mannerly, classy, and just was not at all interested in being with him. He knew the story about Jeff, and had no desire to compete with a dead guy.

Katrina's graduation brought Danny and Kathy to Pennsylvania. This was the moment they all prepared for long in advance. Their pride and joy had grown up. She had turned eighteen in April, and was now considered an adult. She was Valedictorian, having kept up her 4.0 grade point average all the way through school. She was sitting on the patio trying to compose her speech, when her brothers interrupted her.

"Let's take a break, Kid. We want to buy you lunch." Michael had her left hand and Danny had her right hand, and they were pulling her out of the chair. "There are five letters from colleges sitting there for you. Before you open any of them, we need to talk, okay?"

"When did they come?" She wanted to know.

"Just today. Some may not be acceptances, we don't know, but we still want to talk to you." Danny was doing the talking.

"Well, okay. Let's get to lunch, then."

They ended up at Bear's for burgers. Katrina thought of taking them to the restaurant where Clara worked, but knew she would not be able to handle it. She wasn't sure that she could ever go to that restaurant again.

They ordered burgers and fries, and Katrina commanded that they talk.

"Kat, what do you want to do with your life? I mean, you have everything going for you. Do you want to be an artist, or a dancer, or a musician, or a business woman? Your options are open, Kiddo." Danny was once again the spokesperson.

She looked from Michael to Danny, and then back to Michael again. She sighed, and quickly formed her thoughts. "Art is my field, I know that. I want to learn how to manage my financial affairs. I make money from my artwork, and I want to know how to handle that money wisely, create a portfolio, et cetera. Also, I want to develop and pursue my comic strip character, 'Kit-Kat'. Jeff believed in me. He felt that one day 'Kit-Kat' would be a household word. I never said this before, but I think I want to be a cartoonist. I want my own comic strip."

"So where do you really want to go to school?" It was Michael's turn to speak.

Katrina sighed. "I wanted Carnegie Mellon as long as Jeff was alive and at WVU, but Mike, Danny....it's too painful for me here any more. I still hurt over Jeff. Life just isn't the same with him not in it."

"I know that, Kat. I see the pain in your eyes every time you see anything that reminds you of him. He was a great guy, Kat. He loved you, we all know that. And we know how it hurts not to have him here. That's why we think you need a change. Don't say anything to Mom and Dad, but we think you should consider the school in Florida, if they are accepting you. You love Florida, it will be a fresh start for you, and Danny and Kathy will be there for you. Not to mention, I may end up down there, too." Michael winked at her.

"Well, what about the gallery?"

"Close it. The lease is up in another month anyway." Michael reminded her. "Hey, you can open one anywhere. People in Florida like art, and there are a lot of big spenders there, also."

They ate their burgers and fries, and headed home to those envelopes from the colleges. She was accepted at all of those she applied for, except one small one up in Northern Pennsylvania. She sent an application there simply because it was a Liberal Arts School. She chose the University of South Florida. She immediately sent off her letter to them, and her letters declining the other acceptances. She had to work on her speech, so she returned to the patio. She knew what she wanted her speech to convey, and somehow she had to get something into it that honored Jeff. The speech had to do with perseverance and following dreams and goals, but also being a role model in the community. On the podium on graduation night she stood to deliver her speech. She spoke her words clearly and deliberately...."And no one is a hero unless someone else thinks so. Jeff Hall was my hero. He lived his life righteously. He had goals, he had dreams, and he achieved....but he never hurt anybody in order get where he wanted to be. He lived by this belief, and I quote: 'My gain is not worth someone else's pain.' He was a good man. So I say to all of you.....go forth, be successful, pursue your dreams, achieve your goals, but above all else, always achieve without hurting someone else along the way. Thank you." She left the podium with the applause in her ears and tears on her cheeks.

Nathan

21

Rose and Al Perletti had been married almost eleven years before Rose conceived. They had almost given up hope of ever having children, when Rose realized that she was pregnant. Of course, Al knew it would be a son. It *had* to be a son. He always wanted the opportunity to raise a son, teaching him to fish, to play ball, and go camping. These were all the things his father never did with him. He would be a good father, he knew. He envisioned himself as a little league coach, football coach, a mentor, or anything that would be part of his son's growing up. His own father never participated in anything with him. The only time there was ever any interaction between him and his father was when he was beating him. He would *never* be that kind of father to his son. When Rose brought it up that it could be a girl, Al would have none of it. He was having a son. Secretly, Rose would have loved to have a little girl, but she knew that if Al wanted a son, it had better be a son.

Al got his way. Nathan Alphonse Perletti was born on July fourth in the year of 1975. He weighed almost ten pounds and looked much like a three-month-old baby in the nursery, rather than a newborn. Al chose the name Nathan, after his grandfather and Alphonse, of course was his formal name. Little Nathan had jet black hair and rich brown eyes, just like his daddy. There was no doubt that he would grow up to be a strapping six-foot replica of his father. Al had dreams of a son who was athletic and proud, strong but gentle, intelligent but down-to-earth, decent and responsible, a good man like himself. From the day Nathan came along, Al began developing him into that kind of man.

As soon as Nathan was able to sit up in his car seat, Al began taking him everywhere he went. It never ceased to make him feel proud when someone would say to him, "He's just like his old man," or "he's a chip off the old block". Indeed, Nathan was beginning to look more and more like Al as he got older. By the time Nathan was two, he had the same straight, 'Mediterranean' nose that was so prominent in the Perletti family.

When Nathan was three, Al brought home a plastic bat and ball for him, and rushed him outside to try it out. Nathan actually hit the ball when Al gently tossed it toward him and yelled 'swing'. "Rose! Rose! Come out here and watch this!"

Rose had been preparing dinner, but came to the back door, wiping her hands, to watch Al's little protégé hit the plastic ball with the plastic bat. "Good!" She said the word of praise through the screen door. "He's going to be a ball player, Al." Al beamed.

On a warm Saturday morning right after Nathan's fourth birthday, Al and Nathan were returning from the lake. It was the first time Al had taken Nathan fishing, and he was excited that Nathan's line actually snagged a small fish. They were hurrying along the path and were almost home when Rose appeared at the screen door. "Hi, Mommy…." Nathan raised his little hand and waved to Rose. "I caught a fish!"

"You did? Are we going to cook it for dinner?"

"Had to throw it back….too small." was Al's response.

He walked around the side of the house to be put the fishing tackle and poles away, and Rose grabbed up Nathan and took him in to wash up for lunch.

"I have a secret." Rose whispered to Nathan.

"What is it?" Nathan impatiently wanted to know.

"We'll wait for Daddy to come in and have lunch, and then I'll tell you, okay?"

Nathan nodded and said, "Okay."

Rose picked him up and carried him to the kitchen and sat him in his booster seat. He had long outgrown the high chair. Al came in and sat down while Rose served the lunch of diced chicken and wide noodles in light gravy, served over toast. It was one of Al's favorite lunches, and Nathan liked it, too. Nathan piped up. "Mommy has a secret." He looked at Al as he said it, and then looked expectantly at Rose.

"She does, huh? No secrets from me, remember?" He smiled at Rose. "So what's the secret, Honey?"

"Nathan is going to have a baby brother or sister."

Al dropped his fork. "Really? For sure? When did you find out?"

"I saw Dr. Gold yesterday and he called me to confirm my suspicions today while you were fishing. Maybe we will have a girl this time." She smiled at her husband as she rested her chin on the heel of her hand. He leaned over and kissed her cheek, and nodded.

"Can I have a brother, Mommy? I would like a baby brother." Nathan was excited by the prospect of having a baby brother in the house.

"Well, we have to take what we get. A baby sister would be nice, too, don't you think?" Rose was wiping his chin for him. "You could be her big brother and watch out for her."

Nathan thought about this and agreed that it would be okay if it were a baby sister.

"But I'm going to be a big brother, right?"

"Right..." Al and Rose agreed in unison.

Five months later, on December fifteenth, Steven Andrew was born to Al and Rose. He was two months premature, so he was a much smaller baby. Dr. Gold told Rose that he would be her last child, and that was okay with her, considering she was already just past thirty-six, and Al was thirty-seven. The birth had not been an easy one, and there were complications. The baby was stuck in the birth canal and the doctors were concerned. There was a possibility that he could have suffered brain damage. Little Steven had breathing problems right from the beginning, and he stopped breathing more than once on his first night outside the womb. Rose and Al were deeply concerned, but Rose was especially concerned. Sometimes she resented the closeness that was developing between Al and Nathan, and she felt shut out. Maybe another baby would put an end to that closeness and she would once again, have her husband all to herself. It wasn't that she didn't appreciate the time Al spent with Nathan, because she did. It gave her time to herself when Nathan went with Al.

Steven had to remain in the hospital a few days after Rose was released. She and Al and Nathan went to the hospital every night to visit him. Nathan stared at his little brother thoughtfully. "He's so small. Will he get bigger?"

"Of course he will." Rose assured him. "Maybe he won't get as big as you, but he will get bigger. You'll be able to ride bikes together, and play ball together, go fishing with Daddy....all kinds of things." This made Nathan smile. "I'm glad he's a brother and not a sister, then. Girls can't do those things."

"Oh yes, they can! Sometimes they can do those things better than boys!" Rose corrected him. She did not want to be raising any male chauvinists. "Isn't that right, Al?" She looked at Al for support.

"Sometimes, yes, that's right. They have names for girls like that, though." He chided.

"Hush! You know I don't want them growing up thinking women are only good for cooking, cleaning, screwing, and birthing!"

"Well aren't they?" He caught her deadly look, and retreated. "Just kidding! Of course, I want them both to have respect and consideration for women. I hate a man that abuses and disrespects his wife. You know that."

Finally Steven was allowed to go home. Nathan was fascinated with him, and sat there watching him sleep for long periods of time. One day right after New Year's Day, Nathan called to his mother, "Mom, Steven is breathing funny. MOM!! Steven is turning purple!"

Rose ran into the room in time to see Nathan pulling Steven out of his crib, saying, "Come on, Steven, breathe!" Rose grabbed up Steven and told Nathan to go get the telephone. Nathan ran for the phone and dialed 911 before he took the phone to Rose. "My baby brother isn't breathing!" He said into the phone. Rose snatched the phone from him and began to talk into the phone fast. In a matter of minutes, the sirens could be heard, getting closer and closer. The ambulance took Steven, and Rose called Al on the job and agreed to meet him there at the hospital. Rose and Nathan got into Rose's car and headed for the hospital.

Rose asked Nathan, "Why were you taking Steven out of the crib?"

"I was going to put him on the floor like they do on TV, and give him CRP."

"I think you mean CPR. But you can't just do that, you have to be trained to do that. You know what? I think we all should get trained to do that. If Steven is going to have problems breathing we all need to know what to do, right?"

Rose glanced at Nathan to see if he was paying attention and saw that he clung to every word.

"Right.....I want Steven to get big and play ball with me."

At the hospital they were told that Steven had asthma and he would need special attention and special care. Rose cried. Al just stared at the floor and held Nathan in his lap. They were permitted to take Steven home once his breathing became even, but there were prescriptions and restrictions for him. For once, Rose was happy that Al spent so much time with Nathan, because a lot of her time was going to be spent with Steven. At home, Rose put Steven to bed, and Al took Nathan outside to build a snowman in the newly fallen snow. January in Northern Ohio was a bitter cold time of the year, but Al and Nathan didn't seem to mind it. They worked on their snowman and talked about what happened to Steven.

"Daddy, Steven could have died, couldn't he have?" Nathan wanted to know. He stared up at Al waiting for a response.

"Yes, I suppose he could have, Pal. I'm glad he didn't."

"Me, too. Daddy, will he ever be able to play like I do?"

"N-no, probably not. You'll have to watch out for him from now on. He will be very fragile...do you know what that means?" He asked Nathan.

"Breakable....right?" Nathan answered.

"Right."

22

Nathan turned five in July, and started kindergarten in September. He was excited about going to school like the big kids, but he was also concerned about leaving Steven at home. He felt responsible for Steven and felt that it was his job to be there in case something happened to him. There hadn't been a real asthma attack since the one in January, but Nathan remembered that one all too well.

Al took Nathan to school on his first day. He held his hand crossing the street, but Nathan insisted that he should not hold his hand walking down the sidewalk, since he was a big boy now. When they stood in front of the school, Nathan squared his shoulders and walked through the doors, with his hands as his sides. 'That's my boy!' Al whispered to himself.

They found Nathan's room and they got as far as the door, when Nathan turned to Al and said, "I got it from here, Dad."

Al had to turn away so Nathan didn't see the tears that had sprung up in the corners of his eyes.

"Okay, Nathan. Either mommy or me will be here after school, so you don't go anywhere with anybody else, okay? You look for us, okay?"

"Okay, Dad, I won't. Dad?"

"What, Buddy?"

"I love you."

Al smiled and sighed. He ruffled Nathan's hair and said, "Hey, I love you, too, my Buddy. See you later."

* * *

Nathan did quite well in kindergarten, and the school year ended all too soon. In that summer between kindergarten and first grade, Nathan turned six years old. Al surprised him with a small two-wheel bike and a ball glove. Al was delighted when Nathan picked the ball glove up first. "Wow! Dad! This is great. I want to be a ball player some day."

Those words could not have made Al happier, or prouder. His son was growing up healthy and happy, and he loved sports. Al began to think of Nathan as his son, and of Steven as Rose's son. Not that he didn't love Steven; it was just that Steven hung around Rose more, while Nathan preferred to be with him. Beside that, Nathan was the healthy one, and Steven was always ailing. He was small and underweight and he wheezed constantly. Rose was always fussing over him, wiping his hands and face, changing his shirt, or checking his forehead for fever.

The two boys' personalities were as different as night and day. Nathan was good-natured and always trying to be helpful, while Steven was whiny and demanding.

When he became old enough, Nathan joined little league baseball. Al never missed a game his son's team played, and eventually became the coach. Nathan was a strong hitter and he preferred to play second base. His fielding average was outstanding for a little leaguer. Although Nathan was delighted that his dad was there at every game, even coaching the team, he was disappointed that his mother never came. Rose explained to him that Steven could not be around dust because it brought on an asthma attack, and she certainly couldn't go and leave him at home. Nathan said that he understood, but nevertheless, he was disappointed. Al had a few discussions with Rose about it. He felt that she coddled Steven way too much, and that if she let him get out and do more, his asthma would be less severe. From what Al had read about asthma, many times the attacks were less frequent as a child got older.

At the age of ten, Nathan made the all-star team in little league. Since very few ten-year-olds made the all-stars, it was a big deal with Al and Nathan. It meant that he was an exceptional ball player. Nathan would be traveling with the All-Star team for a series of six games. Al planned vacation time around these games, and spoke to Rose about attending some of them. Rose protested that Steven could not be subjected to the dust, or whatever else might be lurking around to cause an attack.

Al slammed his breakfast dish into the sink, where it shattered. "Well, I'll travel with my son, and you stay home with your girl!" Al sneered at the last word.

"That's not fair! Steven has a medical condition. He can't be exposed to things!"

"Well, the last time I checked, you had two sons....but you neglect the needs of one of them, and give all of your attention to the other! Maybe you should let him be a little boy for a change. Let him get dirty, for Chrissake! Let him play like a normal kid! And above all, try to remember that you have another son! You're hurting him! He's not stupid! He has played ball for two years now...and you have not even seen one game! NOT ONE! Do you know how disappointed and hurt he is? Yeah, he loves having me there, but he would love to have his mother show up once in awhile!"

"You have your nerve telling me I neglect Nathan and give Steven all my attention! What do you do? JUST THE OPPOSITE!! You forget about Steven most of the time. What do you do with him?"

"What do you want me to do? Sit home and color?"

With that remark, Al stormed out of the house, jumped in his pickup truck and left for work.

Nathan and Steven were in Steven's room at the time the argument was taking place. Nathan was coloring with his six-year-old brother, and they both heard their parents yelling at each other. Steven began breaking his crayons one at a time, and Nathan was trying to make him stop.

"Don't do that, Steven! You won't have any crayons if you break them all! Come on…don't!"

"I hate daddy!" Steven spat out.

"No, you don't! Don't say that! Want to go downstairs and watch cartoons?"

Steven stared at Nathan for a few moments. "No! I hate you, too!" He screamed it at him, and began tearing up his coloring book and throwing the torn pieces on the floor.

Rose heard the commotion and ran up the stairs to see what was causing it. She saw Steven in a frenzy, just tearing pages up, and Nathan standing there staring at him.

"Steven! Nathan, why did you let him do this? Why didn't you stop him? You know this could bring on an asthma attack!!"

"I'm sorry, mommy. He's mad at Daddy and he's mad at me. He said he hates us." Nathan looked so dejected by these words. "I didn't do anything to him, either."

Nathan ran out of the room and into his own, where he sat down and pulled out his baseball cards and began reading them for the umpteenth time. When he knew Steven was napping, he went outside to practice fielding balls. He threw the ball against the brick chimney wall and caught it, over and over again. He never tired of practicing baseball.

At dinner that night, the air was stiff and formal, with Al and Rose saying only the minimal to each other. After dinner, Al went out to sit on the porch and watch Nathan oil his baseball mitt with saddle soap, the way Al taught him to do. After Rose did the dishes, she came out onto the porch with Steven.

"Why don't you let Steven try on your baseball mitt, Nathan?"

"Okay…here Steven, want to try it on?" Steven nodded.

Steven sidled over to Nathan and took the mitt from him. He wriggled his hand into the mitt and stood there looking down at the mitt on his hand. In one motion, he tore the mitt off of his hand and threw it from the porch, into the dirt.

"Steven!" Al jumped up and grabbed Steven by his arm. "Now you go get that! That was wrong!"

Immediately, Steven started crying and wheezing at the same time. His breathing became labored, and Rose grabbed him and rushed him into the house, to where she kept his inhalers and medications. Al walked into the house and slammed the door behind him, leaving Nathan standing outside, holding his dirtied baseball mitt, and wondering what had happened. He sat down on the porch step and rested his chin in his hand; his baseball mitt was in his lap.

"He all right?" Al leaned into the bathroom and watched Rose administer Steven's medicated inhaler to him.

"He'll be okay. You just startled him when you grabbed him."

"Are you okay, Steven?" Al looked down at him sitting on his mother's lap. Steven nodded.

Al gave Rose a serious stare.

"We need to talk." Was all he said, and went back downstairs and outside to the porch again.

* * *

Al and Nathan did the all-star circuit together, leaving Rose and Steven at home. There had been a terrible argument between Al and Rose the night before they were scheduled to leave for the first all-star tournament. Al accused Rose of spoiling Steven, and that Steven was turning into a spiteful brat. Earlier in the day, Steven had gone into Nathan's room and tore up all his baseball cards. Nathan was devastated.

"Well, maybe you should have put them away, Nathan. He couldn't have gotten them if they were put away!" Rose said this to Nathan when he discovered the cards.

"FOR FUCKING CRISSAKES, ROSE!! THEY WERE IN HIS ROOM!! STEVEN HAD NO BUSINESS GOING IN THERE!!"

"OH, YES, ALWAYS MAKE IT STEVEN'S FAULT!!"

"IT *IS* STEVEN'S FAULT!! HE WENT INTO.... TRESPASSED....INTO NATHAN'S ROOM AND DESTROYED SOMETHING THAT BELONGED TO NATHAN!! IS THIS THE WAY IT'S GOING TO BE? STEVEN CAN DO NO WRONG AND NATHAN IS ALWAYS ON THE LOSING END? WHAT... IS...HAPPENING....HERE?"

Al spat the words at Rose, pounding his fist on the table. He reached out with his foot and kicked over a kitchen chair, got up and walked outside. There he found Nathan, trying to piece together what was left of his cards.

"We'll see about replacing some of 'em, okay, Buddy?" Al patted his son on his back, and Nathan nodded.

Rose leaned out of the doorway, and in a deadpan voice, said to Al, "And by the way, I won't be going with you tomorrow."

"Yeah, well, no shit!! Like I couldn't figure that out already. You never had any intention of going." Rose disappeared into the darkness of the house, and slammed the door.

The following morning Nathan and Al got up early and went to meet the rest of the team to drive to their first destination of the tournament, which was a town on the outskirts of Cincinnati.

* * *

Nathan was the first batter when his team came in from the field. He let the first pitch go by for a strike, but on the next pitch he hit a line drive right past the pitcher and ran to first. He was a fast runner so he was able to steal second base. The second batter hit a fly ball that bounced off the right field fence, and Nathan scored the first run of the game. Nathan's team won the first game of the tournament, with Nathan scoring the last run of the game. The game ended at six runs for the Tigers, and four runs for the opposing team, the Falcons. They were now on the road for Dayton, and wanted to be there by dark to get checked into the hotel, eat, and relax for awhile. Nathan and Al shared a room as did most of the families who traveled with the tournament. Those boys whose parents weren't able to go had to share rooms with other families where there was room. Bobby Jenkins and Derek Pates shared the room with Nathan and Al. Al ordered pizza for them when they settled into the room for the evening. There was a ballgame on television and they all watched until it was lights out. After the boys fell asleep, Al stepped outside for a cigarette and sat down on one of the white resin chairs placed strategically in front of the motel doors. Tom Faloni saw him sitting there and decided to join him. After lighting up and sitting down in the chair next to Al's, Tom asked him why Rose hadn't come.

"Well, to tell you the truth, Tom, I could make up an excuse that Steven was sick so she decided to stay home with him, but that's not the way it is. Steven is *always* sick, and Rose is *always* catering to him. I think that if she let him be a kid he wouldn't be as sick all the time. He has asthma, but lots of kids have it and manage to live a normal life. Well, anyway, she's spoiling him. Whatever he does she defends. He destroys things of Nathan's and she yells at Nathan for not watching him. It's starting to put a hell of a strain on our marriage. You know what I mean?"

"That's really too bad, Al. Have you tried talking to her?"

"Yah, 'til I'm blue in the face." Al snorted a small laugh. "There is a lot of tension between us, but what makes it even worse is it seems like one kid is hers and one kid is mine. Does that make sense to you?"

"Sort of. I guess Nathan is yours and Steven is hers?"

"Yep, that's the way it seems."

"Any way that could be possible? I mean....don't take offense."

"No, none taken. I don't think that's a possibility. Well, I hate to say this, but Rose always wanted a girl, so she has the next best thing.... a frail little boy. Who knows? Maybe he'll grow up to be queer, or something."

"Nah! Don't say that. He's just not as healthy as Nathan is, that's all. I'm going to go get some sleep. See ya in the morning."

"Yeah, g'night, Tom." Al crushed out his cigarette and went in to bed.

* * *

The Tigers won the game in Dayton by eight runs. Nathan hit two singles and walked once. He scored all three times he was on base, but what he was most recognized for was the double play he made at second base. Not only was he fast on his feet, but the play showed that he had a strong arm. Al made a mental note to try him out as a pitcher next season.

The next stop was just west of Columbus. The caravan of cars arrived way before dark, so after washing up and changing clothes, the team went to McDonald's for dinner. Al sat with a few of the adults and Nathan sat with some of his team members at another table. The boys were having a rowdy conversation about the last two games and how they were going to be the state champions. Al watched Nathan and Bobby Jenkins engage in a high five, grins across their faces. Nathan was a year and a half younger than Bobby, but they seemed to get along. Al noticed that all of the team members got along with Nathan. He had that easy manner about him that made him popular with other boys. Al knew that same easy manner would eventually make him popular with girls, as well. Hell, he had looks, too. Those rich brown eyes with the long thick lashes and the thick jet black hair were going to make him a heart throb some day. Al just knew it. 'A chip off the old block' was what people said, Al was thinking. 'He had an easy time with the girls when he was younger, that was for sure. Sometimes he wondered why he ended up with Rose. Oh, she was a looker back in the day, but she never really had any sex appeal. No pizzazz. In fact, as of late, she was downright dowdy. Never put on make-up, didn't fix her hair, and most of the time, didn't care about what she was wearing, either. Maybe the problem wasn't just Steven....'

"Dad? Didn't you hear me?" Nathan was asking him.

"No, Buddy, sorry, I was thinking about something. What's up?" Al smiled at his son.

"I wanted to know if I could get another burger. I'm still hungry."

"Well sure, get a Big Mac if you want. Here's a five; go get what you want."

Tom Faloni leaned over toward Al. "Are you okay? You seem 'out there'."

"Yeah, just day dreaming about how we're going to sweep the tournament, that's all." With this, he laughed.

Tom looked at Al for a moment, and then turned away. 'No way was he thinking that,' Tom thought to himself.

The game in Columbus was delayed by rain twice, and the field was muddy and wet. The game went on with the Tigers victorious by one run. The next game was held in Steubenville. Because of the rain delays, the caravan arrived in Steubenville later than they originally planned. It was another pizza night. This time they all gathered at the park across the street from the motel. Al and Tom did the pizza run while the others stayed behind to supervise the team. After the pizza was eaten, they were all ready to turn in for the night. It had been a rough day for everybody.

Steubenville proved to be an easy win. The Tigers won by twelve runs. In fact, the score was thirteen to one. The team packed up and headed to Youngstown. They were victorious once again, and were looking forward to the final game in Akron. Al was proud of his team, and particularly proud of his son. Nathan was one of the youngest on the all-star team, but he held his own on the playing field.

The team was pumped up by the time they reached Akron. They felt that they were invincible. Because this was the last night, they were taken to a restaurant for dinner, with the understanding that they had to be civilized. That didn't last very long once they were inside the restaurant, and Al felt sorry for the other diners. Later on in the motel rooms, it took forever to settle them down and get them to sleep.

They were outplayed by the team in Akron, and consequently, they lost the game. The season was over for Nathan and Al, and they were going to return home in the morning. They had been gone for ten days, and all Al could hope for was that the war zone at home would be at a 'cease fire'.

23

School began in September. Nathan went to the fifth grade and Steven went to kindergarten. Rose walked with them to the school since it was Steven's first time. Nathan talked to Steven for the entire two blocks.

"Steven, school is fun. Wait 'til you see all the kids you're going to have to play with! They have swings and a slide in back of the building. That's where you go for recess."

Steven said nothing. He walked beside Nathan, staring straight ahead. When they stopped in front of the school, Steven turned to Rose and whined, "I don't wanna go to school!"

"Well, Steven, it's the law. You have to go to school. Besides, it will be fun. You'll make new friends, learn new things, and...."

"But I hate school!"

"How do you know if you haven't been there yet? And don't say 'hate'." Rose was becoming agitated.

Nathan spotted a couple of boys in his grade and waved to them. One called out that they were in room 207 this year.

"Mom, I'm going to go to my classroom, okay?"

"In a minute, Nathan. How about you walk with me and Steven to his classroom?" Rose looked to Nathan for his support.

"Okay, but class is starting soon, so can we hurry?"

The three of them started toward the door that led into the hall. Steven stopped abruptly. "NO! I don't want to go!"

"Steven, Honey, you *have* to! Everybody has to go to school!"

"NO! I don't want to, and *you* can't *make* me!"

Mr. Wolfe, the school principal appeared at the entrance when he heard the commotion that Steven was creating. "Can I be of some assistance?" He asked Rose as he looked at Steven.

"H-he's just scared...... his first day and all. He's going to go into his classroom now. Aren't you, Steven?"

"NO! I'M NOT!" Steven spat the words out at Rose and Mr. Wolfe. Nathan just stood there quietly.

Mr. Wolfe told Nathan to go ahead to his classroom; that they would handle it. Nathan slowly walked to his class, looking back at his mother, Steven and Mr. Wolfe a couple of times before he turned the corner, entering another corridor.

Mr. Wolfe, with the help of the school guidance counselor, managed to get Steven into his kindergarten classroom. Rose promised Steven that she would be back at noon to pick him up. Steven would not look at her or speak to her.

Mr. Wolfe and Miss Banes, the guidance counselor asked Rose if she had a few minutes to spare; that they would like to speak with her. She agreed, and followed them to the school's main office, where she was led into Mr. Wolfe's office. She sat down in the chair that they indicated for her.

"I'll get right to the point." Mr. Wolfe began. "I've seen children like Steven before. He's going to be a real discipline problem here at the school. I can see that already."

"He's not a bad kid, you know." Rose became defensive.

"He doesn't respect authority." Mr. Wolfe stared down his nose at Rose as the guidance counselor placed two folders in front of him. He looked down at the first folder and opened it. It was the larger of the two. "This is your son, Nathan's file." He paused to read for a moment. "Good grades, well-liked by fellow students and teachers.... here's a note here that one of his textbooks, along with his class project, was destroyed last year....by Steven."

Rose interrupted him. "Nathan left it out instead of putting it away. Steven saw it and cut it up. Nathan shouldn't have left it sitting on his desk like that."

"In his room, I take it." The Principal countered.

Rose nodded.

"Well, Mrs. Perletti, if everyone has to keep everything under lock and key so Steven won't destroy it, that's a problem. I mean....where do you keep your kitchen knives?"

Rose gasped. "Mr. Wolfe, he's not dangerous!" She was becoming more and more upset.

"But he tends to be violent....deliberately destroying another's belongings is a sign of violence, Mrs. Perletti, and the fact that he gets away with it teaches him that it's okay to do it. Behavior like that only gets worse."

"So what are you saying?" Rose was trying to keep her voice under control. This pompous man was insinuating that her Steven was a monster!

"I'm going to recommend special education classes for Steven." Mr. Wolfe looked toward Miss Bates, who had been quietly sitting there all this time, for support. "Of course, I want him to go through a battery of tests, including psychological profile tests."

"The school district has a wonderful program for troubled children, many of them having special needs." Miss Bates offered. "He does have asthma, doesn't he?"

"Yes, but he hasn't had many attacks in the past year."

Rose was horrified. These people were talking about Steven as though he were.....retarded, or something.

"Miss Bates, with all due respect, my son is not....mentally..... retarded...." Rose trailed off.

"No, we don't believe he is, but we believe that he may be emotionally disturbed." Miss Banes kept her words as monotone as possible, since she knew how people sometimes reacted to hearing this.

Rose started to protest, but Mr. Wolfe put his hand up to stop her. "Let's do the testing first before we make any further decisions." And with that he stood up, indicating that the meeting was over. "Of course, you should tell your husband what we are planning to do. He will have to be involved in this, too. Once we set up the testing schedule, we will notify you at home. Agreed?"

Rose nodded, and stood up. She was mentally preparing herself for the fight she would have on her hands when she told Al all of this. Suddenly the outer office filled with shrieks and screams, and loud voices. Mr. Wolfe quickly opened the door to see what was going on. The kindergarten teacher had Steven by the arm, and was holding onto the hand of a little blonde girl. The girl was responsible for the shrieking and screaming.

"What's going on here?" Mr. Wolfe's voice was raised over the commotion.

"This boy.....this boy......urinated on her!"

Rose was shocked. She looked down at Steven who just stood there with a smirk on his face. He showed no remorse at all!

Mr. Wolfe went into action. He took Steven's arm and led him to Rose. "Please take him home and we will call you as soon as we can get the testing set up." The guidance counselor took charge of the screaming little girl.

Rose and Steven walked home hand in hand. "Steven, that was wrong to do that. You know that, don't you?" Steven didn't answer.

* * *

Nathan was in his room doing homework and Steven was in his own room coloring in his coloring book. They both had their doors closed to muffle the yelling coming from downstairs. Rose related the morning events to Al and he was furious.

"JESUS CHRIST! HE'S NOT JUST A BRAT NOW!! HE'S A REAL NUT JOB!! I BLAME YOU! I TOLD YOU WHAT ALL THAT CODDLING WAS GOING TO CAUSE! *You…should…. have….listened to me.*"

Al lowered his voice and fell into a chair. "So when does this testing begin? OH, STOP WITH THE CRYING, DAMN IT!"

"YOU COULD BE A LITTLE COMPASSIONATE!" Rose screamed back at him. "You act like I'm not even your wife any more!"

"You haven't been a wife. You haven't been a good wife to me or a good mother to Nathan ever since…….Steven…..was born."

"THAT'S NOT TRUE!" Rose shouted at him; tears running down her face.

"Isn't it? Think about it. When was the last time you put me first, or Nathan first, over Steven?" Al's brown eyes had gone black with anger, as they bored into Rose's eyes.

"But Steven is not healthy! He needs me more"

"More than what? Your husband? Your other son? Do you know how many times I have thought about leaving you? Do you know why I don't? I'LL TELL YOU WHY! Because if I left, you would have custody of both of the boys, and that would give you the chance to destroy Nathan!"

Al hissed these hurtful words at her, and Rose looked as though he had slapped her. She sank down onto a kitchen chair and cried silently. "So what are we going to do? I mean, us."

"I don't know, Rose. I don't know. Oh, we'll stay married…..for the boys' sake. But I want you to understand…..if you *ever, EVER* do anything to hurt Nathan…"

"I wouldn't hurt Nathan!" Rose cut him off.

"Oh Yeah? Well, you have been hurting him for five years now. I hope you know that."

Rose wiped her eyes with a tissue, and shook her head. "How? How have I hurt him?"

"Neglect.....for starters.....lack of affection. You try to make him responsible for Steven and for Steven's actions, for another thing. You ignore Nathan's accomplishments. You never praise him for good report cards, or for being a good ball player, or have you told him lately that you love him?" Al looked at his wife with contempt in his eyes.

Rose stared down at the table, not knowing what to say at first. "Nathan knows I love him."

"Does he? How would he know that? You know, Rose, you always say that you want your sons to grow up having love and respect for women. Do you know how boys grow up to love and respect women? If they get love and positive encouragement from their mothers. I loved and respected my mother, and do you know why? Because she loved me, and she never once hesitated to tell me that. She encouraged me to do well, and she praised me when I did. And, yes, she disciplined me when I screwed up. I grew up loving and respecting her until the day she died. I admired her, and you know what? She admired me! My father was a bastard, you know that, but my mother....my mother made me the person I became. She taught me to love, to care, and to respect others. And by God, I want my sons to be taught the same thing! When my son finds that special woman that he wants to spend his life with, I don't want that woman to ever regret the decision. It's love and be loved, Rose...respect and be respected."

Al stopped talking, covered his face with his hands, and rested his elbows on the table. Rose sat across from him looking miserable and dejected. After a few minutes, Al began again.

"You have to stop punishing Nathan for being perfect."

Rose began to protest, but Al put his hand up and stopped her.

"And you had better start teaching Steven that he can't do what he wants and get away with it. Pissing on a little girl! What the hell, Rose? Is that how you want him to behave?"

"N-no, of course not!" Rose was shocked that Al would even suggest that she thought it was all right.

"Well, then something had better be done about it. If not, he'll do it again." Al started up the stairs to the second floor.

"W-what are you going to do?" Rose asked.

"What any normal father would do when his son does something like that. Beat his ass!"

"NO! Al, NO!"

"Stay out of it. From now on, I take over. You FAILED!"

Al crashed into Steven's room, grabbed him by the arm, and sat him down hard. "What did you do to that little girl today, Steven?"

Steven stared at the floor.

"I'M TALKING TO YOU!" Al was furious again. "WHAT DID YOU DO TO THAT LITTLE *GIRL*?"

"I peed on her." was Steven's reply.

"WHY?" Al tightened his grip on Steven's arm. "WHY?"

Steven shrugged and said, "Because I HATE HER!"

Al grabbed Steven up and threw him over his knee and spanked him hard. When he let him go, Steven just stared at him, with not so much as a tear in his eyes.

"I hate you, too." He simply stated, and turned away.

Al briskly walked down the steps and out the door, slamming it hard. He leaned against his truck and lit a cigarette to calm down. 'The kid's a monster.' He thought to himself.

24

Steven completed the series of tests that had been set up for him. He scored very high on the IQ tests, which pleased Rose, but did poorly on the psychological portion. It was recommended that he enter a school for children with special needs and that he see a psychologist on a regular basis. Rose agreed to all of this, willingly. At this point she would have done anything to save her troubled marriage. She began to pay more attention to Nathan, and the smile on his face told her that Al had been right. She began disciplining Steven when he did something wrong, sending him to his room for bad behavior. She went and got her hair cut and styled, threw out all of her frayed and tattered clothes she had been wearing, and began wearing a little make-up during the day. Al noticed the change and was pleased. He also noticed there was less strain on her face, and he imagined it was because Steven was at school all day and she had time to relax. The house began to take on that spotless look it always had before Steven was born. Life seemed to be returning to normal and once again, they seemed like a happy family.

One day Al came home with flowers for her. When she asked what they were for, he told her they were for her effort. It was the recognition she had been hoping for.

School was ending for the summer. Nathan had just completed his fifth year and Steven was finished with kindergarten. Since Nathan was playing little league baseball once again, Rose asked Steven if he would like to try T-ball that year. He hadn't had an asthma attack since he entered school, so she thought maybe his asthma was going into remission. He wasn't interested, so Rose let it go.

Once again, Nathan made the all-star team. Rose decided that they would all go to the tournaments this year. She got to see Nathan play and had to admit that he was good. She could look at him and imagine him as an adult, playing for a major league team. Al was coaching the team again, so she and Steven sat in the stands together and watched the games. At the beginning of the first tournament, Al asked Steven if he would like to be batboy for the team.

"All you have to do is get the bat from the field when a player hits a ball and runs to first." Al told him. Steven agreed, thus becoming part of the team.

Rose praised her husband. "That was a noble effort on your part, Al. He really feels like he belongs."

"I hate to disappoint you, but it was Nathan's idea. I just hope it works out."

Steven was on medication that was supposed to help him maintain an even disposition. It seemed to be working well, since he had not destroyed anything in the household lately. He didn't seem to be as mean spirited as he once was, and he even stopped using the word 'hate'. For once, Al enjoyed having both of his boys around.

The Tiger team won the tournament. The team, including Steven, received jackets that had the words *'LITTLE LEAGUE ALL-STARS, 1986'* on the back of them. Both Nathan and Steven were proud of their jackets and wanted to wear them everywhere. For once, the brothers seemed to be buddies, which pleased both Al and Rose.

The summer vacation ended too soon, as far as the boys were concerned. Nathan was going into the sixth grade and Steven was entering first grade at the school for special needs children. Rose wanted to try him at the regular school, but Mr. Wolfe vetoed it, with Al backing him up.

"He's doing well there. There has been a big improvement in our household since he started there. Let's not change anything." Al coaxed Rose. She agreed to let him return to the 'special' school as she secretly referred to it.

The year whizzed by. Both boys appeared to be doing well in their classes, and were growing rapidly. Nathan was becoming very handsome and muscular for an eleven-year-old boy. He had his father's physique; that was for certain. Steven, while getting taller, remained on the slim side. He had his father's rich brown eyes, but he didn't have the black fringe of eyelashes like Nathan and his father had. His hair was dark brown; not black like Nathan's and Al's. He was nice looking, but not striking like Nathan. He also lacked Nathan's quick, bright smile and easy manner. He was sullen and rarely smiled. Both Rose and Al chalked it up to 'just two different personalities'.

The school year ended without incident, which was a relief to both Rose and Al. Once again, Nathan was playing little league. He was twelve that summer and he would still have another year in little league. The cut-off date was June 30th. If he would have turned thirteen before June 30th, he would not have been able to play for another year. He missed it by four days. Once again, the All-Star Team traveled the Ohio circuit, with Nathan playing and Al as the coach. Nathan was pitching now. During the practice season, Al tried him out as a pitcher and was amazed at his control. He had a hard fast ball, as well. He managed to learn how to throw all of the pitches required that made a pitcher successful, and he became the top pitcher on the team. Al was proud of him, and so was Rose. Sitting in the stands, she heard comments on how he looked like a major leaguer already. Steven, who was going on eight years old now, remained the batboy on the team. He felt important and that helped his behavior. Rose was asked to join the Ladies Auxiliary that year. She would have to work in the concession stand once a week, but was assured that it wouldn't be while Nathan was playing. That way she would be helping out, yet not miss her son's games. She agreed to this, and felt it was a way to get out alone for awhile and leave the boys with Al. She had not had any time out by herself in years. This would give Steven and Al a chance to bond, like Al and Nathan had bonded.

That summer of 1987 was the best summer they had ever spent together as a family. In one form or another they were all active in the little league baseball program in their little Ohio town. The all-star team lost the first game that year, so the season ended early for Al and Nathan. Al had lots of vacation time left, so he planned a trip to Ocean City, Maryland as a surprise for all of them. The boys had never seen the ocean and Al was looking forward to showing it to them. Rose was looking forward to a few days of relaxation on the beach, hoping to get a nice tan in the meantime. Al told Rose to use the credit cards to get the boys new swimsuits, shorts and t-shirts, and to get herself some new things, too. She and the boys went shopping and she even treated them to lunch at McDonald's. Life was good. She had two healthy, happy boys and a wonderful husband. She only hoped that what she referred to as Steven's darkness was behind them.

They all had a wonderful time at the beach. Al and Nathan tossed a football back and forth, and Steven built a sandcastle worthy of photographing. Rose thought that Steven may have artistic ability, maybe in a sculpture field. The vacation was exactly what the family needed. They returned to Ohio relaxed, tanned, and happy.

Nathan was entering junior high school. "Oh boy, here it comes," Rose thought. "Girls, girls, girls! They will be calling the house, that's for sure." Rose thought to herself, as she watched Nathan tie his shoes. "He's a work of art all in himself," She chuckled at that thought.

He was indeed a handsome boy. Shining black hair like Al's, warm brown eyes with thick, dark lashes, white teeth and tanned from the summer vacation. He had nice features, Rose admitted to herself. His eyes alone were going to melt a lot of hearts. She knew Al's eyes melted her heart long ago when they first met. Nathan had Al's same easy, gentle nature that made everybody feel very special. 'A lot of those melted hearts were going to be broken by him', Rose thought, 'And he won't even know it.'

Nathan picked up his all-star jacket and headed toward the door. He stopped, ran back, and kissed Rose on the cheek. "See ya after school, Mom. Okay?"

"Okay, Nathan. You're not nervous about going to the junior high school this year?"

"No, most of my friends will be there, so I'm okay. See you later." Off he went to a new segment of his life.

Steven was going to second grade. The small bus would be coming to pick him up shortly, and Rose wondered what was keeping him.

"Steven? Are you ready to go?" No answer.

"STEVEN!" Rose started up the steps just as Steven came from Nathan's room into the hallway.

Instantly, Rose smelled the smoke. She ran past Steven and into his room. Nothing. She started toward the stairs and stopped. The smoke was pouring out of Nathan's room! She ran into the room, and was forced back because of the thick smoke. She grabbed Steven and ran down the stairs to the telephone, grabbed it up and called 911. Then she called Al.

"Be right there!" Al yelled into the phone, and hung up. She heard the sirens, grabbed Steven by the arm and forced him outside. The fire engines got there a fraction of a second before Al sped into the driveway.

The firemen worked quickly and extinguished the blaze. Joe, an acquaintance of Al's, came down the steps and out to the back porch to where Rose and Steven were standing.

"There isn't too much damage. Smoke, mostly. Couldn't save those trophies, though. Kid's going to need a new bed, too"

Al appeared on the back porch where Rose and Steven were talking to Joe.

"How did it start?" Al wanted to know, although he had his suspicions.

"Don't know yet. The Fire Marshal will determine the cause." Joe answered.

Al, Rose, and Steven stood on the back porch and waited until everything was clear. The Fire Marshal was upstairs with his assistant when they went back into the house. Joe left with the fire trucks. A police car pulled into the driveway, and Officer Banks got out.

"Everything okay, Al?" He asked when he spotted Al on the porch. "What burned?"

"Nathan's room. Don't know what caught fire yet. The Fire Marshal is up there now."

Al's eyes slid over to Steven as he stared into Officer Banks' eyes.

"So if this fire was set by someone, you're going to arrest someone. Right?"

"I could. It would be arson, then. People go to jail for that. Can get five years in prison or more." The police officer said, matter-of-factly.

They both watched Steven walk down the porch steps and disappear around the side of the house.

"You think he set the fire, Al?" Ken Banks asked, raising an eyebrow.

"I don't know for sure, but I think he might have."

The Fire Marshal walked out onto the porch, and having heard Al's suspicion, said, "Somebody set that fire. I found lighter fluid and matches on the bed. Luckily the can was almost empty, or it could have been a worse fire. Also, it hadn't been burning all that long before we got here."

Al looked over at Rose who had just joined them on the porch. Her face was stark white and her eyes looked like two black holes in her head. "Steven did it, didn't he?" Al's eyes bored into Rose. She conceded that Steven probably did set the fire.

"Where is he now?" It was the Fire Marshal that spoke.

"Ken and I saw him walk around the side of the house." With that, they all went in the direction that Steven had gone. The path led to the wooded end of the property, and they followed it through the trees.

As they walked deeper into the trees, they noticed the presence of a foul odor. It was getting stronger with every step. They reached a clearing and Rose gasped. Hanging with ropes around their necks were several cats, a couple of rabbits and a puppy. They were all quite dead, but it was obvious that they weren't when they were put there. All of them looked like they had been tortured, and a couple of them were partially burned. Officer Ken Banks' eyes wandered up the trunk of a large elm, and made eye contact with the bone-chilling cold eyes of a disturbed eight-year-old. Rose was throwing up and crying. Al looked like he was going to be sick, and the fire marshal looked as though he were in shock.

"Come down from there, Steven." It was Officer Banks who spoke. He looked over at Al. "He needs help, Al. You have to know that."

Al nodded, and went to his wife who was on the verge of hysteria.

25

Al was waiting for Nathan at the school. He saw him come out with some of his buddies, all of them laughing and rough-housing. He tooted his horn and caught Nathan's attention. Nathan grinned, showing his white teeth, and trotted over to the truck.

"Hi, Dad.....What's up?"

"Can you tear yourself away from your buddies? We have to talk." Al looked his son in the eye. "Something's come up."

"Yeah...okay...wait a minute. I'll be right back." He trotted away and gave his explanation to his friends that his dad wanted to talk to him. He ran back and jumped into the truck.

"Let's go to the park, okay?" Al looked at his son and felt so tired.

"Sure.....What's wrong, Dad?" Al didn't say anything until they got to the park.

"Let's just go sit on the bench, okay, Nathan?"

"Sure, Dad....what's wrong? Is something wrong with Mom or Steven?" Nathan felt frightened. "Steven didn't have an asthma attack, did he?"

Al shook his head. "No, I'm afraid it's worse than that."

Al related the day's events to Nathan, while Nathan stared at him, disbelieving.

"Steven's going away, Nathan. He has to. He's a danger to himself, to you, to me and mom, and to anything living and breathing in his way."

Nathan swallowed hard. He had a lump in his throat because he was trying so hard not to cry. His brother was a maniac! Crazy! He destroyed his room, killed defenseless animals, and God knew what else.

"Your mother is taking it very hard. It's hard to accept that there is something mentally wrong with one of your children."

"Yeah, especially when it's your favorite one." Nathan agreed.

Al gave him no argument.

* * *

Steven was taken to a psychiatric facility for children somewhere in the middle of Ohio. Rose and Al visited him on Sundays, but Nathan was not permitted to go. On Sundays he stayed home alone and watched football games. Occasionally, a friend came over to watch the games with him. He didn't really miss Steven all that much, since they really were not very close. He missed his mother, though. Since Steven left, she had become withdrawn and distant. He still had his dad, and he was grateful for that.

Steven was allowed to come home for a visit at Christmas. Al and Rose were instructed to watch him closely. The van to take him back would be there to pick him up at seven PM sharp.

Rose was happier than she had been in weeks. She prepared a wonderful Christmas dinner and she smiled a lot during the day. There were gifts for Steven and for Nathan under the tree. Some of Steven's gifts would have to stay there until he came home, since they were restricted on what they were allowed to have at the facility. The attendant picking him up would decide what he could take back with him. Steven was quiet and subdued. Al and Rose imagined that it was his medication that kept him that way. He and Nathan talked quietly in the living room while Al and Rose prepared the dinner and set the table. The day went without incident, and at seven o'clock sharp the attendant arrived to take Steven back to the facility. He looked over Steven's gifts and picked those that could be taken. Nothing with a sharp edge or with a point was permitted, since it could be used as a weapon. The new clothes were okay, and the card game that was bought for him was fine. Steven put his coat on and Rose hugged him to her fiercely. Al hugged him, too. Nathan tried to hug him, but Steven pulled back. He leaned toward Nathan and whispered in his ear, "I hate you." He disappeared out the door with the attendant.

Nathan looked like he had been slapped. He told them what Steven had said. Rose cried, and Al just stared at the floor. 'Nathan had never done anything to Steven.' Al was thinking. 'Why did Steven hate him so much?' They never told Nathan this, but when they went to visit Steven, he told them he hated Nathan and wished he was dead.

Nathan considered himself a small grown-up, but that night he cried in bed. He had no idea why his brother hated him. Was it because Nathan didn't have asthma and Steven did? He had no idea.

The rest of the Christmas vacation was fun for Nathan, so he was able to put the incident aside. He and his friends played ice hockey at the local pond almost every day. When a new-fallen snow kept his father from going to work the day before New Year's Eve, he stayed home and built a snowman with his dad.

On New Year's Day, his parents went to see Steven, and as usual, he stayed home to watch football. It was dark when his parents came home, and he could tell that Rose had been crying. His parents sat in the kitchen where they thought he couldn't hear them. He lowered the TV volume so he could hear what they were saying.

"Rose, I see no improvement at all. If anything, he's more sullen and withdrawn than ever."

"It's because he wants to come home!" Rose cried.

"Well, his doctors say he's not stable enough, and I won't put Nathan, or you, or myself, at risk. Especially Nathan. For some reason Steven hates him. I think it is jealousy, but it doesn't matter. I won't put Nathan's safety at risk."

"Al, you're talking about your other son! What about him? What about what is right for him?" Rose pleaded.

"What's right for him is that he remains in a place where he can get the care he needs and away from those he can harm. Let the psychiatrists and psychologists help him. We can't, don't you see that? We are not equipped to help him. We can love him, but we can't make him well. Besides, you heard what that doctor said today. Nathan is in danger around Steven."

Al looked up and saw Nathan standing there; his face as white as a sheet.

"How long have you been standing there?" Al asked him.

"Long enough." Then Nathan started to cry. Al got up from the table, went to his son and put his arm around his shoulder.

"I'm sorry you had to hear that, Nathan. I don't know what's wrong with your brother, but whatever it is, it's certainly not your fault." Al tried to comfort him.

"Why…why does he hate me? Does anybody know? What did I ever do to him?"

"Nothing…you did nothing to him. It's not your fault that he feels that way. Hell, it's not even his fault. He's sick. He's mentally ill, Nathan, and there's nothing you or I or your mother can do to help him." With that, he embraced his son so Nathan couldn't see the tears in his own eyes.

Rose was in tears at the table. Nathan let go of his dad and went to her. "Mom, please don't cry. And please don't hate me because I'm not the one who is sick. Please?" His tears were falling onto his chin.

She looked up at him and saw what she had done to him the past few years. She saw the guilt in his eyes that it wasn't he who had the physical and mental problems. "Oh, Nathan…I'm so sorry….I don't hate you….I love you. Oh, Nathan. What have I done to you?" She choked back more tears and reached for her son. She held on to him like she was afraid to let go.

26

Nathan's life improved that year. His mother was showing him the love and affection he had missed over the past eight years. His parents continued to visit Steven on Sundays. He always asked how he was doing when they returned home, and the answer was always the same: "The same."

It was time for baseball season again. Nathan tried out for the Junior Varsity Baseball team and became the proud wearer of the number twelve jersey. He could hit the ball, and he could field the ball, but his number one strong point was his pitching. He had a fast ball and a curve ball that was hard to hit. His coach thought he was a natural on the mound.

Al and Rose tried to make it to all of his games. Coach Phillips waved to them whenever they showed up. He seemed to take a personal interest in Nathan. After one victorious game which Nathan had pitched a no-hitter, the coach approached Al and Rose.

"You have a future major league ball player; you know that, don't you?" His eyes darted from one to the other.

Al responded with a short laugh, and said, "I suspected that we might. I know he's pretty damn good."

"Yeah, he is….and you know what? It just comes to him naturally! It's like a part of him. Just thought I should tell you that. Keep encouraging him. He's a great kid, by the way."

"Thank you, Coach. We already know that." This time it was Rose speaking. Al put his arm around Rose's shoulders and they headed toward the car.

27

Nathan's ninth grade school year began. He was tall and muscular for fourteen. His easy manner and disposition made him popular with other kids and well-liked by his teachers. Rose's prophecy about girls was coming to light this year. Quite a few were calling the house asking for him. He would take the phone and mostly sat and listened to what they had to say. He did very little talking, but was always polite and respectful to them while they were on the phone. He was on the phone when Rose called him to dinner.

"I have to go. My mom has dinner ready. No, then I have to do my homework. See you tomorrow." He hung up the phone.

Al had half of a smile when Nathan sat down. "Is it always the same girl?" He wanted to know.

"No. It's more than one. Actually, it's closer to six of them."

"Interested in any of them?" Al asked.

"No."

"Why talk to them, then?"

"Because I don't want to hurt their feelings. I mean, I don't care if they call. Most of the guys would be really ignorant to them, because if they are nice on the phone, the girls will come up to them in the halls at school, acting like they're going out. Me, I don't care about that. I know whether we are or not. I guess the guys are worried what other people think all the time. I don't care what they think. I know what I'm doing and not doing." He shrugged and reached for his fork.

"Are these girls ugly or something?" Al teased.

"No, not all of them. But the guys like to be the ones picking the girls, not the other way around."

"Well, that certainly hasn't changed much." Rose interjected.

Al snickered. "Not any of them you like?"

"Nah, not really. I mean, some of them are okay, but most of them are too silly."

Both Rose and Al laughed.

"What do you like about a girl? I mean….her sense of humor? Her looks or personality? What?" It was Rose's question.

"I like intelligence. Not nerds, but just someone who is smart. You know, one who laughs when something is funny, not because there is nothing to say. I like girls who can put a sentence together and carry on a conversation without giggling. That doesn't happen too much when they call here. They're always giggling. Sometimes I think they have a girlfriend on the line, listening."

"I remember those days." Rose laughed. "They probably do. My friends and I used to do that. One would call, and the others would listen in. Silly, but true."

Al kept quiet, because he knew what Nathan was talking about. He found it all very amusing.

Christmas was fast approaching, and Al and Rose were wondering about letting Steven come home on Christmas Day. Any more than a day was frowned upon by the psychologist. He said not only was it disruptive in his treatment, but there were still some violence issues that needed to be addressed. Steven attacked and injured a boy the previous week. It had been an unprovoked attack, and the attendants who tried to end it were slightly injured as well. Steven was tall and wiry, but he had a fierce determination to hurt someone when he so desired. He would attack and not stop. It looked like he was literally trying to tear an opponent to shreds.

"You have to watch him every minute if I let him come home for the day. If he goes upstairs, someone must go with him. Above all, do not let him in a room alone with Nathan. There are still some very strong issues there." Dr. Wykoff advised.

Al and Rose agreed to these terms, and now were looking forward to his arrival on Christmas Day. Nathan wasn't sure if he was looking forward to it or dreading it. It had been almost two years since he had seen Steven, and it ended on a bad note that time.

Al heard the van pull into the driveway and went to the door. He watched Steven get out of the van, and saw the attendant intently talking to him. Steven nodded to him, and turned to his father standing on the porch.

"Hello, Dad."

"Hi, Steven. Merry Christmas!"

"Yeah, fuck that, too!"

"Hey, watch your mouth! Don't you dare talk like that in front of your mother. You got it?"

'Already', Al thought. 'He isn't even in the house and he and I are at it.'

"Yeah, I got it." He was as surly as he could be as he walked past Al into the house.

Rose smiled and went to Steven with arms opened for a hug. Steven dodged her arms, said hello, and walked into the living room. Rose was hurt, but she didn't say anything; the smile frozen on her face. She looked at Al, and he shrugged. What could he say?

Steven saw Nathan sitting on the sofa reading what looked like an instruction booklet. He raised his lip in a sneer, and walked over to stand in front of him.

Nathan looked up and smiled at Steven.

"Hi Steven. Merry Christmas. I have a gift for you...."

Steven cut him off. "Still queer?"

"What? Why would you say something like that? Can't you be pleasant for just one day?" Al was standing in the doorway and heard the remark. He felt sick when he spoke to him. "Nathan, why don't you see if your mother needs help with anything, okay?"

"Okay, Dad." He barely whispered it. He, too, felt sick that Steven would say that.

The day didn't end quickly enough as far as Al was concerned. He watched Steven like a hawk. He was afraid to let him near Nathan, and he wouldn't let him go upstairs alone. Al secretly policed the bathroom before Steven got there, making sure there was nothing left in there that he could use to hurt someone. Al let out a sigh of relief when the attendant showed up at seven o'clock. For once, Rose didn't cry when he left. Al felt terrible to be so relieved to see his ten-year-old son go, but every moment was a trial when he was there. Where did that mouth come from? He made a mental note to ask the shrink next time they had a session with him.

2-8

Baseball season began again. Nathan tried out for the varsity baseball team and made it. Al reminded him that since he was only a freshman, he should be prepared to sit on the bench a lot. Nathan told his father that he was willing to accept that, but secretly hoped that would not be the case. He loved baseball and he wanted to play as often as he could. Little did he know that during try-outs, Coach Belinski watched him closely and was especially interested in his athletic ability.

Coach Stan Belinski looked over at his assistant and nodded toward Nathan. "That kid is a natural. He pitches, he can hit, and he has real ability in the field. Within two years, he will be one of our star players...mark my words."

Nathan played in all but two games that first season. Coach Belinski was delighted with his ability and his flexibility. He could put him anywhere and expect favorable results. Nathan was beginning to grow taller and his muscles were developing rapidly. He had speed and control when he pitched, which was unusual for a fourteen-year-old. He was quick on his feet and could handle any play with ease. At bat, Nathan had a good eye for the ball. He wasn't a homerun hitter, but he easily hit at least a single or double every time up at bat. He could have been a homerun hitter, the coach felt sure, but he worked on his pitching more than his hitting.

Nathan received his first varsity letter that year. He attended the awards banquet with Al and Rose where he received his letter for baseball and an award for high honors. He also received the Freshman

MVP award for his team. Al and Rose were so proud they could have burst.

"I guess you have to buy a jacket to go with that letter, huh?" Al looked over at his pride and joy. "Where do we buy it?"

Nathan grinned and produced the order form.

His jacket arrived on the last day of school that year. He carried the box into the house, grinning from ear to ear. He set the box on the table, opened it, and proudly took out his new varsity jacket. The letter had been sewn on for him by the company who manufactured the jackets. The school name was sewn across the back, with the words 'Varsity Baseball' above it. He immediately tried it on and looked at his reflection in the mirror.

Rose came up behind him and smiled. "You look so handsome in it!"

He smiled back at her. "Think so?" He responded.

"Sure do. I'm sure the girls will think so, too." She teased. "So now that school is out, what do you think you'd like to do this summer?"

"I don't know. Have fun maybe. Go swimming. Stuff like that." Since he was still admiring himself in the mirror, he missed Rose's secret smile. She and Al had a surprise for him and she was sure he was going to like it. She promised Al she would wait for him to get home before she said anything.

* * *

Dinner was served shortly after Al arrived home from work. There was the usual banter at the table.

"The Indians won last night, Nate." Al and Nathan followed the major league baseball scores, but were particularly interested in their team, the Cleveland Indians.

"Yeah, I watched part of the game, Dad, but I fell asleep before it was over. Now that school's out for the summer, maybe I'll get to watch a whole game."

"Or maybe not." Al was watching Nathan for a reaction.

"What? Why do you say that, Dad?"

Al looked at Rose and nodded for her to tell him.

"Nathan, your dad and I found a baseball camp that we thought you might like to go to. What do you think? Would you like that?"

Nathan almost choked on his forkful of food. "Really? You mean it?"

"Well, yeah," Al answered him. "Would you want that?"

"Oh, yeah! Big time, Dad! I'd love it!" He could hardly contain his excitement. He knew he could learn so much from a baseball camp, not to mention that he would be playing baseball every day.

"Well, then....done. Camp starts the day after your birthday, July the fifth. We'll celebrate your birthday, maybe go to an Indians game if they're playing at home, and then drive you to the camp the next day. Sound good?"

"Sounds perfect!" He grinned at his parents. "Thanks, Mom and Dad. You're the greatest."

"Well, you're a pretty terrific son, you know." Al said this as he gently placed his fist on Nathan's cheek. He looked at Rose and winked.

The baseball camp dates came at a perfect time. Steven would be coming home for a two-week summer break. Neither Rose nor Al wanted Steven to be around Nathan. They just couldn't trust him. Having Nathan at baseball camp would keep Nathan safe, and give Rose the time to concentrate on keeping a watchful eye on Steven. Even though Nathan was tall and muscular, and Steven was small in stature and slight of build, he was a threat to Nathan. The child was only ten-and-a-half years old, but so full of hate and animosity toward everyone, and especially Nathan. Al agreed to let him come home for two weeks after he spoke with Officer Banks, getting him to agree to stop in at least once a day, if not more. Al didn't like the idea of Rose being alone with Steven. Incident reports from the facility proved that Steven was indeed a menace to society and should not be left unsupervised for any period of time. Al feared for Rose's safety. He chose random vacation days during that two-week period so that he could protect her a little better. The truth was, Al was a little afraid of him, too. He dreaded those two weeks.

* * *

The Perletti family was not able to attend the baseball game, so Nathan opted for Sea World on his birthday, instead. The three of them, and Nathan's friend Bobby, had an enjoyable day visiting all the aquatic animals. Nathan was especially fond of dolphins. He loved watching them play, and hearing their screeching noises. He and Bobby were watching them move across the top of the water on their tails.

"When we went to Florida last year, I saw lots of dolphins in the water. We went on a dolphin watch boat ride, and they were everywhere. Some were just babies."

Nathan looked at Bobby with interest. "Yeah? Florida, huh? Maybe that's where I may end up some day then."

After the day in Sea World, they went to a restaurant for dinner. Al and Rose surprised Nathan with a birthday cake, delivered to the table by their waiter. Some of the wait-staff came over to the table and sang the birthday song to him. Rose couldn't help but notice that one of the younger waitresses couldn't take her eyes off of Nathan. He didn't seem to notice, but Bobby did.

"That chick was checking you out, Nate! She was fine, too." Bobby's voice was full of envy.

"Didn't notice her." Nathan answered him, matter-of-factly, but gave him a sly wink.

Al saw the wink and chuckled under his breath. 'How could my two sons be so different? The Prince and the Dragon. Maybe somebody should write a story with that as the title.' He mused to himself. 'I thank God for Nathan. Steven? Well, I just thank God that there isn't two of him'.

29

Nathan awoke just before daylight. His gear was packed and ready to go the night before, and he could have slept another couple of hours, since they weren't leaving before ten in the morning, but he was too excited to sleep. He was really looking forward to this. He read that there would be a couple of retired major league ballplayers there heading up the program, and he was anxious to meet with them; talk to them and see if he had what it takes to play major league ball. He moved quickly to the kitchen and put on a pot of coffee for his parents for when they awoke, and then he headed into the bathroom to take a shower. As he was drying off from the shower, he glanced in the mirror. He moved closer to the mirror to get a better look. Yep…there they were. A few hairs were growing on his chin. He realized a few days ago that his voice was getting deeper, and now….hairs on his chin. 'Cool,' he thought to himself. He wondered if he should shave them off, but thought better of it. 'They may not come back, so I better just leave them.' He thought to himself again. He looked closely at his chest. There were a couple of hairs there, too. He smiled. "All right, Nate!" This he whispered to himself.

He heard movement in the kitchen, so he headed down in that direction where he found his mother warming up the griddle.

"Good morning, Nathan! Thanks for making the coffee. How about waffles this morning?" Rose was in a good mood.

"Sounds good. Don't know if I'll be able to eat. I'm pretty excited." He looked up at Rose from the table. "Mom, this is a great opportunity for me. Thanks."

"I don't think you're talking about the waffles, are you?" She tried to keep a straight face.

Nathan laughed. "Well…no, but that's good, too."

Al appeared in the doorway of the kitchen. "All ready to go?" He asked. Nathan nodded.

"Don't forget to lock your bedroom door, okay?"

Last night, they told him that Steven would be coming home for a two-week break. Al installed an alarm system in Nathan's room and put a heavy-duty fail-safe lock on Nathan's door. He didn't want Steven going into Nathan's room and destroying anything again. It hurt Nathan that it had to be this way. He really would have loved having a brother he could be friends with, but as it was, he was actually glad that he wouldn't be there while Steven was in the house. The kid was really kind of creepy. He was afraid for his mother, though. Would she be okay? He was slightly relieved when Al told him he had some vacation days planned so Rose wouldn't be all alone with Steven all the time. They were going to try to do things with him while he was home. Maybe he would be better…nicer…if they took him to some nice places. Maybe Sea World would be nice. Nathan hoped it would be a good visit this time; and maybe it would be, since he wouldn't be there. 'Why does it have to be like this?' He thought to himself.

* * *

Al pulled in through the gate to the camp just before noon. Check-in was at one, so they had some time to look around. They checked out the baseball diamond first. Nathan thought it was the best playing field he had ever seen. They were walking toward the office for check-in when Nathan stopped dead in his tracks. He saw a man he recognized from one of the baseball cards Steven had destroyed.

"Dad, look!" Nathan was spell-bound.

"Oh, yeah! One of the greatest pitchers of all time. I didn't know he would be here." Al was pleased with Nathan's reaction. "I guess you'll get to know him, huh?"

Nathan nodded, too keyed up to speak. Another man, holding a clipboard, approached them. Nathan recognized him as well. 'Be cool, Nate.' He silently coached himself.

"Hi!" The ex-major leaguer greeted them with a broad smile. "Name?" He looked at Nathan.

"Nathan Perletti." He responded.

"What position can you play, Nathan...or is it Nate?"

"It's either one. I don't mind either one. I can play infield or outfield, but I love to pitch best." Nathan answered.

"Okay. Well, here we can tell what you're best suited for, so if you want to be a pitcher, you will know by the end of the two weeks whether that's the right position for you. My name is Joe, by the way." He smiled at Nathan and extended his hand, and then shook hands with Al and Rose, as well.

All Nathan could say was 'I know.' Joe's smile turned into a grin.

When Nathan was all settled into his room and had a chance to meet his roommate, Al and Rose got up to leave. Steven would be at the house by five o'clock and they didn't want him showing up before they got there.

"Bye, Mom, Dad...and thanks again." He hugged Al and kissed Rose on the cheek.

"We'll be back in two weeks to pick you up. Learn all you can, and really enjoy the time. Got it?" Al cuffed him lightly under the chin.

* * *

Al and Rose arrived home about forty-five minutes before Steven was due to arrive. Al walked around making things were safe and secure. He checked Nathan's room and was satisfied that he found it locked. He tried to rattle the door but the lock was holding the door securely. He once again checked in the bathroom to make sure there was nothing that could be used as a weapon lying around. He saw a hair dryer under the sink and quickly moved it to the bathroom in the master bedroom. 'This is ridiculous.' He thought to himself. He went back to the kitchen and made sure the knives were in the cabinet where he recently installed a lock. Rose was busily making Steven's favorite meal, which was fried chicken and French fries. She would add a vegetable to the meal when Steven got there. There would be strawberry shortcake for dessert, too. Steven always loved that dessert.

Exactly at five o'clock the van pulled into the driveway. 'How does he do that?' Al mused to himself. 'Always exactly on time.'

Rose looked at Al and smoothed down her blouse. They walked out to greet the van together. The attendant was unloading Steven's suitcase as they stepped onto the porch. Steven was standing beside the van, watching.

"Hi, Steven!" Rose called to him.

"Hi." Steven's response was flat and subdued.

Al and Rose walked up to the van in the driveway, and Rose immediately tried to hug Steven. He stiffened, so Rose pulled back.

"Hey, Kid, how're you doing?" It was Al's turn to break the ice.

"Okay. Where's Nathan? He here?" Al caught the smirk on his face, and knew right then that not much had changed.

"N-no, he won't be here for a couple of weeks." Al answered Steven's question, and caught the look of satisfaction on his young son's face.

"Let's go inside, Steven. I have dinner almost ready. It's your favorite....."

Steven cut off Rose's sentence. "What? Dog shit sandwiches? That's my favorite."

The color drained from Rose's face. Al started to open his mouth when the attendant stepped in. "Now, watch your mouth! That's your mother you're talking to!"

"Sorry. Sorry, Mom." Steven spoke quietly, staring at the ground.

The attendant turned to Al and handed him a packet of papers and a bag full of medications. "The dose instructions are on the bottles. Oh, and this packet of papers is a report for the past two months. There are recommendations, and stuff like that, included in it. The doctor wanted me to make sure you and Mrs. Perletti knew that you should read the contents of the packet."

"Okay, thanks....we'll read it. Thanks for bringing him home." Al took the packet and shook the attendant's hand. Al caught the look of pity in the attendant's eyes when he thanked him. 'Steven must be a real handful at the facility,' Al wondered what was in that report. He would read it after Steven was in bed that night.

Steven ate his chicken and French fries quietly. Rose had opened a package of frozen peas and added them to the menu. Steven ate a few of them.

"So tell us what you have been doing at the facility, Steven. Did you make any friends? How are your lessons going?" Rose attempted to draw him into conversation.

Steven shrugged. He was his usual sullen self all through dinner.

"Anything special you want to do while you're home?" Al asked him. "How about a trip to Sea World?"

Again, Steven shrugged. "Whatever." was his reply.

Al bit his tongue, but thought to himself, 'He's been here for one hour, and already I'm sick of him.'

"Hey, Rose, I'll do the dishes tonight. That way you can spend some time with Steven. Okay?"

Rose's mouth dropped open. "Yeah, sure....that sounds great." She couldn't hide her surprise. Al just smiled at her.

* * *

It was the third day of baseball camp. Nathan was like a sponge, drinking in all the tips he got from the directors and coaches. So far he had not had a chance to show off his pitching. These first three days were focused on base running, signs and signals from coaches. He was learning a lot from these seasoned players. "Remember.... whether you cross home plate depends on what happens after you hit first base." The mentoring coaches constantly reminded the young hopefuls. Tomorrow the batting tips would start. He would like to become a better hitter, so he was looking forward to it.

* * *

Al, Rose and Steven were finishing breakfast before they left for Sea World. Al had spent a good part of the first night of Steven's arrival reading the packet of papers the doctor had sent home with Steven. He hoped Sea World would be a pleasant trip for Steven, at best. According to what he read, Steven hated Nathan for his athletic ability and his good looks. Steven wasn't athletic, but he was good-looking. He was just smaller and thinner than Nathan. But, hell, he was also four-and-a-half years younger. From the information Al read, Steven felt that his parents always did more with Nathan than they did with him. Hopefully, this trip to Sea World would change him a little. He was glad that Nathan was safely at baseball camp and that he and Rose decided not to tell Steven exactly where Nathan was. They just told him that Nathan was at camp.

Al pulled into a parking space and shut the car off. "Well, Steven, are you ready for a fun day at Sea World?"

"I guess." was his short reply.

The day went well. Steven seemed to be having fun, which was a rare occasion in itself. He was fascinated by the Orca Whale, and he loved the water show. Rose and Al were pleased. At last they found something that made their youngest son seem normal. After they left Sea World, they took him to McDonald's and let him order whatever he wanted. He seemed pleased with the special attention. 'Maybe that's it. Maybe I always showed Nathan more attention than I did Steven.' He was annoyed with himself, thinking that he may be part of Steven's problems.

"May I go to the bathroom?" Steven was asking Al.

"Yeah, sure…they're back there. Come right back, okay?" Al couldn't help feeling a little apprehensive. "Do you want me to go with you?"

"No, I can go myself." Steven replied, and got up from the table.

"The day went well, don't you think, Al?" Rose smiled at Al. "He seems almost normal, doesn't he?" Al nodded, but still feeling that little bit of anxiety.

That was when the commotion from the bathroom area began. They heard a child yelp, before they heard a man's voice.

"YOU DISGUSTING LITTLE SHIT! WHERE ARE YOUR PARENTS?"

Al turned to see a man dragging Steven out of the bathroom by his arm. Al stood up and moved quickly to take charge of his son. "What the hell happened?" Al asked the man.

"Your son, I presume? This disgusting little shit just pissed all over my son in the bathroom!"

"Ah, Jesus Christ, Steven….what the hell's wrong with you?" He took Steven's arm and handed him off to Rose.

"Hey, look, I'm sorry. My kid's got some emotional problems. He stays in a facility for kids like him. He's only home for a couple of weeks on a break. I'm really sorry. Can I buy your meal for you, or something?" Al didn't know what else to offer. "Get in the car." He snapped at Steven and Rose.

"Hey, Sir, I'm really sorry for what I called him. My wife has a younger sister who has to stay at a facility like that. I know how rough it must be for you and your wife. Just forget it, huh?"

"Thanks. And again, I'm really sorry for what my son did. I guess I should have gone in with him." Al started to walk away, but then turned back to the man, and said, "You have no idea how long two weeks can be." He sadly walked out to the car.

* * *

One week of baseball camp had passed quickly by. Nathan learned so much in that week! He learned how he could get better hits by changing his batting stance a little. He went from hitting singles and doubles to actually hitting homeruns! He also learned that he could turn a double into a triple just by his speed. In his mind, it had been the best week of his life.

Today, he would show them how he pitched. There had been a classroom seminar on pitching that morning. He absorbed every bit of the information they presented, and he was ready to give it a try.

The pitching coach watched him pitch a few. "That kid's got potential!" He exclaimed to the director overseeing the pitching. The director nodded in agreement.

Nathan pitched quite a few balls that afternoon. The coach was amazed at his control and the speed of his ball. At dinner the coach made it a point to sit at Nathan's table.

"Kid, you got it. You have the makings of a major league pitcher. How old are you?"

"I just turned fifteen." Nathan answered.

"Going to college?" The coach queried.

"Yeah, I hope to, Coach."

"Well, just choose a school with high academics. One that has a baseball team, of course. I think you have what it takes to make it in the big league. I mean that. Just make sure you get a damn good education first. Got it?"

"Yeah, Coach…I got it." Nathan couldn't believe how calm his voice was. He felt like shouting. He couldn't wait to tell his dad.

* * *

Al said very little the rest of the night. He was heartsick. He called off work the next day. No way was he leaving Steven and Rose alone. No matter what they did for Steven, they could do nothing good. It always went back to the same thing: Steven doing some terrible disgusting act to someone or something. Hell, they couldn't even have a dog in the house because of what Steven might do to it. He and Nathan would have loved to have a dog. Steven would probably be allergic to it anyway, even if he wouldn't hurt it. He sat at the breakfast table, staring intently at Steven, without realizing it. Steven boldly met his stare with one of his own. Al had to fight the urge to reach over and smack him in the mouth.

"Aren't you ashamed about what you did to that kid yesterday?" Al tried to keep his voice even.

Steven shrugged.

"That's not an answer. What you did was...horrendous! Why do you do those things?" Al waited for a reply, but all he got was another shrug. He threw down his napkin and got up from the table. "I'll be outside." He told Rose.

Rose thought she would try to get through to him. She sat down across the table from him and began, "Steven, what is it you want? What would make you happy? What would make you a better person? Think about that for a moment before you tell me. I really want to know what it is we can do for you to make you...love us. Just tell me."

"I want you all to fucking die!" He looked her straight in the eye and jammed his fork into the wooden table as he said it.

Rose let out a shriek that brought Al running into the kitchen. Rose was sobbing uncontrollably, so Al turned on Steven.

"WHAT DID YOU SAY OR DO? TELL ME NOW!"

Steven looked him square in the eyes and repeated, "I want you all to fucking DIE! OKAY?"

Before he had time to think, Al reached out and slapped Steven hard enough to knock him down.

"YOU POSSESSED LITTLE BASTARD!"

Al was losing it. He was sick of all they had to put up with from this ten-year-old monster. He was about to reach for Steven again when Officer Banks walked through the door.

"What's going on? I heard the commotion...." He stopped when he saw Steven's bloody mouth. "Hey, Al...calm down. He's just a little kid. Hey, Kid, go sit in your room for awhile." He put his hand on Al's shoulder and led him to a chair. He saw Rose sitting there in hysterics.

"What happened?" The question was not addressed to either of them, but he hoped one of them would answer.

"Is this where I get arrested for child abuse?" Al spoke while staring at the table.

"No, but I would like to hear what happened." Officer Banks looked concerned.

"You know, Ken, I've tried to be a good father to him. I've bent over backwards to make that kid act normal."

"I know. So what went on today?"

Al told Officer Banks about the incident at McDonald's the day before and what Steven had said to Rose just a few minutes ago. "Then he looked me square in the eyes and repeated it to me! What the hell am I supposed to do about it? I just....lost it, you know?"

"Yeah, I think I do." Ken Banks looked sympathetic. "Where's Nathan?"

Al glanced toward the steps to make sure Steven wasn't within earshot before he answered. "He's at a baseball camp. We thought that would be best. Good for Nathan, too."

"Yeah, that's probably best. Nathan's a pretty good ballplayer, isn't he?"

"Yeah, he is." Ken Banks saw the light come back into Al's eyes for a moment.

Banks was thoughtful for a moment. "Funny....how two brothers can be so different, isn't it?"

Al let out a small chuckle. "It's not funny when you have to live it."

"No, I guess not." Banks conceded.

Al's head was pounding. He unlocked the cabinet that held the knives, the pain relief capsules, and anything else that may prove to be dangerous, and took out two Tylenol Extra-Strength capsules, and swallowed them with a half a glass of tap water.

"That's a good idea, keeping all that stuff under lock and key." Ken Banks observed.

"Yeah, the hell of it is that kid has us in our own little prison. We can't live like normal people." Al stopped talking and ran his hand through his hair. He stared at the floor, trying to regain composure.

"Do you mind if I go upstairs and talk to him?" Banks offered.

"No, not at all. Maybe you can...accomplish something." Al moved toward Rose and put his hand on her shoulder and massaged it lightly. She responded by putting her hand over his. She looked up at Al and he could see her eyes were full of despair.

"Hell of a way to live, huh?" He said it mostly to himself.

* * *

Baseball camp was drawing to a close. All that was left was the game between his camp and another baseball camp not too far away. Since he was going to be the starting pitcher, he was looking forward to putting some of the techniques he learned to the test.

At game time he noticed there were several people in the stands. He didn't think to invite his parents, but since Steven was home, they wouldn't have been able to show up anyway. Besides, what if he blew it? He wouldn't want his dad to see that.

Al would have been proud of Nathan that day. He pitched seven innings and didn't give up a hit. He had twelve strikeouts in seven innings. The coaches were impressed, but they took him out after seven innings to give his arm a rest. His team won the game and they went back to their camp to celebrate. Before they left the playing field, a cute blonde girl ran over to him and gave him her phone number. He stuck it in his pocket and nodded at her, but he knew he wouldn't call her. The other boys on the bus teased him all the way back to the camp.

"Coulda got some booty, Nate!" A tall blonde boy who played first base grinned at him with envy. Nathan shrugged it off.

The last day before the camp closed was for fun. The boys went swimming in the pool, played volleyball, and ate pizza for dinner. Nathan was sorry to see the two weeks come to an end, but he had to admit he would be glad to see his parents. He had so much to tell his dad.

* * *

Whatever Officer Banks said to Steven had a positive effect on him. The rest of the two weeks went by without much incident. The psychiatrist called the house a couple of days after the incident. He wanted to see how things were going and also wanted to discuss further treatment with Al and Rose.

"I'm not sure he'll ever get better. All we can hope for is to keep him stabilized so he's not a danger to anyone. I'd like to discuss some options with you, Mr. Perletti. When you come to visit next time, I'd like a little bit of your time." The psychiatrist sounded sincere in his desire to help Steven so Al agreed to a meeting with him.

Rose was putting Steven's things together to put into the suitcase. She bought him some clothes while he was home, so he would have new things to wear. He had grown out of a lot of his clothes, especially his jeans. The van would be there in an hour. Rose felt as though she had to take this opportunity to try to get through to Steven one more time.

"Steven, I really love you. So does Daddy. Why can't you be nice to us? We would like for you to get well and come home for good. Do you think you would like that?"

Steven shrugged, as was his response to most questions.

"It don't matter." He narrowed his eyes and looked at Rose. "Nathan still lives here, so I don't care if I come home or not."

"Why do you dislike Nathan? He's always been nice to you. I remember before you were born how excited he was. He wanted a little brother so bad...." Rose paused as she remembered that conversation with Nathan at lunch so long ago.

"I hate him. I hate you all." There was no emotion in his words. They were just a statement of fact.

Rose sat back and stared at him. She felt truly defeated. Al appeared in the doorway to see what was keeping them. The van would be there soon. He grabbed Steven's suitcase and carried it downstairs and waited for them to come down. As the van was pulling into the driveway, Al handed Steven a twenty-dollar bill.

"That's in case you need anything." He stared at the floor. Since he hit him, Al couldn't look at Steven. He felt terrible that he had done it, but he was also angry that Steven provoked him into doing it.

They waited until the van left the driveway before they went inside. They were both emotionally drained.

"Let's have a cup of coffee before we go get Nathan, okay?" Al was reaching for the mugs out of the cabinet.

* * *

They saw Nathan as soon as they pulled into the parking lot. His grin showed all of his straight, white teeth as he waved at them. He looked so happy and healthy. He came trotting up to the car and opened Rose's door for her. He hugged her and run around to Al's side of the car. Al was just climbing out of his seat when Nathan got to his side.

"Dad, they said I have potential! They said I have a good shot at the major leagues! I pitched seven innings without giving up a hit! This camp is awesome!" Nathan stopped for breath.

"Whoa! We want to hear everything, but not at the same time!" Al laughed and hugged him. "So they say you have a shot?"

"Yep! The coach said to pick a good college that has a good academic program and a baseball team. But he says I'm good…really good!" Nathan was ecstatic. He hooked his arms around both Al and Rose and said, "Come on! They have refreshments inside."

The pitching coach spied them walking through the door. He excused himself from the group in which he was mingling, and headed toward Nathan and his family to greet them. He shook hands with Al and then Rose, and draped his arm around Nathan.

"You got a winner here, Mr. Perletti. I hope you know that. He's headed for the big leagues…I can see that. I've never seen a guy this age pitch like he can. Just make sure he gets educated first. Trust me. He's going to the big leagues."

Al's chest swelled with pride. All the grief of the past two weeks with Steven melted away. Now he understood that Steven's problems were not because of him, or Rose. Maybe it had to do with the difficult birth. Maybe there was some brain damage. He shook off the thoughts of Steven and concentrated on what the seasoned ballplayer was telling Nathan.

"Just take care of your arm, Nathan. Don't ever over-do it. Got it?"

Nathan nodded. "Got it, Coach."

The coach smiled at him. "See ya in the majors, Son!"

Al couldn't trust his voice at the moment. He just hugged Nathan and then after giving himself a moment to regain composure, asked him if he was ready to go.

2-10

Nathan began his tenth grade year. He had matured a little more over the summer. His voice grew deeper and he noticed there were more whiskers on his chin than he had at the beginning of summer. Not enough to shave, but they were there. On his first day of classes, he met up with his buddies from the baseball team. He told them all about the baseball camp and they were both impressed and envious. He left out the part where the coach told him he had potential for the major leagues. That would seem like he was bragging, and he didn't want that.

"I really learned a lot." He told Mike Smith, the team's third baseman.

"Good. Maybe you can teach me a couple of things." Mike countered. "Hey, don't look now, but those girls over there are staring at us and laughing."

"That's because you have a hole in the back of your pants!" Nathan teased.

Mike looked around to the back of his pants. "Asshole! No I don't!"

Nathan laughed. He liked Mike. He had a lot of self-confidence but was not arrogant or conceited. Many of the girls found his blond haired, blue eyed looks appealing, but he never seemed to notice. If the truth be told, Mike would have said the same thing about Nathan, except for the blond hair and blue eyes. Nathan, with his raven black hair and his warm liquid brown eyes attracted just as many girls as Mike, his opposite.

In his fifth period class, Nathan was handed a slip of paper and was told to go to the guidance counselor's office. He couldn't imagine why, since he hadn't done anything to be in trouble. He walked down to the office and sat down to wait for the guidance counselor to call him in.

The guidance counselor was a small man in his forties, with thinning hair and rimless eyeglasses. He gestured for Nathan to sit down, and then went around his desk and sat down as well.

"Nathan, I've been going over you academic record, and I must say, it's impressive." He looked at Nathan over the top of his glasses.

"Thank you, Sir." Nathan sounded relieved.

"Well, what I want to talk to you about is your future. I know you're only in the tenth grade, but there's no time like the present to consider the future. Do you agree?" Again, he looked over his glasses at Nathan.

"Yes, Sir, I do. What is this about, exactly?" Nathan's curiosity was peaking.

"I want you to consider taking some advanced classes. We should have done this with you in the eighth grade, but our school is not as progressive as many schools. You've had algebra, and this year you're taking geometry. I would like to add some science courses, like maybe chemistry or physics, but you'll have to work hard at it. How are you with languages? You should consider a foreign language. I see you had first-year Spanish, last year, and you are taking Spanish II this year. We don't offer a third Spanish class; I'm afraid, but consider a course in French the next two years. This year, I think you can handle an extra course, so how about letting me add a chemistry course to your schedule?"

Nathan thought about it for a moment. 'English, American History, Spanish, Geometry, and....?' He looked up at the guidance counselor. The kids referred to him as 'Geezer', and Nathan could see why. He almost laughed.

"Why not. Yeah, I can add a chemistry course. I can't hurt, I guess." He resigned himself to it.

"No, it certainly can't hurt. I see you play baseball, but you don't belong to any other clubs or participate in any other activities. I would suggest that you find something in addition to baseball. Colleges look at that sort of thing, and so do those who give out scholarships. You also need a humanities course or something in the arts. How about choir? Can you sing?"

"Yeah, I think I can. I need time for baseball practice, though." Nathan reminded him.

"Baseball starts in the spring. How about the winter? Are you planning to play football?"

"No, I don't think so. I'm a pitcher, and I wouldn't want to hurt my arm." Nathan confided to him.

"Good thinking. Well, why don't you go see the choir director, then? Your buddy, Mike is in the choir...." Geezer, or Mr. Hodges, as was his correct name, looked up at Nathan, waiting for a response. "As a matter of fact, Mike also chose chemistry this year. You would be in the same class...." The proverbial carrot dangled.

"Okay, I'll go." Nathan voiced his decision with confidence.

"Go now. She's in the choir room now. I'll give you a slip to get back into class and one for her, too." He scribbled on two slips of paper and handed them to Nathan. "You know, Nathan, it is kids like you that make my job so rewarding. There should be more of you."

"Thanks, Mr. Hodges." Nathan took the slips of paper and retreated.

As he promised, he went right down to the choir room. The director did a two-minute voice test and agreed that he could sing. "Your schedule is free for sixth period, Monday, Wednesday and Friday?"

He glanced at his schedule and nodded.

"Good. You'll have a study period on Tuesday and Thursday. I'm Mrs. Banus, by the way. Your first day will be tomorrow, Wednesday. See you then."

"Thank you, Ma'am." He walked back toward the classroom he left before he was called to the guidance counselor's office. He was studying his new schedule. He still had the seventh period free for when baseball practice started.

* * *

Nathan and Mike met up in the choir room. "Glad you're here, too." Mike's statement sounded genuine. "Hey, this is a good place to hook up with chicks. There are a lot of them here."

Nathan glanced around and saw that Mike was telling the truth about that. There were many more girls than guys. The choir director entered and told everyone to take a seat. Nathan and Mike sat down next to each other and turned their attention to the choir director.

She began talking immediately. "We have a lot to get ready for this year. There will be a Christmas show as well as a musical. Next semester we will turn our attention to the Spring Choral. For right now, we are going to get everybody in their proper areas. The altos are to my right, the tenors are in the middle, in the front....Mike and Nathan, you both are tenors...bases in the back, and sopranos to my left. So everybody get to their correct positions." She pointed to Mike and Nathan. "You two are fine where you are."

The sixth period went rather quickly. Mrs. Banus passed out sheet music and they began learning their parts. Before they knew it, the bell rang to end the period. Nathan and Mike trotted off to their last period, which was a study period. They both completed their homework for the day by the end of that period.

Over dinner Nathan told Al and Rose what had transpired the past two days. They seemed pleased with the guidance counselor's choices for him, and they were glad someone was taking an interest in his academic curriculum.

"So you're going to sing in the choir?" Rose asked.

"Yeah...Mike Smith is in choir, too. It's not too bad. We had our first choir class today and it was okay. Actually it's kind of fun." He glanced at Al to get his reaction, and hopefully a favorable one.

"I think that's great. I used to sing in the choir...did you know that?"

"No!" Rose and Nathan's responses were in unison.

"Yep...and then I sang with a small group. We did gigs at school dances." Al revealed.

"Cool, Dad! Were you any good?"

"Hell, yeah! I was lead vocalist." Al was pleased to pass that information along.

"So you'll come to the concerts I'm in, then?"

"Sure. I'll be glad to." Al matched Nathan's grin with one of his own. Rose looked over at them and couldn't believe how Nathan was beginning to look more and more like Al. She knew how all the women swooned over Al when she first met him, and she imagined the same would be true for Nathan.

* * *

Nathan discovered that he really enjoyed singing in the choir. His voice was good and strong, so the choir director asked him if he was interested in a bigger part in the school musical. He was hesitant since there would be some acting involved, and he wasn't sure he could pull that off. Mrs. Banus assured him that the acting was not what was important, and all he had to do was act naturally. He agreed to a bigger part, especially after he heard who would be playing opposite of him. Tanya. Tanya Griffin would be his counterpart in the musical play. How was that for luck? She was one of the best looking girls in school. She had the bluest eyes, and he was a sucker for blue eyes. It got even better when she called him after school that day.

"Hi, Nathan…it's Tanya." She started the conversation.

"Oh, hi…..What's up?" He hoped he sounded cool and calm, because he sure wasn't feeling it. She actually called him!

"Well, I was wondering…since we are playing opposite each other in the musical…would you like to get together and rehearse some of our songs? Over the weekend, I mean. I always have too much homework to do much after school." She held her breath and waited for his response.

"Hey, that might be a good idea. Might as well be the best at it if we're going to do it at all. The musical, I mean." 'I sound like an idiot,' he thought to himself.

"Yeah, that's just what I was thinking." She responded. "Maybe you could come over Saturday evening. We don't live all that far from each other."

"Okay. That sounds good." He wondered how she knew they didn't live far from each other, but didn't ask her.

"Is seven o'clock good for you?" She asked.

"Yeah, that's fine. I guess I'll see you tomorrow at school in case there are any changes. By the way, where do you live?" He needed to wrap this conversation up before he said something stupid.

She gave him her address, and she was right—they didn't live too far away from each other. The Perletti family lived in the last house, on the very last street on the edge of the town. Their property bordered the woods, which eventually turned into farmland. Their house had been erected far enough from the street that when the trees had their leaves, the house could not be seen by passersby. He was surprised to find out that Tanya lived two streets away and that her house was situated in the same spot on her street. He must have ridden his bike past her house hundreds of times over the past six years. He never saw her.

She said something into the phone, and he refocused his thoughts back to her. "I'm sorry….what?" Okay, now he sounded like a jerk.

"Oh, nothing....I just said we can order pizza on Saturday if you want..." She hesitated. "I mean..."

"That would be great. I gotta go. Mom has dinner ready." He didn't know if Rose had dinner ready or not, but he had to end this before he *really* sounded like a fool.

"Okay." She purred into the phone. "I'll see you tomorrow... okay?"

"Great...bye." He hung up the phone, raised his arm up and clenched his fist. He brought it down in front of him and, with an excited whisper, said, "Yes!"

"Who was that?" Rose asked.

"Some girl." He responded.

* * *

On Saturday, Nathan helped Al do some yard work and then they tackled the garage. By four o'clock they were both exhausted and in need of a shower. Just as they finished the garage, Nathan told Al that he was going over to Tanya's that evening to rehearse their parts for the musical. While he was in the shower, Al relayed that information to Rose.

"Al, have you had the talk with him yet?" Rose looked meaningfully at Al.

"What talk?" Al poured himself a glass of cold water from the refrigerator.

"You know....the talk...about sex." Rose stared at Al and bit her lower lip.

"Oh, *that* talk.....no, I haven't. He's not into that."

"Al, all boys are into that. Think back. Tonight he's going over to a girl's house...I mean....." Rose stopped talking and looked toward the stairway, not wanting Nathan to hear her. "He's fifteen, Al. What were *you* doing at fifteen?"

"Yeah, okay." Al chuckled softly. "Does it have to be tonight?"

"Well, what if her parents aren't home?" Rose countered.

Nathan yelled from the top of the stairs. "Her parents will be home!"

Rose looked sheepish, and Al...just looked relieved.

Rose looked into Al's eyes and stood her ground. "You're not off the hook. You better get to that talk soon." She whispered.

Al nodded and headed into the shower. Maybe he and Nathan could go fishing tomorrow. They could talk then.

* * *

Nathan walked up to Tanya's door exactly at seven o'clock, and rang the bell. Tanya answered the door. "You're right on time! We can rehearse in the game room, and then order pizza later. Is that okay with you?"

Nathan nodded, and followed her down the steps to a huge nicely furnished game room, complete with a pool table.

"Nice room." He spoke as he looked around the room, the walls, and then up to the ceiling where a fan had been installed.

"Yeah, thanks....my dad built it. He does it for a living." She sounded pleased that Nathan liked it. "Want something to drink?" She asked him.

"Sure. Whatever you got will be fine."

She left and came back with two cans of Pepsi, and handed him one of them.

"Thanks. Should we get started on some of the numbers we have to do?"

Tanya nodded, and reached for the sheet music. "Sorry. No piano...so we have to sing without."

They began with the first song they would do together, and they sounded good. Their voices blended nicely and at the same time, complimented each other's. They stumbled over the words in the next number, and ended up laughing at themselves. Mrs. Griffin came down the steps with a bowl of potato chips and dip.

"Tanya, we have to go see Grandma. We won't be late, okay? Nathan, you can stay until eleven, if you want. At eleven, out the door, okay?"

"No problem, Mrs. Griffin. I told my parents I'd be home before eleven-thirty. Thanks for letting me come over." He saw where Tanya got her blue eyes. Mrs. Griffin's eyes were exactly like Tanya's.

"It was nice meeting you, Nathan."

"Same here, Mrs. Griffin."

Mrs. Griffin disappeared up the steps and they heard the door shut. In a few minutes they heard the car in the driveway start, and then pull out.

Tanya fell onto the cushion of the loveseat, and patted the space next to her. "Come sit. Let's read these words and get them right, okay?"

Nathan sat down next to her, and they both poured over the sheet music, repeating the words until they became more familiar to them. Nathan was sure he knew the words. He was about to tell Tanya that, but when he turned toward her, she surprised him by meeting his lips with hers. She was kissing him, and within a second he was kissing her back. It was a long, drawn-out kiss that left them both breathless. He adjusted himself on the loveseat so that he was leaning toward her, and put his arm around her shoulders.

"Wow!" He tried to hide his surprise.

She put her hand on the side of his face and pulled him towards her, and again met his lips. This time the kiss was more ardent, more passionate. He felt her tongue slide into his mouth and he knew instinctively how to reciprocate. He stopped, put his hand on her face, and then kissed her again. He felt her unbuttoning his shirt, and briefly wondered what she was up to. She was running her hand over his bare chest, and he began to feel himself growing and hardening even more than he was already. He kissed her neck and she moaned. She took his hand from her face and placed it on her breast. He could feel her nipple harden as she unbuttoned her blouse. She unhooked her bra and offered the breast up to him, and he quickly drew her nipple between his lips, running his tongue over the top of it. Tanya was fumbling with his zipper so he turned slightly so she could slide the zipped down easily. Her hand went down into his underwear where she grasped his member, slowly sliding her hand up and down the shaft. It felt so good that he thought he was going to explode. She removed her hand and started to force his jeans and underwear down off his hips. Nathan raised his hips and helped her by sliding them down easily. She stood up and pulled up her skirt. She wasn't wearing underwear at all!

"I don't have any....protection..." His voice was raspy.

"You don't need any. I've been on the pill for a year now." She moved to his lap and straddled herself over him and slid down onto him, slowly at first. She sank down until he was deep inside of her, then moving slowly, rose up, then down again. Up and down, again and again, each time moving faster. He was holding a breast in his hand, running his thumb over the nipple, when he felt his explosion deep inside her. She cried out and fell against his chest, wrapping her arms around him. They stayed that way for several minutes, both breathing heavily at first; their breathing slowly returning to normal. She was the first to speak.

"So much for rehearsal, I guess. I'm hungry. Let's order pizza." She spoke matter-of-factly. "What do you like on your pizza?"

"Whatever you want will be fine." He got up and went to the bathroom that was built off the game room, shut the door, and leaned against it. He took in some breath and let it out slowly. After using the toilet, he rinsed his face and ran his fingers through his hair. He studied himself in the mirror to see if there was any tell-tale sign of what just transpired. Hopefully she wasn't lying about being on the pill. What would his parents think? He began to rinse his face again, when Tanya knocked on the bathroom door.

"Did you fall in, or something?" Nathan opened the door and she was standing there, looking like nothing had happened. "Pizza is on its way. Come on, let's put the TV on."

He followed her out into the game room and leaned against the arm of the loveseat. He watched her as she went around the room making preparations for the soon-to-arrive pizza, getting out napkins and paper plates. Nathan insisted on paying for the pizza when it arrived. They took it down to the game room and ate in semi-silence. He was silent and she chattered on about everything and anything. It was obvious that what they had done prior to the pizza had no effect on her. Nathan, on the other hand, was a wreck. At five minutes to eleven he got up to leave. She walked with him up to the front door and put her arms around his waist.

"Thanks, Nathan. It was fun. Maybe we can do it again sometime." She gave him an alluring smile and closed the door.

"What the hell?" He said to himself as he walked down the sidewalk of the connecting street between their houses. Although it was his first time, it definitely wasn't hers. He wondered how many times she had done that before. Then it struck him. 'How was I? Awkward? Did I do okay? I wonder if she knew that was the first time I ever did it.' He saw his porch light through the trees and quickly made his way down the driveway, and opened the front door. His parents were watching the news on the television when he came through the door.

"How was the rehearsing?" Al called through the hallway.

"Okay. We sound good together." Nathan answered him and headed toward the refrigerator.

"Hey, Nate, what do you say we do some fishing tomorrow?"

"Okay, Dad, I'll be up early."

Nathan took a can of soda off the shelf of the refrigerator door and carried it upstairs with him. He undressed and stretched out on his bed and stared at the ceiling, his hands behind his head. He stayed there in that position for what seemed like hours. He knew other guys would be throwing themselves a party if they could have been in his shoes tonight, but somehow, he just didn't feel right about it. Oh, it felt great, he had to admit that. Something was missing, though. That 'something' made what they did all wrong. How would Tanya react to him on Monday? He wondered about that before he fell asleep.

* * *

Al and Nate were sitting on the small pier at the edge of the lake. The fish weren't biting today, so their lines from their poles were only in the water as an obligation to fishermen everywhere. They sat side-by-side, just watching the ripples of the lake. Al cleared his throat.

"Nate, how much do you know about….what goes on between…. men and women…in the bedroom?" Al was fumbling for the right way to phrase it.

"What do you mean by that? You mean…sex?" Nathan looked at Al, wondering if he could tell anything.

"Well, yeah, sex. Sex is sex. Everybody learns how to have sex…. but do you know things like…..how important sex is? Or when to have sex? And when not to? Do you know about protection? Do you know what your obligation to the woman you….have sex with…sleep with…is? When you have sex there is a responsibility you take on. Do you know anything about that?" Al was embarrassing himself. He could always talk to Nathan, but this was a subject he was finding hard to talk about. To him, Nathan was still a baby—his young son—but he was growing up.

"I think I know what you're talking about, Dad." Nathan was staring at the water.

"Okay…then you tell me." Al looked at Nathan and studied his face.

"Well, I think what you are trying to say is…..control myself. Think of the consequences before….I….get myself into something I may…regret."

"Exactly! Now when you find someone that you're….attracted to….you have to think about what is best for *her.* You're a guy. You always know what's best for you. When the hormones rage all you can think about is….relief. But if you care about the…girl—woman… you're with, you have to think about how she feels, what consequences will she have…that kind of stuff. Now if you find a girl that has never had sex….a virgin….you have to be extra considerate of her. If you have sex with her, you will have taken something from her. You have to consider what that will do to her. You have to take on a certain responsibility toward her. Make sure it's right, you know what I mean?"

"Yeah, Dad, I do. What happens when a girl throws herself at you and practically forces you?" Nathan's mind went back to the night before. "That happens, you know. Girls aren't like they were when you were my age. Some of them expect you to….do it."

"Yeah?" Al cocked his eyebrow and looked at Nathan with interest.

Nathan nodded.

"I should have been so lucky. So has this happened yet?" Al's curiosity was peaked.

Again, Nathan nodded. "Last night. Tanya's parents went to go visit her grandmother and she was all over me. It definitely wasn't the first time she ever did it, that was for sure."

"Oh God, did you have any….."

"Protection?" Nathan finished the sentence. "She's on the pill, she said."

"Oh, Christ! I would have demanded to see the evidence of that." Al was worried now. Rose was right. This talk should have happened long ago. "What about diseases? There are plenty of them out there, you know."

"I didn't think about that. Dad, I'm telling you, she was all over me, and I'm just human. I didn't go over there for that. Up until last night, I never even kissed a girl." Nathan paused for a moment. "Do you know what was...weird, actually? It didn't affect her. She acted like...nothing happened...nothing at all. She ordered pizza after it was over and...just talked and talked about school, the choir, her friend Linda....everything. I was the one who was a mess! Something was....missing. To her, there was nothing special about it. She acted like it was just one of those things. Do you know what I mean?"

Al was visibly upset.

"Yeah, I think I know what you mean....sort of, anyway. Apparently she's been around. You'll tell me if you notice anything....different.... down there?"

Nathan nodded, and then looked at Al with widened eyes. "You're not going to tell mom, are you?"

"Oh, hell no....and hear her mouth because I didn't have this talk with you sooner? I'm not crazy. This is just between us, okay? Man to man, or man to almost-man." Al put his arm around Nathan and quickly squeezed his shoulders before he stood up to retrieve the lines from the lake.

As they were walking back toward the house, Al asked Nathan, "You said something was missing. Do you know what it was?"

"Yeah, I do. Feelings. There was no emotion, certainly no love." Nathan quickly looked away.

"Good boy...you got it. So now what about this Tanya girl? Is she going to be a girlfriend? Somebody you will be taking places, or bringing to the house?"

"I don't know. Before last night I thought I was pretty lucky that she wanted me to come over, but now....I just don't know. I think I'll just see how she acts toward me. She's really good-looking, you know? I may have asked her to go out with me, maybe to a movie or something. I won't ignore her if she still wants to...you know, hang out with me."

"Just be careful, Son. That's all I ask. I think you're turning out to be a really good guy, you know that?" Al smiled at him and took the fishing gear to the shed.

* * *

Nathan entered the school through the front doors on Monday morning. He looked around and didn't see Tanya anywhere, but he did see Mike.

"So what did you do this weekend?" Mike started the conversation.

"Not much. Went fishing with my dad yesterday, and on Saturday, I went over to Tanya's to rehearse our numbers for the musical." Nathan barely glanced at Mike as he said it.

"Get any?" Mike queried.

"Fish? No, they weren't biting." Nathan answered.

"No, not fish. Did you get any from Tanya?" Mike rephrased.

"Why would you think that?" Nathan asked him.

"Well, if you didn't, you'd be the first. She's a nymph. Does it with everybody."

"Her parents were home." Nathan lied.

"Oh, well maybe next time." Mike let it drop. Nathan just felt sick.

2-11

The Christmas holiday season was quickly approaching. The choir was almost ready to perform their Christmas show, which would be held a week after the musical. There were many rehearsals after school for the musical, so Nathan knew his parts well. Tanya was a quick study, so together they performed beautifully and flawlessly. Since that night at her house, Tanya had been cordial to Nathan, but not exactly friendly. On the night of the performance, Al and Rose drove Nathan to the school and dropped him off at the designated entrance. After parking the car, they quickly rushed inside to get good seats.

The cast was assembled backstage, nervously awaiting the cue to begin. Tanya walked over to Nathan and asked him to hook the back of her costume for her.

As he was doing as she asked, she asked him, "You never told anybody about what we did, did you?"

"No, why would I do that? It's nobody's business." He replied.

"Well, aren't you the gentleman, Nathan?" She retorted.

"Did you expect me to?" He put his hand on her arm and stared down at her.

"Well.....all guys like to brag about it. Why not you?"

Nathan shrugged. "I didn't see a need to tell anybody. Look.... Tanya, why do you sell yourself so short? You don't have to do that to get a guy. You have a lot of good qualities about you, so.........."

"Because I like to do it. Okay? I like fucking." She cut him off. "I like it. I could do it twenty times a day. The importance placed on sex is overrated. Sex isn't overrated. Sex is great."

"Aren't you afraid of diseases?" He asked.

"Don't even think about it. Besides, I don't screw anybody unless I know him. It's not like I pick guys up from somewhere. It's just the guys at school. I know I'm the first for most of them, so there should be no worry about diseases."

Nathan was saved a reply by the cue that the musical was about to begin.

The first part of the show went well. Nobody missed a cue or forgot their lines, and the singing was good. During intermission, the cast had some light refreshments waiting for them backstage. Nathan sat on a rolled-up carpet, drinking from the can of soda handed to him, thinking about Tanya and what she said. 'There is something really wrong with her.' He thought. 'She almost thinks like a guy, but even most guys aren't that careless.' He got up to use the restroom before the second part of the show began. When he walked into the men's room, he got quite a surprise. Tanya and Jake Wells were going at it right in the men's room. Tanya was facing the sink and Jake, with his pants down, was hammering her from behind. Nathan retreated through the door quickly, and then stopped and leaned against the wall in the hallway. In a few minutes, Tanya and Jake came out, Tanya first, looking like nothing had happened. Jake stopped in front of Nathan and apologized.

"Sorry, Buddy." He said to him.

"You know, some of us use the restroom to piss." Nathan retorted.

Jake shrugged and walked off.

The second half went almost as well as the first half, save for a line that got dropped toward the beginning of the second half. The audience applauded hard, and there were three curtain calls before they stopped applauding. Nathan met his parents out in the main hallway.

"You were really good, Nathan!" Rose's face showed her pride in him.

"Yeah, not bad, Kid! A chip off the old block." Al grinned at him. "How about we go for a pizza somewhere? Good idea?"

Mike joined them in the hall.

"We're going to go for pizza....want to come?" Al invited.

"Yeah, sure. It's better than that lame stuff they call food back there. We have to grab our coats first."

"Okay, see you back here, then." Al instructed.

When they were out of earshot, Mike asked Nathan, "Did you walk in on Jake and Tanya?"

"Yeah...how the hell was I supposed to know they were in there?" Nathan rolled his eyes.

"Yeah...well, I did, too. Then, after the show, I went back in and she was in there again, with our buddy, Bobby!" Mike snickered. "She doesn't care who it is, or where it is...that chick's psycho."

"I agree. I think I'll stay away from her. She's a disease waiting to happen." Nathan assured Mike. Mike nodded.

* * *

The Christmas Choral Show was beautiful. The choir sang old carols and newer hymns. The school rented red and green choir robes for the occasion and the stage was decorated with holly and evergreen trees, red velvet ribbons, and fake mounds of snow. The lighting crew worked hard to get the lighting correctly for each number. The show was a huge hit with the parents. Al and Rose sat in the third row watching. The smiles never left their faces.

"Rose leaned over and whispered to Al, "I can hear Nathan."

Al nodded. "Me, too. He has a strong voice."

Mike and Nathan decided to go to a party a choir member was throwing after the show. Nathan ran out to tell his parents.

"Don't be too late." Al cautioned him.

"Be home before midnight, Dad." He spoke before he ran to catch up with Mike.

The party was in full swing when they got there. The music was loud and blaring and everyone was dancing, laughing and having a really good time, in general. In the corner, a keg of beer awaited the thirsty. Mike and Nathan opened the refrigerator and found what they wanted—soda. Neither of them had ever tasted beer, but they had no desire for it. They both agreed that as athletes, substances such as alcohol, drugs, and nicotine did not belong in their bodies. They stood in the kitchen watching the action in the other room. Many of the kids already had too much to drink. Many of the girls were hanging onto the guys they were dancing with, mainly because they couldn't stand up straight. There were couples on the couch going at it hot and heavy, many of them had much of their clothing removed. There were three bedrooms in use—one of which was called 'The Tanya Room'. Bobby walked into the kitchen and told them that Tanya was up for grabs in that room, so anybody who wanted her could go in and get it. Both Mike and Nathan declined.

Mike looked at Nathan, and said, "Let's get out of here. Where the hell are the parents? I don't want to get busted if the cops show up."

"Good thinking, Mike. I'm ready." Nathan set the soda can down and began to move toward the door, too late.

Uniformed policemen walked through the door and snapped on the overhead light.

"Oh shit!" Mike whispered to Nathan.

"Okay." One of the officers boomed. "Has anybody here *not* been drinking?" He looked around the living room, and then into the kitchen. Nathan and Mike halfheartedly raised their hands when he looked at them.

"You two haven't been drinking?" He stared at Nathan and Mike.

They both shook their heads.

"We just got here. We drank a soda." Mike showed him the cans.

The officer turned to another officer and said, "Take them out and give them a breathalyzer." Officer number two nodded, and waved for Nathan and Mike to follow him.

The breathalyzer proved to the police that they had certainly not been drinking, but they weren't free to go just yet. Nathan spotted Officer Banks and called to him.

Ken Banks approached Nathan, and asked, "What the hell are you doing here? Don't your parents have enough grief?"

Nathan nodded. "Yeah, they do…but I swear…..I haven't been drinking."

The officer who administered the test confirmed to Ken Banks that Nathan was clean.

"So what are you doing here?" Ken Banks resounded.

"We were in a Christmas show. We got invited to come after the show was over. We didn't expect anything like this…honest." Nathan sounded so sincere that Officer Banks didn't have any trouble believing him.

They could hear a clatter coming from inside the house. Someone was screaming profanities at someone. It was a female voice.

"Oh gees, that's Tanya. She's going downtown." Mike assured Nathan.

Nathan and Mike heard someone yell, "Somebody cover that girl up! Put some clothes on, young lady!" They looked at each other and passed a sly grin.

"Can we go?" Nathan asked Ken Banks.

"Wait a minute….I'll give you a ride home. Are you going to tell your folks about this? Banks asked Nathan.

"Probably….I don't keep anything from them…especially my dad."

"Good boy…go ahead and hop in the squad car."

In the morning, Nathan told his parents what had happened. They were relieved that Nathan wasn't in any trouble, but even more relieved that Nathan knew enough to stay away from alcohol. He swore to them that he hadn't had anything to drink, and they believed him. They were also very glad that he told them about it. It proved that they could trust him. Later that day, Ken Banks came by and corroborated Nathan's story.

"He's a good kid, Al. I guess you know that."

Al smiled and nodded. "You know, he's growing up. So far we've had nothing to worry about with him. You remember when we were his age? We were hell on wheels, weren't we?"

Ken laughed. "Yep, we were." He conceded. Banks smiled to himself as he remembered his youth. He and Al were from the same hometown, and in fact, had gone to school together. They lost contact with each other after high school and were surprised to meet up again in Ohio years later.

"Nathan seems more focused on things like the future, his grades, playing ball. I never focused on that stuff when I was young. You're right....he's a good kid."

Ken finished his coffee and stood up. "Well, I have to go handle real problems now. There was a girl at that party last night....gees! She was in a bedroom, just letting guys take turns with her, one after the other. In my wildest days, I would not have wanted to participate in something like that. Nasty!"

Al instinctively knew Ken was talking about the girl, Tanya.

* * *

Al and Rose were getting dressed to go visit Steven for his eleventh birthday. They had gifts for him, wrapped in birthday paper. Nathan had a gift for him, too, but he wouldn't be going with his parents to see him. Steven wanted nothing to do with Nathan. He made that clear on his parents' last visit, when they asked him if he would like Nathan to come with them next time. Nathan added the anonymous gift to the ones his parents had waiting to deliver.

After they left, Nathan settled down in the family room to watch the football game. The game was in the first quarter, when there was a knock on the door. Annoyed at the interruption, he got up and answered the door. Mike and Bobby stood on the porch, grinning.

"Hey, what's up?" They greeted him.

"Just watching the game. Come on in." He was glad to see them.

They spent the afternoon watching their team lose another one, and then turned to HBO to catch a movie.

"So did you hear about Tanya? Her parents sent her away." Bobby was pleased with Nathan's surprised look.

"Sent her away, where?" Nathan wanted to know.

"Some girls' boarding school. No guys. They have doctors, probably shrinks, for the girls so they can get help. Her parents were sick when they found out about her." Bobby seemed proud of his knowledge.

"I feel sorry for her." Nathan told him. "She's a real good-looking girl, too. I wonder why she did the things she did."

"Doesn't matter. She busted all our cherries for us." Bobby smirked over his crude comment.

"It *does* matter." Nathan countered. "Didn't you ever wonder why she had no respect for herself?"

"Nope, sure didn't. Hey, the chick loves sex. What's wrong with that?" Bobby asked.

"There's a lot wrong with a chick like that. *Don't you know that?"* Nathan was getting angry at Bobby.

Mike stood by listening, and finally decided to step in. "He's right, Bob. Girls aren't supposed to be like that. I think she's sick or something."

Nathan appreciated Mike's input. "Yeah, so let's not talk about her any more, okay?"

"Okay." Bobby answered quietly. He knew about Nathan's brother, and how sick he was. Nathan probably thought about his brother when anybody had mental problems.

Mike and Bobby stayed to watch a movie and then left to go home for Sunday dinner. Shortly after they left, Al and Rose came home, carrying dinner in with them. Nathan immediately set the table for the Chinese take-out and put out drinks for all three of them.

"When will Steven be home for Christmas?" He asked, after they were all seated.

Neither Al nor Rose spoke at first. Finally, Al cleared his throat and spoke.

"Steven won't be joining us for Christmas this year. He doesn't want to come home and his shrink says we shouldn't try to force the issue."

"Do you *have* to say *shrink?"* Rose complained.

"Oh, sorry......his *psych-i-a-trist* said not to push it. So he'll be staying at the facility. We can go visit him there on Christmas if we want." Al picked up an egg roll and studied it.

"Isn't he any better?" Nathan's curiosity was genuine.

"He learned more filthy words. Tried every one of them out on us, too." Al looked disgusted.

Nathan was disappointed. How he would have loved to have a *normal* brother!

* * *

Nathan spent Christmas day playing on his new computer while Al and Rose went to visit Steven. This was his first computer, so he had a lot to learn. He was concentrating on an instruction sheet when the phone startled him, causing him to jump.

"Hey, Nathan, this is Cookie. Merry Christmas." Cookie was one of those girls that had lots and lots of friends, both male and female. She wasn't pretty, but she wasn't ugly, either. Although a little overweight, she wasn't really fat. She was funny and fun to be around, and everyone, including Nathan, liked her. Her real name was Martha, named after her grandmother, but everybody called her Cookie.

"Hey, Cookie! What did Santa bring you?" Nathan teased.

"Socks!" She answered, and then laughed. Seriously....I got a computer."

"Me, too....that's what I was doing when the phone rang...trying to make it work."

"You'll get it. You're super-smart. Hey, I was just wondering if you heard about Tanya....."

Nathan cut her off with a groan. "I told Mike and Bobby to stop talking about her. She's sick, or something."

"Yes, she is, but....she called me and wanted me to ask you if you would write to her. She says you're the nicest guy in school, and you were always nice and respectful to her when other guys weren't. Do you want her address? She's all the way on the other side of Pennsylvania."

"Okay...what is it?" Nathan grabbed a pen and paper and wrote down the address. He never wrote to her.

* * *

Nathan heard the car pulling into the driveway just before dark. He dreaded these times when they came home from visits with Steven. His mother was usually weepy and his father was just angry. Whenever his parents fought, it was always about Steven. This time wasn't any different.

Al walked in, kicked a chair over, and then went into the bathroom. Tear stains were visible on Rose's face. Nathan remained quiet. He heard the toilet flush, but Al did not emerge from the bathroom.

"Are you hungry, Honey?" Rose was speaking to Nathan.

"No, Mom, that's okay. Don't worry about it." He just wanted to retreat to his room.

Finally, Al emerged from the bathroom and Nathan saw the tears in his eyes. He didn't dare ask what was wrong. He knew it was another bad visit with Steven.

Al glanced at Nathan and diverted his eyes to the floor. "That kid is a fucking monster." His words were barely audible. "Merry fucking Christmas." He added, and then went to sit in the darkened family room.

Nathan retreated to his room. He never heard his father talk like that, not even when he was with just guys. Something terrible must have happened. He went back to trying to figure out the computer, and just hoped that everything would return to normal downstairs. Al appeared in his bedroom doorway, about an hour later.

"Can I come in?" He sounded sheepish.

"Yeah, Dad…of course. I'm just figuring this thing out."

"You'll get it, I'm sure. I'm sorry about how I acted before. I guess the rest of the day was ruined for you. No dinner…..no parents to spend the day with. Pretty shitty, huh?"

"It's okay…..I understand." Nathan attempted a smile.

"Well, you shouldn't have to suffer because of….how Steven is. I know I shouldn't take it out on your mother either. It's not her fault…. but I get so tired of seeing her cry over him all the time. You know what I mean? Crying doesn't help." Al sighed.

"I know, Dad. Crying doesn't help Steven, but it helps mom. You kick a chair—mom cries. It's her way of letting it out."

Al looked up at Nathan, and was speechless for a moment. A sudden awareness came over him. "You know….you're right. I never looked at it that way. I wouldn't think anything of it if your mom walked in and kicked a chair over, but she doesn't do that. She cries. You know what, Kid? You're the best thing that ever happened to this family. How did we get so lucky?" Al smiled at Nathan. "I guess I should start counting my blessings. So….anything new since we left?"

Nathan told him about Tanya.

"I told Mike and Bobby that I didn't want us to talk about Tanya any more. I just didn't think it was right, you know? Then Cookie called to tell me she wants me to write to her."

"And will you write to her?" Al asked.

"No, probably not. She doesn't need to have any guys in her life right now." Nathan sounded so wise, Al thought to himself.

"Hey, let's go downstairs and see if we can get some dinner. I think I owe your mother an apology." He hooked his arm around Nathan's neck and pulled him toward the door.

2-12

The second school term began the day after New Year's Day. All of the students were buzzing about their Christmas, the gifts they received, and Tanya. Nathan refused to feed into the conversations concerning Tanya. It wasn't right, he told them. He was focused on his schoolwork, the choir, and the upcoming baseball season. He didn't have time for gossip.

In late February, the coach called a baseball meeting. Nathan felt that familiar pang of excitement when baseball season got close. He and Mike trotted down to the gym after choir, dropped their book bags on the bleachers, and sat down waiting for Coach Belinski to start the meeting. The meeting was brief, with the coach handing out practice schedules along with the schedule of the upcoming games. There were a couple of new players added to the roster, mainly to replace those seniors that graduated last year. The coach introduced him to the newcomers as a starting pitcher, and that made him feel proud. He couldn't wait for practice to start. He was going to start warming his arm up as soon as he got home that night. He would start slowly at first, just as they taught him at the baseball camp.

In mid-March the first practice took place. Nathan's arm was still good. He had his control back immediately, and his fastball was untouchable.

Mike walked off the field with him after that first practice. "If you keep that up, we're going to clinch a title this year. Damn, you can pitch!"

Mike's praise pleased him, since he considered Mike to be an A-one ballplayer. As they exited the field via home plate around the backstop, they encountered three girls, standing there waiting for them.

In unison, they lilted, "Hi, Mike! Hi, Nathan!"

"Fans." Mike winked at Nathan and grinned. Nathan chuckled.

* * *

Baseball season was underway. Al and Rose attended the first game, both wearing heavy jackets. It was the last day of March, and the day was nothing like the legendary lamb. It was only about thirty-eight degrees. Nathan gave up two hits that day, giving his team their first victory, a shutout—seven-zip. The players were ecstatic. Nathan looked up toward the stands where his parents sat, and grinned at them. Al had a grin to match his. Rose smiled and gave him a thumbs-up.

"Let's get something to eat somewhere. Nate, where would you like to go?" Al asked as he unlocked the car.

"Some of the guys and their parents are going to Bumpy's. How about that?" Bumpy's was a local sports pub where the food was good and the draft beer was inexpensive, all surrounded by a nice atmosphere.

"Sounds good to me. Rose? How about you?"

Rose nodded. "That sounds fine."

Many of the team members were already seated when they entered Bumpy's. Mike raised his arm and called out to them to come join him and his family at their table. They went right over. Mike made the introductions.

Mike's father, Alex Smith was an older version of Mike. He looked at Nathan and nodded. "You can really handle a baseball, can't you?"

"I try." Nathan sounded modest.

Mike laughed and boasted, "I taught him everything he knows."

"Yeah....right!" Nathan laughed.

The meal was fun. For Rose and Al, it was the most fun they had encountered in quite awhile. Rose thought to herself, 'I forgot how much fun it is to go out and enjoy the banter of other people. I feel so relaxed.'

* * *

The team took the championship that year. All the students in school went wild over it, since it was a perfect record—all wins, no losses. Nathan pitched five no-hitters, and that made him a star with the team, the coach, and the student body. A sports-writer from the local newspaper did a write-up on him, and it was printed, along with a picture of him holding the championship trophy. Al was bursting with pride. He cut out the article and bought a frame for it. He insisted on hanging it on the wall of the family room, where it stayed for years to come. Every time Steven caused turmoil, Al would go look at that article in the frame and count his blessings, as he put it.

The awards banquet was a great event for Nathan that year. Not only did he earn another letter, but he got recognized for outstanding athletic ability. He also received a pin and a certificate for being in the choir, and another for outstanding academic achievement. Al and Rose sat with Mike's parents again, and both of the mothers had tissues out when their sons accepted their awards.

Not only were Mike and Nathan best friends now, but their parents became good friends, as well. Occasionally they got together to play cards or go to dinner. Sometimes the boys went with them, but most of the time they just hung out together at one or the other's house. Mike's dad, Alex was a foreman on the road crew for the city. Since Al was a foreman for a building construction company, they had a lot in common. Cindy Smith, Mike's mother was a stay-at-home mom but sold Avon for extra money, and Rose became a very good customer for her, as well as a good friend. Mike was the Smiths' only child.

* * *

Nathan was ready to leave for the Spring Choral Concert. He was dressed in a dark grey suit, white shirt and a tie that had red, black and grey stripes going diagonally across. When he came downstairs to the kitchen, Rose took a double-take. He was so handsome! When Al appeared right behind him, also dressed in a suit, Rose thought they reminded her of bookends, they looked so much alike.

"You look beautiful, Honey." Al came up and kissed her cheek. She blushed with pleasure. He had not said anything that nice to her in—well, she couldn't remember when. She was wearing a turquoise dress that she bought for the occasion, and the new make-up she bought from Cindy. She thought she looked nice, but it was wonderful to hear Al say it. She was glad she spent the money on the dress, the make-up and the new hair style. The hair stylist put some highlights in it for her and the cut made her look a lot younger than her age of fifty.

Al turned to Nathan and advised, "Always tell your wife she looks beautiful when she does. Remember that." He added, with a wink.

"How about your mother?" Nathan countered. "Mom, you do look beautiful."

Rose looked at him with grateful eyes. "And you're as handsome as your father."

Al laughed. "Okay....admiration society closed for the day. Let's get going." He ushered them out the door to the car.

* * *

The concert was magnificent. Rose and Al, seated beside Alex and Cindy Smith, were amazed at the quality of the singing. The theme was "Motown" and all the singers sang like their hearts were in it. Nathan and Mike both had a solo part, and they also did a duet. They both had beautiful voices, and they looked and sounded like they were really enjoying the music. Since this was the last event of the school year, there were refreshments in the gym for everyone who attended the concert, as well as the choir members. Most of the faculty attended the concert so they were all present for refreshments as well. Many of them approached the Perletti's and the Smith's. Nathan and Mike were star pupils as well as model citizens, and the faculty didn't hesitate to pass this along to the parents. Rose looked around for the boys and spotted them on the other side of the gym talking and laughing with a couple of the girls who had been on the stage with them. She couldn't help but notice the look of admiration on the faces of the girls as they looked up at both Mike and Nathan. 'Those two are going to be a pair when they start going out with girls,' she thought.

She was pulled from her thought by the feel on a hand on her arm. She looked down at the hand on her arm and moved her eyes from the hand, to the arm, and then to the face of the dark-haired, dark eyed girl who quickly removed her hand.

"Hi there." She smiled at this pretty young girl.

"Hi." The girl hesitated. "Are you Nathan's mother?" She wanted to know.

"Yes, I am." Rose waited for the girl to say something, but the girl just stood there. Rose smiled at her again.

Finally the young girl spoke quietly. "He's gorgeous." She retreated into the crowd.

Rose laughed. She made a mental note to ask Nathan who she was. She obviously had a very huge crush on him.

2-13

Another school year ended, and again, Nathan survived with a 4.0 average. Chemistry hadn't been as hard as he thought it would be. It was one of his easiest classes, in fact. Now he had the whole summer ahead of him to just have fun, maybe go fishing with his dad a little, go swimming, or just hang out with Mike and Bobby. Many of the guys were hanging out at the local diner lately. As long as they spent money, the owner didn't care if they were taking up seats. His business was not as good as it used to be since they built the new Denny's practically across the street.

Mike came home with Nathan that afternoon of the last day. Cindy Smith's car was in the Perletti's driveway when they got there.

"Hey, my mom's here. Avon calling!" He joked. Nathan just laughed.

Cindy and Rose were sitting at the kitchen table drinking coffee and talking, when Nathan and Mike made a beeline for the refrigerator. They stopped talking when the boys entered.

"Uh-oh! We interrupted something. They're probably talking about sending us to military school. Let's get out of here, Nate!" All four of them laughed at that.

Cindy and Rose had been talking about Steven when the boys came in, but the actual reason for the visit was to discuss another baseball camp for both Mike and Nathan. The Smith's were joining them for dinner on the grill that night, and they planned on surprising the boys with the news that they would both be going to baseball camp. Nathan's birthday was July fourth, and Mike's birthday was July second. It would be a birthday gift to both of them.

* * *

Mike and Nathan were ecstatic. Their reaction was the same.

"Really? Both of us?"

The parents nodded.

"COOL!" They said in unison, and gave each other a high five.

"When do we go?" Nathan asked, looking from one parent to the other.

"Same time as last year. July the fifth." Al smiled at Nathan and added, "Your mom and I are going to take a little vacation while you're there. Actually, the four of us are going to go to Atlantic City for a few days."

"COOL!" Nathan and Mike had that word down pat, it seemed. Nathan wondered about Steven, but decided it was best not to say anything. His parents needed some time for fun, after what Steven put them through all the time. He worried constantly that his parents would get divorced over it, so he was glad they were going to get away by themselves—no kids—and have some fun.

"Another thing we wanted to discuss with you two is your birthdays. You're both going to be sixteen, just two days apart. Do you want a birthday party?" Cindy looked back and forth at them, and then added, "Sans alcohol, of course."

Mike and Nathan looked at each other and shrugged. "Yeah…why not?" Nathan looked to Mike and raised an eyebrow. "Think it'd be a good idea?"

"Yeah, let's do it." Mike responded.

Al took over the conversation. "We have a lot of room here. What do you say we have a party here—cookout, maybe. What do you guys think about that? You can each invite a bunch of your friends…"

Nathan stopped him there. "We have the same friends, Dad."

"Oh yeah, I guess you would. Anyway, invite them. Let's plan it for the third, right between your birthdays. Am I getting any favorable vibes here?"

"Sounds really cool, Mr. Perletti….Nate, we can have it outside and the chicks will have halter tops on." Nate elbowed him and laughed.

It was then that Rose remembered the girl in the gym. "Nathan, you have an admirer." She told him the story about the incident in the gym after the concert, and Nathan and Mike laughed.

"She puts love letters in his locker." Mike informed them. "She thinks he doesn't know who they're from. Then she baked him cookies once. Remember those cookies, Nate? Burnt! The bottoms were all charred."

"We couldn't eat them." Nathan added. "I felt bad, because she cried. I ate one burnt one just to make her feel better."

"That was noble of you." Al told him. "I swear, though, there must be something in the water to make the young girls in this town act the way they do." Al thought to himself, 'And Steven must be drinking from the same well.'

* * *

The day was perfect for an outdoor party. There was a slight breeze that kept it from being too hot, but the sun was shining and the sky was blue. The parents were preparing the food and Mike and Nathan were hanging streamers from the porch roof. The first guest to arrive was Cookie. She brought some chips and dip with her.

"You didn't have to bring anything, Cook....we have it all covered." Nathan told her.

"That's okay....I wanted to. You two are like my best friends. Oh, and I have something for both of you. You're going to love it." She went in and set her offerings down on the kitchen table, but carried one bag outside.

"Okay, are you two ready for the best birthday present ever?" She shot them a coy glance.

"Are you going to have sex with us, Cookie?" Mike teased.

"Yeah, I'm balling you both," She snickered as she pulled a baseball out of the bag. "This ball is for you, Nate, and this other one is for you, Mike." She handed them their respective baseball.

"Holy shit! Nate, this is signed by....." he stopped and held it up for Nathan to see.

Nathan was smiling at the one in his hand.

"Look at this." He showed Mike the ball he was holding.

"Cookie, where did you get these? How did you get these?"

She shrugged. "My dad works at the stadium. I went there with him last week, took two balls and got a third baseman to sign one, and a pitcher to sign the other. You have to put them in a case to keep them looking like that."

They both grabbed Cookie and hugged her. "You're the best, Cook." Mike told her.

The three of them went into the house to show off the baseballs to the adults, and then put them in a safe place in the family room until they could get cases for them.

Other guests started to arrive. Al put a tub full of ice and sodas out on the lawn under a tree. "It'll keep them out of the refrigerator, and out of the kitchen." He affirmed. Cindy and Rose carried salads and side dishes out onto the table set up on the porch, while Alex was busily turning burgers and dogs on the grill. Mike and Nathan were hooking up the stereo outside on the other side of the porch. Some of the kids were playing lawn darts, while others were playing tether ball. Many were sitting on the grass or on the porch steps. There were nearly fifty teenagers present.

Cindy looked at Rose and whispered, "I didn't know they had that many close friends, did you?"

Rose shook her head. "Thank God Al over-bought. He said he was thinking that what we didn't use today, we would have to eat at another time…"

Her voice was cut off by shrieks coming from around the side of the house. Mike and Nathan had the hose turned on a group of girls who were sitting there.

"Mike, what are you doing?" Cindy called.

Mike and Nathan came around to the porch. Nathan spoke up. "They lit cigarettes back there. We saw flames and we thought we had better put the fire out."

Both boys had the most adorable smirk on the faces. Rose and Cindy laughed.

Mike went back out around the side of the house. Rose and Cindy could hear him. "Sorry, girls….But Nate and I don't hang out with chicks who smoke. You're taking up our oxygen." Rose and Cindy looked at each other and smiled their approval.

The party ended just past ten, with Cookie being the last to leave. She helped clean up before she went. She hugged Mike and Nathan and told them to have a great time at baseball camp. Both Mike and Nathan made a mental note to bring her something when they came back.

* * *

Nathan and Mike were going into their second week of camp. Mike, who was a good hitter to begin with, began to hit the ball even better because of the tips he was given by the coaches.

"Dude, we're going to have an awesome team again next year." Mike assured Nathan. With my hitting and your pitching, we have another championship."

"Providing the rest of the team does their part, maybe. We can't do it alone." Nathan reminded him.

"I guess that's true enough. Hey, how do you think our parents did in Atlantic City? Think they won any money?" Mike laughed when he said it. "They should be back by now, you think?"

"Why? You miss your mommy?" Nathan teased. "Want to call her?"

Mike flipped him the bird and laughed.

"Hey, I hope our permits are there when we get back. We could have our license by the time school starts."

"Cool." Nathan responded before he headed toward the shower to get ready for dinner.

* * *

Mike and Nathan were packed and ready to leave when Rose's car, driven by Al, pulled into the parking lot. Alex was with him. It was just the two of them. Nathan's first thought was that something was wrong.

"Hi, Dad....where's mom?" He couldn't hide the worry on his face.

"She's at home with Mrs. Smith. There wouldn't have been room for everybody, especially with all your gear that will overflow from the trunk into the back seat, so they stayed back. They're going to some kind of party tonight—Tupperware, or something—so it's just us guys. We get to go out and eat junk food, drink beer...well, Alex and I do, anyway...shoot pool, whatever we want. How does that sound? Answer, then tell us about baseball camp."

"Sounds great!" Mike and Nathan answered in unison. They both began to talk about the camp. Al noticed something uncanny about those two. One would start and the other would finish. They never had to talk over each other. He believed it would be a true and lasting friendship.

2-14

Nathan drove to school on the first day of his junior year. His permit was waiting for him after baseball camp, and he immediately badgered Al and Rose to let him begin driving. He handled a car was well as he handled a baseball, and within weeks, passed his driving test. Rose let him borrow her car for the first day, reminding him that he couldn't take it every day.

He pulled into the school parking lot just as Mike pulled in and parked next to him. Mike had Cindy's car. "Dude, we need to get wheels of our own!" He called to Nathan.

"Yeah, well, we have to get money to do that. How do we get money? We get a job!" Nathan was imitating their English teacher at this point, mimicking her movements and her manner of speaking. Mike cracked up.

"Seriously, though, we can't borrow our mothers' cars all the time. Maybe they wouldn't mind if I drove one day and you drove the next day....until we get cars of our own, that is."

Nathan cocked his head to the side and shrugged. "We could ask, I suppose. It sure beats getting on the school bus every day."

They checked their schedules and were satisfied to find out that they had four classes, plus choir, together. Their first class was History. They threaded through the throngs of students standing on the sidewalk and front steps, and went directly to their homeroom, which also happened to be the same this year. They listened to the announcements, and waited for the bell to ring to go to their first period class, History.

Class began promptly after the late bell rang. Mr. Bartolli called the role. "Is there anyone's name I didn't call?" He asked and looked around the room.

He saw a girl sitting back of the room raise her hand. "And what is your name?"

A sweet-sounding voice answered, "Christa Burns. I just transferred from Connecticut. Here's my entry slip." She got up as Nathan turned around to see who the voice belonged to. He liked what he saw. She was so pretty. She had dark red hair and blue eyes, a delicate looking face, with a serene smile.

"I think I'm in love." He whispered to Mike.

Mike turned around to look at the girl walking up toward the front of the class.

"Nice...definitely nice." He whispered back to Nathan.

* * *

Second period class for Nathan was French, while Mike had Latin. Nathan was disappointed that he and Mike wouldn't be in the same class, but quickly overcame that disappointment when he saw that Christa, the new girl was in his class. As luck would have it, she sat down next to him.

He leaned over toward her and made a suggestion. "You should give the teacher your entry slip before the class begins. Unless you like that individualized attention…" He smiled at her.

"Thanks. Good idea." She smiled back at him.

"You're from Connecticut? Did your dad get transferred here or something?" His question was in earnest.

"It's just me and my mom. My dad didn't come with us. They're getting a divorce. My dad….cheated." She suddenly became embarrassed that she told him that.

"Hey, that's rough. I guess you miss your dad, huh?"

"I miss my mom more." She answered. This puzzled him and it showed.

"I mean, she's there, but she's not there. She's always crying or ranting about what a rat he is. She hardly talks to me any more….." She trailed off, wondering why she told him that. He was, after all, a stranger.

"I can identify with that. My mom did the same thing for awhile. I have a brother who is….sick….with mental problems. My mom was always crying and seemed preoccupied all the time. I felt like she blamed me for it. I actually apologized to her that it wasn't me, instead of Steven, who was sick…" It was Nathan's turn to be embarrassed. He never talked about Steven to anyone, including Mike.

"So it's not just me, then. See, I felt like she blamed me for daddy cheating on her." Christa studied Nathan's face. 'He's gorgeous,' she thought to herself.

"Naw, she doesn't. She's just wrapped up in her own misery right now. Give her time. She'll come around. My mom did." Nathan spoke with sincerity.

"Thanks for the advice." She smiled at him and thought to herself, 'maybe this move won't be so bad after all.'

The French teacher entered the room and Christa handed her the entry slip. Class began.

When class ended, Nathan was already sick of conjugating verbs in French. 'Christa may be the only good thing in this class!' He thought to himself.

As they were gathering up their books, he asked, "Where to, next?" He had English class and was disappointed that she wouldn't be going to that class with him.

"Hey, how about meeting me and my buddy Mike for lunch? We get the same lunch break." He hoped she would agree to that, and was relieved when she did.

"Sure…that sounds great. Where is the lunchroom and where will you be when I get there?" She slung her book bag over her shoulder and waited for his answer.

He told her how to get to the lunchroom and where to look for him. "See ya then?" He hesitated, waiting for her response.

"Okay. See you." She walked off and he watched her go. 'This is going to be a good year,' he thought, as he watched her exit the classroom door.

Nathan met up with Mike as they entered the next class together. "I asked that girl to eat lunch with us." He informed Mike.

"What girl?"

"Christa. The new girl from Connecticut."

"Oh….do you think you might ask her to go out with you sometime?"

"Yeah….I don't know….yeah…I'd like to." Nathan admitted.

"Cool….because I was thinking…maybe we could double. I want to ask Lori Watson to go see that new movie that's playing. This Saturday, maybe. Think you can muster up the courage to ask the new girl? It would be fun. I already asked for the car, and my mom said it would be okay." Mike awaited Nathan's answer.

"Yeah….okay. I'll see if she seems interested first. If she does, I'll ask her." The prospect of asking Christa to go out with him made him both nervous and excited at the same time. He hoped she would say yes.

* * *

It was the first official date for Mike and Nathan, as well as the girls. Nathan had been relieved when Christa agreed to go to a movie with him, and maybe somewhere afterward to eat. Mike told Nathan that he knew it would be a done deal, when he saw how Christa looked at Nathan in the lunchroom. The four of them walked out of the movie theater laughing. It had been a good comedy which was just what Christa needed to lift her spirits. They chose a small casual dining restaurant to eat, and were headed that way. It was within walking distance, so they left the car parked where it was and strolled to the restaurant. Nathan kept looking at Christa when he didn't think she was watching. He thought she was the prettiest girl he had ever seen.

After they were seated at the table in the restaurant and had placed their orders, they began to relax with each other. Nathan wanted to know what Connecticut was like and what she did for fun there.

"We get lots of snow, so winter sports are big up there." She offered.

"Do you ski?" He asked.

"No, but I ice skate." She told him.

"I've never been on ice skates. Have you, Mike, or Lori?" Nathan turned to them.

"No." They answered in unison.

"What do you do in Ohio?" She countered.

Lori answered for them. "Mike and Nathan eat, sleep, drink, and breathe baseball. They're both starters for the school baseball team, and they are both *terrific*! You'll have to see them play when baseball season starts. And, Christa, I'll bet if you ask either one of them, they can probably tell you down to the minute how long it is before baseball season starts!" Lori was proud of her declaration.

"We're not that bad!" Mike laughed. "Well, yes we are. Let's see.... it's probably about two hundred-sixty thousand minutes 'til baseball season." They all laughed.

"So you're good?" Christa asked Nathan.

"He's damn good." Mike answered for him. "He's the best pitcher our school has ever seen. Maybe good enough for major league in a couple of years."

Nathan was grateful to Mike for the boost to his ego because Christa seemed impressed.

"Well, Mike here, plays third base. Nothing gets past him. He's a homerun hitter, too. He hit twelve last year." Nathan returned the compliment.

"So I'm out with a couple of baseball stars, then?" Christa really looked impressed.

"Yep, you are!" Lori answered her.

Christa was impressed, but not with the fact that they were star ballplayers. She was impressed that neither of them bragged about himself. She decided that she liked these two guys, especially Nathan, who seemed kind and understanding about everything. She definitely wanted to go out with him again.

* * *

Nathan and Christa, and Mike and Lori became a regular foursome. They went out on weekends and ate lunch together every day at school. It became known to everyone in school that they were together. Nathan invited Christa to dinner at his house one Saturday, and his parents seemed to like her. He went to her house for Sunday dinner the following week when his parents visited Steven. Christa's mother was a nurse, so she easily found work in one of the local hospitals. Mrs. Burns found a lovely townhouse and she and Christa moved in the first week of October. Christa told Nathan that things were going better between her and her mother and that her mother was healing and moving on with her life. Nathan was glad for her.

Nathan asked Christa to the homecoming dance, and of course, they doubled with Mike and Lori. It was Nathan's turn to drive, so he picked Mike up first and then went to collect Christa. He was standing in the living room talking to Mrs. Burns when Christa came down the stairs. He was mesmerized because she looked so lovely. She was wearing a royal blue sheath gown, very plain and simple, but elegant. Her hair was piled high with a few wisps of curl falling around her face. He had never seen her with her hair up like that, but he liked it. Her mother insisted on pictures, so they posed for a few. Mrs. Burns even took a picture of Mike who was standing there looking impatient to get over to Lori's house.

The homecoming dance was fun for all of them. Christa was a wonderful dancer, and Nathan was grateful to his mother for teaching him how to dance the year before. He could certainly keep up with Christa on the dance floor, thanks to Rose. The last song of the night was playing. Nathan held Christa as they danced and looked into her face. He kissed the tip of her nose and she smiled up at him.

"You're so sweet." He whispered in her ear.

She looked up at him and said, "So are you."

The song ended, they got their coats, and headed out the door toward the car. Nathan and Christa reached the car first, and they sat and waited for Mike and Lori. Christa seemed cold, so Nathan put his arm around her, since the car hadn't warmed up yet. He leaned down and kissed her gently on the mouth. She didn't resist, but instead returned the kiss. They continued kissing sweetly, until Nathan began to feel the familiar urgency in his loins. He pulled back and relaxed his hold around her.

"What's wrong?" She sounded alarmed.

"Uh…nothing….I just…thought I heard Mike's voice." 'What am I supposed to say?' He thought to himself. 'Oh, I just got a boner with no place to put it?'

Luckily, Mike opened the rear car door just then. "Hey, these windows are sure steamed up! What have you two been doing?"

"Nothing." They answered in unison.

2-15

Christmas, along with Steven's birthday, was fast approaching. Steven would be twelve this year. Although Rose and Al visited him every week, Nathan hadn't seen Steven in two years. Because he was his brother, Nathan really wanted to see him, but on the other hand, Nathan didn't want to have to put up with the things that Steven said and did. He really didn't miss Steven. Life was always unpleasant when he was around.

At breakfast, the week before Steven's birthday, Nathan asked his parents if they thought that he should attempt to see Steven on his birthday.

Al cleared his throat. "I don't think that would be wise. We're not sure we are going to go to see him on his birthday."

Nathan got the feeling that something was being kept from him. "What do you mean? You're not going for his birthday? Why?"

Al sighed. "Nate, he doesn't want us there....none of us. I don't know what to say....I feel like such a failure...."

"Don't say that, Dad! You've been great. You told me a long time ago that it's nobody's fault...."

"I know what I told you, Nate." Al sighed again. "But after all this time, my....heart hurts. I feel so defeated. You know what, Kid?"

Nathan looked Al into the eyes. "What?"

Al gave him the familiar gentle fist to the chin. "It's the light in you that makes me able to endure the darkness in Steven."

Nathan gave Al an appreciative smile. "Thanks, Dad....maybe Steven will get well...."

Al shook his head. "The psychiatrist said he didn't think so. All we could hope for is to get him stabilized so that he isn't a danger to anyone. When he gets older, maybe there is a chance for newer treatments. Do you know that he has pissed on everyone at that facility? Actually pissed on them? We are talking staff and patients! Everybody! It's just one of the things he does. Whips it out and pisses on people."

"Is there an explanation for it? I mean....is there something that triggers it?" Nathan was trying to give Steven the benefit of doubt.

"Yeah, he has a dick that can pee." Al snorted his answer at Nathan, and then laughed a little. Al regained his serious face. "No, there's no reason for it. Somehow Steven knows that it's nasty and offensive. He has known that since he was real little. You weren't here last time he was in this house. Nate, he acted like he's possessed by a demon. I hit him...hard. I felt like shit afterwards, but when he said those things to your mom and to me, I just reacted. Officer Banks came in the door right afterward and I thought I was going to be arrested. And you know what? I wouldn't have cared. I deserved it for hitting him. But damn it, he made me see red!"

Nathan absorbed all this like a sponge. 'So this is what they have been keeping from me....Steven isn't going to get well...and, dad hit him. Wow. No wonder they didn't want me to know all this.'

"So what happens now?" Nathan asked, eyes darting from Al to Rose.

Rose and Al both sighed this time. Rose spoke up. "We have to let it up to the doctors, Honey. We won't be going to see Steven unless the doctors tell us he wants to see us. The care givers at the facility say that Steven is exceptionally disruptive after a visit from us. His doctor says that if we go only when he asks for us, it may be better for everybody. So that's what we will have to do. He's the doctor."

Nathan looked to both of his parents, one at a time, as he cerebrally digested this information. "So you just won't go out to see him any more?" Somehow this seemed cruel to Nathan.

"Not unless he asks for us." Al stared at his plate, suddenly not hungry any more. "I'm sorry, Nate. I know how much having a brother always meant to you. Let's face it; you have a brother in name only, just as we have a second son, in name only." Al threw down his napkin and got up and left the table.

Nathan looked over at his mother. He could see she was hurting, not because of what Al said, but because what he said was true. He got up and went around the table and hugged her. She looked up at him, grateful to him for being there.

* * *

Nathan and Mike decided to go shopping for Christmas presents together. This was the first time either of them would be buying a gift for a girl, so they wanted each other's approval in what they bought. They were walking through the mall, just taking in the sights.

"Jewelry? Sweater maybe…I don't know, Mike, what do you think?" Nathan was undecided in which direction they should walk.

"Hell, I don't know. What do girls like? Besides us, that is." Mike, proud of his clever remark, snickered.

"Jewelry…..girls always like jewelry. Let's check out the jewelry store." They rounded the corner and walked into one of the mall jewelry stores.

Nathan found a small gold chain first, but turned away when he saw the price. He had to buy gifts for his parents yet, so he had to spend conservatively. Mike, who didn't have as much cash as Nathan, had the same concern.

Nathan looked at Mike. "Hmm.....Maybe jewelry isn't such a good idea. Stuff's pretty expensive."

Mike nodded. Let's go somewhere and think this thing out. Maybe get a cup of coffee or something.....I have to think."

They left the jewelry store and found a place to get coffee. "What the hell are we going to do for gifts for them?" Mike spoke as he stared into his coffee cup.

Nathan shook his head. "We just have to find something they would like that doesn't cost so much. It's not the cost of the gift, but the thought put into it. And the way I figure it, we are thinking pretty hard right now."

Mike looked up and caught the mischief in Nathan's eyes. "Funny shit, aren't you?" Mike laughed.

"Hey, guys...what's up?" Nathan and Mike looked up to see their friend, Cookie leaning on their table.

"Cookie! Have a seat! We are having a dilemma here." Mike smiled up at her.

"Yeah? What's going on?" She looked from one to the other.

"We have no idea what to get the girlfriends for Christmas. Everything seems so expensive." Nathan sounded frustrated.

"Well..." Cookie thought for a moment. "Buy me a cup of coffee and we'll do some brainstorming. Okay?"

Nathan called the waitress over and ordered coffee for Cookie. She took charge of the quandary. "How about sweaters? They're both about a size five, which would be a size small in a sweater."

"I never even thought about sizes. Good thing you're here, Cook." Mike patted her on her back as he spoke. Cookie seemed pleased that she could help them.

"Or....how about silver jewelry? Silver is much cheaper than gold." She looked from one to the other, waiting for a response.

"That's an idea, Mike. I know Christa and Lori both like silver. They both wear it, anyway. You're terrific, Cookie."

"Thanks, Nate. Glad I could help." Cookie beamed over Nathan's praise. "Well thanks for the coffee, but I have to get going to do my shopping. I'll catch up with you guys later." Cookie slid out of the booth and headed toward the crowds in the mall.

The boys completed their shopping and headed for home. They both had to be ready to go out in less than two hours and they still had to eat dinner at home. They were pleased with their purchases, which ended up being both sweaters and a piece of silver jewelry for each of the girlfriends. They went the sweater route all the way, by getting their parents new sweaters as well. As an after-thought, they bought Cookie a sweater from both of them. There was still money left over for a date that night.

* * *

Nathan spent Christmas Eve at Christa's and Christmas day with his parents. Christa opened her presents while he was there and she seemed delighted with them. She gave him a new sweater, too. He tried it on and she told him it looked great on him. It was a rust brown color that brought out his brown eyes from under the thick, dark lashes. She tried on the sweater he bought her and was pleased with how she looked in it. The green color did wonders for her dark red hair. She liked the silver bracelet, too.

Christmas Day was pleasant. It had been two years since Al and Rose had spent a full Christmas Day at home. They bought Nathan a new stereo and he and Al were busy hooking it up in Nathan's room, when Rose called them for dinner. The banter at the table was light with no unpleasant conversation. Steven was not mentioned. At the psychiatrist's suggestion, they were to ignore Steven for awhile, which meant no visits, no calls, and no presents. The psychiatrist felt that by continuing to communicate with Steven, they were sending him a message that his behavior was acceptable. They kept in contact with the psychiatrist, but had no contact with Steven. It was called 'tough love', but the good doctor thought it was necessary.

Christmas week flew by. Al and Rose were going out with the Smith's for New Year's Eve. They had not gone out to celebrate the New Year in many years, and they were looking forward to it. Mike's girl, Lori was having a New Year's Eve party, so Nathan and Christa were going there. Al allowed him to take the truck, since they would be using the car.

"Just be careful." He warned. "You may not be drinking, but a lot of people out there are going to be. Drive defensively….okay?"

"I'll be careful, Dad. I hope you and mom have a good time." He accepted the keys to the truck, and hugged both Al and Rose, and said, "Happy New Year."

Al watched Nathan pull out of the driveway, and in a low tone, mumbled, "Great kid."

* * *

Nathan held Christa's hand as they walked up onto the porch at Lori's house and rang the bell. Lori opened the door and hugged them. "Mike's already here helping me put out food. Come on in. Our party is downstairs and my parents have one going on upstairs." She took their coats and pointed them in the direction of the stairs that descended to the party noise.

Lori's basement had been transformed into a party room, with colored lights and streamers. There were tables set up for food, and there were benches for people to sit. The stereo was blasting music and the early arrivals were already dancing. Mike came over and gave Nathan a high five. He was holding two glasses of punch in his other hand, which he held out for Nathan and Christa to take from him. Nathan encircled Christa's waist gently and smiled down at her.

"Want to set the glasses down and dance?" He brushed her hair back off her face while he spoke.

"Sure."

They danced to a few songs, and then mingled with the other guests. Cookie came in with a date, which surprised both boys. They never thought of Cookie as someone who actually went out with guys. They loved her, because she was good people. She was their friend.

As midnight was approaching, Lori's parents along with some of their guests appeared down the steps to see how things were going. An attractive lady from upstairs told them it seemed like they were having more fun than they were upstairs, and they had alcohol! She and her husband danced along side some of the downstairs dancers, and then retreated up the stairs. The countdown to the New Year began. At midnight, Nathan took Christa in his arms and kissed her warmly. She kissed him back passionately.

"Happy New Year." Nathan whispered into her ear, as he stroked her hair. Mike and Lori appeared at their side, and Mike kissed Christa on the cheek and shook Nathan's hand. Lori kissed Nathan on his cheek.

"Happy New year," they yelled at each other.

Shortly after midnight, Nathan took Christa home, and then headed for home himself. Al and Rose arrived shortly behind him. After turning on some lights, they noticed the light on the answering machine blinking. Al pushed the play button, and at first there was nothing but some background noise. They waited, and then they heard the familiar voice of Steven.

"FUCKERS!" He yelled into the phone, and they heard the receiver on the other side of the call being slammed down.

The smiles that had decorated all of their faces the moment before were wiped away by that one word. For a moment, they all stood there looking at each other, dumbfounded.

Al was the first to speak. "He sure knows how to ruin a moment, doesn't he?" Al walked up the stairs, his shoulders drooping.

Rose knew that in the morning she would have to call the psychiatrist to tell him about the call.

* * *

School began after the New Year. Nathan and Mike were antsy, because it was only a matter of time before baseball season would begin. Valentine's Day was around the corner, and practice started two weeks later. They usually held practice in the gym until the weather turned decent enough to go outside. Inside practices were mostly to get the body in shape for the season.

Nathan asked Christa to go to the Valentine's Day dance. She readily accepted, and as usual, they would be going with Mike and Lori. She bought a new dress for the occasion, and hoped Nathan would think she looked really sexy in it. She believed she loved him and she wanted him to fall in love with her. 'If only I were a baseball,' she said to herself. She discovered that what Lori said was true. Baseball was the most important thing in the world to Nathan.

"Well, maybe this dress will change that." She said aloud to herself in the mirror. She dressed extra carefully, spending time on her hair and her make-up until it was just perfect. Her dress was red, strapless, and short in the front, with the back a little longer, almost like the tails on a tuxedo. She slipped into high-heeled silver sandals and stepped back to get a full view in the mirror. She was satisfied that she looked exactly the way she had hoped she would—sexy.

Nathan's face made all her extra pains worth it. He almost dropped the bouquet of roses he was holding. He whistled softly.

"Wow! You look really gorgeous. Sexy dress!"

"Thanks...you look really handsome. Nice suit." She countered.

Nathan was wearing his grey suit with a white shirt and a red tie, courtesy of Rose. She picked it up for him the day before the dance, knowing it would be appropriate for the evening. A red mock handkerchief just slightly emerged from the outside breast pocket—again, courtesy of Rose. He looked very handsome, indeed. Christa's mother took pictures and promised to get double prints so he could have a copy for himself.

They were the first to arrive, after picking up Mike and Lori. Lori was also wearing a sexy red dress, but not nearly as sexy as the one Christa was wearing. Mike had a red tie and handkerchief to go with his dark blue suit and white shirt. Nathan wondered briefly if their mothers had been shopping together. After checking the coats and finding a table, Nathan led Christa to the dance floor. She wrapped her arms around his neck and moved in close to him as he wrapped his arms around her waist. Their cheeks were touching and she could feel his breath in her ear. It was a pleasant sensation, making her feel slightly dizzy. As they danced, he was gently rubbing his hand up and down her back, and she snuggled even closer to him. He was beginning to feel those familiar stirrings again and knew it was time to back off. When the music ended, he led her to the table to sit for awhile.

"Let me get us something to drink. I'll be right back." He kissed her cheek, and walked toward the refreshment table. When he returned to the table, Mike and Lori were already seated across from Christa. Nathan draped his arm around Christa's chair and took her hand in his free hand. They sat at the table, talking and laughing, and sipping on their beverages. The four of them, all good dancers, danced quite a few more dances. Soon it was the last dance of the night. Once again, Christa wrapped her arms around Nathan and moved in close. While they were dancing he kissed her, softly and gently. She responded with open lips. The stirrings within Nathan returned, but this time he didn't pull away.

The dance ended, and Mike was asked to help fold tables. Nathan and Christa told him they would wait in the car. The car windows were frosted. Nathan started the car and turned on the defrosters, and Christa snuggled close to him. He put his arm around her and she turned her face to his and kissed him. Their kissing turned passionate and Nathan was fully aroused. He nuzzled her neck and kissed her ear, and moved back to her mouth. His breathing was becoming ragged as was hers. She took his hand and placed it on her breast, and he moaned. He stroked her nipple through her dress with his thumb and felt it harden. He felt her hand on his abdomen and sucked in his breath. She was unzipping him. He reached around had pulled down the zipper of her dress, exposing her breasts. His mouth found her breast, and he took it into his mouth, while she stroked his penis. He reached under her dress and found her pantyhose. He began sliding them down and she lifted her hips to help him. He pulled them to her knees and quickly found what he was groping for. He stroked her mound and then entered her with one of his fingers. She gasped, but didn't stop him. His mouth returned to her breast and he teased her nipple with his tongue, while he slid his finger slowly in and out of her. He was losing control.

They both jumped when Mike pounded on the trunk of the car. Christa wrapped her coat around her and Nathan quickly zipped his pants. Mike and Lori climbed into the back seat and Nathan put the car in gear and drove away.

"It's hot in here!" Mike exclaimed. "Can you turn the heat down a little? Or is that all from you two?"

Nathan silently gave him the finger with the hand he had draped across the back of the seat, while Christa kept her head on his shoulder. He dropped Lori off first, and waited while Mike walked her to her door. Nathan helped Christa back into her dress and she pulled up her pantyhose while they waited.

"Got everything together?" He whispered. She nodded and looked up at him.

He smiled at her and kissed the tip of her nose. "Vixen." He teased.

She returned his smile with a weak one. "I didn't want to stop."

"Me neither. It's a good thing we did....I mean, I don't have anything...protection, I mean."

"Oh." She looked at the floor of the car for a moment. "You should get some. Just in case it goes that far again." Nathan nodded.

He took her home before Mike. It was Mike's turn to sit in the car and wait while Nathan took Christa to the door. He kissed her slowly and held her.

"Call you tomorrow, okay?" She nodded.

Nathan slipped behind the wheel and put the car into gear.

"Did I interrupt something?" Mike asked.

Nathan looked at Mike and smiled and raised his eyebrow. "Like what?"

"You know what I'm talking about." Mike snickered.

"Hey, I don't kiss and tell. You know that."

Mike started laughing. "I knew it! I knew it! When you said you didn't do Tanya you were lying! Fucker!"

"What's Tanya got to do with anything? Damn, that was almost two years ago."

"One thing about Tanya....all she wanted from you was your dick....nothing else. You knew where you stood with her. Seriously though, Nate? Be careful. Not everybody is like Tanya. Most girls expect something more than just sex. You don't want to end up with a kid or something. Your whole life would be ruined."

"Yeah, I know....but you know what? I thought Christa was a virgin. I mean, I still think she is....but man, tonight? She made all the moves. I never even thought about things going that far. I'm just human, though. She touches the right places and I'm human putty."

"Wow. Maybe you better make a stop at the drug store before you take her out again, Putty-boy." Mike advised.

"I don't know if I want the responsibility." Nathan sighed.

"What are you talking about? Somebody better take the responsibility unless you want to end up with a papoose strapped to your back."

"It's just something my dad said to me once. He said if you do a virgin, you have a responsibility to her. I don't know if I want that." Nathan admitted to Mike.

"Bring on the sluts then!" Mike started laughing and Nathan joined in. Nathan stopped the car to let Mike out in front of his house, and drove the short distance to his house laughing to himself, thinking about Mike's remark.

2-16

Mike and Nathan trotted to the gym for their first baseball warm-up practice of the season. They left choir practice in a hurry to get there and start warming up. They knew there would be no outdoor practice, since there was six inches of new-fallen snow on the ground from the night before.

Nathan pulled open the door to the gymnasium, with Mike right behind him. "We should live somewhere like California or Florida where we can play baseball all year." Mike grumbled. Nathan agreed.

They met Coach Belinski in the locker room as he was coming out of his office. "You guys ready for a good season this year?"

"Hope so, Coach. I know we're ready to play. Been waiting all year for it. Mike and I went to baseball camp last summer. Mike's going to kill the ball this season." Nathan grinned and clapped Mike on the back.

"Yeah? Well, good....let's see lots of homeruns this year, then." Coach Belinski honored them with a quick smile. He liked these two boys.

Mike and Nathan started tossing the ball back and forth, sometimes overthrowing it to make the other jump high, or throwing it short so the other had to dive for it. The coach watched them for awhile, noting that the smiles never left their faces. 'The love of the game,' he spoke under his breath.

* * *

The first game took place during a sudden thaw. The temperature was in the low sixties, but there were some strong gusts of wind. They were playing the first game at home, so the stands filled quickly with those who were willing to brave the wind. Lori and Christa sat in the stands, and shortly before game time, Cookie joined them. Both Nathan and Mike's parents, equipped with coats and blankets, sat behind the girls in the third row. Nathan was the starting pitcher. The first half of the first inning ended quickly with Nathan striking out all three batters. Christa had never been to a baseball game, but she knew ability when she saw it. Nathan was good.

The game ended in a victory; the winning run brought in by Mike when he put one over the fence in the fourth inning, making the ending score 1-0. Nathan gave up two hits that first game, but each time he gave up a hit, he struck out the next two batters. Christa watched him run off the field at the end of the game and her heart leaped. 'He's so gorgeous!' She thought to herself.

The Perletti's and the Smith's ended the day at Bumpy's, along with the girls, including Cookie. A lot of the spectators from the game were there, and many came up to congratulate them on their win. There were lots of compliments for Mike on his homerun and just as many for Nathan concerning his pitching. Al and Alex split the tab between them, telling everybody to put their money away. Throughout the meal, Rose kept noticing Christa's look of adoration when she looked at Nathan. 'She's crazy about him. He better be careful.' She worried.

* * *

It was the last game of the regular season, and they were the only team that was undefeated. This last game was just for fun, they all said, so they relaxed and just played the game. Nathan didn't start the game, because the coach wanted him ready for the championship playoffs. Even without Nathan as their starting pitcher, they won the game by two runs. The boy who pitched in Nathan's place gave up three runs, but other than that, he did a nice job. Nathan told him this after the game.

They won the championship! Nathan and Mike were ecstatic, along with the rest of the team. They were taking the girls out to a nice restaurant to celebrate, and also to make amends for all the dates they had to back out of since baseball season began. The coach didn't want them going out a lot; he said girls broke their concentration, and booty kills their game! Since they respected Coach Belinski and believed everything he told them, both girls were 'put on ice' for the season. They still called them, and ate lunch in school with them, and occasionally spent an evening with them, but going out every weekend ceased all through the season. Lori didn't mind so much, but Christa seemed upset by it. 'That's the way it is,' Lori told her. Lori actually didn't quite understand why Nathan even liked Christa. She was pretty, but there wasn't much else there. She was quiet and sullen a lot of the times, and lately she didn't even join in on their conversations. And she was 'clingy.' Always clinging to Nathan--always had to be touching him in some way, either holding his hand or having her hand on his back, or something. She didn't give him any breathing room, and Lori knew that was a kiss of death.

They met at the restaurant in separate cars, since Mike and Lori were meeting her parents at a family gathering afterward. Christa warmed up over dinner. She talked and she was friendly to Lori and Mike, and even cracked a couple of jokes. The restaurant was one of the best in the area, with excellent food and beautiful décor. They finished the meal off with spectacular desserts, the first desserts for Mike and Nathan since baseball season started. They left the restaurant happy and well-fed, and drove off in separate cars.

"It's still early, Nathan. Let's go for a drive, okay?" Christa leaned her head on Nathan's shoulder.

"Yeah, sure. Where to?" He put his arm around her and she snuggled next to his shoulder.

"Well, you could show me some of the city lights. I've been here for over seven months and have never seen the city lit up at night."

Nathan looked at his watch, and then agreed to going to the overlook to see the night's skyline, with all the lights of the city coming up to meet it. It was still early enough. He parked the car at the overlook and asked her if she wanted to get out and walk a little bit. She agreed, but soon wanted to get back in the car because she felt chilly. The nights were still not warm enough for being outdoors for any length of time.

In the car, she put her head on his shoulder, and sighed.

"I'm sorry about neglecting you during the season. It's mandatory, though." Nathan squeezed her shoulders, pulling her closer to him.

"I know. The season's over so we can make up for lost time." She threw him a quick glance. "Right?"

"Uh, yeah, right. Christa…." She cut off his words with her lips, kissing him passionately and urgently.

"I've missed you." She whispered, but it came out more like a whine.

"Yeah, I've missed you, too." He tried to keep his tone casual.

She was running her fingers lightly along his neck, his ear, and the nape of his neck, sending shivers down his back. The old familiar arousal came back. She kissed him again, this time teasing him with her tongue. Her hand was on his thigh, slowly creeping up toward his groin. She began rubbing his penis through his clothes, and he felt like he was drowning. He went to unbutton the front of her dress, but she beat him to it. Her breasts were already exposed to him. He kissed both of them, and drew one into his mouth and gently sucked on it. She unzipped his pants again, and put her hand into his briefs and began massaging him. He moaned and adjusted himself so she could reach it better. He kissed her again. He was hot and breathing rapidly when he pulled her pantyhose down. She spread her legs a little so he could insert his finger into her. He could feel her wetness and knew at that moment he could take her. They slid down onto the seat and she worked her way under him, and opened her legs for him. He hesitated and looked down into her face.

"Please." She moaned. "Take me. I belong to you…..I want you so bad. I love you."

Those words hit him like ice water. "No. You don't love me. You don't even know what love is." He moved off of her, and tried to sit up. She grabbed him and tried to pull him back down. He removed her hands from around his shoulders and quickly sat up, pulling her partially up with him. He adjusted himself and zipped up his pants, without saying a word. She sat up and began redressing herself as well, moodily staring at the dashboard.

"So what is it? I'm not pretty enough?" She blurted after she finished buttoning up her dress.

"Don't talk stupid." He retorted.

"Well, what is it? Why don't you want me?" She had tears on her cheeks.

"Oh, I want you. Christa, have you ever had sex before?" He looked into her eyes as he asked it.

"No. You're the first boy I ever wanted to....do it...with." She confessed.

"Well, we can't. I have a responsibility to my parents, my grades, and most of all, to baseball. I don't want another responsibility...not yet."

"What the hell are you talking about?" She sounded angry.

Nathan sighed. "If we....you know....I would have a responsibility and an obligation to you. I don't want that. I want to be with you, go out with you, but I don't want to be with you because I feel responsible for you and obligated to you. Whatever happens in the future, I can wait for it."

Christa didn't speak for a moment. "That's stupid." She said after awhile.

"Yeah, well, I don't think it is." He started the car, put it in gear, and drove her home. They didn't speak all the way to her house, where she quickly said goodnight and got out of the car. He sat there watching her until she was inside, before he backed out and drove home. His mind was in turmoil all the way home. 'Maybe I should talk to dad again.' He thought. His mind was made up that he would talk to Al about all this again.

* * *

At breakfast in the morning, Nathan sat quietly while he listened to his dad talk about the new construction project he had going. When Al finished, Nathan found his chance.

"Dad, want to do some fishing today?" Nathan looked at Al, hoping he would see his need to talk to him.

Al picked up on it right away. "Sure, I'll get the gear out of the shed. Do you mind, Rose?" Rose said she didn't.

At the lake, they cast their lines in the water and sat down beside each other. Neither of them spoke for a few moments.

"So what's on you mind?" Al asked him. "Something wrong?"

"Well, no…not actually…" Nathan began. He related the incident to Al, leaving out some of the more intimate parts. "Dad, what you told me about the responsibility kept coming into my head. I kept hearing your words. That's what made me stop. Anyway, Christa thinks it's stupid. She's actually pretty pissed at me."

Al rubbed his chin in thought for awhile. "First of all, where do you find these girls? When I was your age, the brain in my head hadn't developed yet, but the other brain was fully developed and working overtime. The girls had the brains in their heads. I don't ever remember a girl in high school coming on to me like they do to you. Times have changed. That was the sexual revolution, I guess. The responsibility part still holds true, though. Nate, you don't want some girl relying on you to be there all the time. It will hold you back. Another thing…. women make it a habit to make you feel guilty. You sure as hell don't want that."

"Are you suggesting that I stop seeing Christa?"

"No." Al began rubbing his chin again. "Nate, I'm going to tell you something I have never even told your mother. This is between you and me…okay?"

Nathan nodded in agreement.

"When I was seventeen and in high school, I was dating a pretty brunette. We got hot and heavy, and before you knew it we were going at it every Saturday night. We thought we were in love. Before I was eighteen, we broke up….my fault. I found someone else I liked even better. Well, the brunette took it hard and she cut her wrists. She didn't survive. I still carry that guilt around. Now, she had to be unstable to do that, but never-the-less, I know why she did it. She called me that day and begged me to come back to her."

Nathan was stunned. He thought about it and began to feel uneasy. Christa depended way too much on him. He decided to 'cool it' for awhile. Al got a bite on his line and they dropped their conversation and brought in a large trout.

"Dinner." Al grinned. They walked back to the house feeling closer than they had ever been.

Christa didn't show up in school on Monday. Nathan was both relieved and worried. It was final week and she was going to miss the French final. He called her house and got no answer, so he went in and tackled the French final alone, putting Christa out of his head for an hour. Mike and Lori asked about her at lunch, and Nathan told them he didn't know if she was sick or not. He tried to call again, but there was still no answer. He was really beginning to worry. His thoughts kept going back to what Al told him.

He got home and called her house again, and this time she answered. "Where the hell were you all day?" He asked.

"I just didn't feel good. I slept all day."

"Are you okay now? You missed the French final."

"It figures that would be all you're worried about."

"Hey, I was plenty worried about you all day. What's wrong?"

"Nothing." She was short with him. "I gotta go." She was crying as she hung up.

Nathan sat staring at the phone. He wondered if he should go over there to see her. Yes, he should, he decided. He went to the kitchen and asked Rose to borrow the car for an hour.

"Just be home by dinner time, okay?" He nodded and left for Christa's.

She looked terrible when she answered the door. "Hey, Honey… what's the matter?" He tried to put his arms around her and she pushed him back.

Nathan was truly puzzled by her behavior. "What is it? Tell me."

She started to cry again. "I…I thought you really loved me….or at least liked me a lot…"

"I do!" 'Where was this coming from?' he wondered.

"But you pushed me away! I wanted you and you pushed me away, like you're not even attracted to me."

"That's bullshit! Of course I'm attracted to you…and I really care about you. We don't need sex to prove that!" He couldn't believe he was having this conversation. "Look…" He thought about what he was going to say to her, and sighed. "I don't want your life or my life ruined, that's all. I don't want to quit going out with you. You're the only one I want to be with….just not that way….for now. We have a whole life ahead of us. Come on, let me hold you."

He put his arms around her and this time she didn't push him away. She clung to him, sobbing; her shoulders heaving up and down. He stroked her hair and rocked her back and forth and just held her. He kissed the top of her head, and held her a little longer.

"I'm sorry, Nate…."

"Shhh…..it's okay. Now smile for me." The corners of his mouth turned up a little, hoping to get a smile out of her. "You're still my girl…..aren't you?" She nodded and finally smiled back at him. The next day she returned to school and made arrangements to take the French final. Everything between them turned back to normal.

* * *

Because of a late spring lake-effect snowstorm, the prom had been postponed until the Friday after final week. Most of the students were glad, because parents weren't going to permit them to drive cars during the snowstorm. Nathan and Mike picked up their tuxedos after classes on Friday, and were heading home to get ready. They stopped at the floral shop to pick up their corsages first. Nathan ordered daisies mixed with yellow tea roses since Christa's gown was yellow as was the trim on his tuxedo. Mike's corsage and trim were turquoise to match Lori's gown. Al was picking up a rental car for them so they would have a nice ride for their dates.

Nathan came down the stairs ready to go, and Rose gasped when she saw him, tears welling up in her eyes. "Oh my God….how handsome you look!" He rewarded her with a smile and she reached for the camera. "Will you come back here so we can get pictures of you *and* Christa?" He nodded.

After picking up Mike and Lori, and then Christa, he stopped back at his house so Rose could get all the pictures she wanted, and then headed for the prom. The ballroom at the hotel had been professionally decorated for the occasion, and it looked magnificent. Soft pink lights hung everywhere, and spring flowers were strategically placed among the tables and the pillars standing around the room. The backs of all the chairs had been covered with pastel linens, custom-made for them.

Music was playing when they arrived, so they found a table quickly and immediately went to the dance floor.

"You look really beautiful, Christa."

"Thanks. You don't look too shabby either." She gave him a smile, a wink, and quick squeeze. He laughed.

When they sat back down, there were ballots sitting on their table.

"Who do we vote for?" Christa asked.

"Well, who do you want to win?" Nathan countered.

"Us." She laughed when she said it.

"Well, then....that's who you vote for. Actually, I'm voting for me and Mike. He can be the queen." Nathan looked over at Mike and grinned. Mike gave him the finger and returned the grin.

When the votes were counted, neither of them won. Much to their surprise and delight, Cookie and her date won. Nathan and Mike were so happy for her. She won because everybody loved her. They went up to congratulate her and were touched by the tears in her eyes. Nathan asked her for a dance, and then Mike took his turn. They loved seeing Cookie this happy. She introduced them to her date, a boy named Aaron who went to a neighboring school. He seemed like a good guy, but in order to ensure Cookie's safety, both Mike and Nathan flanked him and told him how important Cookie was to them and that if anybody hurt her they would take it personally. Aaron got the message.

The last song was playing and everyone was dancing to it. Nathan ended the dance with a soft kiss on Christa's lips. She looked up at him, dreamily, and sighed. They walked back to the table with their arms around each other. The night ended without incident. Nathan took Lori home first, and then Christa. He and Mike decided they were going to do something together after the prom, but they didn't let the girls know. It was nothing special, but they just wanted to hang out together for awhile.

They ended up at Bumpy's, just sitting at a table talking and drinking sodas. They still had their tuxes on, but had loosened the ties.

"Have you thought about college yet, Mike?" Nathan was staring into his soda glass.

"Well, yeah....as a matter of fact, a lot lately. You?"

"Yeah, I want to go. I've been meaning to ask you....are you thinking about becoming a doctor?"

"Yeah! How did you know that?" Mike couldn't hide the surprise on his face.

"Chemistry….Latin…it was just a hunch."

"Well, I think that's what I want to be, anyway. It's a lot of school… eight years, to be exact." Mike held onto the base of his glass, turning it between his thumb and forefinger. He looked up at Nathan. "And what do you want to be when you grow up?"

Nathan laughed. "I don't know, exactly. I've been going online a lot and I always end up in the finance Web sites. I love reading the financial stuff….stuff like stocks, bonds, mutual funds. I think maybe financial planning and investing may be my strong points….besides pitching, that is. I read the financial pages in the paper, too."

"I just read the comics." They both laughed. "Seriously, Nate? I've been thinking about Ohio State."

"Yeah, me too. And if you go to med school, where would you like to go?"

"Pittsburgh. Good medical school." Mike spoke with conviction.

"You've done a lot of thinking on this, haven't you?" Nathan was impressed.

"Yeah, I guess I have."

"Well, hell….we should have these talks more often. That's how we learn about each other." Nathan grinned at Mike and he nodded, grinning back.

"Well, look at you two!"

They both looked up to see who was interrupting their conversation. An attractive girl, probably in her early twenties was standing there leaning on their table. She obviously had too much to drink.

"Wait right here….I'm going to get my friend." She held up her index finger, and disappeared.

"We should go." Mike spoke quietly. Nathan nodded.

It was too late. The girl was back with a friend. "Can we sit here with you?"

"We were just leaving, so you can have the table." Nathan told her.

"I don't want the table....I want you." She said to Nathan, as she touched his nose with her forefinger and slid down into the seat next to him. Her friend sat down beside Mike and immediately grabbed his hand.

"My name is Mandy and this is my friend Allison." She looked at Nathan and asked, "What's yours."

"Nathan, and that's Mike. We have to go."

"Aren't they adorable, Ally?" Ally agreed. "So where were you tonight? Wedding? Prom?"

"Prom." Mike answered this one.

"And where are you dates? Oh, yeah, I forgot, curfews." She leaned her head on Nathan's shoulder and giggled. "We don't have curfews. We can stay out all night." She giggled again.

"That's nice." Her head on his shoulder was starting to annoy him. He looked over and saw Ally running her hand through Mike's hair.

"What do you want, ladies? We have to go." Mike was equally annoyed.

The one named Mandy looked at Nathan and crouched down like a cat. "I want to fuck your brains out." She hissed, and then giggled some more. Nathan thought she was obnoxious.

"So do you guys have monkeys to go with these suits?" She was fingering the jacket of Nathan's tuxedo.

Mike piped up. "Yeah, I have a monkey for you. A one-eyed trouser monkey."

She let out one of her obnoxious giggles again. "Oh, that's cute. Prove it. Ally, how about some young stuff tonight?"

"Works for me." Ally chimed in. "Let me buy you boys a drink."

"No." Mike and Nathan said flatly, at the same time.

"You guys aren't gay, are you?" Mandy taunted.

"No, just picky." Mike spoke as he was trying to remove Allison's hand from his hair.

Nathan stood up and Mike followed. They almost made it to the car before Mandy and Allison caught up with them.

"Let's see that monkey." Allison grabbed Mike by the arm, and swung around in front of him, smashing up against him. She immediately put her hand between his legs. "Ooh. It's there. I feel it."

Nathan was taken by surprise. When he stopped walking, Mandy came up from behind, put her arms around him, and went for him between his legs. "That feels nice. Give me some." She whispered into Nathan's ear.

Nathan looked over at Mike. He was holding onto Ally, kissing her, and fondling her breast. "Let's go get into my car." He heard Ally say to Mike. Mike nodded.

"This your car?" Mandy was holding onto the door handle of the rented Buick. Nathan nodded. "Well….? Don't worry, your girlfriend won't find out."

Nathan opened the door and Mandy jumped in. Nathan went around to the driver's side and Mandy already had his door open. He slid into the seat, and she was there, her hands all over him. She kissed him hard, choking him with her tongue. Nathan smelled the alcohol on her breath and tried to ignore it. Her hand was fumbling with his zipper until she finally got it down.

"Ooh….your friend may have a monkey but you have a hell of a nice organ." She laughed at her wisdom. Her head dipped down and she took him into her mouth. Nathan almost went through the roof.

"Oh my God!" He moaned.

"You like that?" She smirked at him. He nodded.

She fumbled with her pantyhose and got them off quickly. "How about this?" She moved with the agility of a cat, quickly straddling him, and then sinking down onto his penis, swallowing it up. She glided up and down rhythmically and slowly, and then moving faster. Nathan held back, waiting for her. Suddenly she cried out, and then he released himself into her. He held her tightly and waited until the spasms stopped.

"Wow…that was good. Now if my husband was that good I wouldn't be here with you."

Nathan jerked his head up and stared at her.

"Your husband? What the fuck? You're married?"

"Yeah, so is Ally. We married for money, both of us. Our husbands are old men, past fifty. Neither one of them can keep a hard-on. You have no idea what it's like for us."

"You could have said something." Nathan was feeling guilty.

"Hey, don't feel bad. Nobody will know. You'll go home and call your girlfriend in the morning and everything will be fine. I'll go home a happy camper, for once."

"So how often do you do this?" He saw a red flag in his head.

"You're the first one, but you won't be the last. I forgot how great sex can feel." She was adjusting her clothing and putting her pantyhose back on as she spoke. "How old are you, anyway?" It sounded like an after-thought.

"Sixteen."

"Oh gees! I should be feeling guilty. But you're a man down there. What you got is pretty nice, do you know that?" She tweaked his penis lightly, and hopped out of the car. She leaned back into the car for a moment. "By the way, you're one of the best-looking kids I've ever seen." Then she was gone. Nathan sat in the car, and waited for Mike. He felt emotionally drained.

Mike hopped in the car within a couple of minutes after Mandy hopped out. "I don't think those were the kind of girls your dad was talking about." Mike sounded out of breath.

"They're married women." Nathan spoke flatly.

"Naw…they aren't…..are they?"

Nathan nodded. "She said they're married to guys past fifty…. married them for the money. We just screwed a couple of married women. Shit." He started the car and they headed for home.

Nathan stopped the car in front of Mike's house. As Mike opened the door to get out, he looked over at Nathan and reminded him. "At least the responsibility part doesn't apply."

Nathan shook his head, and drove home. His parents were in bed, thank God. He ascended the stairs quietly, undressed and got into bed. He lay on his back with his hands under his head, just staring up at the ceiling. Eventually he fell asleep.

2-17

School was officially out for the summer. On the first day of summer vacation, Nathan took Mike fishing at the lake.

"Do you catch a lot of fish here?" It was Mike's first time to go fishing.

"Well, yes....and no. My dad and I use this as a place to talk about stuff. This is where I got my "birds and the bees" talk. Sometimes we catch a trout. If it's big enough we take it home, my dad cleans it and cooks it."

"So did you bring me up here to tell me about the birds and the bees?" Mike joked.

"Yeah....birds shit and bees sting. Now you know."

Mike broke up laughing. "Hey, you didn't tell your dad about Mandy and Ally, did you?"

"Oh, hell no! There are some things that are better left unsaid."

"Yeah, no shit....I just wondered. I was afraid if you had, he would tell my dad. My dad and I don't have that same kind of thing like you and your dad. I mean....my dad's great and all...but he's not....cool, like your dad is."

"No way could I tell him I screwed a married woman. He'd kill me, or at least take my driving privileges away. Same thing, I guess. Let's walk back to my house and see if my mom has lunch for us. The fish aren't biting." Nathan grabbed the poles and reeled in the lines.

"Hey, our birthdays are coming up pretty soon." Mike reminded Nathan. "What do you want to do for them?"

Nathan shrugged. "I'll have to think about it."

* * *

For their birthdays, the girls decided to cook them dinner. Christa's mother was working the evening shift and she granted permission for the four of them to have the dinner at the townhouse, providing they would clean up after themselves. The girls bought steaks, baking potatoes, asparagus, salad fixings, and a cake mix for a birthday cake. Christa picked up a couple of movies from the video store for after dinner. Mike picked up Nathan and they were on their way.

"Do you think they can cook?" Nathan laughed as he spoke.

"Don't know. Hope you have money for McDonald's if they can't" Mike responded.

"Christa doesn't even have a dog to feed it to under the table if the food's no good. We may be in trouble."

Dinner turned out fine. The boys ate everything and complimented the girls on their effort. The birthday cake, decorated by Lori, was a big hit. They ate it while watching one of the movies Christa picked up. The four of them had a lovely evening together, and Nathan and Mike left happy. Of course, the big birthday event was going to be the next day, when Al and Alex took them to an Indians game. Al picked up box seat tickets, the best seats he could get.

At the stadium, they were searching for their seats when Mike grabbed Nathan's arm. "Don't look now, but Ally and Mandy are sitting over there. I think that must be their husbands."

Nathan froze. "Are you sure?"

"Yep."

Nathan slowly slid his eyes in the direction Mike indicated, and sure enough, it was them. To make matters more uncomfortable, their tickets were for seats directly behind theirs.

"Maybe they won't recognize us." Nathan hoped they wouldn't, but when they were seated, Mandy turned around and smiled at him.

"Nathan and Mike….how nice to see you. How the hell are you guys?"

"We're fine. How about you?" Mike tried to sound casual.

"Good. Oh, this is Gerald, my husband. And this….is Arnie, Ally's husband." She turned in her seat and touched the other man's shoulder. Mike and Nathan nodded and raised their hands in a greeting.

"Who the hell are they?" Gerald demanded.

Mandy was slick. "Oh, these are the two boys who helped us when our car wouldn't start that one night we were out so late."

"Oh." He turned around and stared at Mike and then Nathan. "Thanks for your help."

Mike and Nathan were relieved. They enjoyed the game and didn't give Mandy or Ally, or their husbands another thought.

Mandy didn't fool Al. 'My ass…." He thought to himself. "Nathan and Mike….ace mechanics. Right. That's got to be one of the stupidest grown men alive."

2-18

Nathan's SAT scores came on Saturday in mid-August. Nathan opened the envelope at the table where he and his parents were eating lunch. He smiled and set the results down in front of Al.

Al stared at the paper set in front of him and let out a low whistle. "Wow! Great scores, Nate. Our boy's going to college, Rose." He choked back tears as he handed the paper to Rose.

"Oh, Nathan! I'm so proud of you!" Rose got up and went around the table and hugged Nathan, and she didn't even try to hide her happy tears.

"So where are you going to apply? It's time to start, you know." Al tried to keep his voice even.

"I know, Dad. I think I want to go to Ohio State. I got an application the other day."

"Well, let's fill it out then! Just in case, send a couple more out to different schools....just to be on the safe side. Your mother and I have dreamed about you going to college, Nate. We have some money put away for you. Maybe not enough, but hopefully you can apply for some scholarships." Al reached over and ruffled Nathan's hair. "Damn, Nate, I'm so proud of you!"

Nathan grinned at Al, and ran to answer the ringing telephone. It was Mike.

"Hey, Dude! I got my scores today! They're good, too!"

"Dude, I got mine, too. I'm pretty happy about mine. I'm gonna do the application for Ohio." Nathan waited for Mike's response to that. He hoped Mike was going to choose Ohio State, too.

"Yeah, me, too, Nate. Maybe we'll both get there, huh?"

Nathan and Mike ended their conversation with plans to meet up later. Nathan thought about calling Christa but remembered that she was still in Connecticut visiting her father.

* * *

School began two weeks later. Both Nathan and Mike sent off applications to three colleges apiece, and would now wait for the responses from them.

Mike picked Nathan up on the first day of school. "Did Christa make it back?" He asked Nathan.

"Don't know. I tried to call her yesterday and there was no answer. Maybe she decided to live with her dad."

"And you're okay with that?" Mike glanced over at him.

Nathan shrugged. "If that's what's best for her, then yeah…I'm okay with it."

"Cool. I just thought maybe you'd be….I don't know, bent up about it…."

"She's not forever, Mike. I like being with her, but she's just not the one I want to spend my life with, or anything."

"How do you know that?"

"I just do. Did you ever think that there may be someone out there that you haven't discovered yet? Someone that's right for you?" Nathan shrugged again. "I don't know….maybe it's crazy, but I just feel that some day I'm going to meet *her*. It's like she's somewhere waiting for me and I just haven't met her yet."

"Very poetic, Dude. Hey, who's to say you're wrong? Maybe you're not. I guess it's something to look forward to." Mike shrugged and grinned at Nathan. "Let's go do our senior year!"

Christa returned from Connecticut and entered her senior year a week later. She was very cool to Nathan, and that puzzled him. He wondered what he did wrong. She sat at their table at lunch but was not very talkative.

"What's the matter, Christa?" Lori asked her.

"Nothing. Just tired. It was a long flight. We had two layovers."

"Oh." Lori let it drop.

"So….do you want to go out Friday night? How about the football game?" Nathan was still puzzled over her coolness.

"Sure, why not? Are you two going?" She looked mostly at Lori when she spoke.

"I guess we are. Mike?"

"Yeah, if you want, Lor." Mike slid his arm around Lori's shoulders.

Lori and Mike were in Nathan's next class, but Christa went to another. Nathan asked Lori if she noticed Christa's attitude.

"Yeah, Nate, I did. What's her problem?" Lori's face showed concern for Nathan.

Nathan shrugged. "I don't know. Maybe she met someone up in Connecticut. Maybe she really doesn't want to go out with me any more and she's afraid it'll hurt my feelings."

"Will it?" Lori asked him.

"Yes and no....I mean..."

"She's not his 'forever' is what he's trying to say." Mike answered for Nathan.

The one thing that bothered Nathan most about Christa is that she didn't join anything. No clubs or sports; not even the choir when Nathan asked her to try out for it. He liked a girl who was independent and did her own thing once in awhile. Christa seemed to cling to him, and whatever he was interested in, she developed the same interest. If Christa would have joined anything, Nathan would have supported her in it.

Nathan didn't see Christa for the rest of the day. When he got home he thought about calling her, but decided against it. He wasn't up for a moody conversation.

* * *

One Saturday in early October Christa called Nathan and asked him to come over. It surprised him, since other than the football game they attended together right after school started, she declined every time he asked her to go out. He quit asking her after the third time she turned him down. He agreed to be there within the hour.

"So Christa, what's up?" He came right out and asked.

"Nate, do you love me?" She came right to the point.

Nathan stared at her for a moment before answering. "I'm very fond of you, Christa. You know that. Love....well, that's something that has to wait. I have a lot to focus on, things to accomplish before I can even think about the L-word. Why is this so important to you? I'm *with* you. I don't go out with anybody else. Why can't you just let things be the way they are? Enjoy what we have? Why do you have to hear the word 'love'?"

"Because I'm pregnant." She blurted out.

"What? You and I....we never did anything. What are you saying?" Nathan felt sick.

"It's someone I met in Connecticut this summer. I...." Christa was crying.

"Well, then maybe you should tell *him* you're pregnant." Nathan turned and walked out, slamming the door. He swung the car out of the driveway and peeled off a layer of rubber from the tires as he sped away.

Nathan stopped the car in front of Mike's house and found Mike in the garage cleaning the grass off of the lawnmower blades.

"Hey, Dude, what's up?" Mike grinned, looking up from the upside down mower.

"Christa's pregnant."

"Oh, man. I told you to make a stop at the drugstore, Dude."

"It's not mine."

"It's not?"

"No. We never did anything."

"Well, whose is it?"

"She said it's some guy in Connecticut. I told her to go tell him. We're done...obviously."

"Hey, I'm sorry, man....I don't know what to say."

"It's all right. Don't worry about it. I'm already over it. She could be a pain in the ass at times anyway. There's a lot of other chicks out there." Nathan grinned to show Mike that it really was okay.

* * *

On Monday, Nathan saw Christa in the hallway but avoided talking to her. She didn't show up at their table in the lunchroom, and Nathan was glad of that. Lori was shocked when Mike and Nathan told her about Christa's plight.

"I think she was trying to trap you into that situation. I thought that all along."

"I think maybe you're right, Lori. She sure as hell wanted to do it." Nathan just looked down at his plate, no longer hungry.

Christa left school and returned to Connecticut. Nathan never heard from her again, and realized that he didn't miss her either.

Mike and Lori were making plans for the homecoming dance. They encouraged Nathan to ask someone so they could make it a foursome. He ended up asking a girl named Stephanie Lewis. She was pretty and it was obvious that she was delighted to be going to the dance with Nathan. They had a lot of fun at the dance, and Nathan asked her to go out with him the next day. The weather was still warm, so they made plans to visit the zoo. Mike and Lori agreed to go with them. When the girls went to the ladies room behind the zoo's concession stand, Stephanie asked Lori what happened to Christa. All Lori told her was that Christa went back to Connecticut to live with her father. Stephanie let it drop, just happy that Nathan was taking her out now.

The following Saturday, Nathan and Al went fishing.

"Something you need to talk about?" Al knew his son well.

Nathan told him about Christa.

"Are you okay? How do you feel about it?" Al studied Nathan's face.

"Yeah, I'm okay. Wow, you know....she really wanted that to happen, I think. I'm just glad it didn't happen with me."

"Me too, son.....me, too." Al put his hand on Nathan's shoulder and tightened his grip a little. "You know, I'm glad we have these talks. It lets me know that I can trust you, and that you trust me. I just won't ask about Mandy and Ally." Al gave Nathan a sly grin.

"Oh, gees! That was a mistake. No, it was rape, I think. Mike and I didn't have a chance. We didn't know they were married until....it was too late. What a sad pair they are, huh, dad?"

Al nodded.

"Dad?" Nathan waited until he had Al's undivided attention. "This may sound a little weird, but....I just have a feeling that somewhere out there is a girl...just waiting for me. And she's 'the one'....know what I mean? I haven't met her but I can feel her. Does that sound... stupid?"

Al sat rubbing his chin and stared at the water. After a moment, he said, "No, it doesn't. She's your soul mate...that's why you feel her.

I'll bet that wherever she is, she can feel you, too...but she just doesn't know who you are. When you two find each other, you'll both know. That's your true love." Al was quiet for another moment. "You have a beautiful soul, Nate...you really do."

* * *

Nathan got his acceptance letter to Ohio State. He couldn't have been more ecstatic. He trotted to the telephone to call Mike, but the phone rang before he could dial. It was Mike.

"We're going to OSU together?" Nathan was grinning into the phone.

"Yep! We have to go down there and check out the campus. Wanna go over the weekend? Our parents can go, too. We go in one car and they go together in the other. Sound good?" Mike was hoping it would work out that way.

"I have to check with my parents, but hell yeah, it sounds good!" Nathan was pumped up over the prospect of college. He really hoped there would be a scholarship to go with the acceptance. There was still time to earn it.

It turned out the way the boys wanted it. The families went down to the campus the following weekend, with Mike and Nathan driving down together. Nathan followed Mike's parents' car all the way down to the campus.

Mike looked over at Nathan. "Hey, do you think there's a chance for any kind of scholarship?"

"We have to apply for some. Hey, there's baseball, there's even scholarships for choir. We should be able to get something. Both of us have good grades and good SAT scores."

They arrived at the campus and spent the afternoon wandering around, checking everything out. They met with a man from the dean's office and he told them a little about the school. He seemed to like both of them, and said he was there to help if they had any questions. After they left the campus, all six of them decided they were hungry, so they found a nice restaurant and enjoyed a delicious dinner. Life was good for all of them.

2-19

December brought bad weather. The first snow occurred on the first day of the month, and it seemed like it snowed every day. The Thanksgiving holiday was behind them, and Christmas was approaching—Christmas and Steven's birthday. On Thanksgiving, Nathan, Al, and Rose traveled to Nathan's grandmother's house to spend the holiday with her. Nathan loved his Grandma Perletti, and she adored him. He was her favorite grandchild, probably because he was the one she got to see the least. All of Nathan's cousins lived near her, just outside of Fort Wayne, Indiana. Al and Rose lived there at one time, too, but moved to Northern Ohio when Al was offered a lucrative promotion and relocation with his company. He took it and Rose and he moved away from the family. When the company cut back and closed Al's division, they were already established in their community, and Al quickly found work with the company in which he still worked. Financially, he was doing quite well. Steven's illness was very costly, but his company insurance covered quite a bit of it, and that was a blessing. He was still financially able to maintain a decent lifestyle and put money away for Nathan's college as well as retirement for himself when the time came.

Nathan enjoyed Thanksgiving with his grandmother and his aunts, uncles, and cousins. He began to feel like an only child, with Steven being gone, so he loved the big family atmosphere. Plans were made for his Uncle Joe and Aunt Betty, along with his two cousins, Joey and Linda, to come to Ohio the day after Christmas and stay through New Year's. Joey was only six months younger than Nathan and Linda was two years behind him. It was going to be great having family around, and Nathan looked forward to it.

Steven's thirteenth birthday—December fifteenth—was approaching. Al and Rose wanted to see him, but he told them to "fuck off". That got him time in the 'quiet room' at the facility. They sent a birthday gift, addressed to the psychiatrist, and wondered if Steven would accept it. Apparently he accepted the gift, but nothing changed. A week after his birthday, he sent a thank you letter that was brief and to the point—all it said was "Thanks for the birthday present.

Suck my dick. Die, Nathan. I hate you. Steven." Rose tore it up and threw it away, sobbing.

Nathan and Mike took the girls to the Christmas dance, promising their parents that they would be very careful on the icy roads.

"Remember, pick up the girls, go straight to the dance, then come straight home afterward, okay?" Al was worried about the bad roads.

"Okay, Dad. You have my word." Nathan told him.

"Remember, if you have a problem, just call me…okay? Promise me." Al kept looking outside.

"I promise, Dad. Hey, I don't want anything to happen to me either."

Al looked at him mischievously. "It's the car I'm worried about." He gave him the familiar soft punch on the chin. "By the way, you look good."

Nathan was wearing a black and white tweed suit that looked custom-made for him. Rose produced another new tie for him. He was wearing a light gray shirt, and the blue, gray and red striped tie looked good with it. Stephanie was wearing a red velvet dress that complimented her blond hair and green eyes, and accentuated her small waist. Of course, they went with Mike and Lori. At lunch one day, Lori laughed when she told Stephanie that Mike and Nathan were attached at the hip. "Sometimes I feel like the other woman." She joked.

The dance ended early because of the snow. Nathan and Stephanie danced the last dance, he kissed her on the dance floor, then they made a beeline to get their coats and drive home. Already, it looked like a foot of snow had come down. The ride home was treacherous and Nathan drove very carefully. When he finally pulled into his own driveway, he was relieved. The lights were on in the house, so he assumed his parents must have been worried.

When he came in through the door, Al called out to him. "Nate? Everything okay?"

"Yeah, Dad, everything's fine. The roads are really bad. The dance let out early because of the snow. I didn't have to be told twice to drive straight home. This is where I want to be right now. I'm freezing."

Rose was standing in the doorway to the family room. "How about some hot chocolate?"

"Couldn't think of anything I would want more right now." Nathan smiled at his mother.

"Good. Go get out of the wet clothes and I'll have it ready in a few minutes. How about some for you, Al?"

"Good deal. See you all in the kitchen." Al folded the newspaper in front of him. He had been staring at it, but hadn't been able to concentrate on it. He just wanted Nathan home safely.

They met in the kitchen where Rose had the pot of cocoa cooking on the stove.

"Just in time. It's ready. So let's hear about the dance, especially Stephanie. Did she look pretty?"

"Yeah, she did. We had fun. Stephanie has a good sense of humor. She wants to be an actress, so she belongs to the drama club at school."

"When do we get to meet her?"

Rose was curious about this one. She always thought that Christa was too sullen and quiet for Nathan. She was nice, but not much fun. She wondered what Nathan saw in her, besides the fact that she was very pretty.

"You would have met her last week if the Christmas concert hadn't been canceled. She was going to go to it…just to hear me sing, of course." Nathan smiled. "Maybe Christmas. If the roads clear up, I'll bring her here sometime on Christmas Eve…if that's all right."

"That's fine, Honey. We'd like to meet her." Rose looked at Nathan and smiled.

'He's a great kid.' She thought to herself.

* * *

By Christmas, the roads were clear. Nathan had plans to pick up Stephanie early on Christmas Eve and take her to his house to visit with his family. After that, they would go back to Stephanie's and spend some time there with her family. Christmas Day was reserved for their families.

Nathan ushered Stephanie through the front door. "Mom? Dad?"

"In here, Nate. Come on in….it smells good in here!" Al was sitting at the kitchen table drinking a cup of coffee and sampling some of the cookies Rose had been baking for the past three weeks. Rose was standing at the stove stirring a pot of something that smelled delicious.

"Hi, Dad, Mom….this is Stephanie." Al stood up and extended his hand to this pretty blond girl. "Here, sit down. Do you drink coffee?" He got up and pulled out a chair for her.

"Yes, I could use a cup of coffee. It's freezing outside!" Stephanie looked grateful for the offer as she sat down.

Rose set a mug of coffee in front of her, and put one in front of Nathan. The cream and sugar were already on the table. "Hi, Stephanie, it's nice to meet you. Merry Christmas."

Rose gave her a winning smile and then a quick smile of approval to Nathan. She placed a plate of homemade cookies down in the center of the table.

"Thank you. And Merry Christmas to you. Thank you for having me over."

"Nathan tells me you're in the Drama Club. You want to be an actress?" Al liked this girl. Nathan could tell by how easily his father spoke to her.

"Hopefully, I will be. I work hard at it, but there is so much competition." She liked Al immediately. He was a little like her father; she could tell.

"Why don't you show her the tree, Nathan? Stephanie, Nathan did the tree on Sunday. It's just beautiful."

"Okay, Mom. Want to see the tree, Steph?" Nathan stood up and waited for Stephanie to stand.

They went from the kitchen to the family room. Al and Rose could hear her exclaiming over the beautiful tree. Al looked at Rose, and nodded. "Better." Rose knew that Al just compared Stephanie to Christa.

After having rejoined Al and Rose in the kitchen and having a second cup of coffee, a couple of cookies, and lots of small talk, Nathan and Stephanie got up to leave for her house. Nathan grabbed gifts he bought for Stephanie from under the tree, and they left to go visit with her parents.

Nathan was received warmly by Stephanie's parents. Mr. Lewis, Stephanie's father took Nathan into the living room where the tree stood. "What do you think of the tree?" Jay Lewis was a friendly guy, open and easy-going. He was talking to Nathan like he was an old friend.

"It looks good. It's a lot bigger than ours, I think." This observation made Mr. Lewis beam with pride.

Stephanie came into the living room with a tray of eggnog and the inevitable cookie assortment. Some were the same kind of cookies that Rose made, but there were some different ones that Nathan had never seen before.

"Sit! Sit! Mrs. Lewis will be in shortly. She's getting something out of the oven." Jay Lewis patted the back of the sofa as an invitation for Nathan to sit there.

Louise Lewis came into the living room with another tray of baked goodies. "Hi! I'm Stephanie's mom, and you have to be Nathan."

Nathan started to answer, when Stephanie interjected, "Does he have to, Mom? Can't he be Bob or Bill if he wants to?"

Nathan laughed. "Yes, I'm Nathan. It's nice to meet you, Mrs. Lewis."

"Isn't my daughter a smart aleck? That's where her younger brother and sister get it, I think." She smiled warmly at Nathan.

Nathan looked at Stephanie with surprise. "I didn't know you had a brother and sister."

"I don't like to talk about terrible things, so I don't. I have a brother who is older than I am. He's in college. Then I have the twerp. He's thirteen. My sister is fifteen."

"Where are they now?" Nathan was curious as to why they weren't around. Stephanie called her younger siblings terrible things. She had no idea. His brother was a terrible thing.

"Oh, they'll be popping in at any moment. Samantha's ice skating with her friend and Cody is next door at the Silverman's house. He's enthralled by their menorah. Jason, our oldest is at his girlfriend's house. He may or may not be home soon."

"Well, you two enjoy the cookies and pastries. I have some last-minute wrapping to do, and my wife has some things cooking in the kitchen. We'll rejoin you probably when the younger ones get home." Jay smiled and nodded at them and darted up the stairs.

"How about opening your presents, Steph?" Nathan bought Stephanie a watch when he noticed she didn't wear one. He hoped she liked it. His other gift to her was a sweatshirt from Ohio State. He brought a box of chocolates for the rest of the family, and hoped that was sufficient. It was a small one pound box he purchased before he realized that there were so many of them.

Stephanie reached under the tree and grabbed a wrapped package for Nathan. "You have to open yours, too."

He handed her the larger package first. She quickly opened it and exclaimed, "Ohio State! That's where you're going to college! Oh, wow! Thank you! Now I'll have it when you're away and I'll think about you every time I wear it. Now open yours."

Nathan was taken by surprise. It was a sweatshirt, also. This one had the logo of Carnegie Mellon University on it. She was watching his reaction and smiling up at him when he looked at her. "That's where I've been accepted."

Nathan couldn't have had a wider grin. "Really? Hey, Steph, that's great! I'm happy for you. Great school! You have to open the other one now. Go for it."

"At CMU I can continue my drama classes. Do you know that? They have a wonderful liberal arts program…." She was talking while she took the wrapping off of the smaller package, and then she stopped. "Nathan….oh, Nathan….this is beautiful! Thank you! Thank you so much!" She slid over to him and put her arms around his neck. "I really love it. I broke my other watch and…….."

Her words were cut off by his lips. "Merry Christmas," He said softly, when the kiss ended.

She smiled at him and tugged on his hand. "Come on, we have to do this legally."

"What? What are you talking about?" He was caught off-guard by her declaration.

Stephanie pointed up at the ceiling fan. "Mistletoe." She laughed and dragged him up to stand under the mistletoe. They grinned at each other and then he took her face between his hands and kissed her ever so sweetly once, and then kissed her again.

"Ahem." Nathan heard a masculine voice behind him, and let go of Stephanie, slightly embarrassed.

"Hey, it's okay. That's what mistletoe is for." Mr. Lewis was standing there wearing a grin of his own.

* * *

Christmas Day was quiet at the Perletti's house. Nathan opened his gifts while Rose and Al opened theirs from Nathan and from each other. They invited Mike to have brunch with them when he showed up to wish them a merry Christmas. There was no mention of Steven, or of a visit to Steven. Nathan wondered about that, but decided not to say anything, since it always brought tension into the house. It was getting so that he barely remembered Steven. He hadn't seen him in three years. The day moved too slowly for Nathan. He was looking forward to seeing his cousins the next day.

The holiday week was a whirlwind of activity. Nathan loved having his cousins around. He and Joey became good friends that week, and Linda obviously had a crush on him. The house was full of chatter and constant laughter. Nathan couldn't remember ever hearing that much noise coming from their house. Mike came over to visit, and Linda's attention immediately turned to him. Alex and Cindy Smith came with Mike and the adults claimed the family room as theirs for the evening. Al mixed drinks in the blender and Rose put various hors d'oeuvres and snack foods on the tables. The younger crowd cloistered themselves in Nathan's room with the stereo blasting. Lori and Stephanie joined the crowd in Nathan's room, and soon they had their own party going. Stephanie brought her brother, Cody, and soon Linda focused her attention on him.

The week ended too soon. Nathan felt like they were a normal family, for a change. Not that they were abnormal, but it was just the three of them, with Steven lurking in the shadows all the time. The three of them lived together in peace and harmony, but the chaos seemed more like a normal atmosphere.

New Year's Eve was at the Perletti house. Rose and Al invited the Smith's and a few other friends, and Nathan was permitted to have a few of his friends at the party, as well. Al, Nathan and Joey brought the stereo down from Nathan's room and hooked it up in the family room. Rose and Betty, along with Linda's help, prepared food. Al and Joe made a run to purchase beer and liquor and mixers. Mike, Nathan and Joey drove to the local discount store and purchased noise makers and various New Year's hats and leis for everybody. They also found plastic champagne glasses, and Rose congratulated them for their good thinking.

The party was what the Perletti's needed. They enjoyed entertaining their friends, one of which was Officer Ken Banks and his wife Sherry. He quietly told Al that he was glad to be there on a happy occasion for a change. Al just nodded. At midnight, Nathan grabbed Stephanie and kissed her. Everyone was kissing their partners, and then the round of kissing and hugging started among the partiers. Al hugged Nathan and whispered, "This is your year, Nate. Happy New Year. I love you, son."

"I love you, too, Dad." He hugged his father back and consequently, missed the tear running down Al's cheek.

2-20

The new year brought the last semester of high school for Nathan. He planned on enjoying it, and then enjoying the summer before going off to college. Of course, that old familiar antsy feeling was coming over him by now. It was less than two months until baseball season. He enjoyed life all year, but he lived for baseball season.

He met up with Mike and Lori in the lunch room. Stephanie quickly joined them.

"Great party, Nate." Mike and Lori had talked about it all day long on New Year's Day. "Your cousins are pretty cool."

"Yeah, I was sorry to see them leave yesterday. We had a good time all week." Nathan reached for Stephanie's hand and interlaced his fingers through hers. "Did Steph tell you her news?"

"What news?" Mike and Lori asked simultaneously.

Nathan looked at Stephanie and nodded. "Go ahead. Tell them."

"I got accepted at CMU—Carnegie Mellon University." Stephanie was proud to make the announcement.

“Great!” Again, Mike and Lori were simultaneous.

“We have to celebrate all of our acceptances. I just got accepted at Michigan State.” Lori beamed as she told them.

“COOL! Too cool!” Nathan raised his hand for a high five from Lori. They made plans to go out to dinner on the following Saturday in order to celebrate their collective acceptances.

* * *

At the end of the school day, Mike caught up with Nathan. “I guess we’re losing our women. They’re both going to different colleges. They’ll probably end up meeting some grad students and we’ll be history.”

Nathan shrugged. “Whatever is best for them....and us. If we’re meant to be together, we’ll see each other again....after college.”

“You have got to be the most unselfish person I have ever met. You’re also strange. You like Stephanie, don’t you?”

“Yeah, I do. But......I don’t think she’s.......”

“Your ‘forever’, I know. Maybe you should write poetry, or something.”

“Bite me.” Nathan laughed. “Mike, is Lori the one you want to spend the life of your life with?”

Mike thought for a few seconds. “Hmm.....I don’t know. Maybe.... but then I haven’t seen who else is out there.”

“Well, that’s the point. Lori is here now, but you may meet someone who you like better. You don’t know that yet, because you haven’t been anywhere to find out. If it’s right for you and Lori, you’ll come back and find her. It’s that simple.”

* * *

Coach Belinski called the first practice of the season. It was bitter cold outside so the practice would be held in the gymnasium as in other years. As usual, Mike and Nathan were the first ones in the locker room, ready to get out there and practice.

The coach called to them. "Mike, Nathan, come in my office for a minute."

They looked at each other, wondering if they were in trouble for something. Inside his office, the coach pointed to two chairs and closed the door. Nathan and Mike looked at each other, puzzled.

"Okay, now that I have your undivided attention, I just thought I'd tell you I'm working on setting you guys up with baseball scholarships. This season there will be people watching both of you. I'm pushing for you to get scholarships. You're both going to Ohio State?"

They nodded.

"Okay, I'm working on it for you. Let's hit the gym."

"Thanks coach," They yelled over their shoulders as they headed out toward the gym, grinning at each other; both of them full of hope.

* * *

Nathan was not the starting pitcher for the first game. He sat on the bench and groaned as Tyler, the starting pitcher walked his first and second batter. The third batter hit a single, loading the bases. By the end of the first half of the first inning, the team was losing by two runs. Nathan's team was at bat, and the first two batters struck out. Bobby batted third, and hit a triple, and that brought the spectators to their feet. The fans sat back down when the fourth batter struck out, ending the inning with the team still behind by two runs. In the second inning, Tyler gave up two hits, and a walk, which loaded the bases again. The coach called 'time' and waved for Nathan to come to the mound. The next three batters were struck out with no wasted pitches. This brought the crowd to their feet again, cheering Nathan on. They got their two runs back, plus two more, when Mike hit one over the fence with a runner on base. Nathan didn't give up a hit, so the game ended 4-2, their first victory of the new season.

As had become their pattern, everyone congregated at Bumpy's for after-game burgers, fries, and drinks. Baseball season was underway. Nathan and Mike were now in their element, and couldn't have been more motivated.

* * *

The season was already half-over, and the weather was still brisk, but warming. So far, the team remained undefeated, and the season looked like it would be a repeat of the previous year. Nathan and Mike had all but forgotten about Coach Belinski's said intention to get them scholarships.

At the end of the twelfth game, they ran off the field, victorious once again. Mike and Nathan trotted into the locker room, giving each other a high five. Nathan pitched another no-hitter, and Mike had blasted two homeruns over the fence, scoring a total of five of their eight runs. As they entered the locker room, Tyler passed them, saying, "Coach wants to see you two in his office—now."

Nathan and Mike didn't give it another thought. They immediately went to the back of the locker room to Coach Belinski's office. There appeared to be a crowd in his office when they got to the door. The office was small, and at the moment, quite full. Three men were sitting around the coach's desk.

"Come on in, boys." The coach waved them into the small space. Belinski introduced them to Nathan and Mike as scouts from Ohio State. Nathan felt a little jolt in the pit of his stomach, and he was sure Mike felt the same thing.

The designated spokesman, Mr. Cox looked Nathan in the eye, and then stared at Mike. "I'm going to get right to the point. Do you boys have an interest in playing baseball for Ohio State?"

"Yes!" Nathan and Mike answered in unison. Nathan's heart was pounding.

"We've looked over your transcripts and your participation in school activities, and we also checked into your backgrounds. You both turned up squeaky-clean—that's good. You both appear to be gentlemen of high character. I need for you both to fill out these apps, and get three letters of recommendation…and none can be from your girlfriends. I'm sure you both have plenty of those." He ended his quick rundown of their investigation with a quick wink

"Coach, get these things collected and back to me within a week. Then we'll review, and let you know." At these parting words, all three men got up and briskly left the office and walked toward the exit.

Nathan and Mike were grinning at each other first, and then at Coach Belinski. "Thanks, Coach." Nathan smiled at Belinski, giving him the benefit of seeing all his straight, white teeth.

"Don't thank me....you're only getting what you deserve." Belinski clapped them both on the shoulders. "Now get the hell out of my office and get those apps done. I want them, along with the three letters, by Monday." Coach Belinski was already pulling on his jacket and turning out the lights.

Nathan and Mike jumped in Rose's car and headed toward Bumpy's, where the parents were waiting.

"What the hell took you so long?" Al greeted them when they walked through the door. Both boys were still wearing their uniforms, as well as the grins of the century.

They quickly related what had happened, both talking at once, and then finishing each other's sentences. Neither of them lost the grin on his face though the entire retelling of the meeting. Nathan and Mike gave each other another high five, and then the rest of the families joined in, giving high fives all around the table. Food was ordered and the party was on, with everybody laughing and talking.

Al looked over at Nathan for a moment, and then softly said to him, "It's happening, Nate. Just like I knew it would. You're going to make it. Damn, Kid....you're going to make it. I feel it!" Al took a deep breath to regain his composure. He concentrated on his plate of food in order to keep from embarrassing himself by bawling in front of everybody. Damn, he loved this boy!

2-21

Nathan and Mike were scheduled to sing in the Spring Concert. It was the end of April, and this would be the last time they would sing with the choir. They both admitted that it had been fun, and they were glad they joined the choir, but they contended that they would rather be playing baseball.

Nathan, wearing his grey suit, was ready to leave for the concert. He joined Al and Rose in the kitchen, where they were enjoying coffee and conversation. "Ready?" He stood in the doorway observing them.

"Ready!" They exclaimed.

Nathan performed a solo that night. Rose sat with a tissue in her hand, smiling up at the stage, mesmerized by her son's beautiful voice. It had gotten stronger over the last couple of years, and he really began to sound like a professional singer.

The concert ended with the choir director naming the seniors and commending them on their fine participation through their high school years. She wished them luck and happiness as they go on toward their endeavors. Rose needed a new tissue.

Nathan and Mike appeared at their parents' side after the final curtain. Al put one of his hands on Nathan's shoulder, and the other on Mike's. "What do you say we go somewhere and have a late supper? All of us....my treat."

* * *

There were four events left on the agenda before Nathan was no longer a high school student. There was the prom, then the awards banquet, and then graduation, but most importantly was finishing the baseball season in victory.

There were two games left, and the team was once again undefeated. The talk around the school was that Nathan and Mike should get all the credit for the undefeated season. Mike hit at least one homerun in every game, and Nathan continued his winning streak, never having lost a game. He had the best record in the history of the school's baseball team, and that record probably went beyond his own school.

On Monday, before the next to the last game, Nathan came home and found an envelope waiting for him. He noted the return address and tore it open. As soon as he read the first tow lines, he let out a whoop, which brought Rose running. He grabbed Rose and picked her up and swung her around, still holding the letter in his hand.

"What? What is it?" Rose was laughing. Nathan had never done that before.

"I got it!! I got the scholarship!! Mom, I'm playing for Ohio State on a scholarship!"

"Oh, Nathan! Wait until your dad gets home. He's going to be thrilled! Oh, Nathan....I'm so proud of you!" Tears were welling up in Rose's eyes, but she was laughing. "My son, the ball player. I knew it from the time you were three."

Nathan grinned at her. "Yeah?"

"Yeah." Rose responded, and her thoughts drifted back to that day when Nathan hit the plastic ball in the front yard. Al had called her out to see him do it. She came out of her reverie when the phone rang. Nathan grabbed up the phone. It was Mike.

Rose could hear him whooping it up even though Nathan was holding the phone. "I guess Mike got a scholarship, too?" Grinning, Nathan nodded to her.

Al pulled into the driveway and Nathan was there to intercept him. "Dad! I got it!! Me and Mike….we both got 'em!"

Al jumped out of the truck and grabbed the paper from Nathan's hand. "Well, I'll be a son-of-a-bitch!" This time it was Al who picked Nathan up and swung him around. "You didn't think I could still do that, did you?" He and Nathan were both laughing. "Mike got one, too? Rose, call the Smith's. We're all going out tonight."

There was much celebration at the steakhouse that night. Mike and Nathan had not stopped grinning yet. The two sets of parents were extremely proud of their sons, and didn't hesitate to let the entire restaurant in on the news. Many people congratulated the boys while they ate their steak dinners. Mike and Nathan shared another of many high fives. Life was good.

* * *

The next two games were victories. Nathan and Mike were carried off the field at the end of the last game. There would be divisional, sectional, and then the state championship game, but for right now, all they cared about was the sweet taste of a victorious end to high school baseball. They clapped Coach Belinski on the back and shook his hand, and then shook hands with all of their teammates. The word was out about the scholarships and many of the players congratulated them, telling them they deserved it. Tomorrow would be a day of well-earned rest for them. The day after that, they would start preparing for the prom. Mike was taking Lori and Nathan was taking Stephanie. They agreed to sit at the same table with their old friend, Cookie and Aaron.

Aaron had been upgraded from just a date to being her boyfriend, and Cookie was in love. They all looked forward to prom night when they would all be together as friends, maybe for the last time.

* * *

Nathan looked incredible in his powder blue tuxedo, with the ivory cummerbund and bow tie. Stephanie's gown was ivory with powder blue trim, and the combination would prove to be a stunning match. Nathan had Stephanie's corsage made up of powder blue flowers entwined with ivory ribbons. Since Al had rented the car the year before, Alex Smith agreed to cover the rental for this year. Mike picked up Lori, then picked up Nathan, and headed over to collect Stephanie. They would make a stop back at Nathan's house so Rose and Al could get some pictures.

Stephanie was standing in the living room when Nathan arrived. She looked lovely, and Nathan didn't hesitate to tell her so. "You're beautiful, Steph.... really beautiful."

They endured the photo shoot at Stephanie's house, and then returned to the Perletti house so Al and Rose could have their shots.

This year the prom was held at the country club. Professional decorators worked all day to achieve a glamorous look, and they succeeded. Everything was done in white and blue, the school colors, and the ballroom looked incredible. Nathan, Mike, Stephanie, and Lori looked for Cookie, and decided she hadn't arrived yet. They found a table to accommodate six to eight people and settled into the seats. Cookie and Aaron arrived shortly after they sat down. Something was happening to Cookie, Mike and Nathan noted. She lost her baby fat and was becoming very attractive. Nathan thought to himself that it was probably her inner beauty finally coming to the surface.

When the music started, they all went to the dance floor and danced the first dance, each with their partner. For the second dance, they formed a circle and danced with their arms around each other. The feeling was bittersweet for Nathan. He loved these people who were his dearest friends, but he was anxious to get on with his life; begin new adventures.

Nathan and Stephanie were the crowned royalty of the prom. For the first time in his life, Nathan felt embarrassed and awkward. It was a reaction he never expected in himself. He self-consciously accepted the crown and he and Stephanie danced the royal dance together. For Stephanie's sake, he was glad they were chosen. She seemed delighted by it and it helped her end her high school career on a high note.

* * *

The prom was behind them. All that was left was the awards banquet and then graduation.

Nathan, Al and Rose arrived at the awards banquet before Mike and his parents, and were already seated when they got there. To Nathan's and Mike's delight, Cookie and her parents would be joining them at their table. Cookie was receiving an award for outstanding citizen and also for being the editor of the school newspaper. Nathan spotted Cookie coming in the door with her parents and waved her over to their table. Something was definitely different about Cookie these days. She was curvaceous and pretty. Mike whistled at her as she and her parents joined them.

"Oh, stop it! I always knew you had the hots for me." She punched Mike's arm as she spoke, but she couldn't hide the pleased smile on her face.

Nathan and Mike received their pins for choir participation, and awards for academic achievement. Cookie was next to go up on stage to get her award for her work as editor. Nathan and Mike applauded her and made cat calls when she left the stage. Cookie's parents took it all good-naturedly, and in fact, seemed to be enjoying the attention their daughter was getting from two of the best-looking boys in the school. At the end of the clubs and groups awards, Cookie was called back up on stage to receive her award for being an outstanding citizen. Since the entire school voted on who should receive this award, it was an honor to receive it. Cookie's parents were pleased, and Cookie couldn't hide the tears in her eyes when she accepted it. Nathan and Mike stood up when they applauded her, and the rest of the audience followed suit. Both boys kissed her on each cheek when she returned to the table.

"I love you guys. You know that, right?" She hugged them both.

"We love you, too." Nathan assured her.

Sports were the next category of the evening. The football team received their letters and awards, and then it was time for baseball. Nathan and Mike each got their final high school letters for baseball, and the announcement was made concerning their scholarships. The final baseball award was the four feet high trophy for most valuable player.

Coach Belinski stepped up to the podium to present it. "By unanimous decision, this trophy for most valuable player goes to..... Nathan Perletti!"

The applause was deafening. Rose was wiping the tears from her eyes when she looked at Al. This time Al didn't try to hide his tears. "God, Rose....I'm so damned proud of him! I'm making a fool of myself, but I can't help it."

Alex Smith leaned over toward him and patted his shoulder. "You don't look like a fool, Al. You look like a man who is so damned proud of the son he loves. Congratulations! Nathan deserves it. He's a great kid."

When Nathan came back to the table carrying the trophy, Mike shook his hand, gave him a high five, and then grabbed him up in a bear hug. "Congratulations, Buddy! Nobody deserves that more than you." He gave Nathan a sly smile. "Not even me."

"Hey, Mike, you and me together were a great team. This should be cut in half. Hell, it's big enough." Everyone at the table laughed.

"Hey, Al, are you going to raise the ceiling in your family room?" Alex asked, laughing.

The conversation was interrupted by photographers from the school paper and the local evening paper as well. They wanted pictures of Nathan holding the trophy and a couple of Nathan and Mike together since they both were awarded scholarships. Both papers requested a short interview with Nathan. After the interview, they were free to go home.

Alex fell in beside Al as they were walking toward the parking lot. "You know, Al, you have a really great kid there. Even though he was the best pitcher the school has ever seen, he never took the credit during that interview. Did you notice that? He praised his teammates and brought Mike into the picture all through it. He's going to be an awesome man."

Al just smiled, but he thought to himself, 'I couldn't have said it any better myself.'

* * *

Mike dropped Nathan off at home after they completed the last of their finals. Graduation was just one week away, so there were no more classes. Nathan planned on hanging out around the house and helping Rose and Al get some things done. For his first project, he planned on fixing the garage door for Al. He looked over at Al's truck when he got out of the car, and frowned. What was his dad doing home from work so early? He hoped he wasn't sick.

"Dad? Hey, Dad, you're home early. Everything okay?"

Al and Rose were sitting at the kitchen table drinking coffee. "Nate, come in here and sit down. There's something we have to talk about."

Nathan looked at his parents and saw that Rose had been crying again. Rose looked up at Nathan helplessly. "Al, maybe we shouldn't….."

"He has to know, Rose. He has a right to know."

"What is it? What do I have to know? Dad?" Nathan grew worried as he looked from Al to Rose. "What's going on?"

Al sighed heavily. "It's about your brother." Al ran his hand through his hair and quickly covered his face with both hands. "Nate, Steven has really done it this time."

Nathan sank into a chair across from Rose and looked at Al. "What happened?" He asked quietly.

"He's not even fourteen….fourteen! He committed his first criminal act yesterday." Al raised his lip in a sneer.

"What? What did he do?" Nathan was gripping the side of the table, not sure if he even wanted to hear it.

"Your brother tied a twelve-year-old child to the bed, taped her mouth, raped her, and then…..tore off the tape and pissed in her mouth…." Al couldn't go on. He began sobbing. "Oh, God! Where did we fail him, Rose? Has that shrink been wrong about the treatment all this time? Should we have been there every week and on holidays instead of ignoring him, like the shrink advised?"

Rose couldn't speak. Nathan thought she looked like she was going to be sick. He thought that he might get sick, too.

Al looked at Nathan through red-rimmed eyes. "The little girl is in the hospital. She almost drowned in....Steven's piss." Al jumped up from the table and ran to the bathroom. He was the one to get sick. Nathan could hear him heaving behind the bathroom door.

"Is....is she going to be all right?" Nathan stared at Rose. She didn't answer.

Al rinsed off his face and returned to the table. "Don't cry, Nate. I'm sorry you had to hear this."

Nathan didn't realize until Al spoke to him that he was crying, too.

"Dad, will the girl be okay?"

"She'll live....but will she ever recover from this? I mean, mentally and psychologically she will *never* be the same. Steven destroyed the life of another human being, Nate. He'll be fourteen....and....anyway, the girl's in intensive care in a catatonic state. She shut down, probably as a defense mechanism. She's in bad shape."

"So what will happen to Steven?" Nathan was almost afraid to hear the answer.

"Steven will be moved from that facility. Because he committed a felony, he will be moved to a place where he will be monitored closely for the next four years. That's until he turns eighteen. Then, when he reaches eighteen, a decision will be made, based on his progress or lack of progress. Basically, he will be behind bars for the next four years. He will have treatment and the best of care, but he will not be allowed to move around freely. Right now he's heavily sedated. He fought the attendants when they tried to...get him away from....the girl. He fought hard, too. One of the attendants ended up with a broken nose. Big guy, too."

"Dad, did they ever tell you why Steven is....the way he is?" Nathan had to force words past the lump in his throat.

"No, they don't know why. It could have been something that happened during birth. They don't know. All I know is that something went terribly wrong somewhere...." Al stopped and looked at Rose.

"Rose, please don't look like that. It's not your fault." He reached over and took Rose's hand between his and held onto it.

Nathan reached over and took Rose's other hand, and placed a hand over top of Al's. The three of them sat in silence.

* * *

Mike showed up just as Nathan was finishing the garage door. "Hey, want to take the women out tonight?" He was referring to Lori and Stephanie.

"No, I don't feel like going out very much." Nathan was frowning as he put the tools away.

"Why? What's wrong?" Mike looked worried. He could see something was wrong. Nathan never frowned.

Nathan sat down on his father's workbench and Mike joined him. At first Nathan just sat and didn't speak. Mike waited patiently. Finally, Nathan sighed and told Mike everything about Steven. He knew Mike knew some things but not everything. Mike sat and listened quietly, and for once, didn't find anything funny.

"Wow….that's a hell of a load to be carrying around. How's your mom and dad taking it?"

"Pretty bad. They keep wondering what they did wrong. I don't know….they think it's their fault."

"Their fault? How could it be their fault? They're both pretty cool people. And anyway, look at how you turned out. It can't be their fault."

"Yeah, I know. They think that somehow they failed him. They're taking it pretty rough. I'm not doing too well either. I can remember really wanting a little brother….before he was born. I got Steven. He hates me, you know."

"He hates you? Why?"

Nathan shrugged. "I don't know. Nobody does. He has been kept away from me for years, for my safety. He's four years younger….but dangerous. He set my bed on fire once. That's when they found him in the woods with all the dead animals hung by their necks."

Mike couldn't hide his shock. "Gees, that's…..scary, I guess is the right word. I wish there was something I could say or do to make this easier. It's all pretty fucked up."

"Yeah, I know. Sorry to lay it all on you like that."

"I wish you would have told me all this sooner, Dude. That's what friends are for." Mike's words were genuine.

* * *

Graduation day….the day Nathan and Mike had been waiting for was finally here. The week went by slowly. They hung out together most of the week. Nathan was glad he included Mike in on the family nightmare. It was a lot easier for him to cope with it now that he had someone in which he could confide. They did take the girls out on two occasions that week, and Mike worked at keeping the evenings light and fun. He knew Nathan was anguished over his brother, and he did his best to be there and help him through it. He was a good friend.

Al and Rose were ready to go to the graduation ceremony. They were determined not to let Steven's trouble ruin one of Nathan's most important days of his life. Earlier in the day, Al hid a new Ford Ranger truck in the garage. Nathan wasn't expecting anything so expensive, so Al knew it would be a big surprise. While Nathan was upstairs getting ready, Al pulled the truck out of the garage and parked it in the driveway where it was hidden on the other side of his full sized truck. He couldn't wait to see Nathan's face when he saw it.

The situation with Steven was a little brighter since they found out that the girl was responding to the people around her. Al had already told Nathan the news and he could see the relief on his face. At least they could enjoy the excitement of Nathan graduating a little easier. He was a great kid and he deserved their undivided love and affection on this special day.

Nathan was wearing a new navy blue suit when he came down the stairs. Rose thought he looked incredibly handsome in it. Her pride in him showed when she looked at him and smiled. Al came down the stairs, wearing a suit very similar to his son's. Both of them were breathtaking. At least they took Rose's breath away. Al had that familiar sly smile on his face when he looked at Nathan.

"You handsome devil, you! You look just like me." He lightly cuffed him on the chin. "How about giving me a hand with something before we go?"

"Yeah, sure, Dad....what do you need?"

"There's something blocking my steering wheel in my truck. Can you help me see what it is?"

"No problem. Let's go take a look. What's it doing?" They walked outside together and Nathan saw Al's truck, but it was obvious he couldn't see the other one.

Al was playing his game well. "I don't know but I couldn't pull it to the side when I parked it. See if you can see anything on the passenger side."

Nathan walked around the front of Al's truck and stopped dead.

"Congratulations, graduate." Al was grinning at Nathan, just waiting for a response.

"Are you serious? Dad...is that for me?"

"Uh-huh. Thought you could use some wheels to get to and from college."

Al was almost knocked over when Nathan grabbed him and hugged him.

"Dad, I don't know what to say. Thank you, for starters....gees, Dad. I love you, Dad. You know that, don't you?" Nathan was close to tears.

"Yeah, I know that. No more than I love you, son...I promise you that." Al was in the same condition as Nathan.

Rose stood behind Al, just watching them together. 'He's everything you ever wanted him to be, Al. You wanted a perfect son and that's what you got.' Rose had a lump in her throat as she thought this. Nathan came up to her and hugged her.

"Thanks, Mom. I know it's from you, too." He looked down at Rose and smiled at her. "I love you, Mom."

Rose nodded at him. "I know. And I love you, too. Nathan, I want you to know this. I have cried so much over the past thirteen years, I know I have. But I want you to know that every time I cried over you it was always tears of joy. You have been the joy in our lives since the day you were born. Your dad and I couldn't love you more."

"Enough of the mush." Al's voice was ragged. "Let's go graduate!"

* * *

Nathan and Mike graduated with high honors. Al and Rose and Alex and Cindy sat together and watched their sons receive their diplomas, and they couldn't have been prouder. Cookie was the valedictorian of the class, with Nathan and Mike running a close second behind her.

Cindy leaned over toward Rose and commented, "Isn't it funny how those three are such good friends and they have the highest grades in the class? Birds of a feather, I guess."

Rose grinned back at Cindy. "I guess." She responded.

The closing exercises were mercifully short, and there was an explosion of graduation caps rising up toward the sky. The newly graduated class spent a few minutes hugging, kissing, and shaking hands. Nathan and Mike gave each other their usual high five and then just stood there staring at each other grinning.

"Nate…." Mike had an unusually serious look on his face. "No matter what…no matter where we end up….we're friends….for life.

"You got it, Buddy." Nathan grinned at his best friend.

They were soon joined by Cookie. As they entered in a three-way hug, Cookie added, "We're all going to be friends for life. Remember that." Cookie's mascara was starting to run.

The three graduates walked away, arms around each other, leaving that chapter of their lives behind.

Katrina and Nathan

1

Katrina clicked on the send button and leaned back in her chair and waited for the transmission to go through. It would take a few minutes for a confirmation receipt to be returned to her, and a little longer for the confirmation fax to come through. She picked up a couple of envelopes, opened them and read the contents while she waited. She smiled to herself. Although she didn't get a lot of it, her fan mail, mostly from the under-thirteen crowd, could be very entertaining at times. The letter she was holding was from an eleven-year-old girl in Kansas. The childlike scrawl stated that her name was Rebecca and that she loved Kit-Kat and wished she had a cat just like her. Katrina picked up a pen and addressed an envelope large enough to hold an eight-by-ten picture of the sleek white cat with the big pink bow around her neck and the small pink bow around her tail. In the bottom right corner, there was a pre-stamped paw print with the words "Love, Kit-Kat" above it. She slid the picture into the envelope and sealed it just as the transmission was completed. Within less than a minute her confirmation of receipt popped up on the screen. She got out of her chair and walked to the fax machine, knowing that the faxes confirming that her work had arrived would be coming through at any second. The bell on the fax rang, signaling that she was receiving the confirmations. She waited until the pages came through, removed them from the fax machine and filed them in her log. Her work for the week was now in the hands of the newspaper publishers.

It was still early in the morning; not quite eight-thirty. Katrina poured herself a cup of coffee and sat down at the dinette table. She had an appointment at the salon at eleven o'clock to get her hair trimmed, followed by an appointment for her nails and a pedicure. She had some time to kill so she scanned the headlines of the morning paper, and then opened it to the comics page to see her beloved 'Kit-Kat' in print. Her three live cats, she noticed, were stretched out on the living room floor taking their usual morning nap. She smiled as she observed them. The ringing of the telephone interrupted the morning serenity. She looked at the caller ID, and her smile broadened as she reached for the receiver.

"Hi, Morgan, what's up?"

"You and that caller ID….I can never surprise you." Morgan laughed. "Kat, you'll never guess who came in here for an interview yesterday."

Katrina smiled into the phone. She and Morgan were still the best of friends even though they had been out of high school for ten years now. Morgan graduated from IUP with a Bachelor's degree in Actuarial Science and was working for a financial planning company in the heart of Pittsburgh. Katrina hadn't seen her since her wedding, but they talked on the telephone often. When Morgan and Kevin got married, Katrina flew to Pennsylvania to be Morgan's maid of honor. Kevin had just completed his degree in pharmacy when they got married, and now, two years later, he was the head pharmacist at a local hospital.

"So since I probably won't guess, why don't you just tell me? Who?" Katrina knew this would be good.

"Candy." Morgan rushed to get the name out.

"*The* Candy? From high school? What kind of a job did she come in for?"

"We're looking for an administrative assistant. Our receptionist set up the interview. Boy, was she shocked to see me! Oh, and she asked about you."

"Yeah? She must really want the job." Katrina couldn't help but laugh. "What does she look like now? Fat, I hope."

Morgan broke up laughing. "Old….she looks old. She's not fat, but she has lines in her face like she's really had a rough life. She's not married….divorced, actually. She's been working as a secretary, a receptionist, and a file clerk. She really does need this job. You know, she didn't go to college. I was surprised about that."

"Any kids?" Katrina's curiosity was aroused.

"None that I know of."

"Is she going to get the job?" Katrina couldn't imagine Candy working in the same office with Morgan.

"It depends on how well she did on the tests we gave her, and on how well the others did. I'll let you know. If it were up to me, she definitely wouldn't. But it might be fun to make her life miserable." Morgan giggled. "So tell me....what's new?"

"Nothing. Same old—same old." Katrina already knew what the next question was going to be.

"Seeing anyone?"

"Nope. It's still just me and the kitties."

"So when in the hell are you going to start dating someone? Damn, Kat! Your life is passing you by. Why don't you get out and start mingling with people? All that beauty going to waste!"

"Oh, I've been out once or twice. Went to dinner with a real jerk just last Friday. He's someone I met at a newspaper cocktail party. I have to attend those things once in awhile. Anyway, I met this guy there. His name was Rob. He seemed nice at first, so when he asked me to go to dinner with him, I agreed. What an ass!"

"Why? What did he do?"

"Well, he is good-looking, well-dressed and obviously has a decent career going for him, but....absolutely no table manners! Totally grossed me out."

"I can't say I blame you for that one, then. Seriously, Kat...what are you looking for? What would be the perfect man for you?" Morgan lowered her voice a little. "I mean.....what would he have to be like for you to fall in love with him?"

Katrina sighed. She knew the answer.

"Like Jeff. He'd have to be like Jeff. Sweet and gentle, yet strong. He'd have to be kind, loving, tender, caring, considerate, and protective. And he would have to be funny. Jeff always made me laugh. God, Morgan, I always felt great when I was with Jeff. That was the happiest time of my life, and you know, I *always* had a great life. Nobody could ever replace him, but somewhere there must be someone like him."

Morgan was quiet for a moment. "Jeff was one in a million, Kat. I know that. I just wish you would find someone you could love. You've been through college and out of grad school for almost four years, and I'll bet you can still count on one hand the number of men you have gone out with."

"That's true, actually." Katrina laughed quietly.

"Kat, please tell me you're not still a virgin."

Katrina was too quiet for too long.

"Oh my God, Kat! You are, aren't you?" Morgan was almost whispering.

"Well, I just haven't found anybody that I want to wake up next to, that's all." Katrina defended herself.

"So make him get up and leave before daylight!" Morgan teased.

Katrina laughed.

"Morgan, he's out there somewhere. I know it. I can wait. Sometimes I feel him, but I don't know who he is." Katrina thought she sounded lame.

"Okay, Cinderella, some day your prince will come. So what do you have planned for the day?" Morgan changed the subject quickly.

"I have a hair and nails appointment at eleven. That's my one luxury."

"And the brand new Mustang in the driveway?" Morgan chided.

"That's my other luxury." Both she and Morgan laughed.

"Well, that's not really a big luxury, you know. I could have bought a BMW or a Mercedes. That would be a luxury. I guess because my first car was a Mustang, I just stick with them. But I just *love* Mustangs."

Katrina didn't know why she felt she had to defend her choice of cars. She always drove the car she liked and was not interested in purchasing a 'status car." Besides, she liked 'Buying American,' as her dad put it.

"Oh, I almost forgot. I saw Sean last weekend. He asked about you."

Katrina faked a yawn. "This conversation is becoming boring."

Morgan laughed. "He's not married yet. He just bought a condo. I didn't know he actually played in the NFL for awhile. A knee injury knocked him out of the game permanently. He owns a car dealership now, and apparently, he does all right."

"Well good for him. I'm sorry about the injury, though. He really was a good football player." Katrina held no malice toward Sean. What happened between her and Sean happened a long time ago.

She and Morgan said their goodbyes and promised to talk soon. After Katrina hung up the phone she jumped into the shower, dressed and headed toward the strip mall where her hair stylist and manicurist awaited her.

* * *

The Florida weather was beautiful this time of year. There wasn't a cloud in the sky, Katrina noticed as she pulled her new red Mustang into a parking space. She could have parked closer, but she always felt that it was better to walk the few extra yards than to take a space from someone who needed to be closer. Pulling the keys from the ignition, she slid out of the car, shut the door, and locked it from her key ring. She hit the button once more to engage the factory installed car alarm, and turned in the direction of the salon.

Katrina's long shiny copper hair gleamed in the sun. She toyed with the idea of getting more than a trim, but she decided that she just wasn't ready to give up her long hair. Three inches was the most she would have taken off, and she would allow the hair stylist to shape the hair so it would flow evenly down to her waist.

She tucked her car keys into the pocket of her shorts. She was wearing her favorite shorts outfit. The peach colored top, simply styled, and loose fitting, came down just to the waist of the peach shorts. The shorts were also loose fitting and hung like a mini skirt just to her mid thigh. It was a simple outfit, but very comfortable and looked good with her hair color. As she got to the crosswalk, she suddenly remembered the date. It was Friday, the eighth of April. Her twenty-eighth birthday was next week. She thought about her phone conversation with Morgan. Twenty-eight and still a virgin.... no wonder Morgan was flipping out about it. Totally engrossed in her thought, as she waited at the crosswalk for a couple of cars to pass by, she didn't notice the old green van or the man behind the wheel staring at her. She crossed at the crosswalk and went into the salon. The van pulled into a nearby parking space.

* * *

Two hours later, Katrina exited the salon. Her hair was neatly trimmed and beautifully shaped, and her fingernails and toenails were done in a French manicure. She felt gorgeous. An elderly lady dropped her purse and Katrina stooped to pick it up for her, before she got to the crosswalk. There were no cars approaching the crosswalk, so Katrina walked across into the parking lot of the strip mall and headed toward her car.

As she was coming out of the salon the green van that had pulled in earlier came to life. As she got to the other end of the crosswalk the van pulled out of the parking space and headed in her direction, moving very slowly. The driver was moving at a snail's pace behind her as she passed by in front of other cars on the way to her Mustang. 'What is this guy's problem?' she thought to herself. 'He has plenty of room to pass by me.'

The van did pass her. The driver sped up and drove by her. 'Finally.' She thought.

The van stopped directly in front of her Mustang. The driver got out and went around to the sliding door of the van and opened it. Katrina ignored the activity as she stuffed a couple of bills from her change into her purse. As she reached into her pocket for her keys, a hand clamped down over her mouth and an arm went around her waist like a vise, trapping her arms against her sides. She tried to scream, but the hand on her mouth prevented it. She began struggling, struggling with all her strength to free herself, but the arms were strong and powerful. She tried to bite his hand but it was clamped down too tightly. He half-carried and half-dragged her to the open van while she struggled to free herself. For an instant his grip over her mouth loosened and she bit him.

"Fucking bitch!" He hissed, and brought his hand down hard on her mouth. She tasted blood in her mouth. He removed his hand from her mouth long enough to get a better grip on her as he threw her body into the van. She screamed. She continued screaming after he slammed the door shut.

The elderly lady she had helped turned around when she heard the scream. She gasped and ran into the salon to get someone to call the police.

As Katrina tried to get up pain seared down her left side and she gasped. She pushed herself into a sitting position with her right arm, went for the door and stopped. The inside door panel was missing. There was no way to open the door from the inside! She couldn't hold back the tears and she sat there sobbing for a moment. The driver's side door opened and she jumped. The driver slid in behind the wheel and laughed at her through the rear view mirror. He put the van in drive and shot forward, knocking her down. He laughed again.

She lay there trembling for a moment, before she pushed herself back up into a sitting position. "What do you want? Why are you doing this?" She choked out the question.

The driver laughed again. "Scared, my beauty? Terrified, I hope. I love it when people are terrified of me." He let out a low blood curdling laugh that caused goose bumps on Katrina's arms.

"Where are you taking me? Please…..don't do this! Who are you?" She couldn't keep the tremors out of her voice. The driver laughed again.

"Who I am will never be of any importance to you, Bitch. 'Cause you're not going to be around to remember. First I'm going to fuck you, then I'm going to torture you, and then I'm going to kill you….. painfully." He laughed. He laughed like it was the funniest thing he ever said.

"Why? What did I do to you? Please…..I never hurt anybody…."

"Shut the fuck UP! Women! They should learn to keep their fucking mouths shut! Like my mother. Steven, I made your favorite dinner. Steven, what would you like to do today? Steven, what would make you happy? Stupid bitch! Didn't she realize that what would have made me happy was to be able to cut her up in little pieces and feed her to rats? Her, my dad and that fucking Nathan."

Katrina was shaking uncontrollably as she tried to wipe the tears from her face. Her hand came away covered with blood.

2

Nathan pulled the yellow Thunderbird into the driveway, pushed the button on the garage door opener, and then neatly backed the car into the three-car garage in between the dark red Hummer and the silver Corvette. He grabbed his valise and briefcase out of the back seat and sifted through his keys to find the front door key.

He hadn't expected to return home for another day, but he closed the deal on his latest investment sooner than he thought it would take. Every detail had been worked out with no problem, so he wrapped it up last evening, got a good night's sleep, and then headed for home this morning. He called Marie to tell her he would be home today instead of Saturday, knowing that she would have something in the refrigerator ready to pop into the microwave if he should be hungry.

He unlocked the door and set down his briefcase and valise on the floor of the entryway. He spied the white sheet of paper on the end table, and he instantly knew it was a note from Marie. He read the contents written in her neat handwriting:

Nathan-

There's lasagna in the fridge. Charlie called.

Mike called.

And your dad called.

Call me if you need me. Hope you had a good trip.

See you tomorrow.

Marie

Nathan smiled at the note. Marie was the best housekeeper anyone could ever have. She was efficient, leaving nothing undone, and trustworthy. Sometimes she reminded him of his mother, the way she looked out for him. Granted, he paid her well, but in his mind, she was worth it. He knew he was lucky to have her. She had been his housekeeper for over a year now. He remembered how difficult it had been to find someone he could trust and one that he could rely on. He had interviewed quite a few women and even one man, none of which were to his liking. He had about given up when he ran across Marie by accident. He thought about that day often, and somehow he knew that meeting her was meant to happen.

It was a rainy day in March. He pulled into the grocery store parking lot and braced himself against the downpour as he climbed out of the car. He spied a small lady two cars away struggling to force the window up on her car. She was soaked to the skin. He made a beeline to her car and helped her get the window up. 'You really should get that fixed.' He told her.

"Maybe I will....someday. Just can't afford it right now. You wouldn't know anybody that was hiring, would you?"

It became a perfect arrangement. She told him about her husband who was disabled and confined to a wheelchair, and how his disability checks just weren't enough. She also told him that she really had no skills, and that all she had ever done was keep house. This was music to Nathan's ears. He offered her the job as his housekeeper, telling her that all he expected was that she treat his house like her own. He told her he was willing to pay $1600 a month and she almost choked. All he asked was that she sometimes be willing to put in a couple of hours of extra time once in awhile to help out with entertaining guests. It didn't happen real often, he promised. In fact, it didn't happen at all. In the year Marie had been there, Nathan had not entertained anyone.

Marie started the following Monday and had been a faithful employee ever since. Sometimes he thought of her as a friend as well as an employee. They talked sometimes. He told her about Steven; he told her about his girlfriends; and he told her about his baseball career. He even went so far as to tell her about his belief that there was someone special waiting for him somewhere. She thought that was romantic and sweet. After getting to know him better, she began to believe that, too, since only a special person deserved a wonderful guy like Nathan. He was easy to work for, and very understanding. He encouraged her to bring her husband with her once in awhile so the man wouldn't have to sit at home alone all day. He could tell that Harry loved coming there. He sat on the patio and soaked up the sun or just sat in the family room watching the big screen television. He loved the light airy rooms Nathan's house held, since every room had floor to ceiling windows. Harry called it a glass house. The arrangement worked for all concerned.

* * *

Nathan rifled through his mail, separating the envelopes that had checks in them from the ones that held bills, and tossed the junk mail in the trash. He was not tired but he didn't want to do much tonight except sit in front of the television. He felt he needed some down time, with just himself and his TV. He thought about calling his dad back, but decided to put it off until tomorrow. After all, he wasn't supposed to be home until then, anyway. He went into the kitchen and looked in the refrigerator; and sure enough, there was Marie's lasagna, as promised. He might heat some up later, but he really wasn't hungry at the moment.

He unbuttoned his shirt and glanced outside at the pool. It looked inviting. Maybe he would dip into it in a little while, just to cool off. The day started off cool, but true to the weatherman's prediction, it had hit eighty-five degrees by four o'clock, Florida time.

He leaned against the kitchen counter and wondered what was wrong. He couldn't put his finger on it, but something.....something wasn't quite right in the world, at that moment.

3

Katrina sat in the back of the van, trembling. The van had been moving for what seemed like hours. He had stopped the van once, when he reached back and grabbed her by the hair. He dragged her to the back of the front seat by the hair while she struggled and screamed. He laughed that maniacal laugh. He slapped her several times, and then tried to kiss her. She screamed and struggled, and he hit her again. He tossed her away from him like she was a rag doll. When she looked up at him he extended his tongue and wiggled it at her.

She was afraid to say anything. She was afraid.....no......she was terrified. She felt his eyes on her in the rear view mirror. She looked up to meet his eyes....his cold, dead eyes.

He threw his head back and laughed. "I'm going to fuck you, and then I'm going to piss in your mouth. You're going to drown in my piss. How does that sound?" He laughed even harder.

'Oh, my God....he's insane!' She realized. 'He's really insane! What am I going to do? God, help me! Please, God, help me!' She silently prayed. She tried to wipe her face, but the blood had dried on it. All that came off onto her hand were a couple of dried clots. She touched her swollen lip and her tears began falling again.

He slammed his fist down on the dashboard, making Katrina flinch. "I asked you a fucking question! Answer me! HOW—DOES—THAT—*SOUND*, Whore? You fucking whore!"

"I-I'm *not* a.....whore." She whimpered.

"I DIDN'T FUCKING ASK YOU THAT! OF COURSE YOU'RE A WHORE! ALL WOMEN ARE WHORES! NOW..... answer my question."

"I-it doesn't sound good at all. Why would you want to do that to me?" Her voice had become hoarse.

"Why would you want to do that to me?" He mimicked. "Because I *can*....that's why. Think you're special because I chose you? You're not. You're just another fucking bitch who needs a cock one last time before she dies."

Katrina squeezed her eyes shut and prayed. She thought about Danny and Mike, and her mom and dad. 'Oh, God....if anything happens to me....they'll be devastated. Please, God...help me." She felt his eyes on her again, but this time she wouldn't look up. He laughed again. 'Women and their games.' He thought.

The van jerked to a stop, which sent a whole new surge of fear through Katrina's body.

"Honey, we're home." He sang. He jumped out of the driver's side door and quickly moved around to the other side of the van and tore open the door. Katrina shrank back, but not fast enough. He had her by the arm in a flash and dragged her out of the van.

He was speaking to her as he dragged her. "The guy who lives here? I'd like to be around to hear him explain the dead girl in his pool. That will be a gas! Mr. Perfect. Too bad he's not home. He could watch me fuck you"

The light hurt her eyes and she winced. They were in front of a big beautiful house. 'Who owns this house?' She wondered, inanely. Her head was pounding as he dragged her off the pavement onto the grass and threw her down. He grabbed her clothes and tore them half off of her body and she screamed. He slapped her hard across the face and she screamed again. She kept screaming as he fell on top of her, struggling to get his zipper down. Katrina knew she was fighting for her life. She had to find the strength she needed. Without thinking, she moved fast and brought her knee up into his crotch. He screamed, jumped back, but then, surprisingly, he recovered quickly.

"Oh, so you want to really get hurt, huh?" He balled up his fist and drew his arm back. Katrina screamed once more.

Out of nowhere came a third hand, locking onto the arm that was drawn back. The driver of the van was jerked up and flung backwards.

Nathan stood poised, ready for him to come at him.

"What the hell do you think you're doing? Get off my property."

"Well, if it isn't my dear brother." Steven snarled at him.

"Get off my property." Nathan repeated.

"If I go, she goes, too." Steven taunted.

"*NO*!" Katrina gasped. She sat up and tried to cover her naked breasts with her arms.

"She came with me…" Steven looked at Nathan defiantly.

"*NO*!" Katrina's teeth were chattering in the eighty degree heat. She couldn't control her trembling.

"She's my girlfriend." Steven tried to make his voice sound reasonable.

"*NO*! I'm *not*! Ask him my name! Go ahead, *ask him*! He doesn't know it!"

Nathan glanced at Katrina and looked away. He took his shirt off and gently tossed it to her so she could cover herself. She struggled with the shirt, but the pain in her ribs made it difficult to maneuver into the shirt. She gave up and draped it across her chest.

"What's her name?" Nathan drew his attention toward Steven.

"Sandy…I don't know…she's just some fucking prostitute I picked up."

"I am *not*!" Katrina sobbed.

Nathan looked at Katrina for a moment. "She doesn't look like a prostitute. Now get off my property."

Steven raised his lip into a sneer. "Is that any way to treat your brother?" He asked.

"You were never a brother to me. We hardly know each other. Now…get…off…my… property." Nathan reached into his pockets and pulled a cell phone out of the left one and a revolver out of the right. He flipped open the cell phone and pointed the gun at Steven.

"What the fuck are you doing, Nathan?" Steven stepped back.

Nathan heard the fear in Steven's voice. He remembered reading one of the reports concerning Steven. He was terrified of guns, which is why Nathan got one.

"Calling the police." Nathan stared at his brother as he dialed the number on the cell phone.

"Okay. I'm going." Steven threw his hands up. "The gun…is it loaded?"

"Absolutely." Nathan responded.

"You wouldn't shoot your own brother, would you?"

Nathan responded by cocking the trigger. Steven backed up and jumped into the van and sped away.

Nathan watched the van speed out of the driveway and turn east. He finished dialing and waited for the phone to be answered on the other end.

"Detective Delaney, Please. Oh, Brian, it *is* you. It's Nate. Listen…. can you come over here?"

"Sure, Nate….what's up?" Brian Delaney's voice came over the other end of the phone.

"Well, my crazy, sick brother roughed up some girl pretty bad. She's here. I think maybe you should talk to her."

"Does she know him? I don't want any kind of domestic squabble on my hands."

"No, I don't think so. He didn't even know her name. She's pretty shaken up."

"Okay, I'll be there in a few."

Nathan turned his attention to Katrina. She was a mess. Her swollen lip had been bleeding, and now there was dried blood covering her chin. She had bruises on her cheeks and her eye was almost swollen shut. She had been crying and the tears left tracks through the dirt on her face. Still, Nathan could see that she was a really beautiful girl. He walked over and looked down at her. There was the look of terror in her eyes.

"I think you saved my life." She said in a small, trembling voice.

Nathan nodded. "Are you hurt….badly, I mean? I can see you're hurt."

She started to shake her head, but slowly nodded instead.

"Where?" He asked.

"My side. I think my ribs may be cracked, or broken."

"Can you get up?" He extended his hand to her and she tried to raise herself up. She couldn't.

"Okay…..listen, I'm going to try to pick you up without hurting you some more, okay?" He studied her face.

She nodded. "Okay."

"If I hurt you, tell me, okay?"

She nodded an agreement.

He put his arms under her and lifted her up off the ground, and carried her into the house. He didn't stop at the living room, but instead walked straight up to his bedroom and gently put her down on the bed. She was crying again.

"Are you in a lot of pain? Maybe I should get you to a hospital…"

"No, please, I don't want to go to a hospital if I can help it. I don't want this to get around. It wouldn't be good for my…image…" She trailed off. "I'm sorry; I know you don't understand, but…"

"Okay, then let me call someone to come here. One of my friends is a doctor. He'll come here, and maybe….well, let me call him, okay?"

Katrina agreed to let him call his doctor friend.

Nathan dialed Dr. William Harding's number and he answered on the second ring.

"Dr. Harding."

"Doctor, my ass. What does a duck say?" Nathan laughed lightly into the phone.

"Nathan! How the hell are you? What can I do for you?" Dr. Harding was obviously glad to hear from Nathan.

"What are you doing right now?"

"Nothing, Nate….what do you need?" The doctor's voice got serious.

"Can you come over here and bring your bag of magic tricks? My idiot brother roughed up some girl. Apparently he abducted her, from what I'm gathering. Anyway, she needs medical attention and doesn't want to go to a hospital. Maybe, if she's not hurt too badly, you could patch her up here. I mean….if you think it's more serious, you'll have to persuade her to go to emergency."

"Yeah, okay, Nate….I'll be there in about fifteen minutes."

The call was disconnected as the door bell rang. "That will be the detective. I'll be right back." He hesitated a moment, and smiled at her. He thought she tried to smile back, but her lip was too swollen. He went to answer the door and quickly returned, leading the way with Detective Delaney following. Delaney was an attractive man in his mid-thirties. His dark hair and blue eyes reminded her of Sean.

"Hi. I'm Detective Delaney. What's you name?" The detective smiled at her, pulled up a small footstool to sit on, and opened his notepad.

"Katrina….Katrina Kitrowski." She answered him, her voice shaking.

"Tell me what happened." His voice was quiet and reassuring.

Katrina looked over at Nathan. "Can I have a drink of water?"

"Oh, of course. Hold on….I'll get it." Nathan left the bedroom and returned within moments of her request.

Katrina gratefully took the glass of ice water from him and sipped a little of it. It tasted like blood, but it was wet.

"Okay, now tell me everything from the time you first encountered the….man." He was careful not to say anything that would send her into hysterics.

Katrina told how he grabbed her and threw her into the van. "He kept saying awful things….."

"What things? Tell me."

"I can't say some of them, but he said he was going to kill me, and that the person who lives here was going to have to explain a dead girl in his pool." She was crying again. Nathan handed her a couple of tissues, and she looked at him gratefully.

"Did he say he was going to….rape you?"

"Yes, but he said the F-word, not rape. He said he was going to…. piss in my mouth and that I was going to drown in his…piss." Katrina covered her face, her shoulders were heaving up and down.

Nathan looked sick. He remembered the girl at the facility where Steven grew up. Steven had done that to her.

Detective Delaney asked Nathan about the vehicle. Nathan gave him a description of the van and a partial Ohio plate number. "It may or may not be registered to Steven. I don't know."

The detective nodded and made a phone call. He was having the department run a check on the van with the partial number. "Oh yeah?" Nathan and Katrina heard him say into the phone.

When the call ended, he looked at Katrina, and then Nathan. "Well, what do you know? There's a report at the station about a girl being dragged into a green van outside of a strip mall around two o'clock today. Would that be you?"

He looked at Katrina and she nodded. Suddenly, Katrina tried to sit up. "My purse!" She exclaimed. "He still has my purse, with my ID in it. He could go to my house…" She broke up in tears again, giving up the struggle to sit up. The pain in her side forced her to stay down. Then she remembered the cats.

"Oh my God….my cats are there….alone." Nathan couldn't mistake the terror in her voice. If she only knew how much danger her cats were in.

He nodded his head toward the door and walked out of the bedroom. Detective Delaney followed. "Brian, my brother loves to torture things. If he gets to her place, he will find those cats and torture them to death."

"I'll get someone over to her place to keep an eye out. Maybe plant someone inside." He went back into the bedroom and asked Katrina. "Is there any way to get into your place? I think I want an officer to be inside your home tonight."

Katrina hesitated, and then reached down and felt her pocket. The keys were still there. She pulled out the key ring and handed them to Detective Delaney. He took the keys and nodded at her.

Nathan appeared with Dr. Harding, and then followed the detective out of the room. "Okay, I'm going to get someone to get her car and drive it home, and then spend the night there, watching." He looked down at his notepad and noted the address she gave, and then went to make a phone call from the desk in Nathan's den.

Bill Harding began examining Katrina. "Let's get some ice on some things here. Nate!"

Nathan appeared at the bedroom door. "Hey, Nate, can you make me up a couple of ice packs somehow? Ice in a towel, wrapped in a plastic bag will work." The doctor didn't look up as he studied the bruises on Katrina's face. He spilled some alcohol on a couple of cotton balls and began wiping the blood off of her lip and chin, and then surveyed the damaged lip.

Nathan came back with three homemade ice packs. "Is she going to be okay?" He asked.

"Yeah, I think so. Her ribs are probably cracked, but not broken. I'll tape them for her. I don't think she'll need stitches in the lip, which is a good thing." The doctor lifted Nathan's shirt off of Katrina's side, and Nathan winced when he saw the deep purple bruises over her ribs on her left side. After listening to her lungs through the stethoscope, Dr. Harding looked down at Katrina. "You know, Katrina, I'm a big fan of yours. My daughter loves Kit-Kat."

"Thank you." She said, simply.

Nathan's curiosity was tweaked, but he didn't ask any questions.

"Nate, I'm going to leave something to help her sleep, and some antibiotics as well. Is she going to stay here? At least, until Steven is caught, I mean."

"Yeah, she can stay here. She doesn't look like she eats much." This brought a small laugh from Katrina, and she winced in pain.

The doctor pulled a couple of pills out of an envelope in his bag, and then a bottle holding a red liquid. "Do you have a shot glass, Nate?"

"Yeah, I'll get you one." Nathan found one behind the bar in the family room and brought it back to the bedroom.

The doctor opened the bottle and poured the red liquid into the shot glass, until the glass was three-quarters full. He smiled down at Katrina. "I don't usually do things like this. I usually have a more sterile environment. Drink this when you're ready to sleep tonight. I want you to stay awake for a couple of hours, anyway. Make Nate tell you bedtime stories, or something, okay?"

Katrina nodded.

"Make sure she keeps the ice on her lip and her eye for awhile. The ribs....maybe an hour. Watch for the swelling to go down. You can apply moderate heat when the swelling goes down. It will make the bruises go away faster. I'll check back with you in the morning." Doctor Harding got up to leave and Nathan followed him out.

"You said you were a fan. Who is she?"

Dr. Harding stared at Nathan for a moment. "You don't know?"

Nathan shook his head.

"She's Katrina Kitrowski, the creator of Kit-Kat, one of the best cartoons in the comic strips. My daughter loves that cartoon. You don't read the comics?"

Nathan shook his head. "Not as a rule. Actually....never."

Harding snickered. "You're missing something, then. Anyway, she was on the television on one of those morning shows about a week ago. I walked through my waiting room and my patients were watching it. I stopped and looked because I heard one of them talking about how beautiful she is. She's kind of messed up now, but I can tell you....she is beautiful."

Nathan looked at his friend. "I can see that she is. I feel really bad about what my crazy brother did to her. I hope I can make it up to her, at least a little bit. By the way, this outrageous fee you'll probably be charging is on me, okay? I'll pay you."

"That's fine, Nate. For you, it's doubled." He laughed and patted Nathan on the shoulder. "See you in the morning." Nathan saw him out and then went back to check on Katrina. He found her crying again.

"Hi." He spoke softly and he pulled up the footstool that the detective and the doctor had used. "How are you feeling?" He asked as he handed her more tissues.

"I'm just....I don't know....I was so.....*scared.* He was going to kill me." New tears erupted from her swollen eyes.

Nathan stroked her hair for a moment. "I'm so sorry this happened to you. Wait a minute....maybe this will make you feel a little bit better." He dialed the number written on a small slip of paper, using the phone beside the bed. He waited for someone to answer. "Hi, this is Nate Perletti. Officer Grey? Are you in?"

"Yeah, I'm in. Hey, should I feed these cats? They're climbing all over me."

Nathan laughed through his nose, as he looked at Katrina. "Officer Grey is in your apartment. He wants to know if he should feed the cats. They're climbing all over him."

"They're probably hungry. If he wants to, I'd be grateful. The food is in the bottom right cabinet next to the stove. Some dry and a can split three ways."

Nathan repeated this information to the officer, and was satisfied that he would take care of the cats for her.

"By the way, your car is in your driveway now. An officer drove it there for you."

Katrina looked up at Nathan, grateful for his help. For the first time since she got there, it dawned on her that he was extremely handsome. His rich brown eyes with the dark lashes were quite a contrast to her light blue ones, and his black hair had a casual look that could only be achieved by an excellent cut. His features were manly, yet soft. Katrina noticed the slight dimple in his otherwise strong-looking chin, his straight nose and his even, white teeth behind his perfectly shaped lips. She concentrated on his voice and what he was saying.

"So you have your own comic strip, huh? Kit-Kat….hmmm, Katrina Kitrowski, I get it. That's really cute." Nathan frowned slightly. "Is there someone I should call for you?"

Katrina shook her head.

"Nobody?"

"Well there are a lot of people you could call, but I don't want to worry them. My two brothers, and my parents. If you call my brothers, they'll hunt your brother down. My brother Mike is an FBI agent."

"Really? What does the other brother do?" Nathan was working at keeping her awake, as the doctor advised.

"Danny's a lawyer, here in Florida. Mike lives in Maryland at the moment, but he will be moving wherever they decide to send him."

"Hmmm, a lawyer, a lawman, and a cartoonist."

Katrina smiled. "I got the artistic gene, I guess. I've been drawing since I was about four. Cartooning isn't the only artwork I do. I have a gallery not too far from where I live. My work gets sold there.... hopefully."

Nathan chuckled over her last word.

"Paintings?" He asked.

"Paintings, sketches, and photography. It pays the bills." She added modestly. The truth was that it more than paid the bills. She was becoming quite financially sound by her artwork. "Can I go to sleep now?"

Nathan looked at his watch and nodded. "I think it will be okay. I'll check on you from time to time, so don't get scared if you wake up and see me in here, okay?"

She nodded.

"Oh, here, you have to drink this." Nathan picked up the shot glass holding the red liquid, and then set it back down again. "Let me help you up for a minute." He reached under her and helped her sit up. She winced and grabbed her head for a moment.

"This should help that." He picked up the glass and handed it to her, and she drank it down quickly. He helped her lie back down and covered her with a comforter. "You'll feel better in the morning." He patted her shoulder and watched as she drifted off to sleep.

He stood up and went out to the living room. 'No use in delaying the inevitable.' He thought to himself.

He picked up the phone and dialed.

Al picked up the phone on the first ring.

"Hi, Dad."

"Nathan! I tried to call you." Al sounded relieved to hear Nathan's voice.

"Yeah, I got the message. Listen, Dad....there's a problem....."

"It involves Steven......right?"

"Yeah, how did you know?"

"Is he in Florida? He was here. I caught him looking through the address book your mother keeps in the drawer by the phone. He put it back, but I looked at it later and the page he was on was creased. That page had your address on it."

"Well, he's Florida, all right....and he's in *big trouble.*"

"What kind of trouble? What did he do?" Al dropped down into a chair and braced himself for what he was about to hear.

Nathan quickly related the story to Al. He imagined Al's body tightening with tension when he got to the part where Steven told Katrina he was going to piss in her mouth. He knew how it affected his father the first time he heard that. Al didn't say anything for a few moments. He was having difficulty swallowing.

"How's the girl?"

"She's pretty badly banged up. Cracked ribs, black and blue face, cut lip, and one eye is swollen shut. Emotionally....well, you can imagine. Bill Harding came over and treated her. She didn't want to go to a hospital. Dad, he was going to rape her, kill her and put her in my pool. He told her that." Nathan began to feel sick, on top of the disgust he already felt.

"How did she end up with him in the first place? Steven isn't exactly the dating type."

"He abducted her. There's a report at the police station about a girl being dragged into a green van. It was her. Who owns the van?"

"He bought it. Paid three hundred dollars for it. He should have never been released. I told them.....they wouldn't listen. He got out two months ago. We didn't know it until about three weeks ago. I don't know where he was from the time he got out until he showed up here. He ate here a couple of times, but he never stayed here."

"Well.....Dad, from what he said to the girl, he indicated that she isn't the first one he grabbed."

"Oh, God." Al covered his forehead with his free hand. "There could be others?"

"Yeah, I think so. Are you going to tell mom?"

"I can't keep it from her. I wish I didn't have to tell her. Where is he now?"

Nathan told Al about chasing him off with a revolver and that the police had an APB out on him. "They are going to hunt him down, Dad. There is an officer staying at the girl's apartment. She's here, terrified. Steven has her purse with all of her ID in it. She has cats, and…well, you know."

"Yeah, I remember too well. Does she know about him and small animals?"

"Oh hell, no! I couldn't tell her that. She'd freak out for sure."

"Yeah, she probably would. Hey, listen, I want to pay for the medical bills, Nate. Okay?"

"I already took care of it. Don't worry about it. You just have to worry about what to tell mom." Nathan reminded him.

Nathan promised to keep him informed before he hung up. He went in to check on Katrina and found her crying in her sleep. He sat down on the footstool and stroked her forehead.

"Shh. It's okay. You're safe. I'm right here." He soothed.

Katrina touched his hand and mumbled, "Jeff." She relaxed and her face took on a look of serenity. Nathan wondered briefly who Jeff was, before he got up and returned to his living room.

Nathan sat on the sofa and picked up the TV remote, then thought better of it, and set it back down. He didn't want the sound of the TV to muffle any other sounds that might be detrimental to his or the girl's well-being. 'So much for my night of television.' He thought. Instead, he opened his briefcase and began looking over proposals for possible new investments.

* * *

Nathan's body jerked awake and he looked at his watch. The dial showed that it was eleven-thirty. He stood up and listened for any noises that would be out of place, and he heard nothing. 'She must be still sleeping. I'd better check on her.' He reminded himself.

She was sleeping quietly when he entered the room. In the darkness of the room, he focused on her face. He felt a sadness creeping into him. 'How could Steven hurt such a beautiful girl like this?' He felt a sob catch in his throat and quickly tried to recover. He stared down at her for a moment, and she opened her eyes.

"Are you okay?" He asked her. She nodded, and then drifted back off to sleep. He straightened the comforter, and then pulled an overstuffed wing chair up to the foot of the bed, grabbed a pillow from the other side of the bed, and sat down. He propped his feet up on the bed and quickly dozed off.

The phone was ringing at six in the morning. He got out of the chair and ran into the den to answer it, congratulating himself that he remembered to shut off the bell on the phone in his room. The ringing didn't disturb her, he noticed, as he glanced at her before he went through the doorway. He grabbed up the phone and spoke his greeting into it.

"Nate? Brian." It was Detective Delaney. "We got him. He showed up at her place about four this morning. He's a strong bastard. It took four uniformed officers to put him on the ground. He's in custody now. We'll charge him with assault and battery, abduction, attempted rape, assault with attempt to kill, and attempted murder as well. Resisting arrest will be thrown in, too. I'll be over there in about an hour. How is she doing?"

"She's sleeping now. She's got some really bad bruises."

"I'm sure she does. That son-of-a-bitch is powerful. She was no match for him. Oh, and I have her purse. Everything is still in it, except for her driver's license, which we found on the floor in the front of the van. I'll bring it over. I'm glad she remembered that he had her purse. We may not have thought about looking for him at her place.... I mean, since he grabbed her at a strip mall. I'll be going over there today to see if I can find anybody who saw anything."

"Okay, see you in about an hour, then?" Nathan heard the back door opening and knew it would be Marie. He hung up and went to the kitchen to greet her, and let her know about the events of the day before.

Marie's face showed real concern. "The girl's here now?"

"Yeah, she's sleeping in my bed. I thought that would be the most comfortable for her. She's pretty banged up. Can you help her when she wakes up? She'll probably want a shower."

"Oh, of course....then I'll make breakfast for both of you. I see you didn't touch the lasagna."

Nathan laughed lightly. "I guess I forgot to eat with all the excitement. She's got to be hungry, too. I don't know when she ate last. I'll go check on her to see if she's awake."

Nathan walked into his bedroom while Marie stood outside and waited. Katrina opened her eye—the other remained shut.

"Good morning. How do you feel this morning?" He spoke quietly, and Katrina detected sadness in his voice.

"Like I was hit by a truck." Her voice was hoarse.

"No doubt. Marie, my housekeeper is here. Thought maybe you might want to take a shower. She's here to help you."

"I would love a shower. I know I need one. Thank you."

Nathan waved Marie into the room, and her first reaction was a gasp.

"I know. I look really terrible, don't I?" Katrina tried to help Marie recover from the shock of seeing her banged up face.

"Dr. Harding says everything will be fine. Your face won't show any permanent damage. He'll be here about nine this morning to check on you." Nathan spoke up to assure Katrina that she would not be permanently disfigured.

Katrina was relieved to hear that there would be no permanent damage. That meant she was—just bruised and swollen—no permanent scarring.

"I'm sorry." Marie apologized. "It wasn't how you look that made me gasp, but who you are. You're Kit-Kat's creator, aren't you?"

Katrina nodded. To Nathan she said, "Now do you see why I didn't want to go to a hospital? Too many people could recognize me."

"I see. I think I'm the only one in Florida who didn't recognize you. Everyone who came in here last night knew who you were. Don't worry…they're all discreet people. No word of this will get out." Nathan assured her. "Let's see if we can get you out of bed and Marie can help you into the shower. It's a walk-in shower, so you don't have to climb over the side of a tub. I'll get you something to put on. Your clothes are ruined."

Nathan reached into his closet and found a white terrycloth robe. "I think you'll look smashing in this." He held it up and pulled out the bottom of it like he was trying to sell it to her. She laughed a little.

Between the two of them, Marie and Nathan got her out of bed and into the bathroom. Nathan took his leave and left Marie behind to help her. While Katrina used the toilet, Marie went to round up some things for her shower. She came back with shampoo and even some conditioner, and some nice smelling soap. "Mike's wife left this stuff here the last time they visited. Mike is Nathan's friend from high school. They grew up in Ohio. Oh, and here is a new toothbrush. I buy them when I find them on sale. There is toothpaste in the drawer."

Katrina thanked her and then turned toward the mirror to survey the damage to her face. "Wow….I look really bad, don't I?" Her eyes welled up with tears again. "I was never so…*terrified*….I'm still terrified." She reached for a tissue and dabbed her eyes.

"You're in good hands. Please don't judge Nathan by his brother. Nathan is…just a wonderful person. There aren't any better than he is. He's very compassionate….and decent. He would never hurt anybody….not like Steven. Steven is evil. It's amazing how two brothers can be so different."

Katrina nodded in agreement to that.

* * *

She was sitting on the edge of the bed, wrapped in Nathan's terrycloth robe. It was miles too big for her but it was comfortable. She felt better after her shower. The detective tapped on the door and asked if he could come in.

"We caught him. You're safe now." Delaney assured her.

Katrina began to cry and the detective reached for her hand.

"He's in jail now, and he's going to stay there." He handed her a couple of tissues as he spoke. "You may have to testify….think you'll be up to that?"

She nodded. "Thank you. I'm just so glad you caught him." She wiped the tears from her eyes.

Delaney held out her purse for her to take.

"Everything is there, except this." He pulled her driver's license out of his breast pocket.

The significance of this dawned on her. "He went to my place, didn't he?"

Delaney nodded. "That's where we got him."

Katrina felt dizzy for a moment, just knowing that her fear was justified. "Are my cats okay?"

Again, Delaney nodded. "The officer who stayed there will never be the same, though. All he talked about after we made the arrest were those cats. I think he's going to go out and get one for himself. He said he never realized cats could be so loving and affectionate."

"They grow on you. But it's like that with almost any living thing. They give what they receive. They get love, they give love. People aren't always like that, though. Sorry."

"No, you're right, unfortunately. Well, I have lots to follow up on. We want this wrapped up soon so we can give it to the prosecution." He stood up, nodded at her, and walked out of the room.

Dr. Harding appeared within minutes after Brian Delaney left. "Good morning, Katrina. Let's see how well you're doing this morning." He nudged her onto her side and opened the robe to see the ribs. He pressed on them lightly and she winced.

"Hurt?" He quickly removed his fingers and brought his hands up to her face. He checked her lip, and then got a small flashlight out of his bag. For such a small item, it had a really bright light, and she winced again when he shined it in her eyes.

"Keep cold compresses on the eye all day today. No ice, just cold water. It'll help. You're going to be fine. It will take awhile for all these bruises to go away. Do you need a note to stay home from anywhere?"

"No, I work from home. Maybe a note to keep my brother from coming over and seeing me like this. How about something that says I'm highly contagious?"

Harding laughed. "Why don't you want your brother to see you like this?"

"He's…both of my brothers…..they're very protective. World War Three would start right here in Florida. He'd go ballistic if he saw me like this."

"I can understand that. If I had a beautiful sister like you I'd want to protect her, too." Dr. Harding stood up, signaling that the exam was over. "I want to see you again on Monday. In my office. I have an x-ray machine there, so I can get pictures of your ribs, just to be sure. You can come in around eight. My staff doesn't get there until nine. I'll be there alone, so nobody will see you. Oh, get a ride in. I don't want you driving yet." He scrawled out a couple of prescriptions on a prescription pad and set them on the nightstand. "Have these filled, and take them according to the instructions. My address is on the top of the prescription. See you Monday." He left the room quickly.

Marie came in as the doctor walked out. Katrina got the fleeting impression that there was a line outside the door, all waiting to enter, one at a time. She laughed internally.

"Hey, I'll bet you're hungry. I made breakfast. Nathan is having his on the patio. Would you like to join him?"

Katrina nodded.

"Good. I'll get him to help you out there." Marie exited and came back in with Nathan behind her.

Nathan helped her stand.

"You know, I never thought of it, but you probably haven't had anything to eat in quite awhile. I'm sorry."

"That's okay. I probably couldn't have eaten anything anyway. I'm hungry, but I'm not sure I can get food past this fat lip."

Nathan laughed and said, "We'll cut it up in tiny bites for you." He held on to her as they made their way to the patio, where Marie had the table set and was already placing food onto it.

The patio overlooked the pool. Katrina stared longingly at the pool. "Your pool looks so inviting."

"You can use it any time you want. I'll give you a swimming pass."

Katrina laughed but stopped quickly and held her lip. "You have a beautiful home."

"Thank you. I bought it from an elderly gentleman about two years ago. He had no family left and he went into a nursing home. I paid him a fair price for the house so he could pay for his nursing home care for about twenty years. He was seventy-nine when I bought the place."

"Is he still alive?"

"I think so, yeah. I always promise myself that I'm going to go see him, but I never make it there. I send him a Christmas card and a birthday card, though."

"That's nice." Katrina sincerely meant it.

"Katrina, about my brother…..first of all, I'm so sorry for what happened to you. Steven has spent most of his life in institutions. My dad realized that there was something wrong with him when Steven was five years old. He did terrible things for a five year old. My mother tried to…work it out, you know….make him act normal, but it didn't work. I won't tell you all that Steven did, but I will tell you that my brother is a very sick person—always has been. He set my bed on fire one time."

Katrina gasped. "Were you in it?"

"No, I had left for school already. He destroyed my baseball trophies and some other things, though. The point is we're not the same. We really weren't even raised together. Like I said, Steven grew up in an institution. He proved to be dangerous at an early age. My parents wouldn't ever let him alone with me. Even though I was four years older, they feared for my safety."

"That must have been terrible for you."

"It was. I wanted a brother so badly. They don't know what went wrong with Steven. My parents are good people. I turned out okay, I think."

Katrina nodded. "You seem….normal."

Nathan grinned at her. "I'm glad you think so."

Katrina didn't realize how hungry she was until she saw the delicious-looking breakfast foods placed in front of her. She ate with great difficulty, but she enjoyed the food. Nathan watched her as she ate. He was trying to imagine her face without the swelling and bruising.

Marie appeared when they were finished eating. "Katrina, I found something suitable for you to wear. Nathan, remember when Mike was here, they left some things behind? I think she could wear that sundress Mike's wife left here. I washed your underwear with a load of clothes I had to do, so you'll have clean undies."

Katrina blushed a little. "Thank you."

"Everything is laid out on the bed. Yell for me if you need anything."

Katrina thanked her again, and watched her walk through the sliding glass door.

"Marie's a gem." Nathan broke the silence. "She was quite a find…. and she's the best housekeeper anyone could have."

“I can see that.” Katrina sipped coffee from the good side of her lips. “Can you give me a ride home? Now that it’s safe to go there?” She watched Nathan with her good eye.

“Yeah, you bet. Besides, I want to meet these famous kitties....if that’s okay.”

“Do you like cats?”

“I like all animals. I never had a pet. Couldn’t have one with Steven around.”

He caught the look on her face when he said that. “I mean, along with everything else, Steven had asthma. Allergic to things.”

“Oh.” She seemed relieved, and that made Nathan glad he didn’t tell the entire truth.

“Do you want me to help you into the house?”

“Maybe a little help, I guess. I’ll have to manage on my own at home, though.”

He came around to her side of the table and held out his arm so she could pull herself up. He held onto her arm as they went inside.

* * *

“Make a left here.” Katrina told Nathan. “The apartments are halfway down the road. Turn in the first driveway.”

Nathan turned into the driveway and brought the Thunderbird to a stop. Katrina looked toward her apartment door, hesitantly. A new wave of terror spread over her, and Nathan picked up on it.

“Don’t worry, he’s in jail. By the way, you look really pretty in that dress, even if it is a little too big. Blue suits you.”

She smiled and thanked him. She knew that he was only being nice, and she was grateful to him for that.

“I’ll help you out of the car. You’re going to let me come in to see those kitties, aren’t you?”

“Yes, of course. They love attention.”

Nathan got out of the car and went around to her side, opened the door, and offered his hand. She eagerly took it and pulled herself up and slid out of the door. Nathan took her keys out of her hand, unlocked the apartment door, and walked in first, with her trailing him. He was satisfied that nothing seemed to be wrong with the apartment.

"So where are they?"

"Kitties!" She trilled. All three cats came running from the back of the apartment, two of them meowing. She gingerly stooped down to pet them, and Nathan followed suit.

"They sure are pretty. Hey, I think this one likes me." Nathan was petting Angel, a short-haired white cat with amber colored eyes. Angel was rubbing her face up against Nathan's hand.

"That's Angel. She's deaf. This one is Victoria." Katrina pointed to a long haired white cat. "And the other one is Lacey." Lacey's coat was tan and cream colored. The two colors blended together looked somewhat like a marble finish. The odd thing about this cat was that she had big blue eyes.

"They're all really beautiful. And Officer Grey was right—they are affectionate. Can I help you feed them?"

Katrina started to get up and hesitated. She held onto her side as Nathan helped her rise, slowly. "You may have to feed them for me. I don't think I can bend down to get the food or pick up the bowls."

"No problem. I'll be glad to." As he spoke, Nathan reached for her arm and guided her to the sofa. "Sit. I'll do it. Just tell me what to do."

She watched as Nathan followed her instructions and fed all three cats. Angel looked up at him and meowed as he set the bowls back on the floor.

"That was fun. Why is Angel deaf? How did that happen?"

"She was born that way. It sometimes happens with white cats. Actually, they are born deaf a lot."

"Really? I never heard that before." Nathan was impressed with her knowledge of cats, which was something he knew nothing about.

He looked around the living area of the apartment for the first time since he entered.

"This is a nice apartment. It's pretty big. You have it decorated really pretty, too."

"Thank you. I think it's the artist in me." She smiled as she watched him look around.

He walked toward her Spinet piano and tapped a key. "Do you play?"

"Yes."

"Talented, aren't you?" It was actually an observation more than a question. He looked up at the pictures on top of the piano and on the wall above it. He spied several pictures of her, and pointed to one of them. "Drill team?"

"Yes." She answered.

"And prom queen? Were you homecoming queen, too?" He was looking at two different pictures where she was wearing different dresses, and she donned a crown on both of them.

"Yes and yes." She was a little embarrassed by his observations.

"Was this your high school sweetheart?" He was pointing at the picture of her and Sean.

"He was my first boyfriend. The other one was my high school sweetheart. Sean and I broke up because he couldn't keep his hands where they belonged."

Nathan laughed. "This other one…would his name be Jeff?"

Katrina was taken by surprise. "Yes…..how did you know that?"

"Last night….when I went in to check on you….you were crying in your sleep. I rubbed your forehead for a minute, trying to soothe you. When I told you I was there, you took my hand and called me Jeff."

"Oh." Katrina suddenly felt a wave of sadness, but pushed it behind her.

"Where is he now?" Nathan was studying her face from across the room.

"He died in a car accident. He came home for homecoming, and on his way back to school there was an accident. He was killed instantly."

"Oh, I'm so sorry! Was he….a pretty good guy?"

"Yes, he was. He was the best. I-I don't think I ever quite got over the…..tragedy of his death."

As she said this, Nathan felt an unfamiliar tug in the pit of his stomach, and he couldn't quite explain it.

"Want me to look around….check out the rest of the place…. before I leave?"

"Okay. I guess I'd feel better about being here alone if you did."

Nathan went down the hallway and checked out the bathroom and the two bedrooms. As he stood inside her bedroom, he had a warm comfortable feeling. The third bedroom door he found locked. "Is this door locked for a reason?" He yelled toward the living room.

Katrina got up and walked down to the third bedroom door and reached up on the door frame and took down a key. "Yes. This is where I work. I don't allow the cats in there, but I also keep it locked in case somebody breaks in. I don't want my equipment or my work destroyed." She opened the door so he could see inside, and then she walked into the room with him behind her.

"So this is where Kit-Kat is created every day?"

"Yep. But I do a week's worth of work in one day and submit it. I don't have to work again until Friday."

Both Nathan and Katrina were delaying the inevitable—Nathan's departure. She was afraid to be alone, and he didn't want to leave her alone.

"Hey, I have an idea. I know you won't feel up to making dinner tonight, so why don't you let me take you out?"

"I can't go out like this." She was surprised that he would even suggest it. Who would want to take her anywhere looking as bad as she did?

"Oh, right." He forgot about how badly she must feel with her face all banged up.

"But, you know, I have a nice barbeque grill on the patio. If you wanted to, I would let you come over to barbeque something. If you wanted."

Nathan grinned at her. "Okay....but promise me that you won't do a thing. I'll bring everything. All you have to do is be hungry. Deal?"

"Deal." Katrina nodded and smiled with the right side of her mouth.

"Okay....I'm going to go home, take a shower and a nap. I didn't get a lot of sleep last night. I'll have Marie make up some fantastic side dishes and I'll bring them over....in a picnic basket. I'll cook steaks on your grill....you will do nothing. Okay?"

"Okay. Around six?"

"Perfect. Take a nap, too, okay? Remember to put the cold compresses on your face, and give me your prescriptions. I'll get them filled and bring them with me." Nathan was heading toward the front door and Katrina got the prescriptions out of her purse.

"Yes sir!" She answered playfully, with a military salute.

He rewarded her playfulness with one of his best grins. "See you at six."

Nathan drove home annoyed about something he couldn't put his finger on. What was bugging him? He pulled into the driveway but didn't open the garage door since he would be leaving in a few hours. He opened the car door, got out slowly and leaned against the car. Suddenly the realization dawned on him—he was jealous of Jeff! Katrina talked so highly of him.....he must have been a great guy. Was she still in love with him? Why did he care if she was? He knew the answer.

He entered the house by the back door and found Marie cleaning the stove. She greeted him with a smile.

"Did she get into her apartment all right? How is she feeling?"

Nathan sat down on a stool at the counter and said, "Yeah, she got in okay. She's still pretty shaken up. I met the cats...they're gorgeous... and affectionate."

"Yeah, I like cats myself." Marie confided.

"Marie, there's a problem.....I kinda.....no, it's not a good idea, I guess."

"You're attracted to her. Am I right? You want to start seeing her."

"Yeah, I do."

"So what's the problem? Ask her to go out." Marie was secretly overjoyed about the prospect. She was a sweet girl and Nathan deserved a girl like that.

"I don't know....what do I say? Sorry my brother beat you up, planned on raping and killing you...but hey, would you like to go out sometime? Nope...I don't see that happening. She's really special.... I can see that just from seeing her in her own home. She's also very talented.....and.....she's everything I could possibly want."

"Well then...why not go for it? You have a lot to offer a girl. I'm sure she knows that you're nothing like Steven. And besides, what do you have to lose? Two days ago you didn't know her. Nothing ventured—nothing gained."

"I told her I would take her dinner tonight....with your help, of course. I'll get the steaks out, but do you think you could put together some side dishes for me?"

"Absolutely, Nathan. Just remember to stop and buy a small bouquet of flowers...something simple, like daisies. Tell her it's to dress up the table for dinner."

"Marie, you're a genius. Good idea. I'm going to take a nap for a couple of hours."

"I'll have everything ready when you get up. Don't forget to get the steaks out. There are some filets in the freezer." Marie was already reaching for pots out of the cupboard.

Nathan pulled two nice sized filet mignons out of the freezer and set them on the counter. He knew he could rely on Marie to take care of them for him. He went to lie down for a nap until it was time to get ready to leave for her place.

* * *

Nathan slept fitfully for almost two hours. When he awoke, he felt well rested and was anxious to get ready to go. After showering and dressing, he dropped by the kitchen just as Marie was packing her side dishes into the picnic basket.

"Your steaks are in there. Bottle of wine?" Marie was holding a bottle of red wine in her hand, ready to put it into the basket.

"I don't know if she drinks wine. I doubt that she drinks at all." Although he was undecided about the wine, Marie put it into the basket anyway.

"Can't hurt." She laughed.

* * *

At exactly six o'clock, Nathan tapped on Katrina's door. She looked through the peephole, and then opened the door when she saw that it was Nathan. She had taken a nap after he left and had awakened an hour before he was due to arrive. She showered and changed into one of her own sundresses—a pastel pink and blue voile that flowed softly just past mid-thigh. It was a much better fit than the one she wore home.

"Meals on wheels." He announced. She laughed gingerly.

"These are to dress up the table." He handed her the pastel colored daisies he remembered to get when he filled her prescriptions.

"How pretty! How did you know that daisies were my favorite flower?"

"Just a hunch….lead me to the grill. Feeling any better?"

"Yes, actually. I took a nap like you told me and I used the cold compresses." She spoke as she led him to the patio where the gas grill stood.

"Great…now sit down and watch the master of steaks at work."

He lit the grill and went back to the kitchen to arrange the side dishes that needed to be heated in the microwave, and opened the container that held a garden salad. She followed him into the kitchen and brought a fruit salad out of the refrigerator.

"I have everything we need….." He saw her holding the bowl of fruit salad. "Except I forgot the fruit salad."

She laughed. How noble he was!

"You weren't supposed to do anything, remember?" He scolded.

"Well, I had the fruit and I don't like to let things go bad, so I sat at the table and peeled and cut it up."

"You're forgiven. What cupboard has the dishes? By the way, I do dishes, too, so you don't have to do anything."

"I have a dishwasher."

"Better yet." He grinned at her. He thought it was going well.

Dinner was delicious. The steaks were done to perfection and Marie's side dishes were amazing. She even had a homemade cheesecake for dessert. Nathan offered Katrina wine, of which she took only half a glass. She still had a hard time eating, so her food was cut up in small bites. They talked through dinner.

Nathan studied her for a moment when they sat down to eat. "Has there ever been a Mister Katrina? A husband, I mean?"

"No—never. I....really don't date all that much."

"You must have offers all the time..." He trailed off, hoping the answer was a negative.

"There was Jeff, the guy in high school. We had plans....but they....didn't happen. I've dated a couple of guys, but nothing serious. This is going to sound a little.....Pollyanna, but I just always felt that there was someone special waiting for me. I just haven't found him yet. When I was young, like around twelve, I told my mother that. She believed it was true."

Nathan couldn't believe he heard what she just said. She said almost the exact same thing he had said to his father almost half a lifetime ago.

"Did you ever think that you could feel him but you just didn't know who he was?" He held his breath waiting for her answer.

"Yes! How did you know that?"

He smiled at her.

"So what about you? No Missus Nathan?"

"No. There was one I thought I was going to marry, but it didn't work out."

"Why not? Oh, I guess I shouldn't ask that."

"It's okay. I'll tell you. I was a major league pitcher for about five years. I met her one day after I had pitched a no-hitter. She kind of hung around the field chatting with all the ball players, but she really hit on me. She was pretty, but shallow. I was in love, or at least thought I was, so I overlooked that part about her. I spent a lot of money on her. She always wanted something, and I had the means to get whatever it was she wanted. I bought her an engagement ring and asked her to marry me. The date was set and everything. Then I threw my arm out. Doctors advised me not to pitch any more after that. Fortunately for me, I had a degree....in finance and investments. I had applied my knowledge for the whole five years I pitched. I was making a lot of money from my endorsements and TV commercials then. When I stepped down, I was financially well off, so I didn't need to worry about money and how I was going to make a living. Well, she didn't know my net worth, thank God, because she may have stuck around. Anyway, she ended the engagement when my career ended. She didn't think she could be with a has-been. I let her go and I learned a valuable lesson."

"What's that?" Katrina was engrossed in his story.

"Pretty packages don't necessarily make nice gifts." He simply stated.

Katrina stared at him not sure of what to say. Of course, he was right, but how sad for him.

"Okay, I told you about Julie…now tell me about…what was his name? The one who couldn't keep his hands to himself."

"Sean. He was really good looking and a football star. All the girls were in love with him. We ended badly. After that, I never spoke to him again. Jeff rescued me that night, and from then on it was Jeff and me."

"So what happened?" It was Nathan's turn to be engrossed.

Katrina told him the story about the night she and Sean broke up. He laughed at the part where she punched Sean. His reaction to the rest of the story was not much different than Jeff's.

They talked for hours. He told her about Tanya, and then Christa. Then he told her about Mike. She told him all about Morgan. They talked about their education. Nathan was impressed that she had gone on for a Master's degree. He asked about her piano lessons, and she told him of her dancing lessons. He shared with her his passion for baseball and about how he went to baseball camp in the summer.

"My love for baseball was my greatest love of all. When the coach said no girls, Mike and I didn't see our girlfriends. We lived for baseball." There was a wistful note in his voice.

"Did it hurt to give up baseball?" She had to ask.

"Very much. It's all I ever wanted. But I'm not stupid. My talent only went as far as the arm went. I left the game a winner. Can't ask for more than that. I miss it, though. I still watch it, but every time I do I feel a yearning to play the game. I could have coached, probably, but it would have hurt not to play."

"What about Mike? What happened to him?"

"Mike went to med school. He's Doctor Mike now. Oh, here's a happy story….we've done nothing but tell sad ones."

"I'm ready for a happy one. Go ahead." Katrina tucked her hands under her chin.

"Well, Mike and I had a really good friend, Cookie. She's a great person. In high school she was very popular and well liked, but not exactly gorgeous. Kind of chubby with skin problems. Very short hair with no shine. But Mike and I loved her. She was a good friend to us. Our birthdays are two days apart, so for our birthdays, Cookie gave us signed baseballs—signed by the Cleveland Indians. I still have mine, and I'm sure Mike does, too. Well, anyway, in about our senior year, Cookie started to change. She lost all her baby fat, her skin cleared up and she let her hair grow. She became very attractive. Well, after Mike got out of college and med school, they met for lunch one day. Cookie's a chemist and they work near each other. Well, the way Mike tells it, they were having a nostalgia session and they hugged each other. The next thing they knew, they were kissing—passionately. They got married about two years ago. She's the best wife a man could have. They're really happy and I'm really glad for them. I'm glad because they both deserve someone special, and I can't think of two more special people."

Katrina was smiling. Nathan could see that she was delighted with the story.

"What a wonderful story! Any kids yet?"

"No, not yet....but they're thinking about it. Hey, it's time for me to get the dishes started. What do ya think? You sit. I promised this was my turn at bat."

"I'll just move to the stool at the counter and watch. How's that?"

"Fine. I see you cheated and made coffee. Want some while you watch?"

She nodded and got up and moved to one of the stools that stood in front of her countertop bar. She sipped her coffee and watched him stack the dishes in the dishwasher, then wipe off the counters. He added soap to the dishwasher, turned it on and helped himself to a cup of coffee. As he sat down on the stool next to her, he glanced at the clock. It was eleven o'clock. Where did the time go?

"Your face is starting to heal already. Not much swelling in your lip and your eye is opening again. You look like a raccoon, though." He looked at her and smiled, hoping to get a smile back. She complied.

"The picture over there on the end table....is that you and your brothers?"

"Yes. We took that at Christmas last year. We all managed to make it home for Christmas, and my parents were delighted. They insisted we get the portrait done."

"Nice family. Are your brothers married?"

"Yes, both of them are married. I was in both of their weddings. Mike and Kim don't have any kids, but Danny and Kathy have a boy and a girl. The boy is five and the girl is three. I'm Aunt Kat and I spoil them every chance I get." Katrina's face lit up when she talked about her niece and nephew.

"I'll bet you're a wonderful aunt. What about you? Do you want marriage and kids?" Nathan hoped she did, because he sure did.

"Oh yes....I would love to have kids...but I think I have to find the marriage part first."

"I agree. I want kids, dogs, and cats." He hoped she liked dogs as well as she liked cats.

"Sounds perfect." She meant it, since it was what she would like to have as well.

An old memory came into her mind just then—Jeff's picture of the two of them with five kids. She pushed it out of her mind and concentrated on Nathan's face. He was staring at her.

"Are you trying to see what I look like without all the decorations?" She teased.

"Oh, I can see by the photos on the wall. I was just noticing how blue your eyes are. Most people have to wear contacts to get eyes like that."

"They're like my father's. I have been asked if I wear contacts, though."

They were making small talk now, prolonging the time when he would get up to leave. Katrina was nervous about staying alone, but more than that, she didn't want him to go. He didn't want to go, but he knew it was the right thing to do. He stood up and asked to use the bathroom. Damn, he wanted to hold her.

Katrina knew it was time for him to leave. It was the right thing to do. When he returned from the bathroom, he announced that he should go.

"It was a wonderful evening. I mean that." He sounded sincere.

"Yes, it was....and I mean it, too." Her mind was screaming 'don't go', but she only smiled at him and stood up to walk him to the door.

He put his arms around her and gently hugged her, and she hugged him back. The cats appeared from nowhere and rubbed up against him. Katrina laughed. "Very social, aren't they?"

"Yes, they are. Remember, if you need anything, just call me. I'll be here." Nathan wondered if he sounded as calm as he thought he did. In fact, he felt like electricity was running through his body. He wanted to put his arms around her again, but dared not. "Lock the door, okay?"

She nodded. They stood there in awkward silence for a few moments. Finally, he leaned over and kissed her hair that fell over her forehead. "Sweet dreams." He was out the door, fearing that if he stayed another second, he would make a fool of himself. She watched his headlights until they were out of sight, and then locked the door. She started to turn the porch light off, but thought better of it. 'To hell with the electric bill,' she thought.

Katrina lay in bed staring at the ceiling. When she closed her eyes, all she could see was Nathan's face. She tossed and turned, shifting into several positions before she drifted off to sleep. She dreamed of Jeff....no, it was Nathan. She awoke from the dream around four in the morning. She remembered the dream quite well. She and Jeff were kissing and when they stopped kissing she looked up at him. But it wasn't Jeff—it was Nathan she had been kissing. She saw Jeff across the room, and he was talking to her. "It's okay, Honey. He's like me." Jeff was saying to her. Katrina awoke with a start and felt the tears on her face.

"Oh, Jeff." She whispered into the darkness. She thought about the dream and realized that Nathan was a lot like Jeff. Was Jeff releasing her? Is that what the dream meant? She finally fell back to sleep and didn't awake until dawn.

* * *

Nathan, likewise, could not fall asleep. He stared at the ceiling in his room, and eventually got up and made his way to the living room and turned on the television. He stared at some mindless comedy with B rated actors until he could watch no more. He went into the den and turned on the computer. When his online screen came up he typed in 'Kit-Kat" and clicked on the search button. The search engine produced a number of entries to choose from, most of which had to do with the candy bar. Toward the bottom of the page, he found what he was looking for. The words 'comic strip' showed up in the search engine's description. He clicked on it and there was a sample of the famous 'Kit-Kat" cartoon. There was a small blurb about the creator as well. That would be Katrina. There wasn't much more on the page, so he got out of the screen, and then got off line. He wondered through the house, stopping to get a glass of wine. He was not much of a drinker but he hoped that a little wine would make him sleepy. The wine served its purpose and he returned to bed and fell asleep.

He dreamed of Katrina. She was crying and he wanted to touch her, but he was being held back by something, or someone. He couldn't move his arm. He looked down to see why he couldn't move his arm and found a baseball in his hand. He looked up and saw Steven hit Katrina, and he threw the ball at him. Steven had a bat and he hit the ball with it. The ball sailed back at Nathan and he ducked. Steven laughed. Nathan jerked and the motion awoke him. He turned on the light beside the bed and sat up. It was four in the morning. He wondered if she was sleeping. Of course she was—it was four A.M. He lay back down and tucked his arms under his head. Eventually he drifted off to sleep and awoke for the day at dawn. He quickly showered and put on clean rust colored shorts and a tan polo shirt. Marie was coming in the back door as he got to the kitchen.

"How did it go?" She didn't mask her interest.

"Okay. Dinner was great. Thank you for the effort." He smiled at her sincerely.

"No problem. So? Are you going to see her again?"

"Hopefully. She's really amazing. Interesting, really. We talked for hours. It's obvious that she comes from a good, loving family."

"So do you have anything in common that can keep it going?"

"I think so. We both want the same things."

"Well, then don't stop trying. Did it ever occur to you, although the circumstances weren't the best that it was fate that she ended up here?" Marie waited for Nathan's reaction to this thought.

"No, it never did. Do you think that?"

"Maybe. I mean what are the odds that Steven would come down to Florida and abduct a girl and she end up here in your house? And she turns out to be someone you're attracted to. Sounds like fate to me, regardless of the horrible circumstances. Now…do you want some breakfast?"

Nathan's brain was working on what Marie had just said. He reached for his keys, and answered her. "No, I think I'll go out for breakfast." He grinned at her as he left through the back door.

He drove to the bagel shop and picked up a few bagels and some cream cheese, and then dialed her number on his cell phone. She answered on the second ring, so he knew she was already up and awake.

She had been up since dawn. Twice she walked to the phone to call him, and then thought better of it. Maybe he didn't want to spend Sunday morning with her. Maybe he had things to do. Once, she picked up the phone to make sure there was a dial tone. She fed the cats and had looked wistfully at the phone, willing it to ring. She showered and put on the colorful caftan that Danny and Kathy had brought back from Mexico last fall. Once the coffee was started, she retrieved her Sunday paper from the front porch, and was about to open it when the phone finally rang. She saw his name on the caller ID and tried to sound calm when she answered.

"Hi. Do you have any coffee made? I have bagels." He tried to sound nonchalant.

"I just put a pot on. Bring on the bagels." She tried to sound calm, but there were butterflies in the pit of her stomach. She was smiling when she hung up the telephone. "This is crazy." She whispered aloud.

* * *

Nathan arrived before she had time to change clothes, so she was still wearing the brightly colored caftan when she let him in the door.

"That's real pretty on you." He stood back and smiled at her. "You wear it well."

She thanked him with her eyes, at least the one that was fully opened. "Thanks. It matches my face, I think."

Nathan laughed as he went to the cupboard and reached for two cups. He placed the cups and the bag of bagels on the dinette table, poured the coffee for them, and then got a plate for the bagels and two small plates, one for each of them.

"What time do you have to be at Harding's office tomorrow? I plan on taking you, if that's okay."

"Yes, it's okay. He did say he didn't want me driving." She was so glad he planned on taking her, since she was still nervous about going out. Steven may be in jail, but the memory was running around alive and rampant. "I have to be there at eight."

"I'll be here at seven-thirty then. Where are the kitties?"

"Sleeping on my bed. They have a rough life." She snickered a little. "The truth is, they play all night, and then take a morning nap right after I feed them."

"Humans should have it so lucky. So what do you plan on doing today?"

Nathan was trying to figure out how to prolong his stay. He knew they couldn't sit and talk small talk all day, but he didn't want to go any time soon. He also knew she still wouldn't go anywhere with her face all bruised up. He thought of inviting her to go to his place to swim in the pool, but he knew that was a bad idea, since her ribs were probably fractured.

"Clean, I guess. I usually go over the apartment every day. I haven't done it since Thursday, which means there is a ton of cat hair on everything."

Nathan had a brainstorm.

"Well, the place looks clean….but I'll tell you what….you aren't supposed to do anything strenuous, so I'll do it for you."

Katrina burst out laughing, and then stopped and covered her lip with her hand.

"You're going to clean my apartment? That's too funny!" She was laughing again, and it was hurting her lip, but she couldn't help it.

"Well, yeah....I know how to clean. I didn't always have a housekeeper, you know. I do windows, too. You're not supposed to do anything like that. Bill said nothing strenuous, and that means cleaning. Come on, it'll be fun."

"And what will I do when you're cleaning? I'm not sure I could sit and watch."

A light went on in Nathan's eyes. "I know....you could play the piano for me. I'd love to hear you play. Please?"

"Oh, all right...let's finish off these bagels first. But you have to promise me that when I'm all better you'll let me do something for you....like maybe cook you dinner, or change the oil in your car.....or something. Deal?"

"Deal. Just show me where everything is, and I promise that while you are serenading me, I will make the place spic and span. I'm going to enjoy it, too. I promise."

Nathan, true to his word, cleaned her apartment. She sat down at the piano and began playing while he cleaned. She began with a classical arrangement, and then switched to something more modern. He was impressed with her ability, as he stopped to watch her fingers fly over the keys. Katrina played for quite awhile, and then drifted over to the sofa to rest. After he finished up the cleaning, he sat down beside her.

"Your playing was amazing! No, it was spectacular! You are truly one talented girl."

"Thank you. It took a lot of hard work and a lot of practice. My art talent I was born with....that took training."

"Training that has paid off, I'll say that." He cocked his head and studied her beautiful profile. Yes, she was beautiful, and talented and obviously intelligent, yet, she was so modest about it all. She had a quiet confidence about her, and yet she was very sweet. Perfect....that was the word that came into his mind. She was perfect. He was awed by her, and yet he wanted to protect her, take care of her, but most of all he wanted to kiss her. Being that close to her was driving him crazy. Nathan stood up.

"I could go for another cup of coffee. How about you?"

She nodded.

"Sounds like a good idea. The place looks better, don't you think?"

"If you say so. It looked fine before." He walked over to the counter and poured them each a fresh cup of coffee. While he waited for her to join him he made his way to her massive book shelves. "Have you read all these?"

"Well, most of them. The top shelf holds all my text books, and the next two shelves are all the books I have read. Those on the bottom shelf are ones I plan on reading."

He reached up and pulled a text book off the shelf. "Economics Today." He read the title aloud.

She made a face and said, "Not my favorite subject, but it was a required course."

He smiled and replaced the book. It *was* one of his favorite subjects, but he couldn't play the piano like she could. 'We all have our strong points.' He thought to himself.

He left the book shelves and sat down at the table with her, just as the cats were making their way out of her bedroom.

"Hi, kitties!" He seemed glad to see them. Angel, the one who seemed to take to him the day before, meowed to him and ran to rub up against his legs. He reached down to pet her. The other two gathered around him, waiting for their turn to be petted.

"They like you." Katrina felt good about the cats liking him; since cats didn't take to people they couldn't trust. She knew that if the cats liked him, she could trust him.

The silence was broken by the ringing of Nathan's cell phone. He took the call since it was Detective Delaney.

"Hi Brian, what's up?"

"Nothing. I just called to see how Miss Kitrowski was doing. Is she feeling any better? I called your house and Marie said you might be at her place."

"Well, she's doing a little better." He looked at Katrina and mouthed the word 'detective' to her. She nodded.

"That's good. Hey, and remind her that the plate on her car expires this week. I noticed that when we looked at her registration card."

"Okay, I will. Keep me posted on what's going on. You know, with Steven."

"Will do…talk to you."

Nathan disconnected the call and relayed the message about her registration.

"Oh, yeah, I have the new tag here, but I didn't get a chance to put it on yet. Would you mind?"

"Look, lady, I cook, I clean, I do dishes, but I have to draw the line at that. I will *not* stoop down that low to put your sticker on your license plate."

Surprised, Katrina jerked her head up at him in time to see that he was about to break up laughing. She burst out laughing. Their eyes locked as they stared at each other in awkward silence.

Nathan was the first to move. "Where's your tag? I'll do it right now."

She pointed to the top of the refrigerator, not trusting her voice at the moment. He grabbed it and went out to the driveway.

When Nathan came back in, he turned his chair around and straddled it backwards and sat down. "Okay, you're holding out on me." He was smirking at her.

"Wh-what do you mean?"

"Well, Old Nate here knows that your registration expires on your birthday…so come on, tell me. When is it? I know it's got to be this week."

Katrina tilted her head back and laughed. "Okay, you got me. It's Thursday."

"And how old will you be?"

"I'll be twenty-eight. How old are you, and when is your birthday?"

"I'll be thirty on the fourth of July. I celebrate my birthday with a bang every year." He grinned at her, and she laughed.

"So what are you going to do for your birthday?" He cocked his head and smiled at her.

"Well, the first thing I'm going to do is try to find a way to get out of going out to dinner with my brother Danny and his wife. I can't let them see me like this. Danny would go ballistic, and it wouldn't be pretty. Then he'd call Mike and tell him, and that would be even less pretty. My brothers don't take too well to someone hurting me."

"I can't say I blame them. So how are you going to get out of going out with them?"

"I don't know. I'm thinking about telling them that the queen has summoned me to England that day."

It was Nathan's turn to jerk his head up at her. She had a mischievous look on her face, and Nathan thought she looked adorable. He laughed at her remark.

* * *

Nathan was up at six in the morning. He had left Katrina's around four the previous afternoon, with the promise that he would be there to take her to the doctor's office at seven-thirty the next morning. She said she planned on getting some work done so she wouldn't have to do it all on Thursday to have it ready to submit on Friday morning. The time with her had been delightful, and they parted on a good note, with Nathan hugging her at the door. He still had not attempted to kiss her since it was obvious that her lip was still too sore. He hoped that Bill Harding would have good news to report after he examined her.

She was ready when he got to her apartment, her purse in one hand and a brown envelope in the other. "What's that?" He asked her.

"Oh, it's an autographed picture of Kit-Kat. Dr. Harding said his daughter loves her, so I thought she would like to have a picture of her."

"Can I see it?" Nathan was amused at the idea of a comic strip character having autographed photos to pass out. He took the envelope and pulled the picture out of it. "This is Angel."

"Yes, it is. But who says Kit-Kat can't have a stand-in?"

Nathan laughed and put the picture back into its envelope. "Very cute." He meant it, too. He thought it was *very* cute.

* * *

Doctor Harding was waiting for them when they got there, and as he had promised, none of the staff were there yet. He set her up for an x-ray of her ribs and some of her face just to be sure that no facial bones were broken. While he was waiting for the x-rays to develop, he examined her. "I notice the bruises are fading. That's good." He shined that god-awful bright light in her eye and it hurt a little. "Doesn't look to be any damage to the eyeball. That's good news, too. You probably should see an eye specialist to be sure, though." The bell rang signaling that the x-rays were developed.

Doctor Harding hung them up over the light to read them. "Here, and here." He said to Katrina and pointed to two of her ribs. "That's where the fractures are, but they're healing already. You must be in excellent health. Your body mends fast."

Katrina was studying the x-rays, but for the life of her, she couldn't see what he saw. She just took his word for it that her ribs were fractured.

"Okay. Now I want you to take it easy for a couple of weeks. Nothing strenuous. If you start to feel pain, severe pain, that is, I want you to call me immediately. You should be okay. Continue with the antibiotic and the pain pills as needed, but you won't need many of the pain medication, I don't think."

She thanked him and handed him the envelope she had set down under her purse.

"Here…this is for you daughter." She smiled at him.

He looked into the envelope and smiled, really smiled, at her. "She's gonna love this."

Katrina met Nathan in the waiting room and they hurried out the door before the soon-to-arrive staff began showing up.

As Nathan pulled out of the parking lot, he glanced at her.

"Breakfast? At your place, I mean. Have anything I can make breakfast with? Eggs? Pancake mix?"

"Eggs…and bacon…and bread for toast. Will that do?"

"Absolutely." He responded.

Nathan cooked again, and she was feeling quite spoiled. What a good man he was! She hoped he was doing things for her because he wanted to and not because he felt guilty about what his brother did to her. She wondered. He seemed to like her, and she hoped she was right about that.

He rinsed the dishes and stacked them in the dishwasher for her. He ran out of reasons to hang around…all but the obvious reason, that is.

"Well, I guess I should get going." He turned toward the door, and Katrina felt a tug of disappointment.

Nathan suddenly changed his course, moved back toward the kitchen, and sat down on a stool at the counter. "I don't want to go. I'm sorry, I know I don't have any right to say this, but….I want…you. I want to be with you. I can't stop thinking about you. If you don't have a boyfriend, I want to be him. No…that didn't come out right. Damn it, I can be such a jackass sometimes." He covered his eyes with his hand and stared down at the floor.

Katrina couldn't help but laugh, but she laughed quietly. She thought that what he said and the way he said it was just so damn cute. She quietly went and stood in front of him. "Yes." She stated simply.

He looked up at her. "Yes? Yes, what?"

"You can be my boyfriend….but only if I can be your girlfriend." Her blue eyes were shining brilliantly as she smiled at him. "I thought you'd never ask."

Nathan looked into her eyes and gently touched her face. He wanted to kiss her very badly, but was afraid to hurt her.

Katrina seemed to be reading his mind. She nodded, and whispered. "Very gently. Very, very gently."

He slid his arm around her shoulders, and gently held her face in his other hand. They shared their first kiss. He kissed her gently and softly. When the kiss ended, he studied her face, and brushed back a few strands of her hair off her forehead. He kissed her gently again.

"That was nice." His voice caught in his throat and he had to swallow in order to continue. "Thank you for being you." He kissed her lightly on her left cheek and then on the other. He kissed her swollen eye, and then kissed her lightly on the swollen lip.

Katrina looked up at him with half a smile on her face.

"What was that all about?"

"I'm kissing the boo-boos to make them all better." He had a playful look on his face, which made Katrina laugh.

They spent the afternoon talking about everything and anything. They never ran out of things to say. He wanted to see her photo albums.

"Only if you promise to show me yours sometime." She waited for a positive answer before she went to get them.

They laughed over some of the pictures, but Nathan saw so much beauty in those pictures. There were pictures of every occasion and event in which she participated.

"You were the prettiest girl on the drill team." He stated it as a fact, not as a compliment. "So you've been beautiful all your life, then?" He was teasing her.

Katrina laughed.

"No nose job, no facelift, no plastic surgery anywhere."

"All of these....your baby pictures, your school pictures, every picture in here....you look beautiful in every one of them. These ones of the prom are just gorgeous. My prom dates were pretty but nothing like this." He tapped the picture of her wearing her crown. It was taken just after they crowned her and Jeff that night. He stopped and studied the picture of her and Jeff. He saw the love in their eyes and he felt that little pang of jealousy creep up. 'I wish I could have known her back then.' He thought to himself.

"Jeff was a good-looking guy. He wore the crown well. I looked like a dork with that crown on my head."

"You were prom king?" 'Of course he was. I should have known that.' She thought.

"Yeah, it made Stephanie happy. I was glad for her sake. Lori thought it should have been me and Mike though, since we were inseparable most of the time." He laughed and Katrina laughed with him.

It became late in the afternoon, and they both were feeling rather hungry.

"Let's order some spaghetti dinners from that Italian place two blocks up. They deliver.

7

They had just finished eating the delicious spaghetti dinner, and Nathan was tying up the trash bag to set outside, when someone knocked at the door. Katrina was in the bathroom, so Nathan answered the door.

"Who the hell are you?" It was Danny and Kathy.

"You must be Danny."

"Yeah, I know who the hell I am, but that wasn't my question. Who…."

Danny was cut off by Kathy's shriek. Danny followed Kathy's line of vision and saw Katrina standing there, her face a mess.

"Kat, what happened? Who did that to you?" He turned on Nathan. "Did *you* do that? I'll kill you!" Katrina saw Danny's hands ball up into fists.

"Danny, no! Danny! Stop!" Katrina started crying.

"No, I didn't do that. I would never…."

"What the fuck happened to her? Kat…somebody better start talking…..NOW! What the fuck happened to her face?" Danny was facing Nathan again, and shouting at him.

"Danny, stop….stop now, and listen!" Katrina was on the verge of hysteria. She fell into a chair at the table.

Kathy went to Katrina and put an arm around her.

Nathan stared at Danny, put his hands up, palms down and started toward Katrina. "You're upsetting your sister, can't you see that?"

"Yes, *my sister*…..I still haven't gotten who you are…."

"*Danny*!"

Nathan went to Katrina and stood behind her with his hands on her shoulders. "I think you better tell him what happened to you. He'll find out eventually anyhow." He squeezed her shoulders gently, letting her know he was there for her.

"Yes, I think somebody better tell me…whatever it is." Danny glared at Nathan. "You better not have anything to do with it…"

"Danny, Nathan saved my life!" Katrina took a tissue from Kathy and waited for Danny to calm down. He stared at Nathan, mellowed a little, and sat down in front of Katrina.

"What happened?" Danny took Katrina's hand between his two hands. "Tell me, Kat. Tell me what happened to you."

Katrina told Danny and Kathy the story. Danny's eyes were dark with anger. "Where is this bastard now?"

"He's behind bars." Nathan answered for her.

Danny looked up at Nathan. "Is she safe?" Then he looked at Katrina. "Are you safe from him? Will they keep him there? Did you see a doctor?"

"Yes." Katrina and Nathan answered together.

"Are you going to be all right?"

"Yes. It's not as bad as it looks. My ribs are fractured but they're healing already."

"And so Nathan stopped the attack before..."

"Yes. He came out of nowhere. All I saw was a third arm and then the guy was flung backwards."

"Did you go to a hospital and be checked out?"

"No, Nathan's friend is a doctor. He made a house call. I couldn't go and chance it getting into the papers. I mean, I would have if my injuries were life threatening, of course...but, they're not. Nathan called the police and....well, they caught him. He had my purse in his van and they caught him....here. He had my ID and my address."

"Where were you when he came here?"

"At Nathan's. He took care of everything for me."

"Very resourceful." Danny regretted his tone immediately. "Hey, I'm sorry. I should be grateful to you. Thanks. I came over here because Katrina didn't return my calls. I knew something wasn't right, and when I saw her....well, I kind of went nuts, I guess. So you've been looking out for her since the attack?"

Nathan nodded.

"It's more than that, but yes, I've been looking out for her."

Katrina placed her hand over Nathan's hand, which was still resting on her shoulder.

Danny understood. "I got it." He extended his hand to Nathan. "I'm Dan Kitrowski, and this is my wife, Kathy."

"Nathan Perletti." Nathan answered as he accepted the handshake from Danny. "I think I better tell you the rest."

"Okay. Let's hear it." Danny waited for Nathan to start.

"Her attacker....is my brother. I'm telling you because I know you'll find out eventually. But I want you to understand that we weren't raised together. I hadn't seen him in years. He's mentally ill and spent most of his life in institutions. He found his way to Florida after the last one released him. He *is* dangerous. He would have killed her if I hadn't gotten there in time. He planned on putting her in my pool. Thank God I came home from my business trip a day early."

Danny sagged into the chair, a sickness developing in the pit of his stomach. He held onto Katrina's hand and squeezed it. "Oh my God, Kat!"

"Nathan pulled a gun on him...." Katrina told Danny.

"Yeah, and I would have used it if I had to. Like I said, we weren't raised together and there's no love lost there. I only got the gun because I read in one of the reports on him that he was terrified of guns. If he had the chance he would kill me; I know that. So I got a gun, and learned how to use it, to protect myself."

Danny sat in his chair quietly digesting what Nathan had told him. "So you called the police?"

"I have a friend who is a detective. I called him and he came right away. Once he took over, the police force acted on it. While Katrina stayed at my place that night, an officer stayed here in her place. There were unmarked cars in the area, so when he showed up they took him down. Katrina will probably have to testify....but I'll be right there with her."

"You'll stand by Katrina against your own brother?" Kathy spoke up for the first time.

"Absolutely. Steven needs to be kept locked up, but more than that.....I.....care for her...a lot."

"Kat?" Danny was almost smiling. "And you, Kat?"

Katrina looked right into Danny's eyes and answered. "Ditto."

All the fire and anger left Danny's body, as he sat back and stared at them. He looked over at Kathy. "How about making some coffee? This man wants my sister. We'll need a pot of coffee to drink while I interrogate him." The tension broke as they all laughed lightly.

* * *

Nathan left Katrina in the charge of her brother. He knew they needed some time together, so he bowed out for the evening to give them that. 'That is one protective brother.' He thought to himself. He couldn't blame him, though. After seeing Katrina's photo album he knew that she was the family's pride and joy. He saw the love in the eyes of those who were photographed with her. He had only known her a couple of days, and he knew he was head over heels in love with her. He could imagine what it must have been like watching her grow up, developing her talents, and achieving her goals. Everything he had learned about her in three days' time awed him. He knew there was so much more to learn about her, and he was sure that whatever else he learned would be equally as awesome. She was truly amazing.

He swung by the bar where he went to hang out with a couple of friends once in awhile, mainly his friend Charlie. The bar was more than just a hangout for him. He actually owned fifty percent of it. Jack Dooley ran the place, with Nathan being a silent partner. He let Jack keep eighty percent of the profits for all his hard work, while Nathan took only twenty. It wasn't his usual business venture, but Jack needed money to get into the place. He was a good guy, so Nathan helped him out. Jack was honest, so Nathan never questioned whether he was getting his full percentage. He didn't need the money anyway. His part of the profits he referred to as 'chump change'.

Charlie's car wasn't in the parking lot, so he drove by. He knew Marie would be gone for the day, and it sort of disappointed him. He wanted to tell her that he and Katrina were going to start seeing each other on a more than 'just friends' basis. The thought made him light headed and he grinned to himself. He pulled into his driveway, left the car where he stopped, and ran into the house to call Mike. It was still early enough.

"Hey, I hope I didn't get you two out of bed." Nathan teased as soon as Mike answered the phone.

"Hey, Buddy, what's up? How's everything going?" Mike signaled to Cookie that it was Nathan. Cookie stood by Mike trying to hear Nathan on the other end of the line.

"I found her, Mike."

"Found who? What the hell are you talking about?" Mike had forgotten Nathan's dream of finding 'the one'.

"My Forever. I found my Forever." Nathan was smiling as he spoke.

There was silence on the other end of the line. Finally, Mike responded.

"No shit? Who is she? Wait…I have to put you on speaker phone. Cookie's about to tear my arm off."

Nathan waited until he could hear them both.

"Tell us. Give us the details. What does she look like? What's she like? What does she do? How did you meet her? Nathan….speak!"

Nathan was laughing. He knew it would be like this.

"She's beautiful, talented, intelligent, and she's fun to be with. Oh, and did I mention that she's beautiful?"

"Yes, you did." It was Cookie who answered. "Give us some details like hair color, eyes, the bod. Come on, don't keep us in suspense."

"I love torturing you two. Okay….she has beautiful light copper colored hair all the way down to her waist, and the brightest blue eyes I have ever seen. They sparkle. Those eyes are gorgeous. Her hair is the same as a brand new copper penny. She doesn't wear any eye make-up and she sure doesn't need it. Anyway, she's about five feet, six and maybe a buck-twenty in weight. I say that much because of the excellent muscle tone. She's had years of dancing lessons to get that way, not to mention high school drill team. Oh, and she plays the piano like a professional."

"Sounds like someone spent a lot of money giving her the best of everything. So how does she earn her way through life?" Mike asked.

"You're going to love this. Cookie, do you still read the comics in the newspaper?"

"Yeah, please don't tell me she's Cathy."

"No, have you ever seen the comic strip called Kit-Kat?"

"Oh, hell yeah…it's one of my favorites."

"That's hers. She's the creator."

"No shit! Wow! I'm impressed!"

"She also paints. She owns an art gallery down here that apparently does quite well selling her artwork. Like she says, it pays the bills for her."

"So you're in love?" Mike's voice was soft and emotional. He was happy for Nathan.

"Yeah, I am. I waited a long time for her…and she is definitely worth the wait."

"So what's her name? You haven't told us her name." Cookie pressed.

"Katrina. Katrina Kitrowski." Nathan said it almost with reverence.

"Kit-Kat! How definitely cool! That's where the name of the comic strip comes from! Nathan, when do we meet her?"

"Give me awhile to get to know her. Then you will."

"So how did you meet her?" Mike asked.

"Well, that's kind of a terrible story, but I might as well tell you." Nathan told them the story of that night. They quietly listened except for a few "Oh, my Gods" from Cookie. He told them that Steven was in jail and that Katrina would have to testify against him, and he confided that he would stand beside her against Steven. It sickened him every time he thought about the things Steven had said to Katrina, not to mention the injuries he inflicted.

"But anyway, that's how we met. If I hadn't have come home a day early we would not have met while she was alive."

"So is she okay? I mean, he must have hurt her." Mike sounded deeply concerned.

"Well, she's banged up, fractured ribs and all. I haven't even been able to kiss her except for a few gentle kisses. She's starting to heal, but it's going to take awhile."

"So no sex yet?" Cookie's inquiring mind was controlling her mouth.

Nathan laughed. "No, she's still pretty fragile. That will be worth waiting for, too. God, she's so *sweet!* Every time she smiles at me I want to wrap myself around her and just hold her forever. She's all I could ever want. Oh, I met one of her brothers tonight, by the way."

He told the story about how Danny flipped out when he saw Katrina's face all banged up. But it all ended on a positive note, he told them.

And it had gone well, he thought. Danny asked him lots of questions and seemed to be studying him when he answered. 'Well, he is a lawyer, after all,' Nathan reasoned. He wondered how soon it would be before he was secretly being investigated by the other brother.

He wasn't worried because he knew he could pass any investigation with flying colors. If that would put their minds at ease, so be it.

After he hung up, he went into his den and began working on proposals.

Nathan picked up the phone to call Katrina. It was close to noon and he had just come from the kitchen where he told Marie his good news. Marie was delighted. Katrina was perfect for Nathan. When Marie asked how Katrina was doing physically, Nathan assured her that she was healing, but he only hoped that psychologically she would be okay. He could see that she was still traumatized by the incident.

Katrina answered on the third ring.

"Hi, did I get you away from something?" Nathan immediately smiled when he heard her voice.

"I was just working on my strip. My week's work is almost done and ready to submit Friday morning. Sorry about the inquisition last night. My brother really gave you a hard time. He's like that when it concerns me, and Mike is even worse."

"That's okay, I didn't mind. I'd go through fire and brimstone for you....so that was a piece of cake."

"So let me guess....you went home and called Mike."

"Yeah, how did you know?"

"Because if Danny and Kathy hadn't stayed so late I would have called Morgan; which I will do today if I have time. Next time, maybe you'll get to meet the kids. Cara and little Danny were with a sitter last night. That's why they weren't here. I'm glad because I know my face would have upset them, not to mention their dad going off like that."

"I look forward to meeting them. I wondered where they were last night. I am *glad* they didn't have to witness any of that, too. So how soon do you think Mike will start his investigation on me?"

Katrina laughed.

"I'm sure it's already underway. Danny probably called him either late last night or the first thing this morning. So if you so much as made out with a girl in your car, Mike will know about it by the end of today."

Nathan laughed, but a fleeting image of Mandy crossed his mind. He knew she was deliberately exaggerating Mike's powers, so he put that annoying night out of his head.

"So are you worried? About the background check and all your dark secrets?" She was teasing him; he could tell.

"Not in the least. I've been a good boy all my life." He smiled as he tried to picture what she looked like at that moment. Did she have pajamas on or was she dressed already? Was her hair pulled back?

"Well, you should probably hide your little black book, just in case."

"I threw that book away the day after I met you. Actually, I never had one." He thought for a minute, and then teased back. "I never needed one."

She got his little joke and she laughed.

"Hey, I'm feeling a lot better today. My eye is open and I actually touched my ribcage without flinching. My lip looks almost normal, too."

"That's good news. I can't wait until I can take you somewhere."

"Like where?"

"Anywhere. Just out…to dinner maybe. I'd love for you to meet some of my friends."

"Friends like Mike?"

"Well, him, of course. But he lives in Ohio. I mean friends, like Charlie and his girl Lisa, Jack, and a couple of others I hang out with sometimes."

"I'm not quite ready for that. I'd feel really embarrassed. Your friends would think they were witnessing a freak show or something."

"You don't look that *bad…really!* But it can wait. I want you to be comfortable." He meant it. "So day after tomorrow is the big day. Anything special you want to do?"

"Well, that's actually the 'next time' I mentioned earlier. Danny and Kathy want to come over with the kids, bring food and cake and ice cream. They are going to tell the kids I got hit in the face when some little kid threw his toys at me. They're having a problem with Danny throwing things, especially at Cara. I think they're hoping for shock value. Anyway, I guess they're expecting you to be here, too. They plan on bringing enough for them, me and you. Think you can handle attorney appetizers and lawyer lasagna? That's what I call their food, since they are both attorneys."

"I'd be honored and delighted. Can I bring anything?"

"Nope. Just you. So what are you up to today?" She was hoping that she was included in his plans sometime during the day.

"Well, I'm going to the gym, for one thing. I have a little workout room here, but no weights, so I'm going to lift for awhile. Gotta keep the bod looking good, especially since I met you. Thought maybe dinner? There's a place that has home cooked meals for takeout. It's not too far from the gym. Interested?"

"Sounds great. So around five?"

"Perfect."

9

It was Thursday, Katrina's birthday. She answered the door for the floral delivery and while she was being handed the large bouquet of spring flowers, another delivery truck pulled up. The first flowers were from Danny and Kathy, and the second were from Mike and Kim. Both were spring arrangements, but one came in a basket and the other came in a vase. Yet another truck pulled up with more flowers. These were from Nathan, and they were the most beautiful of all. A dozen red roses with white daisies and baby's breath mixed through them, all contained in a beveled crystal vase. Her heart skipped a beat when she saw them. The delivery man set them down for her and commented on how popular she must be. It was obvious he was staring at her bruised face, though.

"I'm sorry; can I help you with something?" She became agitated.

"Uh, no...were you in a car accident?"

"Yes. Last week." She lied.

"Hope you feel better." He mumbled as he left.

The telephone started ringing and she immediately looked at the caller ID. Morgan. She had tried to call her two days ago but she was out of the office and out of town as well. Katrina grabbed up the ver. She had to sit through the 'happy birthday' song before they actually talked. Katrina laughed at her best friend.

"You're nuts, you know that?"

"Yes, I do. So happy birthday, Kat. I got your message but I just planned on calling you today anyway, so I waited. What's new?" Morgan always asked that.

"Nathan."

"Huh?"

"Nathan's new."

"Who's Nathan?" Morgan was holding her breath. Could it be?

"The one....the one I've been waiting for all my life." Katrina waited for Morgan's response.

Morgan squealed on the other end of the phone.

"No! Really? Kat, details, please! I can't stand it! Who is he? Where did you meet him? What's he like? Come on, don't keep me in suspense!"

Katrina was laughing. "If you come up for air, I will tell you. Morgan, I think I'm in love. He's everything I've waited for. He's wonderful."

"So he's kind, considerate, strong but tender, sweet, good, and funny?" Morgan remembered most of Katrina's requirements for falling in love.

"He's all that, and a bag of chips." Katrina quipped. "Oh, and did I mention that he's gorgeous?"

"No, you must have forgotten that part. I really don't remember that being a requirement."

"It really never was, but it's a bonus."

Morgan laughed at Katrina's terminology.

"So where did you meet him, and how did you meet him?"

"Well, get ready for a true horror story with a happy ending, okay?"

Katrina told Morgan all the gory details of the day Steven abducted her. She could hear Morgan crying at some point of the story. Katrina knew that Morgan was feeling her terror at the time of the abduction. She finished the story by telling her about how Nathan rescued her and took care of her afterward. Then she told Morgan that Steven was Nathan's brother.

"His brother? Oh, my God!"

"Well, they really weren't even raised together, since Steven spent most of his life in institutions. Nathan says he has spent his whole life being sick over things that Steven has done."

"Wow! That's too bad. Hey, I just thought of something. Is 'must rescue you' a requirement of yours, too?"

"Why? What do you mean?"

"Well...if I remember correctly, you and Jeff got together when he rescued you that night...."

"Oh, my God! I never thought about that...." Katrina's eyes went far away for a moment, as her voice trailed off. She told Morgan about her dream of Jeff.

"Do you think that was Jeff's way of....you know, letting me go?"

"Yes." Morgan averred simply. "Jeff has watched over you all these years, I'm sure. I really believe that was his way of telling you to go for it. I might be nuts, but I really do believe that."

"Yeah, I kinda do, too. So I guess we're both nuts."

"Does your family know about him yet?" Morgan knew about the brothers always having her in 'protective custody' as she called it.

Katrina related the story about how Danny and Kathy showed up, and how Danny lost it when he saw her all bruised and swollen.

"So have you done....?"

"Come on, give me a break! He can barely kiss me without it hurting me!"

"Is it that bad?"

"Well, yeah. My ribs are fractured, and my face is a mess. My eye just opened back up yesterday. The swelling in my lip went down, but it still hurts. I have bruises everywhere else, too. But if will ease your mind a bit, I fully intend on that happening, even if I have to initiate it myself."

Morgan really laughed. "Good girl! I'm happy for you, Kat. I can't wait to tell Kevin."

"So tell me, did Candy get the job?"

"Yeah, can you believe it? I get to tell her what to do, too. Aah, some rewards are better than others." Morgan laughed at her own remark.

Katrina chuckled at that one, too. "So is she working out okay?"

.eah, she's doing the job. She keeps asking about you."

"Well, don't tell her anything."

"Oh, you know I won't. I just say that you're fine every time she asks. And now I know that I'm telling the truth. Have a great birthday. Gotta run. Bye."

In less than a minute after she hung up, the phone rang again. This time is was Michael.

"Happy birthday, Kat. So what made you think you could hide things from us? My God, Katrina! I've been going out of my mind ever since Danny told me. Are you all right?"

"I'll live."

"Yeah, but from what Danny told me you could be dead now." Katrina heard the catch in his throat when he said it. "Now tell me about…what's his name? Nathan?"

"Oh, come on, Mike. Who are you kidding? You know his name. How has he checked out through your investigation?"

Mike laughed quietly. "Okay, you got me. He passed. He played major league baseball? From what I read, he was an incredible pitcher, but he threw his arm out and stepped down."

"All that jives with what he told me. Anything else you would like to bestow on me?"

"He's worth a bundle. Owns several different businesses and has his hands in many more. Has some good investments, too. He's a brilliant money-maker. All legitimate."

"Now *that* I didn't know. We don't talk about money. He doesn't know my worth at all, and until now I never even thought about his net worth. I can see he lives well, but then so could I."

"Oh, and I checked on the brother, Steven. Sad case, really. The Perletti's are good people. Al Perletti, Nathan's father is a good man and a hard worker. Steven is the only blemish on that name. There's a major juvenile file on him, but it's sealed. But all in all, I can't find a thing wrong with Nathan. So I'll let you go out with him." Michael waited for the response he knew he was going to get.

"I will go out with him because I want to go out with him. I'm twenty-eight years old."

Michael laughed. Her response was right on target.

"Thank you for the flowers, by the way. They're gorgeous. Mike? You haven't said anything to mom and dad, have you? I mean, it's over and done, and I'm going to be okay. Why worry them?"

Michael was quiet for a moment. "I haven't told them. Kat, they have a right to know. I'll tell you what….I won't tell them and neither will Danny, providing you tell them yourself, in person. You're right about worrying them, but I don't like keeping things from them either. So do you promise to tell them when you see them? They will see that you really *are* okay if they see you, and the horror of the incident won't totally freak them out"

Katrina hesitated and thought for a moment. "Okay, I promise." She agreed, reluctantly.

She returned the telephone receiver to its cradle in time to answer the door again. This time it was Fed-ex and UPS both standing there. The one was a gift sent by her parents, but the one from UPS had nothing to do with her birthday. It was what she had been waiting for: A stuffed version of Kit-Kat for her approval. The manufacturer who won the contract to make them agreed to send her one for her to approve. She had signed a contract allowing her beloved Kit-Kat to be sold as a stuffed animal, but she insisted that it be written in the contract that she must approve the final product. If at any time after her final approval, the design changed, she had the right to pull the product, and sue the manufacturer. That was the only way she would agree to letting Kit-Kat be sold as a toy to the public.

Katrina quickly tore open the box and reached through the packing material to pull out the example of Kit-Kat. She sucked in her breath when she got Kit-Kat out of the box. "It's perfect! Perfect!" She said aloud. "Or should I say 'purrfect', spelled p-u-r-r-fect?" She laughed to herself, dialed her agent's phone number, and gave the approval to go ahead with the manufacturing. 'Kit-Kat would be in many homes across America, just like Jeff said.' She closed her eyes for a moment and tried to visualize Jeff. In her mind, she saw his face. Quietly, she spoke to him. "Thank you, Jeff. Thank you for believing in me." Suddenly Nathan's face appeared in her mind, and she felt a longing she hadn't felt in years.

* * *

"Aunt Kat! Aunt Kat! We got you presents!" Katrina and Nathan heard them before they made it to the door. Laughing, Katrina opened the door to let the munchkins in, Danny and Kathy bringing up the rear.

She stooped down to hug her niece and nephew, unmindful of the soreness in her ribs. Little Danny stared at her face, unsure of what he should do. "That kid who threw his toys at you is bad, Aunt Kat. He hurted you."

"Yes, he did. That's why you shouldn't throw anything. You can hurt people."

"I won't throw anything any more." He promised her.

Cara started to cry.

"Does it hurt, Aunt Kat?" She touched Katrina's face lightly.

"A little. I'll be okay. Now let's see what you brought me to eat. I'm starving."

Danny, Kathy, and Nathan stood back and watched Katrina with Cara and little Danny. 'How they love her!' all three of them were thinking. Danny looked over at Nathan and caught the love shining in his eyes as he watched the display in the middle of the living room. 'This guy is okay.' Danny realized. He had spoken with Mike earlier, so he knew all about the background check. Kat found a good guy, thank goodness.

Little Danny looked up at Nathan. "Who is *that*?" He asked, pointing his index finger at him.

"Uncle Nate." Nathan jumped in quickly. He looked at Danny Senior and whispered, "Hopefully."

"Oh, Hi, Untul Nate." Katrina laughed at Danny's pronunciation.

Kathy put out the food, which consisted of fried chicken, potato salad, cole slaw, and a birthday cake with ice cream for dessert. The kids insisted that Katrina blow out her candles, and then they had to have them lit again so that they could blow them out. Nathan enjoyed every minute of it. He laughed at the kids' antics and eventually ended up playing with them. The deafening squeals and laughter coming from the living room were proof that they were having a wonderful time with him.

Katrina leaned over the sofa and asked, "Do you want some coffee, Untul Nate?"

Nathan roared with laughter, making the kids laugh, too. "Yes, coffee is a great idea. But you know what else is a great idea?" He put his index finger up for the kids' benefit.

"Aunt Kat should open her presents!"

"Yeah!" The children screamed in unison. "Aunt Kat, you have to open your presents! Okay? Aunt Kat, open mine first!" Cara begged.

Both Katrina and Nathan laughed and laughed at all the chaos. Katrina opened her presents for the kids' benefit and made a fuss over the gifts they gave her. When all the gifts were unwrapped, Nathan said, "I have one for you, too."

Both kids started in. "Where is it? What did you get Aunt Kat?"

Nathan reached into his pocket and produced a small box wrapped in pink, and handed it to Katrina.

Katrina gasped when she opened the box and saw it. It was a diamond pendant. The teardrop-shaped diamond looked bigger than a full carat. "Oh, Nathan! It's beautiful. But you shouldn't have gotten such an expensive gift."

"Why not? That's your birthstone, isn't it? I just got you a birthstone pendant."

Katrina looked at Nathan, her eyes shining. "Thank you."

The kids were scrambling to see the gift. "You have to kiss him, Aunt Kat. That's what you do when you say 'thank you'. You always kiss us and we didn't never give you a present that pretty." It was little Danny's logic behind the voice.

"Yeah, kiss him, Aunt Kat, but don't hurt her face, Untul Nate." Cara ordered.

Katrina leaned over and kissed Nathan half on the cheek and half on his lip. This satisfied the kids.

Kat remembered the surprise she had for everybody tonight. It had been so chaotic that she had forgotten about Kit-Kit in her office.

"Okay, thank you all for my presents. Now I have a surprise for all of you. You, too, Untul Nate. You don't know about this either. Wait right here."

In a flash she returned with her surprise, a towel draped over it. "Okay, is everybody ready?" The kids were squealing, and the adults were curious as to what was under the towel.

"Meet Kit-Kat!" Katrina pulled the towel off of the stuffed version of her comic strip character.

"Kit-Kat! Wow!" The kids were jumping up and down.

"Well, so what's this?" Danny looked puzzled, as did Nathan and Kathy.

"Kit-Kat is now a toy that will be sold in stores across America. I approved the final today. My Kit-Kat will be in stores in time for Christmas."

"Holy shit, Kat!" Danny was staring wide-eyed at her. "Do you have any idea how much that may increase your net worth? If that takes off, you may end up a multi-millionaire over it."

Katrina shrugged. "It's not the money. It has never been the money with me. I do what I do because it's in my blood. I'm an artist, and Kit-Kat has always been my pet project. I created her in high school. Yeah, it's nice making the money, but it's the recognition of being a talented artist that's always been important. Making everybody know and love Kit-Kat is important. She's my creation, from my mind to my hands, to the public. Artist's names are very rarely known until they are dead, but their works are known throughout their lifetimes and after their deaths."

As Danny and his family were getting ready to leave, little Danny made an announcement. "I think I should stay here in case that kid comes back."

"What kid?" Kathy asked him.

"The one who threw the toys at Aunt Kat!" He looked at his mother like she should have known what kid he was talking about.

"Yeah, Kathy.....duh!" Katrina laughed. To Danny Senior she said, "What are you teaching him? I don't *need* another body guard!"

10

It was more than two weeks after her birthday, and many of her bruises had gone away. There were some traces of bruising on her eye and around her ribcage, but her lip was healed. Nathan called her bright and early on Saturday morning.

"Want to do something today? It's a gorgeous day."

"Yes, I do. I've been cooped up long enough."

"How about jet skiing? I notice you have one. Does it work? I can come get it for you. I have one, too so we can race."

"Great idea! Sounds like fun! And yes, my jet ski works."

"Okay. Here's the rest of it. We jet ski on the gulf where my house sits and have a picnic on the beach there. How's that sound?"

"Oh, wow! I love it!"

"Good. I'll be there around noon. By the time we get to my house and launch the jet skis it will be after one. I'll have Marie make up a basket of goodies for us. See you in awhile."

He arrived at noon and backed the Hummer into the driveway in order to hitch up her jet ski. "You have a Hummer? I didn't know that!" She stared at the dark red Hummer in awe.

"Yeah, I got the dark red one since it didn't seem as macho as the other colors. I really didn't buy one to be the biggest vehicle on the road. I got it because it comes in handy a lot. Ready?"

"In just a second. There's something I want to do first." She went to him and stood close, put her arms around his neck, and met his lips. The kiss was long and passionate.

"There. My lip doesn't hurt any more."

Nathan smiled down at her. "I'm happy. Ready now?"

She nodded and smiled back at him.

He was correct about the time. They had the jet skis in the water just before two o'clock. After starting them, they cruised around in a wide circle for a few minutes. "Want to race?" He asked her.

She nodded. He quickly designed the course for her and they took off. She outran him the first time. They raced several more times, each of them being victorious a few times. Nathan was delighted with her competitiveness. He was surprised at how well she could handle her jet ski, without fear of capsizing it. They played on them for a few hours until they both became hungry. Nathan looked out over the horizon and saw a storm rolling in.

"We may have to take our picnic inside. Look at those clouds forming." He watched for a moment as lightning struck in the distance. "We better get off the water. Lightning."

They worked at getting their jet skis out of the water and hooked up to the hitch on the Hummer, and then Nathan drove them into the driveway. The wind was picking up and the rain would not be far behind. They secured the tarp covers on the jet skis just as the rain hit, followed by a loud crash of thunder. Nathan grabbed the picnic cooler out of the vehicle and they ran toward the house, the rain pelting them as they went.

Both Nathan and Katrina were soaked and shivering when they entered the house. Nathan went into his room and got Katrina the robe she had worn after her shower the day after they met.

"I'm going to jump in the shower for a moment. You can, too. It will take the chill off of us. You can use my shower and I'll use the one down the hall in the main bathroom. Okay?"

She agreed. She showered quickly since she didn't like the idea of showering while there was lightning in the sky. He must have felt that way, too because he was out before she was. She came out, snuggled in his terrycloth robe, and met him in the living room. He was wearing a navy blue terrycloth robe exactly like the one she wore. He had the coffee table all set up with their picnic food on it, and two large pillows on the floor behind it for them to sit on. She grinned at him and sat down on one of the pillows. He joined her.

Outside, the storm raged. Rain pelted the windows, the wind howled, and lightning lit up the sky. After a loud crash of thunder, the lights went out. Nathan was glad he decided to put lit candles on the coffee table. The room immediately became bathed in a glow of candlelight. Nathan looked at Katrina. She looked good by candlelight. Actually, she really looked good today. The day had brought color to her face, and the exercise must have been exhilarating for her. She glowed in the semi-darkness of the room, and her eyes sparkled in the light. She was so beautiful.

They ate the picnic food Marie had prepared, and talked about their college days. Nathan had so much more fun in college than Katrina did. She laughed at some of the stories he told her. He must have been popular in high school and in college. She was popular in high school, but when she went to college, she stayed to herself, and accepted no offers to go out. At first there had been many offers, but after so many refusals, guys just quit asking. All she wanted from college was an education. Nathan, on the other hand, lived his college days in fun, fraternities, and finals, as he put it. He hadn't gone on for a Master's degree as she had, but instead was picked up by a ball club. She guessed that they both got out of college what they expected. She had no regrets and she was sure he didn't either. They gathered up the remains of the picnic and Nathan took it out to the kitchen. He came back with two glasses of wine.

"Well, I guess TV is out of the question." He laughed as he slid his pillow closer to hers so that they were sitting side by side. "My guess is that whatever that lightning hit will keep the electric off for awhile."

"Thank goodness for candles, then."

"You're not afraid of the dark, are you?" He had to ask, but he somehow doubted it.

"No, but I like to see someone when I'm talking to him. I can't believe how dark it is. It's not really that late."

"It's close to dark, I think. Almost seven-thirty, actually. Time flies when you're having fun, right?"

She turned and positioned herself to face him, and their eyes met. His hand touched her face and slowly their lips came together. He slid his arm around her and held her face in his other hand and looked deeply into her eyes. They kissed again and again. The kisses became passionate as their bodies fell onto the pillows and they were lying side by side. Nathan kissed her neck, and then her throat. He felt like he was drowning. Katrina undid the tie of the robe and let it fall away, exposing her nude body.

He looked into her eyes, and studied her face. "Yes?" He whispered.

"Yes." She whispered back.

His hand trailed down her body lightly, as he delicately teased her nipple with his tongue. She shivered. He went back to her mouth and she accepted his tongue when he slid it past her lips. His hand moved down to her pelvis and he felt her pubic hair. Her legs parted a little and he teased her clitoris. She gasped. His mouth went back to her throat and to her breast as he inserted a finger into her. He felt her wetness, but was momentarily puzzled by how small she was down there. She moaned as he touched her in places nobody had ever touched before. He moved on top of her as she pulled him towards her. Slowly, he began to penetrate her, and stopped as he felt himself push up against the membrane. 'My God, she's a virgin.' His mind was screaming at him. He looked into her face.

"Yes." She repeated.

He slowly and gently rocked back and forth until he felt the membrane give way. She made a noise and dug her hands into his back has she clung to him. He looked into her face to see if she were all right. Gently, he began to move again, studying her face as he moved. She smiled up at him and he kissed her again. Suddenly she cried out and he felt her spasms. He waited for her orgasm to end before he continued. Slowly and gently he moved and then she began to move with him, keeping the same rhythm. Her hands were on his back and she was still digging the heels of her hands into him. She moaned and he felt another wave of spasms. He could hold back no more and so he released his sperm into her. He stayed in her until he went soft, and then he rolled off and gathered her into his arms. They fell asleep.

* * *

Nathan awoke at three in the morning, when the electric came back on. Katrina was sleeping soundly and didn't stir when the lights came on. He stared at her for a moment, overwhelmed by his feelings for her. Gently and slowly he freed his arm from under her so as not to awake her. He got up and the picked her up and carried her to his bed and gently lay her down with her head on the pillow and covered her with a comforter. He returned to the living room and blew out the remainder of the burning candles and went around turning out the lights. He noticed the stain on the large pillow on the floor. He picked it up and carried it to the bedroom closet, and then joined her in bed. Once he was under the comforter, she immediately rolled over to him and draped her arm across his chest. He tucked his arm under her and around her shoulders and held her close.

'Perfect.' He whispered to himself, and drifted off to sleep.

It wasn't daylight yet when he felt her get out of bed and go into the bathroom. When she returned he rolled over to face her.

"Is everything all right?" He searched for her face in the dark.

"Yes." She answered.

"It was your first time." It was a statement rather than a question.

"Yes."

"I wish I had known...."

"Why?"

"Well, I might have done something....I don't know, different. Did I hurt you?"

"No....well, maybe just a little....but I'm okay."

Nathan moved close to her and propped his head up with his hand, his elbow bent. He traced her jaw with his index finger.

"You're the one, aren't you?"

"What do you mean?" Katrina thought she knew what he meant, but wanted to hear him say it.

"The one I've been waiting for all my life. You're the one I always felt but couldn't see. I've waited so *long* for you."

"And I've waited a long time for you." She moved closer to him and ran her hand up his back, feeling his powerful muscles under his flesh.

They made love again. This time is was much better for her now that the barrier was gone. Once again they fell asleep in each other's arms and didn't awake until daylight.

* * *

Nathan was the first to awake. With a slight smile on his face, he stared down into her face. He remembered the talk he and his father had so many years ago. 'I will gladly take the full responsibility for this girl, Dad.' He thought to himself. She opened her eyes.

"Hi." She smiled up at him.

He smiled back and kissed her forehead.

"Hi." He was quiet for a moment. "Hey, I have an idea. Want to go to the zoo today?"

"Yes!" She responded with a grin that made her look like a little child. "But I want to spend some time with the cats, though. I've been neglecting them lately."

"Okay. How about this? We shower here and eat breakfast. Then we go to your place so you can change. I'll feed the cats while you're changing. Then we go to the zoo, and afterward, we go back to your place and spend the evening with the little tigers and lions. We can order pizza for dinner, rent a movie, and sit on the couch with the cats in our laps. How does that sound?"

"Sounds perfect. I have some clothes in the Hummer. Clothes to wear home, that is. All I have in this house is my swimsuit and your robe."

While Katrina showered Nathan ran out to the Hummer to get her clothes for her. He stopped by the kitchen to let Marie know that there would be two for breakfast.

"Katrina's here?" Marie's face lit up.

Nathan nodded.

"We're going to the zoo today." He started toward the bedroom, but turned around and ran back to Marie and hugged her, grinning.

Marie was elated to see Nathan this happy. She was looking forward to seeing Katrina for the first time without bruises, too. Nathan told her just yesterday how Katrina's face had healed.

Marie served them breakfast on the patio. She stared at Katrina and thought about how beautiful she was. She thought they made a beautiful couple.

* * *

They followed Nathan's plan and by noon they were walking around the zoo, looking at the animal exhibits, oblivious to the rest of the zoo patrons. They laughed at the monkeys and were awed by the big cats. Walking hand in hand, they visited every exhibit with interest, reading the facts regarding the animals they watched. Katrina's yellow shorts set and Nathan's white shorts and pale blue polo jersey accentuated their good looks. Passersby stopped to stare at the breathtaking couple who appeared to be so much in love, and smiled their approval. Without their knowledge, a small man in horned rim glasses was photographing them. He followed them around and took pictures of them from all angles.

Nathan found a cotton candy stand. He bought some and fed Katrina pieces of the pastel colored spun sugar while they watched the bears roll around in their man-made waterhole. She pulled some off the stick and fed it to him, as well.

Late in the afternoon, they started toward the exit, arm in arm. Just before they reached the exit, the little man with the camera stepped in front of them.

"Hi....my name's Aaron Shultz." He produced a business card and handed it to Nathan. "I hope you don't mind, but I've been photographing you two all day."

"What! What for?" Nathan put a protective hand on Katrina's arm.

"Read the card, sir. I'm a photographer...free-lance. I got some good candid shots of both of you. All I want you to do is come to my studio in a couple of days and look at the photos. I'm hoping you'll buy some of them. I know I should have asked you first, but I wanted the photos to be of a pure quality—nothing posed. All I'm asking is that you come see them. You make such a beautiful couple...."

"You're right; you should have asked us first. I could call a cop and turn you in."

"I know, and I'm sorry. Please come to my studio and see the pictures. You won't be disappointed. Maybe, if you like my work, you would hire me as your photographer at your wedding."

Nathan and Katrina started laughing.

"We're not even engaged!" Katrina laughed even harder.

"Well, maybe not yet...but come see the photos and you'll see how right you are for each other. Thank you....you have my card." The man darted away.

Nathan smiled at Katrina. "The guy probably doubles as a Justice of the Peace."

Katrina smiled up at Nathan and laughed once again.

* * *

They finished their pizza and were engrossed in their second of three movies. Curled up on her sofa, with the cats around them, they laughed at the comedy they had chosen. The movie ended and Nathan hit the rewind button and got up to stretch his legs.

He pulled a couple of sodas out of the refrigerator and handed one over the back of the sofa to Katrina.

"So when is your lease up here? You have a lease?"

"Well, no…I don't have a lease."

"You just live here month to month?"

"No….well, actually I do. I own the building."

"Really? You are just full of surprises."

"The other tenants don't know that. If they did, every time something went wrong, they would be knocking on my door. A realtor handles my rentals and when something breaks, they call the real estate agency and it gets fixed."

"You're so *amazing!* Any other surprises?" He leaned over the back of the couch and she tilted her head back to look up at him. He kissed the tip of her nose. "Ready for the third movie? I guess we saved the chick flick for last. I got to see guns and violence, so I'm ready for the chick flick now."

They both fell asleep watching the movie that was full of love and romance. It was past midnight when they awoke and made their way to Katrina's bed. In lieu of making love, they just held each other all through the night.

Nathan swung the Corvette into the parking lot at Jack's Place. He hadn't been to the bar in quite awhile, since he had been spending every free moment with Katrina. The evening was warm, even for late May. Charlie's car was parked there in its usual spot. He pulled in next to it, shut his car off and quickly entered the bar from the side door. Before Charlie saw him, Nathan was standing beside him at the corner of the bar.

"Well, look who *finally* showed his face! How the hell are you? Where have you been?" Charlie punched Nathan's arm lightly.

"Been around. Just haven't been around here." Nathan punched Charlie back playfully.

"Hey, Lisa has been asking about you. She has a girlfriend she wants you to meet. I think you'll like her. Good-looking." Charlie looked at Nathan hopefully. He and his girlfriend, Lisa were always trying to fix Nathan up with someone.

"Nah…forget it." Nathan waved him off.

"Why not? What have you got to lose?" Charlie was getting persistent.

Nathan shook his head.

"I met someone."

"Yeah?" Charlie looked surprised and interested at the same time.

"Yeah. There's no one like her. She's all that, and more. When I met her, I met my wife."

"Gees! You love her?" Charlie stared at Nathan like he couldn't believe his ears.

"Absolutely. She's the one, Charlie." Nathan looked Charlie in the eye when he said it.

"So are you going to bring her around? I'd like to meet her."

"Yeah, Friday night, actually. Are you and Lisa going to be here?"

"Where else do we go?" Charlie laughed.

Holly, one of the regular bar patrons appeared beside Nathan.

"Hi, Nathan. Ain't seen you around lately. Where you been hiding?"

"I don't hide, Holly. I stay home sometimes." Nathan was short with her. He didn't really like girls like Holly, who spent so much time sitting at the bar trying to look tempting. She wasn't bad looking, but she had nothing going for her.

"Oh." Holly answered him and walked to the other side of the bar.

"She has the hots for you. I guess she'll be disappointed."

Nathan laughed. "She would be disappointed, Katrina or no Katrina. She's not my type."

"So the girl's name is Katrina?"

"Yeah. God, she's so beautiful! She's everything I could want."

"I can't wait to meet her. You deserve a great chick, man. You're a good guy."

Nathan smiled and looked around the place. It looked good. The lighting was not too bright, nor was it too dark. The floor plan divided the bar area from the restaurant area in the back. The food that was served was edible, and in fact, pretty good. When he put up the money for the place, he insisted on there being decent food served in a nice atmosphere. In the far corner of the restaurant area there was a small stage where a disc jockey offered Karaoke on Friday and Saturday nights. The bar held a good sized crowd and there was rarely any trouble. Nathan's presence in the bar always ensured that. Everybody who came in there knew him as one of the owners and they were careful not to do anything that would get them barred from the place. He was held in high esteem by all the patrons.

Jack set a beer in front of him.

"Hi, Nate. How's it going?"

"Jack, life is good. How about you?"

"Can't complain. Business is good. You should come around more often. I miss ya." Jack meant it sincerely. He felt he owed Nathan a lot. Without Nathan he would be nowhere.

"I'll be in Friday night. Make sure the place looks good....I'm bringing a lady."

"Yeah? Someone special?" Jack raised one of his eyebrows at Nathan.

"Very special." Nathan finished his beer and set a couple of dollars on the counter. "See you Friday."

* * *

Katrina was dressed in a simple yellow dress with thin straps that tied at the shoulders. The princess-style skirt of the dress flared to just past mid-thigh. She chose matching yellow sandals, bare-toed with a small inch-and-a-half heel. The front of her shiny, coppery hair was pulled back and clasped at the crown while the rest of her mane fell down to her waist. She was nervous, since this would be the first time she would be meeting any of Nathan's friends as his girlfriend. She knew that Detective Delaney and Dr. Harding were friends of Nathan's, but they met her under professional circumstances and she wasn't his girlfriend then.

Nathan came through her door and stopped dead, just staring at her. He let out a low whistle. "Wow! You look gorgeous! Ready to go? No, let's just stay here. I don't think I want to share you." He teased, as he put his arms around her, and kissed her. "But I promised everybody at the bar that I was bringing you, so we better go." They left her apartment with their arms around each other's waist.

There were already quite a few cars in the parking lot when he pulled in and took his usual parking space. He went around the Corvette, opened her door, and took her hand. They walked into the bar, her hand in his. A hush fell over the crowd when they entered. Nathan had never brought a girl to the bar, much less one that looked like Katrina. When he introduced her to Jack it was obvious that Jack was overwhelmed. It amused Nathan that Jack became tongue-tied and just stared at her. Jack wasn't the only one. Many of the patrons with whom Nathan was acquainted gawked at her. Holly, who had spoken to Nathan the night he came in during the past week, got off her bar stool and walked to the juke box with attitude.

He led her to a table in the restaurant area, where they sat down and opened menus.

"Charlie and Lisa should be here soon. Let's order food. It's actually pretty good here. I insisted on it when I invested in the place."

"It's a nice place. Kind of reminds me of Bear's Place, where we used to go after football games."

While they were perusing the menu, Charlie and Lisa entered the bar. Charlie asked Jack where Nathan was sitting.

"In the back." Jack used his thumb as a pointer in the direction of the restaurant section.

"Does he have somebody with him?" Charlie asked.

"Oh, yeah. He's got someone with him. And she is *some one!"*

Charlie and Lisa headed toward the restaurant tables and Charlie stopped dead when he saw Katrina. "Oh my God! She's *fabulous!"* Charlie whispered to Lisa.

Lisa just rolled her eyes at Charlie. "Try not to make a jackass of yourself. Remember she's Nathan's date."

Nathan looked up and spotted them, and waved them over. He made the introductions and was annoyed that Charlie couldn't take his eyes off of Katrina. Lisa was doubly annoyed, which made her automatically hate Katrina.

Katrina was an angel all evening. Charlie kept trying to divert her attention from Nathan with his constant banter and jokes. Both Katrina and Nathan took it in stride. It was Lisa who was deeply offended. Charlie asked Katrina questions about herself, but also wanted her opinion on everything that came to his mind. Katrina was polite and answered him, but tried to draw Lisa into the conversation. Lisa excused herself from the table and returned a few minutes later. She was quiet and sullen as she lit a cigarette and sipped her drink. She got up to leave when a cab driver came in asking who had called for a cab.

"Where the hell are you going?" Charlie asked her, obviously annoyed.

"Home, maybe. Or maybe to another bar." Her lips were drawn tightly as she spoke.

"Why? We're just getting started."

"Because you're an asshole." She abruptly turned and left.

Katrina looked at Nathan. "Did she leave because of me?"

"No, she left because of me. You heard her—I'm an asshole." Charlie was looking toward the door Lisa had exited, smirking.

"Why do you have to be so insensitive?" Nathan asked him.

"She has issues." Charlie defended himself. "I can't talk to another girl. She gets pissed when I do."

"Well, maybe you shouldn't, then." Katrina spoke up.

"Yeah, maybe you shouldn't, Charlie. You're just as bad. Any guy talks to her, you're ready to fight. Your double standard sucks."

Katrina began to feel uncomfortable and she was glad when Charlie sauntered up to the bar and stayed there.

Nathan put his arm around Katrina's shoulders and rubbed his cheek against her hair.

"They really do care about each other, but the whole relationship is so unhealthy."

"Well, he came with her and he should not have spent the entire time talking to me. I don't blame her for being angry. It was just rude."

"I agree." Nathan kissed her hair as the music started. "Want to dance?"

It was the first time they danced together. Nathan held her close and kept his lips on her temple. "You're a wonderful dancer." He murmured to her.

"Years of dancing, remember? You're a good dancer, too." She sighed and lightly kissed his chest.

* * *

On the way home from the bar, Nathan's cell phone rang. It was Lisa.

"Nate, I'm sorry for being such a bitch. It's just that…well, if a guy talked to me all night like that, Charlie would be pissed off. Anyway, I felt ignored and that I should just leave. When a beautiful woman comes around, Charlie acts like I'm not even there. By the way, Katrina is very beautiful. She seems nice, but with Charlie's eyes all over her, I really didn't get a chance to…"

"I know, Lisa. We both told him about it. Lisa, Katrina is a wonderful person. If you could just get to know her, you'd see that." Nathan looked at Katrina and smiled and winked at her. She smiled and winked back.

They spent the night at Katrina's and made love for hours. Katrina was completely comfortable with Nathan as her lover and she had started to explore his body, applying techniques she had only read about. Without Nathan knowing, she got herself on birth control, which made her even more uninhibited. Their lovemaking started with Katrina lightly kissing Nathan's chest, and then moving down to his stomach and abdomen. She took him into her mouth and he went crazy with desire. He lifted her on top of him and she slid down onto his penis and began moving slowly. His hands went to her breasts and he lightly massaged her nipples with his thumbs. She cried out as her orgasm started, and he rolled her over and got on top of her. He penetrated her deeply and waited until her spasms stopped, and then slowly and deliberately they moved together, rhythmically up and down, bringing her to another orgasm, and then another. When he could hold back no longer, he cried out as he released his sperm into her. They lay there spent, for almost an hour before they made love again. It was almost daylight when they fell asleep in each other's arms.

12

The ringing telephone woke Nathan out of a sound, dreamless sleep. The clock on the nightstand showed that it was five-thirty in the morning. Annoyed, Nathan reached for the phone, but suddenly realized that it might be Katrina. Alarmed, he grabbed the receiver and spoke into it.

"Nate, Brian Delaney. Got some bad news. Steven escaped."

Nathan sat up in a panic.

"What? When and how?"

"He killed a guard and managed to get past the gates. They say it was about an hour ago. He's on the run somewhere. We have the entire force out looking for him."

"Jesus, Katrina...."

"We already have a couple of cars on the way over there. There is one outside of your place, too."

"Brian, I'm going to go get her." Nathan hung up, grabbed a pair of jeans and a tee-shirt, quickly put them on, and slipped into a pair of loafers. He ran out the door, opened the garage door, and started the Hummer. He drove out of the driveway, tires squealing, closing the garage door from his remote. He saw the police car sitting on the side of the road, in his rear view mirror.

On his way to Katrina's, breaking speed limits, he called Marie and told her to stay home, that Steven was loose.

He spun the Hummer into Katrina's driveway and ran and pounded on the door. He tried the door bell as well. Katrina heard the sounds and jumped out of bed and stood in front of the door, not knowing who was out there.

"Katrina! It's Nate. Open the door!"

She slid back the dead bolt, unlocked the door, and opened it.

"Nathan! What's wrong?"

Nathan was out of breath. "Steven broke out of jail."

He watched the terror creep into her eyes.

"Get dressed and pack a bag. I'm getting you out of here."

"Nathan, the cats!"

"They're going, too. That's why I brought the Hummer. Do you have something to carry them in?"

"Yes, there's a big carrier in the spare bedroom."

"I'll get it. You get some stuff together. Quickly!"

Within minutes he had the cats in the carrier, and went down the hall to collect her. "Come on, whatever you need, we'll buy. Let's go now." He grabbed the bag she was putting things into and zipped it shut. He ushered her out, and made her wait by the door while he made sure it was safe. He put the cat carrier into the back of the Hummer and helped her into the front seat from his side. He quickly shut her apartment door and locked it with her key and jumped into the Hummer and sped away.

Katrina was crying and he reached for her hand. "You'll be safe now. I'm here." Nathan relaxed a little when he saw an unmarked police car sitting halfway up the block.

"There's a cop sitting in that car, Honey. They'll find him. In the meantime....we're going on a little road trip."

She was silent, tears rolling down her cheeks.

"Don't you want to know where?"

"Where?"

"I own a hotel in Orlando. We're going there. Which reminds me...." He snapped open his cell phone and dialed. When the line was picked up he spoke. "This is Nate Perletti. Have the penthouse ready for me. I'll be staying there a few days, maybe." He listened into the phone for a moment. "Very good. I'll be there in about an hour and fifteen minutes." He disconnected his call.

They arrived at the hotel and Nathan parked in a reserved space. He opened the back and grabbed the cat carrier while Katrina got her small suitcase. They took the penthouse elevator up to the top and Nathan keyed the lock so that the elevator couldn't be used by anybody. Katrina was awed by the spacious penthouse suite. She walked around looking at the spacious three rooms, and then checked out the bathroom. It was a huge bathroom that held a luxurious Jacuzzi. She longed to climb into it, just to ease the tightness of the muscles in the back of her neck.

Nathan pressed a button on the wall and a door slid out, closing off the elevator and creating a small hallway between it and the suite. He opened the carrier and let the cats run free. Immediately, they ran to look out the floor to ceiling windows, quickly spying birds flying by. Katrina stretched out on the bed and stared out at the skyline. The sun was up and it looked like it would be a beautiful day.

Nathan lay down beside her and draped his arm over her. "Hey... are you okay?"

She looked over at him and started to cry again. "I'm scared."

"No need to be, now. Steven doesn't know about any of my assets, other than my house. He won't even think of looking for us here, if he even plans on looking for us. Remember, he's a mental case. He may not even remember you. I just got you out of there as a safety precaution...and get you into my penthouse." He pulled her close to him and held her. "You know....if you're real good....we could go to Disney World."

She looked up at him and saw the mischievous look of expectation on his face as he waited for her response.

"Okay....I'll be good." She closed her eyes and dozed off.

* * *

While Katrina slept, Nathan called his father at work to tell him about Steven. He let his father know that he was in Orlando and that the police would keep him posted. Al immediately asked about the safety of the girl Steven abducted before he was arrested. Nathan assured him that the girl was safe. Both he and Katrina thought it best not to reveal to his parents that they were seeing each other. Nathan wanted to wait until his parents met her before her identity was known, if they had to tell them at all. Nathan promised to keep Al posted on any new information. After he disconnected the call with Al, he called Brian Delaney to see what was happening. Delaney told Nathan that they were still hunting Steven and would let him know as soon as something changed. His next phone call was to order food from room service. It was close to ten o'clock and neither he nor Katrina had eaten breakfast, so he was getting hungry.

Katrina awoke and looked around for a moment, disoriented. She remembered where she was, and quickly looked around for Nathan. She got up off the bed and went into the living area. Nathan was relaxing on the sofa with the newspaper in his lap. He looked up when she entered.

"Hi. How are you doing?" Nathan stood up and went to her.

"I'm okay, I guess. Any news?" She looked at him hopefully.

At a knock on the door, Katrina flew into Nathan's arms, and he wrapped them around her and momentarily held her. "This is fun….. but that would be room service." He unwrapped his arms from around her and padded to the door while Katrina sank down onto the sofa. Nathan looked through the peephole to be on the safe side, and then opened the door to a table of food capped in stainless steel covers. The smell of the food made Katrina realize she was hungry. Nathan handed the young gentleman a few bills and ushered him out.

"How did he get up here?" Katrina had a slight frown on her face as she asked.

"The back elevator. Don't worry; it can only be accessed from the kitchen. Come on…the food's hot."

The food was hot and tasty. Katrina ate a small portion but found that she really couldn't eat very much. Her stomach was in knots.

"Want to go shopping after we have breakfast?" Nathan looked at her, hopeful that she would relax.

"*You* want to go shopping? Men don't shop." She chuckled a little.

"Sure they do…when they want something."

"And what do you want?" Her curiosity was tweaked.

"Well, let's get you what you didn't manage to get packed. For one thing, this place has a wonderful pool, and I know you didn't think about packing a swimsuit. Am I right?"

"Yes, you're right. Will it be okay, Nathan? I mean….I'm just so…scared he'll show up. Oh, Nathan….the things he said to me….. they were so horrible…" Katrina started to cry again.

Nathan slid his chair over to her and held her. He stroked her hair while he tried to swallow the lump in his throat.

“I know, Sweetheart. I know. I’ll never let him get to you. I promise.” He whispered. He regained his composure and held her at arm’s length. “So what about the shopping?” He studied her face and waited for her answer.

“How can I resist?” She smiled weakly at him.

* * *

Katrina was thrilled with all the stores Nathan led her through. He spied a white bikini that he thought she had to have, and he bought it for her. Next, he picked up a pale green full length sheath made of a frothy light-weight material. He visualized her in it and knew he had to buy it. She remembered that she forgot to pack underwear so she picked up a couple of pairs that were much more provocative than what she normally wore. Nathan was already up at the cash register when she took her selections up. When she reached for her credit card, he pushed it back into her purse and paid for her items himself. They walked out of the fifth store, each carrying a bag. His was much larger than the one she carried, and she wondered what he had bought. They found a little café and decided to have lunch.

“So what did you buy?” She asked when they were seated.

“You’ll see. Some things for you. I like them and I hope you will, too. I enjoyed shopping for you.” He reached over and touched her cheek.

* * *

The Jacuzzi was hot and Katrina was ready to climb in and sit for awhile. They had spent the rest of the afternoon at the hotel pool, swimming and soaking up the sun. The hot tub was just what Katrina needed. She lay back, closed her eyes and let her mind drift. The heated water felt so good and she felt herself starting to relax. Nathan was beside her and they just sat with their eyes closed, their fingers entwined.

Katrina opened her eyes and looked over at Nathan’s handsome face, and was overwhelmed with desire for him.

"Hey....I'm going to take a shower." She started out of the Jacuzzi and turned and looked at him mischievously. "Care to join me?"

A surprised Nathan looked up at her.

"Oh, *hell* yeah!" He said as he got up and followed her to the shower.

They soaped each other and kissed. They rinsed off the soap and kissed, and then soaped each other again. They teased each other until they were both swimming in desire. Katrina hoisted herself up, wrapped her arms around Nathan's neck, her legs around his waist, and kissed him passionately. He entered her as he pressed her against the wall of the shower. They had simultaneous orgasms, and she cried out and held onto him tightly. Nathan held onto her as he tried to control his ragged breathing, his face against her cheek. He carried her to the bedroom, water dripping over the carpet, and made love to her again. Hours later, Nathan returned to the shower and turned off the icy cold water. He returned to the bed and curled up against her, facing her back, and draped his arm across her waist.

* * *

It was dusk when they returned from Universal Studios. Katrina was carrying a huge stuffed lion that Nathan had bought for her. She set it down on the floor and aroused the cats' curiosity. She laughed when they hesitated and stretched their bodies outward to get a better look. Nathan shook it from behind and the cats jumped in the air. They both shared a laugh over it. Katrina was so happy and relaxed that she was able to forget about why they were hiding out in the hotel. She was wearing one of the new outfits Nathan had secretly bought for her the day before, which was a one-piece white shorts and top combined, with blue piping for trim. The top tied over her left shoulder, leaving the other shoulder bare. Nathan thought she looked beautiful in it. Besides the lion, they brought cooked grouper fish and fries for dinner. Nathan set the bag of food down on the small table near the glass wall facing the sunset.

"I'm starving. How about you?" He looked over at her and couldn't help noticing her radiance in the light from the setting sun.

They ate and talked about the fun they had during the day, remembering some of the day's events and laughing. The plan for the evening was to curl up on the sofa, watch television, and enjoy the cats. Nathan didn't forget them while he and Katrina were at the park. He had three small, furry toy mice, one for each of them, in his pocket. He planned on bringing them out of hiding when they settled down for the evening. Katrina started toward the bedroom to change clothes when Nathan's cell phone rang. She stopped.

Nathan flipped open the phone and answered it.

"Nathan Perletti."

"Yeah, Brian. Uh-huh. I see." Nathan's face changed as he listened to the caller's voice. "So what happened? Where was he?"

Nathan listened intently, and sank down onto the sofa. "Yeah, I'll call them. Thanks, Brian. I know you did what you could. I'll see you when I get back."

Katrina moved to the sofa and sat down, staring at Nathan. He ended the call and sat staring at the floor without speaking. Finally, he looked up at Katrina.

"The nightmare is over......for everybody. Steven's dead."

Katrina gasped, and then searched Nathan's face for a sign of... something.... grief, possibly. She caught a glint of a tear in his eye, and quietly reached for his hand. He stroked the back of her hand with his thumb for a moment.

"Give me a couple of minutes, Honey. I have to call my parents."

He disappeared into the bedroom and she could hear him talking. She waited in the darkening room until he returned. He sat down next to her and pulled her close, laying his cheek on the top of her head. They sat in silence until he began talking.

"He killed a cop....choked the life right out of him. That's when they shot him." He was silent again and Katrina felt his pain. She reached for his hand again and held it. Nathan began again. "He was a monster....I know that. But he was my brother. You know what I mean? I can remember how much I wanted a brother, but....I never really had one. I always hoped that one day he would be well, and we could be friends. Go fishing together, play ball together....all those things that two brothers do. I tried, Katrina. God knows, I tried."

They sat in silence, holding onto each other, until Nathan started speaking again. He told her of all the things Steven had done, and how it almost broke up his parents' marriage. He told her about the girl Steven raped at the facility, just before they shipped him to a maximum security institution. He told her everything, and she sat and listened. Nathan's tears ran down his cheeks to his chin, and then dropped onto her cheeks. They were mixed with her own. She felt all his years of grief and disappointment surfacing from within him, and she quietly held him. She knew he was grieving for the brother he never had, rather than for the brother he just lost.

"We'll have to leave in the morning. I have to accompany the body back to Ohio. You understand, don't you?" He leaned over and looked at her through red-rimmed eyes.

"Yes, of course."

"I'd love to have you beside me to support me through this, but I don't think it's a good idea. Not yet, anyway." He was stroking her cheek as he spoke. "Besides, Steven has brought you enough pain... you don't need any more."

She agreed with him, but only nodded.

13

Nathan left for Ohio early the day after they arrived back from Orlando. He told her he would call her to let her know when he would be back, and asked if she would be all right. She assured him that she would be fine. Although she was still nervous about being alone, she didn't say anything to him. The danger to her was over. She decided to go shopping for groceries, since she hadn't done so in quite awhile. As she walked through the produce aisle, she spied a familiar figure and walked toward her.

"Lisa?" The girl turned around.

"Katrina. Hi. I heard about Nate's brother. How is he? Nate, I mean."

"He's in Ohio with his parents. I guess they will have the funeral tomorrow. Nathan said he'd call me when it was over. He's okay, but he's grieving."

"Why didn't you go with him?"

"Well, we both thought that it wasn't the right time for me to go up and meet his parents for the first time, under these circumstances."

"Oh. Yeah, right. Listen, Katrina....I want to apologize to you. I acted pretty badly that night I met you, and I'm sorry."

"No need to apologize. I didn't blame you for being angry. Listen, Nathan speaks very highly of you. What do you say we give friendship a shot? Come on over to my place. I could use the company...."

Lisa thought for a moment and then smiled. "Yeah...I think I would like that. Have any coffee? I could use a cup."

"Sure do. Just come on over after you've finished shopping. For some girl talk...or whatever." She gave Lisa her address and quickly checked out to get home to make a pot of coffee.

Lisa arrived shortly behind her. Katrina put out chocolate chip cookies and poured coffee. They sat down at the dinette table and soon they were talking about everything and anything. Lisa told her about her problems with Charlie, and how he took her for granted.

"I'm supposed to meet him at the bar tonight, but I really don't want to."

"So don't go." Katrina advised. "I mean, why should you be where you don't want to be, just because he wants you to be there? You're a person...you have a brain."

"I don't know, Katrina. Charlie acts like I should feel lucky that we're together. The bad part is that I do. I really love Charlie. I just don't think he loves me as much. At least not like Nate loves you. I could see it in his eyes when he looked at you. If only Charlie would look at me that way..."

Katrina sat back and sighed.

"Well....then let's work on making him love you as much as you love him."

She smiled at Lisa as she formulated a plan in her head.

* * *

Katrina picked up Lisa at her apartment early Saturday morning. She had all day, since Nathan told her when he called that he wouldn't be home until Sunday evening. He sounded okay, but he said he missed her. She certainly missed him, but she knew he had to be there for his parents. She was glad to hear that Mike and Cookie were there for him.

"So where do you want to start?" Katrina asked Lisa when she climbed into the Mustang.

"The mall, I guess. What time is the salon going to see me?"

"I got you an appointment at four, so we have hours to shop."

"How did you manage to get me an appointment on such short notice? I know that salon is hard to get into."

"Well, I'm a good customer, so they accommodate me when I ask. I'm getting my hair trimmed and my nails done, too. You, however, are getting the works."

Lisa grinned at Katrina.

"Nate's right about you. You *are* terrific!"

They ran through all the stores that were Katrina's favorites. Katrina helped Lisa pick out clothes that were slightly sexy and more feminine than what she usually wore.

"Stay away from severe colors, if you can. Go softer." Katrina advised her. "Also, subtle is better than dramatic. Here, try this." Katrina held up a simple sundress in pale aqua. "This is a good color for you. It'll bring out the green flecks in your eyes, which, by the way, are beautiful. They look like opals."

Lisa gave Katrina a look of gratitude. She was right about the dress. It was a perfect color for her.

"How do you know all this? I mean, how do you know what will look good on me?"

"I'm an artist, remember. I have an eye for color."

They picked out a few outfits, all with Katrina's approval, and then went to buy shoes.

"Go with simple, always. Small heels, light straps look best. Wait until you get the pedicure. You'll love how these look on your feet." She was holding up a pair of white, low-heeled sandals. Lisa smiled at her.

"I'm spending a fortune! I'll be paying for it all for months, but I really need this, so I don't care." Lisa's mood was buoyant.

"Well, the hair and nails are on me, okay?"

"Oh, I can't let you do that! You've already done enough just by giving me all the tips."

"I have plenty of money, so it's no big deal. I insist." Katrina was happy to be helping out. She liked Lisa and wanted her to improve her relationship with Charlie. He was Nathan's friend so they could end up seeing a lot of each other.

After the mall, they visited the salon, where Lisa was transformed into a princess. Her lovely dark hair was styled to frame her oval face, and shaped in the back so that it fell evenly just past her shoulders. Lisa had never gotten her nails done, nor had she ever had a pedicure. She appreciated how much better her hands and feet looked.

Lisa invited Katrina into her apartment when they returned from the salon.

"So what other advice can you give me?" Lisa asked as she put on a pot of coffee.

"Well, can I be honest?"

"Of course. I value what you have to say."

"Okay. First of all, drop the language. Be more demure. Also, be discreet. When Charlie acts like he's interested in another girl, ignore it, or laugh about it. That's even better. Act like it doesn't matter. Believe me, if you act like it doesn't matter, he will wonder why it doesn't matter. By the way, when you didn't show up last night, what did he say about it today?"

"Oh, that was funny. He called me and left a message. A nasty one, at first, but the second message he left was kind of sweet—for Charlie. He asked if I was okay."

"See? Now wait until he sees you. You look gorgeous!"

"Thanks, Katrina. So tell me…is all this advice how you won Nate?" Lisa was not being malicious, but she was curious. Nathan was so obviously in love with Katrina. She must have done something.

"I don't know. I just act like myself. Nathan isn't like Charlie. He's sensitive, for one thing. But….it's something else. It's like we were searching for each other, you know? For years, I felt someone, but I never knew who it was. He felt the same thing. It was just a matter of us finally meeting. I know….it sounds crazy, but it's…true."

"I believe you. So do you love him a lot?"

"Oh God, yes!" Katrina looked dreamy for a moment.

"Charlie and I have been hoping Nate would find someone. Charlie always worries about some girl just using Nate for his money. Like that girl he was engaged to when he played baseball. He told you about her?"

"Yeah, he did. Tell Charlie that he doesn't have to worry about me. I have my own money. I love Nathan for Nathan. He's so.... wonderful." She smiled as she spoke.

Lisa was satisfied that Katrina truly loved Nathan and wasn't after his money. She was so happy for Nathan, and Katrina as well.

14

Nathan sailed through the baggage claim and found his way to his car in long-term parking. He paid the attendant and drove out of the lot, straight to Katrina.

It was a little after six when Katrina changed into the green dress Nathan bought for her in Orlando. She had spent most of the day working, but also managed to call her parents and then Morgan. She gave Morgan the details of Steven's death, but to her parents, she said not a word regarding Steven or Nathan. She wanted them to meet Nathan before they knew about him. She had made Danny and Michael promise not to say anything to them, telling them that she was going to surprise their parents and didn't want it ruined. Reluctantly, they agreed to keep it all a secret....for now.

Katrina heard Nathan's car pull up and she opened the door before he could knock. In an instant they were in each other's arms.

After the first kiss, Nathan was holding her, lightly kissing her temple.

"God, I missed you."

"I missed you, too. Are your parents okay? And you? How about you?" She lightly kissed his chest.

"They'll manage. They loved Steven because he was their son, but he made their lives miserable. Like me, they're grieving for what they never had with Steven."

He rubbed his hand up and down her back and kissed her again, holding her face in his other hand. He lightly planted kisses on her cheeks, the tip of her nose, and then back to her temple.

He kept his lips on her temple and murmured, "You look beautiful in this dress. Too bad it's going to come off."

She gave him a throaty laugh, and began to unbutton his shirt. Nathan was amazed that a simple act like undoing his buttons could cause such an arousal in him. He slid the shirt off his shoulders and let it fall to the floor. When he reached for her, she stepped back and slid the dress off her shoulders and let it drop to the floor with his shirt. She undid his belt and unzipped his jeans and pulled them down. He weakened into jelly and sank to his knees, and she followed. On their knees, they wrapped themselves around each other, kissing passionately. They toppled over onto the carpet. He took her there on the living room floor. She clung to him, moving with wild abandon. She arched her back as he deeply penetrated her. His thrusts became urgent as Katrina wreathed under him. Together, they exploded into ecstasy.

They lay on the carpet, arms loosely around each other, looking into each other's eyes. Katrina smiled at him and said, "Welcome home." They both broke up laughing.

There was so much to tell each other, so she got up off the floor and walked to the kitchen in the nude, and put on a pot of coffee. He came up behind her and suggested she put a robe on, or they would end up back on the floor. She laughed at that, but went to get her colorful caftan, and slipped it on over her head.

Over coffee, he told her about seeing Mike and Cookie, and how they stayed by his side through the entire ordeal of the funeral. They agreed with him that it wouldn't be a good idea to tell his parents about Katrina yet, so they were careful not to say anything.

She told him about running into Lisa, and all they had done together. Nathan seemed pleased about that.

"Wait until you see her, Nathan! She looked beautiful when we left the salon. Not to mention the great new clothes! I also told her about her language."

Nathan laughed. "You didn't! Well, it needed to be said, I guess. I can't stand to hear trash coming out of a girl's mouth. I'm not being sexist, either. I don't talk like that. It sounds terrible coming from a man, but it sounds worse coming from a woman. Anyway, you've done your good deed for the year. I just hope it improves things with them."

15

Fourth of July—Nathan's thirtieth birthday—was a couple of days away. It would be a three-day weekend for most people. Katrina called Nathan to ask what he wanted to do for his birthday.

"Well, it is the thirtieth....that's kind of a big one, I guess. I was thinking of having a poolside party here at my place. What do you think?" He knew she would go along with it, since she held a person's birthday in high esteem. If that was what he wanted, it would be okay with her. What she didn't know was that he had a couple surprises up his sleeve for her. Her surprise to him was an oil portrait of the two of them. She had worked on it for weeks and it was finally finished. Since he had everything, she knew that giving him something she created would mean more to him than anything she could buy. She agreed to go along with the party.

Marie, along with some extra hired help, would be doing everything that needed done for the party. Nathan wrote down a list of people he wanted to invite, including Danny and Kathy. Katrina thought that was a nice idea. She hadn't seen them since her birthday in April. She called them and they agreed to be there. He spent a couple of hours calling people to invite them, and then called her to see about going out to dinner the night before.

Everything was in place for the party when Nathan left to pick up Katrina for dinner the evening before. They went to a beachside restaurant and enjoyed a quiet candlelight dinner. Katrina looked lovely in an ivory dress that was held up by elastic above her breasts and went around under her arms to her back. She was wearing the diamond pendant he had given her for her birthday. Nathan dressed up in Florida style, for the evening, wearing a pale yellow short-sleeved shirt and a tie of olive and tan stripes. Katrina thought he looked wonderful like that.

After dinner, he suggested a walk on the beach, but first had to make a trip to the car. She waited for him on the restaurant deck. When he returned he held what looked like a book in a brown paper bag. They walked on the beach, away from the crowd of the restaurant and watched the last of the sunset. He spied a bench and led her to it, and they sat down. He put the bag in her lap.

"What is this?" She asked as she looked down at it.

"Open it." He was smiling at her.

She pulled the book out of the bag. It was not a book, but a picture album. She opened it and exclaimed, "These are of us!" Then she remembered. "The man at the zoo! You went to his studio! These are…wonderful! What made you go?"

"Curiosity. When I saw them I knew I had to buy them from him. And he was right. Look at these, Katrina! We belong together."

Nathan slid off the bench and down on one knee. He looked into her face.

"I love you, Katrina. I have only said that one other time. At the time I thought I meant it, but since I met you….I know I didn't even know what love was. I love you with all my heart and soul. Katrina Kitrowski, will you marry me?"

He reached into his pocket and produced a solitaire diamond ring of about three carats. Katrina sucked in her breath. She was speechless.

"Katrina?" Nathan was holding his breath, waiting for her answer.

She squeezed her eyes shut and then opened them. Tears were running down her cheeks. "YES! Oh, Nathan….YES!"

He scooped her off the bench and held her as he spun her around, planting kisses on her cheeks, her nose and finally her mouth. When he stopped he was breathless. He looked into her eyes and he spoke, his voice raspy. "You said 'yes'…..that's the best birthday present I could ever have. You're all I ever wanted."

He sat her down on the bench again and took her left hand. He knelt down and slid the ring onto her third finger, and then kissed her fingers. The joyful tears were flowing again.

"Oh, Nathan….I love you." She took his face between her hands and kissed him. Still holding his face, she looked into his eyes. "I really *love* you."

He helped her up from the bench and they started walking toward the light of the restaurant, arms around each other's waist. "What do you say we go to Jack's Place and show off that ring?" Nathan couldn't wait to tell people. As they walked toward the car, he stopped everyone he saw and told them Katrina said 'yes'. People smiled and nodded.

At Jack's Place, they were congratulated by everyone…except the lovelorn Holly. She glared at Katrina and then pouted at the corner of the bar for the rest of the evening. Lisa was happy for them. She was wearing the dress that Katrina picked out for her and she looked gorgeous. She led Katrina to the bathroom to tell her that things were better between her and Charlie. She thanked her for the excellent advice, and then hugged her.

"Again, Katrina, I can't thank you enough."

"Not a problem, Lisa. Hey, I figure if you can't improve him, just improve yourself. It's a positive feedback system." They laughed together.

* * *

The party was well underway when Danny and Kathy showed up. Katrina hugged them and thrust her left hand into their view. Kathy gasped when she looked at the ring.

Danny took Katrina's hands in his. "Are you absolutely sure, Kat? He's the one for you?"

"He's the one, Danny. He's the one I've waited for all my life. I'm positive."

"Then I'm happy. So where is my future brother-in-law?"

Nathan appeared as if he had been summoned.

"Congratulations, Untul Nate!"

The four of them laughed, remembering the kids' name for him. Most of the guests were seated with plates of catered food in front of them. A disc jockey was setting up equipment on the far end of the patio, and waitresses were serving drinks. When the DJ had the microphone ready to go, Nathan took it from him.

He spoke into the microphone, his voice coming across loud and clear. "Can I get everybody's attention, please?" A hush fell over the patio.

"I'd like to thank you all for coming here to celebrate my thirtieth birthday. So thank you. But I also have an announcement to make." The guests waited.

"I'm happy. I'm happier than I have ever been in my life. Those of you who know me well know that that's got to be pretty damn happy, right?" There was some laughter.

"Well, the reason why I'm happy has to do with this little red head, here." He pointed to Katrina. She gave me the only thing that could have made me happier than I already was. She said 'yes'. So I want all of you to meet my future bride, the love of my life, Katrina." He took her hand and drew her to him. He kissed her as the guests applauded. He raised a glass of champagne to her and toasted, "To you, my love. To us."

Katrina fell into his arms. "Oh, Nathan…" She wiped her tears with the heel of her hand.

Danny and Kathy were sitting at a nearby table, watching with tears in both of their eyes. Danny looked at Kathy and wiped his eyes. "That guy is a real class act."

16

Nathan and Katrina were marking the wall to hang the portrait she gave him.

"Honey, this is beautiful. I want everybody who ever walks into this house to see it as soon as they enter. Your work is awesome."

"Maybe the subjects are awesome. It's easy when you have good material to work with." She teased.

He hung the portrait while she stood behind him, looking to make sure it was straight. "There. That's perfect."

He climbed off the ladder and stood back with her, admiring her work.

"It stays there forever and ever. Just like us." He grinned and hugged her.

"There's something I want to talk to you about." Nathan sounded serious.

"What is it?" She questioned him.

"Well, we have to tell our parents. We can't just send them a wedding invitation. That would be insensitive. I want you to meet mine and I want to meet yours. I think we should take a trip up north. What do you think?"

* * *

Katrina was packing for their trip. It was agreed, at Katrina's suggestion, that they would fly to Cleveland and spend a couple of days there, and then rent a car and drive to Katrina's parents' home, just southeast of Pittsburgh. From there, they would drive the rental back to Florida. Danny had arranged for a house sitter to stay with Katrina's cats and take care of them while she was gone. He assured her the girl was responsible and would take good care of the cats. He promised to check in on them once or twice while Katrina was away. She had worked extra hard, turning in three weeks' worth of work to her agent so there would be no interruptions in the Kit-Kat strip. Danny arrived to drive them to the airport right before Nathan got there. He was glad to have those few minutes alone with his sister.

"Remember, Danny, I'm surprising mom and dad, so don't go telling them."

"Hell, Kat, I didn't even tell Mike. Just remember your promise, though. You'll tell them what happened to you?"

"Yeah, I promise."

Katrina finished writing the instructions for feeding the cats when the house sitter arrived. She showed Beth to the spare room and then took her in and introduced her to the cats. The cats liked her instantly, so Katrina felt at ease about leaving them in her care. She explained that the computer in the spare room had Internet access and a Microsoft Office program if she needed it for school work. She also explained the locked bedroom door.

"It's where I work. I don't allow the cats in there so the door remains locked. Do you have any questions for me?" Katrina asked her.

"Do you mind if I have company while I'm here?"

Katrina smiled at that question. "No, not really. Just no parties or anything like that. My neighbors would get very upset."

"Oh, I don't do that kind of thing anyway. I'm a law student and I really don't have time for parties. I work in the law firm where Danny works, so I'm very busy. I just meant someone to study with."

"No problem, then." Katrina smiled at her. She liked this girl.

Nathan arrived with his luggage and asked if they were ready to go. They filled Danny's trunk with suitcases and climbed into the car, after Katrina kissed the cats.

17

From the moment they walked into the baggage claim area, Al knew that Katrina was the girl for his son. He was struck by her beauty, but there was something else. The word 'Quality' came to his mind. He watched them together before Nathan spied him standing there. They looked like two people, obviously in love, joined as one. Every move between them was smooth and in tune with each other. Nathan saw his father standing there and grinned at him.

"Dad, this is Katrina."

Al took her hand with a grin that matched Nathan's. "I'm really happy to meet you. I was beginning to think my son didn't like girls." He had a twinkle in his eye, which both Katrina and Nathan caught. They laughed with him.

"Just one girl, Dad. It's all I need." Nathan's love for Katrina was obvious in his voice.

On the ride from the airport, Al kept looking at Katrina. She was certainly the most beautiful girl Nathan had ever brought home; if not the most beautiful girl Al had ever seen.

"Katrina, we know nothing about you. My son has kept you a secret. What do you do? Where are you from?"

Katrina obliged his questions. "I'm an artist, originally from a small town outside of Pittsburgh."

Nathan's arm was over the back of the seat and he squeezed her shoulders lightly.

"Tell him the rest. You know, who you're famous for."

Katrina laughed. "I'm hardly famous, but I'm the creator of Kit-Kat, the comic strip."

"My wife reads that comic every day! Your mom may embarrass you and ask for an autograph, Nate." Al was obviously impressed.

"I'll give her one, then." Katrina laughed again.

"Dad, Katrina's Kit-Kat is going to be on the market as a stuffed animal. Make sure mom gets one."

"Yeah? That's very impressive. You will be famous, then." Al liked this girl more and more.

Rose was waiting anxiously for them to get there. Nathan engaged! She couldn't wait to meet her. She was beginning to give up hope of ever seeing Nathan happily married. She heard the car pull into the driveway and quickly smoothed her hair and then her blouse. The coffee pot stood ready for them at Nathan's request, and there was a plate of pastries in the center of the table. She heard the banter and the laughter as they came through the door, Nathan carrying their luggage.

"Mom, this is Katrina." Nathan made the introduction.

Rose stared at her, taken back by her beauty. She took in her gorgeous copper colored hair, her amazing blue eyes, her lovely features, and her well-proportioned body all at once, forgetting to speak.

Katrina smiled at her and said, "Hi."

Rose snapped out of it and smiled back at her. "Hi. What a pleasure to meet you."

Al put his arm around Katrina's shoulders and smiled at Rose. "And when you find out who she is, it will be an even bigger pleasure."

Rose looked at Al, and then at Katrina, waiting to hear the rest.

"She creates your favorite comic strip."

"Kit-Kat? You write Kit-Kat? Oh, my gosh, I'm honored to have you in our home!" She spoke breathlessly when Katrina nodded, confirming Al's information.

Nathan was amused by his mother's excitement. He led Katrina to the kitchen where the coffee was waiting. "Coffee, Kat? Mom makes good coffee."

They spent the afternoon at the kitchen table; the Perletti's asking questions and learning all about Katrina. She was a hit with them. Both Rose and Al saw the love in their eyes when they looked at each other, and they couldn't have been happier about it. Nathan told them about how well Katrina played the piano and about her dancing ability.

"Do you sing, too?" Al teased.

Katrina shrugged and answered, "Yes."

Nathan looked at her with surprise. "You do? I didn't know that! Do you sing well?"

Katrina told him about winning first prize with her singing voice in the third grade and then told him about singing the National Anthem at football games.

"I was in the high school choir all through high school." She informed him.

"So was I! I did several solos during concerts. I had no idea you sang, too." He looked at Al and Rose and declared, "I'm still learning amazing things about her. She's so modest about everything she does."

"You've always been like that, too, Nate." Al told him. He turned to Katrina and told her about the time when he received the MVP award; about how when he was interviewed for the newspaper, he gave all the credit to his teammates. Katrina smiled at Nathan and their eyes locked with that look of undying love they felt for each other.

Nathan took Katrina into the family room to show her his trophies and memorabilia on the wall.

When they left the kitchen, Al looked at Rose and said, "Best." Rose knew what he meant. It was his comparison of Katrina to every girl Nathan had ever brought home.

* * *

"Nathan, Dad put Katrina's luggage in St—the spare room. Show her where it is."

Nathan led Katrina up the stairs and she hesitated outside the bedroom. "It's Steven's room, isn't it?"

Nathan nodded and pushed open the door. "For what little time he spent here, yeah."

The room had been redone to look more like a guest room than a child's room, as Nathan remembered it. Katrina said nothing, but she was uneasy going into that room. It was obvious that the furniture that Steven once used had been replaced and that all of his belongings had been removed, but she still felt queasy. She shook off the feeling, realizing she was being silly. He was gone.

She lay in bed awake for what seemed like hours. She just couldn't feel comfortable in that room. Finally, she fell asleep, and she dreamed about Steven. In the dream she heard his wicked, insane laugh. She jerked up into a sitting position, gasping.

Nathan was in a restless sleep, when he thought he heard her. He got up out of bed and crept to the doorway of Steven's room, and listened. He could hear Katrina crying softly, so he opened the door and went to her. He held her until she stopped trembling, and then he wiped her tears with his thumbs. She told him of the dream and how it brought her awake.

"He can't hurt you again, Sweetheart. Steven's gone."

"I know. I'm being such a baby."

Nathan shrugged. "You're *my* baby…"

Al heard them talking and got out of bed to see if everything was all right. He stopped in the hallway when he heard Steven's name, leaned against the wall and listened. He crept back into bed. He knew.

Nathan and Katrina quietly went down to the family room and turned on the television. Al found them sleeping on the couch in the family room in the morning.

* * *

"So what do you say we show Katrina the lake today? Nathan and I used to fish in the lake. It was our spot for quiet time and talks." Al winked at Katrina.

"I know. Nathan told me. I'd love to see it." She gave Al a winning grin.

Katrina was impressed by the beauty of the lake and its shores. Everything was so green this time of year, and the water was clear and clean looking. They walked to the edge of the pier and looked down into the water. There were fish coming to the surface. Katrina bent down to get a closer look at them, delighted to be so close. Al was studying her features as she watched the fish. He gave her a history of the lake, telling her it was man-made and that they stocked it with fish every year. She listened with interest, her blue eyes sparkling. Al became quiet and stared at the water.

"You're that girl, aren't you? The one Steven abducted." Al stared at her intently.

Katrina was taken back for a moment, and then let out a resigned sigh. "Yes." She looked Al in the eye and said, "I'm sorry."

"You have no reason to be sorry. I'm sorry. I'm sorry my son hurt you." Al looked at her, trying to imagine the damage that had been done to her face. There were no traces of injury.

"So how is it that you and Nathan are together? I mean, did you know him or Steven before....that day?"

"No, I....well, Nathan...after he came to my rescue, kind of took care of me and looked after me. I was in no condition to do much for myself."

Nathan came up from behind and heard their conversation. "I did what I could to help her, Dad. By the second day I knew her, I realized I was attracted to her, battered face, broken ribs, and all. I never thought she would even have anything to do with me after what happened. But I kept finding reasons to see her. I even cleaned her apartment for her, just to be near her. Believe me; I would have loved to have met her under other circumstances. But we fell in love. It just....happened." Nathan hesitated briefly, and then looked straight into Al's eyes. "Remember the time when I told you that I could feel someone waiting for me, but didn't know who she was? It was Katrina, Dad. She's the one I've always waited for."

Al kept silent, rubbing his chin with his thumb, as was his habit when he was pensive. He was trying to imagine what it must have been like seeing this girl after she was beaten by Steven. It was time to say something that would let them know that he accepted this union. He stood up and leaned against the railing of the pier, and then cleared his throat.

"You know, Katrina...we lost Steven a long time ago. Long before he was shot and killed. From what I understand, you had nothing to do with that, anyway. He killed a cop with his bare hands. He was strong—strong and dangerous. The police shot him because he killed one of their own. For all the wrong and all the evil in Steven, I would like to think that he did one good deed in his life. I believe he did.

I know the circumstances must have been terrifying for you, but he brought you to Nathan. That was the only redeeming deed he ever did in his life. He couldn't have delivered you on a silver platter—that wasn't his style. He did what he did best—hurt someone. But by some wicked twist of fate, he brought Nathan a lifetime of happiness—you. That's what I want to believe. You have my blessing."

Nathan put his arm around Katrina. He didn't have to look at her to know that she was crying. Al put his arms around both of them. "Now….suppose you two switch rooms tonight? We'll tell your mom that the mattress bothers Katrina's back." The three of them laughed.

* * *

Katrina was dressing to go to Mike and Cookie's house. She was excited to finally be meeting them, since she had heard so much about them. Nathan appeared in the doorway to see if she was ready, and gave his approval on how she looked in the pale blue jumpsuit.

They arrived at the large white colonial style house after stopping to pick up a bottle of wine.

Mike answered the door before they knocked. "Hey, man…good to see you. And this must be Katrina. Holy hell, man, can you pick 'em! You're much better looking than he said you were. What happened to the big wart on the tip of your nose? He said you only had one tooth!"

Katrina was laughing already, and she hadn't even gotten inside the door. She liked Mike instantly. She immediately took in his blonde-haired, blue-eyed good looks, mentally noting that Mike and Nathan were a perfect duo.

"That's his other fiancée. I'm the stand-in he takes in public."

Mike appreciated Katrina's humor, kissed her on the cheek, and grinned at Nathan. "I like her. Katrina, are you sure you want to marry Nate? I could use a second wife."

"Hah! You can't handle the first one!" Cookie made her appearance, swatting Mike on his behind. She hugged Nathan and then turned to Katrina. "Hi! I'm Cookie. You have my deepest respect. You have done what no woman has been able to do—turn this man's head. And I can see why…you're absolutely gorgeous!"

Katrina laughed and smiled warmly at Cookie. She could already see that she was everything Nathan said she was, but was having a hard time picturing this attractive woman as Nathan had described her when they were in high school. In the present, she was positively stunning. They were going to be friends.

Cookie was an excellent cook and a marvelous hostess. The four of them enjoyed good food and good conversation all evening.

"So when's the date?" Mike asked.

Nathan looked across the table at Katrina and cocked his eyebrow. "Whenever she says. Tomorrow, if she wants."

Katrina laughed and thought for a moment. "We haven't even discussed it. I know what I want for a wedding, though."

All eyes were on her. "So…go. We're waiting." Cookie urged.

"I want to get married on the beach. So that would mean sometime before hurricane season and after the rainy season, I guess."

"So that would mean between March and June, sometime, right?" Nathan looked at her with anticipation. He was a little disappointed that they would be waiting that long, but he wanted her to have a nice wedding.

"A wedding on the beach….how romantic." Cookie tucked her hands under her chin and smiled dreamily. "Well, we have some news." She looked at Mike and waited for the 'go-ahead' sign. "We're pregnant!"

"No shit?" Nathan's face broke out in a wide grin. "I thought for awhile that maybe you were going to need my help with that, Buddy!"

Mike laughed and flipped him the bird. The four of them broke up laughing.

"When are you due?" Katrina asked Cookie.

"The end of February, but maybe sooner. It might be twins."

Nathan looked at Mike, astonished. "You have to do two at once? Always were a show-off, weren't you?"

"Hey, don't look at me…the twins run in her family." Mike was beaming with pride.

* * *

"They're both terrific, Nathan. They're just as you said they were. I really like them."

"Good…I'm glad. They are my oldest and closest friends."

Al and Rose took Katrina and Nathan to see the Rock 'n Roll Hall of Fame, and then to dinner at one of their favorite restaurants. Afterward, they stopped at Bumpy's, as promised by Nathan. Katrina was enjoying their trip immensely. She liked Nathan's parents and she was fairly sure they liked her. Bumpy's reminded her of Bear's Place, and Jack's Place, as well. Quite a few of the patrons at Bumpy's seemed to know Nathan. As they came by the table to greet him, many of them gawked at Katrina. He introduced her to many of them, and he could tell that they appreciated what they saw. As they were getting ready to leave, he heard someone call his name.

"Nate! Nate?" He turned around and saw Stephanie with a man he presumed to be her husband.

"Steph! How are you?" He hugged her quickly and kissed her cheek.

"Great! Nate, this is my husband, Jerry. Nate was one of my boyfriends in high school." She told Jerry.

"Stephanie, this is Katrina—my fiancée."

"Hi, Stephanie. I remember seeing your prom picture. It's nice to meet you."

"Same here. So you're engaged, huh? It's about time!" She looked at Katrina for a moment. "But I can see why you held out so long. Finding someone like this one couldn't have been easy." She turned to Katrina. "He's a great guy, but I'm sure you know that."

Katrina laughed. "Yes, I do, and thank you for the compliment."

"I like her, Nate." Stephanie smiled at the two of them. "Best wishes to you. I hope you'll be very happy."

"Thank you," they both answered.

* * *

They were saying their goodbyes on the porch. It had been an enjoyable visit. The Perletti's had a cook-out the day before, and Katrina met Mike's parents, and Cookie's Parents, as well. Katrina felt welcome and comfortable around all of them, and she truly felt like part of Nathan's family.

Nathan had gone with Al earlier that morning to pick up a rental car, and he was putting their luggage in the trunk. Katrina called her parents and asked what they were doing.

"I'm in Cleveland. I can be there in about two to three hours....if you want the company..." She teased. It was a Saturday and she knew both parents would be there when she arrived. She hadn't told them anything about Nathan. It was going to be her surprise. They didn't know he was coming.

Al and Rose kissed Katrina and then Nathan.

"Thanks for everything, Mrs. Perletti."

"Mom...please." Rose instructed her.

"And I want you to call me Dad." Al hugged Katrina. "We love you already."

"Okay, Mom and Dad....we'll see you real soon."

They left in the rental car, waving to Al and Rose, who stood on the porch, arm in arm. Nathan was smiling. It was so good to see his parents happy and together. He was giving them a wonderful daughter-in-law and hopefully, a few grandchildren, down the road. He knew they would be thrilled to have grandchildren.

They motored down the interstate, just enjoying the sights and being together. Nathan hoped her parents liked him as well as Al and Rose liked Katrina. He would soon find out. When they threaded through the traffic of Pittsburgh, Katrina asked if she could drive, since she knew how to get there. He pulled over and let her get behind the wheel.

It was almost noon when they pulled into the Kitrowski's driveway. Mary heard the car door and ran to the front door to open it. Katrina and Nathan barely stepped inside before Mary grabbed Katrina into her arms in a hug. Ed was jogging down the hall to get to his precious daughter, too. He stopped when he saw Nathan standing behind Katrina.

"Oh, how I've missed you, Baby!" Mary was saying to Katrina, and then she spied Nathan. She dropped her arms and looked up at him. "Oh." Was all she could say.

"Mom, Dad, this is Nathan. We're…well, look." She held up her left hand to show them the ring.

Mary gasped at the ring. "Oh, Honey! I-I'm speechless."

Ed offered his hand to Nathan. "I'm Ed Kitrowski, Katrina's father."

"Nathan Perletti." Nathan took Ed's offered hand and shook it.

"The ball player?" Ed asked, surprised.

"Used to be. I pitched…"

"Damn right, you pitched. You were a hell of a pitcher. I saw you pitch once. Struck out twelve batters in a row. It's good to meet you."

Ed hugged Katrina. "You're engaged? To this guy? I guess you'll be having some artistic, dancing pitchers for kids." He laughed at his own joke.

Mary, on the other hand, was still speechless, tears rolling down her face. "I-I guess I should say something. I'm so…so overwhelmed."

"Well, you know how I like to surprise you, Mom. How am I doing?" Katrina hugged Mary again.

"Well, you surprised me. Nathan, I'm glad to meet you. Now that I have my voice back, I can ask. How about some coffee? Are you hungry? You probably are. I have lunch made."

Mary had the dining room table set for three, but quickly got an extra place setting for Nathan. They sat down to lunch.

"So tell me everything. How did this all happen? Last I heard you weren't even dating anyone. Sorry, Nathan, my daughter can be so secretive at times."

Katrina and Nathan looked at each other. "Before we tell you, Mom, do you remember that time when we talked in the kitchen? I was about twelve. Remember I told you about feeling that there was someone and something special for me some day?"

"Yes, Honey, I remember that."

"Mom, it was Nathan I was waiting for; I'm sure of it. He's all I could ever want. Before we give you the details, I wanted you to know that."

Mary set her fork down. Somehow she knew that she would be hearing something very upsetting. Katrina began telling the story, with Nathan interjecting in certain places where Katrina seemed to be unclear. Mary felt faint a couple of times. She was horrified, especially at the part where Steven told her he was going to kill her. Mary felt sick, and at points, she felt like her insides were crumbling. Her hands were shaking.

"Mom, if it hadn't been for Nathan, he would have killed me."

Mary couldn't help crying. "Oh, my baby....Oh, God!"

"Where is this son of a bitch now?" Ed hadn't spoken until now.

"Dead." Nathan answered for Katrina.

Ed rested his elbow on the table and put his hand over his forehead, rubbing his temple. He let out a long breath. "Good. So let's hear the connection from that to the two of you getting engaged."

Katrina looked at Nathan, and Nathan answered. "The guy was my brother."

Both Mary and Ed gaped in shock. Nathan told them about Steven, and how they had been kept apart most of their lives by Steven's mental illness.

"He was really never a brother. I would have killed him to save Katrina, and yet I didn't even know who she was. I could just see what he had done to her and I wasn't going to let him do any more. All I know is that when I picked her up and carried her inside, my heart was aching that my brother could do that to anyone. She didn't want to go to a hospital, so I called my friend, who is a physician, and he came to my house to treat her. That was after I called the police. Because Steven had Katrina's purse with her ID in it, the police posted cars around her apartment, and an officer spent the night in her apartment. She stayed at my place. They captured him there, at her place."

"But you said he's dead..."

"He is. He managed to escape. Killed a guard and then killed a cop with his bare hands. They shot and killed him."

Ed was visibly shaken. Mary ran to the bathroom to empty her stomach. She held herself up at the bathroom sink, trying to calm her breathing.

"So....you looked after Katrina....and what? You two just fell in love?" Ed looked from one to the other.

"To make a long story short, yes." Nathan answered.

Mary returned to the dining room and stood behind Katrina's chair. She bent down and surrounded Katrina with her arms. "Nathan, I don't know you very well, have never even heard of you, but because I can look at my daughter alive and happy, I love you….and I will be eternally grateful." Tears rolled down Mary's face and she sobbed as she spoke, holding Katrina like she was afraid to let go.

Katrina held one of Mary's arms. "I'm glad you didn't see me all banged up, Mom. I can imagine your reaction."

"Are you okay now? No permanent damage?" Ed asked her.

"I'm fine. The ribs are mended and obviously, all the bruises are gone. Mom, Nathan cleaned my apartment for me." She was smiling when she said it.

Mary relaxed a little and let her breath out in a small laugh. "Well, I guess it's a hell of a way to meet your soul mate. So this is it for you, huh? He's Mr. Right?" She smiled into Katrina's blue eyes and whispered.

"Yep, he is." She awarded Nathan with a beautiful smile.

"So when this…Steven escaped, did you take any precautions to protect Katrina?" The ever-questioning Ed looked Nathan in the eye.

"I took her to one of my hotels in Orlando. Took her to Universal Studios, went shopping, anything to keep her mind off of Steven. We stayed there until Detective Delaney called me to tell me Steven was dead. Of course, I had to go back and make a positive identification, and then accompany the body back to Cleveland. We buried him, and then I returned to Florida."

"Cleveland. You're originally from there?"

"Yes. We just came from my parents' home. They met Katrina for the first time."

"Do they know who she is?"

"My dad does. He figured it out. Well, they put Katrina up in Steven's old room, and she had a bad night because of it. I went in to comfort her and my dad heard us talking. Look, Mr. Kitrowski..."

"Ed."

"Ed…my parents are good people. They cried plenty of tears over Steven. They don't know what happened with him. Nobody does. Somewhere there was some brain damage, or something to cause his illness. They raised me, and I think I turned out all right."

"Oh, I know. I'm not judging. I just ask a lot of questions. It's my way of sorting things out. My wife and I are both in shock over hearing this news that my daughter might have been murdered. I thank God for you, Nathan. You can't imagine how much I love this girl of mine."

"Oh, I think I can." He looked at Katrina, his love for her flowing into her eyes.

Ed laughed. "Well, maybe you can. So let's put all of that behind us and move on. Welcome, to the family, Son."

Mary let go of Katrina and went to Nathan and hugged him. "Thank you….thank you for having the good sense to love her." Mary smiled widely at Nathan. "You have excellent taste in women."

"Yes, I do." Nathan hugged Mary back.

"Oh, Honey, Mike and Kim are on their way up. Do your brothers know any of what happened?"

"Yeah, they both know. I made them promise not to tell you. They agreed, only if I promised that I would tell you. I just wanted you to see that I was okay. I knew how crazy you'd get if you couldn't see that I was fine. That's why I waited until now to tell you."

"I can see your reasoning. I guess I went kind of nuts anyway, huh?"

"Yeah, but I know you love me. And since you love me so much…. can we eat at Bear's tonight? I promised Nathan the best burger in the state of Pennsylvania."

"I think that can be arranged." Ed answered for Mary.

"Let me go call Morgan. She's dying to meet Nathan."

Morgan answered her phone immediately. She was sitting on her patio reading a financial report when the phone rang.

"Morgan! I'm in town!"

"Kat! Oh, my God! I gotta see you! Hold on, let me get Kevin. Wait…do you have that Nathan guy with you?"

"Uh-huh."

"Then I'm there! Wait a minute."

She heard her calling Kevin's name, so she waited until Morgan returned to the phone.

"Okay, we're coming over. Okay?"

"Yeah…hey, wait….we're going to Bear's for dinner. Why don't you and Kevin plan on going with us?"

"You betcha!" Morgan hung up.

While she was on the phone with Morgan, Mary was showing Nathan all of Katrina's pictures and accomplishments.

"You have got to be bored by all of this." Katrina laughed when she returned from the phone call.

"I never get bored of seeing anything that concerns you." Nathan reached for her hand and laced his fingers through hers. "Would that be your brother Mike pulling into the driveway?" Nathan was looking past her out through the window.

"That's him. Ready for round three?" She laughed.

"Three?" Mary asked.

"Danny has already met Nathan. In fact, Danny saw my face when it was all beaten up. He went off on Nathan like it was his fault. Well, you can imagine how Danny got. It all ended well, when we explained everything. Actually, Danny and Kathy came to Nathan's birthday party in July."

"Oh." Mary was surprised Danny hadn't said anything, but chocked it up to secrets between siblings.

Surprisingly, Michael wasn't harsh on Nathan at all. He seemed to rather like him. Kim pulled Katrina aside and whispered of how handsome Nathan was. Both Kim and Michael exclaimed over the ring.

"Couldn't you get it any bigger?" Michael joked to Nathan.

Nathan just laughed. "I wouldn't have been able to carry it." He joked back to Michael.

Morgan and Kevin were hurrying up the walk to the front door, and Ed answered it before they knocked. "Hi, Morgan, Kevin. Come on in."

Mary was elated with having a houseful of people. "It's like old times, right, Ed"?

"Sure do miss those times." Ed answered wistfully.

Morgan squealed when she saw Katrina, and immediately hugged her. "My God, he's gorgeous! She whispered in Katrina's ear.

Katrina produced her left hand, and Morgan screamed. She hugged Katrina again, this time with tears. *"Oh, Kat!"*

Katrina waved Nathan over and introduced him to Morgan and Kevin. Nathan shook hands with Kevin.

"You're that ball player. You pitched, didn't you? How many no-hitters did you have?" Kevin was awed.

"Quite a few, I guess." Nathan answered modestly.

Ed put out more chairs and they all gathered around the dining room table, each having their own set of questions for Nathan. There was talk, jokes, and laughter in the Kitrowski household again. Mary and Ed loved every minute of it.

* * *

The eight of them clamored into Bear's place and took the largest table in the place. Ed ordered beers for himself, Michael, Nathan, and Kevin. The ladies ordered wine coolers, something that had been added to the beverage list at Bear's.

Morgan nudged Katrina and said, "How cool! We're old enough to drink with your parents." Katrina laughed.

It was fun being home again and Katrina hoped that Nathan was enjoying himself. After the initial 'tell all' everything seemed fine. Nathan urged Katrina to tell her family about Kit-Kat's new fame. Ed and Mary were delighted to hear it. Mary said she knew what everyone was getting for Christmas that year. Katrina laughed. She and Nathan sat next to each other with their hands linked together. The group ordered another round of drinks before they were ready to order dinner. When it was time to order, Michael asked Nathan if he were going to try the burger Katrina raved about.

"Of course. She says it's the best, so it probably is."

"Whipped already, huh?" Michael laughed, and then Nathan laughed with him.

They heard someone calling out their name. Michael looked up and saw Officer Parks smiling over at him.

"Kitrowski. How are ya?" Katrina looked around behind her and he spotted her. "Hi, Katrina! Long time no see! It's good to see you, and you're as beautiful as ever."

"Thanks, Mr. Parks. It's nice to see you."

"So are you married with about six kids?" Parks was teasing her, and she knew it.

"No. This is my fiancé, Nathan. Officer Parks."

Nathan shook his hand and said, “Nathan Perletti.”

“You’re a lucky man, Nathan.”

“I know, sir.”

Parks patted Katrina on the shoulder and then saluted Michael. He nodded to the rest of the party, and left Bear’s Place.

“I always liked him and Mrs. Parks.” Katrina told Michael.

Michael nodded. “Yeah, they’re nice people.” He started to say something about their jackass son, but changed his mind. Maybe Katrina hadn’t told Nathan about Sean.

Their burgers and fries arrived. Katrina waited for Nathan to bite into his, and then asked, “Well? Am I right?”

“Mmmm….yes, you’re right. It *is* one of the best I’ve ever had. I should go back and see how they make ‘em, and then take the information back to Jack’s Place.”

“Good idea.” Katrina laughed.

The banter at the table continued through the meal. The question about the date came up, as it did with Mike and Cookie.

“I’ve been thinking…..Nate, how does April the eighth sound?” Katrina smiled into his eyes.

“Too far away. But if that’s what you want, that’s what it will be.” He put his arm around her shoulders and kissed her cheek.

Morgan piped up. “Oh my God! Kat, don’t look now but guess who just walked in.”

Katrina looked up and there stood Sean in front of their table.

“Kat….hi. How are you?” Sean was staring at Katrina, but glanced at Nathan.

“I’m fine. How are you?”

Sean nodded, and glanced at Nathan again.

Oh, Sean….this is my fiancé, Nathan Perletti.” Neither Sean nor Nathan offered his hand to the other.

Sean nodded at Nathan and looked back at Katrina. “Take care. It was good to see you.” He walked to the back of the restaurant.

“Well, that was awkward.” Katrina snickered at Morgan.

Nathan watched Sean walk away. “Is that the guy you punched?”

“Yes.” She looked at Nathan and smiled.

Michael looked over at Nathan. “And do you know how badly I still want to punch him?”

Nathan laughed. "Hey, I didn't even know Katrina back then, but I want to get up and punch him."

"Well, hell—let's go then." Michael started to get up.

"Sit down, Michael." Kim spoke up in a flat tone, keeping her eyes on her plate.

Nathan roared with laughter, and then Michael joined in, followed by the rest of the party.

* * *

The visit at the Kitrowski's ended too soon. On Sunday, Mary cooked a big dinner for Katrina and Nathan. Morgan and Kevin were invited over, and they obliged. Michael and Kim, unfortunately, had to return to Maryland, so they wouldn't be there for dinner. The talk at the dinner table was of the wedding.

"Morgan, you will be my matron of honor, won't you?"

"You got it, Kat. Just tell me what you want me to do."

"I have an idea for dresses. You know how I am about color and perfection. Well, I have an idea for the colors in my wedding. As soon as it's more than an idea, I'll let you know."

"What color will *I* wear?" Nathan teased Katrina.

"Maybe pink." She teased back.

Nathan and Katrina planned on leaving early in the morning and taking a couple of days to drive back. They got to bed early in order to get up early. They wanted to see Ed before he went off to work in the morning.

* * *

Katrina hugged Ed when he got up to leave for work. He held her for a moment, and then took her hand as they walked outside. "I'm so glad you came home, even if it was a short visit. Maybe we'll be coming down that way soon, okay?"

"Please do, Daddy. I miss you and mom."

"By the way, Honey, I like him." Ed smiled at her. "He kind of reminds me of Jeff."

Katrina smiled and nodded. "I know."

Nathan was carrying the luggage down the stairs when Mary called him for breakfast. "Come on, Nathan, you can't drive all day on an empty stomach."

Nathan sat down. "You don't have to call me twice. Where's Katrina?"

"She's saying goodbye to her father. They're outside; so if you want to, you can run out and say goodbye to him."

Nathan got back up and went out the back door to say a few words to Ed. He stopped for a moment and watched Ed with Katrina. He could see the love Ed had for his daughter. It was beautiful.

"Nathan." Ed waved at him. "I'm glad I got to meet you. We plan on visiting Florida soon. You'll be around then?"

"I'm going to be around a *long* time, Ed. Your daughter is the love of my life."

Ed smiled at Nathan. "Take care of her?"

"Promise. Always." Nathan shook Ed's hand, and he and Katrina watched him drive out of the driveway. "Your mom has breakfast ready for us." He didn't miss the tear running down Katrina's cheek.

After they ate breakfast, they said their goodbyes to Mary. Nathan knew this would be a tearful event, so he braced himself when mother and daughter hugged each other, sniffling.

"Honey, promise me you'll plan on coming back sooner next time. Daddy and I will be visiting you in Florida, but we want you to come home more often."

"We'll see, Mom. I'll try."

"Nathan, I'm counting on you to bring her home once in awhile." Mary's voice got quieter. "I'm also counting on you to take care of her; keep her safe."

"Absolutely." Nathan returned the hug that Mary gave him.

* * *

They had been on the highway for almost two hours. Nathan glanced over at Katrina, and then reached for her hand. "Are you all right?"

"Yeah, I don't ever realize how much I miss my parents until I see them...that's all."

"You know, Sweetheart, I have plenty of money. If you want to fly up and visit them once a month, you can do it. We can both go, or you can go by yourself if you want."

Katrina looked over and smiled at him. "Thanks. That's why I love you so much. You care when I'm upset, and you always try to fix it."

"When you're happy, I'm happy. That's the way it is." Nathan squeezed her hand lightly and then put both hands on the wheel to maneuver a sharp turn.

They were silent until he got through the turn.

"You know...." Katrina began. "When I knew that Steven was going to kill me, I thought about my family...and how it was going to hurt them. I visualized each of their faces, and I was hurting for them. I have always known how much they all love me."

"They're a great family, Honey. I enjoyed being there with them. And you passed with flying colors with my parents. You know that, don't you? Mom loves you and Dad thinks you're perfect for me. He's disappointed that I didn't tell him about you sooner, but he understands why I didn't. He knows it was wise to let him meet you first."

"Your dad is a very wise man, Nathan. Very intuitive."

Nathan nodded. "So where would you like to go from here? We have time to do a few tourist-type things."

"I always wanted to go to Chattanooga, Tennessee and see the caverns and things they advertise."

"Then that's where we're headed." Nathan engaged the cruise control and relaxed his hands on the wheel. Life was good. The only way to improve it was to marry this woman he loved so much.

* * *

They found a nice hotel for the night and checked in. They entered their room and shut the door, and immediately fell into each other's arms. After following the protocol of sleeping in separate rooms in each of their parents' homes, they were hungry for each other. Their lips were locked together in passion as they quickly undressed each other, and then fell onto the bed, and made love with an urgent frenzy.

After releasing their pent up desires, they lay side by side, drinking in the love from each other's eyes. Katrina ran her index finger down Nathan's cheek and traced the outline of his jaw. He reached for her finger and kissed the tip of it, and then placed it on her lips. They joined together again, slowly and tenderly this time. When the love making ended, they drifted off to sleep, weak from spent passion.

At dawn, Nathan and Katrina awoke feeling hungry, for food this time. They had skipped dinner in lieu of lovemaking the night before, and both were ravenous. After showering and dressing, they found a breakfast diner and ordered large portions of food. They looked at tourist brochures while eating and chose a few sights to visit for the day.

In two days, they covered most of the sights they wanted to see, and planned on heading south the next morning. It was a wonderful vacation for them, and they felt like they were the only two people in the world, even though everywhere they went was overly crowded.

Back on the road, they chose to stop in Atlanta for a day, and then a night, before heading toward home. In Atlanta, they found a zoo, so they spent their day wondering around looking at the animals in captivity. Katrina made a quick phone call to check on the cats, and was satisfied that everything was okay. She talked to Danny briefly and told him everything went well with both sets of parents, and that she would see him soon.

18

They had been gone almost two weeks when they returned home. Because she knew her house sitter would be at the house all night, they spent the night at Nathan's. She called her in the morning to tell her she was back home and that she could drop off the key and pick up her belongings later. Katrina checked out her apartment and found that everything was to her satisfaction. Beth had done well as a house sitter. Katrina stuffed a few hundreds in an envelope and set it on top of one of Beth's books. The cats followed her around the apartment for the first few hours she was home, letting her know that they had missed her.

She was alone for the first time in over two weeks. She shifted through her mail, and then checked the refrigerator, and then decided to make a pot of coffee. Nathan would be over later, but he had some paperwork to do during the day. Katrina called her agent to let him know she was home, and then called Mary to tell her they got back safely.

"Honey, I'm so glad you called. I wanted to tell you that I really like Nathan. Daddy does, too. Surprisingly, Mike likes him."

"Well, he passed Mike's background check, Mom. You know Mike ran a check on him, right?"

"Yes, he mentioned that. But he says Nathan is squeaky clean, to put it in his words."

Katrina laughed. They talked for a few minutes before hanging up, with the promise to talk again soon.

Next was a call to Morgan. "Hey, Kat! It was so good to see you. Nathan is a hunk! He's gorgeous!"

"Yeah, isn't he? I'm in love, that's for sure."

"I told Candy about you being engaged to a gorgeous hunk. I hope that's okay…"

"Yeah, I'm over Candy. I don't care."

"She wanted to know when you were getting married. I asked her why, since she wouldn't be on the guest list."

Katrina burst out laughing. "You didn't!"

"Yeah, I did. She says because she wishes you well, and that you were always so nice to her. So I told her 'Yeah, Candy, and you repaid her by sleeping with her boyfriend!' You should have seen her face."

"Oh, Morgan! You're horrible!"

"I know. Don't you just love it? Anyway….she said she was young and stupid. It was a stupid mistake. I told her it was a mistake that cost her lots of friends, and she agreed. She said Sean was just so easy. I asked her if she knew how easy it would have been to turn him down, and she didn't have an answer."

"I couldn't believe Sean walked into Bear's Place. He looks very sad, Morgan. Don't you think?"

"Yeah, he does. He still carries a torch for you. Maybe now that you're engaged he can put the torch out. I doubt it, though. Did you notice that Nathan didn't even know him, but there was friction there immediately?"

"Yeah, I did. Sean must rub a lot of people the wrong way."

Morgan had to hang up. She had a meeting to go to. She told Katrina she would call her soon, gave her love, and hung up.

Katrina unlocked her office door and aired it out for a few minutes. She got a cup of the freshly brewed coffee, returned with it, and pulled out a fresh canvas and set it up to start working on a portrait of her parents. Their anniversary was soon, and this would be a nice touch to their dining room or over the fireplace.

* * *

The six o'clock news was coming on, so she stopped her work and went to the living room and snapped on the television. The news was all about a hurricane heading into the gulf. "Oh, Lord." She said into the air, and sat down to watch. It was Hurricane Katrina, projected to hit New Orleans within five days, and it was a violent one. She jumped when Nathan knocked on the door.

"Look at this, Nate! Satellite views of this hurricane. It looks wicked."

"Yeah, and it shouldn't be named after you. You're not violent."

He helped himself to the coffee and sat down with her to watch the progression of her namesake hurricane. "If it hits New Orleans there will be major damage. They're already below sea level. That's why I never made any investments in that area."

After the local news came the World News. There was also talk of the hurricane. They watched the game shows after all the news and checked out the movie listings for the evening. Beth, the house sitter came to collect her things and leave the key while the game shows were on. She told Katrina she was willing to house sit for her any time she needed her, and she was quite surprised by the amount of money Katrina paid her.

"It's worth it to know that my cats were well cared for, Beth. They mean a lot to me."

Katrina returned to the television with Nathan after Beth left. They watched a movie and then went to bed.

* * *

They sat glued to the television staring at all the destruction caused by Hurricane Katrina. "My God, Nathan…How awful."

Katrina was holding onto Nathan's arm as they watched. He pulled her close to him, feeling the tension coming from her. He knew how badly she was affected by other people's misery, so he held her. Days of broadcasts telling of destruction and loss filled the television. Telethons were held to raise money. Deeply affected, Katrina and Nathan donated money. There were other hurricanes forming during that time. One in particular was named Nathan. Katrina sat down in Nathan's lap.

"Hurricanes Katrina and Nathan—named after us. Hmmm…..I can think of times when we were like a couple of hurricanes…"

Nathan quickly kissed her and answered, "Yeah, like within the next ten minutes."

Within moments they were in each other's arms on the bed. Katrina went wild as she rolled on top of him, and forced herself down onto him. She clenched his hands above his head as she kissed him passionately, moving her hips forcefully up and down. He climaxed. Within moments her orgasm began. They lay together, trying to control their breathing for several moments.

"Wow! You vixen! And to think I taught you everything you know." Nathan teased.

19

It was the first Monday in October when her agent called. She and Nathan had just returned from bike riding when the phone rang.

"Hey, Kat….Russ. I just wanted to remind you about the convention in Chicago next week. I have your plane ticket and your ticket to the banquet."

"Oh, Russ, I forgot all about that. Hey, listen, I'm engaged now. Any way I can get my fiancé a ticket to go with me?"

"Afraid not. This is a closed convention. Maybe the one at the end of next April….he can probably go to that one. You can live without each other for three days, can't you? You have to be there, Kat. You're up for a recognition award. By the way, Kit-Kat will be on the shelves in two weeks. That's got to excite you."

"It does. Send a courier over here with the tickets, I guess. Thanks, Russ." Katrina hung up and turned to Nathan to tell him she had to go to the convention.

"Well, I guess I'll find something to do. Clean the garage, or something. I'll look after the cats for you."

"That will make me happy. I know you'll take good care of them."

* * *

Nathan drove Katrina to the airport. He had her itinerary, so he knew when to pick her up. He kissed her goodbye at the farthest point he was allowed to go before security took over.

"I'll miss you. Knock 'em dead, Sweetheart."

"I'll miss you too. I love you." She walked toward the metal detectors and waved at him.

He rushed home. He had gotten a brainstorm the day after she told him she had to go to Chicago and he was putting his plan into action. In the house, he went to the small room next to his den. The room was too small to do much with, but he knew what would be perfect for it. The designer and the carpenter were already measuring when he opened the door to the room. He had drawn a crude sketch of what he wanted in the room, and the designer looked at him like he was a nut case. He explained the purpose and the designer relaxed a little.

"Can we do this in three days?" Nathan asked the two of them.

"With some help, yeah." The carpenter answered.

"Well, get all the help you need. This has to be complete in three days."

He looked at the designer. "Get whatever materials you need. No expense spared."

* * *

Katrina hated Chicago, mainly because Nathan wasn't with her. The convention was loud and raucous, but the treat to the day spa made up for it. She felt great when she left the spa and went to her hotel to dress for the banquet. The hotel was full of comic strip and cartoon writers, artists and creators, some of whom she recognized. They waved to her as she got on the elevator up to her room. She called Nathan before getting ready.

"Hi! I'll be going to the banquet soon, so I just wanted to give you a quick call. How is everything? I miss you."

Nathan smiled into the phone.

"I miss you, too. That's how everything is. Cats are fine. I bought them some treats, but I can't teach them any tricks."

Katrina laughed. "And I thought it was just old dogs."

It was Nathan's turn to laugh. "I guess I'll see you at the airport tomorrow. I told Charlie we'd meet them at Jack's. Is that okay?"

"Yes, that's fine. I got Lisa something anyway. I got you something, too. See you tomorrow."

She kissed the phone and hung up the receiver, and then went to get dressed.

The banquet was an elaborate black tie affair. Katrina chose to wear an off-white off-the-shoulder gown. It was a simple sheath that showed off her curves. Her hair, done by a professional at the spa, was swept up on top of her head, with curled tentacles falling in front and at the sides. She looked magnificent. She was seated at the table with Russ and four other comic strip writers, all of whom congratulated her on her successful comic strip. She was among the youngest in the room, but just as successful as the seasoned comic strip writers.

She received the award for best loved comic strip, and was required to go up and give an acceptance speech. She had nothing prepared because she really didn't think she would win. Those words became the bulk of her speech. She told the audience how much she loved her Kit-Kat character and that the comic strip's success went to Kit-Kat. Then she thanked everybody, with a special thanks to her agent, and left the podium. She shook a few hands on the way back to her table.

* * *

The plane touched down right on time, and Katrina knew within minutes she would be kissing Nathan. She hurried off the plane straight to the baggage claim, and there he was, standing there waiting for her. She unabashedly threw her arms around him and kissed him in front of onlookers. He held her and kissed her back.

"Have you no shame, woman!" He teased. He hugged her tightly and kissed her again. Come on; let's get your luggage before the vice squad shows up."

She laughed and wrapped her arm around his waist.

They went straight to her place to drop off her luggage and so she could see the cats. Nathan appeared to be nervous or excited about something. He kept drawing her toward the door, instead of sitting back while she gave out affection to her cats. She got the gift for Lisa out of her suitcase, and then she called Nathan into her bedroom to see his gift. It was a soft robe from the hotel, the hotel emblem sewn onto it. For Lisa, she brought a tank top from the spa.

"Ready now?" He asked anxiously.

They drove off toward the bar, but then he veered in the opposite direction.

"Where are we going? I thought we were going to Jack's."

"We are, but we have to stop at my place first." He grinned at her, hardly able to contain his excitement over something.

He led her through the front door, and then put his hand over her eyes. "I have a surprise for you. Keep your eyes closed."

She giggled for a moment. "Where are you taking me? What's the surprise?"

"Shhh....you'll see. Are your eyes closed?"

She nodded. She could hear a door opening and the light switch being flicked on. His hand was over her eyes.

"Okay....voila! The cat's gymnasium!"

She opened her eyes and looked around the room. She burst out laughing. All around the room there were cat walks and carpeted posts for climbing. There was a set of carpeted steps up to one level. Tunnels led to the cat walks. Over in the corner was a large built-in box with carpet on top and doors with round holes in them. She walked over to it and looked in. Obviously it was for litter boxes, big enough to hold three. The small closet contained three soft-looking beds. The door to the closet had a large rounded opening in the bottom, like a large mouse hole that one sees in cartoons. Of course, the outer wall of the room was floor to ceiling glass, like most of the house. The cats would certainly enjoy that.

"Nathan, this is truly amazing! What made you do this?"

"I don't know. The idea just came to me. I thought the cats would like to have their own room when you all move in here."

"You're wonderful! They will love it. I love it!"

"Of course, they will still have the run of the house, but for those times they want to be human-free, this is for them. The room has never been big enough for much, but it's perfect for them."

"You're right. It is perfect. Like you." She hugged him around the waist and kissed him.

* * *

Lisa loved the gift Katrina brought her. It was only a simple tank top with the Chicago spa's logo embroidered on the front, but Lisa appreciated the thought. Nathan led Katrina to a table in the back, and Charlie and Lisa followed them. The waitress brought them their drinks and asked if they would be ordering from the menu. All four of them wanted food.

Nathan leaned toward Katrina and asked, "Are you going to try Karaoke tonight? I'd love to hear you sing."

"Maybe. I will if you will." She challenged.

"They have all heard me sing, so I guess I can. I'm just anxious to hear you."

Katrina laughed and warned, "Be careful what you wish for."

The song selection books were set out, and Nathan grabbed one for them, so that they could browse through it. Katrina said nothing as she filled out one of the request slips. Nathan took his and hers up to the stage. They would be called when it was their turn. Katrina was called up first. She gave a marvelous performance, singing 'I Will Survive". Nathan hugged her and held her tightly when she came back to the table.

"That was fantastic! You *can* sing! Is there anything you *can't* do?"

Katrina's answer came quickly. "Yeah, I can't pitch and I can't build cat gymnasiums." She grinned at him as his name was called.

Nathan could sing, too. His song was meant for her, and she developed a lump in her throat as she listened to his tenor voice singing 'The Way You Look Tonight'. She wanted to do another song, just for him. She remembered how well she could sing 'My Guy', so she made it her next performance. They had fun doing another one together, and then Nathan insisted she do her 'New York, New York' song. Charlie and Lisa looked on at the fun Katrina and Nathan were having together, making Lisa a little envious that she and Charlie couldn't be like they were. Charlie had improved in how he treated Lisa, but he had a long way to go in order to make Lisa truly happy. Charlie tried, and that was Lisa's concern. Nathan didn't have to try; it wasn't an effort for him to treat Katrina like she was the only one who mattered in the whole world. Lisa could see that as far as Nathan was concerned, Katrina *was* the only one in the whole world.

20

It was nearly Thanksgiving when Nathan called Mary without Katrina knowing. At first Mary was frightened when she heard Nathan's voice, thinking that something had happened to Katrina.

"No, everything's fine. Honest. I just wondered if you would like to have us as house guests for Thanksgiving."

"Oh my, yes!" Mary responded quickly.

"Good. I'll make the arrangements and let you know the details. Katrina doesn't know anything about this. I'm surprising her." Nathan told Mary.

"Oh, Nathan.....I see why my daughter loves you. I think you're.... wonderful!"

Katrina squealed with excitement when Nathan told her they were spending Thanksgiving with her parents. She threw her arms around Nathan's neck, squealing and laughing.

"I have an idea. Why don't we see if your parents will have Thanksgiving dinner with my parents? They will get to know each other. Let me check with my mom first, okay?"

Katrina got the okay from Mary. "Honey, that's wonderful idea. Call them and see if they'll come, and then call me back."

Nathan called and spoke with Al. He checked with Rose and they agreed to go to Pennsylvania for Thanksgiving. Katrina called Mary back and told her that the Perletti's would be there. Katrina now looked forward to Thanksgiving, just knowing that it would be a wonderful holiday.

* * *

Nathan and Katrina arrived at the airport the night before Thanksgiving. Ed was there to meet them, giddy with the excitement of having Katrina home for the holiday. Once they made it to the house, Katrina immediately delved into the preparations for the dinner. Ed asked Nathan to join him at Bear's for a couple of beers. He wanted to build a rapport with him, since Nathan would be marrying his beloved daughter. This gave Katrina and Mary a chance for some mother-daughter talk.

"So Honey, I assume you and Nathan are sleeping together."

Katrina's face burned. "Mom!"

"Oh come on....I know you're twenty-eight years old. I only hope that you two have a normal, healthy relationship in that area. Any problems?" Mary asked her, candidly.

"No....none. I really love him, Mom. He's everything I ever wanted. I waited a long time for him to come along."

Mary smiled at Katrina. "I know you did. He's a lot like Jeff, isn't he?"

"You see it too, huh? Dad sees it, and so do I. Mom, Jeff and I....we didn't....we never went that far. I never went that far with anyone...until Nathan. But it's right....with us. When we first... slept together, I wanted him as much as he wanted me. I feel kind of embarrassed telling my mother this...."

"But I'm glad you can tell me. It's okay, Honey....you're not a child any more. It's....healthy to want to make love to the man you love. And I'm glad you love Nathan, because it is *so* obvious that he loves you." Mary smiled and reached over and patted Katrina's hand.

"You know....if you have any questions about anything, you *can* ask me. You do use birth control, don't you?"

Katrina nodded, ready for the awkward conversation to end. She told her mother about the cats' gymnasium. Mary laughed and remarked on how thoughtful Nathan was.

* * *

Ed and Nathan sat at the bar and ordered a couple of beers. Ed told him how the bar was supposed to be named The Bear's Den, but since everybody knew Bear, they always called it Bear's Place. The sign outside carried the proper name. While Ed was relating the story he secretly marveled at Nathan's composure and confidence. 'The trait of an honest man' Ed thought.

They talked about sports, and Nathan's short baseball career. Nathan told Ed about some of his investments, and Ed listened with interest. Ed had made some investments over the years, but nothing that brought anywhere close to the yield that Nathan's had. Ed recognized that Nathan was a smart investor and a wise businessman.

"So, Nathan, it's pretty obvious that you really love my daughter. It's good to see that kind of love. My wife and I have it, and so do my sons and their wives. You know, I look at Mary and I see the beauty I married many years ago. From the day I met her I never looked at another woman. Didn't need to. She was all I wanted."

"That's exactly how I feel, Ed. I love everything about her, including the cats." Nathan grinned at Ed.

"Oh yeah, the cats. How many? Three?"

"Yeah, three. I never knew cats had personalities until I met hers."

Nathan and Ed both laughed. Nathan told Ed about the gymnasium he had made for the cats. Ed was impressed with his sensitivity. He knew Nathan would be a good husband to Katrina.

"You know, Ed...when you come to Florida you can stay at my house rather than a hotel. I have five bedrooms."

"Sounds like a big house. How many rooms do you have?"

Nathan thought for a minute.

"Well, there are five bedrooms and four baths, living room, dining room, kitchen, den, family room, workout room, and then the little gym for the cats. It's a huge house." Nathan told Ed about how he acquired such a large house.

Nathan looked into the mirror that ran the length of the bar. "There's that jerk, Sean. He just walked in. I still can't get over how he left her and went home. I laugh every time I think about her punching him...." Nathan stopped as Sean approached them.

"Mr. Kitrowski....how're you doing?"

"Fine, Sean." Ed answered him, but made no attempt to ask Sean how he was doing. He couldn't care less how Sean was doing.

Sean studied Nathan. "You're Katrina's fiancé, aren't you? I guess I don't have to tell you how lucky you are."

Nathan glared at him, and Sean retreated to the other end of the bar.

Ed laughed. "I think you intimidated him."

"Yeah, well....he rubs me the wrong way."

"You and everybody else who loves Katrina." Ed finished his beer and suggested they head for home.

Nathan got off the bar stool and was putting on his jacket.

"You know, I don't know what his deal is. He had her, he didn't treat her right, and he lost her. He needs to accept that and move on."

Ed nodded in agreement.

* * *

Nathan's parents arrived right after noon. Katrina and Nathan greeted them at the door, and Ed helped them with their coats. Mary came from the kitchen to be introduced and invited Rose to come on into the kitchen with her. The conversation in the kitchen was light and easy as was the conversation between Ed and Al in the living room. The parents seemed to like each other, to the delight of Nathan and Katrina. Nathan joined the men and Katrina went to work in the kitchen with Mary and Rose.

When dinner was ready they all reunited in the dining room, with Nathan and Katrina on one side of the table, Al and Rose on the other, and Ed and Mary at each end. Katrina and Nathan's hands were joined all through dinner. Since Katrina was left-handed and Nathan used his right hand, they often ate their meals that way.

Dinner was superb. Rose brought a vegetable casserole and home-baked bread as her contribution to the Thanksgiving turkey feast. When everyone could not put another morsel into their mouths, the table was cleared and the dishwasher was put to work. Mary, along with Nathan, asked Katrina to play something on the piano. She sat down at the piano and played Mozart's Piano Concerto Number 21, and then quickly switched to something more contemporary. Then she played a couple of tunes from the fifties, much to the parents' liking. Al and Rose were deeply impressed by her talent.

Mary called everyone for dessert, and even though they all thought they couldn't fit another bit of food into their stomachs, nobody refused the desserts. The talk at the table soon turned to the plans for the wedding. The date was set for April the eighth, just six days before Katrina's twenty-ninth birthday. Katrina told them that she had an appointment the following Tuesday, with a seamstress for her gown and the bridesmaids' gowns. The wedding would take place on the beach in front of Nathan's home and the reception would be at the Holiday Inn not far from the house. There was so much to do, but Katrina knew it would all work out. After all, hadn't her brothers had nice weddings on short notice?

21

Katrina entered the seamstress' shop armed with all of her bridesmaids' measurements neatly written on a piece of notebook paper. She only hoped she could find the material she had in mind. The seamstress brought out books and books of swatches of material for her to consider. She poured over the books with no luck. She knew what she wanted; all she had to do was see it. She had about given up when she found what she was looking for. In the very last book of swatches the seamstress produced out of desperation, Katrina found what she was looking for. It was gauze material in colors that faded from one color to another. The materials came in different colors of the rainbow so she could choose which color she wanted. 'Perfect.... this is perfect!' she thought to herself. She knew that each bridesmaid was going to wear a different color.

She showed her selection to the seamstress. "I want this material.... one in blue to lavender, then one in pink to blue. I want another one in yellow to green, and the last one has to be in lavender to purple. I want the same material for my dress in white."

"Are you sure?" The seamstress looked a little dubious about her selections.

"Yes, I'm sure. Can you do it?"

"Well, of course...it's just that those selections are....a bit different for a wedding."

"Yes...and I'm a different kind of person. Trust me, I'm an artist and I know what I want."

"Do you have all the measurements?"

"Yes, I do. Can we look at styles?"

Dolly, the seamstress got out books of dress styles and patterns. Again, Katrina knew what she was looking for, and found it. Off-the-shoulder elastic neckline with a bodice that narrowed at the waist and then slightly flared out, with the skirt dropping to the floor. The skirt was full with three tiers, and the neckline had a long overlay. It was an old-fashioned peasant style, just perfect for a wedding on the beach. The bridesmaids would wear wide-brimmed hats with flowers that matched each of their gowns. She would have a veil with flowers that would sit on her head like a crown. Her plan was to have the groomsmen's cummerbund and tie the same color as their partner's dress. She asked Dolly if it were possible to make them as well as the dresses. The answer was favorable. Satisfied with that, Katrina pulled the measurement list out of her purse.

Morgan would wear the blue to lavender; Kathy would wear the pink to blue, Lisa the yellow to green, and Kim the lavender to purple. She gave Dolly the measurement list and wrote the colors above each measurement grouping.

"In order to have all the different colors, it may cost you a bit more." Dolly cautioned.

"It's what I want, so I'll pay the extra cost. The wedding is April the eighth."

Dolly sucked in her breath. "That's short notice. I'll need to have extra hands working on these dresses."

"Again, Dolly, whatever it takes. I'll pay for it. How much do you want down?"

They agreed on a figure and Katrina gave Dolly cash and asked for a receipt. Dolly took Katrina's measurements herself so she could get started as soon as possible. They agreed that Katrina would come back on February First to check on the progress. Satisfied that she had the dresses covered, Katrina left the shop and headed home where Nathan was waiting with the cats.

He had coffee made when she got there. After pouring their coffee, she and Nathan sat down to look over lists and details that needed to be taken care of. They also worked on the guest list. They both wanted their wedding to be perfect. Money was no object, since they both had plenty of money to spend, and Ed and Mary had given Katrina a sizable check to help with the wedding expenses, when she and Nathan were in Pennsylvania for Thanksgiving.

22

Christmas was approaching. Katrina was excited because it was the first Christmas she and Nathan would have together. They went Christmas shopping together, going to the toy stores for Danny Junior and Cara, first. One of the hot items of the year was Kit-Kat. Katrina was happy to see that the display shelf holding Kit-Kats was fairly empty. Many people had already purchased her.

"Aren't you going to buy any?" Nathan asked her.

"No....the manufacturer sent me a dozen of them, so everybody will get one."

Nathan took two off of the shelf and put them in the cart. "You never know who you might have overlooked." He grinned at her.

They bought toys for Danny and Cara and headed toward the department stores. Inside, they found gifts for almost everybody on their gift list.

"What do *you* want, Love?" Nathan asked as he put his hand on her shoulder.

"I have all I ever wanted." Her answer came with a sweet smile.

Nathan already knew what he was getting her. He saw a Baby Grand Piano inside a music store one day while he was browsing the stores. He put a deposit down on it and arranged to have it delivered to his house on Christmas Eve. He pictured her face when she saw it and could hardly wait for Christmas to arrive. Likewise, Katrina had Nathan's gifts bought and put away where he wouldn't see them. Besides the usual array of clothing, she bought him a black leather full length coat, a diamond and gold ring, and all the fishing gear and equipment she could find. She knew he liked to fish, so he would have the best fishing equipment money could buy.

Satisfied that they had most of their Christmas shopping complete, they decided to eat at the new mall restaurant that had recently opened in time to accommodate the Christmas shoppers. They found a table and Nathan took their packages out to the car while Katrina waited for a waitress to take their orders for beverages. The waitress arrived just as Nathan returned from the crowded parking lot. They ordered their food and ate heartily when it was in front of them. Exhaustion set in, and they were glad to get out off the mall and home to a quiet evening of television and perhaps, lovemaking.

* * *

Christmas was a week away. Katrina spent the morning on a ladder decorating the porch of her apartment with blue twinkle lights mixed with blinking white lights. Wreaths were hung in every window and a large wreath with a blue silk bow was placed on her front door. Inside, she outlined all the door frames with green pine garland that was intertwined with little blue twinkle lights. She was just putting the finishing touches on her tree when Nathan's car pulled into her driveway.

"The place looks like Santa's house in the North Pole." He stopped and stared at her Christmas tree, all done in little white twinkle lights and blue and silver bows and ornaments, placed strategically in all the right places.

"That tree is a work of art." He exclaimed.

Katrina went to him and slipped her arms around his waist.

"Could that be because I'm an artist?" She teased as she smiled up at him.

"Could be. It's really beautiful, Honey. By the way, at your request, I decorated my house, too. Well, that's a lie. I paid people to decorate it. I don't have your talent."

"Well, next year you'll have me and my talent. I'll save you the money and do it myself. I would have done it this year, actually."

"What? And spoil your surprise of seeing it? Not on your life!" He leaned down and kissed her cheek as he encircled her waist with his arms. "I'll bet you were cute when you were little and believed in Santa Claus. You did believe in him, didn't you?"

Katrina thought for a minute.

"I don't know. I guess I did. I never really needed him. My parents and my brothers always gave me so much all the time….Santa Claus couldn't compete with them."

"Well, now he has to compete with me…and I'm hard to compete against, too. Maybe it's because you're loved so much. Not even Santa could love you as much as I do." He cradled her in his arms and kissed her, making her feel all the love he had for her.

* * *

On Christmas Eve, Nathan arrived to pick up Katrina at six o'clock. She had dressed in a green silk jumpsuit she had gotten especially for this night. They were going to spend Christmas Eve at his house, where Marie had prepared a special evening supper for them, and then go back to her place to spend the night with the cats. Katrina felt that they were part of her family and they shouldn't be left alone all night on Christmas.

Nathan ushered her in through the back door, since he didn't want her to see the piano yet. He had a decorated tree in the family room which led to the patio and pool. She exclaimed over the decorated house on the outside, and was even more thrilled at the decorated family room and the big beautiful ten-foot tree. He had placed wrapped gifts for her under the tree. She carried in her wrapped parcels and added them to the others. Marie had the small table in the family room all set up for dinner, including red tapered candles in the center. The food was left in the warmer and smelled heavenly when they walked in. Nathan served the meal while Katrina watched him, her eyes shining in the light of the candles.

"All that's missing is snow." She said wistfully.

"That's what you think." His eyes were twinkling as he stepped out onto the patio. He flipped a switch on a contraption she hadn't ever seen before, and she gasped as 'snow' began to fall onto the patio.

"I thought of everything." He grinned at her.

"Yes, you did. Thank you. Nathan, I love you so much!" She grinned and giggled as she watched the man-made snow fall and melt as soon as it hit the stone patio.

They ate and talked and laughed until the meal was done. He opened a bottle of champagne and they toasted each other in a "Merry Christmas", the first of many to come. He was in a hurry for her to open her presents, so they sat in front of the tree and began to unwrap their gifts from each other. He loved the leather coat and the ring, and seemed happy with the clothing she picked out for him. He exclaimed with delight at the fishing equipment. She loved the outfits he had chosen for her, and especially liked the emerald earrings and pendant. When all the gifts were unwrapped, they shared a long kiss. She laid her head on Nathan's shoulder for a moment before he jumped up.

"Listen, did you hear that?" He feigned excitement.

"Hear what?" She was puzzled since she heard nothing.

"Bells. Sleigh bells. Didn't you hear them?"

"Nathan, maybe you had too much champagne." Katrina's laugh was delightful.

He took her hand and pulled her up.

"We have to go see. I think I heard Santa Claus."

Katrina was still laughing. "Okay. Let's go see."

He led her in through the kitchen, down the hall into the living room and looked around. He snapped on a light and faked a surprised gasp. There, standing in the far corner of the living room inside an alcove, was the Baby Grand Piano with a large red bow mounted on top of it. Katrina screamed.

"Oh my God! Nathan! Oh!" Tears were streaming down her cheeks as she threw herself into his arms. "Oh, Nathan….I-I—don't know what to say! I can't believe it. You bought me a Baby Grand Piano? Oh, Nathan!"

"Not me....Santa Claus brought it." He was laughing as he led her to the piano. "Now you know what you have to do, don't you?"

Laughing and crying, she looked up at him.

"What?"

"Play some Christmas carols! Will you?"

She sat down at the piano and ran her fingers up and down the scale a few times. She began to play carols, beginning with "Joy to the World". They sang carols together as she played, ending in "Silent Night". As they sat together on the piano bench, she snuggled against him and whispered, "I will love you with all my heart, forever and ever. That's a promise."

* * *

They awoke in Katrina's bed on Christmas morning. The cats were all snuggled around them. Katrina planned on making Nathan a special Christmas breakfast, and then giving the cats their presents. Nathan had things for them, too. She ran to the living room and plugged in the lights on the tree, and then started the coffee. When she heard Nathan coming out of the shower, she started breakfast. They had a leisurely breakfast in the quiet of her apartment. Since they were going to Danny and Kathy's for Christmas dinner, they appreciated the quiet they shared now. The kids would maul them when they got there, thus terminating the quiet of the day.

Katrina showered and dressed to go to Danny's while Nathan made the bed and stacked the dishwasher. The cats were busy with the toys given to them by both Katrina and Nathan. He watched them playing with them after he started the dishwasher.

They stacked the gifts for Danny, Kathy, Cara and Danny Junior in the car and drove across the bridge to Danny's house. Christmas was perfect. She and Nathan looked forward to many more Christmas holidays just like this one, in years to come.

As expected, Danny Junior and Cara besieged them when they got to Danny's house. It was a whirlwind of flying wrapping paper and ribbon, and earth-shattering squeals as they saw what their 'Aunt Kat' and 'Untul Nate' bought them. Danny was trying to hand out drinks, stepping between kids and toys on the floor. Kathy took it all in, grinning. Katrina joined her in the kitchen to help prepare dinner, while Nathan and Danny helped the kids assemble their new toys. Katrina smiled at Kathy, and Kathy returned her smile.

"You look so happy, Kat. I'm so glad to see you this way."

"I am happy, Kathy. Life…with Nathan in it…is perfect."

23

Katrina and Lisa stepped inside Katrina's favorite clothing store.

"Trust me, Lisa….if you don't find the perfect dress in here, it doesn't exist."

Katrina went right to the cocktail dresses and began looking.

"You're about a size seven, right?"

"Yeah! You're good!" Lisa marveled.

Katrina pulled a dress off the rack and held it up, but quickly put it back. She looked at a couple more, and then moved on to another rack. Suddenly she gasped.

"Lisa, this is perfect for you!" She was holding up a black dress, simply styled, with one shoulder bare. The other side covered the shoulder and had a long, tightly-fitted sleeve. The entire outline of the dress was studded with rhinestones. "Try this one on! I guarantee you'll love how you look in it."

Lisa took the dress to the fitting room while Katrina found one for herself. She chose another black dress with simple lines. This one was cut very low in the front and the back, with narrow straps at the shoulders. She entered the fitting room and went behind the curtain next to Lisa. When she came out in her dress, Lisa was admiring herself in the one Katrina had chosen for her.

"You're right. This dress is perfect for me." She looked at Katrina through the mirror. "And *that one* was made for you! This was easy!"

"Yeah, after this, we have time to get shoes! Nate and Charlie gave us two hours!"

Nathan and Charlie were sitting in the restaurant enjoying beers and companionship while the girls shopped. They hadn't spent much time together lately. Charlie sipped his beer and stared at Nathan. He looked so happy these days.

"Nate, I have something to show you." Charlie reached into his pocket and produced a small box. "I'm going to ask Lisa to marry me." He opened the box, revealing a diamond solitaire. "Right after midnight, on New Year's."

Nathan grinned at him. "It's about time, Asshole. Lisa's a great girl. You should stop being such a dick and start treating her right. I wouldn't blame her if she turned you down."

"I hope she doesn't. It's a surprise, so don't say anything, okay?"

"My lips are sealed. Congratulations!"

Nathan called the waitress over and ordered them each a shot of bourbon to celebrate.

Katrina and Lisa met up with them in record time. Katrina had already taken their purchases to the car, so they appeared empty-handed.

"No new dresses?" Nathan asked as he kissed Katrina's cheek.

"Already in the car, along with new shoes."

"Hey, you're fast! I thought we would be drunk by the time you got back here."

Katrina laughed. "You know I always know what I want. I don't waste time; I just go get it. I'm starving....feed me." She joked, and he handed her a menu.

* * *

The plan was to spend New Year's Eve at Jack's Place. Katrina and Lisa had an agenda that she hoped Nathan would be okay with.

"Honey, do you mind if Lisa gets ready at my place with me, and we meet you and Charlie at Jack's? I promised to help her look extra nice. Charlie could pick you up and I could drive the T-Bird. That way we could each have our own cars to go home. Do you mind? She's really counting on making Charlie's head turn when he sees her. She's really going to look gorgeous!"

"No, that's okay. It will be kind of fun to see Charlie's face when she walks in all dressed up. Uh, Kat....don't say anything...but Charlie's giving her a ring tonight."

Surprised, Katrina smiled up at Nathan. "Perfect!"

* * *

Charlie and Lisa picked Nathan up at Katrina's. Nathan left his Thunderbird in the driveway and he and Charlie left together. Lisa and Katrina, dressed in bathrobes, worked on their hair. Katrina used her curling iron on Lisa's hair, giving her a more glamorous, dressy style. Then she did her own, pulling it back and adding curls. She did Lisa's make-up, keeping it subtle. They put on their new dresses and shoes and left to meet their men already at Jack's Place. They both looked wonderful.

Nathan and Charlie were sitting at the bar, waiting patiently for them. Holly sauntered up to Nathan and sat down next to him.

"All alone tonight? What happened to what's-her-face?" Holly's question was sarcastic.

"*Katrina* will be here....any minute, actually. Holly, you have one hell of a piss-poor attitude."

Holly looked as though Nathan slapped her. She quickly got up from the bar stool and moved to the other side of the bar.

Jack began to laugh. "I guess you put her in her place, Nate. Where are the girls, anyway?" Jack looked up toward the door and exclaimed, "Holy *shit!*"

Nathan looked into the mirror behind the bar and saw what caused Jack's reaction. Katrina and Lisa stood in the doorway; both of them were breathtakingly gorgeous. All around them, men were gaping. Nathan quickly swung off his bar stool and made his way to Katrina's side.

"You're exquisite!" He whispered into her ear and immediately encircled her waist and kissed her cheek.

Charlie appeared at Lisa's side. "Wow! You're beautiful, Baby! Really beautiful!"

Lisa caught the small wink from Katrina and she smiled lightly and winked back. Nathan and Charlie ushered them to a table in the back. Nathan knew that Katrina was the most beautiful girl in the room, but he was also impressed with how beautiful Lisa looked.

He set about teasing Charlie. "Charlie, you know....you're kind of an ugly guy. What does this beautiful girl see in you?"

Charlie flipped Nathan the bird, and laughed as he did. Nathan asked Katrina to dance, and was happy to see that Charlie also asked Lisa. Maybe he *was* going to start treating her better.

The four of them danced, sat out a few, joked and laughed, and then danced some more. Nathan held Katrina close, loving the smell of her perfume. He kept his lips on her temple as they danced. He whispered 'I love you' against her temple and she smiled up at him, her eyes sparkling. Midnight was near.

The countdown to the new year began. "Three....two....one! Happy New Year!" The crowd roared. Nathan and Katrina embraced and kissed each other in a long, slow meaningful kiss.

"Happy New Year, my Love. Hey, we get married this year!" He grinned down at her. "I can't wait."

"Me, neither. Nathan, I love you so much. You rock my world!"

Nathan laughed. "I couldn't have said it better. Let's get food and watch when Charlie gives Lisa the ring."

They came back to the table with plates of food and found Lisa sitting at the table alone.

"Where's Charlie?" Nathan asked her.

"Can you believe it? He offered to get my plate for me!" Lisa looked happy.

Charlie came back with two plates of food, and placed his down first. He bent to set Lisa's plate down, and kissed her quickly, to distract her, then slipped into his chair. He waited, and said nothing. Lisa picked up her fork and looked at her plate to see what to attack first. She spied the ring, in its box, in the center of her plate, and she stopped, fork in mid-air. She looked at Charlie, a tear sliding down her face.

"Well? You're going to make me ask, aren't you? Lisa, will you marry me?"

For a moment, Katrina thought she was going to say 'no', simply because Lisa said nothing at all. Nathan laced his fingers through Katrina's, and they both stared at Lisa.

"Lisa?" Charlie looked at her anxiously. "Will you?"

Lisa was in a full cry.

"Y-Yes, I will. Oh my God, Charlie....YES!"

Charlie's next move was quite out of character for him, and it surprised Nathan. He got down on one knee and slid the ring onto Lisa's finger. Katrina wiped her own tears with the heel of her hand. Nathan slipped his arm around her and leaned his head against hers, as they watched Charlie and Lisa kiss. Champagne arrived, and they toasted the New Year and then toasted the newly engaged couple. The party broke up at two in the morning. Charlie and Lisa left together, and Katrina and Nathan went home to her apartment.

24

It was mid-January. The Christmas holidays were behind them and their wedding was getting closer. Katrina and Nathan were asleep in his bed when she suddenly jerked awake crying.

"Honey, what's wrong?" Nathan reached for her and held her tightly. "Hey....what's the matter?" He was clearly concerned.

"Oh, Nate....it was a bad dream. It was horrible! I was dreaming that I was....dead. I kept trying to....come alive again, but I couldn't. You were yelling for me and....I kept trying to....c-come to y-you.... b-but I couldn't...." She was trembling, her shoulders shaking as she cried against him.

He held her tightly. "It was just a dream, Baby. I'm right here and so are you. We're together. Shhh.....it's okay." Nathan was disturbed by her dream. He shivered a little at the thought of anything happening to her. He found her lips in the darkness and lightly kissed her. She clung to him as they made love in the darkness in the middle of the night.

* * *

As planned, Katrina went to the seamstress' shop on the first day of February. Kathy and Lisa took the time off work to go with her, in hopes that their dresses would be ready to try on. It was obvious that Dolly had her staff working overtime, since all five dresses were almost complete. Kathy and Lisa came out of the fitting room wearing the dresses that were created especially for them. Katrina was pleased to see that she had picked the right colors for both of them. The dresses looked gorgeous on them. Kathy's would need a hem, but Lisa's was a perfect fit. They were pleased with how they looked in them.

"Katrina, you are a genius with color." Lisa remarked.

Next, it was time for Katrina to try on her wedding gown. In the fitting room, she slipped the gown over her head and down onto her body. She adjusted the dress and stood back to look into the mirror. It was perfect. She came out of the fitting room to hear the 'oohs' and 'aahs' from Kathy and Lisa.

Kathy's eyes welled up. "Kat, you look beautiful."

Dolly helped Katrina with the veil she had painstakingly made especially for her.

"Oh, Kat!" Kathy was overwhelmed when she saw Katrina in the net veil with the ring of flowers that surrounded the top of her head like a crown. "You look like the angel you are! All you need is wings!"

Katrina shivered a little at that remark, remembering the dream of a couple of weeks ago. She mentally shrugged it off and smiled at Kathy. "Do you think it looks okay?"

"Kat, it's perfect! It's so *you!*"

Dolly assured Katrina that the small alterations that needed to be done would be completed in no time. Kim and Morgan were flying down the following weekend to try on their dresses, and Dolly, again, assured Katrina that she would accommodate them when they got there.

Lisa had to return to work, but Kathy went with Katrina to order the wedding cake and pick up the invitations. Nathan had gone to Aaron's photography studio to arrange for Aaron to take the wedding pictures. After seeing his work, they both knew that he had to be the one who photographed their wedding. They were all going to meet Danny for lunch at noon.

They met Nathan in the parking lot of the restaurant at just five minutes past noon. Danny was waiting inside.

As they slipped into the booth Danny had obtained for them, Nathan told Katrina that Aaron would be their photographer. Kathy, still teary-eyed, told Danny how beautiful Katrina looked in her wedding gown.

Nathan reached for Katrina's hand. "I think she'd look beautiful in a burlap sack."

Danny laughed. "Spoken like a man who's truly in love."

"Guilty." Nathan grinned at Danny and kissed the cheek of his bride-to-be.

* * *

Katrina was sitting at her desk in her office looking over her finances. The Kit-Kat sales over Christmas had put her over the million dollar mark. She shook her head, blinked, and stared at the figures again. She was a millionaire! She couldn't believe it. Life was too perfect. In three weeks, she was marrying the man of her dreams, her work was nationally recognized, and she was now a millionaire at twenty-eight. She heard Nathan come in through the front door. He called to her.

"In here, Honey!" She called back.

"What are you looking at?" Nathan peered over her shoulder and let out a low whistle. "Are those figures right?"

Katrina nodded. "Can you believe it? I definitely jumped up a tax bracket or two."

"I should say. Hell, you'll be supporting me before long." He kissed her neck.

"Well, I guess I'll be able to pull my own weight; don't you think?"

"I guess. Honey, I know I've never discussed my finances with you, but I can tell you this....as long as we live, we will never want for money. With or without yours. Now, tell me...how does Hawaii sound for a honeymoon?"

"Perfect! Oh Nathan...in three weeks we'll be married...." Katrina gasped and looked like she had seen a ghost.

"What? What's wrong?" Nathan looked at her, puzzled.

"Oh my God, Nathan....I just realized something. Our wedding date is the same date we....met. I wonder why I never thought of that..."

Nathan wrapped his arms around her shoulders and thought for a moment. He sighed. "Honey, I know that date has a lot of horrific memories for you, but some good *did* come out of it. We found each other. Try to look at it that way, okay? I think it's the perfect date to get married. April the eighth will only have happy memories from now on, okay?"

"Okay. I like the way your dad put it. I have to remember that."

25

Katrina stood beside the white limo parked in the loading zone and waited for Ed and Mary to come out with their luggage. When she saw them exit the doors from the baggage claim she called to them and waved them over. The limo driver quickly got out and reached for their bags, opening the back door to the limo at the same time.

"What's all this, Honey? The limo, I mean." Ed was obviously taken by surprise.

"It's Nathan's idea. He insisted that my parents and his parents be chauffeured in a limousine while you're here. He owns the company, so he has use of as many limos as he wants all weekend. It's great inside! Wait until you see!"

Ed and then Mary hugged their daughter, both of them noting that she looked radiant, but a little tired, too. All week she and Nathan had been moving some of her things to his house, in between taking care of last minute wedding details. They picked up their marriage license, and then, on Tuesday, met with the Reverend who would be performing the ceremony. After their meeting, they went to the caterer's to approve a new side dish and then on to the disc jockey's residence to pick out special songs they wanted played. Wednesday was spent moving the bulk of Katrina's clothing and personal items. She had four weeks of her work completed, so they dismantled the computer and fax equipment to be taken up to the house and into the room Nathan, with the help of the designer and carpenter, had turned into an office especially for her.

Wednesday night, they transported the cats to their new home. Nathan carried them in their large carrier and took them directly to their gymnasium. When he opened the carrier to let them out they hesitated and looked around. Gingerly, they began walking around sniffing everything. Marie came into the gym to meet them, since she would be taking care of them while Nathan and Katrina were on their honeymoon. Katrina relaxed when she saw that all three cats went right to Marie and rubbed up against her. They would be in good hands while she was gone.

Katrina directed the driver to take them to the Holiday Inn near Nathan's house. "I thought you would like to stay there, since the reception will be held there. Nathan's parents will be staying there, too."

"When will they be in?" Mary asked.

"Tonight. Mike and Cookie will be on the same flight. Their parents are coming, too. But they won't be here until tomorrow. Do you know when Mike and Kim will be here?"

"Danny said he will be picking them up around ten tonight. Do you think it will be around the same time?" Ed, leaning back against the limo's seat, was studying Katrina. She looked so happy.

"I don't know, Daddy. Oh, Morgan and Kevin are driving down; did you know that? She called me a little while ago and they just got into Georgia. Nathan reserved a block of hotel rooms for everybody, and a large suite for me and the bridesmaids the night before the wedding. He's at the Holiday Inn now checking on the reception preparations. We're going to meet him there." Katrina's face lit up every time she mentioned Nathan. Mary and Ed couldn't have been happier for her.

The limo pulled into the Holiday Inn drive and stopped. Like magic, Nathan appeared to greet them.

After the hellos, Nathan told them he had a table reserved for lunch. "After you settle into you room, we can have a nice leisurely lunch. Everything seems to be taken care of." He reached for Katrina's hand and followed Ed and Mary into the hotel lobby.

* * *

Thursday evening was a whirlwind of activity. Al and Rose, along with Mike and Cookie arrived at the hotel. Danny, Kathy, Mike and Kim were right behind them. They all hugged Katrina and told her she looked radiant. All that was left to arrive was Morgan and Kevin, who were just passing through Gainesville, and would be there around midnight. Charlie and Lisa joined the party just before midnight.

The hotel lounge was nearly empty when the families decided to take their party inside. Everyone seemed to be having a wonderful time. Ed took to Mike instantly. They talked about sports mainly, but Ed was impressed that Mike was a physician.

"Where are the babies?" Katrina asked, referring to Mike and Cookie's two-month-old twin boys.

"My mother won dibs on them for the weekend. She couldn't wait for us to go." Cookie smiled and then laughed. "The kids will never be the same." She added.

Mike looked at Nathan and laughed. "I can't believe you're finally getting married."

"Yep…one day and a wake-up…I'm ready." He grinned at Mike, and lifted Katrina's hand to his lips and kissed her fingers.

It was past midnight when the doors to the hotel lounge opened to a flurry of excited chatter. "There they are!" Morgan took Kevin's hand a dragged him toward the Perletti-Kitrowski gathering. Katrina and Nathan got up and met them halfway, where Morgan and Katrina hugged each other tightly.

"I'm *so* happy for you, Kat! Look at me….I'm crying already!"

"Oh, Morgan…..I'm so happy I'm delirious." She led Morgan to the table and introduced her to those who didn't know her. Nathan did the honors with Kevin. They fit right into the party where everyone remained until the lounge closed up for the night.

* * *

When everybody got into their hotel rooms, Nathan and Katrina left for the house. Exhausted, they fell into bed, with Katrina resting her head on Nathan's shoulder. He smiled at her, kissed her temple, and sighed.

"You know….I see you as a gift. I don't know, but I feel so lucky to have you. I love you so much." Nathan smiled at her tenderly.

It was Katrina's turn to sigh. "I think we are each other's reward. We knew we were out there for each other and we waited. We're both good people. I've never hurt anybody in my life and neither have you. We deserve each other. Doesn't that make more sense?"

"Yeah, Sweetheart….it does. It makes a lot of sense."

They fell asleep in each other's arms, overwhelmed by the love they felt for each other.

* * *

Nathan opened his eyes and looked at the clock beside the bed, his slight movement awakening Katrina.

"What time is it?" She asked.

"Eight-ten. We have a lot to do today." He rolled toward her and wrapped his arms around her.

"Yeah, we do. What time are the caterers coming here?" She asked as she positioned herself under him.

"Eleven. I told the families to be here around then, too." He was kissing her neck as he spoke.

"We still need the limos to pick people up from the airport, right?" Katrina nibbled his ear as she whispered into it.

As he entered her he answered, "Right."

Her orgasm came quickly and fiercely as did his, surprising them both. Katrina's breathing was uneven as she held onto him.

"Are you okay?" He asked.

"Yeah....I just know that I want you again....right now."

"Yeah?" He looked down and saw that he could accommodate her, and entered her again. Once again, their orgasms came quickly, forcefully, and simultaneously. They both lay there getting their breathing under control for a few moments.

"Wow....that was incredible." She was looking up at him, her eyes sparkling. "I guess we better get up and start the day."

They rolled out of bed, each heading for a shower, and then met in the workout room, dressed for a light workout. It was ten o'clock when they decided on a quick swim in the pool together. After swimming for a half hour it was time to get ready to greet the guests who should be arriving within a half hour. The caterer would be there soon, bringing brunch and lunch, all in one. Nathan had the day planned for everybody. The catered pool party would be going on most of the day, followed by the rehearsal at six, and then on to the restaurant for the rehearsal dinner. At the moment, there were construction workers down on the beach erecting a small platform and steps to be used as an altar, and a walkway where the bridal party and guests would walk. Electricians were putting in wiring for speakers and the rented organ that would be delivered first thing Saturday morning. Long benches for guests to sit on would be arriving later that day. Katrina insisted on sturdy benches rather than folding chairs. All construction was temporary and would be removed the Monday after the wedding. Expense was not spared; both Katrina and Nathan wanted the ceremony to be perfect.

The first limo was rolling into Nathan's driveway, bringing the Perletti's and the Kitrowski's. Nathan and Katrina greeted them together at the front door, and led them through the living room toward the back of the house. It was Ed and Mary's first glimpse of where Katrina would be living, and they were not disappointed.

Marie had coffee pots set up in the family room, and the coffee was ready. Al poured two cups, sauntered over to where Ed sat down, and set a cup in front of him. He eased into the chair next to him, where they both watched Katrina and Nathan working together.

"They're perfect together, aren't they?" Al was watching Ed's face.

Ed glanced at Al, and turned back to watch his daughter and her fiancé. "Yeah....they are. She's so beautiful, isn't she?" Ed looked at Al.

"Yeah, she is, Ed. She's a beautiful girl."

Ed smiled. "You know how hard it was to let her grow up? My sons....well, it didn't bother me to see them become adults...but Katrina....I remember the first trip we made to Florida to see my oldest son, Dan. Mary let Katrina buy a bikini. She was fourteen at the time. My sons, and me....almost lost our minds. She looked so damn good in that bikini I just wanted to cover her up." Ed got quiet, reliving the memory.

He began again. "I wanted to protect her forever. I always wondered what kind of a person she would marry, and would I be able to handle it. I knew whoever it was; he would have to be pretty terrific. I'm so glad it's Nathan. He's a terrific guy, and he obviously loves her."

"Thanks, Ed. Nathan is a terrific guy. He was a terrific kid, too. Never caused us anything but joy. I know you know all about Steven. Well, I was able to cope with the darkness in Steven because of the light in Nathan. If it hadn't been for Nathan I think Rose and I both would have lost our minds." It was Al's turn to get quiet. He sat there observing Nathan and Katrina and marveled at the way they worked together. They were talking to each other as they were putting table cloths on the tables, and continued talking as they made their way to the bar to put out bottles, ice, and mixers. They never missed a beat.

Nathan smoothed out the corner of the tablecloth while Katrina set down a small floral centerpiece. He smiled over at her.

"What came over us this morning?" His eyes were warm and tender as he watched her face.

"I don't know....but wasn't it incredible?" Her eyes lit up and she smiled at him.

"Yeah....it was. It should have been impossible on my end. Nothing like that has ever happened....wow...that's all I can say."

Katrina grinned at him. "Maybe we're aliens and the mother ship flew over....and it was either have fantastic orgasms or swing into the sun...or something."

Surprised, Nathan turned to her and burst out laughing. How he loved her zany sense of humor.

The caterers arrived and there was a flurry of activity as they began setting up their food trays and hot foods. Rose and Mary joined the group in the family room.

"We've been to the cat gym. What a clever idea, Nathan." It was obvious that Mary was delighted with Nathan's design. "Those cats seem so happy in that room."

Ed got up and suggested to Al that they go check it out as well. "When Nathan told me he did this for Katrina's cats, I knew he was the one for my daughter. I really want to see the room."

Morgan, Kevin, Mike, and Cookie arrived by limo, with Danny's car following close behind. From where Katrina and Nathan stood they could see the activity going on when Danny's car door opened, and it wasn't long before they could hear it.

"Is Aunt Kat here? Is this Untul Nate's house? Is he here?" The kids came running up the walk yelling for their Aunt Kat and Untul Nate.

"Aunt Kat, are you going to live in this house with Untul Nate? Can we swim in the pool? Where's the kitties? Do they live here now?"

"Yes, yes, and yes!" Katrina and Nathan were laughing and hugging the children as they fielded their questions.

Katrina looked up at Danny and smiled. "Why don't you take them in the pool for awhile before they eat? Wear them out a little?"

Danny laughed and yelled for the kids to go swimming, and Katrina ushered the newly arrived guests back to the family room to where they could all observe the activity out at the pool. Nathan handed Katrina her cell phone after he answered it. It was the seamstress on the line letting her know that the dresses would all be delivered to the Holiday Inn around four that afternoon. Katrina gave her the name of the person to contact there so that the dresses could be taken to the suite of rooms for the bridesmaids. The cummerbunds and ties were going to be dropped off at Nathan's house after that. Each one would have the assigned name on it. Nathan had taken care of the flowers, so it looked like all was done and it was time to relax and enjoy the families. Morgan sidled up to Katrina and hugged her.

"This house is fabulous. How about a tour?"

They were quickly joined by Kathy, Kim and Cookie as they walked through the rooms. Katrina took them into the master bedroom and showed them her massive closet for all her clothes. Morgan flopped down on the bed. "So this is where it began, huh?" Morgan was patting the bed.

Katrina laughed. "No, not exactly. It all began on the floor in the living room, during a storm. The electric was out, and we were eating by candlelight, and well....things progressed."

Morgan laughed and hugged Katrina. "How perfect for your first time!"

"Shhh!" Katrina was embarrassed.

Although nobody said anything, the women present caught the significance of what Morgan had said. It was then that they all realized that Katrina had waited and had given herself to only one man—the man she truly loved—the man she would marry the next day. It was so beautiful that each of them was moved to a tear or two.

* * *

The day wore on. Everyone was enjoying the pool and the catered food. Charlie and Lisa arrived after work in plenty of time for the fun, and immediately changed into swimsuits to take a dip in the pool. It was close to five o'clock and time for the minister to arrive for the rehearsal. He was right on time. Behind him came the musicians—the plural surprised Katrina. It was learned that they came together and played together at a one-price arrangement. The one played the organ and the other played the violin. It would be fine, she was assured.

Katrina made a quick change into a white two-piece dress and white sandals and headed down to the rehearsal. The rehearsal took all of twenty minutes and they were ready to climb into the limousines and head toward the restaurant. Danny told them he'd see them there, but first he had to take the kids to the sitter for the night.

Many toasts were made during the dinner. Nathan sat through them, feeling like a king with his queen. He knew that tomorrow would be the happiest day of his life and he looked forward to every day after that. He felt that Katrina must have read his mind, for she turned to him immediately and whispered, "Forever."

Charlie took the floor after the meal ended. "Okay, guys…get ready. We're all going to Jack's Place. We get to take Nate out one last time as a single man. Is that okay with you, Kat?" Charlie looked toward her and she shrugged and smiled.

Nathan laughed softly and looked at her. "Do you mind, Honey?"

"Of course not. Go ahead. I think the bride and bridesmaids will be busy, too. You can just go on back to the house after Jack's and get a good night's sleep. I'll feel secure in knowing that you're riding in limos rather than driving, so go ahead and have fun."

"Mr. Perletti and Mr. Kitrowski? You're going to go, too; aren't you?" Charlie was waving them on.

"Go ahead, Daddy. Mom will be with me. And so will Nathan's mother. You two go and keep these guys under control."

Al and Ed shrugged and got up to go.

Nathan hesitated for a moment. "Wait a minute, Charlie. Before we go anywhere, let's get something straight. I *don't* want a lap dance…. I *don't* want a hooker….I *don't* want a stripper. This is just good clean guys' night, right?"

"Yeah, yeah, yeah…okay. Shoot pool, darts, maybe, drinks, cigars. I got it."

Nathan kissed Katrina and said, "I'll be good."

She grabbed his head between her hands and said, "After this morning, I'm sure of it."

Their eyes locked for a moment and Nathan nodded. The men headed out the door, leaving the women sitting there.

"So what are we waiting for?" Katrina asked them. "Let's go up and shake out the dresses and then hit the lounge ourselves. I'm entitled to a last night out, don't you think?"

They hurried to the suite to hang the dresses, and then quickly made their way to the hotel lounge. After a round of drinks were finished and another arrived they were all laughing and in good spirits. Katrina glanced around to make sure everyone was enjoying themselves and was glad to see that they all seemed to be like old friends.

Morgan glanced up toward the corner of the room and said, "Oh, Kat-rina!"

Katrina followed Morgan's line of vision and discovered Morgan's find—a piano.

"What do you say? A sing-along?"

"Do you think they'll let me?" She grinned at Morgan.

"I'll go ask." Morgan trotted up to the bar and came back smiling. "He wanted to know if you could play. I bet him twenty that you could. Let's go!"

The entire entourage of women headed toward the piano, with Katrina seating herself on the bench. She began with a classical number as she usually did, and it quickly turned the few heads of those patrons sitting at the bar. The women began giving Katrina requests and she complied with them. Soon they were singing songs they all knew and a couple of people from the bar joined in. Rounds of drinks were sent over to them when it was learned that they were part of a bridal party. Morgan began to encourage Katrina to sing a couple of songs solo.

"Don't you have a song that you're going to sing to Nathan tomorrow?" Morgan asked.

"Yeah, during the ceremony, as a matter of fact. An old Debbie Boone song, "*You Light up my Life.*"

"Do it, then. Please?" Morgan begged.

Katrina nodded and all got quiet and waited. As usual, Katrina's clear voice brought emotion out of everyone. Mary dabbed her eyes, and she was not alone. Morgan's tears were flowing down her face.

"Oh, Kat...." Overwhelmed, Morgan hugged her best friend. "You deserve all the happiness in the world. I think you truly found it."

A tear slid from Katrina's eye, and she nodded. "Yes, I have. Life, with Nathan in it, is perfect. I love him so much, Morgan. And I know he loves me. I have never doubted it. Now let's rock this place!"

The women let out peals of laughter and Katrina started banging the piano keys with a rendition of "Shout!" with everyone joining in. Other patrons began to dance. The ladies were having the time of their lives.

* * *

The men were assembled at Jack's Place, all sitting at a table near the pool table. Charlie had ordered shots for everyone, and beers were passed around. The waitress stopped at their table and smiled at Nathan.

"Big day tomorrow, huh? I never saw a man glow before! I'm so happy for you, Nate."

"Thanks, Sal. I'm pretty happy."

"Hey, she's a great girl, Nate. Gorgeous, too."

Nathan nodded his agreement.

Kevin looked over at Nathan. "You know, Nate....I have known Kat since she was in the ninth grade. I have never known her to ever be unkind or say anything unkind about anybody. Even after what that prick, Sean did to her....she never, ever said anything bad about him. It's just not in her nature."

Mike Smith looked at Nathan. "You were always like that, Nate. I remember how you wouldn't let anybody talk about Tanya. You never said anything bad about her or anybody else. That's just one thing that makes you and Katrina perfect for each other."

Danny looked over at his brother, and added his thoughts. "Our sister is very special. She has always been special. Nate, I'm glad you two found each other, because I can't think of anybody else I'd rather see her with."

Nathan looked at Danny with gratitude. "I'll take care of her. I'll never hurt her or let anyone else hurt her. You have my word on that."

"And we'll hold you to it." Came Michael's reply.

Ed cleared his throat to get everyone's attention. "Nate, I'd like to say something if I may."

"Sure, go ahead." Nathan nodded at him.

"Tomorrow I turn over to you my most prized treasure—my beautiful daughter. I know that you will love and cherish her, because I can see that you do now. All I ask is that you always keep her safe. Can you promise me that?"

"Absolutely, Ed. Without a doubt. I make that promise wholeheartedly."

Ed raised his glass. "Then I make this toast to you. To Nathan, my son-in-law. You are now a member of my family."

All the men raised their glasses to Nathan, and he beamed.

"Uh-oh!" Charlie said under his breath. "Here comes Holly."

Annoyed, Nathan glared at Charlie. "So? What is it with her? I never even dated her."

Charlie shrugged as Holly approached the table full of men, her eyes never leaving Nathan. "So tomorrow you're getting married, huh?"

Nathan grinned and nodded. "Yep. Can't wait either."

Holly nodded. "Well, good luck." She turned to walk away.

"Thanks, Holly. Hey, Holly?"

She turned back around and looked at him.

"Ever think about going to school? Enhancing your education?"

"No, I never did."

"Maybe you should think about it."

She nodded at Nathan and walked away.

"Old girlfriend?" Danny asked.

"No, not at all. She just hangs out in here all the time, every night."

"She has always had the hots for Nate." Charlie chimed in. "He never even gave her the time of day."

Al looked over at his son's crass friend. "Nate has never liked women who hang out in bars. That's why he's marrying Katrina tomorrow. He likes class."

"Absolutely, Dad. And Katrina has plenty of that."

Al raised his glass. "To Katrina." He toasted.

"To Katrina." They all repeated.

It was time for their party to break it up, since it was well after midnight. The limos stood waiting outside for the men to fall inside of them. Even Nathan had one too many drinks. The plan was for the entire male wedding party to stay at the house, except for Al and Ed who chose to go back to the hotel to their wives. A limo stood waiting to make that departure after one last nightcap at Nathan's house. Al watched Ed embrace Nathan, and then he hugged Nathan and clapped him on the back.

"I love you, Son."

"I love you, too, Dad."

* * *

Al and Ed entered the lobby of the Holiday Inn all set to head up the elevator to bed. As they passed by the lounge, they heard a beautiful singing voice and they stopped.

Ed looked at Al and grinned. "That's my Katrina."

Ed pushed open the doors to the lounge and looked around. The place was half full of people sitting around listening to Katrina sing. Around the piano was the entire bridal party, including Mary and Rose and Cookie. They seemed to be having the time of their lives.

Al grinned at Ed. "Well, let's go join them." And he sauntered over to the piano.

Al sat down next to Katrina. "Hey, how about singing one with your new father-in-law?"

Katrina grinned at Al. "Sure! What should we sing?"

They chose several old Motown numbers, since Al knew them the best. Al and Katrina stole the show, since they both could sing well. Rose was surprised that Al was that good. He told her he sang, but she never actually heard him. Katrina was certainly going to put new life into the family; that was for sure. Rose looked over at Katrina and smiled. 'She's so perfect for Nathan.' She thought to herself.

It was time to break up this party. All of the women had hair and nail appointments in the morning. Katrina's favorite salon was reserved for the entire morning. They paid their tab and headed upstairs for the night. The bridesmaids, all a little tipsy, giggled in the elevator all the way up to the suite. Mary and Rose followed them up to the suite, promising their husbands to be gone only a few moments. The girls had a gift for Katrina and wanted to give it to her tonight.

On the bed in the suite was a lovely set of luggage. Katrina was surprised.

"Thank you! All of you!" She wiped a tear away.

"Oh, but that's not all! Open them!" Morgan squealed.

Katrina complied. The luggage was filled with sexy underwear and nightgowns. Katrina laughed and hugged all of her friends. "It's great…all of it. I'm going to wear it all on my honeymoon…..just don't tell my mom!" She joked. "And now…since you're all here…. let me give you your gifts. Cookie, I have one for you, too, so don't go away."

She handed each of the women in the room a small wrapped box which contained a diamond pendant dangling on a thin chain of white gold, and matching earrings.

"These are for you all to wear tomorrow. Remember, diamonds are forever. My marriage is forever, and you are my friends and family forever." She ended with a warm smile bestowed on each and every one of them.

"We better get some sleep. We are going to look terrible tomorrow." Morgan laughed.

"I'm so excited, Morgan. I'm not sure I can sleep. Let's sit outside on the balcony for awhile." Katrina wanted to tell Morgan about the love-making session she and Nathan had that morning.

"It was incredible, Morgan. For both of us."

"Kat….does he…..I mean….do you…..do it…..do you have oral sex?"

"Oh, of course. He drives me wild when he does it, just like he goes crazy when I do it."

"See what you've missed all those years?"

"I didn't miss anything. That could only happen with Nathan."

Morgan conceded that she was probably right.

26

"Morgan! Morgan! Wake up! It's my wedding day!" Katrina was gently shaking Morgan's shoulder, trying to get her to respond.

Morgan rolled over and opened one eye.

"What time is it?" She growled.

"It's half past eight. I'm going to get into the shower. Want to be next?" Katrina hopped off the bed and headed toward the bathroom. Morgan heard the water from the shower begin, and she rolled over and went back to sleep.

Once she was out of the shower, Katrina called room service to get pots of coffee for everyone. She worked on getting Morgan awake again. Finally, she won, and Morgan got up and headed toward the shower. Kathy and Kim staggered into Katrina's room, yawning.

"Coffee is on its way." Katrina assured them.

Right behind Kathy and Kim, Cookie and Lisa appeared.

"You look radiant, Kat!" Lisa grinned at her.

"Thanks. Could be because it's my wedding day; do ya think?" She grinned back.

The house phone rang, and Morgan quickly grabbed it up. "Kat, it's your mom. She wants to know what time we have to leave to get our hair and nails done."

"In an hour." Katrina came back from the door after letting room service in. "Okay, here is our coffee. I think we all need it. Morgan, ask my mom if she wants to come up for coffee."

Morgan nodded, and spoke into the receiver. When she hung up she told Katrina that Mary would be having coffee with Ed, and the Perletti's, and they would see them downstairs in an hour.

The limo stood waiting to take the women to the salon. Once everyone was seated, the driver drove effortlessly through the light Saturday morning traffic. He smiled at the banter from the rear of the vehicle. The women appeared to be good friends and family of the bride. Mr. Perletti's bride was certainly beautiful, and also very sweet. He didn't mind spending his weekend driving her around, since she made it all so pleasant. He knew he would be well compensated for giving up his weekend, too, so it was all worth it.

* * *

Ally, Katrina's hair stylist finished her work on Katrina's hair. After trimming off about three inches, she pulled her hair high on top of her head and fastened it there, letting it fall down Katrina's back. Many curls were added with the curling iron and the finished product was magnificent. When everybody's hair and nails were done, the limo appeared in front of the door to drive them back to the hotel. Katrina tipped all the stylists with fifty-dollar bills and stepped out onto the sidewalk. As usual, she felt that inevitable twinge of uneasiness that she experienced every time she left the front door of the salon during the past year. She quickly shook it off and jumped into the limo. Inside the limo, she inspected everyone's hair.

"You all look beautiful!" She exclaimed.

"And so do you!" The response was unanimous.

Ed and Al were waiting for them in the hotel lobby, hoping to have lunch with everyone when they returned. There had been a lunch buffet set up in one of the small banquet rooms especially for the Kitrowski-Perletti guests. Katrina was famished, and so she led the entire group into the banquet room. Everyone grabbed plates and filled them with food and sat down to an enjoyable lunch together. Since the wedding was to begin at five o'clock, the limos would start lining up at four, to transport guests. The bridal party would be among the last of those to be driven to the ceremony, with Katrina, Ed, Mary, and Morgan being in the last car. With all the planning done and everything taken care of, Katrina was free to enjoy this time with her friends and family.

Mary and Ed sat watching her as she laughed and joked with Morgan and Lisa while they stood at the buffet table. Katrina looked wonderful in her white jeans with the wide blue leather belt and white tank top that came just to her waist. 'She is going to be such a beautiful bride,' Mary thought to herself. She glanced at Ed, wondering if he were going to be able to keep it together when he saw her in her wedding gown for the first time.

* * *

Katrina set her fork down to answer her cell phone. Judging from the grin on her face, it had to be Nathan.

"Hi!" She beamed into the phone.

"Hi back! We get married in four hours!"

"Oh, is that today?" She teased.

Nathan chuckled. "Remind me to start beating you after we get married."

"Okay, sounds like fun." She quipped. "Hey, I'm excited."

"Me, too. Hey, do you know where my dad is?"

"Right here beside me. Do you want to speak to him?"

"No….I want to hear your voice. Just relay this to him. Uncle Joe, Aunt Betty, Joey and Jessica, and Linda and Buck are landing at the airport right now. I sent a limo, and they should be getting to the hotel by two or two-thirty. Tell my dad to make sure that the rooms are there for them, and that they don't pay for them. I will. Okay?"

Katrina relayed the information to Al, and he nodded. "Tell him I'll take care of it."

Katrina turned back to the phone. "Anything else?"

"I love you." Nathan smiled as he said it.

"I love you, too. See ya soon?" She asked.

"Oh, did you plan on seeing me today?" He knew he got her back for her smart remark, and he grinned to himself. Katrina laughed, kissed the phone and disconnected the call.

"Wow, I'm surprised Joey and Jessica are coming." Al told Katrina.

"Isn't Joey Nathan's favorite cousin?"

"Well, yeah, but Jessica is nobody's favorite anything. She's a miserable person most of the time. Joey isn't allowed to even be around his family. She's such a shrew."

"Why? Why do you think she is so unhappy?" Katrina was curious.

"I don't know. Joey works hard but he doesn't make enough money to please her. He helps out with the housework, but he doesn't do enough to please her. She doesn't work and feels that she shouldn't have to. We avoid her most of the time because all she does is bitch and complain. I'm surprised she allowed Joey to spend the money on plane tickets."

Katrina knew that Nathan bought the tickets online and sent the vouchers to Joey, but she didn't say anything. Maybe that was the reason they were coming. She didn't want to prejudge anyone, but it sounded as though Joey's wife Jessica needed an attitude adjustment. She really wasn't looking forward to meeting her as much as she wanted to meet Joey. Nathan talked about Joey a lot.

* * *

All the bridesmaids were gathered in the suite to get ready. Katrina was sitting cross-legged on the bed watching them inspect their dresses. Each bridesmaid, along with Katrina, would be wearing white ballet slippers, mainly for comfort, but also because it was easier to walk on sand in them. When the bridesmaids slipped into their dresses, Katrina put her veil on and fixed her hair around it. Morgan stopped to look at Katrina, and made an adjustment to the veil. Katrina was ready to put on her wedding gown. All of the bridesmaids waited. The dress was perfect. The three tiers of pleated gauze had a heavy lace ruffle sewn in between them. Katrina referred to the heavy lace as tablecloth lace. The overlay that hung from the elastic off-the-shoulder neckline was the same type of lace. The dress was beautiful, and Katrina looked beautiful in it. It was time for the bridesmaids to go downstairs to the limo. They kissed Katrina's cheeks before they left and wished her good luck. Only Morgan and Katrina were left in the room, where they waited for Ed's knock on the door. Morgan let him in when she heard him knock. Katrina was standing in front of the mirror and she turned when Ed came in. Stunned by how beautiful she looked, Ed choked out a sob, and reached for his handkerchief to quickly wipe his eyes.

"Honey, you look.....just so beautiful." He couldn't hide the tears in his eyes.

"Thanks, Daddy. It's four-forty-five....are we ready?"

"As ready as I'll ever be to give you away, Sweetheart." Ed smiled at her and offered her his arm. "Your mom is already downstairs in the lobby, waiting for us."

Katrina smiled back and said, "Daddy, at least you know that I'm marrying the best."

"I have to agree with that, Baby. Nathan is a wonderful person."

Katrina, on Ed's arm, and Morgan on her other side, headed toward the elevator and down to the limo that would take her to her destiny.... and the man she loved.

27

The limo with Katrina in it pulled up into the driveway of Nathan's, and now Katrina's, house. It had been a quiet, short ride. Mary, Ed, and Morgan didn't trust themselves to speak during the ride; every one of them afraid to break down in tears. Katrina was a vision in her wedding gown and she was so happy. Her happiness was infectious.

The driver of the limo leaned back and said, "I think we are supposed to wait here in the car until someone comes to tell you to get out. Nathan is still in the house. He'll be walking out in a minute or two. You'll be able to see him, but he won't see you through the tinted windows. Here he comes with the groomsmen now."

Everyone in the limo was quiet as Nathan and his groomsmen passed in front of them. Nathan looked so handsome in the pale gray tuxedo. Katrina saw him look over at the limo. She knew he couldn't see her but she felt his love as he went by. She smiled as she watched him walk down the slope toward the beach where everything was set up for their marriage to take place. She was remembering the day they rode on their jet skis before the storm hit, and...what happened afterward. How sweet and tender he was with her! Her thoughts were interrupted by a knock on the limousine window.

Ed lowered the window to hear Mike Smith say it was time to walk Mrs. Kitrowski to her seat. Mary kissed Katrina and quickly got out of the limo, taking Mike's arm. Ed inhaled and quickly exhaled. In a matter of minutes his baby girl would become Nathan's wife. He had to get his composure! He had an important role in this!

The limo driver opened the driver's side door, and turned around to see them. "Okay, this is it. Maid of Honor, then Katrina and her dad. Everybody ready?"

He opened the rear door and offered his hand to Morgan, who accepted it and slid out of the limo. Ed came out next and offered his hand to Katrina. They stood outside the limo smoothing down their clothes and inspecting each other to make sure everyone looked perfect.

The driver escorted Morgan to the top of the slope, while Ed walked with Katrina behind them. They stopped at the slope and waited for their cue. The music started and the bridesmaids began their descent down the small slope to the runway that had been built for them. Soon it was Morgan's turn to walk down the slope. Ed and Katrina waited for their cue, which would be the beginning of the Bridal March played by the organist. The organist hit the beginning keys and all the guests stood up.

Ed looked at Katrina and smiled. "Are you ready to go get married?"

She nodded and smiled back.

"Yes, Daddy, I am." They started their descent.

All eyes were upon her as she came into view. She looked directly up to the front and locked eyes with Nathan, her blue eyes sparkling as she made her way past the guests toward him as he stood at the top of the risers in front of the minister. She and Ed stopped at the bottom of the risers. As planned, Katrina sang the song she had sung for the women the night before; her sweet voice bringing out the tissues among many of the guests. At the end of the song, Nathan stepped down to the first step of the risers and reached out for her hand. She kissed Ed's cheek and put her hand into Nathan's and walked up to the top with him. They stood under the archway of pastel flowers, their hands still joined. The minister began by asking who gives this woman to this man.

Ed answered, "Her mother and I do."

Nathan and Katrina had prepared their own vows, neither of them knowing what the other was going to say. Nathan went first:

"My Katrina....my beautiful, sweet Katrina. I waited a long time to find you. I promise you that I will love you always. I promise to cherish you and cherish every day we spend together. I promise to protect you. I promise to keep you safe. I promise to put you first before myself, my friends, and my family. I promise to always do what is best for you. I promise to always think of your needs, your wants, and your desires. I promise to never hurt you, and I promise to never make you cry. You are the love of my life. You are my world. You are my forever."

Tears welled up in Katrina's eyes and one slid down her cheek. She couldn't speak as her sparkling eyes looked into Nathan's.

"I think I just broke one of my promises." Nathan reached up under her veil and wiped the tear from her cheek with his thumb. A small murmured laugh went through the seated guests. "Are you okay?" Nathan smiled down at her.

She nodded. "That was just so beautiful," she whispered.

Ed and Mary, as well as Al and Rose, thought so, too. All four of them had to wipe the tears from their eyes. Katrina's bridesmaids had their tissues out now, too. Nathan's beautiful words of promise moved quite a few of the guests and a box of tissues was being passed around. Nathan's cousin, Joey looked around and saw all of the tissues out and quipped to himself, "Now I know the meaning of a white wedding."

It was Katrina's turn:

"Nathan.....I waited for you my whole life. When we met I knew you were 'the one'. The one I waited for; the one I felt waiting for me. You are my Soul Mate. You are the love of my life. My promise to you is that I will be a loyal, faithful wife. I promise I will stand beside you. I promise I will be there for you, no matter what. I promise to love you and be good to you, and to our children. I promise to laugh at life, never forgetting what is really important. Nathan, I *can* promise you forever. You are my love and you are my life. You are my best friend."

Everyone but Katrina missed the tears in Nathan's eyes. She looked into his eyes and silently reassured him that everything she said was true. The minister whispered for the rings.

"With this ring I seal my promises…." Nathan slid the ring onto Katrina's finger.

Katrina slid the ring onto Nathan's finger. "With *this* ring I accept your love and your promises. And I return a promise of undying love and affection for the rest of our lives."

"You may now kiss your bride." The minister whispered.

Nathan lifted Katrina's veil, seeing for the first time, the beautiful bride he just married. They came together in an embrace and then kissed their first kiss as man and wife.

"Ladies and Gentlemen, May I present to you….Mr. and Mrs. Nathan Perletti."

The guests stood up and applauded. Katrina choked on a sob and looked at Nathan.

"Oh, Nathan....I'm so happy!"

Nathan grinned at her. "So am I, my Darling....so am I. I think we have to walk past all these people now."

Katrina laughed and agreed with him. As they walked up the aisle as man and wife, the guests threw rice. One hundred pastel balloons floated up into the sky as the organist and violinist played the traditional wedding music. Cameras clicked from every direction. Their own photographer was clicking away as they went. He was pleased with some of the shots he had gotten and knew they would be, too. The posed shots would be taken inside the hotel, since the outdoor lighting would darken all the faces. Katrina and Nathan stood at the top of the slope waiting for the rest of their bridal party to catch up. A receiving line would be formed there for the guests to congratulate them. Aaron, the photographer saw a perfect shot. The sun was starting to drop and it was a perfect backdrop for a silhouette shot of the bride and groom. He quickly positioned them in front of it and got his shots. He knew those pictures would be among their favorites. The guests were starting to come up the slope now, parents first. The bridal party was assembled for the receiving line. Mary was the first to pass through the receiving line. She hugged Katrina and held onto her for a moment, and then turned to Nathan.

"I'm so happy for both of you. And Nathan....welcome. You are now a member of my treasured family....I have another son."

Nathan smiled at her, gratefully. "I promise to be a good one."

Ed came through the line next. He had regained his composure as long as he didn't speak. He grinned at Katrina and hugged her. He shook Nathan's hand, and then hugged him. He caught up with Mary before he lost it again. Al and Rose were not so composed. They both knew how happy Katrina made Nathan, and that is all they ever asked for. They both hugged Katrina and called her 'Daughter'. Al hugged Nathan and held onto him. He leaned over to Katrina and whispered, "He has been my world since the day he was born. I now give my world to you."

Katrina grinned at Al. "I promise to share him with you. Is that okay?"

Al, not trusting his voice, nodded and went to join Rose.

All of the guests were filing through the line. Katrina's Aunt Cecelia pinched Nathan's cheek and told Katrina he was 'a keeper'. Many of Katrina's relatives showed up, some of which she barely rememberd. Joey and Jessica came through the line, and Nathan introduced them to Katrina. They were both polite and cordial, but Joey whispered to Nathan that Katrina was a 'knockout'. Nathan just smiled at him, hoping Jessica hadn't heard that. If she did, Joey was in for a terrible time at the reception. Linda and Buck passed through; both of them hugged Katrina and told her she looked beautiful. They were a delightful couple, full of fun and laughter. It was quite a contrast to Joey and Jessica. Soon all the guests were through the line and were climbing into the awaiting limousines to be driven to the banquet hall at the Holiday Inn. The bridal party hung back for more pictures. The largest limo with the 'Just Married' sign on it was set aside for them when the pictures were done and the guests had disbursed. They made a stop into the house before they got into the limo. Nathan had something he wanted to show his bride. In the family room that overlooked the pool, Nathan had a sign hung over the bar. The sign read "Nathan and Katrina's Pub". Katrina kissed him and smiled. "How about a quickie?" She whispered. He sucked in his breath and stared at her, disbelieving what he heard. She was kidding; he saw it in the twinkle in her eyes. Life was never going to be dull with her in it. He held her face and kissed her as they waited for the rest of the bridal party to get ready to leave. After the bridal party had used the facilities, straightened their ties, and hair, they got ready to get into the limo to take them to the reception.

Michael and Danny hugged Katrina once more before they got into the limo.

"You look beautiful, Kat." They both told her. They turned to Nathan and added, "Take care of her."

Nathan took Katrina's hand and answered. "I promise I will."

* * *

Nathan and Katrina followed the bridal party into the ball room at the hotel. They were introduced as 'Mr. and Mrs. Nathan Perletti' for the second time. Upon their arrival, the reception was now underway. Nathan and Katrina started the line at the buffet table, followed by the rest of the bridal party. The guests filed in line behind them. When all were seated with their food, Mike Smith tapped his champagne glass with his fork to get everyone's attention. Mike stood up to give his expected speech.

"Can I have everyone's attentions, please?" Mike began. "This is truly a happy day. I have known Nathan for more than fifteen years. We've done a lot together....high school, college, baseball, double-dating. We hung out together a lot. We've been best friends for more than fifteen years." Mike paused. Well, in those fifteen years, both of us dating a variety of different girls, I can remember Nathan always saying one thing: 'She's not my forever.' So when he called me last year and said, 'Mike I found her. I found my forever.' I knew without even meeting her; that Katrina had to be very special. And she is." Mike nodded to Katrina. "I'm so happy he found you. I propose this toast to Nathan and his bride, Katrina....his 'Forever'." Mike raised his glass and the guests followed his lead in a toast to the newly married couple.

Next, it was Morgan's turn to grab the microphone. After a squeal from the sound system, Morgan asked, "Can *I* get everybody's attention, now?" The crowd got quiet again to hear Morgan.

"Well, I have known Kat as long as Mike has known Nathan. Katrina *is* special; you're right about that, Mike. Well anyway, Katrina always said that somewhere there was someone very special waiting for her....and she waited to find that person. The day she told me about Nathan, I knew she had found that one person she had been waiting for. And to see them together is to know that they are perfect for one another." Morgan turned to Katrina and Nathan, and raised her glass. "To Katrina and Nathan....you made the right choice. You belong together forever."

Once again all the glasses were raised in a new toast. Katrina and Morgan shared a teary-eyed look and a hug, and then Morgan quickly hugged Nathan.

The music started with Nathan and Katrina dancing together for the first time as man and wife, and the bridal party joined in. As was the tradition, the parents danced with the bridal party, and everybody changed partners until Nathan and Katrina became partners again. The rest of the guests soon took to the dance floor and the party was underway. Nathan took the microphone and got everyone's attention. Katrina looked over at her parents and shrugged.

"I have no idea what he's going to say!" She smiled up at Nathan.

"How is the food? Is everybody enjoying it?" He waited for the response, which was all favorable.

"Well, one of the many things I adore about my bride is that she is unpretentious. When we went looking for caterers, the first one we went to was trying to talk us into foods we never even heard of. Katrina wanted cabbage rolls and I wanted pasta. The caterer made a remark to the effect that our taste was very low-class and we obviously couldn't afford him. Well, my Katrina stood up and looked him square in the eye and said, 'We can afford anything you have to offer. We want Polish food and Italian food...because that is what we are!' And with this, she took my hand and led me out of there. We went to another caterer and got what we wanted. So I really hope you all enjoy the food."

The guests all laughed at Nathan's story. Katrina laughed, too, since she had actually forgotten her response to the first caterer they saw. Now she remembered how angry he made her feel.

Charlie caught the garter and Lisa caught the bouquet. Nathan and Katrina agreed that was perfect. They cut the wedding cake and fed each other a piece of it without incident, even though Charlie kept urging Nathan to smear it in Katrina's face. One final dance was to be danced before Nathan and Katrina left for the night. Before the dance, Nathan again took the microphone.

"You are cordially invited to have brunch with me and my bride here in the small banquet room tomorrow morning. After brunch, there will be limos to take you to tourist attractions or to take you to my, *our* house, I mean, for swimming and relaxing. We will be there all day after our brunch here. We leave for Hawaii on Wednesday morning. Enjoy the rest of the evening."

Nathan stepped away from the microphone and reached for Katrina's hand. They danced to the song they had chosen for their dance together before they left the reception. When the song ended,

Nathan lifted Katrina into his arms and carried her out of the banquet room to the awaiting limo outside.

"Wh-where are we going?" Katrina was puzzled.

"Shhh…..it's a surprise. I don't like keeping secrets from you, but I didn't want this one to get out. Now kiss me, wife."

Katrina giggled and complied. The limo pulled up to one of the most exquisite hotels of the Gulf beaches. The driver got out and opened their door for them, letting Nathan get out first, and then Katrina.

"We're spending the night here?"

"Um-hmm. Presidential suite, no less. I had to ask the president not to come here this weekend." He winked at Katrina and smiled. She giggled.

The lobby was crowded when they entered. People stared and smiled at them as they made their way to the elevator. Many offered them congratulations and best wishes as they hurried past them.

"Do you think it's the dress that makes them say it?" Katrina's mouth was set in a mischievous grin.

"Maybe." Nathan answered, as he put his arms around her when the elevator doors closed. The elevator doors opened while they were kissing, and a woman and her daughter entered the elevator.

"We're busted." Nathan laughed.

The woman laughed with him. The daughter, who was about eleven or twelve, just stared at Katrina. They got off the elevator a floor below Nathan and Katrina's, and wished them the best.

When the doors opened, Nathan took Katrina's hand and led her to the door of the Presidential Suite. He slipped the key card into the slot, pushed open the door and picked up Katrina and carried her inside, kicking the door closed with his foot. He didn't put her down until he got to the sofa, where he sat her down gently. He called room service and ordered a bottle of sparkling burgundy and strawberries. Katrina got up to explore the suite while he was on the phone. Behind a wall leading to the bathroom was a roomy bath with steps leading into it.

She looked out at Nathan and grinned. "I know we're taking a bath tonight." He laughed at her bold declaration. She wondered into the bathroom itself, and then out into the sleeping area. She saw that her wedding-night luggage, along with Nathan's, had been deposited in that room. She wondered when he had managed to do that, but was thrilled that he had. Katrina heard the water running into the tub as room service arrived. She stood there in the sleeping area for a few minutes until the room service waiter left. It was a moment of shyness for her. When she was sure he was gone, she went out to see what Nathan was up to. He was filling the bath with warm water and adding bubbles to it. 'Perfect', she thought to herself. He looked up at her and smiled as though he had read her mind. He had already taken off his jacket to his tuxedo and had begun to unbutton his shirt.

"No." Katrina said and shook her head.

"No?" He looked over at her, half smiling.

Katrina shook her head again, and walked toward him. "I'll do it." She unbuttoned his shirt and removed it. He sat down and she removed his shoes, and then his socks, and then his pants. She stepped back and waited. He came to her and kissed her while he removed her dress, and then her undergarments. She sat down and he removed the ballet slippers she wore, and massaged her feet. Together, hands joined, they walked into the bubble bath. Nathan had set the ice bucket holding the burgundy and the bowl holding the strawberries next to the bath. They fed each other strawberries dipped in whipped cream and they drank the burgundy. Katrina thought it would be fun to see what Nathan would look like with white hair and beard, so she formed a beard and hairline on Nathan's face, using the bubbles. They laughed together, especially when he did the same thing to her face. Leisurely, they played in the bath, neither of them being in a hurry to do anything else. They had the rest of their lives together. Katrina leaned back against Nathan and closed her eyes. Nathan wrapped his arms around her and leaned his head against hers.

"So how many kids are we going to have?" He asked.

"I don't know. How many bedrooms do we have?"

"Five, including ours." Nathan laughed as he answered.

"We'll start with one first, then we'll see. Okay?" She replied, and then turned her head to see his face. "How soon do you want to start a family?"

"That's up to you. I get the easy part." Nathan kissed her forehead upon answering. He was silent for a moment. "You know....I want kids, but I hear giving birth is no picnic. The idea that it could cause you pain makes me think...."

Katrina put her index finger up to Nathan's lips. "Shhhh.......I'll be fine. We both want babies so one of us has to go through childbirth. I think I'm the logical candidate....besides; they have stuff to take the pain away. Let's start our family soon. Okay?"

"Okay." Nathan smiled at her and tightened his arms around her. "If we have a girl, I hope she looks just like you....because if she looks like me, she would probably have to shave every day."

Katrina laughed. "If we have a boy, I want him to be just like you."

They dozed off in the bath and awoke when the water cooled. Nathan grabbed the extra-large bath towels he had set down next to the bath earlier. When Katrina emerged from the bath Nathan, wearing one towel around his waist, wrapped one around her and pulled her close to him.

"I love you." He whispered. "I can't think of anything I'd rather do than hold you in my arms."

Katrina got that mischievous look in her eyes. "Nothing? How about pitching against the Yankees in a World Series?" She was smirking at him.

"Well.....only if this is what I had waiting for me afterward. You're the only one in the world that has ever been more important to me than baseball."

"I'm honored.....and I'm flattered....and flattery will get you everywhere with me." She grinned up at him and winked

They stared into each other's eyes and then melded into a kiss that soon became passionate. For the third time that night, Nathan picked her up.

28

Nathan and Katrina awoke to sunlight streaming through the window. She rolled over onto her stomach, feeling the coolness of the blue satin sheets against her skin. Nathan glanced at the clock on the night stand. It was only half past seven. He rolled onto his side toward Katrina, put his arm over her and fell back asleep.

Fully awake, they arose at nine. Katrina quickly showered while Nathan called for room service to deliver coffee and then called the limo driver and asked him to pick them up at ten forty-five. Katrina emerged from the bathroom, snuggled in a voluminous robe, just as room service brought the coffee.

"Isn't there a minimum when you order from room service?" She quizzed him.

"Well, yeah, usually....but room service comes with this room. You pay for it automatically, whether you use it or not. I know you got coffee delivered to you at the Holiday Inn, but I got that taken care of in advance." He grinned at her as he handed her a cup of steaming coffee.

While he was in the shower, Katrina dried her hair and picked out clothes to wear to the brunch. She chose a shorts set that was pastel blue and trimmed in white lace. She brushed her hair and decided to just let it hang down her back with no curls today. She found a pastel blue headband that matched her outfit perfectly, and added it to her outfit. She heard Nathan shut off the water in the shower and heard him open the bathroom door to let out the steam.

"Can I watch you shave?" She called.

"Yeah, I guess. It's not real exciting, but you can watch if you want." He called back.

Katrina smiled and ran into the bathroom, still wrapped in her robe. She sat down and watched as Nathan shaved his face.

"So what's the attraction of me shaving?" He asked her.

"I just never saw a man shave before. I wanted to watch; that's all."

He smiled at her through the mirror. Her eyes were sparkling as she watched him, drawing him to distraction.

"You're going to make me cut myself. I can't keep my eyes off of you."

"Okay. I'll go back out there and drink more coffee. See ya in a few..." She kissed his back as she passed by him.

He felt that familiar feeling and looked down. "Lie down." He whispered to himself, and finished shaving.

The limo delivered them to the Holiday Inn at exactly eleven o'clock. They walked into the small banquet room, hand in hand, smiling at everyone. Many of the guests were already seated, waiting for the buffet tables to open up. Ed and Mary were sitting across the table from Al and Rose. The table was a long one, so it was shared with Nathan's Aunt Betty and Uncle Joe, as well as Linda and Buck, Michael and Kim, and Danny and Kathy. Joey and Jessica were sitting alone at a small table, and obviously not speaking to each other, or to anyone else. Nathan and Katrina made a bee-line to their table and sat down.

* * *

"Did you two enjoy the reception?" Nathan asked them. "Did you do any dancing?"

"The reception was nice. We didn't dance though." Joey answered, while Jessica stared at her hands.

"Linda and Buck seemed to have a good time. They were on the dance floor more than they were off." This time it was Katrina who tried to get them to warm up.

"Yeah, they're like that. Always the life of the party. *They* are happily married." Joey emphasized '*they*'.

Nathan and Katrina began to feel uncomfortable.

"Are you going to be tourists today or are you coming to our house for a pool party?" Nathan smiled as he asked. "Actually, I guess you can do both. The limo drivers can always drive you to our place when you're tired of sight-seeing." He added.

Jessica spoke for the first time. "*I'm* going to sight-see. I don't get to go anywhere, so I *have* to take advantage of it when I can." She glared at Joey. "Don't forget to give me some money and a credit card before I leave."

Joey nodded. He looked at Nathan and gave him a quick half-smile. "I'm going to your place. I haven't seen you in quite awhile. Thought we could spend some time catching up....if that's okay with you, Katrina."

"Sure, Joey, that's fine. We are glad to have you. Jessica, you *will* come to the house when you're done sight-seeing?"

Jessica shrugged and nodded.

Nathan and Katrina made their way to the table where Mike, Cookie, Morgan, Kevin, Lisa and Charlie sat.

Cookie leaned over to Katrina and asked, "What is up with that miserable bitch?" Katrina shrugged. "Something's wrong, somewhere."

Morgan smirked over at Katrina, and asked, "How was your night?"

Nathan jumped in with an answer. "We played gin all night."

"Well, I guess you can call it whatever you want." Morgan grinned at Nathan and then laughed.

"So what are you all doing today? Our place or the tourist industry?" Nathan looked around the table, including them all in his question.

Mike told Nathan he and Cookie were going to the house, while Morgan and Kevin said they wanted to go find souvenirs first, and then go to the house. Charlie and Lisa were going home first, and then would be over to the house by two o'clock. Katrina and Nathan already knew that their parents were going directly to the house. Linda and Buck were going to sight-see for awhile, but would be over later. Uncle Joe and Aunt Betty were going directly to the house.

"Swimming in April....unbelievable!" Uncle Joe had exclaimed. Nathan and Katrina laughed.

The limos were lining up at the door as the brunch was ending. Danny stopped by Nathan and Katrina's table and asked if he could go get the kids.

"Absolutely! I'm officially their Untul Nate now!" Nathan grinned at Danny.

* * *

The guests were filing into the house as yet another group of caterers were setting up for snacks, lunch and dinner. Katrina watched the caterers at work and couldn't help thinking that the first caterer she walked out on missed out on a huge paycheck. All of this was costing a fortune, but Nathan told her not to worry; they could afford this and much more. She met Nathan at the bar and began helping him put out bottles of liquor, ice, glasses, and mixers. Beer and sodas were stocked in the refrigerator behind the bar. Jack Dooley showed up and offered to tend bar. Even though his offer was declined, he stepped in and took over. Katrina saw Joey come in and sit down. He looked so miserable, that she quickly went over and sat down beside him. Nathan joined her. She could see that Joey needed to talk, so she left Nathan with him and went to mingle with other guests. Charlie and Lisa arrived, both in swimsuits. Katrina led them out to the pool, and Charlie quickly picked Katrina up and threw her into the pool, fully clothed. Nathan appeared within seconds to help her out of the pool, glaring angrily at Charlie.

"Are you okay, Baby?" Nathan asked her, still glaring at Charlie.

Katrina nodded.

"Hey, it was all in fun, Nate!" Charlie defended himself.

Katrina walked up to Charlie and said, "Yeah? Well, have fun with this!" She pushed him into the pool, ruining the pack of cigarettes in the breast pocket of the unbuttoned shirt he wore above his swim trunks. Lisa laughed for the first time and gave Katrina a high-five.

Katrina went into the house to change out of her wet clothing.

As the day wore on, those who went to see tourist attractions began showing up. When Morgan and Kevin arrived, Morgan grabbed Katrina and whispered that she had something to tell her. They went to the master bedroom and sat down on the bed. Katrina noted that Marie had placed a vase full of red roses, with daisies and baby's breath mixed in, on the dresser. They must have been bought by Nathan, since he knew how she liked the roses mixed with daisies.

Morgan started right in. "That bitch, Jessica? Kat, we saw her in a bar talking to some guy, and then the next time we saw her, she was kissing him…..in one of the limos!! We started to get in, but when we opened the door, we stopped and backed out."

"Don't let Joey hear that." Morgan jumped when she heard a masculine voice behind her. Nathan's was standing in the doorway.

"You heard what I told Kat?" Morgan stared up at Nathan, seeing the anger in his eyes.

He nodded. "Honey, Mike and Kim want you to come into the family room." He reached out for Katrina's hand. "You too, Morgan. Hey, Joey told me he's going to ask her for a divorce. He knows about what she does. Let's not say anything to add to his misery, okay?"

"Got it." Morgan got up and followed them to the family room.

Mike and Kim were standing in the middle of the room with their arms around each other when Nathan, Katrina, and Morgan walked in.

Mike began by clearing his throat. "Can we have your attention for a couple of minutes? We didn't want to say anything before this, since we didn't want to take the spotlight off of Kat and Nate...but the wedding is over, so here goes......Kim and I.....well, we're pregnant!"

Katrina heard Mary gasp from across the room. Immediately, Katrina moved to hug Kim and Michael, with Nathan right behind her. Mary and Ed and Kathy joined in the hug-fest; Danny missing out since he had the kids in the pool.

"So when are you due?" Mary asked.

"The end of October. I'm going to have a little goblin!" Kim laughed, and Katrina laughed with her.

* * *

Toward evening, many of the guests were ready to return to the hotel, since many of them had flights scheduled for Monday morning and afternoon. Those who would not see them again, kissed Nathan and Katrina and wished them well. Morgan and Kevin, Mike and Cookie, and the parents were staying another day. Katrina and Nathan looked forward to a day with just their parents and their best friends. When the last guest was out of the house and the caterers were packed up and gone, Nathan and Katrina collapsed onto the living room sofa, exhausted.

"The past two days have been wonderful, Nate...but I am worn out. Hey, did you notice that Jessica didn't show up here?"

"Yeah, I noticed. I feel so sorry for my cousin. He's a really nice guy."

"He's sweet. I feel bad for him, too...."

Katrina's words were cut off by the ringing of the telephone. Nathan jumped up and strode across the room to answer it.

Joeys' voice came on the line. "Nathan, have you seen Jessica?"

"No, Joey, we haven't. Are you at your hotel?" Nathan looked over at Katrina and shrugged. "Yeah, if we see her, we'll tell her you're looking for her, but we are probably going to bed soon. We're both exhausted." Nathan placed the receiver back in its cradle and went back to Katrina on the sofa.

"I'm the luckiest man in the world." Nathan declared as he put his arms around Katrina and held her tightly.

29

Katrina and Nathan walked through the front door and dropped their suitcases onto the foyer floor

"Home…sweet home." Katrina sighed as she spoke.

Nathan smiled at her. "Should I have carried you over this threshold? I will, you know."

Katrina laughed. "No, you've carried me over enough of them, I think. We're good."

She looked toward the cat gymnasium and called, "Kitties!"

All three cats came charging toward her, two of them meowing loudly, as usual. Katrina bent down to pet them, Nathan following her lead. "They missed us." Katrina grinned at Nathan.

They had spent a glorious two weeks in Hawaii, sight-seeing, walking on the beaches, lying in the sun, and watching the beautiful sunsets, among many other activities. They paid for surfing lessons, which they agreed were lots of fun, but decided they were not surfers. Riding on horseback up the trails better suited them. Nathan surprised Katrina by having a birthday cake brought to their table at dinner on the night of her birthday. She had completely forgotten about her birthday and was surprised that Nathan remembered. His gift to her was a pair of diamond earrings to match the pendant he had given her the year before. In the evenings, they attended a couple of luaus, wearing their Hawaiian clothes they had purchased during one of their shopping trips on the main island. Katrina took a couple of hula lessons from one of the dancers and participated in the dancing when they allowed it. Nathan loved it. Many sight-seeing tours were available to them, and they took advantage of as many as they could fit in. On more than one occasion during these tours people asked them if they were newly-weds. They met an older couple from California who were newly married. They had dinner with them one night and learned that they both had been widowed a couple of years before they met. The couple proved to be delightful company for the evening. Katrina and Nathan would have liked to have spent more time with them, but the older couple was leaving the island the next morning.

Their two weeks ended too soon. Sitting in their seats before take-off to the mainland, Nathan reached for Katrina's hand. "Are you ready to go back to reality?" He asked as he raised her hand to his lips and kissed her fingers.

"I guess. I love Hawaii. It really is paradise. But then again....our life is like paradise, too; so going back to reality is not so bad." As she had spoken those words to him, her eyes sparkled.

"And we will live in paradise forever." He kissed her fingers again.

Now they were back home, ready to begin their life together. There were quite a few items that had to be taken care of; one being Katrina's apartment. The furniture had to be removed and it had to be readied to rent out. There were stacks of mail for both Nathan and Katrina that had to be opened and attended to. Marie, thank goodness, took care of most everything else. A note from her sat on the end table where she usually left it. Nathan picked it up and read it aloud. Marie had food prepared for them if they were hungry. There was a list of people who had called; among them being Katrina's agent and Nathan's cousin, Joey.

Katrina groaned when she heard Russ had called. "I forgot! There is another convention in four days! He's going to want me to be there."

"Tell him you won't go without me." Nathan suggested.

"I will....but be prepared to fly to New York." She warned him.

Her prophecy was correct. Russ had already purchased tickets for Katrina and Nathan. Four days later, Nathan and Katrina sat on a plane that was preparing for a landing at LaGuardia Airport. Nathan had his tuxedo cleaned and pressed and Katrina had purchased a slinky, black gown for the black tie dinner they would be attending. Happily, the convention was only a two-day affair. They would be back home on Tuesday, May second, and once again, take up where they left off. So many things had to be attended to. There was still the apartment that had to be dealt with. Katrina and Nathan had spent their first four days at home catching up on correspondence and writing out thank you cards for the wedding gifts they had received. Nathan had tried to return Joey's call but the number he had for him had been disconnected. He would have to wait for Joey to call again. Katrina had quite a bit of fan mail that she attended to, sending out autographed pictures of Kit-Kat to young people who wrote letters to the cartoon cat. Nathan had several investment proposals to go over, many of them contained quite a bit of detail and took several hours, if not days, to read through; and understand. After this trip to her convention, they would have to spend some serious time on their business affairs.

* * *

The convention came to a close on Tuesday morning, with the conventioneers being treated to a brunch at the hotel. Nathan and Katrina had a flight booked for two o'clock, and they could barely wait to get home. Still affected by jet lag from the flight home from Hawaii, they were both exhausted. They knew there was a lot of work waiting for them at home, but they also knew that they could fall into bed and sleep a dozen hours first, if they wanted. The convention turned out to be enjoyable. Katrina introduced Nathan to several of her colleagues, who in turn, introduced them to their spouses. She liked these conventions so much more when the spouses were invited.

After brunch, they went to their room to gather up and pack their belongings. It would be a long ride to LaGuardia, so they had just enough time to pack and hail a cab.

"I'm glad you came with me." Katrina smiled at Nathan as they closed their suitcases.

"I'm glad I did, too. I never realized that comic strips and cartoons were such a major business. Maybe I should invest in them somehow."

Katrina giggled. "You did.....when you married me."

Nathan grinned at her. "Oh yeah...I guess I did."

They grabbed their luggage and rode the elevator to the lobby, where Nathan handled the check-out and hailed a cab. They made it to the airport in time for their flight. Both of them slept, hands joined, during the entire flight home.

30

Once again, Nathan and Katrina came through the front door and deposited their bags on the floor.

"Ohh…I'm not leaving this place for at least a month!" Katrina exaggerated.

"Sounds good to me." Nathan responded, as he reached for Marie's usual note.

"Hmmm….Joey called again. Didn't leave a number. What the hell? Maybe I better call Uncle Joe."

"Do you think something is wrong?" Katrina took on a worried look.

"I'm not sure. It's just unusual that he would keep calling and not leave a number. He has to know that the only one I have for him is disconnected."

"Then maybe you should call Uncle Joe." She advised.

Nathan nodded. "Later. I just want to be alone with you…. in our house….just the two of us….and the kitties, of course…. no interruptions, no interference, nobody, nothing. Just us. Any objections?"

Katrina shook her head. "None, whatsoever."

* * *

Without unpacking, they had fallen into bed and immediately fell asleep. It was seven in the evening when they awoke. Katrina stretched and rolled toward Nathan, and he encircled her in his arms.

"Should we get up?" He asked her.

"Let's swim for a little bit. Okay?"

"That's a great idea." He smiled at her, and looked through the curtains. There was still plenty of daylight left and it was very warm outside.

They quickly changed into swimsuits and headed toward the pool. Without hesitation they jumped into the cool water and swam the length of the pool, side by side. Katrina did a surface dive and went underwater, emerged, and went under again. Nathan watched her as she glided underwater with her arms at her sides, before she surfaced again.

"You swim like an otter." He teased.

"Yeah? An otter?" She swam towards him and wrapped her arms around his neck and hoisted herself up, wrapping her legs around his waist. "Well, do you know what I think? I think we 'otter' slip into the hot tub and make love."

Nathan let out a surprised laugh, and nodded his head. "Whatever you say." He hooked his arms around her shoulders and her legs and carried her out of the pool and into the hot tub, dropping her swimsuit top on the walkway.

The water in the hot tub was warm rather than hot. Katrina removed the lower half of her suit and reached for Nathan. He didn't need any encouragement; he was ready for her. They kissed long and passionately before Katrina nudged Nathan toward the ledge on the sides of the hot tub. She pushed him down into a sitting position and then straddled herself over him. She was a tigress, eager with desire, as they made love in the hot tub. When they were both spent, Nathan felt dizzy as he held her tightly, his head resting on hers.

"Is this what it's going to be like for the next fifty years?" He whispered; his breathing still not back to normal.

"Yes....if not, how could I talk you into another fifty?" She whispered back, as she kissed his chin.

They remained in the hot tub, wrapped in each other's arms, until darkness fell. The night air became chilly. Nathan ventured out of the water and retrieved two towels that had been draped over a lounge chair earlier. Katrina retrieved what was left of the swimsuits out of the hot tub, while Nathan picked up the bra from her bikini off of the walkway. Wrapped in towels they entered the coolness of the house, bringing goose bumps to their flesh.

"This brings back a memory, doesn't it? We have certainly come a long way since then, haven't we?" Nathan's eyes twinkled as he smiled down at her.

Katrina nodded. She knew he was talking about their first time when they had to run inside because of a rainstorm. "Want to repeat history?" She asked. "Shower, same robes, food on the coffee table, candlelight...."

"I'm on it." He laughed. "Let's head for the shower."

* * *

Wrapped in the terry cloth robes, they sat on the floor, leaning against the sofa. After they showered, Katrina heated the food that Marie had prepared while Nathan positioned the coffee table and pillows and lit the tapered candles. After the food was eaten, Nathan stacked the dishes and carried them out to the dishwasher, and returned with glasses of red wine. Together, they sat sipping the wine, talking about their recent trips to Hawaii and New York. Nathan smiled at her, leaned forward, and kissed her lightly. The moment was interrupted by the ringing telephone. Nathan sighed and got up to answer. It was Joey. Katrina heard Nathan's part of the conversation as she sat on the floor in front of the sofa.

"So where are you? In Florida…where? Okay….I'll come get you. See you in a few." Nathan hung up the telephone and looked at Katrina and shrugged.

"Joey is here, in Florida. I guess you heard that. I guess I have to go pick him up. Do you want to ride along?" Nathan sounded slightly annoyed.

"No. I'll just clean up here, put some clothes on, and get a pot of coffee started. I have a feeling it may be a long night. I'll get a guest room ready, too"

He smiled at her. "I'll be back as soon as I can."

"You seem annoyed." She stated.

"Well, I am. He just shows up here like it's no big deal. He should have called and asked if it was okay to come here." Nathan scowled as he gave her a quick hug and kissed her.

* * *

Katrina heard the car coming up the driveway, and she retrieved coffee mugs from the cupboard. Nathan entered the kitchen through the back door, followed by Joey, luggage in hand. He set his two suitcases down and hugged Katrina.

"It's good to see you again, Katrina. Sorry to barge in on you like this." His voice faltered as he spoke.

Katrina could see that he was hurting and immediately began to feel sorry for him.

"How about some coffee? I just made a fresh pot. Are you hungry, Joey?"

Joey shook his head. "No....but I would love a cup of coffee." He smiled at Katrina tentatively. If only he had a wife like Nathan's. Katrina was obviously wonderful.

The three of them sat down at the kitchen table, coffee mugs in front of them.

"So what's going on, Joe?" Nathan got right to the point.

Joey stared at Nathan and sighed. "Well, as you know, my marriage is shit. Jessica is a bitch....sorry Katrina. No matter what I have ever done, she did nothing but complain. It was never good enough. Well, when we were here for your wedding, she took up with some guy she met in a bar. I didn't see her until it was time to fly home. Well, then she started calling this guy. Ran up the phone bill into three digits. I confronted her about it and she told me to go to hell. I went and filed for divorce the next day, and then she started fighting with me over what little assets we had. I gave her the house, all the furniture; and she cleaned out the bank accounts. All but one, that is. I had one she didn't know about. I cleaned that one out when I decided to come here. I was staying in a small motel near my job, eating out of cans, and I just decided to pick up and leave Indiana."

"So what about your job? You just quit?" Nathan stared at him, waiting for his response.

"No, I didn't just quit. Jessica started harassing me at work. She came in one afternoon and started pushing me around, slapping me in my face, and the boss saw it. He asked her to leave. Well, then she started calling the company, using fowl language, telling lies about me....the boss got sick of it. He asked me to resign. I got a decent severance pay, and along with the money I had in the bank, I decided I had enough to go somewhere and start over. Thank God I never had any kids with that bitch. Sorry again, Katrina."

"So what are you going to do now?" Katrina's question held real concern for Joey.

Joey shrugged. "I guess find a place to live and find a job down here. I like it here. Hey, I know I shouldn't have just showed up, but....well, I tried to get in touch with you...."

"You didn't leave a number where you could be reached." Nathan interjected. "I tried the only number I had for you, and it was disconnected."

"Yeah, well, when the phone bill is over four hundred dollars and you don't pay it; the phone company shuts it off. I told her I refused to pay that. I gave her money for all the other charges on the bill, which was about twenty-eight dollars. I told her to figure out how to pay for the calls to her boyfriend."

"Does your family know that you came here?" Katrina asked him softly.

"No, but I guess I should call them and let them know where I am. Mom and dad will be worried."

Katrina nodded. "You can call them tomorrow. It might be a little late for you to call them now."

"So what kind of work are you looking for?" Nathan asked pointedly. He hadn't been around Joey in quite awhile, and he wasn't sure what type of work ethic he had adopted. He was certainly not going to let Joey just live off of him and Katrina.

"I'm a carpenter by trade, but I also can do maintenance work. I'm good with machines. Oh, and woodworking. I do some wood carving. I'll do most anything, really."

Nathan was satisfied that Joey was willing to work. He led him up to the guest room that Katrina had readied for him, and returned to the kitchen to help Katrina clean up.

* * *

Nathan was working at his desk in the den when Joey appeared in the doorway. Nathan wasn't aware that he was standing there until he heard Angel's hiss. He looked over at Angel and followed her line of vision to the doorway where Joey stood.

"Good morning. You must not like cats." Nathan acknowledged.

"Not particularly. I have nothing against them. Where's Katrina?" Joey leaned against the doorway and studied Nathan.

"She's in her office, working. She works on her strip every Friday and turns it in. She doesn't come out until it's sent."

"So it wouldn't be a good time to disturb her, then." Joey clarified.

Nathan looked at the clock and said, "No, now wouldn't be a good time. Is there something I can do for you?"

"Well, I have an appointment for a job at nine o'clock this morning. I wanted to know if I could borrow Katrina's car. She said if I needed to use it, I could."

"I have cars, too, you know." Nathan had an edge to his voice. He didn't like the idea of Joey asking Katrina for anything. Katrina was such a soft touch; he didn't want Joey to take advantage of her. "Take the T-Bird. That way Katrina can use her Mustang if she needs it."

"Thanks, Nate. Wish me luck." He gave Nathan a thumbs-up and headed out toward the garage.

* * *

Nathan looked at the clock and realized that Katrina would be finishing soon. Joey had already been gone over an hour. He went to the kitchen and poured coffee into two mugs and carried them down to her office, and tapped on the door. "Can I come in?" He asked, through the door.

"Of course! I just hit the send button. I'm waiting for it to go through. Oh wow! I need a cup of that. Thanks, Love." She smiled up at him as she rubbed the back of her neck.

Nathan moved her hands aside and began to lightly massage the back of her neck, immediately releasing the tension in her neck muscles. He sat down with her to wait for the confirmation. "Joey went on a job interview. Hopefully, he'll get the job."

"I was thinking.....when Joey gets a job and can find his own place, maybe he could rent one of my apartments....at a family discount rate, of course. One of the current tenants wants to rent my old apartment. That would leave a two-bedroom open. I get seven hundred a month for a two-bedroom. Maybe I could let him have it for four. He can use the furniture that is still in my apartment. What do you think?"

Katrina leaned back and laced her fingers behind her head, looking up at Nathan.

"I think you are too generous. I think that figure is too low. I think you are extremely sweet. I think I love you more and more every day. That's what I think. It's up to you, though. You know I don't interfere with your decisions concerning your assets…unless you ask, that is." He let out a small laugh, the warmth in his eyes showing as he stared at her over his coffee cup. "Hey, if he comes home with a job, want to take him out tonight? Maybe go to Jack's Place?"

"Good idea. We haven't been out anywhere since we came home from New York. Let's plan on it. I really hope he gets the job." Katrina stopped as she remembered. "Oh, Uncle Joe called very early this morning. Jessica has been calling their house almost every hour, wanting to know where Joey is. She needs money, she says. Even had the nerve to ask Uncle Joe for some. I hope she doesn't get this number."

"Yeah, me too. I would have to tell her to get a job." They both laughed. "Are you ready for breakfast….or I guess it's brunch now. I'm hungry."

Katrina wrapped up her work for another week and they headed toward the kitchen where Marie already had bacon frying for their breakfast.

31

Jack's was crowded, according to all the cars parked in the parking lot. Nathan's usual space was open, so he maneuvered the Hummer into it. They were all in a good mood, since Joey got the job he had gone after that morning. He returned after the interview and no sooner sat down to brunch with Katrina and Nathan, when the telephone rang. It had been the construction company offering him the job. He happily accepted the offer and would begin working on Monday. They now had a reason to celebrate. They threaded themselves through the crowded bar, waving to those who called out to them, as they made their way toward the back room and found a table. Sal, the waitress appeared at the table immediately.

“Well, it’s good to see you two. How was Hawaii? Or don’t answer that. I’ll be jealous as hell.” She laughed at her own remark. “And who is this good looking guy? He has to be related, Nathan. You look a lot alike.”

“Think so? This is my cousin, Joey. You were at the wedding. You don’t remember him?”

Sal squinted and scrutinized Joey.

“Oh, yeah….wife was mad at you for something. I remember.”

Joey laughed. “Wife was mad at me for everything….all the time. Still is, I guess.”

They ordered food and sat back to watch the crowd. The DJ was beginning to set up for the regular Friday night Karaoke.

“Do you sing, Joey? Katrina sings like an angel. I give it a shot, too.” Nathan grinned at Joey.

“I heard Katrina sing at the wedding. Yes, she does sing like an angel. I can’t even carry a tune in a basket. Don’t plan on me getting up there. I’d have to be real drunk to do it.” Joey grinned back at Nathan.

The DJ started playing right after the three of them finished eating. Nathan and Katrina got up to dance, leaving Joey sitting at the table. He wandered out toward the bar to find the men’s room, and returned to the table after Nathan and Katrina sat back down.

“I was talking to a girl out at the bar….I hope it’s okay, but I asked her to join us back here.” Joey looked warily at Nathan and Katrina.

“Sure. You *are* practically divorced. Just don’t go getting involved with someone too soon. That never works out either.” Nathan advised him.

Nathan and Katrina got up to dance again. Nathan glanced over at the table in time to see Holly joining Joey at their table. “Oh, gees! My cousin sure can pick ‘em, can’t he?”

Katrina laughed. “Let him go, Nate. Holly really isn’t bad looking, and maybe a good man will make a good woman out of her.”

Nathan scowled. “Like Jessica?”

Katrina shrugged as they walked back to the table.

“Hi Nate…Katrina. How is married life?” Holly smiled at both of them, acknowledging Katrina for a change. “I knew Joey had to be related to you. You look like brothers.”

"Cousins." Nathan corrected. "And married life is wonderful, since you asked. Right, Honey?" Nathan smiled over at Katrina, reached for her hand and raised it to his lips.

"Right. When you marry the right one." She smiled sweetly at Holly.

"That's nice. So I hear Joey is staying with you." Holly's eyes darted from Katrina to Nathan, and then back to Katrina. "It's not too crowded?"

"With five bedrooms, I doubt it. The house has about eleven or twelve rooms." Nathan was finding it hard to be friendly to Holly, ever since she referred to Katrina as 'what's-her-face' at the New Year's Eve party last year.

"It's only temporary." Joey added. "I'll be getting my own place in a couple of weeks or less."

"You know you can stay as long as necessary." Katrina offered, and looked to Nathan for his agreement.

"Thanks. I'm really looking forward to getting a place of my own, though." Joey looked at them with gratitude in his eyes.

"I wonder why Lisa and Charlie aren't here. They usually are. Have you heard from Charlie?" Katrina asked Nathan.

"No, I haven't. Holly, have they been in lately?" Nathan turned his attention to Holly, knowing that she was there all the time.

"They went to Vegas. I'll bet they get married while they are there, too. Remember, Lisa has no family, and Charlie's only relative is his mother."

"That makes sense. I guess we'll have to wait until they get back to find out." Katrina responded.

It was close to midnight when Katrina and Nathan got up to leave. Joey sidled up to Nathan and asked if it was okay to invite Holly to the house to swim on Saturday afternoon.

Nathan thought about it for a moment. "Okay, but if she disrespects my wife in any way, I will ask her to leave. You understand?"

Joey nodded, and ran back to the table to say goodnight to Holly, and invite her to the house the next day.

32

Katrina awoke when Nathan got out of bed. It was a beautiful Sunday morning, just two days before Nathan's thirty-first birthday. She heard the shower go on and she rolled over and closed her eyes for a few minutes. Nathan would take his shower and shave before he came back to the bed to see if she was going to get up; so she knew she had time to catch a little more sleep. She felt so tired this morning! They had spent the past couple of days getting Joey moved into one of her apartments. The furniture from her old apartment was moved into the smaller apartment after the tenants moved out and into hers. Katrina, with Holly's help, hung the curtains in Joey's place, and then went shopping to fill the refrigerator and at least one cupboard. In addition to her furniture, she gave him her pots and pans, dishes and silverware, and towels and linens. Katrina was satisfied that Joey had everything he needed to survive, including her washer and dryer.

Nathan tapped her on the shoulder. "Hey, sleepy-head, are you going to sleep the day away? You can, if you want, I guess. Me....I'm hungry. Do you want me to bring you coffee?"

Katrina's stomach lurched. "No...I'll get up. I'll be in the kitchen as soon as I shower." She looked up at him and smiled.

He planted a kiss on her forehead and darted out of the room. She arose slowly, feeling the queasiness begin in her stomach, and waited for it to pass before she stood up and walked to the bathroom. She opened the door under the sink and reached for the box containing a home pregnancy test that she had purchased the previous afternoon. She quickly read the directions and followed them. It was only a moment before the results appeared. Positive. POSITIVE!

"I'm pregnant." She whispered to herself. "Oh, Wow! Nathan... he will be ecstatic!"

She showered quickly, slipped on a lavender sundress, and went to find Nathan. He was sitting at the table on the patio, drinking coffee and reading the morning paper when she approached him. She smiled and sat down on his lap.

"Good morning....Daddy." She smiled and studied his face to see if he understood.

"Good....what? Wait a minute! Are you telling me something?" Nathan's grin was from ear to ear. "Daddy? A baby? Are you telling me we're going to have a baby?"

Katrina nodded. Nathan stood up with her in his arms, let out a whoop, and spun her around. He was laughing with tears in his eyes.

"No...don't spin me. I'll get sick."

"Oh, sorry....morning sickness?"

She nodded again. "And you can't tell anyone yet. It's bad luck. You can't tell anyone until I see a doctor, okay?"

"Okay. I guess." He looked up and saw Marie bringing breakfast out to them. "Marie...just Marie. Please? I have to tell *someone!*"

"Okay, but only Marie." She giggled at him. He was like a big kid.

"Marie.....my wife just called me 'daddy'!" Nathan couldn't wipe the grin off his face.

Marie stopped and looked from Nathan to Katrina, then back to Nathan. She understood immediately, and smiled at them. "Well, congratulations! You haven't seen a doctor yet?"

"No, she hasn't, and she says I can't tell anyone until she does. Are there any doctors who work on Sunday?"

Marie and Katrina laughed and shook their heads. "I'll call tomorrow and get an appointment." Katrina assured him. "In the meantime....we tell nobody. Okay?"

Nathan looked dejected. "Okay....damn!" Katrina and Marie laughed again.

Suddenly, Nathan stopped grinning. "Are you feeling okay?" He asked her. "Are you having a lot of morning sickness? Do you need to lie down? What do I do to make you feel better?"

Katrina laughed at his concern. "Nothing, right now. I'm okay, but I'll let you know." She hugged him and kissed his chin.

* * *

Katrina was lucky enough to get an appointment for Thursday morning. Until then, she and Nathan planned on keeping a low profile, spending his birthday, the Fourth of July, quietly at home. She knew he wouldn't be able to keep their secret if they were around a lot of people, so she planned on just the two of them celebrating together. She made a birthday cake and he grilled steaks in the late afternoon. They swam in the pool together and watched fireworks in the distance. They had been invited over to Danny and Kathy's, but declined, saying they had other plans. The only way to keep their secret was to keep Nathan at home away from other people, but she promised him that he could tell everybody after the doctor's appointment. It was only two days of torture for him.

Nathan insisted on going to the appointment with her. They were sitting in the waiting room leafing through magazines, waiting for her to be called in. Nathan was acting like it was Christmas and he was waiting for Santa Claus. He was excited and impatient at the same time. Katrina chuckled silently to herself as she reached for his hand. Finally, her name was called and they both stood up. The nurse told Nathan to wait there; that they would call for him to come in when they were ready for him. Disappointed, he sat back down to wait. He was the only man in the waiting room, and in Katrina's absence, he began to feel uncomfortable and out of place. He buried his face in a magazine, hoping he wouldn't have to wait too long.

"Mr. Perletti, you can follow me now." A smiling figure in a white coat was standing in front of him. He got up quickly and was led to a small office, where Katrina waited. Behind the desk sat a pleasant-looking man, wearing a white jacket and a blue and white striped tie. He looked to be around forty, give or take a year or two. His graying hair was just beginning to show signs of thinning.

He extended his hand to Nathan. "I'm Doctor Logan. It's good to meet you. Have a seat and let's get right to it."

Nathan became alarmed. What was wrong? Get right to what? He looked at Katrina but could not read anything in her face.

The doctor smiled at him. "You're going to be a father. Everything is fine. Your wife is healthy and so far, everything looks quite normal. Now, I like to spend a couple of minutes with the expectant parents just to get their reaction to this news. This *is* good news, isn't it?"

Nathan had been holding his breath, and quickly exhaled. "Yeah.... it's great news. I can't wait to be a dad." He looked at Katrina. "We can tell everyone now?"

Katrina laughed, and then smiled. "Yeah, we can."

Nathan turned to Dr. Logan. "Is there anything we can't do? Any restrictions?"

"Katrina has all the information. You can read over all the literature I gave her. If there are any questions, don't hesitate to call." Dr. Logan stood up and extended his hand once more to Nathan. "Congratulations! See you in a month."

Nathan felt like he was floating as he left the office. He took Katrina's hand and walked out into the sunlight. He stopped, let out a whoop and lifted Katrina up off the ground. He kissed her lovingly, and then brushed the tears from her cheeks. "We're going to be parents, Sweetheart! Just think…we will be setting the curfews, making rules…."

"Changing diapers, wiping up spit-up…." Katrina interjected, laughing.

They stopped talking and their eyes locked. Without saying anything, they conveyed to one another that they knew this child was conceived out of their love and devotion to each other.

* * *

Katrina talked Nathan into waiting until Friday evening to go to Jack's Place. He wanted to tell everyone their news, but Katrina convinced him that their parents should be the first to know. Katrina used her cell phone to call her mother, as Nathan called his mother on his own cell phone. When they had both mothers on the line, they announced their news in unison.

"We're going to have a baby!" They spoke into the phones together, so both mothers heard the news from both of them at the same time. Mary squealed with delight, and Rose cried. "We leave it up to you to tell the dads." They told them. After assuring both mothers that everything was fine and that Katrina was healthy, they disconnected the calls. Katrina called Danny and Kathy, and then Michael and Kim. There was laughter and tears as they spoke over the telephone. Michael and Danny had mixed emotions over the fact that their baby sister was going to have a baby. Both of them conveyed that feeling to her.

"We don't by any chance have a watermelon here, do we?" Katrina asked Nathan.

"No....why? Do you want watermelon? I'll go get one."

Katrina nodded. "Do you mind if I take a nap?"

"Of course not. You nap; I'll run." Nathan snorted a laugh through his nose. "I'll go buy a watermelon. Do you want anything else? Ice cream? Pickles?"

Katrina shook her head to each question. "Just watermelon." She went to lie down.

* * *

They were on the patio sitting at the picnic table, where Nathan was cutting up the watermelon and Katrina was devouring it. She didn't eat much dinner, but she was stuffing herself with the watermelon. Joey and Holly appeared around the corner of the house and joined them at the picnic table.

"You two want some watermelon....before Katrina eats it all?" Nathan asked.

"You like watermelon that much?" Joey stared at Katrina for a moment.

Katrina looked up at Nathan. "Tell. Go ahead."

Nathan took on his 'I'm so excited' grin, and looked at Joey. "We're pregnant!"

"Oh, wow! That's great! And you're craving watermelon?" Joey's eyes returned to Katrina.

"Yeah, like there may be no more after this. I never even really cared for it all that much until now." Katrina laughed as she admitted it.

Holly spoke up. "So are you going to be one of those indulgent expectant fathers who goes out in the middle of the night to pick up whatever she is craving?"

"Yeah. I would do that even if she weren't pregnant. I *love* spoiling my wife." Nathan answered, as he wrapped his arm around Katrina's shoulders and kissed her temple.

"I've heard that some men actually get labor pains when their wives go into labor. Do you think you'll be one of those?" Holly countered.

"Probably." Nathan answered Holly, but looked into Katrina's eyes. "I hope so, anyway. I want to share everything with her."

Katrina's eyes sparkled as she smiled at Nathan. How she loved him! For a brief instant they both forgot that they had company as they looked into each other's eyes, the love flowing.

Joey cleared his throat, bringing them back to the here and now. "I just remembered why we came by. Dad forwarded this letter to me. It's from Jessica."

Nathan scowled, reached for the letter and read it. The contents were unpleasant and the language was fowl, but the concept was that Jessica needed money and would stop at nothing to get it from Joey. Nathan stared at the writing on the pages for a few minutes, and then smiled as he handed the letter back to Joey. He flipped open his cell phone and searched for a number, and then dialed it. Before there was a connection, he walked out of earshot of everyone at the table. After he disconnected he sat back down, looking satisfied.

"What did you do?" Joey quizzed, almost afraid to know.

"She wants money, she'll get money. I have a few connections here and there. I arranged for a delivery of a thousand dollars, all in change, mostly pennies, to be dropped off at her door tomorrow….in garbage bags. There will be a note attached to it…'small change for a small mind'….get a job.' Maybe she will take a hint. If she does, it's worth the grand."

Joey laughed. "I'll pay you back…some day. I hope there will be no return address."

"No…she won't know where it came from." Nathan grinned at Joey as he pulled Katrina close to him. "More watermelon?"

* * *

Katrina was working on her comic strip on Friday morning, while Nathan worked on a couple of proposals in his office. She made a mental note to call Morgan as soon as she was done. She couldn't wait to hear Morgan's reaction to her pregnancy. Nathan had called Mike and Cookie last night, and he was delighted with their reaction. Cookie squealed into the phone, hurting both Katrina's and Nathan's ears. Katrina smiled as she pictured Cookie jumping up and down, squealing. Katrina pressed the send button when the strips for the week were completed. As soon as the confirmations came through, she would call Morgan. Nathan tapped on the door with the usual mugs of coffee in his hands. They would call Morgan together on the speaker phone.

Morgan answered her direct line on the first ring. "Kat! I was just about to call you! I have some news for you!"

"Me, too! I go first, since I called you....We're pregnant!"

Morgan squealed. "No shit? We are, too!! Kat! We're pregnant together! How cool is that? When are you due?"

"Oh, Morgan! I'm due around February fifteenth. How about you?"

"February twelfth...oh wow! If one of us has a girl and the other has a boy, we can arrange a marriage between them! Then we would be related!"

Katrina was laughing. "Morgan, you're a nut! So how are you feeling? Any morning sickness?"

"Oh, well, a little. Not too bad. How about you?"

"A little more than a little, but not too bad. How is Kevin with this? Is he happy?"

"That nut already bought a football! I asked what if it was a girl, and he said she'd play football. He's excited. And Nathan?"

Nathan spoke up for himself. "I haven't stopped smiling since we found out. I don't care if it's a girl or a boy....I just want to be a daddy." Nathan reached for Katrina's hand. "So what do you say we get together on Labor Day? We'll fly up and spend the weekend in Pennsylvania."

"That sounds great! I'll tell Kevin tonight. Is your mom excited, Kat?"

"Now what do you think?" Katrina laughed.

"Yeah, I guess she is. Will you stay here or at their house?"

Nathan spoke up again. "At their house! I want to sleep with Katrina in her room. Not like last time, before we were married."

"Got it. Hey, I have to run. I have a client coming in a few minutes. Talk to you soon. Love you both." Morgan hung up.

Nathan smiled down into Katrina's face. "I'm so happy, Sweetheart."

Katrina smiled back. "Me, too. But I'm hungry right now. Pancakes with strawberries on top, with whipped cream sounds good. Can we go out for breakfast?"

"You betcha!"

Nathan grabbed her hand and they headed out toward the kitchen to tell Marie they were going out for breakfast.

* * *

Katrina stood in front of the mirror in her bra and panties. "Can you tell anything yet?"

Nathan cocked his head and studied her abdomen. "No, not yet, but your stomach is harder. I noticed that last night. The boobs are harder, too. I can't wait to get to Jack's and tell everybody, so hurry up and get dressed. Joey and Holly better not have said anything. They promised. *I* want to be the one to tell! Damn! I'm thinking about putting an ad in the newspaper."

Katrina laughed at him as she dressed. "You're nuts!"

"Yeah, I am....about you. I wonder what you're going to look like when you're real pregnant."

"I think you'll like the boobs. They will get bigger."

Nathan came up behind her and wrapped his arms around her waist, gently rubbing her abdomen. "I like them now. I love every inch of you, from your gorgeous copper hair down to your beautifully pedicured toenails. You're my woman; my one and only."

Katrina smiled up at him through the mirror. "You're the one I waited for. You have my all. I love you. I love how you look...I love how you feel....I love how you smell...."

"Smell? I smell? Like what?" Nathan chuckled.

"Like fresh laundered sheets with a hint of spice. I think it's the most wonderful smell. Now let me finish getting dressed so we can go." She tilted her head back and kissed his chin.

* * *

The bar was crowded again. Nathan was glad, because that gave him more people to tell. He and Katrina stood at the bar together, trying to get Jack's attention. Charlie was at the other end of the bar.

He yelled across the bar to Nathan. "Hey, Nate, what's up? What's going on?"

"We're pregnant, Charlie!"

As soon as the words were out, a hush fell over the crowd.

Katrina rolled her eyes. "Well, that was subtle." She laughed a squeezed Nathan's hand.

Charlie made his way over to them and grabbed Nathan's hand. "Good job, man! Hey, Lisa! Come here!"

Lisa, coming from the ladies' room, trotted over to them and Charlie told her their news. "And how about our news?" Lisa cocked an eyebrow at Charlie.

"Yeah, we're married. Got married in Vegas."

Katrina hugged Lisa. "I'm happy for you! Even if he *is* a jerk." Katrina whispered to Lisa.

"So when is the baby due?" Lisa changed the subject.

"In February. Morgan is pregnant, too! We're due around the same time."

"That's cool! Your brother's baby will only be a few months older than yours. That will be fun. They can grow up together if he moves down here."

"I've been working on that for years." Katrina admitted.

33

Katrina and Nathan found their seats, sat down and buckled their seat belts. The plane was scheduled to arrive in Pittsburgh just before noon. They planned on renting a car and being at Katrina's parents' house before Ed got home from work. The agenda was to spend Friday night and all day Saturday with Katrina's parents, and then go to Morgan's for a barbeque on Sunday. Morgan and Kevin were planning on going to the Kitrowski's on Monday for a cookout. Nathan's parents were driving down on Saturday to join them at the Kitrowski's, and they all planned on going out to dinner. The holiday weekend would be full of family fun, and they both looked forward to it. Katrina looked over at Nathan and smiled. He squeezed her hand as the plane began to taxi for take off.

"I wish I looked more pregnant. I've only gained a half a pound. That's not very much for being three and a half months pregnant; I don't think." Katrina pouted as she looked at Nathan.

"Well, Honey, You've been so sick. Remember, the doctor said the baby is growing. You're just losing a little weight from being sick in the morning. He said that would end soon. Then…you'll get fat." His eyes held a mischievous look as he raised the corners of his mouth in a quick playful smile. He raised her hand to his lips and kissed her fingers, as he always did when he couldn't kiss her mouth.

"Morgan has gained six pounds. She probably looks pregnant."

"Sweetheart, the more you gain, the more you have to take off afterward. Doctor Logan told you that. So….look at it this way….. already Morgan has to lose five and a half pounds more than you do." Nathan watched for a reaction, and he got the one he had hoped for. Katrina burst out laughing, and then smiled up at him. She leaned back and sighed as the plane leveled off in the air. She quickly dozed off.

* * *

"Hello! Morgan? Kevin?" Katrina hollered through the front door. It was late morning when Nathan and Katrina pulled into Morgan and Kevin's driveway. The past two days had flown by while they were at the Kitrowski's house. Both sets of parents overly-indulged Katrina because of her 'condition' as Ed referred to her pregnancy. Rose brought her a tiny baby sweater that had been Nathan's when he was an infant. Katrina was delighted, as she marveled over the fact that Nathan had once been that tiny. They had dined at a newly opened restaurant and were satisfied with both the meal and the service. The Kitrowski's asked the Perletti's to stay overnight and spend Sunday with them, but the invitation was declined. Joe and Betty were driving in from Indiana on Sunday and they had made plans with them. Nathan and Katrina hugged and kissed the Perletti's before they left and promised to keep them posted on every detail.

Today was the day for Morgan and Kevin's barbeque, and the plan was to spend the entire day at their place, and then go out afterward for some music and dancing. That was if Morgan and Katrina felt okay to go, of course.

Morgan jumped up and ran toward the front door when she heard Katrina's voice. "Kat!" She squealed as she threw her arms around her oldest and best friend. "Nathan, Kevin is outside trying to erect a canopy, or whatever it is. You know, one of those things that covers people in case it rains?"

"Does he need assistance? I'll go see if I can help him." Nathan quickly kissed Morgan's cheek, and then Katrina's, and headed toward the back of the house, out through the sliding glass doors to where Kevin was struggling with canvas and frame.

Morgan took Katrina by the hand and headed toward the bedroom where they could compare stomachs. They laughed as they showed off their barely noticeable tummy bulges.

"You can't even see yours!" Morgan, with her hands on her hips, looked pointedly at Katrina. "How much weight have you gained?"

"Half a pound, but I've been really sick. The doctor says the baby is growing, but I'm losing weight from being so sick." Katrina stared into Morgan's full-length mirror, looking dejected. Morgan was already showing, but Katrina could still wear a bikini if she wanted to.

"Well, you also have much better abdominal muscles than I do. All those years of dancing lessons did that for you. Don't worry; eventually you'll begin to look pregnant." Morgan hugged Katrina. "How about some help in the kitchen? Okay?"

They entered the kitchen just as Nathan and Kevin came in through the sliding door. Kevin looked at Nathan, smiling. "Want to bet they were in the bedroom comparing bellies?"

Nathan laughed, and looked over at the two women. "No contest." He answered. He could tell by the looks on their faces that Kevin was right. He winked at Katrina as he accepted a beer from Kevin.

Kevin and Nathan went back out to finish up in the yard, while Morgan and Katrina settled in the kitchen preparing food. Morgan looked at Katrina, tentatively.

"I have to tell you something. I hope you don't get mad."

"What?" Alarmed, Katrina looked up at Morgan.

"Candy is coming.....I'm sorry, but she sort of invited herself, and....I didn't know how to get out of it. I was inviting another co-worker—a colleague, actually—and Candy overheard me. She jumped on the invitation, and I couldn't tell her she wasn't invited, in front of Angela, my colleague. I'm sorry, Kat." Morgan looked nervously at Katrina.

"Hey, Morgan, I'm over Candy. I don't care if she comes. Hey, maybe she is lonely. Maybe she needs friends and companionship. Maybe you're doing a good deed by letting her come. How many people did you invite, anyway?"

Morgan didn't respond to Katrina's question right away, since she was laughing so hard at what Katrina had said. "Twelve. Besides you and Nathan, I invited twelve." Morgan finally responded, dabbing the tears from her eyes. "Good deed! Oh, Kat! I miss having you around all the time!" They both broke out laughing.

The doorbell interrupted their laugh-fest. Morgan quickly moved toward the door to let in the first guest to arrive. Of course, it was Candy. Morgan led her through the living and dining rooms, into the kitchen, where Katrina sat cutting raw vegetables. She looked up when Morgan and Candy entered.

"Candy....how are you?" Katrina smiled a little. She could see that Candy had not had an easy time after they graduated.

"Katrina, you haven't changed a bit. You still look like you did in high school."

"Oh, well, thanks for saying so, but I think I've aged a little. Not to mention that I'm pregnant now."

"Congratulations. I mean, you're happy about it, right?"

"Ecstatic! My husband and I couldn't wait to start a family. So how have you been?"

"Okay, I guess. Katrina, I wanted to come here to see you today, because....well, I wanted to tell you how sorry I am for....anything that I did to hurt you. I mean, you were always so damned nice....to me, and everybody else. You didn't deserve what I did."

"Candy, if you're talking about Sean, you did me a favor. So just forget about it. Try to enjoy the day. Here....sit.....and you can help us get stuff ready. Look....I moved on. I don't think about Sean.... ever. He and I were never meant to be. You'll see what I'm talking about when you meet my husband." Katrina smiled at Candy and rolled a green pepper in front of her. "Can you cut this up?"

Relieved, Candy nodded and began working on the pepper. Morgan went to answer the door to more guests. Soon the house and the patio were teeming with guests, with plenty of laughter to go around. Nathan spied Katrina carrying a tray outside to the table, and immediately retrieved it from her. Candy almost dropped the tray she was carrying when she looked up at Nathan.

"Honey, you shouldn't be carrying things." He set the tray down and put his arm around Katrina and kissed her cheek.

She smiled up at him. "Nate, this is Candy. Candy, this is my husband, Nathan." She added as she turned toward Candy.

It took Candy a moment to respond, she was so taken in by Nathan's good looks. Nathan took over the conversation, and ended the awkward moment. "You went to school with Kat? She went to school with a Candy and I went to school in Ohio with a Cookie. We think that's kind of ironic." Nathan gave Candy one of his easy smiles.

She smiled back at him. "It's nice to meet you, Nathan. And yes, we did go to school together." Candy opened her mouth to speak, but stopped.

Nathan was smiling down at Katrina. "Honey, Kevin and I are going to run out for more ice. Be right back. Need anything?"

"No, Sweetheart…I'm good. Be careful. Love you." Katrina responded.

"Love you more." Nathan responded back, as he followed Kevin toward the driveway.

Candy stared after him, and then turned back to Katrina. "Yes…. I see what you mean. That's who you were meant to be with. It's that obvious. Wow, he's gorgeous."

Katrina just smiled and nodded in agreement. "Yes, he is. And he's wonderful, too. I waited a long time for him to come along; and he waited just as long for me. When we met, we knew we were meant to be together."

"Do you ever think about Jeff?" Candy asked.

"Of course. I loved Jeff." Katrina responded.

"Does your husband know about Jeff?"

"Yes.....Nathan and I have no secrets. He even goes to the cemetery with me. He knows all about Jeff and how we felt about each other. Nathan hopes that Jeff approves of him." Katrina stopped and laughed a little. "Nathan talked to Jeff at the grave site once. He told Jeff that he was taking care of me in a way he thought Jeff would approve. Nathan is a loving, compassionate man, and he fully understands what Jeff and I had. He also wants to punch Sean." Katrina grinned at Candy. "Listen, Candy....let's just forget about all that. It was years ago. I'm over it. I have a wonderful husband. He's perfect. My life is perfect. We're going to have our first baby. Life is good. Now let's get some of that delicious looking food over there, and you can tell me about your years between high school and now. Okay?" Katrina took Candy's arm and led her to the table full of dishes and trays of food.

34

Katrina awoke with a gasp, and then scrambled out of bed into the bathroom. Nathan was right behind her. She barely made it before she started heaving. Spasms wracked her body as she kneeled in front of the porcelain bowl, sick. Nathan's hand rested lightly on her back. When the heaves stopped, Nathan reached over and flushed the toilet for her. He was on the floor beside her, kneeling on one knee. Feeling exhausted, she rested her head against Nathan's inner thigh on his bent leg.

"Is it over?" Nathan asked her as he stroked her hair.

"Oh Nathan.....Honey....I think this is way above and beyond the call of duty for you. You don't have to sit in on these episodes. It's really gross."

Nathan smiled and kissed the top of Katrina's head. "Well.....I married you for better or worse, in sickness and in health. This is the sickness part. Besides, I'm responsible for this sickness, right?" He leaned down and kissed her forehead. "Are you okay?"

Katrina sighed. "You're only half responsible. I had something to do with it. Nathan....I had the dream again."

Nathan's eyes darkened for a moment. "Do you think that's why you got sick? I mean…it's the first time you've done this since we came back from our Labor Day weekend. That's over two weeks ago."

"Maybe. Maybe it was the sudden motion of sitting up. I don't know."

"What time is our appointment today?" Nathan was speaking very softly to her as he stroked her shoulder and her arm. The recurring dream where she couldn't come to him because she was dead, deeply disturbed him; but he didn't want her to know it.

"It's not until one this afternoon." She answered in barely more than a whisper.

"What do you say we go back to bed and get a little more sleep then? I think you're falling asleep on the floor….in front of the toilet, of all things." Nathan chuckled into her ear as he spoke. She nodded and smiled at him as he helped her up.

Katrina fell asleep immediately once she was under the comforter. She lay cradled in Nathan's arms while he lay staring at the ceiling. He couldn't shake the feeling of impending doom. "Dear, God….please don't let her dream come true. I couldn't live without her. Please don't take her from me." He silently prayed. He looked down at her sleeping face and had to fight the urge to crush her to him as tightly as he could. "Dear God," He silently began again. "She's all I ever wanted. I waited so long to find her, and I love her with all my heart and soul. Please, God….don't let anything happen to her." Nathan realized there were tears running down his face. His feelings were mixed with love for Katrina and the fear that something might happen to her. He wasn't sure why he was so disturbed by the dream. It was, after all…only a dream. He tried to think of more pleasant thoughts. Today they were going to have a sonogram, and if they were lucky, they could find out the gender of their baby…..if they wanted to know, that is. They really hadn't decided if they wanted to wait and be surprised or if they wanted to know and decorate the nursery accordingly. He would let it up to Katrina. Whatever she decided would be fine with him.

* * *

"Okay, up you go. Lie down flat on your back." The ultrasound tech instructed. She made some adjustments on the ultrasound equipment, and then spread the cool gel over Katrina's belly. Within seconds an image appeared on the screen. The tech went about her job, filming the images, adjusting knobs as she worked.

Nathan positioned a chair next to Katrina's head and sat down. He laced the fingers on her left hand through his fingers on his left hand; while he held her face in his right hand, and settled down to watch the screen.

Katrina giggled. "You want to get some popcorn for this?" She teased. "You look like you're getting ready to watch a movie."

Nathan looked into her face, grinning, as he kissed her forehead. They both turned back to the little screen of the ultrasound.

"There's your baby right there." The tech pointed to an image on the screen. Neither Katrina nor Nathan thought it looked like a baby, but neither of them said anything.

"Everything is looking good. Do you want to know the sex of the baby?"

Katrina smiled as she looked up at Nathan. Their eyes connected as they grinned at each other. Katrina nodded. Nathan's grin got even wider. "Yeah. Can you tell?" He asked the tech.

"Oh, yeah….I can tell. It's definitely a boy."

Katrina's breath caught in her throat as she looked up at Nathan. He grinned down into her face, as he wiped the single tear from her cheek. He felt as though he was suspended in air at that moment. "Oh, wow," was all he could muster. A son….they were going to have a son!

The tech watched the interaction between them as she finished up. She cleared her throat to get their attention. "You're all done. Here is a towel to wipe off the gel. I'll have copies of your images for you before you go."

Nathan took the towel from the tech and gently wiped the gel off of Katrina's abdomen for her, and then helped her up when he was done. The tech brought the paper images in to them and told them they were free to go.

She was amused as she looked from one to the other. "Have you two been hitting the magic mushrooms, or what? You both look higher than kites."

Nathan and Katrina laughed. Nathan spoke up in their defense. "It's just that…I don't know….it went from being a baby to being our son."

"Yeah!" Katrina corroborated. "That's exactly right. He now seems more….real, I guess I would say."

* * *

In the early evening, the two of them were pouring over baby name books. They were still in a state of euphoria after finding out the day before that they were going to have a son. Earlier in the day, they had gone to the gallery to deliver some new pieces of art. While Nathan unloaded the paintings, Katrina had gone to the bookstore next to the gallery. She found three books that offered names, their origins, and their meanings. She also stopped at the drug store to fill her vitamin prescription. There, she found a plastic bat and ball and she just couldn't resist. When she saw the award-winning grin on Nathan's face, she knew it was a wise decision.

The care-taker at the gallery had some bad news for her. She was quitting.

"I'm sorry, but my husband got a promotion and they are relocating him to Georgia. I hope you understand. We leave in three weeks, so I'm giving you some time to find someone." Madeline told her. She had worked for Katrina for five years and she was going to be hard to replace. Katrina was wondering how she would find a replacement.

"How about this one, Babe?" Katrina shook off her thoughts and looked at the name Nathan was pointing to.

Katrina laughed, since she knew he was being funny. She couldn't even pronounce the name he was pointing to. "Honey, what's wrong with Nathan?"

"Well, nothing, I guess. I just wanted him to have his own name. Maybe Nathan for a middle name. Certainly not Alphonse. What's your dad's middle name?"

Before she could answer him, the doorbell pealed in the background.

"Wonder who that is." He removed a cat from his lap and stood up to go answer the door.

She could hear Joey talking to Nathan as they were coming back toward the family room. All three cats scattered as they got closer. Holly was with him, carrying four frozen fruit drinks.

"You rock!" Katrina grinned at them.

"I see you're looking at names. Any luck?" Holly asked Katrina.

"Not yet.....there are a couple we both like, but we haven't decided on any. Nathan has an announcement to make." She smiled up at Nathan. "Go ahead. You like to tell all the good news."

"It's a son." Nathan announced, grinning ear to ear.

"Good job!" Joey raised his hand in a high five to the grinning Nathan.

The grin turned into a smile as Nathan turned to Katrina. "Joey wants me to go with him, in the Hummer, and pick up a couple of pieces of furniture. Do you mind, Babe?"

"No, of course not."

"I'll stay here with Katrina if that's okay." Holly looked from Katrina to Joey and Nathan.

"That's fine." The three of them answered in unison. Joey and Nathan went out through the kitchen door, and Katrina stood up to make coffee.

"Holly, I'm going to make some coffee. Would you like something else besides coffee? A drink, maybe?"

Holly shook her head. "Coffee is fine. I don't drink very much any more....since I started going out with Joey. He doesn't drink much, so we do other things instead of going to the bar."

"That's good.....isn't it? You and Joey have been going out for...... what? Four months now?"

"Yeah, about that. I really like him....and we get along really well. He's so....considerate....and sweet."

Katrina smiled. "Well, I can tell you this......the Perletti men know how to treat their women. They're all like that."

"So do you get along with Nathan's parents?"

"Absolutely. They're wonderful people. I love them, and they love me. It's the same with my parents and Nathan. We feel very lucky to have such loving, supportive parents. Both sets of parents have just accepted each of us into their lives as family. Joey's mom and dad are really terrific, too. Have you met them?"

"No, but hopefully I will, soon. I'm moving in with Joey. That's what the furniture move is all about. That's okay, isn't it? I mean, I know it's your apartment building."

"That's fine, Holly. Just make sure it's right for both of you. Joey had a rough time with Jessica. There could be some after-effects. It could get painful for you....for both of you, actually."

"Yeah, thanks for the advice, but Joey is over her. He says he knows all women aren't like her, and he's ready to try another relationship. He's the best thing that ever happened to me. I don't want to lose him."

Katrina smiled at her. "I hope it works out. I mean that. Nathan and I are very fond of Joey, and we want him to be happy. If that includes you being happy, then that's great. Coffee?"

The two women settled down at the table with fresh cups of coffee.

"So, Holly, do you work?"

"Hardly.....I mean...I want to, but the store cut my hours down to twenty-four a week. I can't live on that. I'm looking for another job."

"What do you do?"

"I greet customers and sell them jewelry....if I'm lucky. Sales have not been too great lately. I get seven dollars an hour, plus a five percent commission. I haven't had a check for over two hundred and fifty dollars in weeks. Uh, that's not why I'm moving in with Joey, by the way. I'm moving in because we want to be together."

Katrina nodded, and was pensive for a while. "Holly? Would you like to work for me?"

"Doing what?"

"Well, do you know anything about art?"

"A little, actually. I took an art appreciation course once when I was first out of high school. That's when I had dreams of being somebody. I know I like your artwork. That portrait of you and Nathan is just....."

"I'm looking for a replacement at my gallery. The woman who is there now is moving out of state. It's not a bad job. I would imagine it gets boring though. The hours are ten to five Monday through Friday, and ten to three on Saturday. It pays ten dollars an hour, or four hundred dollars a week. Would you be interested?"

Holly stared at Katrina; disbelieving the opportunity she was being offered. "Are you offering me the job? Really?"

"Yes....now there is no commission, but I do give quarterly bonuses according to the sales that were made. What do you think?"

"My God, Katrina! Yes! I would love to! When do I start?"

"Well, I want you to train, so as soon as possible."

"I'll give my notice tomorrow!" Holly squealed. "Oh, Katrina! Thank you!"

"You can thank me by calling me Kat, like the rest of my friends do." Katrina responded. "I hear the Hummer, so I guess their mission is accomplished." Katrina got up to get more coffee cups out of the cupboard.

35

Holly began her training at the gallery just ten days before Madeline planned on leaving. Katrina and Nathan met Holly at the gallery on her first day to introduce her to Madeline. Holly appeared to be excited as well as impressed with the art that was on display in the gallery. Once Katrina was satisfied that Holly was the right fit for the job, and that she and Madeline would get along well, Katrina and Nathan left for a late breakfast at a local IHOP.

When they were seated in a booth by the window, Nathan smiled at Katrina and reached for her hand. "You know, you are incredibly special. You improve every life you touch. Especially mine, but Joey, Holly, Lisa....even Charlie. And I know how you improved Candy's outlook. You're just......so wonderful."

"Honey, I don't do anything special. I'm just me."

"And I thank God for you." Nathan gave her hand a quick squeeze and smiled at her pensively. "It scares me to think we may never have met."

"Oh, we would have. We were destined to meet each other." Katrina smiled into his eyes, and then grinned at him playfully. "We deserve each other."

* * *

For Nathan and Katrina, life continued to be beautiful. Katrina was starting to look pregnant and she had a glow about her that made Nathan's heart melt every time he looked at her. Every night when they got into bed, Nathan kissed her abdomen. He referred to it as kissing his son goodnight. He would then take Katrina into his arms and kiss her tenderly. Sometimes they made love; Nathan being very gentle. He didn't want to 'hurt anything', as he put it. While they continued to see their friends, the bar became off-limits to Katrina, since cigarette smoke had suddenly started to bother her. Lisa and Charlie came to the house to visit as did Joey and Holly. The latter couple was becoming very close to both Nathan and Katrina. Holly seemed happy with her position at the gallery, and her performance was beyond reproach. One thing Katrina noticed was that since Holly had taken over at the gallery, sales had gone up. It made her wonder if Holly was just a better salesperson, or had Madeline been not a hundred percent honest. She put it out of her mind as water under the bridge, and let it go. She was too happy to dwell on it. Danny and Kathy came around more than they had in the past. Sometimes they brought the kids, and sometimes they just needed a break from the kids. Katrina was always happy to see them, with or without Kara and Little Danny.

It was mid-October. Lisa and Charlie had just left and Katrina was carrying glasses into the kitchen, while Nathan was cleaning up the ashtrays outside. Smoking was absolutely forbidden in the house, but neither Nathan nor Katrina minded if their guests smoked outside on the patio. After wiping off the table, Nathan joined Katrina in the kitchen. He found her standing in front of the refrigerator, holding the door open.

"Looking for something special?" He asked her as he rinsed out the dishcloth he had used outside.

She smiled. "No, I just know I want something."

"Do you want to go out and get something? Ice cream, maybe? It's still early."

"No, we have popsicles. I think that's what I want. Want one?"

"Any banana ones in there?"

Katrina nodded, and pulled out two popsicles, banana for him and blueberry for her. She handed him his as she walked to the sofa in the family room, picked up the remote, and clicked it to turn the television on. Nathan quickly joined her and draped his arm over the back of the sofa behind her.

"Honey, how about a shopping trip? For maternity clothes? You don't have any yet.....don't you need them?"

"Yeah, I guess I do. I just haven't gotten very big, so a lot of my regular clothes still fit. But I guess I should go on a spending spree and buy some. I'll plan on doing that next week sometime. Maybe the nursery could be painted while I'm out shopping; do you think?

Nathan nodded. "That's probably a good idea, since you shouldn't be around paint fumes. So how about a movie? I'm not tired, are you?"

* * *

Nathan leaned toward Katrina and quickly kissed her. "Have a good day shopping."

"Is that the way you kiss your wife? That's the way you kiss your friend's wife. I want a better one than that." She pouted up at him.

Nathan laughed, and then smiled down into her face. "I knew I should have started beating you after we got married. Now you're out of control." They both laughed as he took her into his arms and kissed her warmly, holding her to him. "I love you....so much. If we keep this up, I'll be carrying you upstairs.....except I can't.....Joey just pulled into the driveway."

"Hmmm, that's too bad." Katrina spoke in a hushed voice. "Because, you know....you look really sexy in these cut-offs and your sleeveless tee-shirt. Turns me on."

"Yeah? Maybe I'll wear them more often." He held her chin between his forefinger and thumb, and kissed the tip of her nose. "We'll have the room painted before you get back. When it's all dry, you can put those decals where you want them. Okay?"

She smiled and nodded. "I'll be back in a couple of hours. I love you, too.....and I'll be careful. Hi, Joey!"

"Hey, Kat." Joey grinned at Katrina, hugged her and kissed her cheek, and then turned to Nathan. "You two are married people; you know. You don't have to act like you like each other any more."

Nathan and Katrina laughed at Joey's remark. Katrina waved at Joey and Nathan as she walked toward the Mustang. It was a gorgeous day, so she put the top down and drove away. Nathan and Joey stood together in the doorway watching her go. Joey studied Nathan a moment and then asked, "What's wrong?"

Nathan shrugged. "It's strange....but the whole time Kat and I have been together, I have never seen her drive away from me. It's just a strange feeling."

Joey laughed. "You'll be okay. Let's get that room done. I would like to be home when Holly gets home."

Nathan nodded, but glanced toward the road once more before he shut the door. He couldn't shake the strange feeling that had come over him.

* * *

The two of them finished painting the room rather quickly, with most of the credit going to Joey. He was skilled at tasks such as painting, and Nathan accepted his help gratefully. They talked as they worked, which made the job seem to go much faster.

"So you must really like Holly, huh?" Nathan had asked.

"Yeah, I do. She's not.....well, she's not a bitch. She does things with me, and she never nags or complains. She's a friend to me, a partner. She doesn't find fault with anything I do. I don't know; I like her. I know you don't care for her all that much."

"Well....she was very rude to Kat. At first, that is. She got better when you started seeing her."

"She had a thing for you, Nate; I know that. But she got over it when you brought Katrina to the bar. She told me that she thinks Kat is one of the most gorgeous women she has ever seen, and she's amazed that Kat is so nice. She was jealous of her at first, but when she realized that Kat is a genuinely nice person, she became awed by her." Joey laughed a little. "Your wife is a truly amazing person, but I don't have to tell you that. It's written all over your face every time you look at her or say her name."

Nathan grinned. "That obvious, is it? I feel pretty lucky to have her. You're right; she is amazing. But hey, I think it's a good sign that Holly is so honest with you about that kind of stuff. Honesty makes a good relationship. No secrets. My dad told me that. It's trust. You trust a person with your secrets, and you trust that he or she will accept those secrets, and still love you just the same. You know you're with the right person when you can tell her about your past and it stays in the past. You know what I mean? It's not mentioned again."

"Does Kat know about all of your exes?"

"Yep, and I know about hers. It would be stupid to think that she may not have had boyfriends before she met me. I mean......look at her. I was very surprised that I was her first lover, though." Nathan stopped. He realized that he probably should not have said anything. He verbally jumped over the subject and quickly told Joey about Jeff, and the tragedy of his death.

"Wow, that's too bad. But in a way, I guess it's good. You may not have met her if he hadn't died. She was a virgin when you met her? Wow, I didn't know they still had them."

Nathan laughed at Joey's facetious remark.

"Kat says we would have met anyway. We were destined to be together."

Joey looked over at Nathan and grinned. "Probably true. She loves you; I can tell. And you really love her; I can see that."

Nathan's eyes softened when he looked over at Joey. "With all my heart and soul, forever and ever." He grinned at Joey as he picked up the paint roller to finish. "I'm not afraid to show it, either. To hell with that macho shit; she's my woman. I will take her over everybody. About a month ago, Charlie wanted me to go on a weekend fishing trip. Hell; that may have been fun before I met Katrina, but I have no desire to spend a weekend in a fishing cabin, drinking beer and playing cards all night, when I can be here, dry and warm, curled up with Katrina. Charlie said I was whipped. My answer to him? Absolutely, and damn proud of it. Then I told him that I have never once thought of him and smiled, like I do when I think of Katrina. He had no answer for that one."

Joey laughed, and then his face took on a serious look.

"Nate, do you two ever talk about Steven? I know about how you met Kat. Steven must have really been off the deep end. Did he hurt her really bad?"

"He hurt her. She had marks on her for weeks. Bad bruises. Her whole left side stayed purple for a long time. That's where her ribs were broken. I'm just glad I got there before he raped her and killed her. I remember seeing her all bloody and bruised......I wanted to kill Steven for doing that to an innocent human being. Damn! I get pissed off all over again every time I think about it. I remember picking her up and carrying her inside.....the terror in her eyes....the way she was trembling....crying. You don't know how glad I am that I got there in time." Nathan stopped for a moment, the memory clear in his mind. "But you know.....she immediately put her trust in me. She knew from the very beginning that she was safe with me, even though Steven was my brother."

Joey listened to Nathan's recount of that day when Steven abducted Katrina, and he felt the tension coming from Nathan. "It's strange how one of the worst episodes of your life turned out to be one of the best days of your life, isn't it? I mean....meeting Kat had to be one of the best days of your life."

Nathan laughed. "Yeah, meeting her was the start of the happiest days of my life. I can say that. You know what's really cool about Katrina and me? We're together practically twenty-four-seven, and we have never had an argument. No need to. We agree on almost everything, and there is always a reason why we disagree on something. We always go with that reason why or why not, because we have respect for each other's intelligence." Nathan paused for a moment, and then he confided in Joey. "You know....I sometimes get so scared that something will happen....to her. That....we won't be together forever....."

"Hey, you will be. You will be, no matter what. Look at this.... we're almost done in here. It's only just about one-thirty." Joey continued to work in his nice, easy manner, confident that his work showed quality.

"Nate, I'm going to ask Holly to marry me." When Joey got no response from Nathan, he turned around, only to see Nathan bent over, holding his head between his hands. His face was scarlet.

Joey dropped his paint roller on the paint tray and ran toward Nathan. He glimpsed at Nathan's roller, lying on the carpet, where he must have dropped it.

"Nate! What's wrong?" He reached Nathan and grabbed his arm. "Hey! What the hell is wrong? Nate!"

Nathan's ragged breathing was returning to normal as was his skin color. He let out a breath. "Don't know what happened....I suddenly got this horrible pain in my head. Wow....It was severe. It's gone now."

"Do you feel dizzy or anything? I can finish this up myself."

"I'm fine now. I wonder what it was."

"I would suggest you see a doctor about it." Joey was busily cleaning the spot where Nathan's paint roller fell, until he was satisfied that there would be no stain. He looked over at Nathan, waiting for a response.

"Yeah, I will. Now what were you saying? You're going to ask Holly to marry you? Are you sure?"

"Yep. I'm sure. She's good for me."

"Well, I guess Katrina and I will help you plan your wedding, then." Nathan grinned at Joey, glad that his cousin was happy.

He couldn't wait to tell Katrina. He knew she would be thrilled. He was thoroughly enjoying this time with Joey. It gave them both a chance to voice their thoughts and feelings. He was so happy with Katrina and he wanted everybody to know it. Now that Joey was truly happy, they could openly share their feelings with each other.

* * *

Katrina was standing at the cash register in Mother's Maternity Boutique at the mall. She was holding several selections in her arms, and she was satisfied that she had all she would need for the next few months. The saleslady had been very helpful in finding maternity clothes for her small frame, and had made several suggestions, including underwear and a maternity swimsuit. The woman was ringing up her purchases as Katrina piled everything on the counter and was getting a credit card out of her wallet. The lady smiled at her as she rang up the items. When the transaction was complete, Katrina grabbed the four shopping bags and headed toward the exit of the mall, only stopping in a men's store to get Nathan a couple pairs of shorts. She couldn't wait to get home to show Nathan what she bought. The weather was still perfect, so she put her purchases into the trunk, put the convertible top down again, and drove away from the mall.

The traffic was unusually heavy for the time of day, and Katrina supposed it was because of the construction site on the highway not too far away. Patiently, she drove with the flow of traffic at the slow speed required. The traffic stopped and then started up again, until finally the three lanes of traffic came to a dead stop. She sighed and looked at the clock on the dash. It was almost one-thirty. Hopefully, Nathan and Joey would have the room done by now, and maybe were relaxing with a beer or a swim in the pool. She smiled as she thought of Nathan in his swim trucks. 'He just looks so damn good in them,' she thought. As she sat there, she envisioned his smile, and then his big grin when something really made him happy. 'This baby makes him grin like that,' she remembered, as she gently ran her hand across her belly. She caught a glimpse of her face in the rearview mirror and saw the smile on her lips and the love for Nathan in her eyes. She was truly happy. Life was perfect.

Once more the traffic started to move. She inched her car along, hoping that she could make it to the underpass before she stopped again. It would be cooler there. No such luck...she stopped two car lengths short of it. She sighed again. She looked up at the highway structure that crossed over the highway where she sat. There were flashing red and blue lights, suggesting to her that there may have been an accident up there. A helicopter hovered in the air above. Katrina stared at the helicopter, realizing that it was a life-flight. 'There must have been injuries,' she concluded.

On the highway above where Katrina sat in her car, waiting for the traffic to move, there had, indeed, been an accident. Two cars collided, severely injuring the driver of one of the cars. The accident site was being cleaned up and the traffic was moving slowly through the scene. Suddenly, a blue pick-up truck shot out of the line of traffic and accelerated around the slow-moving cars, just as one of the tow trucks swung out into his path. The driver of the pick-up cut his wheel too sharply, causing the truck to slam into the side of a car. He panicked, jamming his foot onto the accelerator, rather than the brake. The blue pick-up slammed into the low concrete wall, and toppled over the side where the railing was missing.

Katrina's eyes were on the helicopter when the movement above her diverted her attention. Too late, she looked up to see the blue pick-up truck hurling down straight toward her. Her eyes widened, as she protectively put her hand over her growing stomach. She froze before she screamed, "NATHAN!"

The truck landed directly on top of her, instantly crushing Nathan's beautiful Katrina to death......................

37

Deputy Thompson's face was strained; his lips tightened into a fine line. He hated this part of his job. He braced himself for the inevitable reaction to the bad news, as he swung the cruiser into the driveway. Joey was just putting his car into gear to leave when he saw the police cruiser. Putting the car back into park, he sat there and waited for the cruiser to stop. Deputy Thompson got out of the car and walked over to Joey's car.

"Mr. Perletti?" The deputy asked in the most neutral tone he could summon.

"I'm Joey Perletti. My cousin is Nathan Perletti. He lives here."

"Is he home?" The deputy asked.

"Yeah, he's here. Officer, what's this about?"

"Does his wife drive a red Mustang?'

"Uh....yeah.....Katrina's okay, isn't she?"

"I have to see Mr. Perletti. You're his cousin, you say? You maybe should stick around. He may need you."

Joey's heart sank. "Nathan's inside." He led the deputy to the back door, opened it, and called for Nathan.

Nathan trotted into the kitchen. "Hey, Joey....what did you........"

Nathan stopped when he saw the uniformed man standing next to Joey.

"Mr. Perletti? I'm afraid there has been a terrible accident. Your wife, Katrina....was involved."

"Is-is she all right? Where is she? I mean, she's okay, right?"

"I'm sorry, Mr. Perletti." The deputy solemnly shook his head.

"No. There must be some mistake. Katrina's at the mall buying maternity clothes. We're going to have a baby. Joey? It's a mistake, right?" Nathan turned to Joey and saw the mixture of pain and pity on his face.

Nathan could no longer stand. He felt his knees buckle under him, and the deputy was quick to respond, sliding a chair up to catch him. His head dropped into his hands and he was gasping for air. "No. Forever isn't over yet. It can't be." Nathan choked on his sobs. He raised his head and looked directly at the deputy, who stood there shifting from one foot to the other, feeling very uncomfortable. "Where is she? My wife, I mean. I have to see her."

"I'll take you there." Thompson turned to Joey and said, "Call someone."

Nathan was out of the door already. The deputy looked back at Joey and said, "Somebody has to make a formal identification of the body. I don't recommend it be him." Thompson looked down at the floor and then back at Joey. "It isn't pretty."

Nathan climbed into the cruiser and Joey went directly to his car. Thompson handed Joey Nathan's cell phone. "He says her brother's number is in there. Find it and call him. Tell him to meet us at the hospital."

Joey nodded, and flipped open Nathan's cell phone to the phone list. He quickly spotted Danny's office number and entered his code into the phone. Danny picked up on the first ring.

"Dan Kitrowski."

"Dan, Joey Perletti. I have some bad news..........."

* * *

Joey waited for the phone to be answered. Al picked up the receiver on the second ring.

"Uncle Al, it's Joey."

"Well, Hi, Joey. How's it going down there?"

"Uncle Al, Nathan is going to need you.....bad. Katrina was killed in a car accident this afternoon."

There was a moment of silence on the other end of the line. Joey waited for a moment before he spoke again. "Uncle Al?"

"Yeah....Joey, I'm here. I'm......stunned. Oh my God. Jesus! ROSE! Joey, where is Nathan now? How is he? ROSE!"

"He's sitting in the hall outside of where they took Katrina's body. He....they gave him a shot of some kind, Uncle Al. He's out of his mind with grief. They won't let him see her. The officer who came to the house said it wasn't pretty, and that Nathan shouldn't see her. Uncle Al, I think you should get here as soon as possible...."

"Yeah, Joey, we're on our way. Tell him....never mind...we'll be there as soon as we can."

Rose walked into the kitchen just as Al was hanging up the telephone. She caught the last sentence of the conversation, saw the tears in Al's eyes, and stared at him, puzzled.

"What's wrong? Who were you talking to?"

"Rose, come here a minute."

Rose slowly walked toward Al, not knowing what she was going to hear. Al's tears were streaming down his face. He reached for Rose and hugged her tightly.

"Katrina.....was killed in a car accident today. We have to get to Nathan."

Rose began to fall, but Al held her up. Her first sob came out like a hiccup. Al embraced her tightly as she let loose with the tears. "Oh God, Al......Nathan loves her so much."

Al nodded, and then put his hands on Rose's shoulders. "Get some stuff together. We need to get down to the Kitrowski's house. Can you imagine what they must be going through? Let's move fast. I want to be there within the next couple of hours. We can all make reservations on the same flight to Florida. I think those people need all the support they can get right now."

* * *

Dan and Kathy walked into the dark corridor through a door in the back of the hospital. They immediately spied Nathan sitting on a bench, looking like he was totally out of it. Joey stepped up to intercept them. "He's in bad shape. They have him sedated right now."

"What happened?" Danny stared at Joey with red-rimmed eyes. "I called Mike. He's going up to my parents' house now. They can't hear this news alone."

Joey nodded, and then quickly gave them the brief story of what happened out on that highway. "It was instant, the deputy said. She didn't suffer."

Danny's lip curled. "I guess I should be grateful that my sister didn't suffer before her life ended, but somehow that's not much consolation right now." His voice cracked, and then the tears began flowing uncontrollably. Kathy held onto Danny, crying.

"Someone has to formally I-D her." Joey looked at Danny and Kathy. "I'll go in when someone comes for us. Is that alright?"

Danny stared at Joey for a moment. "I don't think I can. Oh God….." Danny covered his face and dropped into a chair.

* * *

Holly parked her car and jumped out in a run. Joey called her and told her to just get there, gave her the directions, and hung up. She ran into the back door and stopped, letting her eyes adjust to the darkened corridor. She looked around for Joey, saw Nathan, and then another couple she didn't recognize. Joey appeared at her side and wrapped his arms around her.

"Joey, what's going on? What happened?" She whispered to him.

"Katrina was killed in a car accident." Joey whispered back.

Holly slid down the wall and sat there in a crouching position. She was stunned and speechless, and suddenly very cold. As she wrapped her arms around herself, she could only stare up at Joey for a moment. She forced herself to look over at Nathan, but she turned away almost immediately when she saw the naked agony on his face.

* * *

A man wearing a lab coat entered the corridor through a door that said 'No Admittance" and looked around. Joey approached him.

"I'm Joey Perletti."

The gentleman cleared his throat, and quickly sized Joey up. "I'm Dr. Greene, a pathologist. Uh, we need a formal identification. Are you....you're not the husband?"

"No, he's my cousin, and I don't think he could handle seeing her right now."

"Were you close to her? I mean, close enough that you wouldn't have any trouble identifying her remains? I want to tell you, it looks like a slaughter more than a car wreck. It may be hard to identify her." Dr. Greene spoke in a hushed tone.

"I think I can. Look around you. Do you see anybody else who is in any shape to go in there?"

Dr. Greene looked around, and conceded that Joey was probably the best choice.

"Well, are you ready?"

Joey nodded, and followed the pathologist.

In the middle of the room, under a wide bright light, stood a gurney with a green sheet draped over it. A man wearing green scrubs was standing beside the gurney, waiting for Dr. Greene to give him the go-ahead sign. Joey stopped and braced himself. He knew he was close to collapsing, but he had to remain strong for Nathan right now. Joey nodded to Dr. Greene, who in turn nodded to the man wearing the scrubs. He slowly drew the sheet down, and Joey gasped.

"It's her. I recognize the rings, and...and the hair....her gorgeous long hair."

Although most of the hair was matted with blood, there was no mistaking the glorious, long copper tresses. The long slender fingers of the delicate-looking hand that held her wedding rings were also undeniably Katrina's.

"That's the outfit she was wearing when she left to...to go shopping today, too." Joey's last sentence was hung up by a sob. He was shaking as he backed away from what was left of his cousin's wonderful, sweet, beautiful wife. He immediately limped to a trash receptacle and vomited.

* * *

Kevin was in the kitchen stirring a pot of stew he had thrown together when he got home from work that afternoon. He had heard the phone ring and he knew that Morgan would pick it up in the bedroom. Morgan's piercing screams coming from the bedroom caused him to drop the spoon and run.

"KEVIN! KEVIN!" It was coming out more like a piercing shriek than a scream. Kevin ran to the bedroom where Morgan had crumbled to the floor at the foot of the bed. He ran to her and grabbed her up into his arms. The shrieks continued as tears streamed down her face.

"Baby, what's wrong?" He took the telephone receiver she clutched in her hand and listened into it. He heard someone sobbing. "Hello? Who is this?"

"Kevin, it's Kim Kitrowski. Is Morgan okay? I'm sorry to lay this on you.....Katrina was killed in a car accident this afternoon. I...."

"Oh God!" Kevin let out an involuntary sob and tightened his arm around his wife.

Morgan's body was racked by sobs as the intermittent shrieks continued.

"Thanks for calling, Kim. I gotta go. Morgan's losing it."

He quickly hung up and sat there rocking Morgan, trying to soothe her. Kevin himself was shaking from the devastating and shocking phone call. He held Morgan tightly for several minutes.

"We should go to Kitrowski's, Babe. What do you think?" Kevin was having a difficult time forcing words passed the hard lump that had formed in his throat. His words brought on the shrieks and sobs again, but Morgan started to move up off of Kevin's lap. Kevin assumed that meant she agreed with him.

* * *

Mary and Ed were just sitting down to dinner when Michael came through the front door.

Mary jumped up from the table. "Mike! Hi! Let me get you a plate, Honey."

"Sit down, Mom." Michael's voice was flat as he held himself up in the doorway, leaning on the frame.

Surprised by his tone, Mary stared him as she sat back down. "What's wrong, Mike? Is Kim okay?"

"She's fine, Mom."

That was all he could muster before the uncontrollable tears began running down his face. He dropped onto a dining room chair.

"There was an accident……Katrina……..she….she's gone."

Mary sat zombie-like in her chair. She thought she could hear sirens somewhere in the distance. When she felt Ed sharply tap her cheek, she realized the siren-like sound was coming from her. Mary fainted. Ed, putting his grief aside, picked Mary up and cradled her body to his. As he held her, his sobs let loose, but he managed to carry Mary into the family room where he gently laid her on the sofa. Michael followed him.

"Mike, do you know what happened?" Ed's voice was uneven, and he was trembling.

"Only what Danny told me…and that was sketchy…..something about a truck going over the side of the overpass, and landing on top of Katrina." This brought new sobs from Michael. "She was killed instantly."

"Where's Nathan?" Ed asked. It dawned on him that Nathan might have been with her.

"I don't know. He wasn't with her when the accident happened. I guess she went shopping for maternity clothes and he stayed home to paint the nursery." Michael stopped to wipe his eyes and nose. "The nursery. The baby….Katrina……both….gone." Michael covered his eyes with his hands and remained quiet.

"Nathan…..he must be out of his mind about now." Ed stared into a place only he could see at the moment. "Nathan loves her like nobody else could; you know that?"

His thoughts were interrupted by the doorbell. He opened the door to Morgan and Kevin, both crying. When Morgan saw Ed, she began her shrieking again, but not as loudly. Ed wrapped his arms around her and held her, while Kevin went to Michael and put his arm around Michael's shoulder. Nobody spoke. Nobody had to. The grief in the house was so thick. Mary came out of the family room where Ed had laid her down on the sofa.

"Morgan.....oh, Morgan." Mary reached for Morgan and held her, while Ed held both of them. They were standing together that way when the Perletti's came through the door.

* * *

Marie stood in the middle of the kitchen wondering why the door was left unlocked. She listened for sounds through the house and was satisfied that she was the only occupant, except for the cats who were probably sleeping. She slid the chair Nathan had collapsed onto back to its rightful place under the table. Something wasn't right. Slowly she walked through each room, looking for any sign that would explain her uneasy feeling. The cats meowed at her when she entered their room. She noticed their dishes were empty and immediately, she filled them. That, in itself, was strange. Neither Nathan nor Katrina would ever allow the cats to go hungry. Where were they? She walked up the short flight of stairs past the master bedroom, and entered the first room beyond—the future nursery. Marie could see that the painting was completed, just as Nathan said it would be. Maybe they went out to eat, and just forgot to lock the back door. She entered the master bedroom and it was just as she had left it when she tidied up earlier that day. She left the house around one in the afternoon to take her husband to his doctor's appointment. Nathan had told her she could have the rest of the day off, but she had come back anyway. It wasn't as though she were ever overworked there. She brought some fresh fruit back with her, which she planned on cutting up and putting it in the refrigerator for Katrina, who just loved fresh fruit.

Marie was cutting up the fruit and dropping it into a bowl when she heard a car in the driveway. She assumed it was Nathan and Katrina, and was surprised when Joey walked into the kitchen, obviously upset about something.

"Hi, Joey...where is everybody?"

Joey stopped and ran his hand over his face. "Marie.....I guess you haven't heard." Joey sighed and backed onto one of the stools that sat in front of the counter. "Katrina.....she was killed in a car accident today."

Marie let go of the knife she was holding and it clamored to the floor. She stared at Joey, wondering if she had heard him right. She saw by the look on his face that she had. She opened her mouth to speak but no sound would come out, so she closed it again. For a moment, she thought she might faint, but she recovered when she thought of Nathan.

"Nathan? Where is Nathan?" She squeaked out.

"He's going to stay at a hotel. He....can't come here right now. I just came to get him some clothes. I'll stay there with him. He's..... taking it pretty bad. We all are, I guess."

Marie nodded. "Has anybody called Mike and Cookie?"

"No, I didn't think about it. I called Uncle Al and Katrina's brother, Dan. I guess we should call Mike and Cookie."

"I'll call. You get back to Nathan. He needs you."

Joey nodded and ran up the steps to get some things for Nathan to wear. He stopped just inside the bedroom doorway. The light smell of Katrina's perfume lingered in the air. Joey looked around and saw a pair of Katrina's sandals in front of the nightstand by the bed; her robe draped over a chair. A dark sadness came over him. She was the love of Nathan's life.....gone.....forever.

* * *

Cookie answered the phone on her way in from their back yard. Mike was still outside in the yard with the twins when Cookie decided it was time to get dinner ready. She saw that the call was coming from Nathan's house and immediately grabbed up the phone with a smile.

"Hi, sexy!" She said into the receiver, knowing that it would either be Nathan or Kat.

"Cookie, it's Marie, Nathan's housekeeper."

"Marie....what's the matter?" Cookie's smile became a frown of concern. "Oh, no....oh my God! Is Nathan....well, I'm sure he's not okay...but where is he now?"

Marie told her that Nathan was in a hotel and Joey was with him, and Cookie was relieved by that. "I'll tell Mike. We'll be there....as soon as we can."

"MIKE! Please come in here! NOW! MIKE? This isn't good!"

Cookie waited until Mike put the boys into the playpen. "You two play quietly for a minute. I have to talk to daddy."

Mike saw the distress in Cookie's eyes. "What's up, Cookie-buns?"

"Katrina's dead." She spoke flatly, trying to stay calm.

"What? No, that can't be right...."

"Marie just called. It was a car accident. Nathan's out of his mind with grief. He can't even go back to his house. She says the doctor at the hospital gave him a shot to sedate him a little...."

"So where is he?" Mike demanded.

"He's in a hotel with his cousin. Joey is going to stay with him."

"Cook, start packing....I'll get plane reservations. We need to be there. He's our best friend, and he needs us. I'll call your mom about taking the boys, and call my partner to take over my patients for a few days. Just get us packed, okay? I'll be up to help you as soon as I get everything squared away." Mike turned toward the phone, and then turned back toward Cookie, who was already halfway up the stairs. "And Cookie? I love you....totally."

She smiled down at him. "Me, too, Hon....totally." She knew what an impact this was having on Mike. Nathan waited for so long to find "His Forever" and now she was gone. 'Oh, God! Poor Nathan!' Cookie lamented as she pulled the suitcases from the top shelf in the spare room.

38

Nathan was so cold. Mourners were making their way away from the gravesite, many of them still crying and holding onto each other. Nathan couldn't move. He felt as though the life had been drained out of him and it was lying on top of the platinum casket, but the pain in his chest reminded him that he was still alive. His heart ached; his chest hurt. Al came back up the hill and put his arm around Nathan.

"Come on, Son. There's nothing you can do here." Al coaxed.

"I don't want to leave her." Nathan's voice was flat and barely audible.

"I know, Nate; I know."

Al saw the pain in Nathan's eyes. He looked away as a sob caught in his own throat.

"I wish I could take some of your pain away, Son; I really do. Fact is, all those people walking down the hill are hurting. They're hurting bad. We all loved her, Son. To know her was to love her. She touched everybody."

Al was visibly crying now. Nathan just stood there staring at his beloved Katrina's casket. Al put his arm around Nathan and steered him down the hill toward the car. Nathan put up no resistance; all his strength was gone.

* * *

A luncheon was put out at Jack's Place. The bar was officially closed for the day, as it has been since the accident. Jack had placed a wreath on the door, turned out the lights, and locked up as soon as he heard the tragic news. After the funeral, he rushed back to the bar and unlocked the door, turned on the lights and started arranging tables. Sal and Patty, another waitress, followed him in through the door, and began getting out the food trays they had prepared the day before. Many people had dropped off bowls and trays of offerings, so there would be plenty of food.

Sal kept stopping to wipe her eyes as she arranged the bowls and trays on the table. She barely knew Katrina but she knew she was a high quality girl, and that Nathan loved her with all his heart.

"Did you see the pain in Nathan's face, Patty?" Sal's voice was husky from crying.

"Yeah, I did." Her co-worker answered her, and sighed. "They were such a beautiful couple. So perfect for each other. So much in love. It's not fair; it's not fair at all. What will Nathan do now? Nobody will ever compare to her. God…she was pregnant, too. They wanted that baby so much. It's so sad, Sal….really sad."

People began to file in just as Patty and Sal got everything put out. The two women couldn't mistake the grief on all of their faces.

"That must be Katrina's parents." Patty nodded toward the couple with the hollow eyes, holding onto each other. Sal nodded. "That blonde was her best friend. She's taking it hard. The two good-looking guys behind the parents are her brothers. The one brother's wife is about to give birth, so she couldn't be here. The other brother is the father of those two cute kids. His wife is the little blonde. Mike and Cookie are here. Remember them from their visits to Nathan?"

Patty nodded.

"What's Holly doing here?" Patty asked Sal.

"She's dating Nathan's cousin, Joey. She also works....worked for Katrina. There....there's Joey with his parents and Nathan's mother. Gees......everybody looks.....bad. Katrina certainly was loved."

"Yes, she was. I have a feeling not much of this food is going to get eaten. Charlie and Lisa just walked in. Boy, Lisa is a wreck." Patty pointed out, needlessly.

Both women quietly observed the crowd for a moment. They watched as Nathan came through the door, accompanied by his father. Nathan looked the worst of all. His eyes were swollen and judging by the dark circles under them, it was apparent he hadn't slept in three days.

Al led Nathan to a chair away from most of the crowd and sat him down. Immediately, Jack appeared next to them holding a small glass of bourbon. He set it down in front of Nathan.

"I don't want that." Nathan glanced at Jack and quickly looked away.

Jack retreated. He had never seen Nathan like this. His pain was coming out almost like a smoldering anger.

"I do." Al nodded at Jack, lifted the glass, and sipped the bourbon out of it. Over the top of the glass, he studied Nathan. Al was worried about him. "Can I get you anything, Son?"

Nathan slowly shook his head. "No, Dad.....there's nothing anybody can get me or do for me."

"Are you going to be okay, Nate?"

"No......I'm never going to be okay again." Nathan stared at the floor as he quietly spoke. "From the day I met her I began living for her. She was my life…..” Nathan stopped to swallow the lump that was building up in his throat. “Just….explain to me. Why? Why did it have to happen? Why was she taken from me?” Nathan's eyes were brimming with tears, so he paused and swallowed hard. “Why, Dad? Say something. Can you say something, anything that will help me understand that right now?”

Al sighed. He could feel the emotional pain that coursed through Nathan's body right then. He knew he had to say something.

“Nathan…..she was so….perfect…..so perfect that God wanted her back. All of us….our time here is only lent to us. He needed Katrina back.”

Al stopped when he saw the stricken look on Nathan's face. Al was unsure if what he said had been the right thing to say. Nathan was quietly staring at the floor again. Al stood up and placed a hand on Nathan's shoulder.

“I'm going to go check on your mother. I'll be back.”

Nathan barely acknowledged Al's departure as he continued to stare at the floor. He wondered why the Kitrowski's hadn't come over to speak to him. Did they hate him now because he broke his promise to keep Katrina safe? He failed them. He failed Katrina. He sat and continued to stare at the floor.

Across the room, Mary and Ed were staring at their part of the floor. Mary's head was on Ed's shoulder as he held her. “Honey, we have to say something to Nathan. He loved her so much.” Ed stroked Mary's arm as he spoke.

“I know. Ed, I just can't. I see his misery, and I know how much….. she loved him. Seeing him that way reminds me that I'll never……see my daughter again.” With this came fresh tears and sobs.

“He needs us, Mary. He needs to know that we don't blame him for anything. He needs to know that we….know he loved her and for that, we love him, and always will.”

Mary nodded. “Let me get a grip for a moment. We'll go over there. I *do* love him, Ed. He made our daughter's life so happy…..” Mary stopped talking as the sobs took control.

Patty filled a plate with food, walked over and set it down in front of Nathan. “Nate, eat something. Katrina wouldn't want you to……” Patty didn't get to finish her sentence.

With one motion, Nathan swept the plate of food off the table. The plate crashed to the floor and shattered, food flying everywhere. "DON'T TELL ME WHAT KATRINA WANTED!"

Patty slowly backed away as he lashed out at her.

"I *KNOW* WHAT KATRINA WANTED! *KATRINA WANTED TO HAVE OUR BABY! KATRINA WANTED US TO BE TOGETHER FOREVER!! KATRINA WANTED TO GET A DOG! KATRINA WANTED TO live.....*" His voice cracked on his last words, and his tears began.

As quick as lightning, little Danny ran to Nathan and sailed onto his lap. He held Nathan's face between his small hands and looked into Nathan's eyes. Quietly and softly he appealed to Nathan. "Untul Nate. Untul Nate! Don't cry. Let me hold you. I'll hold you."

Nathan stared blankly at little Danny and saw the tears brimming in his eyes.

"Untul Nate....I want Aunt Kat back, too." His words came out like he was in agony.

Nathan's eyes focused on little Danny's face and his eyes softened. He wrapped his arms around Danny and held him close, gently rocking him. Little Danny was openly sobbing on Nathan's chest, and Nathan continued to rock him as the tears silently slid down his own face. Quietly, he apologized to Patty, who was still standing just out of his reach. The scene between Nathan and little Danny brought fresh tears and sobs to all of Katrina's loved ones.

Nathan caressed Danny's hair and kissed the top of his head quietly. He felt someone next to him and he looked up into Mary's tear-stained face.

"You're still my son, Nathan. I know how much you loved her, and how much she loved you. You made her life so....happy, Nathan. I'll love you forever for that." Mary put an arm around Nathan's neck and laid her head on top of his. She held him like that until Danny stopped crying.

39

People were leaving....going back to their lives. Nathan felt he had no life left. Al held the door for him as he walked out into the bright sunlight. It was getting close to the evening hours, but the sun was still brightly shining. Nathan wondered how the sun could ever shine again. He knew his parents and Mike and Cookie would be staying a couple of days, and then they would leave, too. He would be alone. Alone to remember what he had....alone to feel the pain of her being gone. Life had been so perfect....

His thoughts were interrupted when he felt the car stop. They were in his driveway, and quietly getting out of the car. He followed. He followed until they got to the walkway that led to the front door. Nathan stopped and turned away.

"Nate, you have to go inside sooner or later." Al coaxed.

"Then later, Dad. I want to be alone right now. Okay? Just a little while. I want to....just be alone in Kat's......in her favorite place down on the beach. She loved it there; you know? She played in the sand like a little kid. Built sand castles. I know if I go there, I'll be close to her."

Al nodded. He believed him. He remembered that Nathan had felt her presence years before he met her. He would feel her close to him in her favorite spot. They were soul mates. He watched Nathan slowly make his way down the slope to the beach, his head down and his shoulders slumping. Al worried, but he had to respect Nathan's wishes. He entered the house and stopped to look up at the portrait of Katrina and Nathan. His heart ached as he followed the sounds of Rose and Mike and Cookie. They were petting the cats, which somehow seemed to know that their owner wasn't coming back. All three of them had a look of unusual concern on their faces and they seemed to stay huddled together.

"They know." Cookie spoke quietly to no one in particular.

"Yes, they do." Marie appeared in the doorway in time to corroborate Cookie's observation. "Hey, I made coffee if anyone's interested. Where's Nathan?"

"He's down at the beach. He just wants to be alone for awhile." Al answered. "Yeah, I'd love some coffee."

* * *

Morgan and Kevin arrived at their front door just before dark. Kevin stooped down to pick up four days' worth of newspapers. Katrina's picture was on the front page of one of the papers. Morgan grabbed that edition and sat down at the kitchen table.

"Oh, my beautiful, beautiful friend. Kat, I will miss you so much." Morgan's eyes once again brimmed over with tears.

Kevin was just grateful that she wasn't shrieking any more. He opened up the most current newspaper edition. This time there was a smaller picture of Katrina, but what grabbed his attention was the picture under it. It was Sean's. "Oh My God. Honey, listen to this."

"The body of Sean Parks was found in his blood-spattered Cadillac late yesterday afternoon. The car was parked on High Road, a dirt road that ends on top of a hill overlooking the city. Clutched to his chest was the newspaper edition of the previous day, when the newspaper ran the story of the death of Katrina Kitrowski-Perletti, the local resident who was famous for the Kit-Kat cartoon. A hand-written note that read 'I never stopped loving her' was taped to the dashboard. Ms Kitrowski and Mr. Parks had once dated in high school….."

The article went on to give the particulars of Sean's life, and stated that the death had been ruled a suicide, one shot to the head.

Morgan stared blankly at Kevin until the significance of the article impacted.

"Wow, Kevin. He really did love her, I guess. He was parked in the same place where Katrina punched him the night they broke up."

"I never doubted that he loved her, Babe. It was his maturity level that was all fucked up. Self-control comes with maturity. He was short on both. That time when we first met Nathan and Sean came into Bear's….remember? I saw the regret on his face then. He finally grew up and he realized what he did wrong and he finally understood why he lost her. I saw that in his face. Now….let's think of some way we can honor our friend. We have to do something in her memory. What do you say?" Kevin hoped that would put at least a little smile on Morgan's face.

It did. Morgan smiled at Kevin with tears still running down her face.

* * *

Nathan walked across the small private beach, unmindful of the sand that was slipping into his leather dress shoes. He stopped halfway across and looked down at Katrina's last sand castle, still partially standing. Crouching down for a closer look, he marveled at the detail she put into it. Nathan's chest began to ache as he ran his finger along the edge of the sand castle.

"Oh my Darling," he spoke aloud, barely above a whisper. "My sweet Darling....you gave a hundred percent to everything you did..... even sand castles." Nathan turned his face up to the sky. "You're up there; I know you are.....and you're watching me. I love you, Baby. I'll always love you."

He turned back to the sand castle. "This is your last work of art, Honey. I wish I could somehow preserve it." Nathan was openly crying now. **"Kat. Oh, Kat! Katrina!"**

Tears were streaming down Nathan's face, and he watched them settle into the sand on top of the castle. As he wiped his tears, he felt the rage bubbling up inside of him....a rage that was becoming so powerful that he was forced to his feet. His head was pounding from the pressure of the anger building up inside.

The sun was dropping into the water and storm clouds were rapidly moving in. The rain from them would wash away Katrina's sand castle. Already thunder was rolling through the clouds and the wind was gathering momentum against the sand on the beach. Lightning struck in the distance. Nathan's breathing quickened as his body trembled. Never had he felt this angry. He raised his arm and clenched his fist and shook it into the air. The pain in his head was getting worse. His handsome face was distorted in emotional pain and anger.

"You...BASTARD! YOU SELFISH BASTARD! WHY? WHY? WHY DID YOU TAKE HER FROM ME? IF YOU'RE UP THERE...TELL ME!! WHY?? IF YOU EXIST, TELL ME WHY! YOU SON-OF-A-BITCH!!!

He couldn't breathe. The pain........his head pounded. He gasped for air but couldn't get any. He sank to his knees. "Why?" He asked quietly. At that moment he could have sworn he felt Katrina's lips on his. He toppled over.

* * *

They found him there just before dawn. Cookie and Mike stood side by side, tears dripping, as they stared down at Nathan's limp body. Mike knelt down and felt for a pulse. There was none.

"He went to Katrina."

Mike looked up at Cookie and started to protest, but changed his mind. He knew that what she said was true.

He nodded. "She was his forever. When forever is gone, there's nothing."

* * *

Note: Official cause of death: Brain Aneurism.
It may have been present for years......the coroner said.

Many thanks to the families for giving me permission to write the story of Katrina and Nathan. May they rest in peace, together forever.

Printed in the United States
84429LV00003B/10-12/A

9 781434 318909